VARNEY, THE VAMPIRE.

VOLUME II

THE ILLUSTRATED

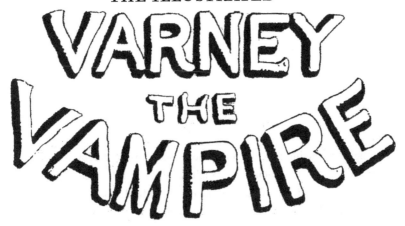

(Varney the Vampyre)

or,

THE FEAST OF BLOOD:

A ROMANCE OF EXCITING INTEREST.

In Two Volumes.

VOLUME II

By

JAMES MALCOLM RYMER

With Thomas Preskett Prest

Edited and Annotated by Finn J.D. John

Pulp-Lit
PRODUCTIONS
CORVALLIS, OREGON

He drew a short dagger from his pocket; at the same moment the figure turned its face towards him. It gave a half unearthly scream as its eyes met those of the baron, who exclaimed, "Now — now's the time — death to the monster!" As he spoke, he threw himself headlong on the prostrate form of the vampyre .... (see page 726)

PART II:

A Disturbance at Anderbury House.

XCIII.

THE ALARM AT ANDERBURY. — THE SUSPICIONS OF THE BANNERWORTH FAMILY, AND THE MYSTERIOUS COMMUNICATION.

BOUT TWENTY miles to the southward of Bannerworth Hall was a good-sized market-town, called Anderbury. It was an extensive and flourishing place, and from the beauty of its situation, and its contiguity to the southern coast of England, it was much admired; and, in consequence, numerous mansions and villas of great pretension had sprang up in its immediate neighbourhood.

Besides, there were some estates of great value, and one of these, called Anderbury-on-the-Mount, in consequence of the mansion itself, which was of an immense extent, being built upon an eminence, was to be let, or sold.

This town of Anderbury was remarkable not only for the beauty of its aspect, but likewise for the quiet serenity of its inhabitants, who were a prosperous, thriving race, and depended very much upon their own resources.

There were some peculiar circumstances why Anderbury-on-the-Mount was to let. It had been for a great number of years in possession of a family of the name of Milltown, who had resided there in great comfort and respectablity, until an epidemic disorder broke out, first among the servants, and then spreading to the junior branches of the family, and from them to their seniors, produced such devastation, that in the course of three weeks there was but one young man left of the whole family, and he, by native vigour of constitution, had baffled the disorder, and found himself alone in his ancestral halls, the last of his race.

Soon a settled melancholy took possession of him, and all that had formerly delighted him now gave him pain, inasmuch as it brought to his mind a host of recollections of the most agonising character.

In vain was it that the surrounding gentry paid him every possible attention, and endeavoured to do all that was in their power to alleviate the unhappy circumstances in which he was placed. If he smiled, it was in a sad sort, and that was very seldom; and at length he announced his intention of leaving the neighbourhood, and seeking abroad, and in change of scene, for that solace which he could not expect to find in his ancestral home, after what had occurred within its ancient walls.

There was not a chamber but which reminded him of the past — there was not a tree or a plant of any kind or description but which spoke to him plainly of those who were now no more, and whose merry laughter had within his own memory made that ancient place echo with glee, filling the sunny air with the most gladsome shouts, such as come from the lips of happy youth long before the world has robbed it of any of its romance or its beauty.

There was a general feeling of regret when this young man announced the fact of his departure to a foreign land; for he was much respected, and the known calamities which he had suffered, and the grief under which he laboured, invested his character with a great and painful interest.

An entertainment was given to him upon the eve of his departure, and on the next day he was many miles from the place, and the estate of Anderbury-on-the-Mount was understood to be sold or let.

The old mansion had remained, then, for a year or two vacant, for it was a place of too much magnitude, and required by far too expensive an establishment to keep it going, to enable any person whose means were not very large to think of having anything to do with it.

So, therefore, it remained unlet, and wearing that gloomy aspect which a large house, untenanted, so very quickly assumes.

It was quite a melancholy thing to look upon it, and to think what it must have once been, and what it might be still, compared to what it actually was; and the inhabitants of the neighbourhood had made up their minds that Anderbury-on-the-Mount would remain untenanted for many a year to come, and, perhaps, ultimately fall into ruin and decay.

But in this they were doomed to be disappointed, for, on the evening of a dull and gloomy day, about one week after the events we have recorded as taking place at Bannerworth Hall and its immediate neighbourhood, a travelling carriage, with four horses and an out-rider, came dashing into the place, and drew up at the principal inn in the town, which was called the Anderbury Arms.

The appearance of such an equipage, although not the most unusual thing in the world, in consequence of the many aristocratic families who resided in the neighbourhood, caused, at all events, some sensation, and, perhaps, the more so because it drove up to the inn instead of to any of the mansions of the neighbourhood, thereby showing that the stranger, whoever he was, came not as a visitor, but either merely baited in the town, being on his road somewhere else, or had some special business in it which would soon be learned.

The out-rider, who was in handsome livery, had gallopped on in advance of the carriage a short distance, for the purpose of ordering the best apartments in the inn to be immediately prepared for the reception of his master.

"Who is he?" asked the landlord.

"It's the Baron Stolmuyer Saltsburgh."

"Bless my heart, I never heard of him before; where did he come from — somewhere abroad I suppose?"

"I can't tell you anything of him further than that he is immensely rich, and is looking for a house. He has heard that there is one to let in this immediate neighbourhood, and that's what has brought him from London, I suppose."

"Yes, there is one; and it is called Anderbury-on-the-Mount."

"Well, he will very likely speak to you about it himself, for here he comes."

By this time the carriage had halted at the door of the hotel, and, the door being opened, and the steps lowered, there alighted from it a tall man attired in a kind of pelisse, or cloak, trimmed with rich fur, the body of it being composed of velvet. Upon his head he wore a travelling cap, and his fingers, as he grasped the cloak around him, were seen to be covered with rings of great value.

Such a personage, coming in such style, was, of course, likely to be honoured in every possible way by the landlord of the inn, and accordingly he was shown most obsequiously to the handsomest apartment in the house, and the whole establishment was put upon the alert to attend to any orders he might choose to give.

He had not been long in the place when he sent for the landlord, who, hastily scrambling on his best coat, and getting his wife to arrange the tie of his neckcloth, proceeded to obey the orders of his illustrious guest, whatever they might chance to be.

He found the Baron Stolmuyer reclining upon a sofa, and having thrown aside his velvet cloak, trimmed with rich fur, he showed that underneath it he wore a costume of great richness and beauty, although, certainly, the form of it covered was not calculated to set it off to any great advantage, for the baron was merely skin and bone, and looked like a man who had just emerged from a long illness, for his face was ghastly pale, and the landlord could not help observing that there was a strange peculiarity about his eyes, the reason of which he could not make out.

"You are the landlord of this inn, I presume," said the baron, "and, consequently, no doubt well acquainted with the neighbourhood?"

"I have the honour to be all that, sir. I have been here about sixteen years, and in that time I certainly ought to know something of the neighbourhood."

"'Tis well; some one told me there was a little cottage sort of place to let here, and as I am simple and retired in my habits I thought that it might possibly suit me."

"A little cottage, sir! There are certainly little cottages to let, but not such as would suit you; and if I might have presumed, sir, to think, I should have considered Anderbury-on-the-Mount, which is now to let, would have been the place for you. It is a large place, sir, and belonged to a good family, although they are now all dead and gone, except one, and it's he who wants to let the old place."

"Anderbury-on-the-Mount," said the baron, "was the name of the place mentioned to me; but I understood it was a little place."

"Oh! sir, that is quite a mistake; who told you so? It's the largest place about here; there are a matter of twenty-seven rooms in it, and it stands altogether upon three hundred acres of ground."

"And have you the assurance," said the baron, "to call that anything but a cottage, when the castle of the Stolmuyers, at Saltzburgh, has one suite of reception rooms thirty in number, opening into each other, and the total number of apartments in the and whole building is two hundred and sixty, it is surrounded by eight miles of territory."

"The devil!" said the landlord. "I beg your pardon, sir, but when I am astonished, I generally say the devil. They want eight hundred pounds a year for Anderbury-on-the-Mount."

"A mere trifle. I will sleep here to-night, and in the morning I will go and look at the place. It is near the sea?"

"Half a mile, sir, exactly, from the beach; and one of the most curious circumstances of all connected with it is, that there is a subterranean passage from the grounds leading right away down to the sea-coast. A most curious place, sir, partly put out of the cliff, with cellars in it for wine, and other matters, that in the height of summer are kept as cool as in the deep winter time. It's more for curiosity than use, such a place; and the old couple, that now take care of the house, make a pretty penny, I'll be bound, though they won't own it, by showing that part of the place."

"It may suit me, but I shall be able to give a decisive answer when I see it on the morrow. You will let my attendants have what they require, and see that my horses be well looked to."

"Certainly, oh! certainly sir, of course; you might go far, indeed, sir, before you found an inn where everything would be done as things are done here. Is there anything in particular, sir, you would like for dinner?"

"How can I tell that, idiot, until the dinner time arrives?"

"Well, but, sir, in that case, you know, we scarcely know what to do, because you see, sir, you understand —"

"It is very strange to me that you can neither see nor understand your duty. I am accustomed to having the dinner tables spread with all that money can procure; then I choose, but not before, what it suits me to partake of."

"Well, sir, that is a very good way, and perhaps we ain't quite so used to that sort of thing as we ought to be in these parts; but another time, sir, we shall know better what we are about, without a doubt, and I only hope, sir, that we shall have you in the neighbourhood for a long time; and so, sir, putting one thing to another, and then drawing a conclusion from both of them, you see, sir, you will be able to understand."

"Peace! begone! what is the use of all this bellowing to me — I want it not — I care not for it."

The baron spoke these words so furiously, that the landlord was rather terrified than otherwise, and left the room hastily, muttering to himself that he had never come across such a tiger, and wondering where the baron could have possibly come from, and what amount of wealth he could be possessed of that would enable him to live in such a princely style as he mentioned.

If the Baron Stolmuyer of Saltzburgh had wished ever so much to impress upon the minds of all persons in the neighbourhood the fact of his wealth and

importance, he could not have adopted a better plan to accomplish that object than by first of all impressing such facts upon the mind of the landlord of the Anderbury Arms, for in the course of another hour it was tolerably well spread all over the town, that never had there been such a guest at the Anderbury Arms; and that he called Anderbury-on-the-Mount, with all its rooms — all its outbuildings, and its three hundred acres of ground — a cottage.

This news spread like wildfire,

awaking no end of speculation, and giving rise to the most exaggerated rumours, so that a number of persons came to the inn on purpose to endeavour to get a look at the baron; but he did not stir from his apartments, so that these wondermongers were disappointed, and even forced to go away as wise as they came; but in the majority of cases they made up their minds that in the morning they should surely be able to obtain a glimpse of him, which was considered a great treat, for a man with an immense income is looked upon in England as a natural curiosity.

The landlord took his guest at his word as regards the dinner, and provided such a repast as seldom, indeed, graced the board at the Anderbury Arms — a repast sufficient for twenty people, and certainly which was a monstrous thing to set before one individual.

The baron, however, made no remark, but selected a portion from some of the dishes, and those dishes that he did select from, were of the simplest kind, and not such as the landlord expected him to take, so that he really paid about one hundred times the amount he ought to have done for what actually passed his lips.

And then what a fidget the landlord was in about his wines, for he doubted not but such a guest would be extremely critical and hard to please; but, to his great relief, the baron declined taking any wine, merely washing down his repast with a tumbler of cool water; and then, although the hour was very early, he retired at once to rest.

The landlord was not disposed to disregard the injunction which the baron had given him to attend carefully on his servants and horses, and after giving orders that nothing should be stinted as regarded the latter, he himself looked to the creature comforts of the former, and he did this with a double motive, for not only was he anxious to make the most he could out of the baron in the way of charges, but he was positively panting with curiosity to know more about so singular a personage, and he thought that surely the servants must be able to furnish him with some particulars regarding their eccentric master.

In this, however, he was mistaken, for although they told him all they knew, that amounted to so little as really not to be worth the learning.

They informed him that they had been engaged all in the last week, and that they knew nothing of the baron whatever, or where he came from, or what he was, excepting that he paid them most liberal wages, and was not very exacting in the service he required of them.

This was very unsatisfactory, and when the landlord started on a mission, which he considered himself bound to perform, to a Mr. Leek, in the town, who had the letting of Anderbury-on-the-Mount, he was quite vexed to think what a small amount of information he was able to carry to him.

"I can tell him," he said to himself as he went quickly towards the agent's residence; "I can tell him the baron's name, and that in the morning he wants to look at Anderbury-on-the-Mount; but that's all I know of him, except that he is a most extraordinary man — indeed, the most extraordinary that I ever came near."

Mr. Leek, the house agent, notwithstanding the deficiency of the facts contained in the landlord's statement, was well enough satisfied to hear that any one of apparent wealth was inquiring after the large premises to let, for, as he said truly to the landlord,—

"The commission on letting and receiving the rentals of such a property is no joke to me."

"Precisely," said the landlord. "I thought it was better to come and tell you at once, for there can be no doubt that he is enormously rich."

"If that be satisfactorily proved, it's of no consequence what he is, or who he is, and you may depend I shall be round to the inn early in the morning to attend upon him; and in that case, perhaps, if you have any conversation with him, you will be so good as to mention that I will show him over the premises at his own hour, and you shall not be forgotten, you may depend, if any arrangement is actually come to. It will be just as well for you to tell him what a nice property it is, and that it is to be let for eight hundred a year, or sold outright for eight thousand pounds."

"I will, you may depend, Mr. Leek. A most extraordinary man you will find him; not the handsomest in the world, I can tell you, but handsome is as handsome does, say I; and, if he takes Anderbury-on-the-Mount, I have no doubt but he will spend a lot of money in the neighbourhood, and we shall all be the better of that, of course, as you well know, sir."

This then was thoroughly agreed upon between these high contracting powers, and the landlord returned home very well satisfied, indeed, with the position in which he had put the affair, and resolved upon urging on the baron, as far as it lay within his power so to do, to establish himself in the neighbourhood, and to allow him to be purveyor-in-general to his household, which, if the baron continued in his liberal humour, would be unquestionably a very pleasant post to occupy.

XCIV.

THE VISITOR, AND THE DEATH IN THE SUBTERRANEAN PASSAGE.

BOUT AN HOUR and a half after the baron had retired to rest, and while the landlord was still creeping about enjoining silence on the part of the establishment, so that the slumbers of a wealthy and, no doubt, illustrious personage should not be disturbed, there arrived a horseman at the Anderbury Arms.

He was rather a singular-looking man, with a shifting, uneasy-looking glance, as if he were afraid of being suddenly pounced upon and surprised by some one; and although his apparel was plain, yet it was good in quality, and his whole appearance was such as to induce respectful attention.

The only singular circumstance was, that such a traveller, so well mounted, should be alone; but that might have been his own fancy, so that the absence of an attendant went for nothing. Doubtless, if the whole inn had not been in such a commotion about the illustrious and wealthy baron, this stranger would have received more consideration and attention than he did.

Upon alighting, he walked at once into what is called the coffee-room of the hotel, and after ordering some refreshments, of which he partook but sparingly, he said, in a mild but solemn sort of tone, to the waiter who attended upon him,—

"Tell the Baron Stolmuyer, of Saltzburgh, that there is one here who wants to see him."

"I beg your pardon, sir," said the waiter, "but the baron is gone to bed."

"It matters not to me. If you nor no one else in this establishment will deliver the message I charge you with, I must do so myself."

"I'll speak to my master, sir; but the baron is a very great gentleman indeed, and I don't think my master would like to have him disturbed."

The stranger hesitated for a time, and then he said,—

"Show me the baron's apartment. Perhaps I ought not to ask any one person connected with this establishment to disturb him, when I am quite willing to do so myself. Show me the way."

"Well, but, sir, the baron may get in a rage, and say, very naturally, that we had

no business to let anybody walk up to his room and disturb him, because we wouldn't do so ourselves. So that you see, sir, when you come to consider, it hardly seems the right sort of thing."

"Since," said the stranger, rising, "I cannot procure even the common courtesy of being shown to the apartment of the person whom I seek, I must find him myself."

As he spoke he walked out of the room and began ascending the staircase, despite the remonstrances of the waiter, who called after him repeatedly, but could not induce him to stop; and when he found that such was the case, he made his way to the landlord, to give the alarm that, for all he knew to the contrary, some one had gone up stairs to murder the baron.

This information threw the landlord into such a fix, that he knew not what to be at. At one moment he was for rushing up stairs and endeavouring to interfere, and at another he thought the best plan would be to pretend that he knew nothing about it.

While he was in this state of uncertainty, the stranger succeeded in making his way up stairs to the floor from which proceeded the bedrooms, and, apparently, having no fear whatever of the Baron Stolmuyer's indignation before his eyes, he opened door after door, until he came to one which led him into the apartment occupied by that illustrious individual.

The baron, half undressed only, lay in an uneasy slumber upon the bed, and the stranger stood opposite to him for some minutes, as if considering what he should do.

"It would be easy," he said, "to kill

him; but it will pay me better to spare him. I may be wrong in supposing that he has the means which I hope he has; but that I shall soon discover by his conversation."

Stretching out his hand, he tapped the baron lightly on the shoulder, who thereupon opened his eyes and sprang to his feet instantly, glancing with fixed earnestness at the intruder, upon whose face shone the light of a lamp which was burning in the apartment.

Then the baron shrank back, and the stranger, folding his arms, said, —

"You know me. Let our interview be as brief as possible. There needs no explanations between us, for we both know all that could be said. By some accident you have become rich, while I continue quite otherwise. It matters not how this has occurred, the fact is everything. I don't know the amount of your possessions; but, from your style of living, they must be great, and therefore it is that I make no hesitation in asking of you, as a price for not exposing who and what you are, a moderate sum."

"I thought that you were dead."

"I know you did; but you behold me here, and, consequently, that delusion vanishes."

"What sum do you require, and what assurance can I have that, when you get it, the demand will not be repeated on the first opportunity?"

"I can give you no such assurance, perhaps, that would satisfy you entirely; but, for more reasons than I choose to enter into, I am extremely anxious to leave England at once and for ever. Give me the power to do so that I require, and you will never hear of me again."

The baron hesitated for some few seconds, during which he looked scrutinizingly at his companion, and then he said, in a tone of voice that seemed as if he were making the remark to himself rather than to the other, —

"You look no older than you did when last we parted, and that was years ago."

"Why should I look older? You know as well as I that I need not. But, to be brief, I do not wish to interfere with any plans or projects you may have on hand. I do not wish to be a hindrance to you. Let me have five thousand pounds, and I am off at once and for ever, I tell you."

"Five thousand! the man raves — five thousand pounds! Say one thousand, and it is yours."

"No; I have fixed my price; and if you do not consent, I now tell you that I will blazon forth, even in this house, who and what you are; and, let your schemes of ambition or of cupidity be what they may, you may be assured that I will blast them all."

"This is no place in which to argue such a point; come out into the open air; 'walls have ears;' but come out, and I will give you such special reasons why you should not now press your claim at all, that you shall feel much beholden to me for them, and not regret your visit."

"If that we come to terms, I no more desire than you can do that any one should overhear our conversation. I prefer the open air for any conference, be it whatever it may — much prefer it; and therefore most willingly embrace your proposition. Come out."

The baron put on his travelling cap, and the rich velvet cloak, edged with fur, that he possessed, and leaving his chamber a few paces in advance of his strange visitor, he descended the staircase, followed by him. In the hall of the hotel they found the landlord and almost the whole of the establishment assembled, in deep consultation as to whether or not any one was to go up stairs and a certain if the stranger who had sought the baron's chamber was really a friend or an enemy.

But when they saw the two men coming down, at all events apparently amicably, it was a great relief, and the landlord rushed forward and opened the door, for which piece of service he got a very stately bow from the baron, and a slight inclination of the head from his visitor, and then they both passed out.

"I have ascertained," said the man who came on horseback, "that for the last week in London you have lived in a style of the most princely magnificence, and that you came down here, attended as if you were one of the first nobles of the land."

"These things amuse the vulgar," said the baron. "I do not mind admitting to you that I contemplate residing on this spot, and perhaps contracting a marriage."

"Another marriage?"

"And why not? If wives will die suddenly, and no one knows why, who is to help it. I do not pretend to control the fates."

"This, between us, is idle talk indeed — most idle; for we know there are certain circumstances which account for the strangest phenomena; but what roaring sound is that which comes so regularly and steadily upon the ear."

"It is the sea washing upon the coast. The tide is no doubt advancing, and, as the eddying surges roll in upon the pebbly shore, they make what, to my mind, is this pleasant music."

"I did not think we were so near the ocean. The moon is rising; let us walk upon the beach, and as that sound is such pleasant music, you shall hear it while I convince you what unpleasant consequences will arise from a refusal of the modest and moderate terms I offer you."

"We shall see, we shall see; but I must confess it does seem to me most extraordinary that you ask of me a positive fortune, for fear you should deprive me of a portion of one; but you cannot mean what you say."

While they were talking they reached a long strip of sand which was by the seashore, at the base of some cliffs, through which was excavated the passage from the coast into the grounds of Anderbury House, and which had been so expatiated upon by the landlord of the inn, in his description of the advantages attendant upon that property.

There were some rude steps, leading to a narrow arched door-way, which constituted an entrance to this subterraneous region; and as the moonlight streamed over the wide waste of waters, and fell upon this little door-way in the face of the cliff, he became convinced that it was the entrance to that excavation, and he eyed it curiously.

"What place is that?" said his companion.

"It is a private entrance to the grounds of a mansion in this neighbourhood."

"Private enough, I should presume; for if there be any other means of reaching the house, surely no one would go through such a dismal hole as that towards it; but come, make up your mind at once. There need be no quarrelling upon the subject of our conference, but let it be a plain matter of yes or no. Is it worth your while to be left alone in peace, or is it not?"

"It is worth my while, but not at such a price as that you mentioned; and I cannot help thinking that some cheaper mode of accomplishing the same object will surely present itself very shortly."

"I do not understand you; you talk ambiguously."

"But my acts," said the baron, "shall be clear and plain enough, as you shall see. Could you believe it possible that I was the sort of person to submit timely to any amount of extortion you chose to practise upon me. There was a time when I thought you possessed great sense and judgment, when I thought that you were a man who weighed well the chances of what you were about; but now I know to the contrary; and I think for less than a thousand pounds I may succeed in ridding myself of you."

"I do not understand you; you had better beware how you tamper with me, for I am not one who will be calmly disposed to put up with much. The sense, tact, and worldly knowledge which you say you have before, from time to time, given me credit for, belongs to me still, and I am not likely easily to commit myself."

"Indeed; do yo think you bear such a charmed life that nothing can shake it?"

"I think nothing of the sort; but I know what I can do—I am armed."

"And I; and since it comes to this, take the reward of your villany; for it was you who made me what I am, and would now seek to destroy my every hope of satisfaction."

As the baron spoke he drew from breast a small pistol, which, with the quickness of thought, he held full in the face of his companion, and pulled the trigger.

There can be no doubt on earth but that his intention was to commit the murder, but the pistol missed fire, and he was defeated in his intention at that moment. Then the stranger laughed scornfully, and drawing a pistol from his pocket, he presented it at the baron's head, saying,—

"Do I not bear a charmed life? If I had not, should I have escaped death from you now? No, I could not; but you perceive that even a weapon that might not fail you upon another occasion is harmless against me; and can you expect that I will hesitate now to take full and ample revenge upon you for this dastardly attempt?"

These words were spoken with great volubility, so much so, indeed, that they only occupied a few very brief seconds in delivering; and then, perhaps, the baron's career might have ended, for it seemed to be fully the intention of the other to conclude what he said by firing the pistol in his face; but the wily aspect of the baron's countenance was, after all, but a fair index of the mind, and, just as the last words passed the lips of his irritated companion, he suddenly dropped in a crouching position to the ground, and, seizing his legs, threw him over his head in an instant.

The pistol was discharged, at the same moment, and then, with a shout of rage and satisfaction, the baron sprang upon his foe, and, kneeling upon his breast, he held aloft in his hand a glittering dagger, the highly-polished blade of which caught the moonbeams, and reflected them into the dazzled eyes of the conquered man, whose fate now appeared to be certain.

"Fool!" said the baron, "you must needs, then, try conclusions with me, and, not content with the safety of insignificance, you must be absurd enough to think it possible you could extort from me whatever sums your fancy dictated, or with any effect threaten me, if I complied not with your desires."

"Have mercy upon me. I meant not to take your life; and, therefore, why should you take mine?"

"You would have taken it, and, therefore, you shall die. Know, too, at this your last moment, that, vampyre as you are, and as I, of all men, best know you to be, I will take especial care that you shall be placed in some position after death where the revivifying moonbeams may not touch you, so that this shall truly be your end, and you shall rot away, leaving no trace behind of your existence, sufficient to contain the vital principle."

"No — no! you cannot — will not. You will have mercy."

"Ask the famished tiger for mercy, when you intrude upon his den."

As he spoke the baron ground his teeth together with rage, and, in an instant, buried the poniard in the throat of his victim. The blade went through to the yellow sand beneath, and the murderer still knelt upon the man's chest, while he who had thus received so fatal a blow tossed his arms about with agony, and tried in vain to shriek.

The nature of the wound, however, prevented him from utttering anything but a low gurgling sound, for he was nearly choked with his own blood, and soon his eyes became fixed and of a glassy appearance; he stretched out his two arms, and dug his fingers deep into the sand.

The baron drew forth the poniard, and a gush of blood immediately followed it, and then one deep groan testified to the fact, that the spirit, if there be a spirit, had left its mortal habitation, and winged its flight to other realms, if there be other realms for it to wing its flight to.

"He is dead," said the baron, and, at the same moment, a roll of the advancing tide swept over the body, drenching the living, as well as the dead, with the brine of the ocean.

The baron stooped and rinsed the dagger in the advancing tide from the clotted blood which had clung to it, and then, wiping it carefully, he returned it to its sheath, which was hidden within the folds of his dress; and, rising from his kneeling posture upon the body, he stood by its side, with folded arms, gazing upon it, for some minutes, in silence, heedless of the still advancing water, which was already considerably above his feet.

Then he spoke in his ordinary accents, and evidently caring nothing for the fact that he had done such a deed.

"I must dispose of this carcase," he said, "which now seems so lifeless, for the moon is up, and if its beams fall upon it, I know, from former experience, what will happen; it will rise again, and walk the earth, seeking for vengeance upon me, and the thirst for that vengeance will become such a part of its very nature, that it will surely accomplish something, if not all that it desires."

After a few moments' consideration, he stooped, and, with more strength than one would have thought it possible a man reduced almost, as he was, to a skeleton could have exerted, he lifted the body, and carried it rapidly up the beach towards the cliffs. He threw it down upon the stone steps that led to the small door of the excavation in the cliff, and it fell upon them with a sickening sound, as if some of the bones were surely broken by the fall.

The object, then, of the baron seemed to be to get this door open, if he possibly could; but that was an object easier to be desired than carried into effect, for, although he exerted his utmost power, he did not succeed in moving it an inch, and he began evidently to think that it would be impossible to do so.

But yet he did not give up the attempt at once, but looking about upon the beach, until he found a large heavy stone, he raised it in his arms, and, approaching the door, he flung it against it with such tremendous force, that it flew open instantly, disclosing within a dark and narrow passage.

Apparently rejoiced that he had accomplished this much, he stepped cautiously within the entrance, and then, taking from a concealed pocket that was in the velvet cloak which he wore a little box, he produced from it some wax-lights and some chemical matches, which, by the slightest effort, he succeeded in igniting, and then, with one of the lights in his hand to guide him on his way, he went on exploring the passage, and treading with extreme caution as he went, for fear of falling into any of the ice-wells which were reported to be in that place.

After proceeding about twenty yards, and finding that there was no danger, he became less cautious; but, in consequence of such less caution, he very nearly sacrificed his life, for he came upon an ice-well which seemed a considerable depth, and into which he had nearly plunged headlong.

He started back with some degree of horror; but that soon left him, and then, after a moment's thought, he sought for some little nook in the wall, in which he might place the candle, and soon finding one that answered the purpose well, he there left it, having all the appearance of a little shrine, while he proceeded again to the mouth of that singular and cavernous-looking place. He had, evidently, quite made up his mind what to do, for, without a moment's hesitation, he lifted the body again, and carried it within the entrance, walking boldly and firmly, now that he knew there was no danger between him and the light, which shed a gleam through the darkness of the place of a very faint and flickering character.

He reached it rapidly, and when he got to the side of the well, he, without a moment's hesitation, flung it headlong down, and, listening attentively, he heard it fall with a slight plash, as if there was some water at the bottom of the pit.

It was an annoyance, however, for him to find that the distance was not so deep as he had anticipated, and when he took the light from the niche where he had placed it, and looked earnestly down, he could see the livid, ghastly-looking face of the dead man, for the body had accidentally fallen upon its back, which was a circumstance he had not counted upon, and one which increased the chances greatly of its being seen, should any one be exploring, from curiosity, that not very inviting place.

This was annoyance, but how could it be prevented, unless, indeed, he chose to descend, and make an alteration in the disposition of the corpse? But this was evidently what he did not choose to do; so, after muttering to himself a few words expressive of his intention to leave it where it was, he replaced the candle, after extinguishing it, in the box from whence he had taken it, and carefully walked out of the dismal place.

The moonbeams were shining very brightly and beautifully upon the face of the cliffs, when he emerged from the subterranean passage, so that he could see the door, the steps, and every object quite distinctly; and, to his gratification, he found that he had not destroyed any fastening that was to the door, but that when it was slammed shut, it struck so hard and fast, that the strength of one man could not possibly move it, even the smallest fraction of an inch.

"I shall be shown all this to-morrow," he said; "and if I take this house I must have an alteration made in this door, so that it may open with a lock, instead of by main violence, as at present; but if, in the morning, when I view Anderbury House, I can avoid an entrance into this region, I will do so, and at my leisure, if I become the possessor of the estate, I can explore every nook and cranny of it."

He then folded his cloak about him, after pulling the door as closely as he could. He walked slowly and thoughtfully back to the inn. It was quite evident that the idea of the murder he had committed did not annoy him in the least, and that in his speculations upon the subject he congratulated himself much upon having so far succeeded in getting rid of certainly a most troublesome acquaintance.

"'Tis well, indeed," he said, "that just at this juncture he should throw himself in my way, and enable me so easy to feel certain that I shall never more be troubled with him. Truly, I ran some risk, and when my pistol missed fire, it seemed as if my evil star was in its ascendant, and that I was doomed myself to become the victim of him whom I have laid in so cold a grave. But I have been victorious, and I am willing to accept the circumstance as an omen of the past — that my fortunes are on the change. I think I shall be successful now, and with the ample means which I now possess, surely, in this country, where gold is loved so well, I shall be able to overcome all difficulties, and to unite myself to some one, who — but no matter, her fate is an after consideration."

XCV.

THE MARRIAGE IN THE BANNERWORTH FAMILY ARRANGED.

AFTER THE ADVENTURE of the doctor with regard to the picture about which such an air of mystery and interest has been thrown, the Bannerworth family began to give up all hopes of ever finding a clue to those circumstances concerning which they would certainly have liked to have known the truth, but of which it was not likely they would ever hear anything more.

Dr. Chillingworth now had no reserve, and when he had recovered sufficiently to feel that he could converse without an effort, he took an opportunity, while the whole of the family were present, to speak of what had been his hopes and his expectations.

"You are all aware," he said, "now, of the story of Marmaduke Bannerworth, and what an excessively troublesome person he was, with all deference, to you, Henry; first of all, as to spending all his money at the gaming-table, and leaving his family destitute; and then, when he did get a lump of money which might have done some good to those he left behind him — hiding it somewhere where it could not be found at all, and so leaving you all in great difficulty and distress, when you might have been independent."

"That's true enough, doctor," said Henry; "but you know the old proverb, — that ill-gotten wealth never thrives; so that I don't regret not finding this money, for I am sure we should have been none the happier with it, and perhaps not so happy."

"Oh, bother the old proverb; thirty or forty thousand pounds is no trifle to be talked lightly of, or the loss of which to be quietly put up with, on account of a musty proverb. It's a large sum, and I should like to have placed it in your hands."

"But as you cannot, doctor, there can be no good possibly done by regretting it."

"No, certainly; I don't mean that; utter regret is always a very foolish thing; but it's questionable whether something might not be done in the matter, after all, for you, as it appears, by all the evidence we can collect, that it must have been Varney, after all, who jumped down upon me from the garden-wall in so sudden a manner; and, if the picture be valuable to him, it must be valuable to us."

"But how are we to get it, and, if we could, I do not see that it would be of much value to anybody, for, after all, it is but a painting."

"There you go again," said the doctor, "depreciating what you know nothing about; now, listen to me, Master Henry, and I will tell you. That picture evidently had some sort of lining at the back, over the original canvas; and do you think I would have taken such pains to bring it away with me if that lining had not made me suspect that between it and the original picture the money, in bank notes, was deposited?"

"Had you any special reason for

supposing such was the case?"

"Yes; most unquestionably I had; for when I got the picture fairly down, I found various inequalities in the surface of the back, which led me to believe that rolls of notes were deposited, and that the great mistake we had all along made was in looking behind the picture, instead of at the picture itself. I meant immediately to have cut it to pieces when I reached here with it; but now it has got into the hands of somebody else, who knows, I suspect, as much I do."

"It is rather provoking."

"Rather provoking! is that the way to talk of the loss of Heaven knows how many thousands of pounds! I am quite aggravated myself at the idea of the thing, and it puts me in a perfect fever to think of it, I can assure you."

"But what can we do?"

"Oh! I propose an immediate crusade against Varney, the vampyre, for who but he could have made such an attack upon me, and force me to deliver up such a valuable treasure?"

"Never heed it, doctor," said Flora; "let it go; we have never had or enjoyed that money, so it cannot matter, and it is not to be considered as the loss of an actual possession, because we never did actually possess it."

"Yes," chimed in the admiral; "bother the money! what do we care about it; and, besides, Charley Holland is going to be very busy."

"Busy!" said the doctor; "how do you mean?"

"Why, isn't he going to be married directly to Flora, here, and am not I going to settle the whole of my property upon him on condition that he takes the name of Bell instead of Holland? for, you see, his mother was my sister, and of course her name was Bell. As for his father Holland, it can't matter to him now what Charley is called; and if he don't take the name of Bell I shall be the last in the family, for I am not likely to marry, and have any little Bells about me."

"No," said the doctor; "I should say not; and that's the reason why you want to ring the changes upon Charles Holland's name. Do you see the joke, admiral?"

"I can't say I do — where is it? It's all very well to talk of jokes, but if I was like Charles, going to be married, I shouldn't be in any joking humour, I can tell you, but quite the reverse; and as for you and your picture, if you want it, doctor, just run after Varney yourself for it; or, stay — I have a better idea than that — get your wife to go and ask him for it, and if she makes half such a clamour about his ears that she did about ours, he will give it her in a minute, to get rid of her."

"My wife! — you don't mean to say she has been here?"

"Yes, but she has though. And now, doctor, I can tell you I have seen a good deal of service in all parts of the world, and, of course, picked up a little experience; and, if I were you, some of these days, when Mrs. Chillingworth ain't very well, I'd give her a composing draught that would make her quiet enough."

"Ah! that's not my style of practice, admiral; but I am sorry to hear that Mrs. Chillingworth has annoyed you so much."

"Pho, pho, man! — pho, pho! do you think she could annoy me? Why, I have encountered storms and squalls in all latitudes, and it isn't a woman's tongue now that can do anything of an annoying character, I can tell you; far from it — very far from it; so don't distress yourself upon that head. But come, doctor, we are going to have the wedding the day after to-morrow."

"No, no," said Flora; "the week after next, you mean."

"Is it the week after next? I'll be hanged if I didn't think it was the day after tomorrow; but of course you know best, as you have settled it all among you. I have nothing to do with it."

"Of course, I shall, with great pleasure," returned the doctor, "be present on the interesting occasion; but do you intend taking possession of Bannerworth Hall again?"

"No, certainly not," said Henry; "we propose going to the Dearbrook estate, and there remaining for a time to see how we all like it. We may, perchance, enjoy it very much, for I have heard it spoken of as an attractive little property enough, and one that any one might fancy, after being resident a short time upon it."

"Well," said the admiral; "that is, I believe, settled among us, but I am sure we sha'n't like it, on account of the want of the sea. Why, I tell you, I have not seen a ship myself for this eighteen months; there's a state of things, you see, that won't do to last, because one would get dry-mouldy; it's a shocking thing to see nothing but land, land, wherever you go."

From the preceding conversation may be gathered what were the designs of the Bannerworth family, and what progress had been made in carrying them out. From the moment they had discovered the title-deeds of the Dearbrook property, they had ceased to care about the large sum of money which Marmaduke Bannerworth had been supposed to have hidden in some portion of Bannerworth Hall.

They had already passed through quite enough of the busy turmoils of existence to be grateful for anything that promised ease and competence, and that serenity of mind which is the dearest possession which any one can compass.

Consequently was it, that, with one accord, they got rid of all yearning after the large sum which the doctor was so anxious to procure for them, and looked forward to a life of great happiness and contentment. On the whole, too, when they came to talk the matter over quietly among themselves, they were not sorry that Varney had taken himself off in the way he had, for really it was a great release; and, as he had couched his farewell in words which signified it was a final one, they were inclined to think that he must have left England, and that it was not likely they should ever again encounter him, under any circumstances whatever.

It was to be considered quite as a whim of the old admiral's, the changing of Charles Holland's name to Bell; but, as Charles himself said when the subject was broached to him, — "I am so well content to be called whatever those to whom I feel affection think proper, that I give up my name of Holland without a pang, willingly adopting in its stead one that has always been hallowed in my remembrance with the best and kindest recollections."

And thus this affair was settled, much to the satisfaction of Flora, who was quite as well content to be called Mrs. Bell as to be called Mrs. Holland, since the object of her attachment remained the same. The wedding was really fixed for the week after that which followed the conversation we have recorded; but the admiral was not at all disposed to allow Flora and his nephew Charles to get through such an important period of their lives without some greater demonstration and show than could be made from the little cottage where they dwelt; and consequently he wished that they should leave that and proceed at once to a larger mansion, which he had his eye upon a few miles off, and which was to be had furnished for a time, at the pleasure of any one.

"And we won't shut ourselves up," said the admiral; "but we will find out all the Christian-like people in the neighbourhood, and invite them to the wedding, and we will have a jolly good breakfast together, and lots of music, and a famous lunch; and, after that, a dinner, and then a dance, and all that sort of thing; so that there shall be no want of fun."

As may be well supposed, both Charles and Flora shrunk from so public an affair; but, as the old man had evidently set his heart upon it, they did not like to say they positively would not; so, after a vain attempt to dissuade him from removing at all from the cottage until they removed for good, they gave up the point to him, and he had it all his own way.

He took the house, for one month, which had so taken his fancy, and certainly a pretty enough place it was, although they found out afterwards, that why it was he was so charmed with it consisted in the fact that it bore the name of a vessel which he had once commanded; but this they did not know until a long time afterwards, when it slipped out by mere accident.

They stipulated with the admiral that there should not be more than twenty guests at the breakfast which was to succeed the marriage ceremony; and to that he acceded; but Henry whispered to Charles Holland,—

"I know this public wedding to be distasteful to you, and most particularly do I know it is distasteful to Flora; so, if you do not mind playing a trick upon the old man, I can very easily put you in the way of cheating him entirely."

"Indeed; I should like to hear, and, what is more, I should like to practise, if you think it will not so entirely offend him as to make him implacable."

"Not at all, not at all; he will laugh himself, when he comes to know it, as much as any of us; the present difficulty will be to procure Flora's connivance; but that we must do the best way we can by persuasion."

What this scheme was will ultimately appear; but, certain it is, that the old admiral had no suspicion of what was going on and proceeded to make all his arrangements accordingly.

From his first arrival in the market town—in the neighbourhood of which was Bannerworth Hall—it will be recollected that he had taken a great fancy to the lawyer, in whose name a forged letter had been sent him, informing him of the fact that his nephew, Charles Holland, intended marrying into a family of vampyres.

It was this letter, as the reader is aware, which brought the old admiral and Jack Pringle into the neighbourhood of the Hall; and, although it was a manoeuvre to get rid of Charles Holland, which failed most signally, there can be no doubt but that such a letter was the production of

Sir Francis Varney, and that he wrote it for the express purpose of getting rid of Charles from the Hall, who had begun materially to interfere with his plans and projects there.

After some conversation with himself, the admiral thought that this lawyer would be just the man to recommend the proper sort of people to be invited to the wedding of Charles and Flora; so he wrote to him, inviting himself to dinner, and received back a very gracious reply from the lawyer, who declared that the honour of entertaining a gentleman whom he so much respected as Admiral Bell, was greater than he had a right to expect by a great deal, and that he should feel most grateful for his company, and await his coming with the greatest impatience.

"A devilish civil fellow, that attorney," said the admiral, as he put the letter in his pocket, "and almost enough to put one in conceit of lawyers."

"Yes," said Jack Pringle, who had overheard the admiral read the letter. "Yes, we will honour him; and I only hope he will have plenty of grog; because, you see, if he don't — D — n it! what's that! Can't you keep things to yourself?"

This latter exclamation arose from the fact that the admiral was so indignant at Jack for listening to what he had been saying, as to throw a leaden inkstand, that happened to be upon the table, at his head.

"You mutinous swab!" he said, "cannot a gentleman ask me to dinner, or cannot I ask myself, without you putting your spoke in the windlass, you vagabond?"

"Oh! well," said Jack, "if you are out of temper about it, I had better send my mark to the lawyer, and tell him that we won't come, as it has made some family differences."

"Family, you thief!" said the admiral. "What do you mean? What family do you think would own you? D — n me, if I don't think you came over in some strange ship. But, I tell you what it is, if you interfere in this matter, I'll be hanged if I don't blow your brains out."

"And you'll be hanged if you do," said Jack, as he walked out of the room; "so it's all one either way, old fizgig."

"What!" roared the admiral, as he sprang up and ran after Jack. "Have I lived all these years to be called names in my own ship — I mean my own house? What does the infernal rascal mean by it?"

The admiral, no doubt, would have pursued Jack very closely, had not Flora intercepted him, and, by gentle violence, got him back to the room. No one else could have ventured to have stopped him, but the affection he had for her was so great that she could really accomplish almost anything with him; and, by listening quietly to his complaints of Jack Pringle — which, however, involved a disclosure of the fact which he had intended to keep to himself, that he had sought the lawyer's advice — she succeeded in soothing him completely, so that he forgot his anger in a very short time.

But the old man's anger, although easily aroused, never lasted very long; and, upon the whole, it was really astonishing what he put up with from Jack Pringle, in the way of taunts and sneers, of all sorts and descriptions, and now and then not a little real abuse.

And, probably, he thought likewise that Jack Pringle did not mean what he said, on the same principle that he (the admiral), when he called Jack a mutinous swab and a marine, certainly did not mean that Jack was those things, but merely used them as expletives to express a great amount of indignation at the moment, because, as may be well supposed, nothing in the world could be worse, in Admiral Bell's estimation, that to be a mutinous swab or a marine.

It was rather a wonder, though, that, in his anger some day, he did not do Jack some mischief; for, as we have had occasion to notice in one or two cases, the admiral was not extremely particular as to what sorts of missiles he used when he considered it necessary to throw something at Jack's head.

It would not have been a surprising thing if Jack had really made some communication to the lawyer; but he did stop short at that amount of pleasantry, and, as he himself expressed it, for once in a way he let the old man please himself.

The admiral soon forgot this little dispute, and then pleased himself with the idea that he should pass a pleasant day with the attorney.

"Ah! well," he said; "who would have thought that ever I should have gone and taken dinner with a lawyer — and not only done that, but invited myself too! It shows us all that there may be some good in all sorts of men, lawyers included; and I am sure, after this, I ought to begin to think what I never thought before, and that is, that a marine may actually be a useful person. It shows that, as one gets older, one gets wiser."

It was an immense piece of liberality for a man brought up, as Admiral Bell had been, in decidedly one of the most prejudiced branches of the public service, to make any such admissions as these. A very great thing it was, and showed a liberality of mind such as, even at the present time, is not readily found.

It is astonishing, as well as amusing, to find how the mind assimilates itself to the circumstances in which it is placed, and how society, being cut up into small sections, imagines different things merely as a consequence of their peculiar application. We shall find that even people, living at different ends of a city, will look with a sort of pity and contempt upon each other; and it is much to be regretted that public writers are found who use what little ability they may possess in pandering to their feelings.

It was as contemptible and silly as it was reprehensible for a late celebrated novelist to pretend that he believed there was a place called Bloomsbury-square, but he really did not know; because that was merely done for the purpose of raising a silly laugh among persons who were neither respectable on account of their abilities or their conduct.

But to return from this digression. The admiral, attired in his best suit, which always consisted of a blue coat, the exact colour of the navy uniform, an immense pale primrose-coloured waistcoat, and white kerseymere continuations, went to the lawyer's as had been arranged.

If anything at all could flatter the old man's vanity successfully, it certainly would be the manner in which he was received at the lawyer's house, where everything was done that could give him satisfaction.

A very handsome repast was laid before him, and, when the cloth was removed, the admiral broached the subject upon which he wished to ask the advice of his professional friend. After telling him of the wedding that was to come off, he said,—

"Now, I have bargained to invite twenty people; and, of course, as that is exclusive of any of the family, and as I don't know any people about this neighbourhood except yourself, I want you and your family to come to start with, and then I want you to find me out some more decent people to make up the party."

"I feel highly flattered," said the attorney, "that, in such a case as this, you should have come to me, and my only great fear is, that I should not be able to give you satisfaction."

"Oh! you needn't be afraid of that; there is no fear on that head; so I shall leave it all to you to invite the folks that you think proper."

"I will endeavour, certainly, admiral, to do my best. Of course, living in the town, as I have for many years, I know some very nice people as well as some very queer ones."

"Oh! we don't want any of the queer ones; but let those who are invited be frank, hearty, good-tempered people, such as one will be glad to meet over and over again without any ceremony—none of your simpering people, who are afraid to laugh for fear of opening their mouths too wide, but who are so mightily genteel that they are afraid to enjoy anything for fear it should be vulgar."

"I understand you, admiral, perfectly, and shall endeavour to obey your instructions to the very letter; but, if I should unfortunately invite anybody you don't like, you must excuse me for making such a mistake."

"Oh, of course—of course. Never mind that; and if any disagreeable fellow comes, we will smother him in some way."

"It would serve him right, for no one ought to make himself diagreeable, after being honoured with an invitation from you; but I will be most especially careful, and I hope that such a circumstance will not occur."

"Never mind. If it should, I'll tell you what I'll do; I'll set Jack Pringle upon him, and if he don't worry his life out it will be a strange thing to me."

"Oh," said the lawyer, "I am glad you have mentioned him, for it gives me an opportunity of saying that I have done all in my power to make him comfortable."

"All in your power to make him comfortable! What do you mean?"

"I mean that I have placed such a dinner before him as will please him; I told him to ask for just whatever he likes."

The admiral looked at the lawyer with amazement, for a few moments, in silence, and then he said,

"D — n it! why, you don't mean to tell me, that that rascal is here."

"Oh yes; he came about ten minutes before you arrived, and said you were coming, and he has been down stairs feasting all the while since."

"Stop a bit. Do you happen to have any loaded fire arms in the house?"

"We have got an old blunderbuss; but what for, admiral?"

"To shoot that scoundrel, Pringle. I'll blow his brains out, as sure as fate. The impudence of his coming here, directly against my orders, too."

"My dear sir, calm yourself, and think

nothing of it; it's of no consequence whatever."

"No consequence; where is that blunderbuss of yours? Do you mean to tell me that mutiny is of no consequence? Give me the blunderbuss."

"But, my dear sir, we only keep it *in terrorem*, and have no bullets."

"Never mind that, we can cram in a handful of nails, or brass buttons, or hammer up a few halfpence — anything of that sort will do to settle his business with."

"How do you get on, old Tarbarrel?" said Jack, putting his head in at the door. "Are you making yourself comfortable? I'll be hanged if I don't think you have a drop too much already, you look so precious red about the gills. I have been getting on famous, and I thought I'd just hop up for a minute to make your mind easy about me, and tell you so."

It was quite evident that Jack had done justice to the good cheer of the lawyer, for he was rather unsteady, and had to hold by the door-post to support himself, while there was such a look of contentment upon his countenance as contrasted with the indignation that was manifest upon the admiral's face, that, as the saying is, it would have made a cat laugh to see them.

"Be off with ye, Jack," said the lawyer; "be off with ye. Go down stairs again and enjoy yourself. Don't you see that the admiral is angry with you."

"Oh, he be bothered," said Jack; "I'll soon settle him if he comes any of his nonsense; and mind, Mr. Lawyer, whatever you do, don't you give him too much to drink."

The lawyer ran to the door, and pushed Jack out, for he rightly enough suspected that the quietness of the admiral was only that calm which precedes a storm of more than usual amount and magnitude, so he was anxious to part them at once.

He then set about appeasing, as well as he could, the admiral's anger, by attributing the perseverance of Jack, in following him wherever he went, to his great affection for him, which, combined with his ignorance, might make him often troublesome when he had really no intention of being so.

This was certainly the best way of appeasing the old man; and, indeed, the only way in which it could be done successfully, and the proof that it was so, consisted in the fact, that the admiral did consent, at the suggestion of the attorney, to forgive Jack once more for the offence he had committed.

XCVI.

THE BARON TAKES ANDERBURY HOUSE, AND DECIDES UPON GIVING A GRAND ENTERTAINMENT.

IT WAS NOT CONSIDERED anything extraordinary that, although the Baron Stolmuyer of Saltzburgh went out with the mysterious stranger who had arrived at the Anderbury Arms to see him, he should return without him, for certainly he was not bound to bring him back, by any means whatever.

Moreover, he entered the inn so quietly, and with such an appearance of perfect composure, that no one could have suspected for a moment that he had been guilty really of the terrific crime which had been laid to his charge — a crime which few men could have committed in so entirely unmoved and passionless a manner as he had done it.

But he seemed to consider the taking of a human life as a thing not of the remotest consequence, and not to be considered at all as a matter which was to put any one out of the way, but as a thing to be done when necessity required, with all the ease in the world, without arousing or awaking any of those feelings of remorse which one would suppose ought to find a place in the heart of a man who had been guilty of such monstrous behaviour.

He walked up to his own apartment again, and retired to rest with the same feeling, apparently, of calmness, and the same ability to taste of the sweets of repose as had before characterized him.

The stranger's horse, which was a valuable and beautiful animal, remained in the stable of the inn, and as, of course, that was considered a guarantee for his return, the landlord, when he himself retired to rest, left one of his establishment sitting up to let in the man who now lay so motionless and so frightful in appearance in one of the ice-wells of the mysterious passage leading from the base of the cliffs to the grounds of Anderbury House.

But the night wore on, and the man who had been left to let the stranger in, after making many efforts to keep himself awake, dropped into sound repose, which he might just as well have done in the first instance, inasmuch as, although he knew it not, he was engaged in the vain task of waiting for the dead.

THE MORNING WAS fresh and beautiful, and, at a far earlier hour than a person of his quality was expected to make his appearance, the baron descended from his chamber; for, somehow or other, by common consent, it seems to be agreed that great personages must be late in rising, and equally late in going to bed.

But the baron was evidently not so disposed to turn night into day, and the landlord congratulated himself not a little upon the fact that he was ready for his illustrious guest when he descended so unexpectedly from his chamber as he did.

An ample breakfast was disposed of; that is to say, it was placed upon the table, and charged to the baron, who selected from it what he pleased; and when the meal was over the landlord ventured to enter the apartment, and said to him, with all due humility,—

"If you please, sir, Mr. Leek, who has the letting of Anderbury-on-the-Mount, that is, Anderbury House, as it is usually called, is here, sir, and would be happy to take your orders as to when you would be pleased to look at those premises?"

"I shall be ready to go in half an hour," said the baron; "and, as the distance is not great, I will walk from here to the mansion."

This message was duly communicated to Mr. Leek, who thereupon determined upon waiting until the baron should announce his readiness to depart upon the expedition; and he was as good as his word, for, in about half-an-hour afterwards, he descended to the hall, and then Mr. Leek was summoned, who came out of the bar with such a grand rush, that he fell over a mat that was before him, and saluted the baron by digging his head into his stomach, and then falling sprawling at his feet, and laying hold of his ankle.

This little incident was duly apologised for, and explained; after which Mr. Leek walked on through the town, towards Anderbury-on-the-Mount, followed by the illustrious personage whom he sincerely hoped he should be able to induce to take it.

It was a curious thing to see how they traversed the streets together; for while the baron walked right on, and with a solemn and measured step, Mr. Leek managed to get along a few paces in front of him, sideways, so that he could keep up a sort of conversation upon the merits of Anderbury House, and the neighbourhood in general, without much effort; to which remarks the baron made such suitable and dignified replies as a baron would be supposed to make.

"You will find, sir," said Mr. Leek, "that everything about Anderbury is extremely select, and amazingly correct; and I am sure a more delightful place to live in could not be found."

"Ah!" said the baron; "very likely."

"It's lively, too," continued Mr. Leek; "very lively; and there are two chapels of ease, besides the church."

"That's a drawback," said the baron.

"A drawback, sir! well, I am sorry I mentioned it; but perhaps you are a Roman Catholic, sir, and, in that case, the chapels of ease have no interest for you."

"Not the slightest; but do not, sir, run away with any assumption concerning my religious opinions, for I am not a Roman Catholic."

"No, sir, no, sir; nor more am I; and, as far as I think, and my opinion goes, I say, why shouldn't a gentleman with a large fortune be what he likes, or nothing, if he likes that better? but here we are, sir, close to one of the entrances of Anderbury House. There are three principal entrances, you understand, sir, on three sides of the estate, and the fourth side faces the sea, where there is that mysterious passage that leads down from the grounds to the beach, which, perhaps, you have heard of, sir."

"The landlord of the inn mentioned it."

"We consider it a great curiosity, sir, I can assure you, in these parts—a very great curiosity; and it's an immense advantage to the house, because, you see, sir, in extremely hot weather, all sorts of provisions can be taken down there, and kept at such a very low temperature as to be quite delightful."

"That is an advantage."

Mr. Leek rang the bell that hung over one of the entrances, and his summons for admission was speedily answered by the old couple who had charge of the premises, and then, with a view of impressing them with a notion of the importance of the personage whom he had brought to look at the place, he said, aloud,—

"The Baron Stoltmayor, of Saltsomething, has come to look at the premises."

This announcement was received with all due deference and respect, and the task of showing the baron the premises at once fairly commenced.

"Here you have," said Mr. Leek, assuming an oratorical attitude—"here you have the umbrageous trees stooping down to dip their leaves in the purling waters; here you have the sweet foliage lending a delicious perfume to the balmy air; here you have the murmuring waterfalls playing music of the spheres to the listening birds, who sit responsive upon the dancing boughs; here you have all the fragrance of the briny ocean, mingling with the scent of a bank of violets, and wrapping the senses in Elysium; here you may never tire of an existence that presents never-ending charms, and that, in the full enjoyment of which, you may live far beyond the allotted span of man."

"Enough—enough," said the baron.

"Here you have the choicest exotics taking kindly to a soil gifted by nature with the most extraordinary powers of production; and all that can pamper the appetite, or yield delight to the senses, is scattered around by nature with a liberal hand. It is quite impossible that royalty should come near the favoured spot without visiting it as a thing of course; and I forgot to mention that a revenue is derived from some cottages, which, although small, is yet sufficient to pay the tithe on the whole estate." *

"There, there—that will do."

"Here you have purling rills and cascades, and fish-ponds so redundant with the finny tribe, that you have but to wish for sport, and it is yours; here you have in the mansion, chambers that vie with the accommodation of a palace—ample dormitories and halls of ancient grandeur; here you have—"

"Stop," said the baron, "stop; I cannot be pestered in this way with your description. I have no patience to listen to such mere words—show me the house at once, and let me judge for myself."

"Certainly, sir; oh! certainly; only I thought it right to give you a slight description of the place as it really was; and now, sir, that we have reached the house, I may remark that here we have—"

"Silence!" said the baron; "if you begin with 'here we have,' I know not when you will leave off. All I require of you is to show me the place, and to answer any question which I may put to you concerning it. I will draw my own conclusions, and nothing you can say, one way or another, will affect my imagination."

---

* *Tithes, in Victorian England, were an obligatory percentage of landholders' revenues, usually 10 percent, that supported the Church of England.*

"Certainly, sir, certainly; I shall only be too happy to answer any questions that may be put to me by a person of your lordship's great intelligence; and all I can remark is, that when you reach the drawing-room floor, any person may truly say, here you have — I really beg your pardon, sir — I had not the slightest intention of saying 'here you have,' I assure you; but the words came out quite unawares, I assure you."

"Peace — peace!" cried again the baron; "you disturb me by this incessant clatter."

Thus admonished, Mr. Leek was now quiet, and allowed the baron in his own way to make what investigation he pleased concerning Anderbury House."

The investigation was not one that could be gone over in ten minutes; for the house was extremely extensive, and the estate altogether presented so many features of beauty and interest, that it was impossible not to linger over it for a considerable period of time.

The grounds were most extensive, and planted with such a regard to order and regularity, everything being in its proper place, that it was a pleasure to see an estate so well kept. And although the baron was not a man who said much, it was quite evident, by what little he did utter, that he was very well pleased with Anderbury-on-the-Mount.

"And now," said Mr. Leek, "I will do myself the pleasure, sir, of showing your grace the subterranean passage."

At this moment a loud ring at one of the entrance gates was heard, and upon the man who had charge of the house answering the summons for admission, he found that it was a gentleman, who gave a card on which was the name of Sir John Westlake, and who desired to see the premises.

"Sir John Westlake," said Mr. Leek; "oh! I recollect he did call at my office, and say that he thought of taking Anderbury-on-the-Mount. A gentleman of great wealth and taste is Sir John, but I must tell him, baron, that you have the preference if you choose to embrace it."

At this moment the stranger advanced, and when he saw the baron, he bowed courteously, upon which Mr. Leek said, —

"I regret, Sir John, that if you should take a fancy to the place, I am compelled first of all to give this gentleman the refusal of it."

"Certainly," said Sir John Westlake; "do not let me interfere with any one. I have nearly made up my mind, and came to look over the property again; but of course, if this gentleman is beforehand with me, I must be content. I wish particularly to go down to the subterranean passage to the beach, if it is not too much trouble."

"Trouble! certainly not, sir. Here, Davis, get some links,* and we can go at once; and as this gentleman likewise has seen everything but that strange excavation, he will probably descend with us."

"Certainly," said the baron; "I shall have great pleasure;" and he said it with so free and unembarrassed an air, that no one could have believed for a moment in the possibility that such a subject of fearful interest to him was there to be found.

The entrance from the grounds into

---

* *"Link" was a synonym for "torch."*

this deep cavernous place was in a small but neat building, that looked like a summer-house; and now, torches being procured, and one lit, a door was opened, which conducted at once into the commencement of the excavation; and Mr. Leek heading the way, the distinguished party, as that gentleman loved afterwards to call it in his accounts of the transaction, proceeded into the very bowels of the earth, as it were, and quickly lost all traces of the daylight.

The place did not descend by steps, but by a gentle slope, which it required some caution to traverse, because, being cut in the chalk, which in some places was worn very smooth, it was extremely slipperly; but this was a difficulty that a little practice soon overcame, and as they went on the place became more interesting every minute.

Even the baron allowed Mr. Leek to make a speech upon the occasion, and that gentleman said,—

"You will perceive that this excavation must have been made, at a great expense, out of the solid cliff, and in making it some of the most curious specimens of petrifaction and fossil remains were found. You see that the roof is vaulted, and that it is only now and then a lump of chalk has fallen in, or a great piece of flint; and now we come to one of the ice-wells."

The came to a deep excavation, down which they looked, and when the man held the torch beneath its surface, they could dimly see the bottom of it, where there was a number of large pieces of flint stone, and, apparently, likewise, the remains of broken bottles.

"There used to be a windlass at the top of this," said Mr. Leek, "and the things were let down in a basket. They do say that ice will keep for two years in one of these places."

"And are there more of these excavations?" said the baron.

"Oh, dear, yes, sir; there are five or six of them for different purposes; for when the family that used to live in Anderbury House had grand entertainments, which they sometimes had in the summer season, they always had a lot of men down here, cooling wines, and passing them up from hand to hand to the house."

From the gradual slope of this passage down to the cliffs, and the zigzag character of it, it may be well supposed that it was of considerable extent. Indeed, Mr. Leek asserted that it was half a mile in actual measured length.

The baron was not at all anxious to run any risk of a discovery of the dead body which he had cast into that ice-well which was nearest to the opening on to the beach, so, as he went on, he negatived the different proposals that were made to look down into the excavations, and succeeded in putting a stop to that species of inquiry in the majority of instances, but he could not wholly do so.

Perhaps it would have been better for his purpose if he had encouraged a look into every one of the ice-wells; for, in that case, their similarity of appearance might have tired out Sir John Westlake before they got to the last one; but as it was, when they reached the one down which the body had been precipitated, he had the mortification to hear Mr. Leek say,—

"And now, Sir John, and you, my lord baron, as we have looked at the first of these ice wells and at none of the others, suppose we look at the last."

The baron was afraid to say anything; because, if the body were discovered, and identified as that of the visitor at the inn, and who had been seen last with him, any reluctance on his part to have that ice-well examined, might easily afterwards be construed into a very powerful piece of circumstantial evidence against him.

He therefore merely bowed his assent, thinking that the examination would be but a superficial one, and that, in consequence, he should escape easily from any disagreeable consequences.

But this the fates ordained otherwise; and there seemed no hope of that ice-well in particular escaping such an investigation as was sure to induce some uncomfortable results.

"Davis," said Mr. Leek, "these places are not deep, you see, and I was thinking that if you went down one of them, it would be as well; for then you would be able to tell the gentlemen what the bottom was fairly composed of, you understand."

"Oh, I don't mind, sir," said Davis. "I have been down one of them before today, I can tell you, sir."

"I do not see the necessity," said Sir John Westlake, "exactly, of such a thing; but still if you please, and this gentleman wishes —"

"I have no wish upon the occasion," said the baron; "and, like yourself, cannot see the necessity."

"Oh, there is no trouble," said Mr. Leek; "and it's better, now you are here, that you see and understand all about it. How can you get down, Davis?"

"Why, sir, it ain't above fourteen feet altogether; so I sha'n't have any difficulty, for I can hang by my hands about half the distance, and drop the remainder."

As he spoke he took off his coat, and then stuck the link he carried into a cleft of the rock, that was beside the brink of the excavation.

The baron now saw that there would be no such thing as avoiding a discovery of the fact of the dead body being in that place, and his only hope was, that in its descent it might have become so injured as to defy identification.

But this was a faint hope, because he recollected that he had himself seen the face, which was turned upwards, and the period after death was by far too short for him to have any hope that decomposition could have taken place even to the most limited extent.

The light, which was stuck in a niche, shed but a few inefficient rays down into the pit, and, as the baron stood, with folded arms, looking calmly on, he expected each moment a scene of surprise and terror would ensue.

Nor was he wrong; for scarcely had the man plunged down into that deep place, than he uttered a cry of alarm and terror, and shouted,—

"Murder! murder! Lift me out. There is a dead man down here, and I have jumped upon him."

"A dead man!" cried Mr. Leek and Sir John Westlake in a breath.

"How very strange!" said the baron.

"Lend me a hand," cried Davis; "lend me a hand out; I cannot stand this, you know. Lend me a hand out, I say, at once."

This was easier to speak of than to do, and Mr. Davis began to discover that it wa easier by far to get into a deep pit, than to get out of one, notwithstanding that his assertion of having been down into those places was perfectly true; but then he had met with nothing alarming, and had been able perfectly at his leisure to scramble out the best way he could.

Now, however, his frantic efforts to release himself from a much more uncomfortable situation than he had imagined it possible for him to get into, were of so frantic a nature, that he only half buried himself in pieces of chalk, which he kept pulling down with vehemence from the sides of the pit, and succeeded in accomplishing nothing towards his rescue.

"Oh! the fellow is only joking," said the baron, "and amusing himself at our expense."

But the manner in which the man cried for help, and the marked terror which was in every tone, was quite sufficient to prove that he was not acting; for if he were, a more accomplished mimic could not have been found on the stage than he was.

"This is serious," said Sir John Westlake, "and cannot be allowed. Have you any ropes here by which we can assist him from the pit? Don't be alarmed, my man, for if there be a dead body in the pit, it can't harm you. Take your time quietly and easily, and you will assuredly get out."

"Aye," said the baron, "the more haste, the worst speed, is an English proverb, and in this case it will be fully exemplified. This man would easily leave the pit, if he would have the patience, with care and quietness, to clamber up its side."

It would appear that Davis felt the truth of these exhortations, for although he trembled excessively, he did begin to make some progress in his ascent, and get so high, that Mr. Leek was enabled to get hold of his hand, and give him a little assistance, so that, in another minute or so, he was rescued from his situation, which was not one of peril, although it was certainly one of fright.

He trembled so excessively, and stuttered and stammered, that for some minutes no one could understand very well what he said; but at length, upon making himself intelligible, he exclaimed, —

"There has been a murder! there has been a murder committed, and the body thrown into the ice pit. I felt that I jumped down upon something soft, and when I put down my hand to feel what it was, it came across a dead man's face, and then, of course, I called out."

"You certainly did call out."

"Yes, and so would anybody, I think, under such circumstances. I suppose I shall be hung now, because I had charge of the house?"

"That did not strike me until this moment," said the baron; "but if there be a dead body in that pit, it certainly places this man in a very awkward position."

"What the deuce do you mean?" said Davis; "I don't know no more about it than the child unborn. There is a dead man in the ice-well, and that is all I know about it; but whether he has been there a long time, or a short time, I don't know any more than the moon, so it's no use bothering me about it."

"My good man," said the baron, "it would be very wrong indeed to impute to you any amount of criminality in this business, since you may be entirely innocent; and I, for one, believe that you are so, for I cannot think that any guilty man would venture into the place where he had put the body of his victim, in the way that you ventured into that pit. I say I cannot believe it possible, and therefore I think you innocent, and will take care to see that no injustice is done you; but at the same time I cannot help adding, that I think, of course, you will find yourself suspected in some way."

"I am very much obliged to you, sir," said Davis; "but as I happen to be quite innocent, I am very easy about it, and don't care one straw what people say. I have not been in this excavation for Heaven knows how long."

"But what's to be done?" said Mr. Leek. "I suppose it's our duty to do something, under such circumstances."

"Unquestionably," said the baron; "and the first thing to be done, is to inform the police of what has happened, so that the body may be got up; and as I have now seen enough of the estate to satisfy me as regards its capabilities, I decide at once upon taking it, if I can agree upon the conditions of the tenancy, and I will purchase it, if the price be such as I think suitable."

"Well," said Mr. Leek, "if anything could reconcile me to the extraordinary circumstance that has just occurred, it certainly is, baron, the having so desirable a tenant for Anderbury-on-the-Mount as yourself. But we need not traverse all this passage again, for it is much nearer now to get out upon the sea coast at once, as we are so close to the door opening upon the beach. It seems to me that we ought to proceed at once to the town, and give information to the authorities of the discovery which we have made."

"It is absolutely necessary," said the baron, "so to do; so come along at once. I

shall proceed to my inn, and as, of course, I have seen nothing more than yourselves, and consequently could only repeat your evidence, I do not see that my presence is called for. Nevertheless, of course, if the justices think it absolutely necessary that I should appear, I can have no possible objection so to do."

This was as straightforward as anything that could be desired, and, moreover, it was rather artfully put together, for it seemed to imply that he, Mr. Leek, would be slighted, if his evidence was not considered sufficient.

"Of course," said Mr. Leek; "I don't see at all why, as you, sir, have only the same thing to say as myself, I should not be sufficient."

"Don't call upon me on any account," said Sir John Westlake.

"Oh! no, no," cried Mr. Leek; "there is no occasion. I won't, you may depend, if it can be helped."

Sir John, in rather a nervous and excited manner, bade them good day, before they got quite into the town, and hurried off; while the baron, with a dignified bow, when he reached the door of his hotel, said to Mr. Leek,—

"Of course I do not like the trouble of judicial investigations more than anybody else, and therefore, unless it is imperatively necessary that I should appear, I shall take it as a favour to be released from such a trouble."

"My lord baron," said Mr. Leek, "you may depend that I shall mention that to the magistrates and the coroner, and all those sort of people;" and then Mr. Leek walked away, but he muttered to himself, as he did so, "They will have him, as sure as fate, just because he is a baron; and his name will look well in the 'County Chronicle.'"

Mr. Leek then repaired immediately to the house of one of the principal magistrates, and related what had occurred, to the great surprise of that gentleman, who suggested immediately the propriety of making the fact known to the coroner of the district, as it was more his business, than a magistrate's, in the first instance, since nobody was accused of the offence.

This suggestion was immediately followed, and that functionary directed that the body should be removed from where it was to the nearest public-house, and immediately issued his precept for an inquiry into the case.

By this time the matter had begun to get bruited about in the town, and of course it went from mouth to mouth with many exaggerations; and although it by no means did follow that a murder had been committed because a dead body had been found, yet, such was the universal impression; and the matter began to be talked about as the murder in the subterranean passage leading to Anderbury House, with all the gusto which the full particulars of some deed of blood was calculated to inspire. And how it spread about was thus: —

The fact was, that Mr. Leek was so anxious to let Anderbury-on-the-Mount to the rich Baron Stolmuyer, of Saltzburgh, that he got a friend of his to come and personate Sir John Westlake, while he, the baron, was looking at the premises, in order to drive him at once to a conclusion upon the matter; so that what made Sir John so very anxious that he should not be called forward in the matter; consisted in

the simple fact that he was nothing else than plain Mr. Brown, who kept a hatter's shop in the town; but he could not keep his own counsel, and, instead of holding his tongue, as he ought to have done, about the matter, he told it to every one he met, so that in a short time it was generally known that something serious and startling had occurred in the subterranean passage to Anderbury House, and a great mob of persons thronged the beach in anxious expectation of getting more information on the matter.

The men, likewise, who had been ordered by the coroner to remove the body, soon reached the spot, and they gave an increased impetus to the proceedings, by opening the door of the subterranean passage, and then looking earnestly along the beach as if in expectation of something or somebody of importance.

When eagerly questioned by the mob, for the throng of persons now assembled quite amounted to a mob, to know what they waited for, one of them said, —

"A coffin was to have been brought down to take the body in."

This announcement at once removed anything doubtful that might be in the minds of any of them upon the subject, and at once proclaimed the fact not only that there was a dead body, but that if they looked out they would see it forthwith.

The throng thickened, and by the time two men were observed approaching with a coffin on their shoulders, there was scarcely anybody left in the town, except a few rare persons, indeed, who were not so curious as their neighbours.

It was not an agreeable job, even to those men who were not the most particular in the world, to be removing so

loathsome a spectacle as that which they were pretty sure to encounter in the ice-well; but they did not shrink from it, and, by setting about it as a duty, they got through it tolerably well.

They took with them several large torches, and then, one having descended into the pit, fastened a rope under the arms of the dead man, and so he was hauled out, and placed in the shell that was ready to receive him.

They were all surprised at the fresh

and almost healthful appearance of the countenance, and it was quite evident to everybody that if any one had known him in life, they could not have the least possible difficulty in recognising him now that he was no more.

And the only appearance of injury which he exhibited was in that dreadful wound which had certainly proved his death, and which was observable in his throat the moment they looked upon him.

The crush to obtain a sight of the body was tremendous at the moment it was brought out, and a vast concourse of persons followed it in procession to the town, where the greatest excitement prevailed. It was easily discovered that no known person was missing; and some who had caught a sight of the body, went so far as to assert that it must have been in the ice-well for years, and that the extreme cold had preserved it in all its original freshness.

The news, of course, came round, although not through the baron, for he did not condescend to say one word about it at the inn, and it was the landlord who first started the suggestion of—

"What, suppose it is the gentleman who left his horse here?"

This idea had no sooner got possession of his brain, than it each moment seemed to him to assume a more reasonable and tangible form, and without saying any more to any one else about it, he at once started off to where the body lay awaiting an inquest, to see if his suspicions were correct.

When he arrived at the public-house and asked to see the body, he was at once permitted to do so; for the landlord knew him, and was as curious as he could be upon the subject by any possibility. One glance, of course, was sufficient, and the landlord at once said,—

"Yes, I have seen him before, though I don't know his name. He came to my house last night, and left his horse there; and, although I only saw him for a moment as he passed through the hall, I am certain I am not mistaken. I dare say all my waiters will recognise him, as well as the Baron Stolmuyer of Saltzburgh, who is staying with me, and who no doubt knows very well who he is, for he went out with him late and came home alone; and I ordered one of my men to wait up all night in order to let in this very person who is now lying dead before us."

"The deuce you did! But you don't suppose the baron murdered him, do you?"

"It's a mystery to me altogether—quite a profound mystery. It's very unlikely, certainly; and what's the most extraordinary part of the whole affair is, how the deuce could he come into one of the ice-wells belonging to Anderbury House. That's what puzzles me altogether."

"Well, it will all come out, I hope, at the inquest, which is to be held at four o'clock to-day. There must have been foul play somewhere, but the mystery is where, and that Heaven only knows, perhaps."

"I shall attend," said the landlord, "of course, to identify him; and I suppose, unless anybody claims the horse, I may as well keep possession of it."

"Don't flatter yourself that you will get the horse out of the transaction. Don't you know quite well that the government takes possession of everything as don't belong to nobody?"

"Yes; but I have got him, and

possession, you know, is nine points of the law."

"It may be; but their tenth point will get the better of you for all that. You take my word for it, the horse will be claimed of you; but I don't mind, as an old acquaintance, putting you up to a dodge."

"In what way?"

"Why, I'll tell you what happened with a friend of mine; but don't think it was me, for if it was I would tell you at once, so don't think it. He kept a country public-house; and, one day, an elderly gentleman came in, and appeared to be unwell. He just uttered a word or two, and then dropped down dead. He happened to have in his fob a gold repeater, that was worth, at least, a hundred guineas, and my friend, before anybody came, took it out, and popped in, in its stead, an old watch that he had, which was not worth a couple of pounds."

"It was running a risk."

"It was; but it turned out very well, because the old gentleman happened to be a very eccentric person, and was living alone, so that his friends really did not know what he had, or what he had not, but took it for granted that any watch produced belonged to him. So, if I were you in this case, when the gentleman's horse is claimed, I'd get the d — dest old screw I could, and let them have that."

"You would?"

"Indeed would I, and glory in it, too, as the very best thing that could be done. Now, a horse is of use to you?"

"I believe ye, it is."

"Exactly; but what's the use of it to government? and, what's more, if it went to the government, there might be some excuse; but the government will know no more about it, and make not so much as I shall. Some Jack-in-office will lay hold of it as a thing of course and a perquisite, when you might just as well, and a great deal better, too, keep it yourself, for it would do you some good, as you say, and none to them."

"I'll do it; it is a good and a happy thought. There is no reason on earth why I shouldn't do it, and I will. I have made up my mind to it now."

"Well, I am glad you have. What do you think now the dead man's horse is worth?"

"Oh! fifty or sixty guineas' value."

"Then very good. Then, when the affair is all settled, I will trouble you for twenty pounds.

"You?"

"Yes, to be sure. Who else do you suppose is going to interfere with you? One is enough, ain't it, at a time; and I think, after giving you such advice as I have, that I am entitled, at all events, to something."

"I tell you what," said the landlord of the hotel, "taking all things into consideration, I have altered my mind rather, and won't do it."

"Very good. You need not; only mind if you do, I am down upon you like a shot."

THE EXCITEMENT CONTINGENT upon the inquest was very great; indeed, the large room in the public house, where it was held, was crowded to suffocation with persons who were anxious to be present at the proceedings. When the landlord reached home, of course he told his guest, the baron, of the discovery he had made, that the murdered man was the strange visitor of the previous night; for now, from the frightful wound he had received in his throat, the belief that he was murdered became too rational a one to admit of any doubts, and was that which was universally adopted in preference to any other suggestion upon the occasion; although, no doubt, people would be found who would not scruple to aver that he had cut his own throat, after making his way into the well belonging to Anderbury House.

The landlord had his own misgivings concerning his guest, the baron, now that something had occurred of such an awful and mysterious a nature to one who was evidently known to him. It did not seem to be a pleasant thing to have such an intimate friend of a man who had been murdered in one's house, especially when it came to be considered that he was the last person seen in his company, and that, consequently, he was peculiarly called upon to give an explanation of how, and under what circumstances, he had parted with him.

The baron was sitting smoking in the most unconcerned manner in the world, when the landlord came to bring him this intelligence, and, when he had heard him to an end, the remark he made was, —

"Really, you very much surprise me; but, perhaps, as you are better acquainted with the town than I am, you can tell me who he was?"

"Why, sir, that is what we hoped you would be able to tell us."

"How should I tell you? He introduced himself to me as a Mr. Mitchell, a surveyor, and he said that, hearing I talked of purchasing or renting Anderbury-on-the-Mount, he came to tell me that the principal side wall, that you could see from the beach, was off the perpendicular."

"Indeed, sir!"

"Yes; and as this was a very interesting circumstance to me, considering that I really did contemplate such a purchase or renting, and do so still, as it was a moonlight night, and he said he could show me in a minute what he meant if I would accompany him, I did so; but when we got there, and on the road, I heard quite enough of him to convince me that he was a little out of his senses, and, consequently, I paid no more attention to what he said, but walked home and left him on the beach."

"It's a most extraordinary circumstance, sir; there is no such person, I assure you, as Mitchell, a surveyor, in the town; so I can't make it out in the least."

"But, I tell you, I consider the man out of his senses, and perhaps that may account for the whole affair."

"Oh, yes, sir, that would, certainly; but still, it's a very odd thing, because we don't know of such a person at all, and it does seem so extraordinary that he should have made his appearance, all of a sudden, in this sort of way. I suppose, sir, that you will attend the inquest, now, that's to be held upon him?"

"Oh, yes; I have no objection whatever to that; indeed, I feel myself bound to do so, because I suppose mine is the the latest evidence that can be at all produced concerning him."

"Unquestionably, sir; our coroner is a very clever man, and you will be glad to know him — very glad to know him, sir, and he will be glad to know you, so I am sure it will be a mutual gratification. It's at four o'clock the inquest is to be, and I dare say, sir, if you are there by half-past, it will be time enough."

"No doubt of that; but I will be punctual."

WE HAVE ALREADY SAID the room in which the inquest was to be held was crowded almost to suffocation, and not only was that the case, but the lower part of the house was crammed with people likewise; and there can be very little doubt but the baron would have shrunk from such an investigation from a number of curious eyes, if he could have done so; while the landlord of the house would have had no objection, as far as his profit was concerned in the sale of a great quantity of beer and spirits, to have had such a an occurrence every day in the week, if possible.

The body lay still in the shell where it had been originally placed. After it had been viewed by the jury, and almost every one had remarked upon the extraordinary fresh appearance it wore, they proceeded at once to the inquiry, and the first witness who appeared was Mr. Leek, who deposed to have been in company with some gentlemen viewing Anderbury House, and to have found the body in one of the ice-wells of that establishment.

This evidence was corroborated by that of Davis, who had so unexpectedly jumped into the well, without being aware that it contained already so disagreeable a visitor as it did in the person of the murdered man, regarding the cause of whose death the present inquiry was instituted.

Then the landlord identified the body as that of a gentleman who had come to his house on horseback, and who had afterwards walked out with Baron Stolmuyer of Saltzburgh, who was one of his guests.

"Is that gentleman in attendance?" said the coroner.

"Yes, sir, he is; I told him about it, and he has kindly come forward to give all the evidence in his power concerning it."

There was a general expression of interest and curiosity when the baron stepped forward, attired in his magnificent coat, trimmed with fur, and tendered his evidence to the coroner, which, of course, was precisely the same as the statement he had made to the landlord of the house; for, as he had made up such a well connected story, he was not likely to prevaricate or to depart from it in the smallest particular.

He was listened to with breathless attention, and, when he had concluded, the coroner, with a preparatory *hem!* said to him,

"And you have reason to suppose, sir, that this person was out of his senses?"

"It seemed to me so; he talked wildly and incoherently, and in such a manner as to fully induce such a belief."

"You left him on the beach?"

"I did. I found when I got there that it was only a very small portion, indeed, of Anderbury House that was visible; and, although the moon shone brightly, I must confess I did not see, myself, any signs of deviation from the perpendicular; and, such being the case, I left the spot at once, because I could have no further motive in staying; and, moreover, it was not pleasant to be out at night with a man whom I thought was deranged. I regretted, after making this discovery, that I had come from home on such a fool's errand; but as, when one is going to invest a considerable sum of money in any enterprise, one is naturally anxious to know all about it, I went, little suspecting that the man was insane."

"Did you see him after that?"

"Certainly not, until to-day, when I recognised in the body that has been exhibited to me the same individual."

"Gentlemen," said the coroner to the jury, "it appears to me that this is a most mysterious affair; the deceased person has a wound in his throat, which, I have no doubt, you will hear from a medical witness has been the cause of death; and the most singular part of the affair is, how, if he inflicted it upon himself, he has managed to dispose of the weapon with which he did the deed."

"The last person seen in his company," said one of the jury, "was the baron, and I think he is bound to give some better explanation of the affair."

"I am yet to discover," said the baron, "that the last person who acknowledges to having been in the company of a man afterwards murdered, must, of necessity, be the murderer?"

"Yes; but how do you account, sir, for there being no weapon found by which the man could have done the deed himself?"

"I don't account for it at all — how do you?"

"This is irregular," said the coroner; "call the next witness."

This was a medical man, who briefly stated that he had seen the deceased, and that the wound in his throat was amply sufficient to account for his death; that it was inflicted with a sharp instrument having an edge on each side.

This, then, seemed to conclude the case, and the coroner remarked, —

"Gentlemen of the jury, — I think this is one of those peculiar cases in which an open verdict is necessary, or else an adjournment without date, so that the matter can be resumed at any time, if fresh evidence can be procured concerning it. There is no one accused of the offence, although it appears to me impossible that the unhappy man could have committed the act himself. We have no reason to throw the least shade of suspicion or doubt upon the evidence of the Baron Stolmuyer of Saltzburgh; for as far as we know anything of the matter, the murdered man may have been in the company of a dozen people after the baron left him."

A desultory conversation ensued, which ended in an adjournment of the inquest, without any future day being mentioned for its re-assembling, and so the Baron Stolmuyer entirely escaped from what might have been a very serious affair to him.

It did not, however, appear to shake him in his resolution of taking Anderbury-on-the-Mount, although Mr. Leek very much feared it would; but he announced to that gentleman his intention fully of doing so, and told him to get the necessary papers drawn up forthwith.

"I hope," he said, "within a few weeks' time to be fairly installed in that mansion, and then I will trouble you, Mr. Leek, to give me a list of the names of all the best families in the neighbourhood; for I intend giving an entertainment on a grand scale in the mansion and grounds."

"Sir," said Mr. Leek, "I shall, with the greatest pleasure, attend upon you in every possible way in this affair. This is a very excellent neighbourhood, and you will have no difficulty, I assure you, sir, in getting together an extremely capital and creditable assemblage of persons. There could not be a better plan devised for at once introducing all the people who are worth knowing, to you."

"I thank you," said the baron; "I think the place will suit me well; and, as the Baroness Stolmuyer of Saltzburgh is dead, I have some idea of marrying again; and therefore it becomes necessary and desirable that I should be well acquainted with the surrounding families of distinction in this neighbourhood."

This was a hint not at all likely to be thrown away upon Mr. Leek, who was the grand gossip-monger of the place, and he treasured it up in order to see if he could not make something of it which would be advantageous to himself.

He knew quite enough of the select and fashionable families in that neighbourhood, to be fully aware that neither the baron's age nor his ugliness would be any bar to his forming a matrimonial alliance.

"There is not one of them," he said to himself, "who would not marry the very devil himself and be called the Countess Lucifer, or any name of the kind, always provided there was plenty of money; and that the baron has without doubt, so it is equally without doubt he may pick and choose where he pleases."

This was quite correct of Mr. Leek, and showed his great knowledge of human nature; and we entertain with him a candid opinion, that if the Baron Stolmuyer of Saltzburgh had been ten times as ugly as he was, and Heaven knows that was needless, he might pick and choose a wife almost when he pleased.

This is a general rule; and as, of course, to all general rules there are exceptions, this one cannot be supposed to be free from them. Under all circumstances, and in all classes of society, there are single-minded beings who consult the pure dictates of their own hearts, and who, disdaining those things which make up the amount of the ambition of meaner spirits, stand aloof as bright and memorable examples to the rest of human nature.

Such a being was Flora Bannerworth. She would never have been found to sacrifice herself to the fancied advantages of wealth and station, but would have given her heart and hand to the true object of her affection, although a sovereign prince had made the endeavour to wean her from it.

XCVII.

THE ADMIRAL'S PREPARATIONS, AND THE VISIT TO DEARBROOK.

IT WAS QUITE FINALLY settled between the admiral and the Bannerworths that he was to have the whole conducting of the marriage business, and he even succeeded in getting a concession from Flora Bannerworth, that he might invite more than twenty guests as had at first been stipulated. Indeed, she told him that he might ask forty if he pleased.

The admiral had asked for this enlargement of his of powers, because he had received from the lawyer such a satisfactory list of people who were eligible to be invited, that he found it extremely difficult to draw any invidious distinction; and, accordingly, he felt fully inclined, as far as he was concerned, to invite them all, which was a piece of liberality he scarcely expected Flora would accede to.

When, however, he got leave to double the number, he considered that he was all right, and he said to Jack Pringle, to whom, as usual, he had got completely reconciled,—

"I say, Jack, my boy, we'll have the whole ship's crew, and no mistake; for, at a wedding, the more the merrier, you know."

"Ay, ay, sir," said Jack, "that's true. I have not been married more than a dozen times myself, at the outside, and I always took care to have lots of fun."

"A dozen times, Jack! you don't mean that?"

"I rather think I does. You know I was married at different ports of India twice; and then wasn't I married in Jamaky; and then after that wasn't I married in the South Seas, in one of the Friendly Islands?"

"A deuced deal too friendly, I should say. Why, confound you, Jack, you must have the impudence of the very devil."

"Yes, I believe ye, I have. I look upon it that it's our impudence has got us on in the world."

"How dare you say "our," you vagabond? But, however, I won't quarrel with you now, at any rate, for I expect you to dance a hornpipe at the wedding. But mind me now, Jack, I am serious — I won't have any drunkenness."

"Well, it's rather a hard thing that a fellow can't get drunk at a wedding; but I suppose I must put up with that deadly injury, and do the best I can. And now, admiral, as you have looked over that little affair of mine, in going to the lawyer's when you didn't want me, I'll make you a voluntary promise, and that is, that I'll only take two bottles all the day long."

"Two bottles of what?"

"Oh, rum, of course."

"Well, that's moderate; for as I have known you, I think, take about five, of course I can't very well say anything to two; so you may take that much, Jack, for I really think you won't be much the worse of it."

"The worse of it! I should think not, sir. It rather strikes me that two bottles of rum wouldn't hurt a new-born baby. It's just for all the world like milk, you know;

it has no effect upon me; and as far as being fond of drink goes, I'd just as soon take pump water, if it had a different taste, and was a d — d deal stronger."

"Well, well, Jack, that's a bargain, you know, so we need say nothing more about it."

"I suppose there will be a fiddle, and all that sort of thing?"

"Oh, don't doubt that there shall be lots of fun."

"Then I am your man. I'll show them a thing or two that will make them open their eyes a bit; and if so be as they wants anything in the shape of a yarn, I'm the proper sort of individual to give it them, I rather think, and no mistake. I'll tell them how you ran away once, with a female savage after you, with a long thing like a skewer, that she called a spear, and how you called to all the ship's crew to come and help you, as if the very devil was at your heels."

Jack very prudently did not wait for an answer to this; for he was rather well aware that it was not the sort of thing that was exactly pleasing to the admiral, who was just upon the point, of course, of getting into one of his rages, which would have produced another quarrel, only, as a matter of course, to end in another reconciliation.

The old man, however, was too well pleased with the unlimited commission he had to do as he pleased regarding the marriage affair, to allow himself to be put much out of the way in the matter, and he bent all his mind and energies towards the completion of that piece of business which he had in hand, and which was certainly the most interesting to him that he had ever been permitted to engage in.

Passing as he did almost the whole of his life upon the ocean, he had never married, and his affection for Charles Holland, who was the only relative he had in the world, was of that concentrated nature which is only to be found under such circumstances.

Charles's mother had always had a large portion of the admiral's regards, and when upon returning home once from a cruise of three years' duration he found that she was dead, and had left behind her an orphan child, he at once avowed his intention of filling the place of a parent to it, and that he had both in the spirit and the letter kept his word, we know that Charles Holland was always most ready to admit.

Perhaps the severest shock he ever experienced was when that letter purporting to be from Charles, but which was really the production of Marchdale and Varney, was produced, and which seemed at the first blush to imply a dishonourable breaking of his contract with Flora; and if anything could have increased his admiration of her, it certainly was the generous and noble manner in which she repudiated that attempt to injure Charles in her esteem, and at once declared her belief that the letter was a forged document.

We may easily imagine, then, from these preceding circumstances, that the marriage of Charles with one whom he so entirely approved of was one of the most gratifying affairs in the old man's life, and that he viewed it with an extraordinary interest.

As we have before stated, he got possession for a month of the house on which he had fixed his fancy, and an extremely handsome and commodious place it was.

It was arranged that after they had remained there for some time they should all move off to Dearbrook together, and as it was only in early infancy that the Bannerworths had seen that estate, they purposed paying it a visit before the marriage ceremony took place.

This was an idea of the old admiral's, for he said truly enough, "You can't possibly know what state it is in till you go there, and it may be necessary, for all we know, to do a great deal to it before it is fit for occupation."

Apart from this consideration, too, it seemed likely enough that somebody might be in it; for of late it had changed hands, and, for all they knew, the Bannerworth family might have to institute a suit at law for its recovery.

The distance was sufficient to make it a whole day's journey; but it was a very pleasant one, for they went in a travelling carriage, replete with every accommodation, and the road passed through one of the most fertile and picturesque counties of England, being interspersed with hill and dale most charmingly, and reminding the younger branches of the Bannerworths of some of those delightful continental excursions which they once had the means of making, but which, for a long time, they had not had an opportunity of enjoying.

It was towards the close of a day of great beauty, for the season, that they reached the village of Dearbrook, close to where the estate was situated, and put up at the principal inn, to which they were directed.

The circumstances under which the Dearbrook property had been left for a long time had been such, that there was likely to be some difficulty concerning it.

In fact, it had been used by Marmaduke Bannerworth as a kind of security from time to time for his gambling debts, so it was probable that hardly any one had had it long enough to trouble himself about rentals.

"If we find any one," said Henry Bannerworth, "in possession, I shall not trouble them to pay anything for the use of the house they have had, provided they quietly give up possession, and leave the place in a decent state."

"Oh, that of course they will do," said Charles Holland, "and be too glad to escape arrears of rent; but it would be no bad thing to ask the landlord of this house what is the state of the property; no doubt he can not only let us know whether it be tenanted or not, but, if so, what sort of people they are who occupy it."

This suggestion was agreed to, and when the landlord was summoned, and the question put, he said,—

"Oh, yes, I know the Dearbrook estate quite well; it's a very handsome little property, and is at present occupied by a Mr. Jeremiah Shepherd, a Quaker—a very worthy gentleman indeed, I believe; but I suppose all Quakers are worthy people, because, you see, sir, they wear broad brimmed hats and no collars to their coats."

"An excellent reason," said the admiral; "but I had a friend who did know something about Quakers, and he used to say that they had got such a reputation for honesty that they could afford to be rogues for the rest of their existence."

"Well, well," said Henry, "we can but call upon him. Do you think that this would be a reasonable hour?"

"Oh, yes, sir," said the landlord; "he is sure to be at home at this hour if you have any business to transact with Mr. Shepherd. He is a very respectable man, sir, and as it is his own property that he lives upon, he is quite a gentleman, and never wears anything but drab breeches and gaiters."

Without waiting to enter into any further conversation with the landlord, who had such extraordinary reasons for his opinions, Henry, and Charles, and the admiral, leaving the rest of the party at the inn, proceeded to Dearbrook Lodge, as it was called, and found as they approached it that it exceeded in appearance their warmest anticipations.

It was a substantial red brick house, of the Tudor style of architecture, and had that air of dignified and quiet repose about it which a magnificent lawn, of the greenest possible turf, in the front always gives to a country mansion.

The grounds, too, seemed to be extensive, and, to take it for all in all, the Bannerworth family had every reason to be well pleased with this first view that they got of their acquired property.

"You will have some trouble," said the admiral, "with the Quaker, you may depend. They are a race that cry 'hold fast' to anything in the shape of pounds, shillings, and pence, and are not very easy to be dealt with."

"Oh, the man will not be so absurd, I should think," said Charles. "It can be proved that the estate was in the Bannerworth family for many years, and your possession, Henry, of the title deeds

will set the question at rest. But see what a stately looking servant is coming in answer to the ring which I have just given to the bell."

A footman, most certainly having all the appearance of what is so frequently advertised for as "a serious man servant," advanced to the gate, and, in answer to the inquiry if Mr. Shepherd was within, he said,—

"Yes, truly is he; but he liketh not to be disturbed, for he is at prayers — that is to say, at dinner, and is not accustomed to be disturbed thereat."

"I regret that we must disturb him," said Henry, "for our business happens to be important, and we must positively see him."

Upon this remonstrance the servant unlocked the gate, and conducted them up a path by the side of the lawn which led to the house, and the more they saw of it the more pleased they were with the many natural beauties with which it abounded, and Henry whispered to Charles,—

"I am quite sure that Flora will be delighted with this place, for, if I know anything of her taste, it will just suit it agreeably and comfortably, and I do sincerely hope that we shall be able to get possession without the disagreeable necessity of a law suit."

They were ushered into a handsome apartment, and then told that Mr. Shepherd would be with them very shortly; and they were not sorry to have a little leisure for studying the place before its reputed owner made his appearance.

"I suppose," said Henry, "the best way will be at once to state that I am the owner of the place, and upon what conditions I am willing to forego any claim that I might otherwise succeed in setting up for arrears of rental during the time that he has been here."

"Oh, yes," said Charles; "you cannot be too explicit; but hush! here he comes, and you will soon know what sort of an individual you have to deal with in this matter."

At this moment, the door opened, and Mr. Shepherd, the present ostensible possessor of the Dearbrook estate, and whose appearance spoke to the truth of the landlord's word, make his appearance.

But as what he said was sufficiently important to deserve a new chapter, we shall oblige him with one.

XCVIII.

THE INTERVIEW WITH THE QUAKER AT DEARBROOK.

THE QUAKER WAS a man of about middle age, and was duly attired in the garb of the particular sect to which he belonged. There was about his countenance all that affectation of calmness and abandonment of worldly thoughts and desires which is mistaken by so many people for the reality of self-denial, when, really, those who know this sect well, are perfectly aware that there is not a more money-loving, grasping people on the face of the earth.

After gravely motioning his visitors to be seated, Mr. Shepherd cast his eyes up to the ceiling, as if he were muttering some prayer, and then he said,—

"Verily, may I ask to what I am to attribute this visit from individuals who, in this vale of unblessedness, are unknown to me."

"Certainly, sir," said Henry; "you are entitled, of course, at once, to such an explanation of us. I have called upon you because I am the proprietor of this estate, to know how it is that you became in

possession of it, and under what pretence you hold that possession?"

Mr. Shepherd slightly changed colour, and staggered back a pace or two before he said,—

"The property is mine, but I naturally decline to produce my title to anybody who may ask for it. Thou mayest go, now; behind thee is the door."

"Mr. Shepherd," said Henry, "I am fully in a condition, as to means and evidence both, to prove my title to the estate, and an action of ejectment will soon force you from it; but I am unwilling, under any circumstances, to do what I fully may do if anything short of that will answer my purpose. I therefore give you fair notice, that if, upon my convincing you that I am the owner of the estate, you go out quietly within fourteen days, I will make no inquiry as to how long you have been here, and will say nothing whatever upon the subject of rental owing to me on account of such occupation."

"I defy thee, friend," said the Quaker;

"and if thou givest me any trouble I shall put thee in Chancery,* from whence thou wilt not get out for the term of thy natural life; so I give thee due notice, and thou mayest please thyself in the transaction; and again I tell thee the door is exactly behind thee, out of which I beg to request thou shouldst at once walk."

"I tell you what, Mr. Quaker," said the admiral, who had with difficulty restrained himself thus far, "I look upon you as one of the greatest humbugs ever I came across, and that's saying a great deal, for in my time I have come across some thumpers; and if we don't make you smart for this confounded obstinancy, you wolf in sheep's clothing, we will know the reason why. If it costs me a thousand pounds I will make you suffer for it."

"Thou mayest be damned, friend," said the Quaker; "possession is a great number of points of the law, and, as I have it, I mean to keep it. I have a friend who is in the law, and who will put thee as comfortably in Chancery, and with as little expense to me as possible. This is a very charming estate, and I have not the slightest intention of giving it up."

"But you must," said Charles, "give it up to the right owner. How can you be so foolish as to run yourself to legal expenses for nothing?"

"Teach thy grandmother, young man, to suck eggs," said the Quaker. "I wish thee all a remarkably good day, and thou mayest all return from whence thou camest, and hang thyselves, if thou pleasest, for all I care; and having made up my mind to live

_____

* *The Court of Chancery, which dealt with matters of equity law such as property rights. adverse possession, and fiduciary duties, was notorious for being slow and expensive.*

and die on this very pleasant property. I shall have to put thee all into Chancery."

"Why, you canting thief!" said the admiral.

"Thou mayest be damned," said the Quaker. "In speaking so to thee, I use the language which I am perfectly well aware thou wilt best understand; so I say unto thee again, thou mayest be damned. Obediah, show these sinners off the premises; and, should they refuse to go with that quickness that shall seem to be fitting and proper, thou mayest urge them on with divers kicks on their hinder persons, and thou mayst likewise call to thy aid, Towzer, the large dog, to bite singularly great mouthfuls out of them."

The Quaker turned, and was walking in a very stately manner out of the room, when the admiral stepped forward, and exhilarated his movements with such a kick, that away he went as if he had been shot out of a gun.

"There, friend," said the admiral, "since you seem found of kicking, I think that is a very good beginning. It strikes me you didn't know who you had to deal with; and now, Mr. Obediah, it's your turn, and we'll manage Towzer when we get outside."

"I thank thee all the same, friend," said Obediah, "but would rather be excused."

"Perhaps you would like your nose pulled instead, then?"

"No, friend, it is quite long enough already; and I shall take myself off to the lower regions of these premises forthwith."

So saying, Obediah rushed from the room with great precipitancy, leaving, most certainly, the admiral and his party masters of the field; and although both

Henry and Charles both disapproved of the assault which the admiral had committed, they could not interfere for laughing, and, as they left the house, which they did now of their own accord, Charles said,—

"Uncle, you may depend you will be pulled up to the quarter session."

"Damn the quarter session!" said the admiral. "Do you think I was going to sit still, quietly, while that vagabond promised to kick me; but, as it is, it's all up with coming to Dearbrook to live for one while to come; for, if he is really as good as his word, and puts the matter into Chancery, there's an end of it. I have heard it's like ducking in head foremost into a hollow tree, with a wasp's nest at the bottom of it; you may kick, but I'll be damned if you can get out."

"Well," said Henry, "I believe that's rather an apt illustration; but we must do the best we can in such a case, and, in the meantime, seek out some other place to reside in. Your friend, the little lawyer in the town, shall have the case to conduct for us, and perhaps, after all, we shall defeat the Quaker sooner than you imagine."

"I long to see the day come," said the admiral, "when that fellow will have to troop out of the place; for, in all my life, I never did know such confounded impudence as he treated us with."

"Never mind, never mind," said Charles; "the time must come, of course, when this pleasant estate, to which we have taken such a fancy, will be ours; and, until then, we shall have no difficulty whatever in finding some sweet verdant spot, full of exquisite and natural beauties, which we can make a home of well and

easily, caring nothing for being a short time only kept from possession of that which, of right, shall, in a short time, belong to us; and there is one thing that I am rejoiced at, which is, that Flora has not seen this place; so that she can have no regret about it, because she don't know of its existence farther than by name, and it can hold no place in her imagination which could make it a subject matter of regret."

WHEN THEY REACHED the inn, they informed Mrs. Bannerworth and Flora of the ill success of their enterprise, and of the obstinacy of the tenant of the house; and on that evening they had a good laugh with each other about the little scene that had occurred between the admiral and the Quaker; so that, upon the whole, perhaps, they were quite as happy — for people can but laugh and be merry — as if they had at once got possession of the Dearbrook estate without any trouble or difficulty whatever.

They determined upon staying there for that night, although they might have got fresh horses and gone back, if it had pleased them so to do; but there was much to tempt them in the romantic scenery, around which they took a stroll, when it was lit up by the sweet moonlight, and everything came out in silvery relief, looking so beautiful and serene, so pensively quiet and so admirable, that it was calculated to draw the mind entirely from all thought of earthly matters, and to completely rid them of even the shadow of an annoyance connected with that Dearbrook property which was so wrongfully detained from them.

"It is at such seasons as this," said Flora, "that contentment steals into the heart, and we really feel with how little we should be satisfied, provided it be sufficient to insure those ordinary comforts of existence which we all look for."

"It is, indeed," said Charles; "and you and I, Flora, would not repine if our lot had been much more humble than it is, provided Heaven had left us youth and love."

"Those, indeed," said Henry, "are dear possessions."

"Well, then," remarked the admiral, "you have got youth on your side, and I once knew a worse looking fellow than even you are; so why don't you fall in love with somebody at once?"

"Don't make so sure, uncle," said Flora archly, "that he has not."

The old admiral laughed — for he liked Flora to call him uncle, and said, —

"You shall tell me all about it, Flora, some day when we are alone; but not now, while these chaps are listening to every word we utter."

"I will," said Flora; "it's a grand secret of Henry's, which I am determined to tell."

"That's very unkind of you," said Henry, "to say the least of it."

"Not at all. If you had trusted me, Henry, it would be quite another thing; but as I found it out from my own natural sagacity, I cannot see that I am bound in the slightest to bestow upon you any consolation on account of it, or to shew you any mercy on the subject."

"And she hopes," said Charles, "that that will be a lesson to you to tell her upon another occasion everything whatever, without the slightest stint or hindrance."

"I stand convicted," said Henry; "and my only consolation is, that I don't mind a straw the admiral knowing all about it, and I meant to tell him myself, as a matter of course."

"Did you?" said the admiral; "that's a very good attempt to get out of it; but it won't answer exactly, Henry, with those who know better; so say no more."

In such light and pleasant conversation they passed some time, until the chill night air, grateful and pleasant as it was to the senses, made them think it prudent to retire to the inn again.

After they had partaken of the evening meal, and Flora and Mrs. Bannerworth had retired to rest, the gentlemen sat up, at the express desire of the admiral, to talk over the affair upon which they were all in common so deeply interested.

A general feeling of anxiety evidently pervaded all their minds to ascertain something of the whereabouts or the fate of Varney, who had so very mysteriously taken himself off at a time when they least of all expected he would have executed such a manoeuvre.

"You all see," said the admiral, "that what is bred in the bone, as I told you, will never be out of the flesh; and this vampyre fellow could not possibly be quiet, you see, for long, but he must be at his old tricks."

"I do not know," said Charles Holland, "but I am rather inclined to think that he has somehow become aware that he had become rather a trouble to us, and so his pride, of which I think we have had evidence enough that he has a large share of, took the alarm; and he went off as quick as he could."

"It may be so," said Henry; "and, of

course, in the absence of anything to the contrary, I feel inclined to give even Varney, the Vampyre, credit for as much purity of motive as I can."

"That's all very well, in its way," said the admiral; "but you must acknowledge that he did not leave in the most polite manner in the world; and then I, for one, cannot exactly approve of his jumping upon Dr. Chillingworth's back, from off a garden wall, as a cat would upon a mouse."

"Be liberal, uncle," said Charles, "and recollect that we are not quite sure it was Varney, for the doctor declines to be positive upon the subject, and he ought to know."

"Stuff," said the admiral; "the doctor knows well enough; but he is like the man that threatened to kick the other for laughing at his wife — he said he was sure he had done it, but if he had been d — d sure, he would have kicked him into the middle of next week."

"Certainly," said Charles, "the doctor seems quite clearly of opinion, that whoever committed that assault upon him, did so with a full knowledge of the worth of the picture, which he believes contained within its extra lining, bank notes to a large amount."

"And which," said Henry, "after all, is but a supposition, and Varney, after such an attempt to possess himself of such a treasure, if it was he that made it, may be actually now a houseless wanderer; but I consider that such has been the notoriety of his proceedings, that if he now attempts any vampyre tricks, he very soon will be discovered, and we shall hear of him."

"From his own account," said Charles Holland, "he has not been the most scrupulous person in the world with regard to the means by which he has, from time to time, recruited an exhausted exchequer; and we can easily imagine that this vampyre business of his would so terrify and paralyse people, that he would have little difficulty in robbing a house under such circumstances."

"You may depend," added Charles, "that he has done one of two things. He has either commenced a much more reckless career than ever he has yet attempted, or he has gone away completely into obscurity, and will never be heard of again. I sincerely myself hope that the latter is the case, for it will be better for him, and better for everybody connected with him."

"Hang the fellow," said the admiral; "I should not like him to starve, although he has given us so much trouble; and I hope that if anything very queer happens to him, he will not scruple to let us know, and he shall not positively want. But come, is it to be another tumbler a-piece, or to bed?"

Bed was voted, for such they knew was the admiral's wish, or he never would have mentioned the alternative; and in the course of another half hour the whole of these persons, in whose fate we profess to have so profound an interest, were wrapped in repose.

We will now turn to a consideration of what this singular and mysterious Baron Stolmuyer of Saltzburgh was about, for that he has some ulterior objects in view, which, by no means, at present, shew themselves, we cannot doubt; and, likewise, there can be no question but that very shortly some of his views and projects will develop themselves.

XCIX.

THE BARON BECOMES MASTER OF ANDERBURY-ON-THE-MOUNT, AND BEGINS TO
CONGRATULATE HIMSELF. — THE DREAM.

IT WAS A WONDERFUL RELIEF to Mr. Leek to find that the fact of a dead body having been found in the subterranean passage of Anderbury House, was really no bar to the baron possessing himself of those premises.

Mr. Leek could not disguise from himself that, to many persons, it would have been a serious impediment, and the very mystery in which that affair was still wrapped up, would have made the impediment greater, because people don't so much think of a murder, which is all found out, and for which the perpetrator suffers; but a murdered body found, and yet no murderer, keeps public curiosity upon the stretch, and is almost certain destruction to house property.

But now, whether the baron bought Anderbury House, or rented it, was much the same to Mr. Leek; for, in the former case, he got his per centage all at once; and, in the latter, acting as agent, he got more, but he got it by degrees.

He waited, therefore, with some degree of feverish impatience to know which way that illustrious individual would make up his mind; and when he said, at length, in his strange calm way, that he would give 10,000 pounds for Anderbury-on-the-Mount, Mr. Leek wrote off, in violent haste, to the owner, advising him to accept the same without delay; and, as the owner never intended again to set foot in Anderbury House,

and, moreover, wanted money, he wrote back again in as violent haste that he would take 10,000 pounds most certainly, and wished the transaction concluded as quickly as it very well could be, promising Mr. Leek, which was a very gratifying thing to that gentleman, not on account of the money, as he himself said, "Oh, dear, no!" but as a matter of feeling, a handsome bonus, in addition to his per centage, if he quickly got the matter completed.

Armed with this authority, the agent showed an amount of generalship which must, if he had been placed in the situation of Field Marshal the Duke of Wellington, have won for him all the continental battles.

He went at once to the baron, and told him that he had received a letter from the owner of Anderbury-on-the-Mount, asking 10,500 pounds for the estate, but leaving it at his, Mr. Leek's option to take 10,000 pounds if he chose.

"Now, my lord baron," said Mr. Leek, "business is business, and I may as well put 250 pounds in my pocket, and your lordship put 250 pounds in yours, as not."

"That is to say," said the baron, "that you are willing to sell your employer's interest to me."

"Oh, why, it isn't exactly that, you know, my lord; only you know, in these transactions, everybody does the best he can for himself; and I am sure I should be very sorry if you thought that—that—"

"Mr. Leek," interrupted the baron, "you need have no delicacy with me, whatever. I believe you to be as great a rogue as ever stepped; so you need make no excuses, only, of course, you cannot expect me to assist you in your villany—that is quite out of the question; so you will understand that I decline giving more than the 10,000 pounds for Anderbury House; and, if that is not accepted in one hour from this time, I will not have it at all."

"It's accepted now at once," groaned Mr. Leek, who found that the baron was too many for him. "It's accepted at once, my lord; and I beg that you will bury the past in what do you call it—oblivion."

"Very good," said the baron. "I presume, if I give you a check for a thousand pounds as a deposit, I may have possession at once, while the deeds are preparing."

"Certainly, my lord baron; oh! certainly."

The baron then gave Mr. Leek, and took his acknowledgment for the same, a check for a thousand pounds on one of the most eminent banking-houses in London; and in two hours from that time, such was the celerity and precision of his movements, he took possession of Anderbury House, and engaged the man and woman who had been minding it to be his temporary servants, until he could get up an establishment suitable to his rank, and the place he inhabited.

It would have been a strange sight to Mr. Leek, and would have made him open his eyes a little with wonder, if he could have seen the baron traversing the apartments of Anderbury House alone.

"And am I at last settled?" he said to himself, as he stood in a large saloon. "Am I at last settled in a home such as I can really call my own?—and shall I not be hunted from it by my enemies? Let me consider—I will be quick in giving such an entertainment here, that it shall be talked of for many a day to come. It shall be such an entertainment as shall present to me all of youth, beauty, rank, and wealth, that can be found in the neighbourhood; and out of them I will choose some one who shall be the baroness, and, for a time, pace the stately halls as their mistress—for a time; yes, I have said only for a time. I wonder if there be a family vault to this property, because, if there be, I may want to use it."

In this purchase of Anderbury on-the-Mount, the ancient furniture of the place had been all included; so that, in truth, the baron had but to walk in and to find himself, if he could make himself so, quite at home.

A costly bed-chamber was prepared for him; the bed-linen and furniture of which was sent by Mr. Leek from his own house; and, no doubt, he fully intended to be well paid for the same.

The baron, after about two hours spent in the examination of his house, sat down in one of the principal apartments, and partook of a very slight repast; and after that, folding his arms upon his bosom, he seemed to give himself up to thought entirely; and from the smile that occasionally showed itself on his remarkable physiognomy, it would seem that those thoughts of his were of a pleasant and felicitous character.

Now and then, too, from a few and unsettled words that fell from his lips, it would seem as if he were greatly felicitating himself upon something which he had achieved that was of a character to give him intense satisfaction.

Perhaps it was the death of this singular man who called upon him, that gave him so much pleasure; and we are inclined to think that was the case, for, after the commission of a murder such as that, one of two feelings were pretty sure to possess him.

Remorse might take possession of him, and he might suffer much mental anguish in consequence of the deed; or the object which he achieved by that death might be of such a nature as to become quite a subject of congratulation, so as, whenever, he thought upon it, to give him the pleasantest and most delightful feelings.

It looked very much as if this was the case as regarded the baron, because it was as clear and evident as the sun at noon day, that he had felt no degree of remorse or regret for that deed; and that, as regards his conscience, certainly the murder he had committed sat as easy upon it as anything well could.

The evening was now drawing on, and the large apartments of the ancient house began to be enveloped in gloom; but, unlike the generality of persons who have committed crimes, and whose consciences are charged with injustice, the gathering gloom of night seemed to have no terror whatever for the Baron Stolmuyer.

But at length, with something of a sense of weariness, he rose and rang for attendance, desiring to be shown to the bedchamber which had been prepared for his reception.

It was a strange thing; but it seemed to be customary with him not to undress when he retired to rest; but, as he had done at the hotel, he only took off a portion of his apparel, and then cast himself upon the bed, and, in a few moments, it seemed as if a deep repose crept over him.

We say seemed; but, in reality, it was a disturbed and anxious sleep which the baron had; and soon he began to toss his arms to and fro restlessly, and to utter deep groans, indicative of mental anguish.

Occasionally, likewise, a muttered word or two, scarcely articulately pronounced, would come from his lips, such as — "Save me, save me! Not yet, not yet — my doom — no — no — the moonlight — the moonlight — kill him — strike him down!"

This state of mind continued for a considerable time, until with a shrill cry he sprung to his feet, and stood in an attitude of horror, trembling in every limb, and exhibiting a most horrible and frightful picture of mental distress.

Then there came a loud knocking at his chamber-door, and the voice of the man Davis, who had been alarmed at the strange shriek that had come from the baron's lips fell upon his ears. The sound of any human voice, at such a time, was like music to him.

"Are you ill, sir?" cried Davis; "are you ill?"

"No — no — it was nothing but a dream — only a dream;" and then he added to himself, "but it was a dream of such absolute horror, that I shall dread to close my eyes in rest again, lest once more so fearful a vision should greet me. It was a dream of such frightful significance,

that it will live in my remembrance like a reality, and be dreamed of again as such."

He sat down, and wiped the cold perspiration from his brow; then rising, he walked with unsteady steps towards the window, and throwing aside the massive curtain which shut out the night without by making a still deeper night within, a flood of beautiful and tender moonlight fell into the apartment.

As the cold rays fell upon his face, he breathed more freely, and seemed more to revive beneath their influence than as if he had suddenly found the bright sunshine beaming upon him in all the refulgence of its mid-day glory.

"I am better now," he muttered; "I am much better now. What a fearful vision that was which came across my heated fancy! Welcome, welcome, beautiful moonbeams, welcome; for deep in my very heart I feel your cheering influence now."

The violent trembling which had seized him passed away, and once more he resumed his wonted composure and calm hideousness of expression, if we may be allowed the word.

Now, for some time, he sat in silence, and then, in a low deep tone, he spoke.

"It was a strange dream! A dream made up of strange fancies and strange impulses! I thought that I stood in a vaulted chamber, and that all around me depicted nothing but gloom and desolation; but, as I there stood, the chamber filled with hideous forms, coming from where I knew not, but still crowding, crowding in, until the shadow of the merest shade could not have found a place.

"And so they crushed me into the smallest possible space; and there I stood, with a hundred grinning faces close around me, and in such a mad paroxysm of terror, that I would have given the world for escape from that dreadful thralldom.

"But they gibed at me, filling my ears with shrieking noises, and then at once there was a proposition — a proposition yelled out with shrieking vehemence by every voice. It was, to place me in the tombs even as I was, a living man.

"'Heap mountains of earth upon him,' cried a voice. 'Endow him with the rare gift of immortality, and then let him lie buried for thousands of years yet to come.'

"They seized upon me, those gaunt and terrific forms, and deep into the bowels of the earth I was hurried — a depth beyond all calculation; and when I thought my fate was sealed, a change came over me, and I found myself in one of the ice-wells of this mansion, cold and death-like, while a crowd of eager, curious faces, illumined by the light of torches, gazed down upon me, but no one spoke; and then they began to cast large fragments of the rocky cliff upon me.

"I called for aid, and asked for death; but still they proceeded to fill up the pit, while I lay, incapable of anything but agonised thought, at the bottom of it.

"Then it was, I presume, that in my despair I shook off that fearful slumber and awakened."

He was silent, and seemed again much to rejoice in the moonbeams, as they fell upon his face; and, after a time, in order, it would appear, that he might feel more of their influence, he opened the window, and stepped out upon a balcony which was immediately in front of it.

The view that he now had was a beautiful one in the extreme, spreading far over, in one direction, a beautiful tract of highly cultivated country; and on the other, as far as the eye could reach, upon the boundless ocean, on which the moonbeams fell with such beauty and power, that, still and placid as the waters were on that particular night, the sea looked like a sheet of radiant silver, broken into gentle irregularities.

It was a scene upon which a poet or a

painter — but painters should all be poets, although poets may not be painters — might gaze with rapture and delight.

Not the slightest breath of air stirred the gentlest leaf upon a forest tree; but such a calmness and such a serenity reigned over all things, that one might imagine oneself looking upon some new and beautiful world, the harmony of which had never yet been disturbed by the jarring sounds of elemental strife.

Strange thoughts and feelings seemed to come over the baron, as he then looked upon that mild and placid scene without, and, after a time, he spoke, saying, —

"And what do I struggle for now?" What is it now but mere existence that is the end and aim of all these anxious thoughts and feelings? Nothing more, nothing more, but the mere liberty to breathe and to be anxious — the capacity to endure pain. That is what I live for — nothing else — nothing else in the wide world; for when and how can I expect that calm contentment of the soul which man takes such pains to cast from him, but which I know the full value of, can ever be mine?"

Once more he cast his eyes around him, upon the great extent of cultivated country, and although he felt he could call the most of it, that lay immediately beneath his observation, his own, it yet gave him but little gratification to do so, and probably he looked with about as much indifference upon his own possessions as any one possibly could.

"This is a new career," he said, "and something tells me that it is my last; so, while it continues, I will not shrink from it, but, on the contrary, enjoy it; and I will endeavour to lose the recollection of those stormy periods of my existence which have passed away in a complete round and whirl of what the world calls enjoyments and delights. I will spend large sums on brilliant entertainments, and this house, which they tell me has been so long deserted by everything in the shape of festivity and hilarity, shall once again ring with joyous laughter, and I will make an endeavour to forget what I am."

He evidently dreaded again to lie down to repose, for, after some time further spent in thought, and in the expression of the feelings that lay uppermost in his mind, he put on again that portion of his apparel which he had taken off.

"In this soft and pleasant moonlight," he said, "which is so grateful to my senses, I will walk in the gardens of this mansion; and, should a sense of weariness oppress me, I shall be able to find, no doubt, some pleasant spot where I can lie down to rest, and I shall not fear horrifying or anxious dreams when I can repose beneath the beams of the moon, which cool my fevered brow."

With a slow and stately step he moved across the long and beautiful corridor from which his chamber opened, and then, descending the grand staircase, and in that house a grand staircase it really was, he made his way across the hall, and, undoing the fastening of a window which opened into a large and handsome conservatory, he passed through that again, and soon found himself in the extensive gardens of Anderbury.

Certainly, if there be any sight more chaste and beautiful than another, it is a highly-cultivated and well-wooded garden by moonlight, and we cannot but admire the taste of the Baron Stolmuyer in preferring it even to the stately bed-chamber he had so recently left, and which, notwithstanding all the advantages and beauties that art could bestow upon it, could never hope to rival, or even to come near, the natural beauties of that highly-cultivated piece of ground.

And there are some flowers, too, that give out their sweetest odours to the night air, and some again that unfold their choicest beauties only when the sun has set, and the cold moonbeams can but look down upon them.

When he got fairly into the garden, he found that there was a light, gentle breeze playing among the shorter shrubs and flowers, but that it reached not high enough to stir the leaves of the trees; but it is extremely doubtful if, completely taken up as this man was, no doubt, with worldly pursuits, he did not, after the first few moments, completely forget the world of natural beauties by which he was surrounded.

Folding his arms, he walked along the stately avenues with a solemn tread, and then, soon banishing from his mind those feelings of melancholy sadness which had oppressed him, he began evidently to indulge in dreams of felicity which, by the manner in which he spoke of them, were evidently but dreams.

"What can I desire or want more than I have?" he said. "Immense wealth — consequently, immense power. Golden opinions may always be purchased with gold, and what is there then really to hinder me pursuing to the full the career which I have marked out to myself? Surely I can surround myself with all that is young, and delightful, and beautiful? Can I not make these halls echo with such laughter, that surely it must awaken, even in my breast, joyous emotions? Then there is the wine cup; why should not that flow with rich abundance, gladdening the hearts of all, and adding even to genius, for the time, a new fire, and a more delightful expression of its thoughts and feelings?

"And music, too: surely I can have abundance of music, to shed the witchery of its charms about me; and, with these inducements and allurements, I must and will succeed in banishing reflection, if I achieve no more."

As he now stood, and turned his eyes towards the east, he fancied he saw that the morning light was beginning faintly to show itself in the far off horizon.

"Another day is coming," he said, "and how much, how very much might be done in a day. I will, with the assistance of that man Leek, who, I can readily perceive, is quite willing to bow down to any idol, provided it be of gold, to commence the career of festivities that I have set my heart upon, and we shall soon see how striking an alteration will take place in the halls of Anderbury."

He entered a small summer-house which was built in the garden, and through the stained glass of which the moon shone with a variegated light, and there he sat down, and, after a time, tasted of that repose which, upon the bed of down that he had left, and surrounded by all the costly litter of his handsome bedchamber he had courted in vain.

C.

MR. LEEK SPECULATES UPON THE BARON'S MATRIMONIAL INTENTIONS.

Mr. Leek pondered deeply over what the baron had said to him regarding his intention to take unto himself a wife, and viewed the resolution in all its bearing, with a view of discovering in what way such a thing could be turned to account, and whether that account might not be managed to his own advantage, which was a matter that Mr. Leek very often considered of paramount importance to himself, as being the pivot upon which things moved.

In Mr. Leek was certainly centered all those notions which usually arise from a desire to benefit oneself, and causing, as far as in him lay, all events to circle around him when they least appeared to do so.

"I must make this move of the baron's matrimonial alliance redound to my own advantage in some way or other, though I cannot precisely say in what way; but, if I have any hand in it, there must be a way, of that there can be no doubt; the only thing is to discover the way."

Mr. Leek set himself steadily to consider the subject in all its various bearings, determined he would not give up the chase until he had discovered what was to be done.

"I have it—I have it!" he muttered—"I have it; who can suggest anything better? I must have something to do in the suggestive style. I will persuade the baron to invite some one with whom I can have a few words in private. I will

have some few words in the way of a bargain with them.

"Yes, yes; I will do my best to make somebody else's fortune; but at the same time they must do something for me in return. I must have a *quid* for my *quo*, as the parsons say. They cannot preach the gospel without they have a full stomach; for who can be pious and hungry at the same moment? I can't, my thoughts would be diverted; but the case holds good in every relation in life; even though whom I would benefit must benefit me, else I lose the natural desire I have to benefit them. This reciprocity is the motto I like to apply in cases of this kind, and very proper too."

Thus did Mr. Leek argue the matter within his own mind, and then, having thus made a resolution, his next step was to consider how he should put it in practice—how he should be able to realize his hopes, and give life and being to the suggestions of his inventive faculties, which were usually of a practical nature.

"Well, well," he muttered. "Let me see—it's difficult to say who's who now-a-days; but that must not cause me to lose a chance, and I think I can make pretty sure of my bargain. I think, if I undertake anything, I can go through it and not fail. I will have so much of security as will prove a bargain, and thus bring shame and disgrace upon them if they refuse to make good the conditions."

Thus Mr. Leek had an eye to the future, and the contingencies that might, under different circumstances, arise by any possibility.

Men like Mr. Leek do not often fail in their endeavours when they take a comprehensive view of any affair in which they might engage, and thus, by contemplating it in all its various phases, insure, as much as may be, success to all their schemes.

The next consideration that presented itself to Mr. Leek was the party. It was all very well to chalk out a plan of action — the mode in which a thing should be done; but it was another to adapt the tools to the occasion, and make them subservient to the purpose he had in view.

He did not choose his tools first, and then adapt his work; no, he saw his object and adapted the means to the end; and, in considering this part of the affair, he came to the following resolution.

"I think I know who to pitch upon," muttered Mr. Leek to himself, in a thoughtful tone. "Aye, she has several children, and is a widow, too. I know she is comparatively poor, and not too much troubled with compunction, or any absurd notions of delicacy upon this matter. I can tell her what I mean better than I could to a good many. Yes, I will go and visit her. I can come to an understanding at once."

This was satisfactory, and he arose to quit the house, and proceeded to the residence of Mrs. Williams, the lady whose accommodating disposition, and whose desire to see her daughters well provided for, would cause her to bargain about matters that many would think too serious and too much a matter of the affections to be permitted to be looked upon in the light of a mere affair of pounds, shillings, and pence.

Now, Mrs. Williams was a lady who possessed something very much like a genteel independence, which is a very mysterious matter, and one which puzzled many people to divine. No one can understand what a genteel independence means.

It is one of those things that enables people to flit about, apparently comfortable in circumstances, with genteel clothes, and fingers on which no marks of toil are observable, but which are white and soft, through often lean attenuated, in consequence of privations.

However, to return to Mrs. Williams. She was a widow, had several marriageable daughters, and was most anxious that they should be settled out in life, so that she might be sure of their future welfare. She was a sharp-sighted, clever woman in some respects; and, in others, she was as women usually are, which is not saying much.

The house the widow occupied was on a pattern of neatness and gentility, and ornamented with woman's work from one end to the other; the ladies were accomplished and well educated, and possessed of some personal charms; and they were not altogether unacquainted with the fact.

"Yes, yes," he muttered; "I will go to Mrs. Williams, and there we can come to an immediate understanding. Helen Williams will, I think, stand a very good chance indeed. I must go and have some conversation with her, and learn her sentiments before I break ground with him; else she may try something without my aid on her own account."

This was a laudable object, and was but, as he said, merely putting another person in the way of making a fortune, and putting something into his own pocket at the same time; which was doing two good things at once, charitable acts of the first class, because charity begins at home, and then it gives to one's neighbours when we have a surplus.

It did not take Mr. Leek very long to reach the widow's house; and it was not without some degree of confidence that he rang the bell for admission; and, when a servant appeared, he said,—

"Is Mrs. Williams at home?"

"Yes, sir, she is," answered the drudge; "do you want her?"

"I wish to see her, else I should not have come here," replied Mr. Leek. "Tell her Mr. Leek desires to speak with her."

"Very well, sir," said the girl, who left the hall, and then walked to the parlour, in which Mrs. Williams was seated, and overheard all that was said in the passage.

"Mr. Leek, ma'am," said the girl.

"Tell Mr. Leek to walk in," said the lady; and, in due form, Mr. Leek did walk in, introduced by the servant, who soon departed, leaving the two worthies in each other's presence.

"Good morning, Mrs. Williams."

"And good morning, Mr. Leek; this visit is unexpected, but valued. I am happy to see you. Will you be seated?"

"Thank you," said Leek, "I will. Unexpected incidents give rise to other unexpected incidents; so, you see, one event gives rise to another, and they follow each other in rapid succession."

"So they do," said Mrs. Williams.

"Well," said Mr. Leek, as if greatly relieved in mind, giving sound to something very much like a sigh, "and how do you find yourself this variable weather — eh, Mrs. Williams?"

"As well as can be expected, you know, at my time of life."

"Your time of life! Upon my word, you are a young woman; and, if I might hazard an opinion, one with no small share of charms; indeed, you are decidedly a beautiful woman, Mrs. Williams."

"Ah! Mr. Leek, I though you were too much a man of business to be given to flattery; but I am afraid of you."

"There is no need, ma'am, I assure you. But how are your lovely daughters? — in the enjoyment of good health and spirits?"

"Yes, they are very well, I thank you, Mr. Leek — very well indeed; they usually are; they are considered to enjoy very good health."

"That is a good thing, I am sure — a very good thing, upon my word; they usually are well?"

"Yes; they have very little that ails them."

"It will be a blessing to you when they are comfortably provisioned off, under the protection of some one who will seek their future happiness as his own," said Mr. Leek.

"Why, as to that," said Mrs. Williams, "I am not so anxious as many might be. I love to see my children round about me; I love to be in their company, and to know that no one can illuse them."

"That is very true," said Mr. Leek.

"And yet, I have, I must say, at times, a wish that I might, before I die, see them comfortably settled in life, and their future happiness secured."

"Certainly; it is quite a mother's wish

that it should be so; that her children might enter the world, and that they might be provided for and subject to none of the disagreeable contingencies of life."

"Those are my feelings."

"I thought as much, Mrs. Williams. Have you heard of the Kershaws lately?" inquired Mr. Leek.

"Yes; I did hear there was a marriage in the family: pray is it true?"

"It is."

"A good marriage?"

"Yes, I believe a very good marriage; one in which a great deal of money is floating about from one to the other; indeed, I hear the gentleman is very rich."

"How did they become acquainted with such a man? I did not think they had any friends who could have brought them into contact with such a person."

"A friend," said Leek.

"Indeed! Why, as I said, I did not know they possessed such friends; but still, I suppose, there was some drawback — either low-bred contracted friendships, or some circumstances or other, that caused him to settle there."

"I believe not," said Leek.

"And what is he then?" inquired Mrs. Williams.

"Why, he was a stranger in those parts; but he had an excellent fortune, and was, according to all accounts, a very excellent match."

"How came they to find him out? who introduced them to him? I should like to know such a person."

"Why, some friend."

"How very disinterested of that friend," said Mrs. Williams.

"Not quite. It was a mutual understanding, I believe."

"How?"

"Why, thus; the friend wanted money, and the lady wanted a husband for her daughter."

"Well, I dare say she did, and I should have thought she was like to have waited long enough."

"And so she would; but an active man of business may have the means of pushing a family's fortune, if they will but make it worth his while; it was in this manner the Kershaws have made their fortune."

"And what did they do?"

"Why, they pushed a daughter into certain company into which she was introduced by the man of business; not by himself, but he managed it so that she was introduced, in a manner that made it appear as if they had no connection, and then he could exert himself in another manner, and so contrived to serve them by spreading favourable reports."

"And that's how Mary Kershaw got her husband, is it?" inquired Mrs. Williams, with a serious air.

"Yes, it is, indeed."

"How very immoral!"

"Eh?"

"How very immoral of a mother speculating in matrimonial matters for her daughter. How could she expect that she could procure happiness for her, when she uses such means?"

"What better could she use? You mistake the motive of the affair altogether, Mrs. Williams; give me leave to say you do."

"Indeed."

"Yes, decidedly. Thus, you don't attempt to buy a daughter's happiness; you only pay an agent; that is all. But it can be no crime that that agent is engaged upon matters connected with the happiness of your daughter, which is the great object of a mother's care."

"Certainly — certainly; how plain all that is," said Mrs. Williams; "but I can't think it is exactly what I should do myself."

"Perhaps not. But I have exactly such a chance, at this very moment."

"You, Mr. Leek?"

"Yes, I. I have the means, I believe, of obtaining a good fortune for the daughter of a very respectable person, of the first respectability, and with natural advantages in her favour. Such a one, if it were worth my while to lose time in carrying such an affair — "

"Why, then, the matter looks a little different to what it did, and certainly who could object to do what was just and right?"

"Exactly. Now, if you were desirous of seeing your daughter Helen, for instance, comfortably provided for, what would you give — making it a suppositious case — what would you give to see your daughter happy and comfortable for life, with a good home over her head?"

"A good deal."

"What?"

"I cannot say; but, of course, that would depend much upon the value of such a prize; but I would not hesitate at a trifle in such a matter as that, come what may."

"Well — well, that is really the best way to consider the affair in all its various branches; you become more satisfied in the end. Now, do you really think you would be able to tolerate such an attempt to benefit yourself and daughter?"

"I do."

"Will you enter into particulars?"

"Yes, Mr. Leek; whenever you please. I am willing to attend to your proposal, and will be bound to anything I may say; for, in matters of this kind, I must consider anything one may say or undertake, as a debt of honour."

"Exactly. But what we agree to now we must put in black and white, because, bye-and-bye, we may not think of it so well as we should when we see it drawn up before one."

"Agreed. But what of this person?"

"Why, I think, if we were to agree, you would find this gentleman very rich and munificent, and living in a princely style; he is, in fact, a man of rank — of title, in fact."

"Is that so?"

"Yes, it is, I assure you, because I know him, and have had business matters to do with him; and, though a correct man, he is not at all nice about matters in which money is the chief ingredient. He pays eight hundred a year for rent, so you may guess he is not at all unlikely to give your daughter a handsome settlement."

"If he will have her."

"Exactly; if he have her; there is the contingency, of course, which, however, cannot affect you."

"Yes, it must, since my daughter does not obtain her husband."

"And you pay no money. If the benefit is contingent to you, it is to me also. I do not wish to bind you to anything that will cause you to be a loser under any circumstances."

"Very well," said Mrs. Williams. "Say what you please; there is pen, ink, and paper; make it out, and I will sign any memorandum you may please, provided it be of the complexion you have mentioned."

"I wish for no other."

Mr. Leek, accordingly, sat down near a table, and produced an agreement, which was, to give him a certain sum of money, provided Helen Williams was married to the baron.

"And who is he, my dear Mr. Leek?" said the lady.

"There," said Leek, "read that, and you will see his name."

And, as he spoke, he pushed the memorandum towards her, and she took it up and read it carefully over, and when she had so done, she signed it, and returned it, saying,—"So he is a baron."

"Yes; I told you he was a man of rank and title."

"You did; and where will he live?"

"At Anderbury House."

"A fine place; I know it. A splendid and princely place it is, too. He must have a large fortune there. It will be a splendid match for Helen. I wonder if there be any prospect of success; it appears almost too great a catch."

"I should say there was every prospect of success."

"But we must not let Helen know anything of our compact. I know her feelings so well, that I am fully persuaded that she would not acquiesce in the arrangement at all."

"Certainly; it may for ever remain our own secret, with which no human being need be acquainted."

"That is precisely what I wish; but now how are we to manage the introduction?"

"That will be easy enough."

"I am glad of it; but how is it to be managed at all?"

"Thus: the baron will give grand entertainments, and as he knows I am very well acquainted with the generality of the gentry about, he has asked me to point out those whom he might safely invite to his splendid banquets."

"Then you will have the kindness to invite us," said Mrs. Williams. "I see through it now. Aye, a very good plan. Then you can say everything that is necessary."

"To be sure I can, and will," said Leek.

"Well, I am glad you have called about this to-day, for we have had some little scheme in view, but unknown to the principal party concerned; however, as this one is in view, I shall prosecute no other."

"It would be dangerous to attempt two such speculations at once, else he would be unlikely to fulfill a promise even after he had gone some way towards doing so."

"I would run no risk in landing such a prize," said Mrs. Williams, who began to have a keen relish for the chance they had in view, such as they had not yet heard of from any quarter.

"Then I may fully rely upon your putting Helen forward upon every occasion that may present itself?"

"You may."

"And in the meantime keep as much to yourself as you can. You must profess to be unbounded in your admiration for all he says or does, and then you will obtain a preference for companionship, and every little is an aid in such matters."

"I shall be careful."

"And in the meantime I will bid you good day," said Mr. Leek.

CI.

THE GRAND ENTERTAINMENT GIVEN BY THE BARON AT ANDERBURY HOUSE, AND HIS ANNOUNCEMENT.

THE BARON MADE quick work of it, for in five days after the one on which he took Anderbury House, he gave his first entertainment. Money works wonders, and in the baron's hands it seemed to have lost none of its magical power; for Anderbury House in that time was furnished like a palace; rich and costly were the decorations — the ornamental plants were bold and florid.

The house and grounds were of a most magnificent character, though they had been viewed as separate features; but when considered as one, as that which was part and parcel of one great whole, it was truly princely.

Great care, labour, and expense had been exerted to make the mansion one befitting the habitation of a prince; and the baron himself was looked upon as little less than a prince; his disregard of money, his liberality, all concurred in making him looked upon as one of the most popular men in that neighbourhood.

Indeed, none such as he had ever been seen or heard of in that quarter. He was safe to be considered as one of the grandees of the day.

Anderbury House was now a theme of conversation with every one in the whole town. His magnificence, liberality, and all things connected with him, were all well calculated to cause a feeling of prejudice to be made in his favour.

When people saw the men that were at work, the loads of articles which were sent there, they were amazed, and could hardly credit their senses. Then they all considered how very rich he must be to be able to spend so much in furniture, in hangings, in beautifying, and in ornamental work, which must have been very heavy.

The baron was fully determined to do all he had intended to do in the way of opening his first grand entertainment with great *eclat*, and in a manner that would take the whole country by surprise.

The day came; the house was furnished, decorated, filled with servants, and everything that could make it appear as though it had been for years in that state.

It is surprising how soon a place can be made to lose all signs of its ever having been uninhabited, and the fact of human beings being in a place soon wears away the look of desolation by which it is otherwise enveloped; but how much easier must it have been, with ample means, for a man like the baron to cause such a house as that of Anderbury House to become what it was.

The great wonder being, not what was done with ample means, but the short time in which it had all been collected together, which was done with such celerity and such small signs of bustle and disturbance, that it appeared as if performed by the wand of a magician, so sudden and so quiet was it done, comparatively.

At the end of five days there was a number of invitations fairly written out and directed, by order of the baron, to the principal inhabitants and gentry of the place to visit Anderbury House, and partake of a grand banquet given by the baron to them and his friends on that occasion.

The day was named, and the information supplied by Mr. Leek to the baron, was of a character that to that individual was extremely valuable, and of which he freely availed himself.

It must not be imagined that the worthy Mr. Leek was in any way oblivious of the promise or obligation into which he had entered with Mrs. Williams, whose name he had taken very great care to insert in the list of invitations that the baron had sent out.

The evening arrived, and the carriages drove up to Anderbury House in rapid succession. There were few or none who knew the baron; they were all, however, anxious, most anxious to see who and what the baron was, who occupied the estate.

The title and name sounded well, and that was what dwelt upon people's minds, and made an impression upon them, and they freely accepted the invitations, especially when they inquired among themselves what was the extent of invitations that had been issued, and they were confined wholly to the *élite* of the place.

What was thought or said upon the occasion, it would be difficult to say, because it was so various, and there were none who could in any way form an opinion at all, that wore any appearance of probability about it.

But there was a rumour spread about that he was a foreigner who had immense riches, desirous of marrying an Englishwoman, and yet unable to obtain introductions in the usual way, or else he was merely acting in accordance with the customs and habits of his own country.

The carriage-drive of Anderbury House was completely occupied by the strings of carriages that had taken up and set down for two hours or more, as rapidly as they could.

The fine apartments that Anderbury House contained, that were destined to be used for the occasion, were indeed a splendid suite of rooms; but they were now lit up with chandeliers, and adorned with glasses, and mirrors, and pictures.

As for the ornamental part of the mansion, it was superb. Nothing had been spared in expense, and by the way in which that was laid out, it was evident the baron was a man of taste and judgment, and had converted a nobleman's residence into a palace.

THE GENTRY CAME dashing up to the door. The place was crowded, and many were announced, and met and welcomed by the baron, who gave them a cordial and distinguished greeting.

There were many persons present; they were astonished at the display of magnificence and wealth of the baron; they were delighted by his reception of them — his conversation, and general manners; and many, too, were much astonished by the splendid entertainment which he had provided for them.

All that art or the season could

produce was there — superb wines and liqueurs — fruits — to an extent they had never before contemplated or thought of.

Anderbury House was without a rival.

The wines were good, and they warmed the blood; and courtesies and civilities of life were by the aid of the alchemy of old port, splendid and sparkling champagne, sherries, Burgundies, and other wines, soon turned into friendships and cordialities.

"Baron," said one of the guests, "you have a superb place, and you certainly are the proper individual to own such a place."

"And why, my dear sir?" inquired the baron, blandly.

"Because you have the taste and heart to decorate and array the place in a manner befitting its extent, and you have the hospitality of one of the ancients of the east."

"Ha! Ha! very good, my dear sir. You are kind, very kind; but I must admit I do like to see neighbours act honestly, and in good faith with each other; besides, I am of opinion that man is a social animal, and one who lives only in society. I cannot be a hermit."

"Right. If the world were all of your opinion — and I believe they are, practice only is opposed — what a state of kindliness and comfort we should all be in — I am sure of it."

"Aye, so am I. Do you like music?"

"I do," was the answer.

"Then you shall hear some. We shall have the dance presently, and then there will be no heart that will not beat in unison with the harmonious strain."

"I think they deserve not to be here in the centre of happiness, if they did not."

"Ho! music, there!" said the baron, as he stamped on the floor of the grand saloon, in which several hundred guests stood.

The call was answered by a loud crash of instrumental music, that came suddenly and startlingly upon the ears of the guests; but then it was followed by a lighter strain, with a pretty but marked melody, such a one, that it instantly communicated to those present, the feeling of being participators, and even actors, in the scene that was about to be enacted upon the floor.

It required but very little exertion to form the dance, where every one was willing and anxious to take their places. There was a slight degree of excitement in the procuring of partners.

Here for a moment the baron was at fault; but, by some means that were not at that moment explained, or even thought of, Mrs. Williams led the beautiful Helen past the spot at the moment. He had spoken to her before, and was well pleased with her. He perceived she was beautiful and amiable. Her mother, too, was with her, and in another moment the baron stepped forward, saying, —

"Madam, if the hand of your daughter is not already engaged, I beg respectfully to claim it for the opening dance?"

Mrs. Williams curseyed with condescension, saying, in reply, —

"Yes, my lord. My daughter is disengaged."

"Miss Williams," said the baron, with much deference, "may I request the honour of your hand?"

Helen Williams curseyed, and said she was not engaged, and accepted of his offer with a smile, but with some diffidence.

The baron immediately led her to the top of the room, where, by this time, there was a perfect lane for them to pass through, until they reached the top.

All had taken their places by an instinctive sort of feeling that was almost universal in the ball-room.

The signal was given, and then the baron led Helen down the first dance, amidst the admiration of all, and the envy of not a few. The giddy whirl of the dance, the throng of beauty, and the sweet but gay notes of the bands, added to the *coup-d'oeil* of the scene — a scene of so much happiness and gaiety, that there were few who could have looked coldly upon it.

The baron, himself, appeared in the highest spirits, and with the greatest hospitality he sought to administer to the wants of his guests, every moment that he could abstract from the present leadership of the dance.

He first visited one, and then the other, until he had made a fair round, and then he found that the night was far advanced, and that, in but a short time, he was convinced that daylight would come.

The guests were well pleased with the splendour of the entertainment, and the profusion that was there. Nothing was wanting. All were well pleased with the arrangements. Great care and great expense had been gone to to gratify and pleasure them, and it had succeeded indeed; if it had not, they would have been captious and ungrateful to an extreme.

The guests, however well pleased with their entertainment, were still unable to bear up against the excitement and fatigue of pleasure for hours, and the animal power fails.

Indeed, there is no one sense which may not be exhausted by an overindulgence; even hearing will, as soon as any other, become invariably tired by listening too long to music; aye, and even become unable to distinguish between the different melodies; and the guests began to flag, and to pay more attention to the side tables, and then to look drowsy, and

some few of the younger spirits appeared to have the dance to themselves.

The baron now saw the proper moment had arrived for dismissing the company; and, causing the music to cease, he advanced to the middle of the room, and, waving his hand, said, —

"My honoured guests, the sun begins to peep over the hills, and the bright car of Phoebus rapidly ascends the skies, telling us that another day has begun. The happiest mortals must part, and so must we. Let me thank you all for this kindness, for thus honouring my banquet with your presence, and let me hope it may often be thus.

"Often, I say. Yes, fair ladies, your presence will always be a distinguished honour. While I am a bachelor, I shall continue these *fêtes* once a fortnight regularly, until somebody takes the arrangement of such matters out of my hands, by legally assuming the title of baroness."

There was a long pause after this announcement, and then a sudden buzz of admiration, which was heard on all sides; and the ladies looked at each other, the baron, and the magnificent place they were in. We cannot tell what passed in their minds, but a shrewd guess might readily be formed, and to the performance of that task we leave the reader.

There were many courtesies before the separation was effected, and an hour had passed before the Baron Stolmuyer of Saltzburgh found himself alone.

CII.

THE WEDDING FEAST. — THE ADMIRAL'S DISAPPOINTMENT.

AND NOW THE DAY arrived, at length, when Charles Holland was to call Flora Bannerworth his bride.

On this most auspicious event, as may be well imagined, the admiral was in his glory, and he declared his intention of dancing, if any very handsome young lady should ask him to be her partner at the ball, but not otherwise; for it had been agreed to have a ball in the evening.

Jack Pringle, too, was restored completely to favour upon the occasion; indeed, as far as the admiral was concerned, he seemed to have granted a general amnesty to all offenders, because he was heard to say,—

"Well, I really should not mind if any poor devil of a Frenchman was to come; he should know what good eating and drinking was for once in his life; or even that vagabond, old Varney, the vampyre. What a fool he was to take himself off before the wedding, to be sure."

Henry Bannerworth had undertaken to take off the old man's hand all the trouble connected with the actual ceremony. That is to say, letting the clergyman know, and so on; therefore he, the admiral, had nothing at all upon his mind but the festivities that were to be gone into upon the occasion.

The numerous guests recommended by the lawyer were invited to a breakfast, which was to be at one o'clock ; while a favoured few, which, together with the family party, made up, altogether, about eighteen persons, were to come to the wedding itself, and to be actually present at the ceremony.

The admiral was rather annoyed at Jack Pringle, about ten o'clock, looking very anxiously at the sky, and shaking his head in a manner which seemed to indicate that he had something of importance on his mind.

"What the deuce is in the wind, now?" said the admiral. "You are always looking for foul weather, you are, and be hanged you!"

"Oh!" said Jack, "I was only a considering what they calls the blessed aspect of the sky, and it seems to me there is a sort of kind of look about things as says that there won't be no marriage at all to-day."

"No marriage!"

"No, not a bit of it; I'm tolerably sure there won't. I was a going on one of my numerous occasions to be married, and there was just that there kind of look in the sky, and I wasn't."

"What kind of look, you lubber? I rather think, after living afloat a matter of forty years and more, I ought to know the looks of the sky rather, and I don't see any thing unusual in it."

"Don't you? Then I does; and there won't be no marriage."

"Why you infernal croaking swab, you are drunk or out of your senses, one of the two. I would bet my head to a bottle of rum, that there will be a marriage."

"I don't mind," said Jack, "betting one bottle to twenty that there won't."

"Done, then—done; and, Jack, for once in a way, you will find yourself regularly done, I can tell you. I know you have got some crotchet or another in your head, by which you think you will get the better of the old man; but it won't do: for I won't stand any quibbling or lawyer-like sneaking out of it."

"Oh! I won't sneak out of it, you shall see. It shall be all plain sailing and above board, I can tell you, admiral."

The old man rather puzzled himself to think what Jack could mean; but after a time he gave it up, and forgot it; for his mind began to be too actively engaged upon what was going on to pay much attention to what he considered was some joke of Jack's, which would turn out to be a mere quibble of words after all.

The admiral was right when he said there was no appearance of anything in the weather to indicate that any stop would be put to the festivity on that account; for a more pleasant, and a more genial, delightful day for the occasion never shone out of the heavens.

Indeed, if anything could have been considered as a gratifying omen of the future felicity which Charles Holland was likely to enjoy in the society of Flora Bannerworth, it was the aspect of that day—a day so replete with beauties that, had it been picked out specially for that occasion, it could not have been more gratifying or delightful.

The house was a large and a handsome one which the admiral had taken, and, since, of course, he considered it to be his own, he was from an early hour in the morning in a perpetual fidget, and here, and there, and everywhere, for the purpose of seeing that all the arrangements were complete for the day's proceedings.

As may be well supposed, he was a great hindrance to everybody, and most especially the servants, whom he had temporarily engaged, wished him at the very devil for his interference.

But, however, notwithstanding all these drawbacks, by ten o'clock everything was in a tolerable state of readiness; and then the admiral vociferously congratulated the first of the guests who arrived, for that was a great merit in the old man's eyes, and, although he did not know the person a bit, he almost terrified him by the cordiality of his greeting.

"That's right," he said; "take old Time by the forelock, and always be too soon instead of too late. I'll tell you some capital stories some of these days about the advantage of being a little too soon—But, hilloa! here comes somebody else. Egad! we shall have them all here soon. Here, Jack Pringle! where are you?"

"Here!" cried Jack; "hard on your larboard bow."

"Pipe all hands among the flunkies!"

"Aye, aye, sir," said Jack.

Producing then a boatswain's whistle, he blew a shrill call, which pleased the admiral, for, as he said, that was the proper way to begin anything like an entertainment.

People know they must be punctual at weddings, and generally are tolerably so, with the exception of those persons who are never punctual at anything; so that, in a short time, nearly the whole of those who had been invited to be present at the ceremony had arrived, and the hour was fast getting on towards that when the marriage was to take place.

The admiral would have been blind, indeed, if he had not perceived that there was a great deal of whispering going on among the Bannerworth family, and he got rather indignant and a little uneasy to know what it could all be about; but, most of all, he began to be annoyed at Jack Pringle, for that individual's conduct was certainly of a peculiar and extraordinary character.

Every now and then he would burst out into such an amazing roar of laughter, apparently at nothing, that it became seriously annoying to the old man; and, finally, taking up a pair of nut-crackers that were upon the table, he gave Jack a hard rap upon the top of the head, as he said,—

"Are you out of your senses? what are you going on about?"

"Oh, nothing," said Jack; "I was only a-thinking. Don't you recollect our wager?"

"Yes, I do; you have laid me one bottle of rum to twenty that Charles and Flora won't be married today."

"Very good," said Jack, "that's quite correct, and mind, I hold you to it."

"Hold me to it—I'll hold you to it. I know well enough it's some stupid joke you have got hold of."

"Very good," said Jack; "we shall see."

The time crept on, and half-past eleven o'clock came, and the guests were assembled in the drawing-room, where, by a special licence, the ceremony was to have been performed; and on the mantle-shelf of which there was a time-piece, indicating the rapid arrival of the hour named for the ceremony.

"You know, Henry," said the admiral,

"I left everything to you. I hope it's all correct, now, and that you have not made any blunders."

"None whatever, I assure you, admiral. I have arranged everything; but Flora has just told me that she wants to speak to you."

"Speak to me! then why the deuce doesn't she speak? I suppose she can speak to me without asking your leave?"

"Admiral," said Flora, "I am extremely anxious to ask you if you will forgive me for something which may possibly annoy you a little, and which certainly I feel myself answerable for."

"What is it?"

"You must promise to forgive me first."

"Well, well, of course—of course I do; what is it?"

"Then, I must say, I would rather not be married to-day."

"What!" cried the admiral.

"I told you so," shouted Jack. "I saw it in the look of the clouds this morning. I never knew anybody get married when there was a light breeze blowing from the nor'-east."

"You be quiet," said the admiral; "I'll be the death of you, presently. What is the meaning of this, Flora? Is it not rather a cruel jest to say such a thing to me now?"

"It is no jest, sir, but a fact; I must beg to be excused."

"And I, uncle," said Charles Holland, advancing, "am of the same mind; and I join with Flora in begging that you will look over the little disappointment this may occasion you."

"Little disappointment!" cried the admiral; "am I awake—am I out of my senses? Jack, you rascal, where am I?"

"Can't say," cried Jack; "but I think as how you are abut two points to the south'ard."

"Flora, speak again. You do not, cannot mean to tell me that any foolish quarrel has interfered to prevent this union, upon which I have set my heart? If you are not jesting, there must be some very special reason for this alteration of intention."

"There is," said Flora, as she looked the old man kindly in the face; "there is a very special reason, sir, and one which I will mention to you at once; a reason which makes it next to impossible that the ceremony should proceed. The real fact is —"

"Well, go on — go on."

"That Charles and I were married a fortnight ago."

"D — n me," said the admiral, "if ever I was so taken in my life. A fortnight ago! shiver my timbers —"

"Go on, old pepper-castor," said Jack; "only remember you owe me twenty bottles of rum."

"I won't look over it," said the admiral; "I won't and I can't; it's treating me ill, Flora — I tell you, it is treating me ill."

"But you know you have looked over it, admiral," said Flora, "and I have your positive promise to forgive me."

"Besides," said Jack, "she won't do so no more; and, as far as I sees of these ere things, it's a deuced good thing as we ain't bothered with any parson coming here this morning, casting up his eyes like a dying dolphin if you outs with so much as a natural 'd — n' or two. I can't stand such rubbish, not I; and its my out and out opinion that we shall be all the merrier; and as for the old man —"

Jack's oratory was put a stop to by the admiral seizing a piece of confectionary that was upon the table, and throwing it with such a dab in his face that he was half choked and covered with currant jam; and he made such a spluttering that the guests could keep their countenances no longer, but burst into a roar of laughter consequent upon that proceeding.

"And you, too, Henry," said the admiral, "I suppose you were in the plot?"

"Why yes," said Henry, "I rather think I was. The fact is, that Flora disliked the public marriage, although she looked forward with pleasure to the meeting with this pleasant party on the present occasion; so, among us, we all cast about for some means for securing the agreeable without the disagreeable, and so, a fortnight ago, they were married quietly and privately, and I plead guilty."

"I thought as much," said the admiral, "I'll be hanged if I didn't; but now just answer me one question, Charles."

"A hundred, if you please, uncle."

"No, one will suffice. I want to know whether you were married in the name of Bell, or in the name of Holland?"

"I took legal advice, uncle, as to the validity of my marriage in the name of Bell; and as I found that a man's marriage was quite legal, let him call himself whatever he pleases, and as I knew that it was your wish I should take the name of Bell, I was married in that name, and Flora now calls herself Mrs. Bell."

"Then I'll say no more about it," said the admiral, "but let it pass so — let's be as merry as possible; and first of all, we will have a bumper all round to the bride."

This affair, upon which Charles really had had some misgivings, being thus

agreeably settled, there was certainly nothing to interfere with the hilarity of the meeting, and as there was an abundance of good cheer, and the guests had been selected judiciously, and were persons who could and would enjoy themselves, an extremely pleasant day was passed.

For about an hour, perhaps, only the admiral now and then exhibited some symptoms of indignation, and shook his head occasionally at Flora; but a smile from her soon restored him, and he did actually contrive to get through a quadrille in some extraordinary manner, by almost knocking every lady down, and ending by falling sprawling himself.

The only great interruption — and that lasted for nearly half an hour — to the proceedings arose from that incorrigible Jack Pringle, who, as usual, did not get a glass too much, but a whole bottle too much; and then an obscure idea seized him that it was absolutely impossible for him to avoid kissing all the ladies, as it was a wedding, or ought to have been a wedding.

Blaming himself, therefore, very much for not having thought of it before, he made a wild rush into the drawing-room, and commenced operations.

A scene of confusion ensued which quite baffles description, and Jack had to be carried out at last by main force, thinking himself a very ill-used person, when he was only doing what was right and proper.

The admiral apologized to the ladies for Jack, calling their attention to the fact that he wasn't such a fool as he looked, and that, after all, it wasn't a bad notion of Jack's, only that he had not set about it in the right way.

"Howsomedever," said the admiral, "I don't mind showing you how he ought to have done it."

This, however, was universally declined, and that with so much decision, too, that the admiral was forced to forego the generous intention; but long before the parties separated for the night, he admitted that it was just as well the marriage business had been all settled before; and it was shrewdly suspected that, from the fact of the admiral singing "Rule Britannia," after he had gone to bed, he had just slightly exceeded the bounds of that moderation which he was always preaching to Jack.

CIII.

DR. CHILLINGWORTH MAKES URGENT INQUIRIES FOR THE VAMPYRE; AND THE LAWYER GIVES SOME ADVICE CONCERNING THE QUAKER.

IF THE BANNERWORTH family and the admiral were inclined to put up quietly with the loss of the large sum of money which Dr. Chillingworth fully believed that Varney, the vampyre, had gone off with, he could not fully divest himself of the idea that it was recoverable.

When he went home, he succeeded in silencing the clamours of his wife, by assuring her that his practice for half-a-dozen years would not at all be equal to what he should gain if he could successfully carry out what he was aiming at; and as everything, to Mrs. Chillingworth, resolved itself into a question of pounds, shillings, and pence, she was tolerable well satisfied, and consented to remain quiet, more especially as he gave her sufficient to keep the household comfortably for some time while again left home.

So thoroughly had he made up his mind not to let the matter rest, that he carefully resolved the best means of setting about, systematically, to inquire for Varney.

He thought it impossible that he could have left the cottage home of the Bannerworths with such great secrecy that no one had observed him.

He was too remarkable a man, too, in personal appearance to escape notice; and if any one saw him, with a grain of curiosity in their composition, they would be sure to look after him with speculative eyes as to who and what he was.

The cottage had not many dwellings near it, and the doctor thought it highly possible that if he visited them all, and made proper inquiries, some one among their inhabitants might be able to tell him that such a man as Varney had been seen.

Accordingly he commenced his tour, and, as luck would have it, at the very second cottage he went to, a woman stated that a tall, dark, singular-looking man had asked leave to sit down for a few minutes, and to be accommodated with a glass of water.

"Had he any parcel or bundle with him?" asked Mr. Chillingworth.

"No," was the reply; "he certainly had nothing of the kind that I could see, and only seemed very weary and exhausted indeed."

"Do you know which direction he went in?"

"I watched him from my cottage door, and after looking about him for some few minutes, he walked away slowly in the direction of the London road."

This was all the information that Dr. Chillingworth could obtain in that quarter; but it strengthened him in his own opinion, that Varney had left that part of the country, and proceeded to London; but with what motives or intentions could not be guessed even, although probably it was with an intention of finding a wider sphere of action.

"If," thought the doctor, "he has gone on the London road, and walked, he must have stopped, in the very weak state that he was, within a very few miles for rest and refreshment; in which case I shall hear tidings of him, if I take myself the same path."

He pursued this plan, and walked on, inquiring at the different inns that he passed, but all in vain, for such a man.

No one had seen anybody resembling Varney; and the doctor, with a sense of great disappointment, was compelled, himself, to stop for rest at a roadside inn, where the mails and stage coaches stopped to change horses.

The landlord of the inn was a good-tempered, conversable man, and was listening, with quiet complacency, to the rather long description of the personal appearance of the individual he sought, that was given by Dr. Chillingworth, when the mail coach from London, which was proceeding to a very distant part of the country, stopped to change horses, and the coachman came to the bar to take his usual glass of refreshment.

While so engaged, he heard something of what Mr. Chillingworth was saying, and he remarked to that gentleman, —

"Do you mean, sir, a long fellow, that looked as if he had been buried a month and dug up again?"

"Well," said the doctor, "he certainly had something of that appearance; but the man I am inquiring about disappeared last Thursday."

"The very day, sir; I was going up with the mail, when he hailed it, and got up on the outside. It's the very man, you many depend; I remember well enough his getting up, but somehow or another when we got to London he wasn't to be found; and so he had his ride as far as it went, and I have not the least idea of how far that was, for nothing."

"I thank you for your information, and I have no doubt that it was the man I seek for. Although he had a large sum of money with him, I think, yet it was not in an available shape to use, and I dare say he would not be very scrupulous about the means he adopted to avoid the inconvenience of any detention."

"Not he, sir, he wasn't very particular. I dare say he got down somewhere in London, most probably at Piccadilly, where there is always a crowd, and I draw up for about five minutes. I don't look to see who gets down, or who stays up, so, as regards that, he might take himself off easy enough, if he liked."

"But you missed him?"

"Yes, I did, when it was too late. Can you tell me who, or what he is, sir?"

"Yes," said Dr. Chillingworth; "it was Varney, the vampyre, of whom, no doubt, you have all heard so much, and who has made such a commotion in the countryside."

"The deuce it was!" said the coachman; "and I have actually had one

of these creatures upon my coach, have I! I only wish I had known it, that's all; I would have pretty soon got rid of such a customer, I can tell him. They don't suit me, those sort of gentry; but I'm off, now; good day, sir. I hope you may catch him."

The coachman got upon his box, and drove away; and Dr. Chillingworth began to think that unless he took a journey to London, which he was scarcely prepared to do, he must give up, for a time, the pursuit of Varney.

Besides, he thought, and justly enough too, that even if he went to the metropolis in search of him, its extent would baffle all inquiry, and make it almost impossible that it could be set about with any prospect of success; so he resolved, before he went any further in the matter, to urge the admiral and the Bannerworths once more upon the subject.

He was firmly, himself, of opinion that something more, and that, perhaps, too, of a very uncomfortable character regarding Varney, would soon be heard, unless they could communicate to him in some manner, and persuade him either to retire from England altogether, or to lead a quiet life with a portion of the wealth he had acquired.

It will be seen with what great pertinacity the doctor clung to that idea which to the Bannerworths appeared such a very doubtful one, namely, that Varney had really got possession of all the money which had been hidden by Marmaduke Bannerworth; but we must leave the doctor for the present inactive, because he felt that, at the period of Flora's marriage, they would be too much occupied to give him the attention he required, and, therefore, he determined to wait until that ceremony, at all events, was completely over.

AND NOW WE MAY as well state at this juncture that the admiral was quite as good as his word, as regarded taking the advice of his friend, the lawyer, concerning the Quaker who still held possession of the Dearbrook estate.

With all the indignation that he felt upon the matter, he laid it before the man of law, explaining how liberally Henry had dealt with him, and what a very uncourteous reception they had met with.

"I am afraid," said the lawyer, "that he may keep you out of it for a year or two, unless you compromise with him."

"What do you mean by compromise?"

"Just this; he knows very well, of course, that he cannot hold possession, and he wants to be paid out, that's the whole of the affair. He considers that you may take friendly advice, and that then you will be told how much shorter, cheaper, and less vexatious a course it is, to put up with almost any amount of imposition, than to get involved in a law suit."

"That's all very fine," said the admiral; "but do you think I'd let that rascally Quaker have a farthing of my money? No, indeed; I should think not. If he expects us to compromise he will be disappointed."

"Well, then, if your determination is to proceed, I will, if you like, take the necessary steps in the name or Mr. Henry Bannerworth. Do you know if he administered to his father's estate?"

"No; I know very little about it. But you had better see him."

"Certainly," said the lawyer; "that will be the best plan. I had better see him, as you say — and I dare say," added the lawyer to himself, "I shall find him more reasonable that you are by a great deal."

THE LAWYER DID SEE Henry; for he called upon him and so strongly advised him to compromise the matter with the Quaker, that Henry gave him full instructions to do as he pleased.

"Your title is so clear," said the lawyer, "that it cannot prejudice you to make the offer, or, rather, to allow me to make it for you; besides, I will take care it shall be made without prejudice, and I dare say you will get possession pretty quickly of the Dearbrook estate."

The lawyer wrote to the Quaker, asking for the name of some solicitor who would act in his behalf, and at once received an answer, referring him to a Quaker attorney, who was tolerably notorious for sharp practice, and who was about as great a rogue as could be found in a profession somewhat notorious for such characters.

The shortest plan and the best was that which was at once adopted by the admiral's friend, the attorney; for he went to town and saw the Quaker upon the subject.

The result of their conference was, that Mr. Shepherd wanted a sum equivalent to two years' rental of the premises he occupied, before giving up possession of them; and in reply one year was offered, and there the matter rested for mutual consideration of the principals.

Henry did not feel exactly disposed to do anything in the affair, in actual defiance of the admiral, so he resolved upon trying, at all events, to persuade him into the compromise, if possible; and the principal argument he intended using was, that Flora had heard sufficient of the Dearbrook property, and that it would be a thousand pities, consequently, to keep her out of possession of it, since, from what they had all seen of it, they felt that it would be a very desirable residence indeed.

The admiral's anger, however, had been so roused by the insolent conduct of the Quaker, that it required great care and tact to introduce the subject to him in such a shape, and Henry set about it not without some fear of the result.

"I have seen, admiral," he said, "your friend, the lawyer, about the Dearbrook property, and we shall not have possession in our lifetimes."

"What do you mean by that?"

"Oh, our ghosts may perhaps haunt its verdant shades; but we shall be all dead long before the Court of Chancery decides in our favour; for, owning to the manner of my father's death, some difficulties may be thrown in the way to protract time."

"What! does he tell you so?"

"Yes, indeed he does, admiral; and then, you see, Heaven knows how many claimants may arise for the estate, if it was known how recently we came by the title-deeds."

"The deuce they would! I can't say but there is some reason in that, after all; but what is to be done? You can't say that the Quaker, Shepherd, is to be allowed to retain possession of the Dearbrook estate, just because there are some difficulties in the way of getting it out of his clutches?"

"Certainly not; but the whole question resolves itself into what is the best means of accomplishing that object, and the great difficulty seems to be this; that he actually has possession, which you have heard, of course, is nine points of the law, and puts a man in such a position that he can give a deal of trouble to any one who is not so fortunately situated."

"Can he; then I tell you what I'll do, Henry; I'll pretty soon alter that state of things."

"But how can you, admiral?"

"By going and taking possession, to be sure; and if possession be indeed nine points of the law, I don't see why we shouldn't have them. I have taken a ship or two from an enemy when they have been under their own batteries, and it ain't the most likely thing in the world that a Quaker, who, in the navy, we call a wooden gun, should stop me taking possession of the house."

"I am quite sure," said Henry, "that if you were to set about it, you would do it,—there can be no doubt whatever upon that head; but it's a very difficult thing to treat the law in that sort of way, and you may depend there would be an amazing fuss made about it, so much so, indeed, that some serious consequences might ensue, and we should perhaps lose the estate altogether."

"Hang the estate! it's the Quaker I want to serve out."

"But you have served him out. Don't you recollect the kick you gave him?"

"Why, yes; I certainly did give him a kick."

"And a good one too."

"You think it was a good one, do you, Henry? Well, I must say, I am very glad of that — very glad of it. It's some consolation, that's quite clear."

"And I think then, after that, admiral—after feeling that you have served him out in that kind of manner, and that he has put up with the degradation of having been kicked by you, you might just as well forego a little of your resentment, and allow me to ascertain if I cannot make something like terms with him."

"Terms with a vagabond like that!"

"Yes. What say you to giving him a trifle, and then let him go; provided he clears out of the estate at once, and gives us no further trouble?"

"I'd ten times rather kick him again."

"Why, yes; and I must confess he deserves kicking most certainly. I admit all that, that a greater scamp you could not find; but, after all, you see, admiral, it comes to a question of pounds, shillings, and pence. Nothing in the world makes a man like that suffer but touching his pocket."

"Very likely; but you propose to put something into his pocket."

"Yes, at first; but it is to save the more, as would easily be found; and, besides, you see how he has been afraid to take any notice of your kicking him."

"To be sure he has; such fellows are always afraid. You didn't expect he would take any notice, did you? and, if you did, I knew better. Afraid, indeed! Ah! to be sure; that's just what he was likely to be—afraid, as a matter of course."

"If you please, sir," said a servant, coming in to the admiral, "here is a gentleman wants to speak to you."

"To me? Who the deuce can that be, I wonder?"

"He says it's on particular business, sir."

"Well, well; show him in here."

A mere youth was shown into the apartment, who, addressing the admiral, said,—"Pray, sir, is your name Bell?"

"To be sure it is; and what of that?"

"Nothing particular, sir; only I have the honour of serving this upon you."

"And what the devil is it?"

Before this question was well out of the admiral's lips the lad had disappeared, and when the old man unfolded the paper, he found that it was a notice of action from Shepherd, the Quaker, on account of the assault which Admiral Bell had committed upon him.

"And this is the fellow," cried the admiral, "that you want me to compromise with. No, Master Henry, that won't do; and, since he has had the imprudence now to commence war with me, he shall not find that I am backward in taking up the cudgels in my own defence, I'll pretty soon let him know that he has got rather an obstinate foe to deal with, and we will see how long he will find it worth his while to persevere."

Henry felt at once that this imprudent act of the Quaker, which, no doubt, was intended to hasten and facilitate a compromise, placed it further off than ever, and that, in the admiral's present state of mind, it was quite absurd to think of talking to him in anything like a peaceable strain, for such could not be done.

The utmost that could be hoped was that he would not actually give way to some act of violence, and that he would, at all events, do nothing more than what the law allowed him to do in the matter.

This was what Henry did not feel quite sure of, and he only hoped it.

CIV.

THE BONE-HOUSE OF THE CHURCHYARD OF ANDERBURY. — THE RESUSCITATION.
— THE FIGHT, AND THE ESCAPE OF THE DEAD. — THE BOAT, AND THE VAIN PURSUIT.

THE CORONER, AFTER THE inquest was over, issued his precept for the interment of the body of the man who was found in the ice-well of Anderbury House, and whose body was deposited at the bone-house in Anderbury churchyard.

There was an end now to these proceedings, though it was much too fresh in people's minds to enable them to forget it; yet, once the coroner's inquiry over, it usually happens that a feeling of satiety, arising from excitement, in the first place, or following that excitement, and induced by the knowledge that all is done that can be towards unravelling the mystery that had caused such a sensation, takes place.

The town of Anderbury was first subsiding to its original quietude, and the only indication of any excitement was that among a few old topers, who met in the early part of the evening, to discuss anything that there might be stirring to talk about, and to do that required but little inducement, to talk being their principal, not to say only, amusement; indeed, to have deprived them of that would have been to have deprived them of nearly their only inducement to work and to live, that they may indulge in their evening conversations at the alehouse.

There was a very general belief among such people that, as the whole affair was unexplained, that it was mysterious, and the nods and winks were numerous; indeed, it was thought that there was more than the usual amount of mystery. However, this has its limit, and when all is said that can be said, there must be an end to the discussion, which is usually dropped for want of fuel to feed it.

THAT NIGHT THE BARON sat alone in his apartment, apparently buried in deep thought; but, now and then, he might have been seen to lift up his eyes towards the east, as if watching for something, and then he would cast them towards a magnificent timepiece on the mantelpiece, and then he would again relapse into thoughfulness.

There were several such fits as these, that were broken in the same manner as before, and, at length, the arose and took a small book off one of the tables, and examined a certain page and a certain column, and then he half-muttered to himself,

"Yes — yes; it is as I thought — the moon will rise in about an hour and a half; that will do. I will now go to the bone-house, and there watch the body, and ascertain if my fears are correct; if not, I shall be well repaid for my trouble; and should they be, why, I must endeavour to make the affair take the best turn I can. I must try and prevent the completion of my own deed from being disturbed in its integrity. The dead must remain so; and, if not, to that condition he must return, and lie where no moon's ray will reach him."

He arose, and, wrapping his cloak around him, went to the door of his apartment, and paused, as if listening.

"No one is stirring," he muttered; "no one is about."

He stole softly out of the apartment, and descended the stairs, making his way towards a small private door, which opened into the garden, which he secured behind him.

Then he walked rapidly but softly through the garden, which he quitted by another private door, and which he also secured after him; and then proceeded quickly and silently towards the church yard of Anderbury church, which was but ill-qualified to keep intruders out of it, seeing that there was but a low wall and a hedge for the purpose of a fence, which could at various places be easily scaled; indeed, there are few country churchyards that cannot be so entered; and it does not appear usually the practice to endeavour to keep out human beings, but rather to keep the yard clear of all brute intruders, for it was open to all who should choose to come.

The scene was not very distinct; the moon was not yet risen, and darkness reigned upon the earth; he could see but a short way, and he cared but little for that.

"If darkness prevents my seeing, it also prevents others seeing me; therefore, it is welcome. The moon will rise soon enough to aid me in my watch, and if it rise not at all, it would be agreeably satisfactory, seeing that there would be no probability of what I suspect happening without her rays."

He hurried onwards towards the churchyard. The sea was close by, and the night breeze, as if swept across the face of the ocean, gave the indistinct roar, which never ceases, but only increases and abates as a storm or calm prevails at the time, and as the wind increases or diminishes, thus increasing or diminishing the intensity of the roar; but it never entirely ceases at any time.

The baron made his way towards the churchyard by an unfrequented path that was well known to him; but as he was about to get over a stile into a field, he thought he heard a voice speaking on the other side of the hedge.

He paused a moment, and crept along the hedge, until he came to the spot where the voice seemed to come from, and then he paused, until he heard them speak again.

"I tell you what it is, Jack; it's a very strange affair — a very strange thing, indeed."

"So it is."

"And one I can't understand at all, though I have endeavoured to do all I can that way. I have thought the matter over very often; but it always comes to this — that it is a very strange affair."

"What can be the cause of it?"

"I don't know."

"Have you seen it?"

"I thought I did once," said the second; "but it was misty and dark; but I think I couldn't be mistaken."

"Nor I."

"You have see it oftener than I; have you not?"

"Yes — yes — I have, several times."

"How did you see it?"

"Why, thus: I was looking out for the lugger, and there away in the east I saw something white coming across the sea. It came very steady and slow, and looked small at first."

"Yes — yes."

"Well, then, after that it came closer and closer, until I saw it changed its shape to a gigantic woman."

"A woman!" exclaimed the other.

"Yes, or may be a man in a winding-sheet; that is most likely though, after all."

"I think so, too," he replied; "as sure as there are dead bodies in Anderbury churchyard, it forebodes some great evil — of that I am very well persuaded."

"What great evil do you think will happen?"

"How can I tell? I am no prophet. I cannot imagine in what shape it should come; but come it will depend upon it; if it comes not now, when it does come, remember my words."

"I will."

"And you will find them all true some day or other, if it don't come too soon to be pleasant; but I think something may happen to the lugger."

"She has not been seen these two days; and it is now past the time when she ought to have been in. Thus it was with the other lugger that the revenue cutter took."

"Did you see the apparition?"

"No; but there was a token, I believe; but I was not in those parts at that time."

"Well; but how did it happen that they let the lugger be taken by the king's men?"

"Oh! they couldn't well help it, you may depend upon that. She was coming from Cherbourg, laden with brandy and with lace, a good cargo, and worth something, I assure you."

"She must have been worth something."

"She was. Well, she had a very good run for a part of the way, when a fog came on. Well, it wasn't well understand what they were to do. Some were for putting back; others for standing where they were, and some few for running in shore.

"'I shall run in shore,' said the captain. 'I know every hole upon the coast; and I know the exact spot where we are, and how to steer. I can run the vessel to an inch.'

"'And that inch may do the business for us all,' said one of the crew; 'but I'm ready.'

"'And I, too,' said the captain; 'and I will run her where there will be no chance of any meeting with the preventive people; but the fact is, we can neither see nor be seen; we are safe, boys. A good run on shore, and a swift voyage home.'

"'Huzzah!' shouted the men; and the vessel was run towards the shore, and, at the same time, they were going under an easy sail safe and secure, and had no thought of any evil.

"There was a look-out, at the same time we could not see two yards beyond the vessel. The watch was alert, but he could see nothing; but suddenly he called out, —

"'Ship a-head! Port your helm!'

"'What ship's that?' inquired a voice, and, in another moment, they found themselves alongside the revenue cutter, from whom they had so long and so often escaped.

"'Board!' shouted the officer on board, and then he called upon our people to surrender; but the captain drew his sword, and called out to the crew to do as he did, and defend the ship; and as he spoke, he cut one man down, but was immediately met by a pistol-shot, which laid him dead on the deck.

"After that there was no resistance; the men didn't want to endanger their lives by resisting men who were doing their duty, and protected by law; they were, moreover, out-numbered by the revenue people, and if they resisted, they would be liable to hanging, whereas they could but imprison them.

"They were all taken, and they were all imprisoned for different crimes — all, however, getting free after a term."

"Did that ruin the owners?"

"Oh! no; they calculated upon a loss now and then, and can well afford it too."

"Well, what do you think of the baron at Anderbury House?"

"Think! Why, I think he's a trump. What a glorious haul there would be there, if we could get hold of it."

"How do you mean?"

"Why, the plate and other things that are valuable. Look you now, if we could load the lugger with the contents of the house, what would they not fetch in Paris?"

"We should not get it if we were to take it there."

"We should obtain a heavier profit than ever we should under any other circumstances; and I think it will be a very good plan, indeed, to take Anderbury House by storm. There's some thousands of pounds' worth of plate and jewellery there."

"So there is."

"Well, what do you say to make the attempt? Attempt, I say; but I shall not call it an attempt, for there will be no attempt at resistance — we shall have only to walk in and frighten a few servants; there will be nothing but to carry away what we can lay our hands on."

"That will do — anything that will pay."

The baron had been an attentive listener. He had, moreover, had some thoughts in his own mind of jumping over the hedge, and seizing the two men; but, upon second thoughts, he believed that this was the worst that could be done.

"I will frighten them, and thus prevent them from putting their designs into practice to my damage."

The baron silently collected several large stones and clods of earth into one space, and then he peeped through the hedge. He saw where they lay, and took up two clods, pitched one on each of their heads, and then he said, when they started up, —

"Miserable sinners! the eye of Heaven is upon you; go your ways and repent while there is time."

The men were for a moment horrified, and stood still, chained to the spot; but suddenly they were released, and in a moment they rushed from the spot with the fleetness of deer.

The baron watched them out of sight, and then he muttered to himself, —

"'Tis well; they are now out of sight; they are gone, and they will make no attempt upon Anderbury House, I'll warrant them they think their design will be penetrated by others, and they will suffer for it should they attempt it. I trust I can make a very good resistance; however, it is worth thinking of."

He paused a few moments longer, and then turned towards the churchyard.

He pursued his way, however, thoughtfully; every now and then, however, he looked around to ascertain if any one were present, but he was satisfied there was none, and thus he was quite and entirely alone in his walk.

There was now light enough to enable him to distinguish objects at a short distance, and he quickened his pace, as he thought of the moon's rising; but a few minutes brought him into view of the church of Anderbury.

The old church was seen to advantage at such an hour, for as the sky was cloudless, and the stars were out, the tapering spire looked like some great and gigantic indication raised there for some purpose pointing heavenward.

There was a deep gloom surrounding the whole place, for there was not a shadow cast by any one object, neither had the church one side that was lighter than the other.

In a very short time the baron reached the charnel-house, or the bone-house, as it was more usually called. It was a small place, attached to the church itself. The wants of the population were not great; and, therefore, all these public places were built with the view only of a limited use.

It was large enough for all purposes, and as large as it is usual for them to be in such places; and the baron, before he attempted to enter the place, took a walk all the way round, to ascertain if there was any one lurking about; but finding none, he returned to the door of the charnel-house with the full intention of going in.

However, there was no key, and he could not, therefore, enter it by the usual way, and he must find some other.

"There is sure to be something or other," he muttered, "to cause a temporary stop to one's career in some place or other; but I will not be deterred by such a trifle — there is a place in the roof somewhere here, I think, where I can get in with but little trouble."

The baron looked about for a place that would enable him to climb up, but he suddenly withdrew his hand, exclaiming, —

"Hilloa! what have we here?"

It was soon settled, and the baron held up between him and the light the key of the charnel-house, which he had found as he put his fingers into a niche to assist him in lifting himself up to the roof.

"This is lucky, and will save me much trouble; but I have not much time to spare."

He put the key into the lock, and found it fitted the lock, and he in another moment opened the door of the charnel-house, and entered its unwholesome precincts.

There were but few who would have entered that place at that hour, knowing, too, that a man was lying dead that had died a violent death; few, indeed, would have done so, but the baron was himself above such considerations; and besides, he had an object in view, which was of some importance.

He desired to watch the body of the murdered man — he desired to stay there, and watch the effects of the moon's rays upon it. He now smelt where he was, for there was that fetid smell of death, which always hangs about the bone-house, which is a receptacle of all the mortal remains of man, which have been once cast into the grave, for which their friends have paid large fees — as well for the ceremony, as for the quiet enjoyment of the home of death; but which bargain must be continually violated, and the bones of a man's ancestor, instead of ornamenting some museum, or his carcass doing some good by way of instruction, lie rotting in the grave-yard, till the sexton digs up the same ground and takes fresh his fees, but burning the bones of the former.

The baron entered the receptacle of the remains of mortality. One after the other have men's bones been thrown in here, or, perhaps they have been mixed together, so that it would have puzzled an angel to have separated them from each other.

What more could mortals expect? their bones, at least, will form a fuel to be sure; but very indifferent fuel, too.

Here, however, the baron entered, and stepped lightly into the place. It was an uncomfortable place at best — cold, cheerless, very bare, save of such things as would remind one of the sexton's duty, and of the nature of the place in which he was.

The first thing the baron did, was to look towards the place where the window was placed, but no light came in. He advanced to it, and gazed out upon the night.

"Well, well," he muttered, "the moon is just rising; there will be time enough, and I can remain in this place as long as any of its rays penetrate the windows."

He paused a few moments, during which he looked out upon the country; but all was wrapped up in gloom and darkness, save where some of the moon's beams fell, and then there could be seen some dark spots more prominent than the rest; and then, after awhile, he could distinguish between the different objects, though he could not always tell their different parts.

"Well," he muttered, "I am here now, and am housed. Faugh! how the place smells. I shall never be able to remain here. I shall never get the scent from my nostrils."

He turned from the window, and examined the place. It was a square room, with bare walls. A few shelves, and some odd lumber thrown into one corner, a ladder, some tools, trestles, and a lot of rubbish in the shape of old pieces of coffins, bones, and other matters that belonged to a churchyard. There was very little in all this, to make the place at all likely to become popular with anybody.

The shell in which the man had been placed was, from some cause or other, upset from off the trestles, and the body had rolled out. It lay in all its ghastly proportions at full length upon the ground, somewhat on one side, and looking towards the window. The posture shewed the body was deprived of life. It was still and motionless — not a sound or motion escaped the lips of the baron, as he gazed upon the victim of the ice-well.

Well did the baron mark the position of the body, and marvel at the singularity of the accident which had exposed the body in the way in which it laid.

"I wonder what could have been the cause of such an accident? Who could have thought it would have happened? I am sure I never could have expected it should have happened."

He took one of the trestles that lay near the body, and placed it so that he could gaze upon the corpse, and out at the window, alternately, without any disturbance to himself.

"Here I can watch the progress of the moon," he thought, "and the body, too; and if I find my conjectures are right, I will soon prevent his quitting this place, and put him in such a position as shall preclude the possibility of the revivifying powers of the moon ever reaching him again. He shall lie till corruption visits his body, and then a return to life be impossible."

Thus muttered the baron, as he gazed fixedly at the body of the man, who had met his death in the manner related, and of whom the baron entertained some singular suspicions.

The moon was rising above the horizon, and shed a soft light over the fields and woods. It was strange and silent, save when the church clock struck out the hours as they fled.

It was a strange sound, and almost startled the baron to hear the hour come booming through the building, and gave such a sound, that it broke the awful stillness of the night which reigned; the moon all the while rising higher and higher in the heavens, until its beams came very near the window.

The baron's patience became somewhat impaired; he saw that the time would soon arrive, when his curiosity must be satisfied, and when the truth would at once break in upon him.

"Can it be," he muttered, "that the dead should ever again rise to communicate with the world, and live to lead a loathsome life? Impossible! and yet 'tis said so by many, who assert they speak but the evidence of their own senses; if it is to be

depended upon at all, it will be as well for me as they.

"Why should I not be satisfied as well as they are? I have, moreover, more than ordinary motives for satisfaction. The human bloodsucker shall not live. I am resolved upon that."

The moonbeams now entered the window of the charnel-house. At first it was but a pencil ray, so small and minute, that the baron himself could scarce perceive it; but he did see it, and kept his eye intently fixed upon it, watching its increase in size and change of position with intense excitement.

There was the moon rising high in the heaven, with all its myriads of stars, and black canopy, studding the vault with innumerable gems; and as it rose, so it gave a far greater change to the aspect of the landscape than would have been expected.

The whole side of the charnel-house was illuminated by the moon's rays, but they fell aslant and only entered the window in one direction, which cast them on one side, near where the baron sat.

He could now see how the place was furnished; the significant appurtenances of the charnel-house were easily discernible, and would have given a melancholy turn to the thoughts of anybody who might have examined them; but not so the baron — he was by far too excited to heed them, though he honoured them with a passing glance.

They are used by the sexton in the prosecution of his business, in the performance of his duties; therefore, there need be but little attention paid to them; they cannot harm any one, but are the means of frightening fools.

To frighten the baron was, however, something more than a mere matter of course; his nerves were strung to the purpose with which he visited the place, and they were not to be disturbed by any insignia whatever. There were plenty of ghastly objects about; bones, legs, hands, arms, and even skulls, were lying about in profusion, or rather they were heaped up in one corner of the place, and there was an attempt to hide them by heaping up old boards in front of them, as if it were done on purpose to prevent the prying eye of man from peeping and seeing the secrets of the charnel-house.

It is strange, but true, being accustomed to such scenes as these causes a diminution of the awe and fear in which such things are usually held. Soldiers and sailors care not much for death; they are used to exposure, and the loss of life does not seem to them so terrible as to those who have never faced danger.

So with the sexton: he turns up the remains of mortality, as if they were so much rubbish, and never had been endowed with life; indeed, it is only necessary to become familiar with the remains of man, and then much of the awe and mystery attending them dies away.

What cares the grave-digger whether the burial service has been read over the remains or not? What cares he if the ground in which they have been placed is consecrated ground? He can't tell the difference, and it matters not to him; he is above such consideration, and so is he and his patrons, as to whether the spot in which the remains lie, has been bought and paid for long ago.

He has no objection to sell again that which has been sold, and that which has been used as the resting-place of some one or other. No matter, they say; the mystery, the freemasonry, and all, have been instituted for the multitude, and not for those who are behind the curtain, and pocket the fees; that is the great object of the conspirators.

However, here they were, all lumped up together, on one side, or rather in one corner, with a few boards thrown over them, as if to prevent their being seen by any incidental intruder.

Here the baron sat, watching the moonlight in its slow progress towards the dead body; and, as it crept towards the object, he felt more and more excited, but yet remained perfectly immoveable. He turned his eyes sometimes from the body to the streak of moonlight that passed through the small window, and then to the small window itself, from which he could see the moon himself, but that was fast rising too high, and was becoming invisible by changing its position, so that the baron could not see it.

"The moon travels fast," he muttered, "and a few more minutes will tell me what I am to expect."

As he spoke these words, he felt in his pocket, and appeared satisfied with what he found there — possibly some weapon.

The moon's rays were now within an inch or so of the body, an all was as still and silent as the grave; no sound, no motion, not even a breath of air stirred to interrupt the silence and stillness of the scene; even the breathing of the baron himself was suppressed, and he strove to watch without motion.

The moonlight appeared to grow more brilliant, more beautifully white, and cast, as he thought, a stronger and more sickly light than usual into the charnel-house. There was nothing that he had ever before seen like it, and he looked around him more than once to assure himself that he was where he was, and that he was alone with the body in the bone-house.

At such moments the fancy is apt to play us strange freaks, and, if not a strong and nervous man — capable of throwing off any extraneous influence, why he would soon be bowed down by the weight of mental terror and agony — that is, nothing short of temporary madness, and which probably would make a permanent impression, and leave the seeds of mental disease for ever.

But the baron was not easily moved; he had not been brought up in schools where the mind is bound, enchained from infancy by artificial means, which seem to bind the powers of the mind in after years, and, in moments of doubt and difficulty, to render it dependent upon any extraneous circumstance, rather than itself.

However, there were few things thought of then by the baron, who sat intently watching the progress of the moon's beams towards the body, which was now touched by them.

The light fell strong, it edged the white garments that were thrown around the body; the baron watched more and more intently, and each moment lessened the space of time when the truth would come out — when he would be assured of the truth of his conjectures.

There was no ray on the body yet, but it slowly and slowly let the light approach the body; the edge was illumined, and then the moonbeams fell more and more upon it; gradually did they enlarge its surface till the whole body was in the light of the moon.

The baron's excitement and expectation were now at the highest, for the whole body was illuminated.

"Now!" he exclaimed, in a muttered whisper; "now is the moment."

No sooner was the whole of the body, the breast, and the face illumined, than there was a perceptible quiver through that form.

"Ha!" exclaimed the baron, with a start.

The features presented a ghastly spectacle; there was a peculiar sickly and horrible expression in the countenance, much of which was caused by the peculiar position in which it was placed; the peculiar colour of the moon's rays and the additional horrors of the place, all seemed to give an effect to an object peculiarly ghastly and horrible.

The body, after a few moments, as if awakening to life and recollection, lifted up its head, and turned over upon one side towards the moonlight; and then, after a moment, it looked up in the moon's rays, which seem to pour down upon the countenance that lifted up towards it.

The baron rose softly and stealthily.

"You shall feel that this is your last hour. The newly awakened life which feeds upon the blood of others, shall never exist to carry on its disgusting career."

As he muttered these thoughts to himself, he drew a short dagger from his pocket; at the same moment the figure turned its face towards him.

It gave a half unearthly scream, as its eyes met those of the baron's, who exclaimed,

"Now — now's the time — death to the monster."

As he spoke, he threw himself headlong on the prostrate form of the vampyre, for such it was; which, as he did so, endeavoured to rise up and escape. The baron, who had aimed a deadly blow at him, as he threw himself upon him, caused him to fall back again; but the fearful being had contrived to ward off the blow, either with its arms, or by means of shifting its position, or something of the sort; the baron missed the blow, and was now in a deadly struggle with the vampyre.

The struggle was fierce; no signs of shrinking on the part of the baron, who carried it on with the full intention of its ending fatally to his opponent, while he was exerting himself to escape the muscular grasp of the baron.

The baron, however, was not a match for the more than superhuman strength of the vampyre, who, endued with all the energy of love of a newly-acquired life, struggled with a desperation scarcely to be conceived.

Had any one looked in, from without, upon the struggle that was going on within, they would have believed that some demons of the dead had suddenly become endued with the power of appearing upon earth, and had chosen that spot upon which they could exercise their malignity in combat with each other.

Suddenly, however, the baron was thrown with great force upon the ground, and he lay for a moment half stunned; then the vampyre, disengaged as he was, stopped to cast a magnificent look of triumph upon his fallen foe, and dashed out of the bone-house by the same entrance as that which afforded ingress to the place to the baron.

In another moment the baron rose up and rushed after the flying vampyre, his defeat by no means extinguishing his courage or ardour.

He soon caught sight of the vampyre as he was flying from the bone-house; indeed, the moonlight was now so strong, that it seemed almost day.

Every object, far or near, appeared distinct and observable; while the waves of the ocean appeared every now and then to throw off the silvery light, like a thousand moving mirrors.

Beautiful as the scene was, there was none there who stood to look upon it. The only living and breathing persons present, were those who were engaged in the chase. Not a soul, save these two, were about — none saw them — none witnessed the fearful efforts of the two.

The place looked like some spot of earth spoken of by the enchanters; all was motionless and still, save these two, and the ceaseless motion of the ocean waves.

The vampyre made for the shore, with the baron a short distance behind him. They strained every nerve; and the baron thought he should succeed in securing him on the beach.

There were some boats that were secured on the beach, and towards these the vampyre sped with the fleetness of the wind; and, no sooner did he reach one, than seizing its head, he caused it to run through the sand by the impetus he had acquired in running, and it was afloat in a moment.

There was no time to lose, for just as he had pushed into deep water, the baron had rushed down almost in time to seize the boat but missed it.

He then made for the boats, and succeeded in reaching one that was afloat, secured only by a rope.

In this he pushed out on the waves in pursuit of the object of his search. Away they both went; the sea was comparatively smooth; they both rowed with velocity, that promised much as regarded their capability as rowers.

The spray of the water was thrown up by their oars and by the boats' heads. The baron, however, had the worst of it; he rowed to disadvantage; because, every now and then, he had to turn his head to see which way the object of his pursuit was rowing; and, therefore, a loss of speed occurred; but yet he kept up well in the wake of the vampyre.

There was, however, no attention paid as to where he was going; as long as it was straight in the wake of the flying, he was satisfied. But he saw nothing else, nor looked at aught else; indeed, the world might have been there, and he would not have been aware of the fact. His whole faculties were bound up in the object before him, to reach which, he exerted his whole strength.

However, upon looking up again, he could nowhere see the vampyre. He looked long and steadily in all quarters, but saw him not. He had eluded him.

CV.

THE BARON PROPOSES TO HELEN WILLIAMS, AND IS DULY ACCEPTED, WITH A COMPLIMENT ON HIS BEAUTY.

THE BARON HAD PUT out to sea in chase of the vampyre, without considering that there was really great danger in so doing, inasmuch as that the elements were not quite in a kindly disposed condition, and there was a heavy sea.

Where he had obtained his skill as a seaman, Heaven only knows; but certain it is he had obtained such knowledge somewhere, for he commenced navigating the boat with the greatest skill, and soon succeeded in getting close in shore.

The moment the keel grated upon the beach, a man rushed into the water, and laid hold of the boat with one hand, and the baron with the other, exclaiming,—

"You are my prisoner! You took my boat, and I don't care who or what you are, I will have justice."

"How much money do you require?"

"More than you will like to pay. I sha'n't let you off under a pound."

"Here are five pounds."

"Lor! Excuse me, your honour; I didn't mean what I said; if so be as your honour is such a gentleman as I now sees as your honour is, it don't make any matter in the world. I hopes as how your honour will always take my boat when you wants one, and no mistake."

The baron made no reply to all these compliments, but walked away at once towards his own house on the cliffs.

"I have missed him," he muttered, "and all my labour has been in vain. I thought that at least I had got rid of that affliction; I thought that he at least would have rotted in the tomb. Curse on the tardiness that left him unburied until the moonbeams had rested upon him. After that all was in vain, unless some new death had come over him."

There was a flush of anger upon the baron's face as he reached his own house, and let himself into it by a garden-gate that he always kept the key of, which would have effectually prevented any of his servants from taking any notice of him, had they met him.

But at such an hour, it was not likely he should meet any one, nor did he do so.

He at once sought his own chamber, where he remained for some time immersed in deep thought. This thought was not wholly devoted to a consideration of his annoyance at the escape of the vampyre; but he took into his most serious thoughts the circumstances attending upon his entertainment.

The question of to marry, or not to marry, was not one that had to be settled by the baron. No, that he had done already; and he had not made the announcement he had to Mr. Leek, of his matrimonial intention, unadvisedly.

What the baron now considered was, whether he should propose to Miss Helen Williams or not.

He certainly had been somewhat struck by the quiet beauty of the young girl; and probably he was aware that he was not just the sort of person to win a young maiden's heart, and that if he achieved such a honour at all, it would most probably be in consequence of acting upon the cupidity of her relations.

As he was determined, therefore, to marry, it became necessary that he should select some one for his victim who, in addition to the personal charms which appeared to him to be a desideratum, should be of so pliant and amiable a disposition as to give way to those solicitations and incessant remonstrances which she was likely to be assailed with if she resisted.

It was fortunate for Mr. Leek that the baron did fix his regards upon Helen Williams; because, from what we know of Mrs. Williams, we can well perceive that it is quite evident she will not let any considerations of her daughter's happiness stand in the way of an equitable arrangement with that gentleman.

And although there might have been, and indeed were, persons at the baron's entertainment whom he would more gladly have called by the name of bride than Helen Williams, yet he was not slow to perceive that those parties had wills of their own, and, if their relatives had pleased to do so, they would not themselves have admitted that they were up for sale to the highest bidder.

The result of the baron's considerations, therefore, was, that Helen Williams would suit him very well, and that the poverty of her family was just the circumstance of all others which insured his success.

"I will wed her," he said, "although I cannot win her. She will be mine, because I shall purchase her; which, to my mind, is a much more admirable mode of embarking in a matrimonial career than the trouble of a tedious courtship, with all its frivolities and follies."

Whether or not the baron was used to matrimonial affairs, we cannot say; but certain it is he did not seem to consider that the proposing for a young lady and marrying her was a matter of very grave or serious moment; but really, by the style in which he considered it, anybody would have thought it one of the most ordinary concerns of life.

During his short stay at Anderbury, he had managed, by the magic power of wealth, to procure everything he required in the shape of servants, carriages, and horses; and now, on the morning after his most strange and mysterious adventure with the corpse of the murdered man, he ordered his carriage, and went out to pay a number of visits to the parties who had been present at his entertainment.

Among those visits he included one to the Williams family, and by about twelve o'clock in the day reached their residence, and was received with such an extraordinary amount of bustle, that it was quite ludicrous to see it; but still it suited him, because it showed how they worshipped wealth, with the exception of Helen, and she did not make her appearance at all.

Mrs. Williams was all smiles and sweetness, paying so many compliments to the baron, that, although he knew nothing of the diplomatic arrangement of Mr. Leek, he yet felt quite certain that he had her with him most completely, and that none of her exertions would be wanting for the purpose of securing his victim.

After these compliments had somewhat subsided, the baron said,—

"Madam, I hope I shall have the pleasure of seeing your daughter Helen, who did me the honour of being at my poor entertainment the other evening, and attracted while there the eyes of all beholders."

"Oh, certainly, my lord baron. I have not the slightest doubt in my own mind but that Helen is quite—quite panting, in a manner of speaking, for the honour of seeing you again."

"You are very obliging, madam; and I can assure you that one of the most gratifying circumstances that have occurred to me during my short residence in this neighborhood, had consisted in the fact of my making the acquaintance of you and your amiable family."

"Will you excuse me for one moment?" said Mrs. Williams; and, after a courteous bow from the baron, she left the apartment, and proceeded to the room of her daughter Helen, whom she addressed, saying,—

"Helen, are you aware that the baron is here—the great baron, the Baron Stolmuyer of Saltzburgh? Good God! how can you be so foolish? He has actually asked for you, and you are not there; when you know as well as I do, Helen, that such a man as that, to whom the expense is no object, might pop in a moment."

"He might what, mother?"

"Pop the question—propose, of course. Don't tell me that you don't know what I mean. I have no patience with such nonsense. Only think how rich he is. You know as well as I that it would be the making of you and the whole family; and I can tell you, Helen, that, if you are not a positive fool, in my opinion, he will pop, for there was quite a particular expression upon his face when he asked for you."

"But I fancy, mother, there is always a particular expression upon his face—a particularly ugly one, I mean; for, beyond all question, he is the most ordinary man I ever saw in my life."

"Now, really, Helen, you are enough to vex a saint. What can a man's looks have to do with his property?"

"But what's his property to me, mother?"

"Oh! good gracious! Have I lived to hear a child of mine ask what a man's property is to her, when he begins to be attentive! I did not expect it—I will confess, I did not expect it. I did think there would be a little consideration on the part of a child of my own, when she knows I have to strive, and strive, and stretch our means like a thin piece of Indian rubber, to make both ends meet."

"But, mother, if I cannot love this man, wherefore should I for one moment entertain the thought of making him my husband?"

"Self, self!" exclaimed Mrs. Williams, lifting up her hands; "nothing but self."

"I cannot suppose, mother, that it is an extraordinary act to decline sacrificing one's whole existence for the sake of marrying a man with money, who one can not only not love, but who is an object of positive aversion as this man is to me."

"Yes," exclaimed Mrs. Williams; "that's right. See me dragged to prison, and see us all without shoes to our feet. That's what you would do, rather than give up your nonsensical notion about people's looks."

"But, why," said Helen, "should these calamities, which have never yet appeared, all suddenly come over us, because I do not feel inclined to marry the Baron Stolmuyer of Saltzburgh?"

"And as for the man's looks," added Mrs. Williams, rather adroitly shifting the argument, and declining to answer the rather home question put by Helen — "as for the man's looks, I am quite ashamed of any daughter of mine talking about men's looks — it's indelicate, positively indelicate."

"I cannot see your argument, mother, and I implore you not to persecute me about this man, whom I really cannot love."

"Persecute, indeed! but I tell you what

it is, Helen, you don't seem to be at all aware, first of all, that I am drowned in debt; secondly, that I shall have to bring your brother Charles home from college to make him a tailor, or a shoemaker, or something of that sort, and you will have to go out as a daily governess, while I rot away by slow degrees in a prison."

"But, mother, if these evils are all about to fall upon us, cannot some fair means be adopted of extrication from them? Your income, I always understood, was a certain one, and surely it almost amounts to criminalty to live far beyond it."

"Not at all, when you expect your daughter to be a reasonable Christian, and to marry decently and respectably. Really, my dear, I must say that I little expected such remarks as you make, from a child of mine, I can tell you."

Mrs. Williams was right enough there, for it was a wonder that such remarks should come from a child of hers, who could not be supposed to have heard any such sentiments, but who must have, from the mere force of a just and admirable disposition, given utterance to them.

"Mother," she said, after a pause, "do not fancy that I would not do much to relieve you from any burthens you may have; and, if difficulties have arisen, they are to be remedied in the best way we can, as well as regretted. But I pray you not to ask me to wed this man, whom I cannot love."

"Well, well. I'm sure you make a terrible fuss, and I don't know what about, for my part. It's nothing, I rather suppose; and, after all, the baron may not be going to propose at all for you, and I may be wrong."

As Mrs. Williams thus admitted the possibility that she might be wrong, she looked with an expression of countenance, as much as to say, "Did you ever, in all your life, hear of such virtue as that, or such self-denial?"

"Then what do you wish for me to do, mother?"

"To see him. You cannot put such a slight — indeed, I might almost say, an insult upon him, as not to see him when he actually calls and asks for you. He is, you know, after all, a gentleman."

Helen found it difficult to say that she would not see the baron, so, although it was done with great reluctance, she followed her mother to the room in which that lady had left him, and where he did most anxiously expect her. He felt that his cause was not quite so good as it had been, and that the non-appearance of Helen got up some serious doubts as to the complying disposition he thought she had.

When, however, he at length saw her, some of those fears were dispelled, and he began to imagine that his suit did not look quite so desperate.

There was certainly about the baron a rather courtly air and manner, which, as Mrs. Williams said, shewed that he lived in the best society; and Helen would not allow her aversion to the man to carry her so far as not to behave to him with politeness, so that for some moments that the conversation proceeded, any one would have thought that those three persons were upon the most amicable of terms with each other.

But Mrs. Williams, like some skilful old general, was well versed in matrimonial tactics, and, after making a few remarks, she deliberately left the room, to poor Helen's great chagrin; for, although she had consented out of ordinary civility to see the baron, she had by no means intended to have a *tête-a-tête* with him.

That was quite another affair, and one may well suppose what a degree of indignation she felt at being forced into such circumstances, and by her mother, too, who, of all persons in the world, ought to have protected her, and to whom she ought to have looked certainly for very different things indeed.

It was a very awkward situation to be placed in for poor Helen, inasmuch as she now really could not leave the baron completely alone without great rudeness; and yet she much dreaded, in consequence of the hints that her mother had thrown out, what the interview would be that was about to ensue.

How devoutly and particularly she hoped that, after all, the supposition of her mother that the baron had any matrimonial intentions towards her was a mistake, and she felt that the first words he might utter would be the means of chance letting her know if such really was the case, or if she was to be what she could not help styling, the victim of his addresses.

Of course the baron knew perfectly well that Mrs. Williams had taken her departure for the express purpose of giving him an opportunity of pressing his suit to her daughter, if he felt so disposed, and as he did feel so disposed, he was not at all likely to neglect the opportunity.

None but a man of great tact and discretion, however, could have made so good use of such an opportunity as the baron; for although he certainly did not succeed in removing from the mind of

Helen Williams a strong feeling that he was an uncommonly disagreeable man, he did not add to that impression.

"Miss Williams," he said, "I have not until now had an opportunity of thanking you for the very great favour you did me, by making one at the party at Anderbury House."

"The obligation," said Helen, "was on my side, sir, and I beg that you will not pay me so empty a compliment as to endeavour to make it otherwise."

"You do yourself a great injustice. The grace which you lent to my entertainment was to my mind its greatest charm. I feel, I assure you, compelled to say so much, because it is the genuine truth, and not for the purpose of paying to you an empty compliment, which I have too much respect for you to do."

Helen was silent, for she knew not very well what to reply to this speech, inasmuch as it was one of those general ones that require no reply, unless the persons to whom they are uttered choose to enter at length into a civil complimentary kind of warfare, for the express purpose of so doing.

The baron waited for some reply to be made, and then, as none came, he spoke himself, saying, after at least two minutes' pause,—

"Miss Williams, you may, or you may not, have heard that my principal intention in settling in this neighbourhood — which I was informed, and I find correctly so, is celebrated for the respectability of its inhabitants — was to marry."

"Sir," said Helen, "I know nothing of that matter, nor do I think it is one with which I ought to be in any way troubled."

"Without explanation, certainly not, Miss Williams; but will you allow me to add, that unless my speech had contained certainly something more than a mere compliment, or a mere desire to give you a piece of gossipping information, I should not have uttered it on any account; but I have something to add to it, which does concern your private ear most particularly, and which I do hope will meet with your favourable consideration."

He paused again, and, as Helen returned no answer, he after a time continued, saying, in a still lower tone,—

"May I venture to hope that no preconceived prejudice will have the effect of diminishing any expectations and hopes with which I have pleased myself?"

It is said, and said most truly too, that there are none so blind as those who won't see, and the same rule may be most unquestionably applied to those who won't hear or understand; and although it was, of course, impossible that Helen Williams could have any doubt as to what the baron meant, she was resolved that he should speak out plainly, in order that she might, without giving room for any ambiguity, likewise speak as plainly to him, in answer to the proposition that was upon his lips.

Perhaps the baron was wise enough to see that much, for he proceeded now with much more clearness to declare what he meant, when he said,—

"I told you, Miss Williams, that my object in coming here was to contract a matrimonial alliance, being tired of the solitary life I had been leading for some years. I should not have troubled you with such a communication, had it not been in my power to add to it another, that will explain why I did so."

Helen merely inclined her head, to signify that she heard him.

"That other communication," he continued, "is to the effect that I have found the person on whom I feel convinced that I can fix my affections, without the possibility of their ever wandering again from the dear object. Amid all the rank, beauty, and intelligence that graced my halls on that occasion which will ever be hallowed in my imagination, I had eyes but for one form, and ears but for one voice."

Still Helen was silent.

"There may be many who, in the possession of much attraction and much virtue, may make many happy homes; but the heart culls its own flower, and will think that it presents the most delicate and most beautiful tints to the eye. That flower, from amidst all the galaxy of beauty, I think—nay, I know, that I have selected. Can you not now guess the purport of my simple words, Helen?"

It was tolerably familiar to call her Helen upon so short an acquaintance, and she drew back, looking some astonishment, which he perceiving, and divining the cause—for no one could accuse the baron of want of tact—replied to.

"Forgive me, if, in conversing with you, my heart seems to forget the distance that is between us, and I think of you by that name which, certainly, it is presumptuous on my part to call you by; but there are persons in whose thoughts and feelings we so deeply sympathize, and who, from the first moment that we see them, become bound to us by so many mysterious links of feeling, that we seem as if we had known them for ages, and as if, from that moment, we could be as familiar—aye, much more so—than with many whom we may have met often in the great world."

This was true, and, what is more, it happened to be a truth that touched a right chord in the breast of Helen Williams; for she felt what he said recall recollections of the past, when there was one whom she had seen, and, from the first moment that she had seen him, had felt that time and circumstances could effect no change in those first dear and delightful impressions which had swept across her heart.

The baron saw the contemplative aspect of her face, and he added,—

"You feel the truth of what I utter?"

She started, for she had indeed felt the truth of the sentiment, although her heart was far away, and for a moment she had completely forgotten the existence of the baron, or that it was from his lips she had heard the sentiment expressed.

It was a mortification to him to see this—for he did see it—and he said,—

"Miss Williams, I hope I have said enough, at all events, to convince you that I am not one of those cold, worldly-minded spirits who have none of what may be truly called the higher and the nobler feelings of humanity; but who can, and who do feel and think that there is much of beauty and much of innocence in life, and that both are the dearest and best gifts of Heaven."

"I have nothing to say in contradiction to what you have uttered," said Helen; "but you will, I trust, now excuse me, sir, from continuing a conversation which can have no good result, and which, between persons who are nearly perfect strangers, is scarcely desirable."

This was a speech which, if anything would, was calculated to bring the baron to the point at once; and, as she rose while she uttered it; as with an intention of leaving the room, he at once said,—

"Nay, as I am here, allow me to utter that which I came to speak, and do not, I pray you, hastily decide upon a question of more importance to yourself and to me than any which can be ordinarily asked. Let me beg of you, Miss Williams, to be seated, and to believe that, in my manner of putting this question to you, there shall be nothing which can, in the slightest degree, prove offensive to you."

Thus urged, it would have been something savouring of ill-manners, if Helen Williams had refused to accede to his request; and, although there was nothing she so devoutly wished as that that interview should be over, and over quickly, she felt that perhaps the surest way of accomplishing that object, was to listen quietly to what he had to say; and accordingly she did so, reseating herself again on the chair she had so recently occupied, and determined in her own mind to give him a decisive answer. He then seemed rather in doubt as to how he should commence, and, as he spoke, there was an air of hesitation and doubt about him such as he, indeed, very seldom wore.

Probably, he felt that it was rather a climax that he had arrived at, and that if he was to accomplish anything in the matrimonial way, it was a very doubtful case as regarded his present application.

"I cannot but feel," he said, "that what I am about to say sounds hasty and premature, considering that we have known each other for so short a space of time. It is not for me to enlarge upon circumstances which, I fear, will have but little weight with you; but still it is my duty to mention that I have a large fortune, and consequently can afford to place the object of my affections in such a position in life as that she shall feel surrounded with everything that can make her existence pleasant and desirable."

"Go on, sir," said Helen; "I am staying to hear you, in order that I might clearly and distinctly answer you."

This was by no means encouraging; but still the baron proceeded:—

"I wish to make you an offer of my hand and heart; and, as the Baroness Stolmuyer of Saltzburgh, I am quite certain that you will add a dignity to that title, instead of receiving one from it."

"Sir," said Helen, "an offer of this kind from any gentleman is a compliment which ought always to be appreciated, and I assure you it is one which I feel highly; but as one's future happiness in a marriage is by far too important an affair to be trifled with, I must beg to decline the honour you intend me."

"Decline!" said the baron.

"Yes, sir, I said decline; and I trust that the justice of the Baron Stolmuyer will effectually preserve me from anything in the shape of a persecution for so declining."

At this moment, and before the baron could make any answer to what was said to him by Helen in this firm and determined manner, the door was flung open, and Mrs. Williams rushed into the room.

"My dear sir," she cried to the baron, "of course you understand these matters perfectly well. Girls, you know, are always so very unreasonable, that you can't expect anything from them but a refusal at first, although they may really mean quite the reverse."

"Mother, is this just or fair?" said Helen, reproachfully.

"Oh, stuff—stuff! don't speak to me about justice and fairness, indeed, when you are so absurd as to behave in this dreadful manner towards the baron."

"But, madam," said the baron, "I fear—"

"Fear nothing, my lord; but if you will have the kindness to step into the next apartment for a few minutes, I will join you, and we can talk this matter over."

Mrs. Williams did not think it at all necessary to make any excuse for having listened to the baron's overtures; and perhaps, indeed, she thought that it was not necessary to do so, and that her interest in the affair was a sufficient extenuation of what certainly was a most abominable proceeding.

Shame and disgust at her mother's conduct now kept Helen silent; and as the baron was perfectly willing to give himself all the chances he could, he made a low bow, and left the apartment, in conformity with the desires of Mrs. Williams, wondering much in his own mind by what miracle she purposed influencing her daughter's decision after the extremely positive negative she had given to his proposal.

He waited with much impatience, as well as curiosity, and as our readers may, as well as the baron, be a little curious to know what arguments Mrs. Williams used, we shall proceed to give them a brief outline of what she said.

"Are you mad?" was the first ejaculation. "Are you thoroughly and entirely out of your senses, that you behave yourself in this extraordinary manner?"

"In what extraordinary manner? A man asks me if I can wed him and love him, and, as he asks me politely, I tell him as politely that I cannot, which is the whole of the affair. Is there anything so very extraordinary in such behaviour as that?"

"Indeed, I think there is something very extraordinary in it. I tell you what it is, Helen, Mr. Leek is firmly of opinion that the baron's income must be at least ten thousand pounds a-year." *

"I do not think I shall marry a man for his income, if it were ten times that amount."

"This is insanity—positive insanity. Have you really the least idea of what you are talking about? But I know what it is well enough; I know very well what it is; of course it's that fellow, James Anderson, that comes between you and your wits. That's the scamp that prevents you from exercising a proper control over yourself, and you know it is; but he is gone to sea, and it is to be hoped we shall never look upon him again. I don't wish to see him, and I am quite sure you need not, so you had better make up your mind to marry the baron at once."

"This is too cruel—much too cruel; and but that I see it with my own eyes, I would not have believed it possible."

She burst into tears as she spoke, and then for a brief moment—but it was only for a moment—the heart of the mother was a little touched. The love of money again assumed its sway, and the happiness of her child sunk into insignificance compared with that worst of passions.

"Listen to me, Helen," she said: "it's

---

* *Worth £930,000 in 2020 currency ($1.2 million)*

all very well to make choice of who you like, and to refuse who you like, when it can be done; but I tell you that, in this case, it cannot be done, for we are all of us on the brink of ruin, and, if you will not by this marriage rescue us from that state, destruction must come upon us all. You can save me, you can save your sisters, and you can save your brother, if you will. In course, if you will not, I cannot make you; and you will have the consolation of knowing that, although you had it in your power to save us all from destruction, you did not do it."

"But why should I be placed in so cruel a situation as to be called upon to sacrifice myself completely for my family? Would it not be nobler to meet difficulties, if they have arisen, with a good spirit?"

"As you please — as you please; I can say no more."

Mrs. Williams moved towards the door; but Helen called to her, saying, —

"Give me time to think — I only ask you to give me time to think."

This was a grand concession, and Mrs. Williams at once acceded to the proposition, that it was prudent to leave well enough alone in such a case, and that, having once seen that persecution would do something, it was highly desirable to leave it to work its way.

She accordingly at once left the room, and proceeded into the adjoining apartment, to which the baron had retired; and where, from his attitude, it seemed highly probable that he had taken example by Mrs. Williams; and, as she had listened to his conversation with her daughter, he had, in like manner, listened to her.

"I have the pleasure to inform you, baron," she said, "that my daughter, although at first taken a little by surprise as regards your offer, now accepts it; and I can only add, for my own part, that it is with great pleasure I contemplate having so handsome and distinguished a son-in-law."

"Madam, I highly esteem your compliment; and I must beg of you as a favour, that you will fix the wedding-day as quickly as you please or can; and that, as it must put you to some expense as well as your other daughters, and as it would be very unjust that, on my account, you should expend one penny piece, you will do me the favour of accepting from me a 500 pound note to cover those expenses."

Mrs. Willams quite instinctively held out her hand, but the baron added, with a bow that damped her expectations a little —

"A sum which I shall have the pleasure of handing to you as soon as the wedding-day is fixed."

It would be doing great injustice to the acuteness of Mrs. Williams, if we did not say she quite understood this to be a bribe for expediting proceedings; and if anything was likely to clench the matter, and to place the marriage of the baron with Helen beyond the shadow of a doubt, it certainly was this fact, that 500 pounds was offered to the mother for what we cannot help calling the sale of her child.

But these kind of things are much more common in society than people are at all aware; and one half the marriages that take place at all, are most unquestionably matters of barter. When the highest bidder obtains the prize, if prize that can be called, which generally consists of a shallow, conceited heart, nurtured in all kinds of selfishness, and full of feelings, not one of which can be considered great or estimable.

It is sad, indeed, when, as in the case of Helen Williams, the victim is made a victim on account of her better and nobler feelings, and where it is not her own selfishness, but the selfishness of others, which she is condemned to be victimized to. Whether she will or will not consent, under the circumstances we have narrated, to become the bride of the Baron Stolmuyer of Saltzburgh, we shall shortly discover; but certain it is that he entertained a strong notion she would,

and that Mrs. Williams thoroughly made up her mind that she should.

Nothing can save Helen but a determination of character, which we fear we cannot say she possesses.

Her correct reason makes her say things which, if she could carry them out, would be as proper and as decisive as possible; but the great fault of her character consists in a weakness of purpose, which effecutally prevents her from carrying out the suggestion presented to her by her own superior intellect.

CVI.

THE PREPARATIONS FOR THE BARON'S MARRIAGE. — THE YOUNG LOVER, AND THE REMONSTRANCE.

SO IT APPEARED that the baron was right, and that with all his disqualifications he had succeeded in obtaining the promise of a wife, because he had the one great qualification which outshone everything to his disadvantage, namely, wealth.

And he was not so blind, or so foolish, as not fully to understand, and to know, that it was to the relatives of the bride, and not to the bride herself, that he was indebted for an answer in the affirmative to his proposition.

Well he knew that although he had dazzled their eyes and awakened their cupidity, he had produced no such an effect upon the young and beautiful being who was about thus to be sacrificed upon the altar of Mammon; and probably if anything could have added to his earnest

desire to make her his, it was that he saw she was untouched by the power of his gold, and therefore he could not but respect, as well as admire her; and he much preferred taking to his arms one for whom he entertained a supreme and sovereign contempt.

She felt that she was a victim, and that if she consented to become his, she must look upon herself as blighted and sacrificed for ever.

But he was too selfish to hesitate on such a ground as that. His feelings were far from being so human as to stop short, because he knew the alliance was viewed by her with hatred and horror. And that she did view it with those feelings, spared him, at all events, as he told himself, some trouble, for it took away from the necessity of keeping up the constant shew and glitter of wealth, for that shew and glitter affected her not, and therefore would have been presented to her imagination in vain.

But far different was it regarded her friends and connections, who had arrogated to themselves the power of deciding upon this matter of life and death to her.

To them he felt that he must shew all the glitter of display that belonged to his extensive means, or they would be disappointed, for they not only wanted riches themselves, but they wanted the worldly reputation contingent upon having so rich a relative.

Therefore was it that he determined that nothing should be wanting at his approaching nuptials to make them most magnificent, and he racked his imagination to discover a mode by which he could spend a large sum of money, so as to get for it the greatest amount of display. This was a matter which a man such as he was eminently calculated to achieve; and, as he succeeded in fixing his nuptials to take place in a fortnight from that time, he had ample time to make all such preparations as he might consider requisite.

It so happened that on the following evening to that on which he had obtained so strange a consent, through another party, to his matrimonial speculation, that the sun sunk upon the coast with every appearance of approaching stormy weather.

Scarcely had its disc sunk below the western horizon, when a furious gale arose, and, for the first time since his residence at Anderbury Hall, he felt what it was to hold an estate so near to the sea-coast.

The sea rose tempestuously, appearing to shake the mansion to its very foundation, and more than one half of the excavation leading from the grounds to the sea-coast was filled with water. The gale blew off the sea, and one or two trees upon the Anderbury estate were torn up by their roots, spreading destruction around them among the numerous shrubs and flowers.

Some of the windows of the mansion were dashed in, and the wind came roaring into the house, whistling up the staircases, opening and shutting doors, and altogether producing a scene of devastation and uproar which would have terrified most persons.

The baron, however, on the contrary, notwithstanding whatever damage was done was of course done to his property, took the matter with the greatest ease and composure in the world; and, in fact, rather seemed to enjoy the fury of the elements than to be awed by them.

He remained out of doors the whole time and although the rain now and then fell in torrents, and drenched him to the skin, he seemed scarcely conscious of that circumstance, or, if he were, he evidently thought it too trivial to take any notice of.

The servants looked at him in amazement, scarcely believing it possible that any one in his senses could be so indifferent to the rage of the elements that was proceeding; but they little knew the real character of the man whom they had for a master, or they would have wondered at nothing, and been surprised at nothing that they saw of him or heard of him.

The storm continued until the night completely set in, and still it showed no signs whatever of anything in the shape of an end; and it seemed but too evident that it was likely to continue in all its wild and ungovernable fury for many an hour to come.

He got as close as he could to the beach, so as not to leave his own estate, and from there he listened attentively to the howling of the blast, seeming rather pleased with the idea than otherwise, that much mischief was being done by that most terrific storm.

A servant brought him a telescope, so that he could look out upon the waste of waters, and see some of the struggling vessels that, with might and main, were endeavouring to keep off the shore, but which, despite all their efforts, were being hurried to destruction — a destruction which they could not avoid, and which must present itself in the most serious aspect, because it appears inevitable, and is invested with all the misery of a protracted execution.

And in particular he remarked one vessel which was drifting onward to certain and inevitable destruction.

He could see the rockets and the blue lights that they burnt now and then through the storm; while, ever and anon, with a booming strange sound over the waste of waters there would come the signal gun of distress, with its awful reverberations, awakening feelings of sympathy in the breast of every one but the baron, and he seemed impenetrable to all human feeling, for he looked on with a strange calmness, a calmness that one might suppose would set upon some man who had nothing to do with human hopes,

human thoughts, or human feelings, but not by any means that calmness of a pure spirit looking upon things which it would aid, if it could, but which are beyond its power of action.

He saw the anxious throng of persons on the beach precisely below his own estate.

He saw them launch a boat, and, with a grim smile, he saw it swamped in the surge, and the brave bold men, who had made the gallant endeavour to save their fellows, met themselves, with but one exception, a watery grave.

And then even the baron smiled, and muttered to himself, —

"What is all this to me? what have I to do with human hopes and feelings? What is it to me whether they live or die, or whether yon ship, that I now see struggling through the waste of waters, reaches its destination, or is engulfed for ever in the foaming surge? What is it to me, I repeat, whether these bold brave men live or die? Will they not be the very persons to hunt me from the face of society? Will they not be the very persons who would declare that I was unfit to live? And shall I trouble myself with one thought as to whether they live or die? Ah! they come nearer, nearer, nearer still, and I shall see such a sight as may not often be observed by one such as I am, and on such a coast as this."

There was a strange, wild, wailing cry, and the ship, which was a large one, struck heavily upon a rock about a mile distant from the shore, and very close, indeed, to where the Anderbury estates commenced.

Now, as if seized with a sudden impulse, although we cannot and do not think it was one of humanity, the baron descended by a large fissure in the rock to

the beach. This took him some time to accomplish, for he had to walk completely through the grounds of Anderbury Hall, and half-a-mile beyond, before he reached it, and then it took him some time to walk down, because he had to do so with extreme caution, inasmuch as the heavy rain that had fallen had made the ground so slippery that it was with great difficulty he could at all keep his feet.

When he arrived in sight of the beach, the ship was gone, but a life boat was being launched, amid the hurrahs of the multitude, for the purpose of picking up some of the survivors of the wreck who were noticed drifting upon portions of its hulk.

The baron had brought his telescope with him, and he placed it to his eye, and took a long and steady look at the boat.

A muttered malediction came from his lips, and, having shut the telescope, he turned, and hastily pursued his path again to Anderbury House.

AFTER THE WEDDING, Jack Pringle really felt himself so upset by the quantity of healths he had drunk, and the general manner in which he had disposed of a quantity of rum, that he told the admiral he found himself not quite so well as he ought to be, and that he thought it was all owing to having been out of sight of water for so many months.

This was a plea which sounded very reasonable to the admiral, and when Jack said,—

"You know it ain't possible to live very long without a glimpse, at least, of an arm of the sea, or something of that sort."

The old man assented to the proposition at once, and replied,—

"Why, that's true enough, Jack, and I shall have to go somewhere myself soon, or else get musty; for, you may depend, it never was intended that human beings should live all their lives on land."

"I should think not," said Jack, and I what I was going to say was, that you must try and take care of yourself, you old baby, for a day or two, while I take a run to the coast. It ain't above twenty-five miles; and mind you don't get into any mischief till I come back."

"Confound your impudence! It's a very odd thing that you can't come into my presence without a lie in your mouth. You know you have been as much trouble to me as a cargo of monkeys in a storm. Be off with ye, and if I never see your face again, it will be a good job."

Jack considered that he had quite sufficiently announced his departure, so he set off at once, and made his way towards the coast, not a little pleased, as he neared it, to fancy that, every now and then, he kept snuffing the sea air; and when the coach in which he went put him down within about four miles of a little village inhabited by fishermen, he walked that distance, although, sailor-like, it was an exercise he was by no means fond of, and, to his great joy, once more stood upon a sandy beach, and heard the murmur of the ocean, and saw the waves curling at his feet.

He was quite delighted, and really felt, or fancied that he felt, which was the same thing, wonderfully invigorated by the change, and quite another thing to what he had been.

Under such circumstances, Jack was sure not to be long in picking up a companion, so, in one of the cottages into which, with all the free and easy manner of a sailor, he strolled, he found an old man-of-war's man, retired there to spend the remainder of his days along with his son and daughter.

We feel that it would be quite impossible for us to do justice to the meeting between those two worthies, for they soon found out the capabilities of each.

Some grog, which Jack thought the sweetest he had tasted for a long time, because it was drunk within sight of the ocean, was produced, and then the tales they set to telling each other of their adventures afloat, would have been enough to stun anyone.

We have rather a fear, likewise, that in some cases, they were not so strictly particular as they might have been had they been upon their oaths, as regards truth; but they seemed to be upon the principle of mutual forbearance, and the implied understanding of "You believe me, and I'll believe you."

Whenever this kind of rivalry, however, commences between inveterate story-tellers, there is no saying to what length they will go, and Jack certainly related some extraordinary things.

They happened both to have been to the same latitude, but, of course, they had not both seen the same sights exactly, or enjoyed the same adventures; so what one did not know or could not invent, the other pretty soon did; so that between them they made up a most entertaining conversation, and one which really would, to any one who was willing to be amused and not very particular about veracity, have had great charms.

"Ah," said the old sailor, "when I was on the coast of Ingee, the hair melted off my head."

"Did it," said Jack. "Oh! that's nothing at all; we had a couple of men roasted at the wheel with the heat, and they didn't know it, till they were both done brown."

"You don't say so?"

"Yes, I does, and, what's more, we always had our meat cooked over again upon one of the gun slides; and, after that, when we were a long way southward, it was so cold not one of the crew shut his eyes for a week."

"Indeed! But you spoke of a man as you called Safety Jack; who was he? I should like all for to know."

"When I was on board the *Fame*, our captain was a know-nothing sort of shore-going lubber, who had been guved a pair of swabs* over better men's heads, and uncommon afeared he was of getting into any danger. He'd always come on deck on a morning, and guving a kind of a hurry-skurry skeared look all round him, he'd say, if so be as he seed no land, —

"'Where are we? Is there any danger?'

"Then our first luff he'd say, —

"'No danger, sir; only a little fear.'

"Then the captain he'd say, all the while looking as skeared as a marine in a squall, —

"'Let us be safe — let us be safe, that's all.'

"So we called him Safety Jack, in consekense o' that peculiarity. Well, you must know as we were running for the Cape, and Safety Jack he wouldn't be persuaded, but insisted upon hugging the coast of Africa all the way, 'cos, as he said, it looked safer to see the land. So, as it happened, when we neared the Cape, we got into a regular north-westerly current, that set clear away south-east, or it might be a few points more southerly. The wind, too, blew in the same direction, and it seemed a bad job altogether. Our luff then says, says he to the captain — that's Safety Jack, you must understand, —

"'It will take us some time to work into the bay with this wind and current, but we can do it.'

"'Is it safe?' said Safety Jack.

---

* *A jocular reference to the fringed epaulettes of contemporary naval officers, which looked somewhat like little golden string-mops.*

"'Oh, yes,' said t'other; 'though I have known a vessel of small draught to be capsised hereaway.'

"Safety Jack at this turns very pale, and he says,—

"'Well, run before the wind a few leagues to the south; it's safer—and—and the gale may go down, and we may get out of the current—and—and—besides, it's safer.'

"Well, everybody grumbled, but Safety Jack would have his own way, and we went spanking along with the wind and current nearly due south.

"But instead of getting out of the current we got further into it, and the gale increased to a hurricane. We went through the water at such a rate that the men who stood facing the wind could not button their jackets, or shut their eyes, and there was the mate and five able-bodied men holding the captain's hair on his head. The men's teeth, too, were all blown out of their mouths, and kept rattling among the rigging like half-a-dozen old shot in a locker. On we went, faster and faster, till all of a sudden we saw the sails flapping against the masts, and the ship was evidently turning round in spite of the helm.

"'We're out of it now,' mumbles Safety Jack.

"'I think we're in for it,' cried the mate. 'This is a whirlpool!'

"And so it was; round and round we flew like lightning, coming nearer to one point at each turn. The men all fell down on the deck as giddy as geese, and Safety Jack he begins screaming. Just to give you an idea of how we went round, there was two of the crew as had a squabble about a bottle of rum, and one on 'em says—'If I

can't have it you sha'n't, and there it goes,' shicing it behind him. Well, you'll hardly believe it—but the ship was going round so fast in a circle of about a mile, that afore the bottle could drop the man as threw it was brought round to it again, and it knocked his eye out.

"Well, presently the ship gives a kind of shivering and stops for half a moment, and Safety Jack he screams again. Then the water opened like a well-hole, and just for a moment we could see it bubbling and lashing like a boiling cauldron. Then down we went into the foaming surge like a lump of lead."

"You don't mean to swear to that?"

"Yes, I do; at any time and any day; I should think so, and rather think I ought to know, as I was there."

"And how did you get saved? That's the question, my boy."

"You ought to be satisfied about that, I should think," said Jack, "by seeing me here. If I had not escaped, I rather suppose I shouldn't have been here to have told you about it."

"That's all very well; but I ask you how you escaped?"

"Oh, that's quite another thing. I floated about for eight weeks upon an empty tar barrel."

"Eight weeks, did you say?"

"Yes; eight weeks, two days, four hours, and three-quarters."

"The deuce you did! How came you to be so mighty particular as to the three-quarters?"

"Because I thought some fool would be sure to ask me.

"Oh, that indeed; but the most odd thing that happened to me, I will say, was when I was once wrecked on an island that we called Flee Island."

"Flee Island; what a rum name! What made you call it that, I should like to know?"

"Oh, a trifling circumstance — there was nothing in it but flees, and they were as big as elephants."

"Very good," said Jack; "I can believe that, because there is nothing outrageous about it. I don't consider myself at all difficult to please, and so long as you stick to such things as that nobody can doubt you will find it all right with me."

"I am very much obliged — but should you happen ever to come across that captain of yours again —"

"Yes, but it were a good while afterwards I was on board a whaler, and I saw something floating that looked like a great lump of chalk, and when we picked it up, who should it turn out to be but Safety Jack, what they call putrified, and turned to something like white coral."

"You don't mean that."

"Yes, I do; we keep him out of curiosity for about a week lashed up to the mainmast, but the men of the night watch were scared at him, and threw him overboard, because they said, when the moonlight fell upon him, he for all the world looked like a ghost, and they couldn't keep their eyes off him, which I dare say was somewhere about the truth."

"You certainly have seen a little service; but mix yourself another glass of grog, and I shall do the same, for I don't mean to turn into hammock to-night."

"What for?"

"Because there is going to be a storm. I have not been looking at the weather for so many years without being able to tell that before it comes. There will be a storm before twenty-four hours are over, and I think it will blow off the sea, so that there will be no end of mischief."

Jack Pringle went to the door of the fisherman's hut, and, although the evening had set in, he cast a scrutinizing glance at the heavens, looked earnestly in the direction from whence the wind proceeded, and when he came back again and sat down by the side of the old sailor, he said, —

"You are right; there will not only be a storm, but such a one too as they hav'n't seen for some time; so I shall no more think of turning in than you do. Who knows but that some vessel may be drifted in shore, and then we who are seamen will be able to do more good than a score of your shore-going fellows, who are afraid if the saltwater gets above their ankles."

"That's true enough; when the wind does rise in this way, and blows a strong gale, it is pretty clear that there will be something in the shape of wreck to look at."

The prognostications of Jack and the old sailor turned out, as we know, to be tolerably correct, for the storm which they anticipated was precisely that severe one which roused the Baron Stolmuyer of Saltzburgh from his lethargy, and induced him to go down to the beach, to see what was likely to be the fate of the vessel from which the signals of distress had proceeded.

So soon as the wind began to howl, and the waves to dash upon the shore, Jack Pringle and the old sailor left the cottage, and stood with great anxiety upon the beach, anxious to render what assistance they could to those who were suffering from the fury of the storm.

We have before mentioned that a

boat that the Baron Stolmuyer saw swamped, had ventured out to the assistance of the crew.

In that boat had been Jack Pringle; and he had refused to allow the old sailor to accompany him, on account of his age.

"No, no," said Jack: "this is a work for youngsters, and they and they only ought to set about it. You remain where you are. We know well enough that your will is good, and let that be sufficient; and now, my lads, who will go with me?"

Jack soon got a few good volunteers, and started out on his chivalrous expedition, to see what could be done towards rescuing some of the crew of the distressed ship.

But, alas! what the baron had said about the fate of that boat was true, although he was incorrect as regarded the consequences of its swamping to all on board; for Jack Pringle, in consequence of being a first-rate swimmer, and possessed likewise as he was of great coolness and presence of mind, contrived to reach shore again, although he was the only one of the ill-fated crew who really did so.

But, as Jack himself said, they died in a noble cause, and as everybody must die some time in some sort of way, he didn't see that they had anything very particular to complain of in that respect.

It was on the second occasion, however, that Jack was going out with a life-boat, that the baron reached the beach, and then, as if indignant that such daring attempts should be made to save what he evidently thought so little of, namely, human life, he retired in indignation again to his home.

But not all the barons in the world would have stopped Jack in his chivalrous enterprize, and so he proceeded at once to carry it out to the best of his ability; and he did pick up a man who was nearly exhausted, and clinging, with but a faint hope of deliverance, to a portion of wreck.

CVII.

THE YOUNG SAILOR SAVED BY JACK PRINGLE TURNS OUT TO BE AN IMPORTANT PERSONAGE.

IT WAS NOT THE LEAST gratifying part by any means of Jack Pringle's going to the sea-side that, in consequence of that occurrence, he had been instrumental in saving the life of a fellow-creature; and when he returned to the cottage of the fisherman, bearing in his arms the apparently lifeless remains of a young man, who had been clinging to a portion of the wreck, the cheer that greeted him from the bystanders was certainly the most grateful music that had ever greeted his ears.

He had a strong impression on his own mind, that the young man whom he had removed from the wreck would recover, and that impression he was wonderfully well pleased to find verified by the fact.

The care and assiduity of the family,

upon whose hospitality the young stranger was thus by the fury of the elements thrown, succeeded shortly in restoring him to perfect consciousness.

He showed a disposition, then, to arise, but this Jack Pringle and the old fisherman would not permit, for they both knew from experience in such cases, how essential rest was; so they darkened the room in which he lay, and left him to himself.

"Well," said Jack, as they sat together; "what do you think of that young fellow? I cannot, for my own part, make out very well what he is, although I can say what he is not, and that's a seaman."

"No, he is no sailor, certainly; and he is more likely to have been a passenger on board the merchantman, than anything else; and if so, it's an odd thing that he should have been the only one saved out of the ship's crew, when there much have been men used to such disasters, and one would think capable of taking care of themselves."

"It is an odd thing; but there is no accounting for it; we shall hear all about it, though, when he recovers sufficiently to speak to us without doing himself any mischief."

"Certainly; and that will be after he has had a sleep, for then he will be all right; for, mind you, I don't think he was insensible on account of having been in the water so much, as because he was so thoroughly tired out, that he didn't know what he was about."

The stranger slept for about four hours; and then he awakened, greatly refreshed by the slumber, and quite able to give some account of himself without fatigue.

After expressing his most grateful thanks for the service that had been rendered to him, to which Jack listened with great impatience, because he really did not consider it a service at all, but one of the most natural things in the world for a man to do, who saw another in distress, he said,—

"I was captain's clerk on board a king's ship called the *Undine*, and we had a smart affair with a nest of pirates on the African coast. We were absolutely attacked by four or five of their vessels at once, and, having sunk three and captured the remainder, during which, however, we lost some officers and a number of men, our captain determined upon sending home a dispatch of the transaction, which he entrusted to my care."

"Hang pirates!" said Jack. "They ought all to be hung up at the yard-arm, without judge or jury; but, I suppose, they are by this time pretty well settled."

"I have no doubt of it, for it was the captain's intention to steer to the nearest port, and there be evidence against them, and get them in due course executed. He put me on board a merchant vessel with my dispatches, and a more prosperous and pleasant voyage we could not have, until the storm which arose off the coast here, and proved the destruction of our vessel."

"Ah!" said Jack, "it's always the case, if anything happens, it's within sight almost of the port you are bound to."

"So it is," said the old fisherman. "All is safe out in the blue waters; but, when you least expect it, and things are looking quite pleasant, and people a-brushing themselves up to go on shore, then, all of a sudden, something will occur, and you will find yourselves a wreck."

"It would seem so," said the young stranger; "and, at all events, that was our evil fortune, whatever it may be any one else's, for we were, indeed, just congratulating ourselves upon being at home, or nearly so, when this terrific storm arose, and, I suppose, I am the only survivor out a crew of twenty-eight men."

"The only one," said Jack, "I am sorry to say. All had sunk before the life-boat had reached you, and, what's more, several brave fellows lost their lives in the first attempt to pick up some of the crew; so it has been a most disastrous matter altogether."

"But cheer up," said the fisherman; "it might have been worse, for I have known cases when a ship has gone down, and not left one survivor to say who or what she was; or tell the tale of her destruction."

"And I too," said Jack.

"On what part of the coast," said the stranger, "am I? for, during the night, we have drifted so far, and been so beaten about by the gale, that whether we came twenty miles or a hundred I cannot tell."

"Why, the town close at hand here is called Anderbury."

"Anderbury!" exclaimed the young man. "Is it possible that my faculties have been so confused by the danger I have been in, as not to know this coast. This is the very place to which I should have proceeded post-haste, directly I concluded my business in London at the Admiralty."

"Indeed. Then you had better stay here at once, and go to the Admiralty afterwards; for, I dare say, that will answer the purpose just as well, at all events. And, I suppose, you have lost your dispatches."

"I have, indeed; but yet it is my duty to report myself, as soon as possible. But, now that I am in Anderbury, I cannot resist the opportunity of calling upon a dear friend, who resides in this town. Do you happen to know a family of the name of Williams?"

"No," said Jack; "I never heard of them, except you mean a Bill Williams, that was once on board the *Ocean* frigate, as cook."

"No, no. I mean a family residing here, one of the members of which is dearer to me than life itself."

"Well," said Jack, "it's good fortune that has cast you here, since that is the case. It is not likely that I should know anything of the people you speak of, because I am a stranger in the place myself, and have come a distance of twenty-five miles, just to have a look at the sea, and nothing else, and good fortune brought me here in time, it appears, to save your life, and I only hope you will find your sweetheart true to you."

"I can have no doubt of that."

"Well, it is a good thing to be confident; but, for my part, I always had very serious doubts, and, when I came off a voyage, I frequently found that my sweetheart had picked up with somebody else, in the course of about a week after I was gone."

"But, in this case," said the young stranger, "I would stake my life upon the fidelity of her whom I wish so much now to see."

"Well," said Jack, "of course you please yourself; but, before you make a fool of yourself, by calling upon her, just satisfy yourself upon the subject, that's all, and get some friend to make an inquiry for you, or else, perhaps, you will be served as I was once."

"How was that?"

"Why, the fact is, when I was younger than I am now, I took a fancy to a nice little creature, of the name of Jemima West, whom I fully intended to marry, and so I told her, before I started upon one voyage that I meant to be my last; for, you see, I had a pretty good stock of prize money, and I meant to set up a public-house at Liverpool."

"And did she prove false to you?"

"A little. When I came home, of course I walked off straight to where she lived. Her father and mother were very respectable people, and amused themselves with selling coals and potatoes. So, in I walked, as I used to do, into the shop, and so on, bang into the parlour, and there sat Jemima, much as usual, neither very clean, and neither very dirty. Well, on the other side of the fire-place was a fellow smoking a pipe, and, when I caught hold of her, and gave her half-a-dozen regular kisses, he takes his pipe out of his mouth, and opens his eyes like an old crocodile.

"'Well, my girl,' I said; 'how are you?'

"'Oh, I don't know,' she said; 'I didn't expect to see you any more.'

"'No,' said the fellow, with the pipe, 'and I'm d—d if ever I expected to see you at all. Who the devil are you?'

"'Who the devil are you?' says I; 'but, however, that don't much matter, for be you whom you may, if you don't pretty quick take yourself off, I'll kick you out.'

"'That's a good joke,' says he, 'to talk of kicking a man out of his own house, after coming in and kissing his wife like a steam-engine. A very good joke.'

"'Wife!' says I. 'Do you say you are this fellow's wife?'

"'Yes,' says she, and she pretended to wipe something out of the corner of her eye with her apron. 'Yes,' says she; 'I thought you were drowned long ago, and so I thought I might as well be Mrs. Juggles.'

"Now you may guess, messmate, what a d—d fool I looked after that, and how glad I was to back out; so, you see, I advise you to make some inquiries just before you take upon yourself to be so positive about your sweetheart."

The young man laughed, as he said,—

"I think I'll chance it; and, notwithstanding your misadventure, I have some reason to believe that I shall not be so unfortunate; but at all events I will take your advice and make some previous inquiries. It shall not be said that I fell into any misadventure of that nature for want of ordinary caution."

"That's right, don't be above taking advice; and, do you know, I sha'n't be at all surprised, that you will find your sweetheart going to be Mrs. Somebody Else; but come, here's dinner will be ready directly."

"Yes," said the old man; "it will as soon as my son returns from Anderbury, where he has gone to buy a bit of fresh meat for you, for I thought you would be tired of fish, and we had nothing else in the house."

"I regret much giving you so much trouble; but I shall have my pay to receive when I reach London, and will take care that you are amply recompensed."

"Oh, don't mention that; and, by-the-bye, here he comes. Well, Tom, what have you brought?"

"A leg of mutton," said Tom; "I ain't a judge of nothing else, but I thought I might venture upon that, at all events. I think somebody told me it was very good with shrimp sauce."

"Rather an odd mixture, that, Tom, and not quite usual I should say."

"Well, the fellow was on the grin that told me, on account of an old woman that had been to them to ask for some more credit for a month or two, because her daughter was going to be married to a baron somebody, who they say has taken Anderbury-on-the-Mount, and is immensely rich."

"Did you hear her name, Tom?"

"Oh, yes; I have seen her before in the town. It's old Mother Williams, and it's her daughter Helen as is going to be married."

"Well, I never!" cried Jack; "I say, messmate, didn't I tell you? The murder is out, now; that's your sweetheart, ain't it?"

The young man turned very pale, and for a few moments he did not speak; but when he did so, he said, —

"There must be some mistake; I could stake my life upon her constancy."

"Then a precious goose you would be," said Jack, "to do any such thing, for I wouldn't stake my little finger upon any woman. Why, man, it's just what you ought to have expected. It's the way with them all, out of sight out of mind, and I am only surprised at a fellow of your sense not knowing that, for you seem to be up to a thing or two."

"It cannot be — it cannot be — I must go myself to seek Helen, and at once put a stop to these rumours, which, I am convinced, arise from some misconstruction, and probably a confusion of names. I know that Mrs. Williams is a selfish woman, and it is possible that she might not hesitate in sacrificing one of her daughters to gold, but that one cannot be Helen, who has pledged her faith to me."

"Well," said Jack, "take advantage of any doubt you can, but it would be very absurd for you to go interfering in the matter yourself. You leave it to me to make the necessary inquiries, whilst you remain here snug and unknown, and I promise you, on the word of a British seaman, that I'll bring you exact news all about it."

"I accept your offer gratefully, for if she be faithless to me, I wish never to encounter her again, but to leave her to enjoy what happiness she can with that other for whom she has broken her faith with me."

"Good," said Jack; "that's the wisest plan, for, after all, you see, in these affairs who's to blame but the girl herself? and you can't very well give her a thrashing, you know; for, as regards the fellow, of course, she don't say anything to him about you, and he can't tell but what she is a regular free trader."

"True — true — and the best thing, therefore, I can do, to make certain of controlling my temper in the transaction, is not to see her, unless I can make certain that she is faithful to the vows she has plighted to me; but let me beg of you, as quickly as possible, to end my state of suspense and doubt."

"I believe you," said Jack; "I'll go at once to find it all out. You sha'n't be in doubt much longer, and, of course, I hope that things will turn out to your satisfaction; although I can't say I expect they will."

"The hope that they will, is life itself to me, and I shall wait here with an impatience bordering upon positive agony for your report."

CVIII.

THE DECISION AGAINST THE DOCTOR, AND MORE NEWS OF VARNEY, THE VAMPYRE.

IT WILL BE REMEMBERED that Dr. Chillingworth, although he had, without doubt, ascertained that Varney had proceeded to London, hesitated about following him there without the full connivance and consent of the Bannerworths; and now, at the very first opportunity he had, when he found the admiral and Henry together, he introduced the subject.

He detailed what he had already done in the way of tracing Varney from place to place, and ended by declaring his conviction the he was to be found in London.

"It is not only of importance," he said, "to discover Varney on account of the property which I think he has taken with him, but it really amounts almost to a public duty to do so, when we consider the evil he has succeeded in bringing upon us, and that some other family may be soon suffering from similar machinations."

"But, doctor," said Henry, "I presume you have no disinclination to admit that the principal view you take of this subject, is as regards its connexion with the supposed sum of money which Varney has taken with him?"

"I freely own," said the doctor, "that I should like to place that money in your hands, because I think you are entitled to it; and, perhaps, that is my principal motive, but it certainly is not my only one; for, as I consider Varney quite a curiosity in a medical point of view, I certainly wish to follow him up, and should be extremely sorry to lose sight of him altogether."

"But you must be aware, doctor," said Henry, "that there really is something like positive danger in following such a man up; and, although he feels himself under such great obligations to you, that I do not think he would willingly do you an injury, yet there is no knowing what so strange and irascible a temper might not be goaded to."

"I have no dread of danger."

"I dare say you have not," said the admiral; "but I give my vote against having anything further to do with Varney."

"And," said Henry, "although I cannot withhold an expression of admiration for the doctor's perseverance, I beg him to think that we oppose his pilgrimage in search of the vampyre, because we feel more for his personal safety than we fear any of the machinations of Varney."

"Well, gentlemen," said the doctor, "since I am in a minority, of course I must give in, and say no more about it. I should certainly have liked to find the fellow; for it is my impression that he certainly has a good many thousands of your money in his possession. But, as it is, I will say no more about it; although I shall retain my opinion that you are ill-advised in not following him up."

"Oh," said the admiral, "it wouldn't do to follow people up always."

"I don't know that. There's that Quaker, for instance, who has got possession of Dearbrook."

"The Quaker!" shouted the admiral. "D—n the Quaker! I'll follow him up while I have a guinea left, or a leg to stand on. What the deuce made you mention him? for you know the very sound of his name is enough to put me in a fever. The Quaker be hanged, an infernal thief as he is!"

It was well known to both Henry and the doctor, and, in fact, to all the family now, that the mention of the Quaker was always enough to drive the admiral nearly frantic; so that we are inclined to think Dr. Chillingworth was actuated by a little spirit of vengeance when he made that remark, and that, on the whole, he was so vexed at the non-participation of the Bannerworths and the admiral in his views concerning Sir Francis Varney, that, on the irritation of the moment, he did not scruple to say something which he thought would be annoying; but his downright good feeling so got the better of anything of that sort, that, turning to the admiral, he said,—

"I do apologise — I ought to apologise for my calling to your attention anything of a disagreeable character; for I have no right whatever to do so; and it was only upon the impulse of a moment, I assure you, that I uttered the words."

"Doctor," said the admiral, "I know all that as well as you can tell me; so just say no more about it, if you please, for I don't want to hear one word upon such a subject."

"Well, then," said the doctor, "now that I stand acquitted of doing or saying anything of a doubtful or disagreeable character, I can only tell you that I shall persevere in my opinion, and that it is just possible, though not very likely, that I may, upon my own account, do something in the matter."

"All of which," said Henry, "I am very sorry to hear you say, doctor."

"But why are you sorry?"

"Because I cannot help anticipating danger. I feel almost certain that it will ensue, and, in that case, no one will more bitterly regret that you mixed yourself up in the affair than I shall."

"Oh, do not presume any such thing," said the doctor, jestingly. "You may depend Varney and I understand each other too well for there to be much danger in my intercourse with him. There is something about the fellow yet that will not permit him to do any deliberate wrong to me; and, strange as the feeling may appear, I cannot help acknowledging that I like him in some things, and that, having been the means of restoring him to life, I feel, somehow or another, as if I were bound to look after him."

"Well, that is rather absurd," said the admiral, "I must confess. But, however, doctor, if you have any such feeling, by all means carry it out — I won't say nay; but by any means find him out, if you like, and if you can make him a decent member of society, in Heaven's name do so."

"I do not expect that," said the doctor; "and if I only keep him out of mischief, I shall be sufficiently satisfied, for that would be accomplishing a great deal with such a man."

"Promise me one thing," said Henry, "in connection with this affair."

"What may that be?"

"It is that you will not take any step in

the matter without letting us know. Of course, you are a free-agent in the transaction, and have as much right as anybody to say or to do anything as regards Varney, the vampyre; but still, knowing so much of him as we do, I, for one, certainly would be glad to be made aware of anything you were attempting concerning him."

"That I will promise you, so you need be under no possible apprehension on such a score, but feel completely at your ease that nothing is being done unless you know of it."

At this juncture, a servant entered the room with a letter, which was addressed to Henry Bannerworth, and, upon opening it, he uttered a sudden exclamation of surprise.

"What is it?" said the admiral; "you seem astonished, Henry."

"I am, indeed, astonished, and I may be. Who do you suppose, admiral, this letter is from?"

"I can't possibly take upon myself to say."

"Why, from no other person than Varney, the vampyre."

"Indeed!" cried Dr. Chillingworth; "and does he offer restitution? — does he offer to return the money he so wrongfully has got possession of? — tell me that."

"I cannot answer you, for I have not read one word of the epistle; I only see by the signature that it is his; but as it is impossible that there can be any secrets between myself and Varney, I shall read it to you aloud, and you shall both of you be able to judge concerning it."

The admiral and the doctor assumed attitudes of attention, while Henry, after glancing his eyes slightly down the

contents of the letter, commenced reading it as follows: —

To Henry Bannerworth:

Sir, —

Probably the last person in the world from whom you might expect to receive a communication, is he who now pens this epistle; but as it is penned with a good feeling towards you and yours, I hope and trust it will be received in a kindly spirit.

Admitting that the circumstances under which I left the protection of your house were such as to require some explanation from me, it is that explanation which I now proceed to give.

Circumstances made it imperatively necessary that I should adopt a course of conduct that should no longer make me a burden to those who had more cause to wish me dead, than to assist me in maintaining existence.

Without, then, the least sinister motive towards you or any one belonging to you, I left your home secretly, and at once, not being willing to listen to remonstrances that I knew would be spoken kindly, but which I knew at the same time could not be very serious, inasmuch as my presence cannot possibly be otherwise than a severe tax upon your kindness and your patience.

I cannot be so besotted as to think for a moment, that you can forget, although a generosity of temper, for which I give you full credit, might enable you to forgive, the injuries you have received from me; but I could not make up my mind to reside under your roof on such terms; and since my recovery from the violence of a lawless mob, the question in my mind has been, not whether I should leave you or not, but how I should leave you, and where I should betake myself to.

At length, finding it impossible to come to any rational conclusion upon these points, and that time was rapidly wearing, so that it became necessary, if I came to a conclusion at all, I should come to it quickly, I resolved to leave without giving you any notice of the fact, and set up my staff, as it were, in the wilderness, and proceed in whatever direction chance might point out to me.

This, I say, was my resolve, and I have carried it into execution. All I ask of you is, to forget me, and not to waste any thought upon the man who will never do any injury to you, or to any one belonging to you, and who hopes you will make no inquiry for him; but, should you meet him ever, you will pass him by as if you knew him not.

These few words come from him who was —

VARNEY, THE VAMPYRE.

THERE WAS A DEAD SILENCE when this epistle was concluded, and all seemed busy with their own opinions as regarded this communication, which certainly was one of a singular nature, and highly calculated to excite their surprise.

Upon the whole, though, there was one extremely evident conclusion to be drawn from it, and that was, that Varney was extremely anxious not to be interfered with.

"Can anything be more transparent?" exclaimed the doctor; "it is just as I say, Varney wants to try some new scheme, and is very much afraid that he may come across us in some way, and be baulked in it, by our exposing what his real character is; and, if anything could give me a stronger impulse than another to follow him and see what he is about, it would certainly be that letter."

"I do not think you need be afraid," said Henry; "for the letter, bearing as it does that signification, is such a one as induces me to believe he is fearful that some circumstances may throw him in our way, and in that case, that we may spoil his sport; and of the likelihood of such a thing occurring, he is, of course, a much better judge than we can be. So I should say, let him alone, and see if anything really turns up concerning him; if it does, we have a fair principle action before us, for we have no occasion, merely because he has asked us, to be quiet and peaceable, if we find him playing any pranks, or attempting to play any pranks."

"That's my opinion, too," said the admiral; "be quiet and take no notice, and it will be an odd thing to me, then, if you don't soon hear something of Master Varney, and that may be a something, too, that may astonish us."

"It that all the letter?" said Dr. Chillingworth.

"Yes, with the exception of these words in a postscript,—

Any communication addressed to V. V., General Post-office, London, will reach my hands promptly.

"Ah! then there's the gist of the matter," said the doctor; "the vagabond wants to be assured that we shall not interfere with him; and then he has got some rascality in hand, you may depend, which he would set to work about in real earnest."

"I shall not write to him," said Henry, "but shall pursue quite a different course of policy, and wait patiently for what may happen, for I am convinced that is the only plan to pursue with any chance of benefit or success."

"And you will bear in mind, doctor," said the admiral, "that the fellow in this letter talks of giving us an explanation, and yet not one word does he say about jumping upon your back from the garden-wall. The deuce a bit does he explain that."

"No," said the doctor; "nor did I expect he would. Such a man as Varney is not likely to criminate himself; and, while there is a doubt about whether he is that person or not, you may depend he will not

be the man to take any pains to dispel it."

"Of course not — of course not."

"Well," said the doctor, "I can only tell you all one thing, and that is, that, whatever you may think or flatter yourselves, this affair is very far indeed from being over, and sooner or later, something yet very serious will occur in connection with Varney, the vampyre. Do not fancy that you have got rid of him, for, most certainly, you have not."

The doctor spoke these words so oracularly, that they sounded extremely like one of those predictions founded upon such a firm basis, that they are sure to be carried out by future facts, and both Henry and the admiral felt as if they had heard truth from some one who knew well what he was uttering, and was not likely to be mistaken.

CIX.

THE PREPARATIONS FOR THE WEDDING OF THE BARON STOLMUYER OF SALTZBURGH.

THERE IS A COMMON ADAGE which inculcates the necessity of striking while the iron is hot, and this was an adage which, to judge from her conduct, seemed to have made a great impression upon the mind of Mrs. Williams, and she thought that, as regarded her daughter's feelings, the iron was hot, and that, if she struck now, she might be able to wring from her a consent, no matter how reluctant, to call the Baron Stolmuyer her husband.

The objects which Mrs. Williams felt certain she should succeed in achieving

by such an union in her family, were far too weighty to be easily dispensed with. They not only comprehended the five hundred pounds which the baron had so judiciously promised her upon the wedding day being fixed, but she had an eye to after circumstances, and considered that the son-in-law who could spare five hundred pounds, as a mere bribe to her, would be an endless source, from whence she could draw her pecuniary supplies.

"And then," thought Mrs. Williams, "there are the other girls to get off, too, and what a famous opportunity it will be to do that, when they can be at all the grand parties the baron will give at Anderbury House."

To an intriguing woman, such as Mrs. Williams was in reality, all these advantages appeared in full force; and, if ever she made up her mind thoroughly and entirely about anything in the world, she certainly did that her daughter Helen should be the Baroness Stolmuyer of Saltzburgh.

She certainly wished, in her own heart, that the baron had chosen one of her other daughters, because then she knew that she would not have had to encounter the opposition she had done, and, perhaps, had still to encounter, in the case of Helen; but, as it was, that part of the business could not be helped, and she, Helen, was to be sacrificed.

If the baron had thought for twelve-months over the matter, he could not have come to a better conclusion, as to the best means of making Mrs. Williams a zealous partisian of his, than by distinctly naming a sum of money that she should have, and when she should have it, for now she considered that each moment's delay was a piece of actual criminality on the part of Helen, inasmuch as it was keeping her, Mrs. Williams, out of a large sum of money.

There was one thing, however, which she did at once; and that was to go to the different tradespeople who had had the awful insolence to stop the supplies, and tell them that her daughter Helen was about to become the Baroness Stolmuyer, and that, if they continued to execute orders, and to wait with patience, they would all get paid within one month.

This positive announcement staggered some of them, for they would hardly have thought it possible that she would have made it, if there had not been some great foundation for truth in it, of some sort, and it was one of these announcements which, as the reader is aware, had been overheard by Tom, the son of the old sailor, and which, when reported, had created so much consternation in the mind of the young man who had been saved by Jack Pringle from the wreck.

On the following morning, the lady received a laconic note from the baron, in which were the words: —

> MADAM, —
> Have you settled with your daughter the day and hour of my nuptials with her? I have drawn a cheque in your favour, and only wait your further proceeding in the affair to sign it, and send it to you.
> "I have the honour to be, madam, yours truly, —
> STOLMUYER.
> MRS. WILLIAMS.

This note put Mrs. Williams into a perfect fury of impatience. The idea, that actually a cheque for five hundred pounds should be drawn in her favour, and only awaiting the signature of the baron, and that, by one word, her daughter Helen could procure that signature, was absolutely maddening.

She rushed, at once, to Helen's room.

POOR HELEN KNEW enough of her mother to feel convinced, from the first, that no possible exertion

would be spared for the purpose of forcing her into that marriage, which had no charms, alas, for her, but which, on the contrary, presented itself to her in the most hideous of all possible aspects.

From the first moment that her mother had broached it, it had seemed in its remembrance to lie at her heart like a lump of lead. She seemed already to feel that, after an unavailing resistance, she would have to yield, and then that her future existence would involve in it all the pangs of despair and regret.

"Alas — alas!" she said; "under what fatal planet was I born, that I should be so unhappy as I now am? What will become of me, and how shall I gather resolution enough either to bear with seeming patience the fate that afflicts me, or to resist the machinations of my mother, who would force me to wed this man whom I cannot love."

The long absence of her lover was so perplexing a source of woe and reflection to her, that already it had sapped much of the joy of her young existence.

"He surely ought," she said, "and might have found some means of communicating to me long ere this. He might well know, and must know, that suspense is, of all feelings, the worst to bear. Oh! why am I thus deserted by all, and left to the mercy of the worst of circumstances?"

With her sisters, poor Helen could have no sympathies in common; either of them would have been delighted to change places with her, as regarded the fact of becoming the Baroness of Saltzburgh, and they had towards her a tolerably cordial ill-will, on account of her superior charms, which made her so much admired, while they were left to "pine in maiden meditation fancy-free." *

But to Helen Williams, this gift of beauty was what it truly has often been described — a most dangerous one, and she would have given the world to have been able to wear an appearance that

would have repelled, instead of attracted, the Baron Stolmuyer.

She was in this desponding state of mind, revolving in her mind her dismal prospects, if she should consent to wed the baron, and her equally dismal ones if she should refuse — for well she knew how painful a position with her family such a refusal would place her in — when her mother entered the room.

Mrs. Williams had so thoroughly determined that this marriage should take place, that she could not be said to have now sought her daughter to persuade her to it; but, on the contrary, to insist upon it. The sisters, too, with whom this unnatural mother — or rather, perhaps, we ought to say, too natural, but too common mother — had held a conversation upon the subject, were anxious, despite their jealousy upon the occasion, that the affair should proceed, because certainly the next best thing to themselves making such an alliance was to succeed in getting it made by some other of the family, and they fully intended making Anderbury-on-the-Mount their home.

"What, Helen!" exclaimed Mrs. Williams — "in tears as usual!"

"Have I not cause for weeping, mother?"

"Well, well; I cannot say much to you beyond the few words I have come to say. I have, I fear, as regarded this affair of the offer that was made to you by the Baron Stolmuyer, behaved precipitately."

"Oh, mother," cried Helen, with renewed hope, "I am rejoiced to hear you say so. Then you will not now ask me to sacrifice myself to a man whom I can never love? Say no more of the past. It is sufficient that you have awakened to

---

* *A line from Shakespeare's* A Midsummer Night's Dream, *Act II Scene I.*

better resolves now, dear mother, and I shall be happy."

Such words as these ought to have softened the mother's heart; but such a woman had no heart to soften; and, after a pause, she proceeded in her plan of operations.

"Well my dear, perhaps it is all for the best."

"It must be for the best, mother, because it never can be for good that I should have consented to plight my vows to one whom, of all others, I cannot look upon with the least affectionate regard. Indeed, mother, so much as I can absolutely dislike any one, I dislike that man."

"There's no occasion to say anything more about it, my dear. I have come to bid you farewell, and Heaven only knows when we may meet again."

"What do you mean, mother?"

"I mean, my dear, just what I say; I am going now at once to a prison."

"A prison?"

"Yes. It certainly is not an agreeable idea; but, as I told you, I was too sanguine, and built too much upon your consenting to marry the baron, so I borrowed a sum of money to pay some pressing debts; but as I have not been able to repay it, I am arrested, and have now only persuaded the man to go away upon giving him my solemn promise that I will, in half-an-hour's time, be at the gates of the town gaol."

Helen heard this declaration with a feeling of perfect horror. She was too little acquainted with the usages of society to see what a transparent lie it really was, and, to her mind, it did not appear improbable that a man who came to arrest anybody should take their word to come to the gaol in half-an-hour.

"Oh! mother, mother," she sobbed, "can this be?"

"I don't know," said Mrs. Williams, "if it can be or not. All I know is, that it is so, and that I am perfectly willing to pass the remainder of my days in a dungeon."

Helen's ideas of prisons were all procured from romances, and she was not at all surprised, consequently, to hear her mother talk of a dungeon; and if she had added something about chains, and bread and water, and a heap of straw merely for a bed, it would have found a ready credence with poor Helen.

No wonder, therefore, that the idea of such a catastrophe presented itself to her in the most terrific colours; and she saw at once all her recent congratulations upon an escape from a marriage with the Baron Stolmuyer of Saltzburgh scattered to the winds of Heaven.

She was so petrified with astonishment and grief, that for some moments she could not speak, and Mrs. Williams took care to improve upon that silence by adding,—

"I am sure I should be the last person in the world to ask any daughter of mine to make a sacrifice; but as I have been so foolish, because I took a pride in my family, as to go into expenses I cannot stand, why, of course, I must take the consequences."

"Oh! no, no."

"Oh! it's all very well to say, 'Oh! no, no,' but it's 'oh! yes, yes'; and all I have to ask of you now is, to say that business has compelled me to leave this part of the country, and after that, the best way will be to say that I am dead."

"Heaven help me!"

"And then, of course," continued Mrs. Williams, in the most martyr-like and self-denying tone in all the world; "and then, of course, people will leave off making any inquiries about me, and you may all of you in time manage to forget me likewise."

"Mother, mother, is not this cruel?"

"My dear, I really cannot say that I think it is. I am, and have been, mistaken, and perhaps I did push the affair of your marriage with the Baron Stolmuyer of Saltzburgh a little too far, and too much counted upon it. I know I am apt to be too sanguine — I am well aware of that. It's a little peculiarity of mine, but I cannot help it; and when we have those little peculiarities, all we can do, is to put up with it as best we may."

"But, mother —"

"Oh! it's no use talking."

"Is the creditor so very inexorable?"

"Yes, and only on one account; he thinks I have deceived him, that's the fact; and having asked me to give a decided answer if the wedding-day was fixed between you and the baron, for nothing else would satisfy him, and as of course I could not say that, he got quite furious, and at once threatened me with law proceedings, which I did not think he really meant; but it appears he did, for here I am arrested."

"But can nothing be done?"

"Not that I see. The baron, when he made the proposal, was anxious for an immediate reply, and then he would have made some very handsome settlement, which would have been soon known, and anybody would have trusted me. But as it is, the only thing that can save you all, will

be for me to go to prison at once, and so disappear."

Helen wept bitterly.

"And therefore, my dear, I beg you won't think anything of it. I am quite willing to go at once, without any more fuss about it. But I have not yet said anything to your sisters, because I thought that the first explanation was due to you in the affair, since you were the most mixed up with it."

"Oh! this is too dreadful — much too dreadful!"

"Farewell — farewell. We may meet again, or we may not. I wish you all manner of happiness."

Mrs. Williams moved towards the door, but before she reached it, Helen sprung after her, and detaining her, cried, —

"No, no. It must not be. If there is an imperative necessity for some victim, let me be it. Oh! let me be it."

"What do you mean, Helen?" asked Mrs. Williams, in pretended surprise.

"I — I mean, mother, that — that I will, to save you, give up all hopes of happiness in this world, and that although I would far rather go at once to my grave, I will, since my destiny seems to point out that it must be so, consent."

"Consent to become the Baroness Stolmuyer of Saltzburgh, &c., &c. Do I hear aright?"

"Yes, yes. Heaven help me! I feel that I have no other hope. The dreadful alternative that is presented to me, leaves me no other course to pursue. I must, and I do consent, if it will at once save you from the prison."

"It will, my dear, if I can succeed in convincing my importunate creditor that you have really consented, and that it is not a scheme of mine merely to escape a prison. But if you write a few words signifying your consent, that will be quite sufficient."

This was an artful proceeding on the part of Mrs. Williams, for although she by no means intended to put the baron in possession of such a document, yet she considered that by having it, she completely protected herself from any reproaches which he might otherwise cast upon her, should any hitch arise in the proceedings, or anything go wrong with the affair, even at the last moment.

The few words in writing, which sufficed, as Mrs. Williams thought, fully to commit poor Helen to the marriage, were freely written, for there was no duplicity in the character of Helen, and what she said she would consent to, she was quite willing to write.

"Well, my dear," said Mrs. Williams, "although you don't feel happy just now about the marriage, you may depend upon it you will enjoy your existence very much; for when you get a little older, you will find that it is, after all, the possession of ample means that is the most important thing to look to."

Helen shook her head, but she made no reply. She did not at all agree with what her mother said, but she felt by far too much depressed to argue the point with her just then.

"You will all your life," added Mrs. Williams, as she left the room, "have the great consolation of knowing that you saved me from a prison, and in so doing, absolutely saved my life, for although I did not say before, I am quite sure I should have died."

CX.

JACK PRINGLE CALLS UPON MRS. WILLIAMS, AND TELLS HER A PIECE OF HIS MIND UPON AFFAIRS IN GENERAL.

JACK PRINGLE NEVER promised anything without an intention of performing it, whether he could succeed or not; and accordingly, when he promised that he would make due and diligent inquiry, for the purpose of ascertaining if Helen Williams was indeed faithless, he proceeded at once to do so in the most direct manner in the world, viz. by calling upon no less a personage than Mrs. Williams herself, and popping the question to her in a manner which almost precluded the possibility of her returning anything but a direct answer.

This was a measure which few persons would have attempted; but having, as it had, all the characteristics of boldness about it, it was not one that he was likely to fail in, but, upon the contrary, calculated in every respect to be eminently successful.

He proceeded to the town in perfect ignorance of its locality, or even of the abode of Mrs. Williams, except so far as a very involved description had been given to him of the route to her house by the old sailor's son, Tom, who certainly was not the best hand in the world at a direction.

But Jack was never at a loss, for, some how or another, by the force of a good-tempered manner that he had, he contrived to make friends wherever he went, and among them he soon found one who was willing in every respect to take pains with him, and to walk with him to the door of Mrs. Williams.

"Thank ye, messmate," said Jack; "and if ever I meet you again you may make up your mind that you have met a friend. And so this is Mrs. Williams's, is it?"

"Yes," said the man; "this is Mrs. Williams's."

"And what sort of a creature is she?"

"Oh, why, as to that, she is not the sort of woman I like; but there is no accounting for tastes, you know, and other people might like her very well."

"You are a sensible fellow," said Jack; "and I should say you have quite wit enough about you, that if you fell into the fire you would get out again as soon as you could."

The man hardly knew whether to take this as a compliment or not; but at all events he bade Jack good-day civilly enough, and took no notice of it.

Jack then boldly knocked at the door, and when the one miserable servant of the Williamses made her appearance, and asked him what he wanted, he replied,—

"Why, I have principally called to tell you what a remarkably fine girl you are, and after that I should like to see Mother Williams."

"Go along with ye," said the girl; "you are only joking, and I can tell you that missus would just as soon give you to a constable as look at you."

"Oh, no, she wouldn't," said Jack; "for good-looking fellows are scarce, and I dare say she knows that as well as possible, and she would much rather keep me herself than give me to anybody."

"Well, I'm sure!" said the girl. "You are like all the rest of the men, and have a pretty good opinion of yourself; but, if you really want to see missus, I may as well tell her at once."

"To be sure," said Jack.

Mrs. Williams, from a room on the ground floor, had heard that some sort of conversation was going on at the street door, and she called out—

"Susan, Susan; how dare you be talking there to anybody! Who is that, I say—tell me who that is immediately?"

"It is me, ma'am," cried Jack.

"And who is me?"

"Why, ma'am, I have come on a delicate mission; I have got something to say to you as is rather particular."

Mrs. Williams's curiosity was excited, and perhaps some of her fears, for when she had told Helen that she was drowned in debt, she had, hyperbolically speaking, not far exceeded the truth, and therefore she dreaded refusing seeing any one who came to ask for her, lest, smarting under the aggravation of such a proceeding, the party, be he whom he might, should leave some message that it would not be quite pleasant to her for Susan to hear.

This was the respect, then, which placed Mrs. Williams positively at the mercy of any one who chose to call upon her, and which induced her to give an audience even to Jack Pringle, who, under ordinary circumstances, she would, as Susan had correctly observed, have not

scrupled to place in the hands of some
guardian of the public peace as an intruder
into her house.

When Jack was shown into the
apartment where the lady waited to
receive him, he made what he considered
a highly fashionable and elegant bow,
which consisted in laying hold of a lock of
his hair in front, and giving it a jerking
pull at the same moment that he kicked
out his foot behind and upset a chair.

"How do you do, ma'am?" said Jack.

"You have the advantage of me," said Mrs. Williams.

"I rather think I have," said Jack, "and I mean to keep it, and an out-and-out thing it would be if I hadn't, seeing the many voyages I have had, when I dare say you was never out of sight of land in all your life."

"I certainly never was," said Mrs. Williams; "and I hope I am speaking to some officer, and not to anybody common."

"Oh, yes, ma'am," said Jack; "I'm a rear-admiral of the green, and what I come to ask you, is, if there is going to be a marriage in your family?"

"Rather an eccentric character," thought Mrs. Williams; "but anybody may see in a moment he is a gentleman, or else he would not be an admiral of the green; I know there are admirals of all sorts of colours; and so I have no doubt he is quite correct.—Yes, sir, there is going to be a marriage in my family, I am proud to say, for my daughter Helen is going to marry what might be called quite a foreign potentate."

"A foreign potato. None of your gammon—don't be poking your fun at me."

"A foreign potentate, I said, sir—a kind of monarch—a potentate, you know."

"Oh, I understands; I dare say them fellows lives on potatoes, and that's why they calls them such. But are you sure it's your daughter Helen, because I was thinking of proposing for her myself?"

"Really, then, Admiral Green, I am very sorry, but she is going to be married to the Baron Stolmuyer, of Saltzburgh."

"The baron what? did you say?

Stonemason and Saltpot? What a d—d odd name, to be sure."

"Dear me, what an eccentric character!" thought Mrs. Williams; "but quite the gentleman."—"Admiral Green, it's Stolmuyer of Saltzburgh is the baron's name."

"Oh, I knew it was something about salt; but, however, it don't matter; and when is the ceremony to come off, ma'am?"

"It is left to me, sir, to fix the day, and I shall do so, of course, at my convenience; and I can only express my great regret, Admiral Green, that you should have been too late; but, you see, the baron's offer was so unexceptionable, and he is really quite a wealthy individual—which his offering me a cheque for five hundred pounds, is a convincing proof—that I really could not think of refusing him."

"What! five hundred pounds?"

"Yes; I assure you, Admiral Green, that he had pressed upon my acceptance five hundred pounds."

"The stingy devil."

"Stingy!"

"Rather. Why, I meant to have asked you to accept of a couple of thousands, and a large estate that I have got, which brings in as much every year, and that I really don't want."

"Two thousand pounds and a estate! Gracious Providence! I don't know what to say to that; really Admiral Green, you are so very liberal, that, upon my word, I am quite puzzled. Two thousand pounds, and an estate worth two thousand pounds a year!—did you really mean that, Admiral Green?"

"To be sure I did. What else could I mean? but I don't want to interfere with a foreign potato and a Baron Saltbox."

"Well, but, my dear sir, stop a moment — let me think."

"No, ma'am," said Jack, "I ain't quite such a humbug as you takes me for. I say nothing, but it's very likely that your baron will turn out to be some half-starved swindler who is going to wind up his affairs by doing you, and sarves you right, too — I wishes you good morning, ma'am"

So saying, Jack, despite the remonstrances of Mrs. Williams, whose cupidity was so strongly excited by what he had said, that she would gladly have thrown overboard the baron, and who now began to look with something like contempt upon the five hundred pounds which she had before thought was quite a large sum.

"How odd it is," she exclaimed, when she was alone; "how odd it is, that after I have been looking about, I don't know how long, for a decent match for some of the girls, all the men should come at once, and want Helen — it's an extraordinary thing to me, very extraordinary. Dear me, if I could but have secured Admiral Green for Juliana, and so got her married on the same day with Helen, there would have been two thousand five hundred pounds for me at once. What a capital thing! I would not have spoken of it to anybody, but I would have paid all the tradespeople about here eightpence in the pound as a composition, and then I could have gone and lived in London quite comfortably.

Thus is it ever with such schemers as Mrs. Williams — success brings with it quite as many evils and distressful feelings as failure, and now the agony of what she thought she had lost, much more than counterbalanced any satisfaction she might have had in procuring her daughter's consent to the marriage with the baron.

This consent, although we know how it was wrung from Helen, we certainly much blame her for giving, because no human power could really force her to marry any one who was not her choice, and the mere fact that her mother represented how deeply she was in debt, ought not to have been sufficient to induce Helen to consent.

She might and ought to have taken a much higher view of the subject — a view which should have excluded a consideration of James Anderson: that view should have been a refusal to commit the perjury of solemnly vowing before Heaven to love and honour a man for whom she entertained such opposite feelings.

But Helen was not a close reasoner, and although all the argument was upon her side, and all the propriety, and all the justice, we grieve to say that she did not avail herself of either to the extent she ought to have done; but, on the contrary, gave up those moments to regret which should have been far better employed in resistance.

When the consent which we have recorded had been wrung from her, she gave herself up to the most melancholy reflections, weeping incessantly, and calling upon Heaven to help her from the pressure of circumstances which she was quite competent to relieve herself from, if she could have persuaded herself to make the necessary efforts.

At last it seemed to her that she had hit upon a plan which might afford her some relief, but in projecting it, she little knew the real character of the man she had to deal with.

This scheme was to tell the baron candidly that she loved another, and, whether that other was living or dead, his remembrance would so cling to her, that she could never love another, and that, in making her his wife, he, the baron, would be laying up for himself a source of regret and disquietude, in the feeling that he possessed one whose affections he could never hope to obtain.

"Surely," thought Helen, "if he be at all human, and if he have any of the natural pride of manhood about him, he will shrink from attempting to continue a suit that must be mortifying in every one of its stages, and which cannot confer upon him even the shadow of happiness."

CXI.

THE WEDDING-DAY FIXED, AND THE GUESTS INVITED.

WHEN SHE WAS TO receive so handsome a reward for the intelligence that she had wrung a reluctant consent from Helen to be the baron's bride, it was not likely that Mrs. Williams would let a long time elapse before she communicated that fact to him, and, accordingly, she started to do so personally.

It would appear that the baron fully expected her, for he made no remark at all expressive of surprise, but received her with that courtly grace which Mrs. Williams attributed to his intercourse with the highest and the noblest.

He did not seem so impatient as any one would have supposed a very ardent lover would have been, and, before he would allow Mrs. Williams at all to enter into the object of her visit, he requested her to be seated, and would insist upon placing before her some of the very choicest refreshment.

Indeed, as often as she then attempted to enter into the subject-matter which had brought her there, he interrupted her with some remark of a different nature, so that she found it very difficult to say anything regarding it.

At length, however, when he had satisfied the claims of hospitality, he said,—

"I presume that I shall have the pleasure of listening to something particularly pleasant and delightful to me, inasmuch as it will convey to me the realization of my dearest hopes."

"Why, my lord baron, I must confess," said Mrs. Williams, "that notwithstanding the extremely liberal offers of Admiral Green—"

"Admiral Green, madam? This is the first moment I have heard of such a personage."

"No doubt—no doubt; but for all that, since we have had the honour of your offer for the hand of Helen, Admiral Green has made one, and such a liberal one that it's quite distressing to refuse him."

"Then allow me to say, madam, that I hope you won't distress yourself about it, but accept of Admiral Green at once. I should be very sorry indeed to stand in the way of any advantageous arrangement, and, therefore, I beg you will close with Admiral Green."

The adage about coming to the ground between two stools forcibly presented itself to the memory of Mrs. Williams, and she replied, in a great hurry,—

"Oh, no, baron, certainly not— certainly not. I have refused the admiral on your account. I told him, most distinctly, I could not think of entertaining his offer for a moment, and I refused him at once."

"Then why trouble me about him, madam?"

"Oh, I thought I would only merely mention it, because the admiral said he would have great pleasure—which, of course, was a very liberal thing of him—in handing me a cheque for two thousand pounds."

"Oh, now I understand," said the baron. "I give you credit, madam, for having a good reason for making this report to me. You think that I may be induced to emulate the munificence of Admiral Green; but when I assure you that I have not the remotest intention of so doing, probably you will think that it would have been just as well if the matter had never been mentioned."

The baron was right; for Mrs. Williams did think so; and she felt all that bitterness of disappointment which wonderfully clever people do feel when they find that some pet scheme has most signally failed, leaving behind it all the consequences of a failure: and, whatever people may say to the contrary, failures do always have bad consequences, and never leave the circumstances exactly where they were.

There was rather an awkward pause of some moments' duration, and then Mrs. Williams thought she would get over the baron completely, for she put on the most amiable smile she could, and said,—

"My dear baron, I am sure we shall all be the most happy and united family that can possibly be imagined; and it is the greatest pleasure to me to be able to give you the intelligence that my daughter has consented to become yours."

"Madam, I am much obliged."

"And, although Admiral Green did say that if I would bring him similar intelligence he would there and then, on the spot, without any further delay, hand me two thousand pounds, I said to him,—'Admiral Green, I am only to get five hundred pounds from the Baron Stolmuyer of Saltzburgh, and that five hundred pounds he has likewise promised to pay me down.' Down—you understand, baron?"

"Madam, I am not deaf."

"But you understand—down?"

"Oh, I begin to see; you want the money. Why could you not say so at once? It's of no use hinting things to me; but if you had said to me at once,—'Baron, I have brought you the consent to the marriage, and now I expect at once the five hundred pounds that I am to receive for so doing,' I should have understood you, and said at once,—'Oh, certainly, madam; here is the money,'—as I do now. You will find that check drawn for the amount."

"What a charming thing it is," said

Mrs. Williams; "what a charming thing it is to do business in such a real business sort of way; but there are so few people, baron, with your habits, and upon whom one can so thoroughly depend, as one can upon you."

"Madam, you do me too much honour. Of course, having promised you this insignificant sum of money, it was not likely that I should but keep my word; and now let me ask, when is to be the happy day?"

"If this day next week will suit you, baron."

"Wonderfully well, madam — wonderfully well."

"Then, we will consider that as settled. I suppose you will have a public marriage?"

"No — no, strictly private. I am resolved, madam, not to have more than one hundred and fifty people, and to keep the expenses within a thousand pounds; so you see, I am going to do it in the plainest possible manner, and make no fuss at all about it."

"Gracious Providence!" thought Mrs. Williams; "what would he call a public marriage, if he considers a thousand pounds' expense, and one hundred and fifty guests, a private one, and making no fuss about it."

"On one of my former marriages —" said the baron, with an air of abstraction.

"One of them?" said Mrs. Williams; "may I presume to ask how often you have been married, my lord?"

"Oh, certainly. Let me see; I think eleven times."

"Eleven! and pray, sir, what became of your wives?"

"Why, really, madam, I cannot say. I hope the majority of them went to Heaven; but there were one or two I most heartily wished at the other place."

"My gracious!" thought Mrs. Williams, "he is quite a Bluebeard;* but, however, things have gone too far now; and I am not going to give up my cheque if he had twenty wives; and, after all, it shows he must be a man of great experience, and of great wealth, too, or so many women would not have had him; but, if that little fact about all his wives should come to the ears of Helen, I am really afraid she wouldn't have him, so I must caution him about it. — My lord baron."

"Yes, madam."

"I think, between you and I, my lord baron, that it would be quite as well to say nothing to my daughter about her being the twelfth wife; but just let her quietly think she is the first, because, you know, my lord, young people have prejudices upon those subjects, and she might not exactly like the idea."

"Oh, certainly, madam, I shall not mention the little affairs that have preceded hers. I assure you I am quite aware that it is likely there should be a prejudice against a man who has had eleven wives; and people will think that he smothered a few of them."

"Good gracious!" said Mrs. Williams; "you don't mean that, my lord baron. I hope that nobody ever accused you of such a thing."

"Nay," said the baron; "how are the best of us to escape censure? You know as well as I, Mrs. Williams, what a bad world

* *A reference to a then-well-known French folk tale of a nobleman who married and subsequently murdered seven young brides..*

it is we live in; and how dreadfully selfish people are."

"Yes," said Mrs. Williams, "that's remarkably true; but it ain't often, my lord baron, that one man has eleven wives."

"No; and it ain't often that such a man would exactly like to venture upon a twelfth."

"Well, no, there is something in that; but I will now, my lord, take my leave, entertaining no doubt whatever, but that this will be an extremely happy marriage, and in every respect just what we might all of us desire."

Mrs. Williams left the baron with these words; but, to say that she believed them, would be to make by far too powerful an experiment upon the credulity of our readers.

When he was alone, the baron smiled a strange and ghastly smile.

"That woman," he said, "is so fond of gold, that she sells her child without hesitation to me. If, upon hearing of my pretended marriages, she had given me back my money, I should have thought some good of her; but no, that she could not do. Money is her idol, and when once in her possession, she could not dream of parting with it. But what is it to me? Have

I not made up my mind to this affair, let the consequences be what they may? Have I not resolved upon it in every possible shape? Henceforward I will cast aside all feelings of regret, and live for myself alone; for what have I now to hope, and what have I now to fear, from mankind?

"Hope! did I say I had nothing to hope? I was wrong; I have something to hope; and it is a something I will have — it is revenge. Yes, it is revenge — revenge! which I must and will have against society, that has made me what I am; and the time shall yet come when my name shall be a greater terror than it is, and that to some were needless, for it is such a terror already, that but to mention it, would cause a commotion of frightful inquietude."

He looked from one of the windows of his house, and he saw Mrs. Williams, as she proceeded down one of the garden walks, take his cheque from out her reticule, where she had placed it, and look at it attentively.

"Ah!" he said, "now she is worshipping her divinity, gold. She knows that that piece of paper carries weight with it, and that, flimsy as it looks, it is sufficient to purchase her. Fool! fool! and she thinks she is buying contentment."

CXII.

THE SINGULAR INVITATION TO THE BARON'S WEDDING.

ABOUT THREE DAYS after the transactions which we have just recorded, the admiral received a call from his friend, the attorney, and that call had a double object.

In the first place, the man of law wanted to tell him how he was proceeding, as regarded the Quaker, and there they had a great tussel about what was to be done, for, when the attorney said to him,

"Now, admiral, as regards this assault upon Mr. Shepherd, all that can be done is to let him prove his case, and then come up for judgment, and move in the court in mitigation. I dare say, you will dragged up to Westminster Hall for judgment, and I should not at all wonder, but you will get off with a fine of six-and-eightpence."

"What do you mean," said the admiral, "by letting him do what he likes?"

"In effect, it is the same thing as pleading guilty, you know, to a charge brought against you, and, by so doing, you, to a great extent, disarm justice."

"Guilty!" roared the admiral; "guilty! You will be a long time, indeed, in convincing me that there is any guilt in kicking a Quaker, and especially such a Quaker as Mr. Shepherd. Why, I'll do it again, and think it, as I do now, a meritorious action."

"Yes; but you misunderstand me. It's called guilt, you know, in law, to do anything contrary to law; and, by pleading guilty, you do no more than just admit the fact that you have kicked the Quaker."

"That's quite another thing. I have no objection to the fact, whatever, but don't call it being guilty, for that's all moonshine, and I won't have it, at any price. Guilty be hanged! I think I see it. Guilty of kicking a Quaker, indeed; I have half a mind to go and kick him again, just on purpose; and I don't know but what I may do it yet."

"Well, well, admiral, now that we have settled that knotty point, I have got something else to tell you, of a more agreeable nature."

"Out with it — out with it."

"It is this. You recollect that, upon the marriage of Miss Flora Bannerworth with your nephew, Mr. Charles Holland —"

"The marriage feast, you mean, for, as far as the marriage was concerned, they all got the better of the old man."

"Yes; the marriage feast. You recollect that, upon that occasion, you gave me leave to invite a number of persons, all of whom were very grateful, and thought very highly of you and the honour of coming into your company."

"A devil of a sensible fellow this lawyer is," thought the admiral. "It's enough to make one take to lawyers, I'll be hanged if it ain't." — "Go on — go on; what of all that? I am sure I was as well pleased to see them all as they were to see me."

"Well, sir, it appears that some of these persons, and especially a family of the name of Clark, have been exceedingly anxious to bestow some civility upon you in return; and, as they have been invited to a wedding, they wish to prevail upon you to go with them, as it will be a very stylish affair."

"Well, I don't mind," said the admiral. "Where is it?"

"It's as far as twenty miles off, at a place called Anderbury, and it is wished that you should bring anybody you like with you, upon the occasion."

"Well, it's civil, at all events, and I don't mind, if Henry and Charles and Flora like it, going. But, when you mention Anderbury, I'll be hanged if I don't think it's the very place that Jack Pringle has gone to, to get a sight of the salt water, for the benefit of his health."

"Well, sir, it will have none the less recommendation to you, I dare say, that it is close to the sea."

"You are right there, and, I can tell you, I was thinking of going myself, because you know, what suits Jack, in those respects, is pretty well sure to suit me; and I thought, as that vagabond was enjoying himself down by the sea-coast, I might as well go and do so likewise."

"Well, sir, then I may consider I have your full consent to the arrangement, and I am sure it will be received by the parties with a great deal of satisfaction, indeed."

"Well, well, somehow or another, you talk me over to things, so I'll go, without making any more fuss about it; and I will take Henry with me, and Charles, and Flora, and I'd take old Varney, the Vampyre, too, if we had him here. It would be a good bit of fun to take such a fellow as that to a wedding."

"He would not be the most welcome guest in the world."

"No; I should think not. But who are our invitations to come from?"

"They will come from the bride's mother, as the people I have told you are so anxious to take you with them are friends of hers."

"Very good — very good; so, as it's all right, I will speak to Henry about it, and Flora, and, I dare say, we shall all manage to get there comfortably enough. Let me see; it's just two stages for post-horses. Well, well, lawyer, you may look upon it as decided; it is to be, and there is an end of it."

I N DUE COURSE, on the following day, there came a note to Admiral Bell, enclosing a card, on which was said,

    Mrs. WILLIAMS *requests the honour of Admiral Bell's company, with his party, to breakfast, on the 10th instant, at two o'clock, on the occasion of the celebration of the nuptials of Miss Helen Fedora Williams with the Baron Stolmuyer of Saltzburgh, &c., &c., at Anderbury-on-the-Mount.*

"The devil!" said the admiral. "This is an odd affair — something slashing, and out of the way, I should say. Breakfast at two o'clock! that's the d — dest piece of humbug in the whole affair. Who the devil is to wait for their breakfast till two o'clock? I never heard anything better than that; but I suppose there will be something to eat, so I shall take the liberty of having my breakfast at seven in the morning, and calling that my dinner, and my lunch I will manage to get at some inn on the road."

With this card of invitation in his hand, the admiral went to Flora, and laid it before her, saying, —

"Here will be fine fun, Flora, for you. This is the invitation I spoke to you of, and they are going to have breakfast at two o'clock, lunch, I suppose, at five, dinner at nine, a cup of coffee at about twelve, supper at four o'clock in the morning, and I suppose they will get to bed at about daybreak."

Flora laughed as she perused the card, and then she said, —

"It certainly promises to be quite a fine affair, uncle; and, at all events, as we are only guests, we shall be able fully to enter into the amusement of the affair, if there be any, and I am inclined to think there will be, by the rather pompous reading of the card of invitation which has been so civilly sent to us."

"If they are ridiculous people," said the admiral, "we will laugh at them, and they cannot expect but that we should; and if they should turn out to be otherwise, they may become very pleasant acquaintances, you know."

"Assuredly; and it will not do to judge of people always by such a trivial piece of evidence as a card of invitation can afford to one; so I will endeavour to go to the wedding with an impression that they are agreeable people — an impression which, considering the complimentary manner in which they have invited us, we ought to cultivate."

"Very good; and do you speak to Charles about it, for I have not had an opportunity of so doing; and as the people have invited us handsomely, I think we ought to go in a manner so as to do them as much credit as possible; and, therefore, I should say that a coach and four, with postilions, will be the plan, and look rather stylish."

"Oh, uncle, you will be mistaken for the bridegroom."

"Shall I? Very well, I am quite willing that I should be, always provided I may chance to admire the bride; but if I do not, you may be sure that I shall take pretty good care to explain the error."

CXIII.

JAMES ANDERSON SEEKS AND OBTAINS AN INTERVIEW WITH MRS. WILLIAMS.

THE REPORT WHICH, in accordance with what he had heard from Mrs. Williams, Jack Pringle felt himself compelled to make to the young man whom he had saved from the wreck, but too surely convinced him that all his hopes were dashed to the ground, and that it was indeed but too true that Helen had consented to become the wife of another.

There could be no mistake in the affair, or the slightest loophole for escaping an entire and complete conviction of the faithlessness of her in whom he had so deeply confided for his future happiness.

The blow appeared to fall upon him with a stunning effect, and for some time he seemed to be quite incapable of thought or action. But Jack Pringle rallied him upon this state of things, and tried hard to induce him to view the matter with the same kind of philosophy that he would have brought to bear upon it.

"Come, come," he said, "don't be downhearted about a woman. Cheer up, my lad; there's many a better fish in the sea than has ever yet been got out of it, you may depend upon that."

"I could have staked my life upon her good faith."

"Likely enough, and so can we all upon the good faith of the woman we happen to love and admire; but what is there in the whole world so common as being jilted by a wench, and when it does happen, a man should whistle her down the wind, and forget her all at once, and for ever."

"I have no doubt," said James Anderson, "that such is good philosophy; but it's a hard thing to tear away from the heart at once an image that has lain enshrined in its inmost recesses for many a month."

"Perhaps it is. But the best remedy in all the world, is to look about for another, I know that from experience in these matters. You do so, and you will soon be able to forget the girl who has jilted you."

James Anderson shook his head, and smiled faintly, as he said,—

"I fear I should never love another as I have loved her. The heart, when once it has loved as I have loved, can never know another feeling. I cannot with any hopes of success undertake such a mode of cure as that which you point out to me."

"Oh! you will think differently in a little while, I can tell you. Time does wonders in these cases, and before you are a month older, you will be in quite a different frame of mind to what you are now."

"I must confess I should not like to be all my life the subject of never-ending regret; but at the same time I do feel, that let what chances may befall me, I shall never feel another disappointment so bitter as this."

James Anderson, upon making these few remarks, shewed a disposition to drop the subject, and as it was one which certainly concerned himself more than any one else, Jack Pringle and the fisherman both agreed to say no more about it, and it rested.

But although he said nothing, the matter was far indeed from being absent from the mind of James Anderson, for it occupied him wholly, and engaged his attention to that extent, that all other thoughts were excluded therefrom most entirely and completely.

Those who had afforded him so kindly a shelter, were not unobservant spectators of this state of his mind, and Jack Pringle strove to move him from it, by calling his attention to his obligations and duties in other respects.

"Come, messmate," he said, "ain't it time you should think of going to London to make your report of how you lost the dispatches that your captain committed to your care?"

"It is so," said James Anderson, "and I shall start this evening."

"That's right, and the best thing you can possibly do, I can tell you. You will get some new appointment, and in the bustle of life you will soon forget all disappointments whatever. If you go regularly into the service, you are young enough yet to rise in it, and you may yet live to have a pair of swabs upon your shoulders, I can tell you."

"At all events," said Anderson, "I can have the comfort of knowing that I have, by being wrecked here, made some acquaintances, which I hope I may always have the pleasure to retain. I feel myself now quite well enough to walk, and I will go into the town and make some preparations for getting on to London, which I am, by your liberality, Mr. Pringle, enabled to do."

Jack made a wry face, as he said,—

"Whatever you do, messmate, don't call me Mr. Pringle—my name's Jack Pringle. It always has been Jack Pringle, and it always will be. I begin to think as something must be the matter when anybody calls me Mr. Pringle, and I don't like it a bit."

"I won't again then offend you by calling you Mr., but you shall be Jack

Pringle, if you like, to me; and I can only say that a more esteemed friend than yourself, it is not likely I shall ever encounter in this world."

Jack was always much more easy under censure, let it come from where it might, than under praise, and consequently he fidgetted about in a most alarming manner, while James Anderson was professing to him his grateful feeling, and at length he said,—

"Belay there, belay there, old fellow—that will do. I don't want any more of that, I can tell you. It's a d—d hard thing that a man cannot save a fellow man's life, without it being at all sorts of odd times thrown in his teeth in this way. Don't say any more about it, I ain't used to being *parsecuted*."

This was no affectation in Jack Pringle. On the contrary, it really was to him a positive persecution to be praised; and, as James Anderson now felt fully convinced that such was the case, he determined upon avoiding such for the future.

TOWARDS THE DUSK of the evening, having attired himself as respectably as the wardrobe of the old seaman and his son would permit him, for his own clothing had been completely spoiled by the salt water, he proceeded to the town of Anderbury.

By so proceeding, Jack Pringle considered that his principal business would be to get some means of quick conveyance to London; but James Anderson had another motive in his walk to the town, which he communicated to no one.

That motive was a strong desire to see Helen Williams, if he possibly could, before he left, in order that he might hear from her own lips what it was that prevented her continuing her plighted faith towards him; for he could not, from all he knew of her character, bring himself to believe that it was the wealth of her new suitor that had had any effect upon her.

"No, no," he said; "I know her far better than for one half instant to do her such an injustice; she must have been imposed upon with some account of my death; or some artful and well-arranged tale of, perhaps, faithlessness upon my part has hurried her into the acceptance of the first offer that has been made to her. If I could but obtain an interview with her for a few brief moments, I should know all, and either be able to take her to my heart again, or to find ample reason for forgetting her."

He knew the way well to that house where he had frequently watched Helen enter and emerge from; but how to send any message to her was a matter which required great consideration.

He had been absent long enough, no doubt, for some changes to have been made in Mrs. Williams's household; so that, although there had been in old times a servant who was favourable to him, and who would not only have taken his message to Helen, but would have told him all the news of the family, she, no doubt, had long since left.

After thinking over the matter for some time, so as to come to a conclusion that the difficulty about getting any message or note delivered to Helen almost amounted to an impossibility, he saw a boy come out of the house, apparently to go on some errand, and with a feeling more of desperation than reflection, he spoke to him, saying,—

"I think you came out of Mrs. Williams's house, my lad."

"Yes, I did," said the boy; "what of that—hit one of your own size; I haven't done nothing to you."

"You mistake altogether, my boy; I am not going to touch you, you may depend; but, on the contrary, I will reward you if you will answer me what questions I shall propose to you, and I assure you they are all such as you may honestly answer."

"Well, I don't know. How much?"

"One shilling for every question."

"That's a rum way of doing business, but it ain't so bad either. Ask away, and you'll soon see how I'll earn the shillings."

"Is Miss Helen going to be married?"

"Yes—a shilling."

"Who to?"

"To the Baron Stollandmare and a Salt Bug—two shillings."

"Will you take a note from me to her if I reward you extra for so doing."

"Oh, I begin to smell a rat. Yes, I will. You is some other lover, you is—three shillings."

"I am—one shilling."

"What do you mean?"

"Why, my young friend, if I pay you a shilling a question, I don't see why I should not charge you at the same rate; so don't ask me anything, and then you will get all the shillings to yourself, you understand."

"Oh, I doesn't see any joke in that; I don't want to ask any questions—not I.—What will you give me for taking the note? I think I ought to have half-a-crown, between you and me and the post;

because, you see, if old Mother Williams was to cotch me, she would serve me out pretty tidy."

"You shall have your own price of half-a-crown, and here is the note, which I charge you mind to deliver into no hands but those of Helen herself."

"Oh, I'll do it; and what shall I get if I bring you an answer back?"

"Another half-crown; so, you see, you will make a very good evening's work of it, indeed, if you are clever and faithful."

"Give me the note; I'll do it. You may always trust me, when there's anything to be got by it. My father brought me up to get my living, and he used to say to me, 'Caleb,' says he, 'always do your duty, Caleb, to those who employ you when you go out to service in a family, unless somebody offers you something more not to do it.'"

"Quite a philosophical maxim," said James Anderson; "I suppose you are in the service of Mrs. Williams?"

"Yes, I am page of all work, I am; I do a little of everything, and make myself generally useful. Where will you wait for me?"

"At this corner; and, with a due regard to performing your part well, be as quick as you can on your mission, for I am rather impatient to see its results."

Caleb, the page of all work, duly promised to be quick, and after completing an errand that he had been sent upon by Mrs. Williams, he returned to that lady's house.

We cannot help thinking that after the principles in which Caleb had announced he had been brought up, it was rather an indiscreet thing of Anderson to trust him with the note that he had already

prepared for Helen, in case an opportunity should present itself of getting it delivered to her; but he was desperate, and, perhaps, did not so accurately weigh the pros and cons of the affair, as he undoubtedly ought to have done.

As it was, however, he had a faith in his messenger, which we are sorry to say was most decidedly misplaced, for Caleb did shew that he had not forgotten the lessons of his paternal relative, but that, on the contrary, he was disposed to carry them out with great tack and perseverance.

Whether or not he would, of his own accord, have set about scheming in the matter we cannot say, but, at all events he was spared that trouble, for Mrs. Williams had seen, from one of the windows of her own house, his interview with one who was a stranger to her; for, although she had once, before he went to sea, seen James Anderson, he was much altered, and she did not recognize him; and when Caleb came in she called him into the parlour and shut the door.

"Caleb," she said, "I insist upon knowing immediately who you were talking to just now in the street, and who gave you a note."

Caleb was rather staggered at this home question, for he did not think that Mrs. Williams had seen him, and, after a moment's pause, he said,—

"What will you give, missus, to know?"

"Give — give! How dare you ask me such a question?"

"It's no use, missus, getting in a passion about it. I've got an opportunity of earning eight shillings snugly and comfortably. If you will give me sixteen shillings I will tell you all about it; and I don't mind saying, beforehand, that I know, missus, as you won't think it dear at that price; no, nor at three times as much, if you could only guess what it was."

"Sixteen shillings! It must be something wonderful, in the way of news, that I would give you such a sum for."

"That's just what it is, missus. Come, now, is it a bargain? because I'm in a hurry, and have got never such a load of things to do."

"Well, well, Caleb; tell me what it is, and give me the note."

"Not till I haves the money, missus. Oh, no; I knows better than that. I've got a hold on the fellow as you saw me with, but I haven't on you. Oh, no; the deuce a bit. I must have the cash first, and then you shall have the information; and, I tell you again, that it ain't dear at the price, as you will own yourself."

The curiosity, as well as the suspicions, of Mrs. Williams were strongly excited; for she began to suspect that something or another was going on in which her interests were involved; inasmuch as, upon mature consideration, she had come to a conclusion, that there was more in the visit of Admiral Green than quite met the eye.

"Well, well," she said, "I have only gold in my purse; but you shall have the amount, you may depend, Caleb, if I promise you."

"I haven't a doubt in the world," said Caleb; "but there is nothing like ready money, missus; so just hand us a sovereign, and here is four shillings change; which will be right, you know, all the world over."

This was vexatious; but, as it was quite clear that Caleb had thoroughly made up his mind not to part with his information without the cash, Mrs. Williams was compelled to hand the amount to him, which she did not do with the best grace in the world, and then she said,—

"Now, I expect you to tell me all."

"So I means, missus. You don't suppose I'd take sixteen shillings of you, and not tell you all as I have to tell you. No, missus; I'd scorn the action."

"Well, well, don't keep me in suspense; but go on at once."

"I will. There's a chap at the corner of the street, as wants me to give this here letter to Miss Helen, and bring him back an answer."

"A letter to Helen! This is news, indeed. And who was he?"

"That I don't know. I was going to ask him, but, somehow or another, I found out it was a great deal better left alone. But I should not wonder, missus, but you will find out who he his, if you read the note. People, you know, usually put their blessed names at the end of their letters, unless they sends what is called a *synonymous* one."

This was a good suggestion of Caleb's, and Mrs. Williams, without the smallest scruple as to the fact of opening a letter addressed to another person, tore asunder the envelope that covered young Anderson's epistle, and read as follows, in a sufficiently audible tone to enable Caleb to hear every word of it; for, in her intense eagerness, she forgot the fact of his presence: —

DEAREST HELEN, —

I can still address you as such, because I have not yet heard from your own lips, although I have from the lips of others, that you have forgotten me. Can it be true, that you are about, in the face of Heaven, to plight those vows to another which were to be mine, and mine only?

I ask of you but to meet me, and tell me yourself that such is the case, and you will meet with neither persecutions or reproaches from me. Tell me that you are oppressed, and you know well that in me you have a defender. Name your own time and place of meeting me; and by the boy who will deliver this to you, let me beg of you, by the memory of our old affection, to send me an answer.

Yours ever,
JAMES ANDERSON.

"I say, missus, that's pitching it rather strong," said Caleb.

CXIV.

MRS. WILLIAMS'S MANOEUVRE TO GET RID OF JAMES ANDERSON.

THIS EXCLAMATION FROM Caleb informed Mrs. Williams of the fact of his presence; and duly indignant was she at that circumstance; for, in her anger, she immediately rose to execute upon him some vengeance; and, had he not adroitly eluded her, by leaving the room, there is no doubt she would have well made him remember indulging in such a piece of impertinent curiosity.

"That wretch," she exclaimed, "has overheard me; and who knows, now, that he may actually go and tell the other. If he would betray him, he would betray me; and what redress should I get for such a circumstance?"

This was a mental suggestion which made it necessary Mrs. Williams should not only look over the fact of Caleb having stayed to listen to the letter, but likewise see him, and hold out some other inducements to him to be faithful to her, however he might chose to behave himself to other persons.

"Caleb," she said, when she had summoned him again into her presence; "Caleb, you may depend I will make it well worth your while to attend to me in this affair, and to no one else. I can, and will, pay you well; and, when the baron marries Miss Helen, I dare say, if you would like it, I should be able to get you some great place at Anderbury House."

"Well, missus," said Caleb, "I looks upon myself as put up to auction, and the highest bidder always has me. I don't mean to say but what you have done the right thing, as regards the sixteen shillings; so what would you like me to do next, missus?"

"I want you to take a note back, in answer to that which you have brought me; but, of course, the young man who gave it must suppose that it came from my daughter Helen."

"How much?"

"What do you mean by how much?"

"How much am I to get, I mean."

"Oh, I understand you. How much do you expect for such a piece of service?"

"Something handsome, I should say. What do you think of ten shillings and sixpence, missus?"

"I think it rather high, Caleb; but, nevertheless, I shall not stop at a trifle in rewarding you, provided always I may depend upon you."

"Money down," said Caleb; "you know, short reckonings make long friends, missus; besides, it's always better not to let these things accumulate; for, if we goes on doing business in this here sort of way, it would come to a good bit in a short time, and then you would think it was too much, and wouldn't like to pay it."

With a bad grace — for Mrs. Williams never liked parting with her money — she produced the sum which Caleb required for this new service, remarking, as she did, —

"Well, Caleb, you will soon grow rich, if you go on this way."

"Likely enough, ma'am," said Caleb; "I likes to be paid, and I don't see why I shouldn't."

Mrs. Williams soon handed him the note, which merely contained the words,

Come at eight o'clock, and ring the door-bell.

These words she wrote as much as possible in her daughter Helen's hand, and, having sealed up this extremely laconic epistle, she handed it to Caleb, directing him to go at once and deliver it to the party who was expecting him, and we must say, that this lad appeared to be one of the most thoroughly selfish rascals the world had ever produced, for he was now quite willing for money to betray Mrs. Williams to James Anderson, if there was any likelihood of his accomplishing such a purpose with safety.

But here some difficulties presented themselves, which Caleb's natural acuteness enabled him very well to see. In the first place, James Anderson, he shrewdly suspected, was not the sort of individual to be trafficked with, as Mrs. Williams was, and, considering that he had already committed an immense breach of trust, in giving the letter to Mrs. Williams, instead of to Helen, he thought, and, we are inclined to think, correctly enough, that it would be rather a hazardous thing to say anything to him about it.

"No, no," he said; "I'll just give him

missus's letter, and then back out of the whole affair, for I don't half begin to like it. That young fellow looks a chap that wouldn't mind wringing one's neck for one — for half a pin; so I'll just leave him alone, and say nothing more about it."

JAMES ANDERSON WAITED round the corner with considerable impatience, for, in consequence of the proceedings that had taken place at Mrs. Williams's, Caleb had been considerably delayed.

When, however, he saw him coming, hope again sprung up in his bosom, and he felt all the agitation of extreme pleasure, as he saw that Caleb had in his hand what was undoubtedly a letter.

When the boy reached him, he advanced to meet him, eagerly exclaiming, as he did so, — "You have the letter — you have seen her, and you have her answer?"

Now, as Caleb had made up his mind to commit himself but as little as he possibly could with the young stranger, he went upon the good old adage of the least said being the soonest mended, and, accordingly, instead of making any remark which might, at a future occasion, be thrown at his teeth, he satisfied himself by placing his finger by the side of his nose and nodding his head sagaciously.

He then handed to James Anderson the letter, in the contents of which that individual became too much absorbed, short as they were, to pay any further attention to the messenger.

Caleb thought this a good opportunity of being off at once, before any troublesome questions should be asked him, so he made a retreat, with all the expedition that was in his power.

James Anderson, when he looked up from the perusal of the one sentence which the letter contained, was astonished to find his messenger gone, considering how very eager he had before been on the subject of the reward which he was to get for that service.

"What can have become of the boy?" he said; "I had a hundred questions to ask him."

So well had Mrs. Williams succeeded in imitating the handwriting of her daughter Helen, that James Anderson was fully convinced the letter was written by the chosen object of his heart.

He certainly did think that it was cold and distant, and that there might have been a word or two of affection, at all events, in it, especially considering how long he had been absent, and with what an untiring affection he had ever thought of her.

"She might have told me that her heart was the same," he murmured to himself, "or else she should have let me known at once that it was so altered I should not know it for the same. But still it is something to look forward to an interview with her. She may not have had the time to write more, or, perhaps, she may have doubted the messenger, and thought it unsafe to utter anything concerning her real feelings in this epistle."

Thus hoping, and trying to persuade himself of the best, did James Anderson anxiously expect the hour when, by the note that had been sent him, he expected once again to look upon the face of her, the remembrance of whom had cheered him in many a solitary hour, and enabled him to bear up against evils and misfortunes which otherwise had been insurmountable.

IT WANTED BUT a very short time to eight o'clock, and, at five minutes before that hour, James Anderson walked, with trembling eagerness, up the steps of Mrs. Williams's house door. His hand shook, as he placed it upon the bell-handle, and told himself that the time was come when all his doubts would be resolved, and he should really know what he had to hope, or expect, or to fear.

There was certainly a something weighing heavily upon his heart, an undefined dread that all was not well, and, during the interval between his ringing and the opening of the door, he felt all that sickening sensation which is ever the accompaniment of intense anxiety, and which renders it so fearfully painful a feeling.

The door was opened by a female servant, who had received her instructions from Mrs. Williams, so that she knew exactly what to say, and, without waiting for the visitor to announce himself, she said,

"Are you Mr. Anderson, sir?"

"Yes — yes," he said.

"Then I am ordered to ask you to step into the back parlour."

"All is right," thought James Anderson; "she expects me, and has prepared for my reception."

He followed his guide implicitly, for he fully believed, as who would not, under the circumstances, that she was in Helen's confidence, and so could be safely trusted.

She led him into the back parlour, where there was no one, and then she said, —

"If you will be seated for a few minutes, sir, my mistress will come to you."

"Her young mistress, she means," thought James; and he prepared himself to wait, with what patience he could assume, and that, under the circumstances, was by no means a large amount; for he had been kept in such a constant worry by what had occurred, that suspense became one of the most agonizing feelings that he could possibly endure, now that his fate was about so nearly to be decided.

It was no part of Mrs. Williams's plan to keep him waiting, for she certainly had no fancy for retaining such a customer in the house as James Anderson; for, playing the double part that she was, she knew not what sudden accident might happen to derange her plans, and, probably, render them completely abortive.

For all she could tell, Helen herself might actually descend the stairs, and enter that very room where she hoped a short conference would suffice to get rid of the troublesome claims of James Anderson for ever.

She was in the front parlour when he was shown into the back, for they communicated by folding doors. She had but to open these doors, and at once show herself to the astonished Anderson, who little expected on that occasion to behold the mother instead of the daughter.

He gave a sudden and violent start of surprise; but, as Mrs. Williams had determined to do the dignified, and to call herself quite an injured person, she took no notice of the evident agitation of his manner, but said, with an assurance that only she could have aspired to, —

"May I ask, sir, under what pretence you write notes to my daughter, at such a time as this? — notes which appear to me to be highly calculated to do her some serious injury, and, consequently, which I cannot but think are intended for that precise purpose."

"Mrs. Williams," said James Anderson, "since it appears that I have been betrayed, and that the messenger I perhaps foolishly trusted, has delivered to you, instead of your daughter, the note I addressed to her, I have only to say, —"

"I beg your pardon, sir," said Mrs. Williams, interrupting him; "but as it was from my daughter I received your note, you may spare yourself the trouble of blaming the lad whom you had to seduce from his duty by bribes and corruption."

"From your daughter?"

"Yes, sir; from my daughter; and I flatter myself that there is too good an understanding between my daughter and me, for her to keep as a secret such a circumstance."

This was a very unexpected blow to James Anderson — a blow, indeed, which he was totally unprepared for; and yet, although he doubted, he had no means of disproving what Mrs. Williams chose to assert in the matter; and she quickly saw the victory she had gained over him, and the difficulty in which he found himself.

"Sir," she said, "if you have anything more to add to what you have already said, my daughter desires that you should inform me of it, and if it consists of such matter as she can properly take notice of, she will reply to it by letter; but she most unhesitatingly declines an interview, which she considers cannot be productive of anything but unpleasantness to all parties, and most of all to her, considering her peculiar situation, and that she is so soon about to alter her condition, and become the wife of the Baron Stolmuyer, of Saltzburgh."

"I'll not believe it," said James Anderson, "unless I hear it from her own lips."

"I suppose, sir, when you see it announced in the 'County Chronicle,' you will believe it?"

"That," said James Anderson, "it never will be; for I cannot, will not, dare not think that one whom I have loved so well could be so false."

"False, sir! What do you mean by that? I shall really have to speak to the baron, if you use such expressions towards his intended wife."

"I'll speak to the baron," said James, "and that in a language he shall understand, too, if I come across him."

"If you threaten, it will be my duty to inform the baron, so that he may take such legal steps as he may be advised."

"I repeat to you, Mrs. Williams, that I will not believe it; and since you force me to such a declaration, I have no hesitation in saying that I think you are quite capable of selling your daughter to the highest bidder, and that the baron you mention probably occupies that unenviable position — a position which no gentleman would, for a moment, wish to occupy, and which he perhaps is not fully aware of. I will see him, and explain to him that there are prior claims to the hand as well as to the affections of your daughter."

This threat rather alarmed Mrs. Williams; for she thought it possible that, if the baron really found there had been a former lover in the case, probably much encouraged by the lady, he might think his chances of happiness rather slender, and decline keeping the engagement which she considered was so suspiciously commenced.

This might or might not be the result; but at all events it was worth consideration, and placed the matter in rather a serious light.

Therefore was it, then, that Mrs. Williams determined to have recourse to her last expedient, and that was the production of the written promise to marry the baron, which it will be recollected, in the excitement and impulse of the moment, she had succeeded in procuring from Helen.

"Well, sir," she said, "since you will not be convinced by any ordinary arguments, and since you doubt my word in this matter, I shall be under the necessity of adopting some means of explaining to you the matter fully, and of showing you that there is abundance of proof of what I have asserted."

"Proof, madam! Nothing but an assurance from Helen herself can come to me in the character of proof in such an affair as this. Let me see her; for the mere fact that you sedulously keep her from me, involves the affair in a general aspect of suspicion."

"Read that, sir, and if you know anything of the handwriting of her whom you affect so much to admire, it ought to resolve your doubts."

James Anderson took the paper in his hand, and glanced upon it, and by the sudden change that came across his countenance as he did so, Mrs. Williams saw that it was having all its effect.

He could not doubt it. He knew that signature too well. He had it to some affectionate documents, which he felt would remain by him to the latest day of his existence.

It was indeed a horrible confirmation of all that had been told him — such a confirmation as he had never expected to see, and which, at one blow, dashed all doubt to the ground.

"Now, sir," said Mrs. Williams, with a triumphant air, "I trust that you are satisfied — at all events, of one fact, and that is, that my daughter had consented to become the Baroness Stolmuyer, of Saltzburgh; and without at all entering into the question of anything which may have passed between you and her upon other occasions, I think you ought, as a gentleman, to perceive that the sooner you go away the better."

"It is enough," said James Anderson. "Falsehood, thy name is woman."

"I really can't see, sir, what you have got to complain of, for people have a right to alter their minds upon the little affairs of life, and I don't see, then, wherefore they should not have a similar privilege as regards things of more importance."

"Enough, madam — enough. What steps I may hereafter take, upon a due consideration of these affairs, I know not; but now I bid you farewell."

Mrs. Williams was very glad to hear these words, or rather the last of them, because she was in perpetual dread, during the whole of the interview, that something would occur by which a meeting would take place between James Anderson and Helen herself, at which some very disagreeable explanation might take place.

It was a wonderful relief to her when he had left the house, and she heard the streetdoor close behind him, and she drew a long breath when such was the case, as she said to herself, —

"Well, thank the fates, that job is

over, and a good thing it is. There is no knowing what mischief might have been the end of it, if it hadn't been stopped as it has. He is not a bad-looking young man, and if he had had a few thousands a year, I certainly should not have made any objections to his being my son-in-law; but I possibly cannot, and will not, have poor people in the family. There is no end of trouble and bother with them; and instead of getting your daughters off hand, it's just taking on hand, in addition, some man for their amusement."

James Anderson went sorrowfully enough back to the fisherman's cottage, where he related to the sympathising old seaman what had occurred; for Jack Pringle was not there, and if he had been, James Anderson knew very well he would have got no sympathy from him on account of the circumstance; for the frailties of the softer sex did not seem to have any material effect upon Jack Pringle or his sympathies, since, by his own account, he had been jilted so often, that he now thought nothing at all of it.

CXV.

THE RETURN OF THE RESUSCITATED MAN, AND THE ROBBERY AT ANDERBURY HOUSE.

THE MORNING AFTER the occurrences that took place in the bone-house of Anderbury broke dimly and obscurely over the ocean in the neighbourhood of that town. For leagues away, as far as the eye could reach, there was a haziness in the atmosphere which the fresh wind that blew did not dissipate.

There was a white light rising in the horizon, which did not cast the warm glow over the bosom of the ocean as it sometimes does; it was dull, cold, and cheerless; there was nothing that could be called beautiful.

The waves dashed about, and came tumbling over each other, their crests now and then covered with foam, which was swept off by the fresh breeze that blew over the ocean. It was just daylight.

There was nought in the landscape save the water and the sky — nothing else to be seen for miles. Yes, there was one object, and that was a boat washed to and fro by the waves as it sat on the bosom of the sea, wafted hither and thither, as the waves impelled the boat, which appeared to be empty, for no oar was used, and no human form was visible.

But that boat, so lonely, and left to its own guidance, or rather that of the waves, contained a living being; it was he who had striven so hard to escape from the baron on the preceding evening.

He sat alone in the bottom of the boat; he was fatigued — he was shivering from the cold. The great exertions he had undergone were followed by a reaction; but he knew not where he was, or in which direction to pull, or where the shore lay.

How long he lay in this helpless condition it is not known; but he occasionally lifted his eyes upwards and across the sea, to watch which way the vessels sailed, and if any should come in sight.

The scene was one of singular desolation and dreariness, in which nothing could be seen that could cheer the eye or gladden the mind of man. Now and then, to be sure, a gleam of sunlight would cross the dreary water, but it seemed to enliven only a small spot, and that but for a very short time, for it soon again became obscure.

There was the dreary ocean with its leaden-coloured sky, and then the boat at the mercy and direction of the wind and waves, both of which seemed in no placid humour, though not absolutely squally.

A VESSEL FROM CHERBOURG, with brandies, for the port of London, was sailing direct for the mouth of the Thames, making for the Foreland, where it would have to round the point, and then enter the mouth of the river.

There were three or four men and a couple of boys on board; when they came near the boat, — "Boat, ahoy!" shouted the man on the look out; "boat ahoy!"

No answer was returned to the shout, and the men on board shouted too, and crowded to the side of the vessel to see what was going on, and who was in the boat. The captain came up; he had been in the cabin, but hearing the shout, he came on deck to see what was the matter.

"What is the matter?" inquired the captain, looking around.

"Boat on the starboard," said one of the men; "nobody in it, I think; she seems to be drifting."

The captain looked at the boat for some minutes attentively, when one of the

men said, — "Perhaps some wreck, and the boat has been swept away by the waves, or the crew hadn't time to get into her, or something of the sort."

"No," said the captain, "she's not a ship's boat — a shore boat, that's what it is, lads. She's got washed out, or somebody's drowned, upset, or rolled out."

"Something of the sort, I dare say, sir."

"Well, we needn't heave to for her — she's no service to us, and we can't spare time."

"I think there's some one in her."

"But the boat's drifting," said the captain; "but she's coming this way, and that will be the easiest way to ascertain the truth of our conjectures."

They steered the vessel so as to meet the boat, which the sea was beating towards them; and in about twenty minutes or half an hour, they came within a couple of score yards of the boat, when they could plainly perceive that some one was sitting in the bottom of the boat.

"Hilloa!" shouted the captain; "boat ahoy! — ahoy!"

The man who was in the boat looked up, and seeing the vessel, he answered the cheer.

"Throw him a rope," said the captain to one of the men who were standing by.

A rope was made fast to the vessel, and then it was thrown by a strong arm to the boat, and came right athwart it, and was immediately made fast by the man who was in it.

He then began immediately to haul up the rope, and so draw his boat up alongside of the vessel, and then he came on deck.

"How now, shipmate, what do you do out at sea in such a cockle-shell as that?"

"Nothing," replied the other.

"Nothing! Well, you have come a long way to do that. What induced you to come to sea, or were you driven out, or how was it you came here?"

"I was driven out against my will," replied the man; "I was rowing about shore, when I fell asleep, thinking myself safe, having secured the boat, as I believed, safely enough."

"Aye, aye," said the captain; "and so you found out, when you awoke, your mistake?"

"I did. My moorings had broken away, which was only a boat-hook and a rope; the tide coming up, lifted the boat hook out, and I have been out to sea ever since, and don't know where I am."

"Why that must have been last night," said the captain.

"Last night it was," said the stranger.

"You have been to sea all night then?" added the captain, taking a long gaze at the stranger.

"Indeed, I have, and I am quite cold and hungry. I had nothing with me. I rowed some time in hopes of getting in shore again, but unfortunately didn't succeed. I suppose I got further out to sea, rather than nearer in shore."

"Well, that is about the fact; you must be about fifteen miles out at sea," said the captain; "you are a long pull away from shore, I can tell you, and how you will get back again, I don't know; but, at all events, you are a very queer-looking fish, and I suppose your being out at sea all night, and no stores, makes you look as you do; though, upon my soul, I don't know what to make of you; but you mustn't starve. Here, lad, bring up some coffee and boiled pork. Can you eat any?"

"Thank you," said the unfortunate being, "I can. I have been out for many hours."

"Well, sit down, or rather go below, and eat; when you have done, come up, and we will tell you where the land lies, though I don't know how you will keep it in sight for the life of me."

The man then went below, where there was some coffee royal made for him — that is, coffee and brandy — and some salt pork was given to him, of which he partook most plentifully, apparently, while the captain muttered to himself, —

"Well, of all the odd-complexioned shore-going sharks as ever I saw, you are the oddest! D — d if I should think he was wholesome — there's a great deal of the churchyard about him." *

"There isn't a very agreeable look about him," said one of the men; "but I suppose he has been so much frightened, that he looks more like a vampyre than anything else."

"Aye; or a revivified corpse."

"Yes, sir."

"But that arises from his being so terrified and starved, as well as fatigued; exposure all night, all added together, has almost changed the current of his blood."

The man came up now, having had sufficient provisions below, and had expressed himself much gratified with the coffee-royal to the cook, who, in his own mind, thereupon declared that he must be a Christian after all, though he had obtained by some means the complexion of a white negro. †

"And now," said the captain, "if you

---

* Referring to the churchyard burying-ground.
† A Victorian term, now obsolete, for an albino Black person.

like to go with us to London, you shall go with us, for, as I said before, we cannot run into any port before we get there, for the wind is favourable and strong."

"I would sooner get back by means of my boat," replied the man, "if I were sure of making land."

"You might, if you could keep in a straight course, but there is the difficulty; you cannot do so very well without a compass, and that you have not got."

"No, indeed, I have not—though with it I have no doubt of being able to reach the land."

"I have," said the captain, "a small one below, a pocket compass; you shall have that, and see what can be done; and if you get ashore, it will have done some service at all events."

"I shall be greatly obliged to you for your kindness," said the stranger; "but I am wholly at a loss to know how I shall ever be able to repay your kindness."

"Say nothing about that; we who get our bread upon the sea, know well the risks we all run, and therefore do not mind lending a hand to each other when in distress and trouble."

"I will endeavour to save some one else in your line of life, if I cannot you," replied the stranger, "and so, if it be possible, make some return."

"Aye, that will do mate; do a Christian's charity to any one whom you may cross, and I shall be well paid for my trouble."

The boat was now brought up alongside the vessel, and, before the stranger embarked, the captain said to him, as he held the compass in his hand,—

"You must place this compass on one of the thwarts of your boat, shipmate."

"I will."

"A precious vessel she is, for a voyage out of sight of land; but, never mind, you are safe enough, unless a sea was to come and roll over you—but that's neither here nor there. Mind you keep your boat's head to the north-west, and, by so doing, you'll make land at the nearest point from where we are now."

"Thank you," said the man.

"Moreover, you must pull so as to keep her head in the direction I tell you. It will be too long a pull for you to get there by rowing—you would get too tired to keep your seat, and you are unused to it, too."

"I am obliged to you," said the man; "if I get to shore safe, I shall be under great obligations to you. You will have saved my life."

"I have ordered enough biscuit, and grog, and cold beef, to last you till night—you will get to shore before that time, I have every reason to believe. In five or six hours you ought to get there; but, in case of accidents, there is enough to last till night."

"You have loaded me with obligations."

"Say no more; be off with you and pull away from the vessel as quickly as you can; for we have slackened our speed for you."

"Farewell; a pleasant voyage to you," said the man.

"Good bye, and good luck go with you," replied the captain. "Keep to the northwest, and all will be well; push off, and keep your eye on the compass."

The man did as he was desired; laid the compass on one of the thwarts; took the oars in his hands, and began to row away with good will.

The crew of the vessel crowded to the

side and witnessed the departure of the boat, and when she was a few hundred yards off, the sails were spread, and the vessel ploughed through the waves, leaving the boat behind, a mere speck on the sea, diminishing each moment.

But yet while the boat was within hailing distance, the captain said to the crew,—

"Give him a cheer—he may meet

with a score of accidents before he reaches shore, any one of which will be sufficient to destroy him."

The crew obeyed, and gave a loud shout to the boat, and the captain added his own voice; the cheering huzza reached the boat, for the occupant elevated his oar, and returned it. The solitary cheer was borne to the vessel faintly but distinctly; however, they gave him one cheer more, and then pursued their way over the trackless waters.

THE BOAT PURSUED its course for some distance, until it was too far from the vessel to be seen, and then, slackening his pace, he contented himself with merely keeping the boat's head in the direction which he had been told, and in which he knew the land lay.

There was no hurry and desire to reach the land, but merely to keep where he was; and when any vessel hove in sight, he pulled so as to keep clear of her and out of hail; and there were a great many who passed near him, and would have aided him had he required any; but that did not seem to be his object.

Midday was passed, and the sun began to decline towards the west, when the boat was gradually brought nearer and nearer in shore.

Not only was the shore visible, but the very houses might be counted, and yet he would not come ashore, but appeared to be awaiting the sinking of the sun before the boat chose to seek the protection of the land.

It was about sun-set that the provisions, which were given by the captain of the vessel, were now consumed, and that while they were being eaten, the occupant of the boat sat still with his eyes fixed upon the town, which was every moment becoming hidden in the approaching denseness of the night; and, at length, could not be distinguished, save by the existence of numerous lights, that shewed the precise position in which it lay.

Darkness now came on, and nothing was to be seen on the ocean whatever, and he remained yet longer at sea; but at length there was no danger of being noticed; he gradually rowed his boat in shore and secured it.

Then jumping ashore, he wandered about the town from one place to another, and, finally, he determined to make his way to Anderbury House.

"There is, at least, plenty of everything there," he muttered; "and, though there are plenty of servants, yet, in so large a place, there is ample room to secret oneself, and plenty to be had for the trouble of taking it."

He came to a small public-house, which he entered, with the view of resting a short time, and of ascertaining what was going on in the town.

There were several people seated in the public-room, and he now seated himself up in one corner of the room, unobserved by anybody.

"Well, well," said one; "there is more than one strange thing of late that has happened. The baron has given some very handsome entertainments."

"Aye, so he has," said one.

"And more than that, they say he's going to keep 'em up till he gets a wife; though I cannot tell why he should leave them off then, because women like that sort of thing too well to make any objection to its being carried on after marriage."

"The baron is very right; if he carried it on then, he would be watched by his wife, who would take good care to rate him for any attention he might pay to any of the ladies; and, therefore, it would only be keeping up the means for being scolded to keep up the balls."

"Aye, it would only be getting into hot water, and keeping the kettle boiling on purpose."

"He would," said another man, "merely be keeping the entertainments on for the purpose of showing off his wife and her self-will, as well as her power over him, and showing them all how she could rule a man — a very favourite pastime with married women, who, when they have a partner who don't like fighting and quarrelling, and who does love peace and quietness, know how to give it him."

"I think better of the baron, who, I think, is a man who wouldn't stand much of that."

"Ah, you don't know what an upas-tree a woman can become, when she pleases." *

"Well," said another, "the strangest thing that I know of is the loss of Bill Wright's boat."

"Oh! what was that? I have heard something about it, though I can't say I have heard the rights of it yet. What was it all about, eh?"

"Why, he says, when he went to bed, he left his boat safe enough moored to other boats and afloat. Bill says he'll swear she couldn't get clear without help; but she did get clear, and there is nothing to

be seen of it now, at all events, and poor Bill is in a devil of a way about it, too, I can tell you, and good reason enough."

"Yes. Bill will scarce be able to get another boat, unless some good friend should give him one, and that is scarce likely, I think as times go."

"There's no ball at Anderbury House, to-night, I believe," said one of the visitors.

"None, that I know of."

"No, there is none," said another, "because I know of several who have got leave of absence; so they are short-handed there, and they would not be so if they had anything particular going on, for the baron does the thing handsomely."

"So he does."

The stranger listened to all this conversation very quietly, for some time, muttering to himself, —

"That is well. It will suit my purpose very well. I will go and see how the land lies in that quarter. I have objects in view, and some of the valuables to be found there, at all events, will aid my projects, and assist in my comfort, and I may as well have them from there as anywhere else; besides, I know more of that place. It suits my taste to do so, and will be somewhat in the shape of revenge."

Calling for his reckoning, which he paid, he left the house, and proceeded towards Anderbury House.

IT WAS NOW NINE O'CLOCK or a little later. No one was about, or scarcely any, and those few the moving figure endeavoured to avoid. He turned out of the usual paths, and walked over the fields and unfrequented ways, keeping near the hedgerows, until he came to the bounds of

---

* An upas-tree is an evergreen with highly poisonous sap, native to Southeast Asia.

the grounds of Anderbury House.

Here he paused, and bethought himself of the best means of entering the house unseen and unsuspected by any one, else his object would be defeated.

However, after a few moments' thought, he determined to proceed, and, for that purpose, he made for a spot where the fence was low, and ran by some trees that had been cut down and grew bushy.

Having reached there, he, by aid of the branches, contrived to get over into the grounds, and then made his way swiftly towards a plantation that ran up close to the house, and by means of which he hoped to reach the house, and perhaps to enter it.

Silently he made his way into the plantation, and just as he reached it, he saw the moon rise in the east; it was just rising above the horizon.

"Thanks," he muttered, looking towards the luminary, "thanks you did not appear before; but now you are welcome, for I can keep under cover of the trees, and the deeper the shadow, the safer I am from observation."

This was right enough.

The moon rose full, but not bright, for some clouds seemed to intervene, or rather some thin vapours, which gave her a strange colour, and, at the same time, increased her apparent size; but she rose rapidly, and as she rose that would wear off, and she would resume her silvery appearance and usual diameter.

He was now safe in the plantation, but, at the same time, it would require some caution not to be discovered, for, at times, even the plantations formed beautiful evening walks, in which many of the inhabitants of Anderbury House had

indulged at various times, and especially when there was what was termed a family party.

On a moonlight night, when there were several members of the family who knew the grounds well, then they would find ample amusement in wandering about.

However, there was no such parties on this evening, and as it followed, he ran no danger. Lightly, therefore, he crept forward, making no sounds save such as it was impossible to avoid.

The foot-fall upon dried leaves — the cracking of sticks, and the rustling of the smaller under-growth, when he came in contact with it.

"How I shall be able to pass the open spaces, I know not," he muttered; "but I have passed worse spots than this, and I may be pretty confident I shall succeed in escaping detection on this occasion; however, it shall be tried. There are few who are about — all is quiet and still — the very watch-dogs are quiet and asleep."

He crept onward now until he came within some hundred and fifty yards of the house itself, when he paused and listened, but hearing nothing, he again came forward and approached to within a few score yards of the house, when he was suddenly arrested by the sound of voices.

He paused and listened; it was a female voice spoke near; she was evidently speaking to a man.

"Now, William," she said, "do you really believe you can get in without making any noise?"

"I am sure of it, providing you leave the window open, and the rope there."

"Yes, yes, I will. Well, that room is empty; pull off your shoes, and creep out of the door; don't let it bang together, or it may alarm some one."

"Yes, yes; I'll take care."

"Well, then, remain in the passage or room until I come to you; but should you be disturbed, you can hide yourself in any of the closets, or go up stairs, which will bring you to the floor on which is my room."

"I'll take care; but don't forget the rope, and to leave the window open."

"I'll not forget. I'll throw the rope on one side, so as to hang among the vine leaves, so that it will not be detected by any one accidentally coming this way, though that is very unlike, indeed."

"I understand; for the matter of that, I think the vine is strong enough to bear me without the rope."

"I would not have you make the attempt lest you fall, and are killed, William; be sure you do not make the trial; what a thing it would be if you were discovered, and all were to come out — I should be ruined."

"Never fear that; I will take care, both for your sake as well as my own."

"Then good-bye."

Some words were then uttered in a whisper, the import of which he did not hear, but it continued for a minute or two, and then the female said, —

"Wait here a few minutes, and you will see me come to yon window, and let down the rope; and then begone as quickly as you can."

"Never fear for me; I will wait here until I see you at the window, and then I will leave."

The female figure he saw glide quickly away, and he watched it until she was out of sight, and then he watched for the signal also. He could see the form of the male figure, who stood within about three or four yards from the spot where he was concealed.

Then, after a time, he saw the female figure come to the window indicated by her, and then throw the rope out of it, and cause it to hang down by the side, or among the leaves of the vine, so that it could not be seen, except it were looked for.

When this was done, and the figure saw the female had withdrawn, he turned from the spot, and walked hastily away further in the plantation, and when he was quite out of hearing, and the stranger could no longer hear his footsteps among the dried rubbish in the wood, he walked cautiously forward to the edge of the grounds, and then gazed up at the house, and listened carefully to ascertain if there was any sound at all indicative of the vicinity of any human being.

Hearing none, he assumed another attitude, and prepared to make a dart forward to the window, as he muttered, —

"The coast is clear, and it will be hard, indeed, if I do not now succeed. Once in the house, I will soon secure myself, and the contents of some of the baron's drawers — some of his gold will be mine."

Again taking a cautious survey, and, being perfectly satisfied that he was unobserved, he dashed across towards the root of the vine, and, in a moment more, he had seized the end of the rope; but he heard the sound of footsteps. What to do he could not tell, but sprang up a few feet, and buried himself among the leaves of the vine, which were very luxuriant.

The footsteps were heard closer and closer, until he could perceive the very female who had thrown the rope out of the window stop within a few inches of him, and then seize hold of the very rope he had been about to seize.

Her object was to ascertain if the rope was low enough to be reached; and, when she had adjusted it to her mind, she exclaimed, in a low voice, to herself,—

"Ah! that will do; he will easily find it, I dare say; and it will be all right. Nobody will see it."

Having satisfied herself of that, she left the spot, and returned the same way she came. It was an awkward situation as anyone could well indulge in without discovery.

"It was a very narrow escape," he muttered. "I had no idea of her coming back in that way; I never dreamed of such a thing. But no matter; I believe I am quite safe now; if not, I shall have some other escape. She must have been next to blind not to see me."

However, he got down, and then pulled down the rope straight; and, by the help of that and the vine, he then pulled himself up to the window, into which he speedily got, and found himself in an empty room.

Here he paused, to ascertain if he could hear any one moving about; but he heard nothing, and at once proceeded to feel his way, cautiously, along to the door, which he approached with a cat-like step.

Opening the door, he paused to listen, before he ventured into the landing to which it opened; but, finding the coast clear, he went through that, and then into the next room, which was apparently a store room, being filled with a variety of things of a miscellaneous character, and which were only of occasional use in the house.

This he closed, and went up stairs, where he came to a suite of servants' bed-rooms, and thence he walked about from room to room, until he came to a portion of the house he recognised, and then he made direct for the baron's own room.

"There," he muttered, "I am likely to meet with what I want; and the carpets are soft, and give no noise. I can sleep for a short time, if I will."

He made at once for the baron's sleeping room, which he opened and entered. It was empty, and he at once closed the door; then he made an instant search about for a place of concealment; and, having found one, he began to make a search for some other matters, that were not of the same, but a more valuable character in the market.

However, he found out the drawers and depositories; but he was unable to open them, because they were locked; and he must wait until the baron had gone to sleep, and then, taking his keys, he would be able to help himself, without any difficulty, to what he most desired.

He had scarcely made this determination, before he was alarmed by the footsteps of the baron, as he ascended the stairs. This produced a necessity for instant concealment; and he immediately flew to the spot which he had chosen; and, scarcely had he done so, before the room-door was opened, and in walked the baron himself, who brought in a light with him.

He remained walking about some time, examining a variety of matters, but appeared as though he never intended to go to sleep. There was every probability of his discovering the place of concealment; which was easily done, had he but turned his head, or moved his hand, under certain circumstances; but, as fortune willed it, the baron did not.

It was near an hour before the baron sought the repose he might have taken, but for the dominion of the spirit of restlessness; and it was even then some time before he fell into a sound slumber, apparently being engaged in deep thought.

However, he did fall asleep, and the tongue of Morpheus spoke loudly — like some human beings, through the nose; and then it was the hero of Anderbury church-yard stole from his concealment, and began to examine the chamber.

"Where are his keys, I wonder?" he thought. "He must carry them about him; but he must have left them somewhere in his clothes; and if I can obtain, and use them, without making any noise, it will be fortunate."

He found the keys, though not without making a slight jingle with them, but that caused no motion on the part of the baron, who lay snoring in his bed.

He stole to the drawers, and the key fitted; he quietly unlocked it and drew it open.

"Fortune befriends me," he muttered.

At that moment the baron turned in his bed and heaved a deep sigh, and appeared for a minute or two restless, and as if on the point of waking up.

The intruder, however, stopped short in his depredations, and paused, and then crouched down, lest the sleeper might open his eyes, and, by a momentary glance, detect him.

Suddenly he spoke, but indistinctly — very indistinctly, and yet loudly enough. The stranger started — he thought himself detected; but he found that the baron was only dreaming. He drew nearer to him, and listened to what he said.

"Ha!" sighed the baron; "she is very beautiful — very beautiful. Ha! her form and face are perfection!"

He paused, and again went on, but too indistinctly. A word or two was heard plain enough now and then, but it was impossible to form any sense of them — they had no connection with one another.

"She is a very beautiful," again muttered the baron in his sleep. "She is lovely — amiable — what a wife!"

Then he again fell into a train of half-mumblings, from which nothing could be gathered.

"Heavens, what a prize!" exclaimed the baron, and again he relapsed, but appeared more composed and quiet.

"I would he were nine fathoms deep below the level of the sea," muttered the robber; "and then I should not be bothered by him. Sleep, or let it alone," he exclaimed, between his teeth. "It would almost be safest to kill — and yet, one cry might bring the whole household upon me."

Turning to the door, he ascertained that it was locked. He turned the key, and, in doing so, made a noise with the lock which had the effect of causing the baron to start in his sleep.

"What was that?" he muttered, in sleepy accents. "I thought I heard the door go; but it can't. I locked it — I remember very well I locked it."

After this speech he fell fast asleep.

"Another escape," muttered the intruder, who rose from his crouching posture, and setting the door open, so that he could, in case of an accident, make his escape from the room.

Then he again turned towards the drawers, and began to help himself to the contents, when he accidentally struck the keys, which fell with a clash to the floor. In an instant the baron started up on his elbow, and pulled aside the curtain, to see what was the cause of the disturbance.

In a moment the light was put out, and the intruder had assumed a motionless posture; but it was too late to escape the quick eye of the baron, who instantly jumped up, exclaiming, as he laid his hand upon a pistol, which he had under his pillow, and cocked it, — "Ah! robber — assassin! Stand, or I fire!"

The sound of the cocking of the pistol was quite enough. It came distinctly to the ear, and suggested the idea of more than ordinary danger with it; and he dashed past, heedless of the command of the baron, who called upon him to stand.

The baron fired, and in an instant the house was filled with a stunning report, which echoed and re-echoed from room to room, filling the inmates with wonder and alarm.

The sensation produced by the sound was of that description that can hardly be described. To be awaked from a sound sleep by such a dreadful, stunning report, which carried such a sense of danger with it, that they remained in an alarming stupor for nearly the space of a minute, until, indeed, they were aroused by the shouts of the baron, was rather terrifying.

Hardly had the stunning and deafening report died away, when the baron leaped from his bed to ascertain if his shot had taken effect.

The intruder heeded not the commands or the shot of the baron, for he dashed out of the room at his utmost speed, making his way towards the lower portion of the house, that offering greater facilities for escape.

The baron, as soon as he had recovered from his first surprise, jumped out, and seizing a heavy cane that was lying across one of the chairs, he rushed after the flying figure, shouting and calling to his people to get up.

"Robbers! thieves!" he shouted. "Here, help — help to secure the robbers who are in the house."

The intruder made for the lower stairs, but was closely followed by the baron, who could just see the dusky form of the object of his pursuit before him; but now, in the lower rooms, where there was no light at all, the shutters being up, he missed him.

The robber had taken advantage of the darkness, and doubled upon his pursuer, and hastened up stairs with the view of reaching the place where he entered.

In doing this, however, he was met by one of the men who was coming down. There was no time for deliberation, and he dashed up, regardless of the blow the man aimed at him, who said, — "Here you are. Here goes for one on 'em."

As, however, the battle is said not always to be with the strong, so in this instance he was unable to accomplish his object, for the blow, by the agility of the robber, was evaded, and the result was, that the serving man was suddenly whirled down the stairs, and being once on the descent, he did not stop until he got to the bottom.

"Murder! murder!" shouted the unhappy individual, as he rolled down stair after stair, until his cries were stilled by a violent concussion of the head.

In the meantime the stranger rushed up stairs at a headlong speed, until he attained the landing which led to the room at the window of which he entered. Securing the door behind him, and then getting out of the window, and seizing the rope, he began to descend very rapidly, fearing he would be intercepted by those below.

He slipped down the rope rather than

let himself down, and before he had got half way down, he met with an impediment, which, however, quickly gave way, and they both came down plump to the earth together.

"My God! my God!" exclaimed a man's voice, in great terror and tribulation. "What's that? what's that? Mercy — mercy! I didn't mean to do any wrong."

The stranger heeded not the words of the terrified swain, who, it would appear, had begun to ascend to reach the dormitory of his fair but frail one, when his flame was so unceremoniously quenched in the way we have related; but dashed away from the spot, and was speedily lost in the plantation, whither the unfortunate individual when he had sufficiently recovered his senses, and released his head from the inprisonment of his hat, soon after betook himself, thankful the affair was no worse.

―――――

CXVI.

JACK PRINGLE FALLS IN LOVE, AND HAS RATHER AN UNHAPPY ADVENTURE WITH A BOLD DRAGOON.

JACK PRINGLE, LIKE OTHER men, was subject to the vicissitudes of the passions, which placed him under a certain string of circumstances that produce results quite at variance with those which are usually anticipated when an individual enters upon the pursuits of the tender passion.

Indeed, Jack could see nothing at all unhappy, or in the least degree unfortunate, in the black eyes and rosy lips of Susan, who was most certainly the "maid of the inn," though not in precisely the same rank as the one alluded to by the song. *

He had taken up his residence at the inn, had Jack. Indeed, he was partial to inns in general — there was usually a greater latitude permitted there than elsewhere; not only each one being allowed to accommodate himself as he pleased, but he could have what 'baccy and grog he chose to order, as long as there was a shot in the locker.

This being the state of affairs, Jack found another inducement to stay where he was, and that was the existence of the before-mentioned Susan, who appeared to be as kind as she was good-natured.

She never refused to answer Jack's call; and when she came, she always said, —

"What did you please to want, Mr. Pringle?"

"Mr. Pringle," thought Jack. "Well, that sounds pretty from such a pair of lips."

Jack scratched his head, and turning his quid in his mouth, was often lost in admiration, and forgot all his wants at that moment, and it was not until the question was more than once repeated, that Jack was aware that he really did not want anything, especially as his grog was not all gone.

―――――

* _Probably "Mary, the Maid of the Inn," a broadside ballad by Robert Southey, written in 1796._

"Well," exclaimed Jack, looking at the glass, "I forgot; but never mind, Susan, I'll have another can while this is going — so I sha'nt hurry you. I wouldn't hurry you, Susan — no, that I wouldn't."

The course of true love never did run smooth — that is, we know, a rule that is as old as the hills — but then it is of constant recurrence, and one that it may fairly be presumed always will, to the end of the world, and possibly after.

However that may be, Jack was not without a rival, and one of a very formidable character; not that Jack valued him a piece of rotten yarn. No; he never did think anything of a landsman, especially a soldier, for it was to that class this rival belonged.

"Susan," said Jack, as he sat in the kitchen, watching the various evolutions to which the hands of Susan were applied, in the performance of her multitudinous duties.

"Well, Mr. Pringle," said Susan.

"Ah!" said Jack; and then there was a pause, during which Jack forgot even to chaw his quid, and was quite abstracted in manner and thought. He had intended to say something, but it had quite escaped him; and it was difficult for Jack to hold his thoughts, as it is for countrymen to hold a pig by the tail when this latter member was well greased, and when it was of that description usually denominated a "bob-tail," a common occurrence.

"What did you say, Mr. Pringle?" said Susan, bustling about. "I am sure you were about to say something."

"Well, I suppose I was," said Jack; "but I don't know what it was now; but perhaps you do."

"How should I know? I can't tell what you are thinking about. What made you think that?"

"Because your black eyes seems to go through me, Susan, like a forty-two pounder. I tell you what, you ought to know what I want to say, because I'm always thinking of you."

"Are you, though?"

"Yes, I am," said Jack; "you're a light craft — a rare pretty figure-head you'd make."

"Lor! Mr. Pringle," said Susan.

"Well, you would, though; and I'll take three dozen and never wink, if there's one to be found half as handsome in the whole British navy, or in any other."

"To think," said Susan, "that I should be called a figure-head! Well, I declare, I never heard the like. Why, what will you not say next? I never thought that of you."

"Why," said Jack, who was very much bewildered, and didn't know precisely what to say — the turn the compliment had taken was one he couldn't understand — "why, you see, Susan, the figure-head is the beautifulest part of the ship, except maybe her rigging, her portholes, her sides, and her trim; but then, you see, them things ain't no manner of likeness to anything human, especially you, Susan."

"Ain't they, Mr. Pringle? Well, you know best; but I dare say it's all right, for you must know best. But my cousin says I am more like the Venus day Meditchy, than anything else."

Jack stared.

"Who?" he inquired, with his eyes opening very wide.

"The Venus day Meditchy," said Susan, speaking in a very slow, emphatic manner, for Jack's behoof.

"Don't know her," said Jack. "I'll go bail there ain't such a ship in the navy. There never was such a thing heard of, unless some of them d — d French craft; but your cousin ought to be well cobbed for saying you were like anything French. Why, you are true blue, and no French about you — is there, Susan?"

"I don't know; but I never heard there was, and I don't know if there is; but that's what he said, and he's been a long way."

"Who is *he?*" said Jack, laying emphasis upon the last word, to indicate that the sound was displeasing.

"Oh! my cousin."

"Well, but who is your cousin?" inquired Jack. "Have you see him very lately?"

"Yes, I saw him this morning; his regiment is quartered only a few miles from this place."

"Oh!" said Jack, "he's a soldier, then?"

"Yes, he is — a horse-soldier," added Susan.

"A horse-marine. Ah! I know 'em afore to-day; they are a rare lot to lie and gallop away. But lord bless you, they never lay alongside an enemy till you've beaten him. No — no — they can't do that."

"He'll be here to-night," said Susan. "You shall see him, Mr. Pringle; he's coming all this way to see me."

"To see you!" said Jack Pringle, who was much displeased with this piece of particular attention in the cousin, and he could not help saying so.

"But he is my cousin," said Susan; "and you know one cannot refuse to see one's friends and relations; besides, he has been at all times very kind and good-natured to me, so that I cannot do otherwise than receive him kindly."

"Oh, to be sure," said Jack; "by all manner of means; only we must understand each other, Susan; there can't be more than one captain aboard at a time."

"How very odd you do talk, Mr. Pringle. My cousin will ask you what you mean."

"Will he now?" said Jack. "Well, he may do so, if he like; but my lingo will be as good as his, I am sure; but we shall see him, however; but, Susan, you don't care anything about him, you know."

"Not a bit, Mr. Pringle; only as a cousin, you know."

"Oh! very well," said Jack; "I don't care about that a bit; but if so be you're going to carry on any games, you know, why, I won't stand it."

"Oh, honour," said Susan, looking tenderly at Jack; "honour, you know. Do you think I could be capable of doing so? No, I never do anything unbeknown to a person. No, I say, let all be fair and no preference."

"Well," said Jack, "but I want all fair, but I should have no objection to a little preference, too. Don't you give no preference to me over a soldier, Susan?"

"Don't know," said Susan; but she gave a look towards Jack that made him suspend the libation he was about to pour down his throat.

"Oh! I see how it is with you, Susy," said Jack, becoming more familiar and pleased, for Susan's black eye had a magical effect upon Jack, and he felt as if Susan must love him as much as he loved Susan; her eyes told him more than her tongue; Jack was quite sure of that.

"When is he coming?" said Jack.

"To-night," said Susan; "and you must

promise me you will be very quiet and civil, and then you shall see him; only you won't take any notice of what he says or does."

"No, no," said Jack; "it's all right; I understand. I won't quarrel with him; no, not even if he were to — but splinter my mainmast, if I could stand that!"

"Stand what?" inquired Susan, demurely.

"Kissing of you," said Jack, striking the table with his fist, so as to make the glasses that happened to be there tremble; "I couldn't; I could stand the cat first."

"Lor, Mr. Pringle! who asked you to do so? I am sure, I would not do such a thing."

"What?" said Jack.

"Why to let him kiss me, to be sure."

Jack looked, perhaps felt, electrified, and, after a moment's pause, took his quid out of his mouth, hitched up his trowsers, and then seized Susan by the waist, and gave her a kiss. It was a kiss; such a one only as a man-of-war's man could give; it went off like the report of a pistol.

"Lor, Mr. Pringle!" said Susan, "I thought you were quite another sort of a man. What would my cousin, the dragoon, have said, if he had seen you? Dear me! you must have alarmed the whole house; I didn't think you were going to make so much noise, though."

A footstep approached, and the landlady thrust her head in; but Susan was busy, and Jack was chewing his quid as grand as an admiral.

"Susan."

"Yes, ma'am," replied Susan.

"What's the matter?"

"Don't know, ma'am. Didn't know there was anything wrong at all, ma'am."

"I thought I heard a plate smash just now. Are you sure you haven't broken anything."

"Yes; quite, ma'am."

"Oh!" said the landlady. "I certainly thought I heard a smash; but, I suppose, it was a mistake altogether, However I am glad of it."

"There!" said Susan, when she had gone; "I told you how you had alarmed the place."

"Well," said Jack, who felt much abashed at what had happened, "I didn't make so much noise, either. But never mind; I'll take more care another time."

THE EVENING CAME round, and with it came the dragoon, as fine a specimen of military dress, discipline, and riotism as can well be let loose upon a decent community; and Susan met him in the passage.

"Ah! my pretty Susan," said the son of Mars, "the star of my destiny, and the hope of my heart. While I wear spurs, I will love you, ever dearest."

"Oh! come, none of that nonsense, you know, Robert; it won't do; you say too many fine things, you know."

"Of course I do; but can I say them without occasion. No; as well might you want day without daylight — the moon without moonlight. You inspire me, you see, and without you I couldn't say anything."

"I dare say not," replied Susan; "you are such a man, that you make one believe what you say."

"You ought, since I speak the truth, and nothing else; but, come, come, we'll go in. I want to talk to you, Susan; I came on purpose to see you. There's the barmaid at the Plough and Gooseberry-bush, quite sulky because I didn't stop there; but I know I promised you I would come, and so I would be as good as my word."

"Are you sure she was sulky?"

"Certain, because she did would not say good bye."

"Well, but now I want to speak to you about something I want to explain."

"Explain, my dear. I'll explain anything that can be explained — I don't mind what it is. You'll never find me backward in coming forward with any amount of explanation that you can by any possibility require."

"That is not what I want. I have a cousin here."

"Aye; I'm not particular. I will pay her every kind of attention. I am sure you will acknowledge I am not wanting in any attentions to you."

"Oh! dear, no; but it is not a female cousin that I want to speak to you about."

"Indeed! I can't tolerate another."

"Yes, but you must. He's just come from sea, and is a very odd man, but an uncommonly good-hearted man, so don't take any particular notice of what he says or does."

"I don't mind him a bit — not the value of a pinch of snuff."

"Yes, but you must do that, only don't do anything to vex him. You can be pleasant company when you please, I know."

"And so I will."

"To please me you will; for though I don't care anything for him more than if he were my brother, yet he's very fond of me."

"That's no recommendation to me," said the dragoon; "a spoony anchor buttons, I suppose."

"You must be civil to him, or I will never see you any more."

"Well, then, my charmer, I will say anything you like to this salt-water fish of yours; but he mustn't lay hands upon you; if he should do so, why, I should be obliged to chastise him."

"But he's a man-of-war's man."

"And I am a man of war myself, my dear."

"Lor!" said Susan.

Upon which she turned her eyes and face towards the dragoon, who could not let such an opportunity slip, and he immediately saluted her in true military style, but he did not commit the same offence that Jack Pringle did, for the former told no tale by the report — it was all quiet; and he followed Susan until they came to the room in which Jack was sitting.

"This is Mr. John Pringle," she said.

"Aye, aye," said Jack; "here am I — Jack Pringle — afloat or on shore, all the same."

"And this," continued Susan, "is Mr. Robert Swabbem."

"How d'ye do," said Jack, "Mr. Swabbem? I dare say it is so; but since we are to be shipmates, we may as well be friends — how d'ye do?"

"Pretty well, I thank you, Mr. Pringle — very well, indeed. Hope I see you quite well, and at home?"

"Yes, quite so — both ways; well, and at home."

"The devil!"

"Yes, we call him Davy Jones; but, then, I suppose, you have one on purpose, in your line?"

"Why, there's a little of the devil in us — that is pretty well admitted on all hands; and that's as much as we have any wish to have in the way of connection with the gentleman whom you name."

"Aye, aye; maybe you'll know more on him afore you are done; but no matter — sit down, messmate, we can discuss a can of grog, I reckon."

"Yes, easily. I can do my duty in any point, friend, you may best please. Facing an enemy, drinking a can, or kissing a lass. What more can you say?"

"I can do the same myself as some I know can testify, if they chose to speak," said Jack, who gave a sly look at Susan; but at the same time she nearly fell a laughing, when reminded of Jack's tremendous smack, which the landlady mistook for a smashing of crockery; "but, howsomever," cried Jack, who had relapsed into a grim smile, "we'll have a can together."

"Very well; Susan, will you do what is needful for us? If the landlady would allow me, I'd wait upon you and do all your work."

"And a pretty bobbery," said Susan, "she would make of it; you would soon get discharged for tasting the grog on its way from the bar to the parlour."

"Ah! well, I might get into trouble if I did that. What do you say, friend Jingle?"

"Pringle," said Jack.

"Oh, ah! Ringle. I have it now distinctly."

"Why, you swab," said Jack in a rage, "I ain't got no such kickshaw names as them — mine's quite different altogether, so say what you like."

"My name," said the soldier, "ain't Swab — but Swabbem, at your service."

"Ah," said Jack, "whether Swab or Swabbem, it don't much matter — we all must fill our place — some are luckier than others, though they might be cousins."

"Cousins! curse cousins, say I."

"Same here," said Jack; and then they both stared at each other, believing each other cousins to Susan, though not to each other.

"I am glad you are here," said Susan; "I have the grog for you; it is extra strong. I know, because I put some more into it; I turned the tap on into each, and she didn't see me do it."

"Ah, Susan, I see you have a great regard for me; but it is not more than you ought, when you come to consider how I respect you," said the soldier.

"The same here," said Jack, who thought this pretty good for a cousin; "I admire Susan — she's got such eyes, and such cheeks — "

"So she has — they are like diamonds set in roses; that they are."

"Yes," said Jack, "and as soft as velvet."

"Damme," said the soldier, "you beat me hollow. I say, messmate, where did you learn to fire your great guns off in that manner, eh?"

"Where!" said Jack, putting the can down; "why, where there were men to fire into us again. I'll warrant you it was none of your field days, where people are tearing their hearts out to look fine — no, no; the lee scuppers ran with blood, and every heart was a true British sailor's."

"Well, that was good; but when I served on foreign service, there was no getting out of the way of danger, behind a wall, stone, brick, or wooden."*

---

*A reference to the "Wooden Walls of England," that

"No, nor even laying on the ground — we had not even that; for as we fought, we destroyed the very building which supported us, and we had the spirits

is, the Royal Navy, a term coined in a poem by Henry Green written in 1773.

of the sea to contend against, as well as the dangers of the fight."

"Oh, it's all very well," said the soldier, "but danger's danger, and there's an end of the matter; only I wish there was no such thing as bad grog."

"That's a great evil. Why, what d'ye think we did at Portsmouth the day after we landed? The landlord gave us bad grog, and how do you think we served him? Why, we made him drink till he was so drunk he couldn't lay down without being afraid of falling, and then we cut his hair all off."

"Well, I recollect a place in Portugal where they brought us some wine which we couldn't drink. It was horribly thin and sour. We had in vain asked for better, but none was to be had at our bidding; indeed, we felt sure there was better, and we determined to have it.

"We called our landlord and told him we were resolved to ruin him if he didn't bring it up — we would have better wine; but he protested he had not got any.

"Now, we were resolved to search, and accordingly we did search until we came upon some beautiful wine — some of the best port ever I tasted, and we made free with it. At all events, we drank as much as we could drink, and then fell fast asleep, and forgot to punish our landlord for the rascality; but I suppose he was well aware of what he deserved, for he endeavoured to excite some of the peasantry about to murder us while we slept, and when we awoke, we found ourselves surrounded by a dozen men.

"There was but three of us, but we were armed, and the peasants had nothing but a miscellaneous description of weapons — old guns, swords, and clubs; but they were not the men we were.

"Well, it came to a hard fight; more blows were struck, however, than did any mischief, because we could make use of our tools, and fought so hard, that they were glad to leave us victors."

"Lor!" said Susan; "you don't mean that — do you?"

"I do, indeed; but that was nothing. I frightened a whole regiment of the enemy."

"Eh?" said Jack; "what, a whole ship's compliment, eh? Well, that will do; go a-head; you beat all the cousins as ever I heard of, if you don't never mind me, that is all about it; a good yarn, well spun, is worth a glass of grog at any time."

"Well, I'll tell you all about it; it's sooner told than done, I can tell you; but never mind, Susan, don't be frightened; it's all past now, though it was true; but the best things must have an end some time or other, and this had one too.

"I was serving in Spain. I fought against the French then; and though I say so, you may depend upon it I took my chance as well as another man. However, I had many inclinations to go a step or two beyond my strict duty, and do more than I was obliged; but what of it? If you succeed, you are sure to be rewarded; and I wanted, if I could, to capture a pair of colours, which would give me a step in my regiment.

"'Charge, my brave boys!' shouted the colonel, as the enemy appeared coming down upon us.

"They were three or four to one, besides a reserve at a short distance. But we thought nothing of that; we had every reason to believe we were outnumbered; but that was all; and we drove hard at them.

"It was a glorious sight to see us full tear at the heavy-armed cavalry, in squadrons; but they had the advantage of weight and number of men; yet our shock was so great, that many of the enemy were thrown out of their saddles, and many more were killed; we hewed and hacked at each other for some time, until, in fact, the enemy began to give way.

"As soon as we began to find out that, we urged our horses on, and ourselves to strain our utmost, and we forced them back, and they began to turn about in right earnest, and show us their heels.

"Unfortunately for us there were no other troops at hand to support us. I say unfortunately, for while we were engaged in beating a larger force than our own, and which even then outnumbered us, we were taken in the rear by the reserve, and many men were cut down before our men could be called off.

"Among those who were taken prisoners was myself. I had received one or two severe wounds, which were, indeed, considered mortal; but which were not so dangerous as they were believed.

"However, as I kept my saddle, I was taken prisoner; indeed, I was unable to offer any resistance; my eyes were filled with blood—"

"Lor! how dreadful," said Susan.

"It was dreadful to think of it, then; but I did not; I was too much occupied with my desire to do my duty, so heated and excited, to think anything about it. I was dragged away.

"Then what became of me, I don't know; but I have some recollection of having a cloak thrown over me; and I rode away in company with them. I know we went away very fast, for they dreaded another charge of our men; and they had succeeded in escaping and reforming, and they were hovering, reinforced, upon our march.

"Well, that night, as I was deemed too badly wounded to give them any trouble, or attempting to make an escape, they let me lie in a stable.

"I fainted away; and, after several attempts to restore me, they left me as a hopeless case; but it was no matter to them, they didn't grieve. I wondered in my own mind, as to the reason of their doing so much; but I suppose it was that prisoners were at a premium with them at that time; and they were anxious to return as large a number of prisoners as possible; and, upon the principle which induced the elderly dame to attempt emptying the sea with a tea-spoon, that every little was a help, they thought that if I lived I should be one more, and where the numbers were small, one was of importance.

"They gave me up as a bad job altogether, and after they had racked up their horses, they sat down for the evening to their meat and their wine. They had been all conversing together, but they were about to lie down and have some sleep, when suddenly I awoke from my trance, and walked out without at all knowing what I did.

"The men stared at me, and shook like so many aspens, but did not stir, till one of them said,—

"'A ghost—a ghost!'

"This had the effect of clearing the place, for they all jumped up and ran away from the spot, leaving me master of the place; and judging that I was alone, I very soon made my way back to the quarters of the English, and got to the quarters of my old regiment, where I was kindly received, my comrades having given me up as lost."

"Well," said Jack Pringle, "you were very nearly gone certainly, though you warn't quite a ghost; but that ain't half so bad as a fire-ship—especially in towing a fire-ship among the enemy. I was once on an expedition of that sort when I was in the Mediterranean."

"Lor, a fire-ship! What's that?" inquired Susan.

"A ship-load of fire, with lots of combustibles," said Jack. "It's a thing that won't do for a plaything.

"Well, the enemy had several, and, as we came up to them, we found they had the wind in their favour, and the first thing they did was to put out several of these fire-ships. But the wind was not direct for them, it was shifting. Well, we were ordered to man the boats, and tow the fire-ships back again amongst the enemy.

"Well, you may be sure they didn't like that, especially when the fire-ships blew up. They did so with a dreadful explosion, setting fire to friend and enemy, and blowing them out of the water.

"This we did, and, as we towed the vessels along, we were fired at at a pretty smart rate, I can tell you; why, the very sea seemed to boil around us."

"Lor!" said Susan, "how dreadful! Why it's horrible here when the pot boils, and Heaven knows what it must have been there. Why, I am sure, I wonder how you escaped being scalded to death."

"Why, some on 'em did get killed," said Jack. "My starboard man was shot through the head, and one or two more went on an errand to Davy Jones."

"It was lucky for them," said Susan, "that they were sent out of the way when there was so much danger going on around you. I am sure I should have been glad."

"May be so," said Jack, turning his quid; "but I know this, them as was sent upon that errand never came back any more; they stayed away altogether; many of them becoming food for the sharks. However, we towed awayed, and, the breeze shifting, we got pretty well among them, and then we left the fire-ships where they ought to be, among the enemy.

"Well, we had a hard pull to get back, there being five or six ships firing broadside after broadside at us; but they never hit the boat. The other boat they did hit, and a shot went clean through her, and she went down in deep water."

"And what became of the poor men that were in it?" inquired Susan, horrified at the detail.

"Some on 'em were drowned, and some we saved," said Jack; "but we had scarcely reached our own vessel, when the fire-ships blew up, setting fire to and damaging several of the enemy, who were near at hand, and covering the sea with bits of burning timber, and many fell into the ships, setting fire to their rigging, and knocking men on the head, and doing a world of mischief besides."

"Goodness me!" said Susan, "what a dreadful thing, to be sure. I should not like to be near a fire-ship. At all events, missus is quite a fire-ship here."

There were but few observations to make. Jack thought he had quieted the dragoon, and had given him a dose of salt water; and, moreover, Jack ogled the "maid of the inn" in such a way that speedily brought the military hero to a sense of his danger, so, curling his moustache with his finger, he said,—

"Well, it's all very well talking of the dangers of the sea, but it's nothing to a storming party."

"A storming party! what's that?" inquired Susan.

"Why, I'll tell you, my dear, and then you'll know all about it. You see, we were at the siege of Bangpowder."

"Never heard of such a place," interposed Jack; "what's the bearing of that outlandish place?"

"Oh, never there, eh?" said the dragoon, contemptuously; "then you don't know it. Talk of danger, you should have been there, and you would have known what danger was. However, I'll enlighten your ignorance.

"You must see, Susan, my dear, that at Bangpowder we were very little use in the way of assisting the siege, except that we acted as outposts — foraging parties — and kept off the light troops of the enemy when they shewed themselves, while the infantry set to work in the trenches to work the guns.

"They did work them above a bit, too. For weeks together there was firing day and night, on our side and on theirs, so the air was never without a strong smell of gunpowder, which you might smell for twelve leagues quite strong."

"Lor!" said Susan.

"Smash my timbers," said Jack Pringle, "if you ain't a-coming it strong this time."

"Well," continued the dragoon, taking no notice of what was said; "well, that was nothing — that was a mere trifle. After some weeks' firing, we made a hole in the wall, which increased day after day until big enough for a man to enter.

"After that, a storming party was ordered; but, after more than one attempt, our men gave it up as a bad job. Our captain, being a dare-devil sort of fellow, and not liking to see men beaten back, said the breach was practicable, and could be entered.

"This was denied by the officers and men who had been defeated, and he said if his own troop would volunteer, he would undertake to enter the place.

"This was told us, and we all at once volunteered to follow him to the devil, if he chose to go.

"He at once informed the commander-in-chief, and we were ordered to mount the breech. To do this we of course dismounted, and went on foot.

"There was some little excitement upon this matter, but we were cheered as we passed, and when we arrived within a few yards of the walls, we were met by a tremendous fire of all arms.

"This, however, did not daunt us, though it thinned our ranks, and we were less in number; but up the breech we went, one man at a time. Six of them, one after another, were knocked over dead as herrings. Well, the men began to look blue over this; they wouldn't have minded rushing on in a body, and giving and taking till they all died; but to get on the top of a brick wall, one at a time, to be shot at, why it was more than they liked, especially as they had not struck one blow, or fired a single shot in return.

"'Hurrah, lads!' said I; 'I'll have a shy, now; come on, and follow me quick.

"I jumped up and cleared the wall, though a thousand bullets were fired, and got over clear without a shot, save one, that shaved some of my whisker off.

"We all got over, and soon after we were followed by some of the other regiments, and the place was our own; but we were nearly stripped naked."

"Oh, lor! how was that?" inquired Susan, interested.

"Why, we had so many narrow escapes, that our clothes were all shot to shreds."

"Goodness!"

"Oh, but it is true," said the dragoon rising, and going out of the kitchen.

In a few moments afterwards Susan left it also, and Jack, after turning his quid, and squirting the tobacco juice on the floor, rose and hitching up his trowsers with a preliminary "damme!" left the kitchen also; but he hadn't got far, when, oh, horror! he perceived Susan in the arms of the dragoon, whose moustachoed lips more than once met hers.

"Sink the ship," muttered Jack, "here's a pretty go — the black-looking piratical thief."

But Jack's peace was soon held, and he listened to an assignation which Jack was determined he would keep himself, to the discomfiture of the dragoon.

Having made up his mind upon this point, he returned to the kitchen, and Susan also in a very few moments; but Jack pretended to be asleep, and wouldn't speak to her, because he thought she hadn't behaved well in this affair of the dragoon; he was resolved, however, in substituting himself for the soldier, or, at all events, of making a row.

The time came and Jack stationed himself upon a position where he could with ease lift the dragoon into the water-butt below, in case he offered any opposition to the substitution before named.

The moment came round, and the dragoon was seen slowly and cautiously mounting the way to the window of Susan. It was a kind of leads just above the water-butt, accessible by means of some wooden steps.

"Avast, there," said Jack, when he got up to the level with the top. "What do you do there?"

"What is that to you?" inquired the dragoon.

"A great deal," replied Jack; "but you don't come here — I heard all about it; but I tell you what, you ain't a coming here, at all events."

"But I am."

"Don't attempt, or I'll sink you. I will, by all that's good — so keep back, and go away."

"I'll see you d — d first," said the dragoon. "I have mounted a worse breach than this before to-day; but I suspect there isn't much danger here."

He ran up, and soon faced Jack, who seized him round the waist, would have lifted him up in his arms, and could have thrown him into the water-butt, only Jack's foot suddenly slipped, and he fell down, the soldier upon him, who in an instant regained his feet, and rolled Jack over and over, until he came to the water-butt.

Into this Jack went, head first, and kicked and floundered about; and if the water-butt had not been very rotten, and gave way, letting all the water escape, it is very doubtful if Jack would not have found a watery grave in the confined space of a water-butt.

As it was, he was more than blind and breathless, and sat down in the midst of the water on the stones, to recover himself from the immersion he had undergone.

CXVII.

THE PROPOSAL OF JACK PRINGLE TO TAKE JAMES ANDERSON TO THE WEDDING.

A CIRCUMSTANCE NOW occurred which soon enabled Jack Pringle to console himself for the misadventure he had had, which he was delighted to think was not known to any of those persons with whom he came ordinarily into contact.

The pleasant circumstance to which we allude, was the reception of a letter from the admiral, and by the mere fact of his writing such an epistle to Jack, it would seem to be perfectly true that he really felt unhappy without the companionship of that worthy.

The letter was to the following effect: —

> JACK, you mutinous rascal, your leave of absence has expired, and you know you ought to have a round dozen when you come back to your ship; but as it turns out you may stay where you are, for a reason that I am going to tell you.
>
> There is to be a wedding at the very place where you are staying, between some odd fish, a Baron Something, I don't know who; but as we have been all invited, we are coming down, the whole lot of us, and shall arrive on Thursday, so that you may look out from the mast-head as soon as you like, and you will see us coming with all sails set.
>
> No more at present from, you vagabond,
>
> — YOU KNOW WHO.

"What an affectionate letter," said Jack; "I know the old fellow couldn't do without me long — he is quite an old baby, that's what he is; and if I wasn't to take a little notice of him, he would be as miserable as possible. Hilloa! What cheer? have you come back?"

These last words were addressed to James Anderson, who at that moment made his appearance in the cottage of the old seaman, he having just left the house of the Williamses, after the painful interview which we have recorded took place between him and Mrs. Williams, during which she had succeeded in convincing him that all his hopes, as regarded Helen, were crushed completely.

The appearance of deep dejection that was upon his countenance was such, as to convince Jack Pringle the nature of the business he had been upon, and he cried, —

"Come, come — cheer up, man. I guess, now, you have been looking after that sweetheart of yours, who is no better than she should be."

"I have, indeed," said James Anderson, "been to extinguish all hope — nothing now lives in my breast but despair. I shall proceed to London at once, to make my report to the Admiralty, as it is my duty to do so; and, after that, I care not what becomes of me."

"Stuff, stuff," said Jack; "I have got some news for you. My old admiral, that I take care of, has had an invitation to the very wedding, as I take it to be, of your old sweetheart."

"What! is it possible — do you mean an invitation to Helen Williams's wedding with the Baron Stolmuyer of Saltzburgh?"

"Yes, I do; that's just what I do mean, and no mistake. Here is his letter which he has written to me to go, and I think I shall let the old fellow, for it will amuse him. Just read that."

Jack handed the admiral's letter to James Anderson, which he read with a great deal of interest, and when he had concluded, he said, —

"Mr. Pringle, a sudden thought strikes me, —"

"About ship," said Jack, "and begin again. I told you before not to call me Mr. Pringle — I cannot stand it. Call me Jack, and then go on telling me what your sudden thought is."

"Well, then, Jack, my sudden thought is this, that your friend the admiral might be induced, upon your representation, to let me join his party, and I would take care to conceal my features and general appearance so that I should not be known, while I had the mournful satisfaction of taking a last look upon that occasion of her who I have loved, before she becomes irrecoverably the wife of another."

"If you wish it," said Jack, "it shall be done. I'll undertake there shall be no objection on the part of the admiral; and as for the Bannerworths, they are good sort of people, and would do all they can for anybody, I am sure."

"I should take it as a peculiar favour; for although I feel now that my hopes are blasted, and I can have no possible expectation of beholding her with eyes of pleasure, I still wish to look upon her, that

I may see if anything of regret is upon her countenance, or if she has quite forgotten the past."

"Say no more," said Jack, "but consider it as done. I'd take care though, if I were you, that she did not find me out; for I wouldn't let the finest woman that ever breathed — no, not if she was seven feet high, and as big as a hogshead — fancy that I cared so much for her as to go to her wedding after she had jilted me."

"She shall not see me," said James Anderson; "she shall not see me, you may depend; for, without doubt, the guests will be very numerous, so that I can easily keep myself in the back-ground, and look upon her face without her being at all aware of the presence of such a person at the ceremony."

"Yes, you can manage that; and, if I were you, just as I was going away, I'd give the baron a jolly good kick, and tell him you wished him joy of his bargain. I wouldn't do anything violent, you know, but a little quiet thing like that would just show them all what you thought of the business."

"A sense of my wrongs," said James Anderson, "should not extinguish a sense of justice; and I have no means of knowing that the baron is at all in fault in this matter."

"Oh, you are too nice by one half. If a fellow takes away my sweetheart, hang me if I care who is at fault."

"Oh, but it is necessary that we should be just at all events; but still, Jack, accept my sincerest thanks for placing me in the way of looking upon Helen. I'd rather see that she was happy and contented with her lot, than I would observe evidences upon her face of any passionate regret.

The former would reconcile me, by making me think I had made a great mistake in the object of my attachment; while the latter would leave in my heart a never ceasing pain."

"Gammon," said Jack.

"I fear I tax your patience, Jack Pringle, when I talk in such a strain as this."

"I'll be hanged if you don't. What do you mean by it? There is lots of women in the world. I have no patience with a fellow that, because one girl uses him ill, goes snivelling and crying about his feelings, and his agony, and his chest, and all that sort of thing. I should recommend a bottle of rum."

"Well, well, Jack, it may happen some day with even you, and then you may feel some of the mental agony of knowing that another has possessed himself of her whom you thought all your own."

This was hitting Jack rather hard, although James Anderson did not know it; so he said,—

"Ah, well, to be sure, there is something in that, after all, and I don't mean to say there ain't; but, however, keep up your heart, my boy, and there is no saying what may happen yet."

"Alas! there can nothing happen that can give me pleasure; all is lost now, and the only hope I can have, is to forget."

Jack would have written a letter back to the admiral in reply to the one which he had received, only that somehow or other he was not a first-rate penman; and as he said it was such a bother to know where to begin, and when you did begin, it was such a bother to know where to leave off, that, taking all things into consideration, he rather on the whole declined writing at all; and, as the appointed day was near at hand, on which the wedding was to take place, he thought it would do quite as well if he kept the look out which the admiral had suggested for the arrival of the Bannerworths.

As for the scheme of James Anderson to be present at the wedding, the more Jack thought of it, the more he liked it, because he considered that it afforded a chance, at all events, if not a good prospect, of as general a disturbance as any that had ever existed.

"Lor! what fun," he said, "if he would but kick the baron, and then if the baron would but fall foul of him, and the girl scream, and old mother Williams go into hysterics. That would be a lark, and no doubt about it; shouldn't I enjoy it above a bit. I'd give them a helping hand somehow or another; and then, who knows but the girl may have been regularly badgered by the old cat of a mother into the match, and may wish for all the world to get out of it."

There can be no doubt but that if Helen Williams, even at that last moment, chose to make any appeal, it would not be made in vain to Jack Pringle, who, with all his faults, and they were numerous enough, had in his heart a chivalrous love of right, and a hatred of anything in the shape of oppression, which nothing could subdue; and such qualities as these surely are amply sufficient to atone for a multitude of minor errors, which were more those of habit and defective education, than anything else.

It very much delighted him to think that the admiral and the Bannerworths were coming down to Anderbury, because such a fact not only prolonged his stay there, which he was pleased it should do, because he was really very much delighted with the place, but it at the same time threw him again into the company he so much liked; and his attachment to the Bannerworth family had really become quite a strong feeling.

He waited quite with impatience until the Thursday came on which the admiral had announced his arrival; and instead of being in the town, or on the outskirts, to watch for him, which would have been but a tiresome operation, Jack walked boldly on to meet them by the high road, which he knew they must traverse.

After he had gone about four miles, he had the satisfaction of seeing, in the distance, a travelling-carriage, manned, as he called it, with four horses, rapidly approaching, and Jack immediately produced a large silk handkerchief that he had purchased, which was a representation of the national flag of Great Britain. This he fastened to the end of a stick, and commenced waving it about as a signal to the admiral of his presence in the road.

At this moment, too, it happened, fortunately for Jack Pringle, as he considered, that a man came across a stile in the immediate vicinity where he was with a gun in his hand.

"Hilloa, friend," said Jack Pringle, "just let me look at that gun a minute."

"I'll see you further first," said the man; "you seem to me as if you were out of your mind."

So saying, he levelled the piece at some birds which were flying over-head, and fired first one barrel and then the other in rapid succession.

"Thank ye," said Jack, "that was all I wanted; and it will answer my purpose exactly; there is nothing like, when you display your flag, firing a gun or two. It's all right — he sees me, he sees me."

The admiral had actually been looking from the window of the carriage, although he had not expected to see Jack quite so soon; but the appearance of the handkerchief, which was made so much to resemble a flag, convinced him of the fact that Jack had come that distance to meet them; and when he heard the gun fired twice, he was quite delighted, and leaning back in the carriage, he cried, —

"Ah, Flora, my dear, it is a great pity that Jack is so given to rum, for he is a remarkably clever fellow. You would hardly believe it, now, but he has contrived to hoist a flag just because he sees me coming."

"Indeed, uncle."

"Yes, my dear, he has; and didn't you hear that he actually managed to fire a couple of guns, some way or another?"

"I certainly did hear the report, but had no idea that we were indebted to Jack Pringle's management for them."

"Oh, yes, I can see him a short distance ahead. He is lying to, now; and, if the wind wasn't against us, we should be up to him in a few minutes, but don't you feel it blowing in your face?"

Nothwithstanding the admiral considered, which he certainly did, that the wind was a real impediment to the progress of the carriage, they did in a few moments reach to where Jack Pringle was waiting, when the admiral called out from the window in a loud voice, —

"Hilloa! what ship, and where are you bound to?"

"The Jack Pringle," was the reply, "from Anderbury, and to fall in with the Admiral Bell, convoy of the pretty Flora."

"There now," said the admiral; "didn't I tell you what a clever fellow Jack was? What shore-going humbug, who had never been to sea, would have thought of such a thing?"

"Well," said Jack, as he walked up to the coach window, for the postilions had been ordered to halt, or, as the admiral had expressed it, "to heave to," "well, here you are, all of you."

"Yes, Jack," said the admiral; "and I was just saying I thought you a very clever fellow."

"I am sorry I can't return the compliment, you poor old creature," said Jack; "I hope you haven't got yourself into any trouble since I have been away from you. What a miserable old hulk you do look, to be sure. There you go, again; now you are getting into a passion, as usual; what a dreadful thing temper is, to be sure,

when you can't manage it."

Jack scrambled up behind into the rumble before the admiral could make any reply to him, for indignation stopped his utterance a moment or two; and, when he did speak, it was to Flora he addressed himself more particularly, saying,—

"Now, did you ever know a more ungrateful son-of-a-gun than that? After I had just told him that I thought him a clever fellow, for him to burst out abusing me at that rate! Now I have done with him."

"Oh, you may depend, Admiral Bell," said Flora, "that he don't at all mean what he says; and I am convinced that he entertains for you the highest possible respect, and that he is only jesting when he uses those expressions which would seem as if it were otherwise."

"Let's just wait," said the admiral, "till the wedding is over, and then I'll let him know whether a boatswain is to make a joke of an admiral of the fleet."

CXVIII.

THE BARON'S PREPARATIONS FOR THE MARRIAGE, AND THE WEDDING MORNING.

DURING THIS TIME neither Mrs. Williams nor the Baron Stolmuyer were idle spectators of the progress of the hours; but, on the contrary, they made the best possible use of the week which was to elapse before the marriage ceremony took place after Helen had given her consent to it.

Five hundred pounds, in the hands of such a person as Mrs. Williams, will go a long way, and produce an amazing amount

of show and glitter; so that she managed, before the day on which the ceremony was to be performed arrived, to make quite certain that herself and her daughters would present a most dazzling appearance; and she thought it not at all improbable that even at the very church some meritorious individual might be dazzled into thinking of matrimony with one of her other daughters, upon seeing what a brilliant appearance they managed to present upon the marriage of Helen.

"I am quite sure that no harm can come of it," she said, "if no good does; and, at all events if no good is done at the church, the baron will soon be giving parties enough to bring out the dear girls to perfection, particularly as I fully intend we shall all live at Anderbury House."

Mrs. Williams considered this as a settled point, whether the baron liked it or not; and, knowing as she did the gentle and quiet disposition of Helen, she did not doubt for a moment of being permitted to rule completely over the domestic affairs of her establishment. All this was amazingly satisfactory to such a lady as Mrs. Williams, and the very thing of all others she would have liked, had she been looking out for what would please her in the marriage of her daughter.

We shall shortly see how these views and opinions were verified by the fact.

All the other preparations were left to the baron; and when he wrote a letter to Mrs. Williams, saying, that he would be ready by ten o'clock on the morning which had been named for the nuptials, and would send one of his carriages for the bride, Mrs. Williams was perfectly satisfied that all was quite correct.

THERE WAS NO VERY GOOD excuse for calling at Anderbury House; but, if she had then called, she certainly would have been astonished at the preparations which the baron was making for that day which was so near at hand.

It was quite terrific the expense he went to; and the gorgeous manner in which he fitted up one of the largest apartments in the house for a dance looked really like expenditure of the most reckless character, and such as indeed it must have required an immense fortune to withstand.

The walls of that apartment were hung with crimson draperies of a rich texture, and such beauty of design that they were the admiration of the very workmen themselves who were employed upon the premises.

Then the magnificent order he gave for a feast upon the occasion, and the wines he laid in, really almost exceeded belief; and such proceedings were indeed highly calculated to give people most exaggerated visions regarding his wealth.

He had indeed mentioned to Mrs. Williams, that he had silver mines on some of his estates abroad; and that fact to her mind was quite sufficient to account for any amount of money he might possess, because, to her ideas of geology and mineralogy, the discovery of a silver mine meant finding a hole of immense width and depth, crammed with the precious metal.

But be this as it may, and whether the Baron Stolmuyer of Saltzburgh owed his wealth to silver mines, or to other sources, one thing was quite clear, and that was, that he had it.

And that was the grand point; for in a highly civilized and evangelical country like this, the question of how a man got his money is not near so often asked, as, "has he got it"; and it is quite amazing what liberality of feeling and sentiment is immediately infused into people by the fact of successful speculation of any kind; while failure immediately incurs the greatest of opprobrium and contempt.

And now the day was so close at hand,

that Mrs. Williams got into a terrible flutter of spirits, and began really to wish it over; for she was completely ready, and each minute became an hour of impatience to her.

She was continually bothering the baron with notes and messages upon different subjects, and he had the urbanity to answer two or three of them; but he soon left that off, and the last half dozen, at the least, were, to Mrs. Williams's great mortification, taken no notice of at all.

Some of these notes were upon the most nonsensical points, and several of them, although they did not actually ask it, pretty strongly hinted that more money would be a very desirable thing.

The baron would not understand any hint, however, upon the subject; so Mrs. Williams became fully convinced that she must make the best of it she could, and put up for the present with the five hundred pounds she had already received.

But when the day had actually dawned on when the auspicious event was to come off, and, upon looking around her, she found herself surrounded by gay apparel and jewellery, she almost dreaded that even yet it would turn out to be some delusion, or a dream, for she could scarcely believe in the reality of such glory and magnificence belonging to her.

But facts are stubborn things, and, whether for good or for evil, are not likely to be got over; so, when she looked out of the windows and saw that a bright morning's sun was shining, and that the life, animation, and bustle of the day was commencing, she told herself that it was, indeed, real, and that she had reached very nearly the summit of her desires and expectations.

"Yes," she exclaimed; "I shall be mother-in-law to a baron; and I dare say I shall have at least twenty servants in Anderbury House to command and control continually."

A more gratifying reflection than this could not possibly have presented itself to Mrs. Williams; for if any one thing could be more delightful than another, it certainly was that kind of petty power which gives an individual a control over a large establishment.

After she had arisen on that eventful morning, she did not allow her establishment many minutes' repose; but, in the course of half-an-hour, all was bustle, excitement, and no small share of confusion.

And while she was thus energetically pushing on her preparations, let us see what the Bannerworths are about, now that they have fairly arrived at Anderbury, and are in readiness, probably, to be present at the ceremony.

BY FLORA'S INTERCESSION, a peace was established between Jack and the admiral; and the former took the latter down to the old seaman's cottage, in order to introduce him to James Anderson; and on the road he made him acquainted with the particulars of the young man's story; at the same time informing him of the wish that Anderson had expressed to be permitted to join their party.

"Oh, certainly," said the admiral, "certainly; let him come by all means, although I must say that he ought to leave for London, at once, with his despatches, or at all events with the news that he had lost them. However, I am not on active service; and, therefore, have no right to do anything more than advise him in the matter."

"Oh, he will go," said Jack, "as soon as he has seen his sweetheart, and perhaps kicked the baron; for though he said he wouldn't, I live in hopes yet that he will be aggravated enough to do it."

The admiral liked James Anderson so much, that he not only promised him he should go to the wedding under cover of the general invitation which he, the admiral, had received, but he proposed, likewise, that he should come home with him at once and be introduced to the Bannerworths; and by home he meant the inn at Anderbury, where they were staying.

The young man expressed himself highly gratified at this invitation, and at once accepted it, so that they walked towards the inn together, and began to make preparations for their appearance at Anderbury House.

Flora and the Bannerworths, as well as Charles, received young Anderson very graciously, and they each expressed to him their sympathy for the painful situation in which the baron's marriage was placing him.

Flora and Charles Holland, as may be well supposed, could both feel, and feel acutely too, for any one crossed in his affection, as poor James Anderson was; and it certainly much damped the satisfaction they had in going to what everybody told them would certainly be the most brilliant wedding that had taken place in that part of the country for many a year.

"Let us hope," said Henry Bannerworth, "that you will find some other, Mr. Anderson, who will be more worthy of your esteem, than she who has treated so lightly your affection and her own faith."

"I know not," said Anderson, "whether to accuse her not; for who knows but after all she may be the victim of treachery, notwithstanding the apparent powerful evidence that has been given to me by her mother?"

THE BANNERWORTH FAMILY were determined, and so was the admiral, that they would bestow what credit they could upon those who had so kindly invited them; and, accordingly, when they started for the Hall in the handsome carriage which had brought them down to Anderbury, they certainly presented a rather showy and attractive appearance.

But still when they reached the entrance to Anderbury House, they found that theirs was by no means the only equipage of the kind that was there to be seen; for although both the entrances were open for the reception of guests, they had to wait a considerable time before they could get up to either of them.

One hundred and fifty guests, sixty or eighty of whom kept equipages, were calculated to make some little degree of confusion; but when the Bannerworth family fairly got within the house, everything else was forgotten in their admiration of the brilliant arrangements within.

The richest carpets were laid down that money could purchase, and servants in gorgeous liveries ushered the guests into an immense hall, in which the marriage ceremony was to take place, and which was decorated with a splendour that was perfectly regal.

And here a new set of domestics glided noiselessly about with various refreshments upon silver salvers, and the place began rapidly to fill with such an assemblage of wealth, and beauty, and rank, as perhaps scarcely ever had been congregated in one place before.

But among those whose beauty attracted much attention, we may need well reckon our friend, Flora Bell, as she was now properly called, and whose sweet countenance was the cause of many a passing observation, couched in the most flattering terms.

It wanted yet an hour to the time of the ceremony being performed, and the Bannerworths, as they saw that their companion, young Anderson, was in a painful state of excitement, all sat down in the deep recess of a large window to wait the coming of the bride and bridegroom.

"I don't think, Mr. Anderson," said Henry, "that your coming here at all was a well-advised step; but since you are here, you should muster up resolution enough not to betray any feeling."

"I will not betray it, although I feel it," said Anderson. "Rely upon it, that I shall look much firmer, and act much firmer when she whom I wish to see is actually here, than I do at present — I am enduring suspense now, and that is the worst of all."

"I do wish," interposed Flora, "that you had seen her whom you love before this ceremony, for in that case, although you might have endured the pang of finding that she was willing to call herself another's, you would have been spared the pain of this day's proceeding."

"I wish to Heaven I had seen her; but I knew not how to arrange such a meeting; and when I was shewn, in her own handwriting — which I knew too well to doubt — a consent to be the wife of another, I no longer had the spirit and the perseverance to ask to see her; and it was an afterthought that made me wish to look upon her face once more before I left her for ever."

"What," said Jack Pringle, suddenly making his appearance, "is he gammoning you with his feelings?"

"Oh! so you have got in, have you?" said the admiral.

"So I have got in — why, what do you mean by that? Of course I have got in; wasn't I invited? I do think you get a little stupider every day; and, in course of time, you won't know what you are about. I should not be surprised to see you take out your handkerchief to blow your eye instead of your nose."

Latterly, Jack, when he made one of these speeches, always walked away very quickly, leaving the admiral's anger to evaporate as best it might; so that he escaped the retort which otherwise he might have received.

CXIX.

A RATHER STRANGE CIRCUMSTANCE AT THE BARON'S WEDDING.

AT LENGTH, THE HOUR came, so anxiously looked for and expected by all the Baron Stolmuyer's guests; and the great clock which was in one of the turrets of Anderbury House proclaimed that the minute had arrived when all was presumed to be ready for the union.

All eyes were directed to a large table that was placed at one extremity of the hall, and covered with crimson velvet, and at which the ceremony was to be performed.

The Bannerworths were a little forward, so that they commanded a good view of everything, and James Anderson was completely hidden from observation behind the bulky form of the admiral. Now, a small door opened, and an Archdeacon Somebody — who had been engaged, as you would engage a celebrated performer, at some theatre, to perform the ceremony — made his appearance, accompanied by several ladies and gentlemen, whom he had brought with him to partake of some of the baron's good things.

In a few moments, from another doorway, came the bride, accompanied by six bridesmaids, but she was covered with such a massive lace veil from her head to her feet, that not the slightest vestige of her countenance was visible.

But, still, Flora thought that, as the bride first came in, she heard from beneath that veil a deep and agonized sob; and she remarked the circumstance to Charles, who confirmed her opinion by at once, saying, —

"It was so, and I don't think it at all likely that we should both be mistaken."

There was a slight murmur of applause and admiration among the assembled guests as the bride took her seat by the table; for although there were many there who had never seen her face, there were likewise many who had; and even those who had not, could not but perceive, by her graceful movements and the delicate outline of her figure, that they were looking upon a creature of rare beauty and worth.

It was astonishing that the bridegroom should be late, and the audience who were present began to be indignant at such a fact, and whispered together concerning it in language not very flattering to the baron, who, had he heard it, would have found that he must mind what he was about, or his rapidly-acquired popularity would soon be at a discount.

Minute after minute thus passed, and Mrs. Williams, who was attired in a richly-flowing garment of white silk, embroidered with flowers, began to be in a most particular fidget.

"Where could be the baron — good God! where is the baron?" and some one or two said, "D — n the baron!" When suddenly the door at which the bride had entered was again flung open, and two servants in rich liveries made their

appearance, one standing on each side of it. Then there was heard approaching a slow and measured footstep, and presently, attired in a court suit of rich velvet, the Baron Stolmuyer of Saltzburgh appeared in the hall, and marched up to the table.

He had but just time to execute half a bow to the assembled multitude, when Admiral Bell called out in a voice that awakened every echo in the place,—

"It's Varney, the vampyre, by G-d!"

YES, IT WAS VARNEY — the bold, reckless, audacious Varney, who had thus come out in a new character, and, with vast pecuniary resources, acquired Heavens knows how or where, was seeking to ally himself to one so young and beautiful as Helen Williams.

We do absolutely and positively despair of giving an adequate idea to the reader of the scene that followed.

Ladies shrieked — the bride fainted — Mrs. Williams went into strong hysterics, and kicked everybody — Jack Pringle shouted until he was hoarse; while Varney turned and made a dash to escape through the door at which he had just entered.

James Anderson, however, by springing over a table, succeeded in clutching him by the collar behind; but Varney turned on the instant, and lifting him from the ground as if he had been a child, he flung him among a tray of confectionary and wine, and from thence he rolled into Mrs. Williams's lap.

Following close, however, upon the footsteps of Anderson in pursuit of Varney had been Henry Bannerworth; but he accomplished nothing, except to strike his head violently against the door through which Varney escaped, and which was dashed in his face, and immediately bolted on the other side.

"He is a vampyre," shouted the admiral — "I tell you all he is a vampyre — Varney, the vampyre, and no more a baron than I am a broomstick. Stop that d — d old woman from making such a noise."

"It's the bride's mother," said somebody.

"What's that to me?" roared the admiral; "it don't make her a bit less of a nuisance. I offer a hundred pounds reward for Varney, the vampyre; and there must be some people here that know the house well enough to catch him."

"Do you mean a hundred pounds for master, sir?" said a great footman, with yellow plush breeches.

"Yes, I do, you hog in armour," said the admiral.

The footman rushed through another doorway in a moment, and then Jack Pringle jumped upon a chair, and, waving his hat, cried, —

"Hurra, hurra, hurra! Three cheers for old Varney! I'll tell you what it is, messmates, he is the meanest fellow as ever you see; and as for you ladies who have been disappointed of the marriage, I'll come and kiss you all in a minute, and we'll drink up old Varney's wine, and eat up his dinner like bricks. My eye, what a game we will have, to be sure. I am coming — "

At this moment the admiral gave such a kick to one of the hind legs of the chair, that down came Jack as quickly as if he had disappeared through some trap-door.

"Hold your noise, will you," said the admiral, "you great brawling brute!"

"I'll settle him," said Mrs. Williams, who had suddenly recovered; and had not Jack suddenly made his escape, it is highly probable she would have make him a regular scape-goat in the affair, and that he alone — for Anderson had pretty quickly escaped her — would have felt the consequences of her deep disappointment.

The confusion now became, if anything, worse than at first, for many of the guests who had looked on apparently quite stunned and paralyzed at what had taken place, now recovered, and joined their voices to the general clamour.

Some, to rush out of the place, took the opportunity of going through the different rooms; while a number, who had heard of the wide-spread fame of Varney, the vampyre, and who were utterly astonished to find him and the baron one and the same person, joined in the pursuit, with the hope of taking prisoner so alarming a personage.

No one knew for some time what had become of the clergyman, until Jack Pringle saw a human foot sticking out from under the table, upon which he took hold of it, and with a pull dragged the archdeacon somebody fairly out, to the great horror of some very religious old ladies who were present, who considered that an arch-deacon must be somebody very wonderful indeed.

"Hilloa! Mr. Parson," said Jack; I suppose you thought it was your old friend the devil come for you before your time; but cheer up, I know him; it's only a vampyre, and that's nothing when you're used to it."

Jack did not seem at all to think that it was necessary he should assist in the capture of Varney, and probably the real fact was, he did not care whether Varney was captured or not, so he walked to one of the tables which were loaded with refreshments, and knocking the neck off a bottle of champagne, he gave a nod to Mrs. Williams, saying,—

"Come, old girl, take something to drink. That red nose of yours looks as if you knew something of the bottle. It's only me, so you needn't be shy. Ah, it's

devilish good wine, though. I do give old Varney credit for getting up the thing decently, which he certainly has, and no mistake."

"Who has seen my daughter? Where is my daughter?" cried Mrs. Williams, as she looked about her in vain for Helen.

"You needn't trouble yourself, ma'am," said the admiral; "she has just walked off with a little fellow of the name of Anderson, who, although he was no match for Varney, the vampyre, I think will turn out to be one for your daughter."

Mrs. Williams was thoroughly thunder-stricken, and she sat down in a chair, and commenced wringing her hands, muttering as she did so,—

"Oh, that I should have lived to see this day. Oh, that I should have existed to be so—so—"

"Jolly well humbugged, ma'am," said Jack Pringle, "with a vampyre, instead of a baron; why, lord bless you, ma'am, nobody in their senses would have taken old Varney for a baron; why, he is a regular old blood-sucker, he is, and a nice family you would have had; but, however, if you are fond of him, you can marry him yourself, you know, now; and I shouldn't at all wonder, but he will consent, for a man will put up with any d—d old cat, when he finds he can't get a better."

"Good God," said Mrs. Williams, "I think I know your voice now; ain't you Admiral Green?"

"Avast, there," said Jack; "I ain't anything of the kind; they calls me Colonel Bluebottle, of the horse-marines."

"The what?"

"The horse-marines. Didn't you never hear of them, ma'am?"

"I certainly never did. But don't try to deceive me, sir; you are Admiral Green and if you will, my dear sir, spare me a few minutes of your valuable time, I shall be able to explain to you—"

"What?" said Jack.

"Why, that really—you will scarcely believe it—but really, Admiral Green, my daughter Julia is, although I say it, one of the best of girls."

"Oh, I dare say she is, ma'am; but I don't know as that much matters to me."

"Excuse me, Admiral Green, but it really does, and you must know—of course it's quite between ourselves this—that she happened to see you when you did me the honour of calling upon me."

"Did she really?"

"Yes, my dear admiral; and, do you know, ever since then she has been positively raving about you; and as you were good enough to say, the baron should not stand in the way of your affections, allow me to recommend Julia to you."

"Oh, that's it, is it!" said Jack. "Well, ma'am, I should not have said no, only that you ain't half particular enough for me!"

"Not particular! Oh, good God."

"No, ma'am, you ain't. Here you would have married one of your daughters to a vampyre, and how do I know what other sort of odd fish you might bring into the family."

"But, my dear Admiral—"

"Oh! gammon. I tell you what, now, I will do—I don't mind standing something devilish handsome, if you will marry old Varney yourself."

"What! the baron that was, and the vampyre that is? I marry him! Oh, dear,

no, I really could not—that is to say, how much would you give, Admiral Green?"

"Ah!" said Jack, "I knew it. Who says, after this, that women won't marry the very devil himself, if they only have the chance. And now, Mother Williams, I'll just tell you what you have done. The fact is, I took a fancy to you myself, and that's why I came here at all to-day. I meant to have proposed to you, and if you had only said you would not have the Baron Vampyre for any money, d—n it, I would have had you myself, and settled a matter of £15,000 a year upon you."

"Oh, gracious Providence! what do I hear?"

"Just what I says. I'm a man of my word, ma'am, and would have done it."

Mrs. Williams was so affected at the chance she had lost, that she quite forgot to look after Helen, but was actually compelled to indulge herself with a glass or two of something strong and powerful, which she said was sherry, but which somebody else said was brandy, in order to recover from the faint feeling that would come over her.

After this, Jack thought he had had about the bitterest revenge upon Mrs. Williams that it was possible to achieve, and he was quite right as far as that went. The old admiral, too, who overheard some part of the colloquy, was quite delighted with it, and again told himself what a clever fellow Jack was, and quite a wonderful character in his way.

"Ah!" he said, "one would have to sail a tolerable lot of voyages before finding anybody as was exactly Jack's equal; and I'll be hanged if I don't forgive him for the next piece of mutinous conduct he is guilty of, on account of the way he has served out that horrid old Mother Williams; for in all my life I never saw a woman I disliked more. Stop, what am I saying? Did I really forget Mrs. Chillingworth, the doctor's wife? That was too bad."

CXX.

THE HUNT FOR THE VAMPYRE IN THE SUBTERRANEAN PASSAGE.

THE INFORMATION THAT had been given to Mrs. Williams respecting her daughter and James Anderson having together left the great hall of Anderbury House, was perfectly correct.

The voice of Anderson, whispering words of affection in the ear of Helen, was sufficient to arouse her from the state of syncope into which she had fallen; and when she recovered and looked in his face, the expression of joy which her countenance wore, at once dispelled all his doubts.

"Helen, dear Helen!" he whispered; "are you, indeed, still, in heart, mine?"

"Still, as ever," she replied.

"Come with me; I have much to tell you; and we need not heed the thoughts and feelings of the throng that is here. If you can walk, place your arm in mine, and lean upon me, and we will get out of all this trouble and confusion."

Helen was but too glad to avail herself of such an offer, and she accordingly at once did so; and leaning for support upon that arm, which, of all others, she most loved to bear upon, they together passed out of the great hall, through one of the numerous doorways leading from it.

Being both of them quite ignorant of what may be called the topography of Anderbury House, they went on till they came to a small but very elegant apartment, in which a table was laid with wines, and some costly refreshments, which, from the fact of an extremely clerical-looking shovel hat being upon one of the chairs, there was no great difficulty in coming to the conclusion that this had been a reception-room, got up purposely for the reverend gentleman who was to perform the ceremony of marriage between the baron and Miss Williams, and in which he had refreshed himself prior to the performance of that dreadfully arduous task, for which, no doubt, as all persons are, he was so very insufficiently paid.

A glass of wine, which James Anderson poured out for Helen, tended much to recover her; and then he said to her in accents of the greatest affection,—

"Helen—Helen! is it possible that you really so far forgot me, as to promise your hand to another?"

She burst into tears as she clung to his arm, saying,—

"I know you cannot, you ought not to forgive me. I did promise; but I did not forget you; and if you know the cruel persecution to which I have been subjected, you would pity, perhaps, as much as you condemn me."

"You did not know that some days since I wrote you a note."

"Me a note? Oh, heavens! no — no. What became of it? To whom did you entrust it? Oh! James, had I but thought you were near me, do you think that for one moment I would have yielded, even to the representations which were made to me?"

"I see it all," he said. "Your mother has carried on this matter with more tact than candour and honesty of purpose. I do not condemn you, dear Helen; and no one shall ever disturb you in your possession of a heart which is wholly yours."

"And can you forget — "

"All but that I love you I can and will forget, Helen."

"I do not deserve this noble generosity, for I ought not to have yielded, James. I feel that I ought to have clung to the remembrance of your affection, and found in that an abundant consolation, as well as abundant strength, to resist the whole world."

"Say no more, dearest, upon that head; but let us, to the full, enjoy the happiness of this meeting, without the drawback of a single doubt."

"We will never part again."

"Never — never."

"But, James, what was the meaning of that sudden exclamation, from one of the guests, as regarded the baron?"

"You allude to Admiral Bell proclaiming him to be a vampyre; and, I must say, it fills me with quite as much astonishment as it can you. I did hear a strange story of that sort from a sailor a short time ago, but I looked upon it as a mere superstition and paid no attention to it. You know what it means, I presume, and that a vampyre is supposed to be a half-supernatural creature who supports a spurious and horrible existence, by feeding upon the blood of any one whom he can make his victim."

"If this horrible superstition," said Helen, with a shudder, "be true, what a dreadful fate have I escaped!"

"It surely must be some error of judgement; but still, dear one, you have escaped a dreadful fate, a fate worse than any vampyre would have inflicted upon you — the fate of being united to one whom you cannot love."

"Yes," said Helen; "that is, indeed, an escape; but how came you, of all persons in the world, a guest here?"

"I came, Helen, under cover of a general invitation, with a most worthy family, to whose kindness I feel myself much indebted, and which empowered them to bring with them whom they pleased. My wish and object was to take one last look at the face I had loved so well before I left you for ever."

"Oh, Heavens!" said Helen, "and I was so near being sacrificed while you were by. Even now I shudder at the dreadful chasm; I feel that you ought not to forgive me."

"Say no more — say no more; all that, Helen, is now past and forgotten, and I can well imagine how your mother would torture you with supplications, because she believed this man to be rich, and consequently the sort of person, above all others, as most desirable for her to have as a son-in-law. We will only consider that a great anxiety and a great danger has passed away, and we will not stop to ask ourselves what it was."

"Ever good, and ever generous," resumed Helen, as her head reposed upon her lover's breast.

"Oh," said Jack Pringle, as he popped his head in at the door; "I beg your pardon, you are better engaged; but we are going to have a grand vampyre hunt through the house, and I thought you would like to join in it, perhaps."

"Stay a moment, stay," cried Anderson. "Do you mean to tell me, really, that this is the person who gave your friends, the Bannerworths, so much trouble and inconvenience?"

"Yes, I do," said Jack; "lor' bless you, he is quite an old acquaintance of ours, is old Varney; sometimes he hunts us, sometimes we hunt him. He is rather a troublesome acquaintance, notwithstanding, and I think there are a good many people in the world, a jolly right worse vampyres than Varney."

"I have no cause to hunt him," said Anderson, "and so, therefore, I feel certainly more inclined to decline, than otherwise, engaging in such a transaction."

"Don't mention it," said Jack; "you are a deuced deal better engaged, and there needs no excuses."

Jack was quite correct as regarded the projected hunt for the unfortunate Varney in Anderbury House; for the liberal offer of reward which the admiral had made to any one who would secure him, was calculated to stimulate every possible exertion that people could make upon the occasion; so much so, indeed, that the Bannerworths, after a brief consultation among themselves, thought that for the protection of Varney it would be much better that they should find him, than now leave him with the character that had been given him as such a dangerous member of society.

The servants, and some of the guests, even, had gone very systematically to work for the purpose of taking Varney prisoner; for, in the first instance, they had secured all the outlets from the house, so that, as the footman with the yellow plush continuations remarked, he must jump over the cliff if he wanted to get away.

The admiral and Henry agreed with each other that they would be foremost in the search, in order to protect Varney from any violence; for although this conduct of his might be considered as very bad, and an outrage upon society in passing himself off as a baron, and endeavouring to effect an alliance with a young and innocent girl, yet they, the Bannerworths, had nothing to complain of in the transaction whatever.

Consequently was it that they felt an inclination to defend Varney from personal violence.

And this was, to a certain extent, to be dreaded, because Anderbury being so short a distance from Bannerworth Hall, it was not to be supposed but that some news of the mysterious appearance of the vampyre had reached the ears of almost every one who happened to be present at the baron's wedding.

And although these persons might be supposed to belong to a class of society not likely to commit acts of violence, yet there was no knowing what, in the excitement of the moment, might be done.

While the search went on, Flora was introduced to Helen Williams, and remained with her, commencing a friendship which lasted afterwards, to the great advantage of Helen, for many a year.

The Bannerworths would have been pleased and interested at going over Anderbury House, under any other circumstances than the present one, for truly the baron had made it a most magnificent abode.

By judicious additions to the antique furniture which had belonged to it when he took it, he had made some of the apartments look gorgeous in the extreme; and while he had not disturbed the character of the decorations, he had certainly shown a very fine taste in adding to them.

But their minds were by far too much occupied with considerations connected with Varney to pay much attention to his house; and, as they traversed room after room in search of him without finding him, they began to think that, with his usual good fortune, he had contrived entirely to escape.

The servants, who knew the place well, perhaps better than Varney did himself, searched for him in almost impossible places, until it began to be the general opinion that he must have escaped.

They were standing by a large bay window, which commanded a view of the gardens, when one of the servants suddenly exclaimed,—

"I see him—I see him; there he goes," and pointed into the garden, where, for one instant, Henry Bannerworth, as well as the admiral, saw Varney, in his rich suit of wedding apparel, dart from among the bushes, towards a summer-house that was in the garden near at hand.

" 'Tis he, indeed," said Henry. "Let us get down instantly, or he may yet effect his escape."

"No, no," cried one of the servants, "he cannot do that; the garden wall is too high, and the men are stationed at the gate. It's quite clear to me what he is about. Look at him; he is going towards the old passage that leads to the sea shore."

"Then he will escape, of course," said Henry, "for no one can hope to overtake him."

"Don't you be afraid of that, sir," cried the servant; "one of my mates has gone round to the beach to watch, and he won't let the door be opened that leads out on to the sands, so he cannot get away by that mode."

"In that case, then, we have him completely entrapped, and, as you say, he cannot escape. It must be the madness of positive desperation that induces him to go to that place."

"Let us be off at once after him," said the admiral; "that is our only plan. Come on at once. The sooner we get hold of him the better, for his own sake as well as for ours."

Thus urged, they all proceeded towards the garden, in which was the mysterious, well-like entrance to the subterraneous passage, which formed so great a feature in the estate of Anderbury, on the moment, and which, at the time that Varney had taken the mansion, had evidently formed to him one of its principal attractions.

To the admiral and his party, as well as to several of the guests, who joined from motives of curiosity in the pursuit for Varney, this place was perfectly new, and it certainly, to look down it, did not present by any means an inviting prospect; for although it sloped sufficiently to take off the absolute appearance of being a downright hole in the earth, yet, beyond a few feet in depth, the gloom had something positively terrific about it.

"Well," said the admiral, "I've been into the hold of many a ship, but never one that looked half so gloomy as this, I can say. What do you say to it, Jack?"

"It's no use saying anything to such places," said Jack. "The only way, if we want to catch old Varney, which I suppose we do, is to pop down it at once and done with it; so come along, I won't flinch if it was ten times worse. Come on, admiral, let's go down after the enemy."

"I cannot say it's exactly the kind of place I admire," said the admiral; "but, howsomedever, if one must go down it, who shall say that Admiral Bell flinched from it? Come on, all of you. Let all who will follow."

The passage did not look a very inviting one; and it was found that the courage of the guests began to cool down wonderfully when, instead of rushing from apartment to apartment, in search of Varney, the vampyre, they found that they had to encounter the gloom and darkness of that underground abode.

Out of the positive throng which had been pursuing Varney, only four, in addition to the admiral and the male portion of his party, ventured to descend into that black-looking place.

"What!" cried Jack, "have we got such a lot of skulkers whenever we come to close quarters with the enemy? Well, shiver my timbers, if I didn't expect as much from a lot of land lubbers, who don't know what they are about any more than a marine in a squall. But who cares? Come along, admiral; and, if we do have all the fighting, we shall, at all events, have all the glory."

"I hope there will be nothing of the one, at all events," said Henry; "for my intention is rather to save Varney from injury than to injure him."

"We must have lights," said the admiral. "I don't mind going down into a queer place to look for Varney, but I must have the means of seeing what I am about when I get there."

"They will be here, sir, directly," said the big footman, who from the first had made himself conspicuous in the pursuit of Varney; that is to say, ever since the reward of £100 had been offered by the admiral to any one who would take him prisoner.

And in a few moments, some of the links, which were always kept in the kitchen of Anderbury House, for the express purpose of descending into the subterraneous passages with, were produced and lighted. By this time, too, the four guests had decreased to three, and two of those seemed to hang back rather a little; while one of them seemed disposed to make up as much as possible for any deficiency of courage on the part of the others, by declaring his intention of ferretting out Varney, let him be hidden where he might.

"I am with you, sir," he said to the admiral, "let this place lead where it may; for I have heard so much about vampyres, and really am so curious to know more about them."

"You don't believe in them, do you?"

"I cannot say that I do, sir. But, at the same time, when we hear such well authenticated cases brought forward about them, it is very difficult, indeed, to say at once, that one has no belief in such things."

"Well, you are right enough there; and if you knew as much about Varney, the vampyre, as we do, I think you would be a little puzzled to know what to say about him; for I'll be hanged if he don't puzzle me above a bit, and I don't know now what to think of him."

CXXI.

THE DEATH OF THE INQUISITIVE GUEST. — THE ESCAPE OF SIR FRANCIS VARNEY.

THE GUEST WHO WAS so valorous, and so very impatient for the capture of Varney, would have preceded everybody in descending to the passage cut in the cliff, but Henry Bannerworth thought not only was it more particularly his concern to do so, but that as he knew Varney better, it was desirable that he should go first.

He thought there would less likelihood of any mischief by adopting such a kind of procedure, for he did not anticipate that Varney would willingly do him any injury; while, as regarded what he might do if any stranger should attempt to seize him, that was quite another affair.

"You do not know him as we know him," said Henry, to the guest. "He is a dangerous man, and in all respects such an one as your prudence might well induce you to keep clear of. Allow me to precede you, therefore, for the sake of preventing the probability of the most unpleasant consequences."

This argument appeared to have its effect and to damp a little the ardour of this individual, which it might well enough do, without casting any imputation upon his courage whatever; for, after all, he could have no strong motive in the pursuit of Varney, since he was in a line of life which would have prevented him, even if he had been the sole captor of Varney, from taking the reward which the admiral had offered for his apprehension.

The sudden change from the daylight, and all the noise and bustle which had animated the scene above, to the silence, the darkness, and the strange atmosphere which reigned in the underground region, could not fail of having some effect upon the imagination of every one present.

This effect would, of course, vary in different individuals, being the greatest in those of a highly excitable and imaginative turn of mind, and the less in those who were of a more matter-of-fact kind of intellect. Probably, Henry Bannerworth felt more acutely than any one else the full effect which such a scene was likely to produce, and he was profoundly silent upon the occasion for some time.

Under even the most extraordinary circumstances, the descent into such a place must have affected the mind to some extent, for it seems like leaving the world altogether for a time, and bidding farewell to everything which we have been in the habit of enjoying and thinking beautiful.

No one ever thought of accusing Admiral Bell of being very imaginative;

but, upon this occasion, although he was the first to speak, what he did say showed that he had felt some of those sensations to which we have alluded.

"How do you feel, Henry?" he said. "I'll be hanged if I don't seem as if I were going into my grave before my time."

"And I, too," said Henry; "but I rather like the solemn feeling which such a place as this inspires."

"Gentlemen," said the tall footman with the yellow plush what-do-you-call-ems, "gentlemen, I think, after all, that I somehow will go back again. I don't seem, actually, in a manner of speaking, to care to catch the baron, somehow; so, if you please, gentlemen, I rather think I'll go back."

"Why don't you say you are afraid, at once, John?" said the admiral.

"Who, me, sir? I afraid? Oh, dear, no, sir. It would take a trifle, indeed, to frighten me, I rather think. Oh! no, no, sir, you mistake me. It's my feelings — it's my feelings, sir."

"Why, what the deuce have your feelings to do with it?"

"Everything in the world, sir. Haven't I drank his beer, sir, and haven't I eat his beef, and his bread, and his *tatoes*, sir, and shall I now hunt him up among his own ice-wells? No; perish the thought — perish the blessed idea. Perish the — the — the — good-bye, gentlemen."

With these words, the chivalrous footman gave up all idea of continuing the chase for Varney, the vampyre, and turning quickly, so as to stop the possibility of his hearing any further remonstrance, he went from the place with great speed.

Still, however, with the departure of this individual, whose courage from the first had had about it a very suspicious colour, they were in quite sufficient strength to have accomplished the capture of the vampyre, if they could get hold of him, and always provided he was not sufficiently armed with powers of mischief to their number, by taking perchance the life of some one of them.

There was one circumstance connected with a search for anybody in that strange region, which spoke much in favour of a successful result, and that was that the passage was narrow, and that there were no hiding-places except the ice-wells, to explore which, at all events, could not be a very difficult task; and as they proceeded, they felt certain that they must be driving Varney before them.

Before they had got very far, Henry Bannerworth thought it would be advisable to announce to Varney the precise intentions of himself and the admiral, always provided he were equally peaceably inclined, and within hearing of what was said to him.

He accordingly raised his voice, inquiring, —

"Sir Francis Varney, you no doubt recognise, by my tones, that it is Henry Bannerworth who speaks to you; and therefore you may feel convinced that no harm is intended you; but you are implored to come forth and meet your friends, who, from former circumstances, you ought to know you can trust."

There was no reply whatever to this appeal, and when the echoes of Henry's voice had died away, the same death-like stillness reigned in the place that had before characterised it.

"He will not answer," said the admiral; "and yet, if the other end of this passage be guarded as it is said to be, he must be here. Let us come on at once — I have no wish of my own to stay in this damp, chalky hole a moment longer than may be absolutely necessary."

"Nor I," remarked Henry; "so let us proceed, and it will be necessary that we keep an accurate watch upon our progress, for I am told that there are ice-wells here of great depth, down which you may fall and come by an awful death when you least expect, unless you are very cautious in looking where you tread."

"There's no doubt of that, sir," said one of his guests. "This place is considered to be one of the most curious that Anderbury can boast of, and I have been told that there are ice-houses, in which all kinds of provisions may be kept with ease and safety in the most violent heat of the summer months."

After a few moments they came upon one of the ice-wells, which yawned terrifically before them, and had they not been very careful and watchful upon the occasion, one or more of them might have been precipitated down the well, and the loss of life must have been the result.

"I scarcely think," said Henry, "that ordinary caution has been used in the construction of these places, or they never would have been left in such a state as they are now in. The ice-well, you perceive, lies directly in the very pathway?"

"Yes," said the admiral, "it does seem so, Master Henry; but if you look a little closer you will perceive that at one time there has been a wooden bridge exactly over this chasm."

"Ah, I do, indeed, now perceive such has been the case."

"Yes, and that made the place both safe and convenient; for no doubt there was a means of lowering down any baskets of wine or other matters that required a low temperature."

The admiral was perfectly right in his supposition, for that was just the way in which the ice-wells of Anderbury House were constructed; and now, since the bridge had been broken down, there was but a very narrow pathway, indeed, by which the well could be passed, unless it was jumped over, which might be done by any active person.

They would not pass this ice-well without an examination of it, and that was accomplished by lying down upon the rough pathway of the passage, and holding a light at arm's-length down it, when the bottom was clearly visible.

"He is not there," said Henry, who was the person who made the experiment; "he is not there, so we must pass on."

They accordingly did so, until they came to another such ice-well, and then the guest which had shown such eagerness in the chase, and accompanied them so far, went through the process of stooping down the chasm to ascertain if it contained anything unusual beyond the debris of broken bottles, old flint-stones, &c, which might fairly be expected to be there.

"Do you see anything?" inquired Henry, as the guest seemed to be looking very intently over the precipice.

He was about to reply something, for some sound came from his lips, when he suddenly, as if he had been impelled to do by some unseen power, toppled over the edge and disappeared, torch and all, into the abyss below.

"Good God!" cried Henry, "he has fallen."

"Good night," said the admiral, with characteristic coolness; "I suspect, my friend, that your career is at an end."

"Listen! for God's sake, listen!" cried Henry; "does he speak?"

There was a strange scuffling noise, and then a low deep groan from the bottom of the ice-pit, and then all was still; and from the character of the sound, Henry was of opinion that this well was of much greater depth than the former one, which he had so successfully examined.

"He has met with his death," said Henry.

"Don't be too sure," said the admiral; "we must have a good stout rope, and somebody must go down; if nobody likes the job, I will go myself."

"If ropes are wanted," said one of the other two persons who were present, "I can show you where they may be found, for I was at the inquest on the body of the man who was found dead in this place some time ago, and I marked that the ropes by which his body had been got out of one of the ice-wells were left where they had been used."

"That, then, said the other, "is further on, and nearer the beach."

"Yes; lend me the light, and I will get the rope as quickly as I can; for I don't think, as well as I can remember, that there is another well between this one and that which is nearer the beach entrance."

This was done, and for a few moments Henry and the admiral were left in darkness while the ropes were being searched for. It was a darkness so total and complete, that it did indeed seem like that darkness which it requires but a little stretch of the imagination to fancy it can be felt.

"Henry," said the admiral — "Henry!"

"Yes; I am here."

"Were you ever in such a confounded dark hole in all your life?"

"Scarcely, I think, ever. It is certainly tremendous, and it is a grievous thing to think that a life had been sacrificed, as no doubt it has, in this adventure."

"Ah, well! we must all go to Davy Jones's locker some day, you — But — but don't lay hold of me so!"

"I lay hold of you! I am not near you, sir."

"D — n it! who is it, then? Somebody has got hold of me as if I were in a vice. Stand off, I say! Who are you?"

"Varney, the vampyre," said a deep sepulchral voice; "who warns you, and all others, that there is abundance of danger in visiting here, and nothing to be gained."

Almost as these words were spoken, Henry suddenly found himself whirled round with such force, that it was only by a great effort that he succeeded in keeping his feet, and he felt convinced that some one had passed him. Who could that one be but Sir Francis Varney, the much dreaded vampyre?

In the next moment the light glanced again upon the walls of the subterranean passage, and the admiral cried, —

"He has escaped, unless some one stops him above. But let us think of nothing else at present, but to find out if the poor fellow who fell down here be alive or dead."

Henry descended by the assistance of the ropes, and found the adventurous guest quite dead. They raised the body from the well, and conveying it, as best they could, among them, they arrived, after some troubles on account of their burden, in the gardens, and, finally, in the great hall of Anderbury House, on a table in which they laid the corpse.

It was quite evident now to the admiral and to the Bannerworths that Varney had escaped, so they could have no desire to remain at the house, over which Mr. Leek was running like a madman, wondering what he should do. Flora had invited Helen Williams to accompany her to the inn, so that the whole party of the

Bannerworths went away together, with the one addition to it of that poor girl who had so narrow an escape of becoming the vampyre's bride. Horrible destiny!

———

CXXII.

MRS. WILLIAMS VISITS THE BANNERWORTHS AT THE INN. — THE MARRIAGE OF

JAMES ANDERSON WITH HELEN.

LET US FANCY NOW, after all these singular circumstances had taken place, the Bannerworth family, with James Anderson and Helen Williams, seated in a comfortable room at the inn at Anderbury, where they had put up when they came to that place, in pursuance of the invitation they had received from Mrs. Williams.

And that lady, probably could she have foreseen what was about to occur, would have taken most especial pains to prevent such an invitation from ever reaching such a destination; but she had fallen a victim to her own love of display, and not being content with inviting people whom she did know, she must, forsooth, give them a *carte blanche* to bring with them people whom she did not know at all.

And this it was that she had been horrified by what had taken place, and had had all her brightest visions of the future levelled with the dust.

When Jack Pringle told Mrs. Williams that he believed she would quite willingly have sold her daughter to a vampyre, he was right; for she would have done so, always provided that the vampyre, as aforesaid, had a good property, and was able to convince her of that most important fact. The only person of all the little party that was assembled at the inn, who looked pale and anxious, was poor Helen, and she certainly did look so; for when we come to consider her novel position we shall not wonder at it.

She had thrown herself completely upon the consideration of strangers, and was severed from all those natural ties which ought to have for ever held her in their gentle bondage. But this conduct, or rather the conduct of that one who ought to have protected her though all trouble and anxieties — her mother — had been such as to deprive her of the feeling that she had a home at all.

Flora saw that her guest, as indeed she considered Helen, looked sad and dejected, and she made every effort within her power to rescue her from such a state of things.

"Do not despair of much happiness," she whispered to her; "but rather thank good fortune, which, at the last moment, rescued you from one whom you could not love. Be assured that now you will enjoy the protection of those who will soon be able to prevail upon your mother to look with a favourable eye upon any new arrangement."

"I am much beholden to you," said Helen — "very much beholden to you, and I feel that I ought to congratulate myself upon my escape. But my heart does feel sad, because the state of things, to avoid which I made myself a sacrifice, may now ensue in all their terrors."

"My dear," said the admiral, who overheard her, "don't you believe any such rubbish as all that. I have no doubt you have been regularly persecuted into the match with the supposed baron, and you would, perhaps, have found out afterwards that one-half of the things you were told, to induce you to consent, had no foundation but in somebody's active imagination."

"Do you think so, sir?"

"Do I think so! To be sure I do. Now, I dare say you were told how, if you married the Baron What's-his-name, you would be doing something wonderful for all your family."

"Yes — yes."

"Oh, of course; I can see through all that clearly enough; and I tell you, my lass, that you have had a most fortunate escape, and that there is, and shall be, no reason on the face of the earth why you should not be married to the man of your choice. He has been to sea, and so, of course, he has finished what may be called his education. If he had been on shore all his life, you might have doubted about the prudence of having him; but, as it is, it's quite another matter."

"Sir, I thank you for your kind advocacy of my cause," said James Anderson; "and I shall ever consider, as one of the most fortunate accidents of my life, the meeting with Admiral Bell."

"Oh, don't say anything about that. I know some of the people at the Admiralty, and when you go to make the report of how you have been shipwrecked, and how you lost your despatches, I will give you a letter of introduction, which, I dare say, won't do you any harm."

"Indeed, sir, this is more kindness than I ought to expect."

"Not at all, my boy — not at all. Don't put yourself out of the way about that. Only I tell you what I would do. You need not take my advice unless you like; but, if I were you, I'd be hanged if I moved an inch anywhere till I had made Helen Williams my wife."

"Can you suppose," cried James Anderson, while his eyes sparkled with delight — "can you suppose, my dear sir, that such advice could be other than most welcome to me?"

"And what do you say, Helen, to it?" whispered Flora.

"What can I say?"

"You can say yes, I suppose?" said the admiral.

Helen was silent.

"Very good," added the admiral. "When a girl don't say no, of course she means yes; and you can make sure of your prize now you have got her, Master Anderson. Let's see; you manage these affairs with what you call a special license, don't you?"

"Yes, uncle," said Flora; "that is the way. You seem to know all about it, and I almost suspect you really must have had some experience in those matters."

"I experience, you little gipsy! — what do you mean? I never was married in all my life, and I don't intend to be."

"Don't make too sure, uncle. But, despite all that, no one could more warmly second your advice to Mr. Anderson than myself."

"Very good. For that speech I forgive

you. And now, Mr. Anderson, just come along with me, for I want to say a few words to you which nobody else has anything to do with."

When the admiral got James Anderson alone, he said to him, —

"Of course you are without funds, so it's no use making any fuss of delicacy about it. I have no doubt but that, with my interest, I shall be able to get you into an appointment of some sort; but, in the meantime, I beg that you will not cross me in my desire to serve you; and mind, I take your word of honour to repay me, so, you see, there is no obligation."

"Sir, this noble generosity —"

"There, there — that's quite enough; for the fact is, it ain't noble generosity at all, so hold your tongue about it, and be so good as to let me consider that as settled. Here are fifty pounds for you, which will enable you to go to London like a gentleman, and to conduct your marriage either here or there, as you may yourself think proper, and as your bride may consent."

"Sir, I would fain make Helen my own here."

"Very good. I don't pretend to understand how to manage these things: but set about it as quickly as you can, and don't be deterred by anybody."

This short but, to James Anderson, deeply interesting conversation, because it relieved his mind from a load of anxiety, took place a few paces from the inn door only, so that they returned at once; but scarcely had they joined the rest of the party, and were considering what they should order for dinner, when one of the waiters of the establishment came to say, —

"If you please, there's a lady who wants to come in. I asked her her name, but she won't give it; but she says she must see everybody."

"The deuce she must!" cried the admiral. "What sort of a craft is she?"

"Sort of a what, sir?"

"My fears tell me," sobbed Helen, "that it is my mother."

The admiral whistled, and then he said, —

"I suppose we shall have a breeze; but the sooner it's over the better. Let the lady come in; and don't you be afraid of anything, my lass. Why, you look as pale as if you expected — here she is."

The door was flung open, and Mrs. Williams made her appearance. Anger was upon her face, and it required but a small amount of penetration to perceive that she came fully charged with all sorts of reproaches. Helen trembled and shrunk back, for she had an habitual fear of her mother, which the imperious conduct of that individual had induced in the mind of so gentle a creature as Helen from her very childhood.

"Well, madam," said Henry, stepping forward; "to what are we indebted for the honour of this visit from one who has not the courtesy to wait for an invitation?"

"Oh! I expected this," said Mrs. Williams, with a shivering toss of her head; "I quite expected this, I can assure you — of course. But I'll pretty soon let you know, sir, what I came about. I have come for my daughter, sir. What have you got to say against that?"

"Nothing, madam; if your daughter chooses to comply with your request."

"Helen!" screamed Mrs. Williams. "Helen! I command you to come home this moment!"

"Mother, hear me!" said Helen. "Consent to my happiness with one whom I can love, with the same readiness that you would have seen me the bride of one for whom I never could hope to feel anything in the shape of affection, and I will accompany you home at once."

"Oh, dear, yes — of course. Consent to ruin — consent to nonsense! Consent to your marrying a scapegrace who cannot even keep himself — far less a wife! No, Helen; you cannot expect that I should ever consent to your marrying such a poor wretch."

"But don't you think," said Henry, "that any poor wretch is better than a vampyre?"

"No; I do not."

"Oh! very good, then," said the admiral; "if that's the lady's opinion, what can we say to her? And, as for commanding Miss Helen, here, to go home, I command her to stay."

"You command her?"

"Yes, to be sure. Ain't I an admiral? What have you got to say against that, I should like to know? I shall take good care that James Anderson is no poor wretch by getting him some good appointment; and, as your daughter is of age, old girl, and so can choose for herself, you may as well weigh anchor, and be off at once, for nobody wants to be bothered with you."

"Do you mean to say you are a real admiral, and have nothing to do with the horse-marines?"

"Nothing whatever, ma'am. Good day to you — we are all waiting for our dinners, and don't feel disposed to talk any more; so be off with you."

Mrs. Williams seemed to be considering for a moment, and then she said, — "Oh, gracious! a mother's feelings must always be excused. I almost think that — just to please you, admiral — I will consent."

"You will, mother?" exclaimed Helen.

"Why, in a manner of speaking," said Mrs. Williams, "I should not mind; but it's quite, you see, a dreadful thing to think of, when we consider what an expense I have gone to in all these matters, and that I have not had so much as one farthing from the baron, although he did say he would pay all the cost I might be put to."

"From resources which, in course of time, industry may procure me," said James Anderson, eagerly, "you shall be repaid all that you can possibly say has been expended for Helen."

"Ah! well, then, if Admiral Bell, here, will say that he will see me paid, I consent."

"Very well," said the admiral; "I'll see you paid. If you had acted generously in the matter, you should have been a gainer; but, as it is, you shall be paid, and we decline your acquaintance."

Mrs. Williams began, from the tone and manner of her daughter's new friends, to suspect that it would have been more prudent on her part if she had behaved in a very different manner towards them, and complied with a good grace with their wishes; for, as regarded the baron, anything in the shape of a more extended connexion with him was clearly out of the question.

But she had gone almost too far for reconciliation, and, although there was no such thing as denying the genius of the lady, she was, for a few minutes, puzzled to know what to do. At length, however, she thought it would not be a bad plan to be suddenly quite overcome with her feelings, and make a desperate scene.

Accordingly, to the surprise of every one, and the consternation of the admiral, she suddenly uttered a piercing scream, and commenced a good exhibition of hysterics.

"D — n it!" cried the admiral; "what does she mean by that? Come, come, I say, Mother Williams, we cannot stand all that noise, you know; it is quite out of the question!"

"Let us all leave the room," said Henry, "and send Jack Pringle to her. I have heard him say that he has some mode of recovering ladies from hysterics by throwing a pail-full of salt water over them, and then biting their thumb-nails off."

"The wretch!" exclaimed Mrs. Williams, suddenly recovering. "The wretch! I'd let him know soon enough what it was to interfere with my nails!"

"Oh! you are better, are you?" said the admiral.

"What's that to you?" shrieked Mrs. Williams. "I'll go at once to a lawyer, and see what can be done with you. I look upon you all with odium and contempt!"

"Ah! words easily spoken," said the admiral; "and just like young chickens they commonly go home to roost."

Mrs. Williams darted an angry look at the whole party, which she intended should be expressive at once of the immense contempt in which she held them, and of her determination to have vengeance upon their heads, which double-dealing look, however, had no effect upon them of an intimidating character, and then she bounced from the room.

"My dear," said the admiral, turning to Helen, who he saw was affected at the proceeding. "My dear, don't you fret yourself. Your mother cannot make us angry; and, as far as regards her own anger, it will all subside, and then we will forget that she has said anything at all uncivil to us. So don't you fret yourself about what is of no consequence at all."

"You may depend," said Henry, "that such will be the fact, and that in a very short time you will find that your mother has completely recovered from her anger, and will be as pleasant with us all as possible. I grieve to say so to you, but the fact is, what you must perceive, namely, that, as regards your mother, your marriage is merely a matter of pounds, shillings, and pence, and when she finds that the baron's fortune cannot be had, she will content herself with reflecting upon the prospects of Mr. James Anderson, who, if he do well, will soon be quite a favourite."

It was humiliating to poor Helen to be forced to confess that this was the correct view to take of the question, but she could not help doing so at all: and, after a time, she did not regret having sufficient moral courage to resist the command of her mother to return home.

In the society of him whom she loved, and upheld and encouraged, too, as she was by Flora, who was just about the best and kindest companion such a person as Helen could have had, the minutes began to fly past upon rosy pinions, and the remainder of that day she confessed, even to the admiral, was the happiest she had known for many a weary month.

THE BANNERWORTHS AND James Anderson fully expected another visit from Mrs. Williams on the morrow, but she did not come; and, although they had expected her to do so, her not coming was no disappointment, but, on the contrary, a matter for some congratulation.

But no time was lost; and, as James Anderson was really most anxious to get to London to report himself at the Admiralty, and as that was an anxiety in which the admiral much encouraged him, so that as it was quite an understood thing among them all that the marriage of the fair Helen should take place before he again left her, a special license was procured, and the ceremony arranged to take place at nine o'clock in the morning, on the second morning after the strange and exciting occurrences at Anderbury House.

This marriage was conducted in the most private manner possible; because, as it had been so well known throughout the whole of Anderbury that Helen Williams was the chosen of the great and rich Baron Stolmuyer of Saltzburgh, who had tuned out to be such an equivocal character, the news of her marriage with any one else would have been sure to have created a vast amount of pubic curiosity.

All this they escaped by fixing the hour at which the ceremony was to be performed at an early hour in the morning, and trusting no one out of their own party with the secret.

Of course, from what the reader knows of the gentle and timid disposition of Helen Williams, he may well suppose how glad she would have been to have had the countenance of her mother at her marriage, notwithstanding the conduct of that mother was certainly not what should have entitled her to the esteem of any one whatever, not excepting her own child.

But this was a feeling which, when she came to consider the new tie she was forming, was likely soon to wear away; and, although, while she pronounced those words which were irrevocably to make her another's, the tears gushed to her eyes, they were far different from those bitter drops she had shed when she considered that, beyond all hope of redemption, she was condemned to become the bride of the baron.

When the ceremony was over, they all went back very quietly and comfortably to the inn, and, after a good breakfast, and many healths had been drank to the bride, James Anderson, according to arrangement, took his departure for London, leaving Helen in the care of the Bannerworths until he should come back to claim her, as he now could do, despite all the plots and machinations of Mrs. Williams, who, as yet, was in a state of blessed ignorance as to the fact of her daughter's wedding, and who had not quite made up her mind as to what she should do next in so delicate and troublesome a transaction.

CXII.

MRS. WILLIAMS TAKES THE INITIATIVE, AND NEARLY CATCHES AN ADMIRAL.

MRS. WILLIAMS, WHEN she reached home after what must be called her very unsuccessful attempt to make a disturbance, and to do the grand at the inn where the Bannerworths were, set herself seriously to think what would be the best course for her to adopt in the rather perplexing aspect of her affairs.

The few words she had used at the inn, indicative of her censure of all the proceedings, had been of rather a strong and energetic character, so that she had a very uncomfortable suspicion upon her mind that she would find it rather a difficult task to pacify her daughter's new friends.

The offer which the admiral had made to repay to her any expense she had been at, impressed her with a belief that he surely must be in possession of what, to her, was the most delightful thing in the world, and comprehended all sorts of virtue, namely, money; and of course her feelings became instantly most wonderfully ameliorated.

"I'm very much afraid I have been too precipitate," she said. "I really am afraid I have, and that ain't a pleasant reflection by any means. What can I do to get good friends with them all, and particularly the dear old gentleman who promised to pay me?"

This was the problem which Mrs. Williams presented to her mind, for the captivating idea of actually having been

paid five hundred pounds by the baron, and thus sending in a bill of the same amount to the admiral, took wonderful and complete possession of her.

This was, indeed, she considered, a masterstroke of policy, and all she had now to consider was, the means of getting on such good terms with the admiral that he should neither question items nor amount of the account she intended to send him in.

"If he only pays the five hundred as well as the baron has paid his, I shall not come out of the transaction so badly," said Mrs. Williams.

While she was in this state of perplexity, she was sitting by the window of her dining-room, which commanded a view of the street, and, as she sat there, she was much surprised to see Jack Pringle, who she still had a lingering suspicion might, notwithstanding his disclaimer of the title, be Admiral Green, on the other side of the way, making various significant movements of his hands and head, as if he had something of an exceedingly secret and strange mysterious nature to communicate to her, Mrs. Williams.

This was quite sufficient to call for that lady's most serious attention, and accordingly she walked graciously so close to the window that her aristocratic nose touched the glass, and nodded to Jack, after which she beckoned him across the way, after the manner of the ghost in *Hamlet*, upon which Jack, with a nod, came across the way forthwith.

In another moment Mrs. Williams opened the street-door herself, and said, —

"Mr. What's-your-name, have you got anything to say to me?"

"Rather," said Jack.

"What is it, then — pray what is it, Mr. What's-your-name?"

"Don't call me What's-your-name, ma'am, any longer; my name is Jack Pringle."

"Mr. John Pringle, I suppose?"

"No such thing; nothing but plain Jack, ma'am; so you see you are mistaken. But I have got something to say to you, ma'am, as you ought to know."

Any one who had known Jack would have seen, by a certain mischievous twinkling of the eyes, that he had on hand what he considered one of the most excellent of jokes in all the world, and was about to perpetrate what he thought some famous piece of jollity. What it was, we shall quickly perceive, from his communication with Mrs. Williams.

"Well, ma'am," he added, "you know Admiral Bell, I believe?"

"Oh, yes — yes; certainly, I do."

"Well, I don't know as I ought to tell you, Mrs. W., what I'm going to tell you; but, first of all, the old admiral, what with prize money, pay, and one thing and another, is so immensely rich, that he really don't know what to do with his money."

"How dreadful!" said Mrs. Williams; "I think I could really suggest to him some few things to do."

"Oh, he is so desperately obstinate, he will listen to nobody; and, you see, as he never married, who as he got to leave it to? At least that's what we have been all

wondering, for I don't know how long; but now what do you think we have found out, Mrs. Williams?"

"Well, that's very difficult, of course, for me to say. Perhaps you will be so good as to tell me."

"You ought to know. He has fallen in love, ma'am — actually in love, for the first time in his life. Yes, he has actually fallen in love, Mrs. Williams; there's a go."

"And with one of my daughters! It's with Julia — I did mention her to him, and I thought I saw a curious expression come across his face. Of course, I'm quite delighted to hear it; for, with the feelings of a mother, I like to get my girls off hand as well as I can; and, as Admiral Bell is so very respectable a person, I can have no sort of objection in the world."

"There you go, again," said Jack; "you are quite mistaken, I can tell you. You never made a greater blunder than that in all your life, Mother Williams — excuse me, ma'am, but that's my way."

"Oh, don't mention it — but where's the mistake, my dear sir?"

"Why, just here, ma'am — just here. The admiral is not so young as he was twenty-five years ago, and he ain't quite such a fool as to think that a young girl can care anything for him. But he is in love, for all that. Only you see, ma'am, it happens to be with somebody else."

"Good gracious! Who is it? — and why do you come to me about it?"

"Because it's you."

"Me! me! oh, gracious Providence, you don't mean that! In love with me! The rich old admiral — he cannot live long. How much money, take it altogether, do you really think he has got? I declare you have taken me so by surprise, that I don't know what I am saying. Of course he will propose a very handsome settlement."

"You may depend upon all that," said Jack; "but the odd thing is, you see, ma'am, that although he is quite over head and ears in love, he won't own it, but walks about like a bear with a bad place on his back, doing nothing but growl, growl, from morning till night."

"Then how can you tell," said Mrs. Williams, "if he never said so?"

"Oh, he does say so. He mumbles it out to himself, and we have heard him say, —

" 'Damn it all! that Mrs. Williams is the craft for my money; but what's the use of me bothering her about it? — she wouldn't have an old hulk like me, so I won't say anything about it to anybody.' "

"What an amiable idea!"

"Very, ma'am, very; and what I have come to you for now is to say, that if you have no objection to the match, you might as well make the old man happy, by letting him know, in some sort of way, that you wouldn't be so hard-hearted as he thinks, but would have him if he would say the word."

"How can I express how much obliged I am to you, Mr. Wingle!"

"Pringle, if you please, ma'am, is my name; and as to being obliged to me, you ain't at all, and I'll tell you how: you see, I and the admiral have sailed with each other many a voyage, and I have a sort of feeling for the old man that makes me, when I see that he has a fancy, try my best to gratify him; and, without thinking of anybody but him, I've come to you just to tell you what I know about the affair, and I must leave it to you to do what you like."

"Still I am very much obliged to you. What if I were to call and ask for a private interview with the old man?"

"A good idea," said Jack. "It was only the other day I heard him say you was his pearl, and the main chain of his heart, I can tell you, and ever such a load more. He will be taking his dinner at four to-day, and after that he usually takes a sleep in an arm chair, in a room by himself, and if you like to come then, you will catch him."

"Be assured, my dear sir, I shall be there punctually to the minute. You will be so good as to receive me, and introduce me to him, and, perhaps, it would remove some of his timidity if I were to let him know that I was aware that he had called me his pearl, and the main chain of his heart."

"Of course it would," said Jack. "You put him in mind of it, ma'am, and if you find him back'erd a little, don't you mind about giving him a little encouragement, because you know all the while he really means it, so you need not care about it."

"Well, Mr. — a — a — Bingle, all I can say is, that I feel very much obliged to you indeed, for letting me know this matter; and my great respect for you and for the old admiral will, I assure you, induce me to consent to what you propose. — A-hem! of course I have many offers, as you may well suppose, Mr. Cringle."

"Damn it," said Jack, "I've told you before that my name is Pringle, and if you can't recollect that, just call me Jack, and have done with it — you won't forget Jack, I'll be bound. Call me that, and I sha'n't quarrel with you about it, ma'am; but don't be inventing all sorts of odd names for me."

"Pray excuse me, my dear sir, I

certainly will do no such thing; and at three o'clock, I hope I shall have the pleasure of seeing you. I believe it's the Red Lion where you are staying?"

"Yes, the Red Lion Inn; and at three I shall be on the look-out for you, ma'am, you may depend; and I only hope you won't mistake the admiral's bashfulness for anything else, because, I assure you, he is mad in love with you, but don't like to own it, ma'am; so just you bring him out a little, and don't you mind what he says."

Mrs. Williams duly promised she would not mind what the old man said, and, from what we know of that lady, we are quite inclined, for once in a way, to give her credit for sincerity in that matter, and the greatest possible amount of candour.

As for Jack, when he left her house, and had got fairly round the corner and out of sight, he laughed to that excess that several passers-by stopped to look at him in wonder, and had he not ceased, he certainly would have had a crowd round him in a very few minutes longer, that would have perhaps thought him out of his senses.

But after a few minutes, the explosion of his bottled-up mirth had subsided, and after giving a boy, who was the nearest to him of the admiring spectators, a good rap on the head, he walked to the inn.

Jack would have been glad to have told someone of the capital joke he was playing off at the admiral's expense, but he was afraid of being betrayed; so he wisely kept the secret of the forthcoming jest all to himself; although Henry Bannerworth and Charles Holland might both, after such a thing happened, or even during its progress, have a good laugh at it, it is not to be supposed, entertaining as they did so great a respect for the old admiral, that they would have lent themselves to the perpetration of such a joke.

As may be supposed, Mrs. Williams was all flutter and expectation, and the idea of at length mending her decayed fortune by an union with the old man, who was reported to be immensely rich, and who had already reached an age when his life could not be depended upon one week from another, was one of the most gratifying circumstances on record to her.

No possible plan could have been devised which was so likely to chime in with her humour as this, and if she had been asked in which way she would like to make money, it would have been that which she would have undoubtedly chosen.

"Now," she thought, "I shall, after all, make an admirable thing of this affair, there can be no doubt. I shall, of course, soon be a widow again, for the old sea-monster cannot live long. I shall insist upon a very liberal settlement indeed, and then I suppose, while he does live, I must keep him in a good humour, so that he may leave me, at all events, the bulk of his property when he dies, and then I can live in the style I like, and make everybody die of envy."

To excite an extraordinary amount of envy was the very height of felicity to Mrs. Williams, as, indeed, it is to many people of far greater pretensions than that lady; and we cannot help thinking, when we see gaudy equipages and all the glittering and costly paraphernalia of *parvenu* wealth, that the great object of it is to excite envy far more than admiration and pleasure.

"There are the Narrowidges, and the Staples, and the Jenkinses," thought Mrs. Williams. "Oh! I know they will all be ready to eat their very heads off, when they hear that I am married, and that, too, so well. Oh! they will die of spite, and particularly Mrs. Jenkins. I am quite sure she will have a serious illness."

These were the kind of triumphs upon which Mrs. Williams felicitated herself, and pictured to her imagination as the result of her marriage with the admiral, which she now looked upon as quite a settled thing; because, if he were willing, she felt perfectly sure that she was; and, therefore, what was to prevent the union from taking place?

What pleasant anticipations these were! Really, we can almost consider them, while they lasted, as sufficient to counterbalance any disappointment which was likely afterwards to take place; and the hour or two which Mrs. Williams devoted to the gorgeous dream of wealth she so fully expected to enjoy, were probably the most delightful she had ever passed. And certainly so far she had to thank Jack Pringle for giving her so much satisfaction, although, as will be seen, she did not feel towards him any great amount of gratitude on the momentous occasion.

Mrs. Williams, no doubt, still thought herself quite a fascinating woman; and when she had failed in guessing that it was to herself that the admiral was, according to Jack's account, devoted, it was not that she entertained a modest and

quiet opinion of her own attractions, but from the force of habit, seeing that so long a period had elapsed without her having an admirer, that she could not believe she had one then, until actually assured in plain language of the fact.

AND NOW, ABOUT half an hour before the appointed time, the lady arrayed herself in what she considered an extremely becoming and fashionable costume, and started to keep her appointment with Jack Pringle, who, in her affections, now held quite a pleasant place, and towards whom she considered herself so much indebted for the kind information she had received at his hands.

The distance from any house in Anderbury to any other, was but short, so that Mrs. Williams was within the time mentioned, when she reached the door of the Red Lion; but she was gratified to find that Jack Pringle was there, apparently on the look-out for her, because it showed that nothing had happened to alter the aspect of affairs, but that the chances of her becoming Mrs. Admiral Bell were as strong as ever.

"I'm glad you have come," said Jack. "They got over their dinner rather quick, and that's a fact; and the old man is fast asleep as usual, so you can commence operations at once."

"A thousand thanks — a thousand thanks, my good friend, and you may depend upon my gratitude."

"Hush! never mind that," said Jack; "I don't want nothing. This way — this way, ma'am, if you please."

CXXVI.

THE ADMIRAL IN A BREEZE. — A GENERAL COMMOTION, AND JACK PRINGLE MUCH WANTED, BUT NOT TO BE FOUND.

To SAY THAT MRS. WILLIAMS was on the tiptoe of expectation, is to say very little that can convey a good idea of what was her real condition, nervously speaking, as she followed Jack Pringle up, not the principal, but a back staircase of the inn, toward the room where the admiral took his nap, which was —

His custom always of an afternoon.[*]

The fact is, that Jack had a great dread of Mrs. Williams being seen by any of the Bannerworth family, because they all knew her; and the nice little plot he had got up for the purpose of holding out the admiral to ridicule, while at the same time he enjoyed the immense satisfaction of having some revenge upon Mrs. Williams.

Hence was it, that, like many a great politician, he went up the back staircase instead of the front, in order to avoid unnecessary observation and remark.

By good fortune, as well as good management, Jack met nobody, but succeeded in reaching the room door, within which the admiral was sleeping, in perfect safety.

"Now, ma'am," said Jack, "don't you be backerd in going forerd, 'cos, as I tell you, the old man is dying by inches for you, and I don't see why you shouldn't have his

half a million of money,[†] as well as anybody else. Ah! and a good deal better, too, when one comes to consider all things."

"Thank you, Mr. Pringle, thank you. I really don't know how to express my obligations to you, upon my word. You are so very kind and considerate in all you say."

"Oh! don't mention it, ma'am. Walk in, and there you will find the old baby. I shouldn't wonder but he's disturbing his old brains by dreaming of you now."

Jack opened the door, and Mrs. Williams glided noiselessly into an apartment, where, seated, sure enough, in an easy chair, with a silk handkerchief over his face, sat the admiral, fast asleep, enjoying that comfortable siesta, which he never for one moment imagined would be disturbed in the manner it was about to be.

"Well," said Mrs. Williams, "there he is, to be sure, just as Jack Pringle said, — asleep, and no doubt dreaming of me. I must make sure of the old fool in one interview, or he may slip through my fingers, and that would not be at all pleasant after counting upon him, and taking some trouble in the matter."

But although she made up her mind that nothing should be wanting, upon her part, to make sure of him, yet she debated whether she ought to awaken him or not;

------

[*] *A line from Shakespeare's* Hamlet *(Act I, Scene V). Refers to Hamlet's father, who was murdered during his customary afternoon nap.*

[†] *£46 million ($60 million) in 2020 currency.*

for she well knew that many old people, especially men, were very irascible if they are awakened suddenly, and from what she had already seen of the admiral, she could very well imagine that such might be the case with him.

This was getting rather a quandary, out of which Mrs. Williams did not exactly see her way; and yet the proposition that the admiral was to be, and must be, awakened in some way, remained as firmly as ever fixed in her mind. And then, too, the idea — a very natural one under the circumstances — came across her that each minute was fraught with danger, and that, for all she knew, the yea or nay of the whole affair might depend upon the promptitude with which it was concluded.

What, if, she asked herself, some of the odious Bannerworth people were to come in and find her there — of course they would awaken the admiral at once, and in consequence of their presence, she would lose all opportunity of exercising those little blandishments which she meant to bring to bear upon him.

This was positively alarming. The idea of all being lost, prompted her at all events to attempt something; so Mrs. Williams thought that the mildest way of awakening the admiral was by a loud sneeze, which she executed without producing the least effect, as might have been expected; for the man who had many a time slept soundly in the wildest fury of the elements, was not likely to awaken because somebody sneezed.

"Dear me, how sound he sleeps. A — hem! — hem! A — *chew!* — a — a — hem! — A *chewaway!*"

The admiral was proof against all this, and Mrs. Williams might just as well have spared herself the trouble of exciting such an amount of artificial sneezes, for the admiral slept on, and it was quite clear that something much more sonorous would be required for the purpose of awaking him.

"How vexatious," she thought; "how very vexatious. But there's no help for it. Awakened he must be, that's quite clear; and if fair means won't do it, why, foul must."

Acting upon this resolve, Mrs. Williams hesitated no longer, but, approaching the sleeping admiral, she dragged the handkerchief off his face, and its passage over his nose, no doubt, produced the tickling sensation that induced him to give that organ a very hard rub, indeed, and start wide awake with an exclamation that was much more forcible than elegant, and that consequently we need not transfer to our pages at all.

"Oh! admiral," said Mrs. Williams, assuming a look that ought at once to have melted a heart of stone; "oh! admiral, can you, indeed, forgive me?"

"The devil!" said the admiral.

"Can you, indeed, look over the fact, that in my anxiety to see that face, I took from before it the envious, and yet fortunate handkerchief that covered it? It was my act, and upon my head fall all the censure, my dear, good, kind admiral."

The old man rubbed his eyes very hard with his knuckles, as he said, —

"I suppose I'm awake."

"You are awake, my dear sir. It is, indeed, no dream, let me assure you, that disturbs you, but a living reality. You are awake, my dear sir."

"Why — why, what do you mean? I begin to think I am awake, with a vengeance; but who are you? Hang me if I don't think you are old Mother Williams!"

"Oh! my dear admiral, you are so facetious — so very facetious; but can you for one moment fancy, my dear sir, that I am insensible to your merit? Can you fancy that I could look with other than indulgent eyes upon a Bell?"

"Upon a what?"

"A Bell — an Admiral Bell. Indeed, I may say — with a slight but pardonable alteration of a word — an admirable Bell. My dear sir, your pearl speaks to you."

The admiral was so amazed at this address, accompanied as it was by most languishing looks, that, with his mouth wide open, and his eyes preternaturally distended, he gazed upon Mrs. Williams without saying a word; from which she inferred that he was beginning to see that she was aware of his attachment to her, and was thinking of how he could best express his gratitude for her taking the initiative in the matter.

Thus encouraged, then, she spoke again, saying, as she advanced close to him, —

"Oh, my dear sir, what a thing the human heart is. Only to think now, that from the first moment I saw you, I should whisper to myself — there — yes, there is the only human being for whose sake I could again enter into that holy state from which the death of Mr. Williams released me."

"Why, good God!" said the admiral, "the woman's mad!"

"Oh! no — no. The world — the horrid, low, work-a-day world, may make invidious remarks about us, but your pearl will recompense you for all that, and in

the sweet concord of domestic life, we shall never sigh for more than we shall have, which will be, of course, if I understand rightly, a large income — I don't know how much a year, and if I ask, it is only out of curiosity, my dear sir, and nothing else. Love — absolute and beautiful love, is all I ask."

"Hilloa!" roared the admiral; "Charles! Henry! Jack! Where the devil are you all? D — n it, you are all ready enough when I don't want you; but now, when I am going to be boarded by a mad woman, you can't come one of you. Hilloa! help! Charles! Jack, you lubber, where the deuce have you taken yourself to, and why don't you tumble up when you are sent for?"

"But, my dear sir, why need you trouble yourself to call so many witnesses to our happiness? Let us be privately married in some rural church."

"Privately d — d first, I'd be," said the old admiral.

"Oh, then, it shall be a public alliance, if you wish it," exclaimed Mrs. Williams, as she made up her mind to clinch the affair at once by a *coup de main;* and advancing to the admiral, she flung her arms around his neck just as a door at the other end of the apartment opened, and Charles and Henry, with Flora, made their appearance, and looked with the most intense astonishment at the scene before them.

"Well, uncle," said Charles, "I certainly should not have expected this of you. I am astonished, I must confess."

"Nor I," said Henry; "why, admiral, I had no idea you were so dangerous a personage."

Mrs. Williams, when she saw what arrivals had taken place, gave a faint scream, and released the admiral, and then she added,—

"Oh, admiral, how could you hold me so when you hear somebody coming? How shall I ever survive such a scene as this? My character will be gone for ever, unless I am immediately married to you, and I have no doubt but that all your friends will at once see the propriety of such a step."

"I do," said Charles.

"And I," said Henry.

"And I," of course, said Flora.

Mrs. Williams burst into tears when she saw this unanimity of opinion; but the admiral's face got the colour of a piece of beet-root, and he was only silent for a moment or two, while he was made the subject of these cruel remarks, until he could sufficiently recover to speak with the energy that did characterise him when he really began.

We are not exactly in the vein to transfer to our pages the violent expletives with which he garnished his outburst of passion, and our readers, if they recall to their minds a large amount of nautical oaths, can have no difficulty in supposing that the admiral uttered every one of them with a volubility that was perfectly alarming.

"D—n it! do you mean to kill me, all of you, or to drive me mad? (Five oaths in a string came in here.) Do you want to cut me up, you—(three horrible epithets)? What do you mean by setting this old woman upon me? Whose precious idea was this, I should like to know, to put an elderly she-dragon upon me, whom I hate and be—(ten oaths at least) when I was enjoying a comfortable nap?"

"Hate!" exclaimed Mrs. Williams;

"did you say hate, you old seducing villain! when you knew you said I was your pearl, you hoary-headed ruffian!"

"That's a thundering crammer," cried the admiral; "you said it yourself; and as for hating you, d—n it, if I don't do that with all my heart."

"And is this the way I'm to be treated before people? Oh! you wicked old sinner, I understand you now. Your intentions were not honourable, and now you find that my virtue is proof against your horrid old fascinations, you want to pretend that it's all a mistake."

"Really," said Charles, "we must confess, uncle, that we found Mrs. Williams and you—ahem!—rather loving, you know; and the gentleman on these occasions is usually asked to account for such things, I take it."

"Of course," said Mrs. Williams; "I'll bring an action against the admiral, and I shall call upon you all to be witnesses for me. Oh! you old sinner, I'll make you pay for this!"

"We certainly can all be witnesses," said Flora, "that the admiral called for help; and when we came we found Mrs. Williams holding him fast round the neck, to which he seemed to have the greatest possible repugnance."

"That's right! hurrah! That's the truth, Flora, my dear. That's just how it was. This horrid old woman come all of a sudden and laid hold of me after awakening me, and then I called for help. That's how it was."

"But these gentlemen," said Mrs. Williams, appealing to Henry and Charles, "will swear quite different."

"Oh, I beg your pardon, Mrs. Williams," said Charles; "if we are brought forward to swear anything, we must be correct; and, therefore, we shall have to say just what this lady has stated; and perhaps your best plan will be to go away and say no more about it; but consider that you have made a mistake."

"A mistake!" screamed Mrs. Williams; "how could I make a mistake, when Mr. John Pringle, who knows the admiral so well, told me that he was dying to see me, and in love with me to never such an extent, only that he was afraid I would not have anything to say to him on such a subject."

The admiral drew a long breath and sat down. Then, clenching his hand, he shook it above his head, saying, in a voice of deep and concentrated anger, —

"I thought as much. D — n it, if I did not. It's all that infernal scoundrel Jack Pringle's doings, I find. It's one of that lubberly, mutinous thief's tricks, and it's the last one he shall ever play me."

"A trick!" screamed Mrs. Williams; "a trick! You don't mean that! Ah, me! what compensation shall I get for the dreadful circumstance which has made me confess the secret of my heart! What shall I do — oh, what shall I do? When shall I hope for consolation! What sum of money, even if you, my dear admiral, were to offer it to me, would be a sufficient balm now to my wounded heart?"

"Madam," said Henry, "it seems that you have been imposed upon, and made the victim of a practical joke, which we nor the admiral can have nothing to do with; and the only consolation we can offer to your wounded heart, is, that we will keep the secret of your attachment most inviolate."

"What compensation is that to me?

I'll bring my action for breach of promise of marriage, if I don't get something, and that something very handsome too. It's all very fine to talk to me about your mistakes; I'll be paid — ah, and paid well, too, or I'll make the whole country ring again with the matter."

"Madam," said Charles, "I dare say the admiral don't care one straw whether the country rings again or not, and you can do just as you please; but since you have commenced threatening, you will, I hope, see the obvious propriety of at once leaving his place."

"I will leave this place, but it shall be to go direct to my solicitor, and see what he will say to a lone woman being treated in this way. I'll swear that he called me his pearl — and if that don't get me a verdict and most exemplary damages, I don't know what will. We shall see what we shall see, and, in the meantime, you wretches, I leave you all to contempt. Yes, contempt."

"Stop a bit, ma'am," said the admiral. "It's quite plain to me that you don't mind how you earn a trifle, so that you do get it; and now I'll tell you, that if you find out that rascal, Jack Pringle, and give him a good trouncing for his share in the business, you may come to me for a reward."

Mrs. Williams, whatever might have been her personal feelings on this head, did not deign to make the least reply to this intimation, but suddenly cried —

"I want to see my daughter."

"She is not here at present," said Flora; "and, if she were, she is Mrs. Anderson now, and therefore would of course decline accompanying you to your home — and she is only waiting some arrangements of her husband's, prior, most probably, to going to London with him."

This speech brought to the recollection of Mrs. Williams, that the admiral had promised her all the expenses that she had been at contingent upon the broken-off marriage of her daughter with the baron, and she began to consider that her action for breach of promise of marriage against him might fail, and that, if it succeeded, it might not bring in half so much as the amount of the bill she could by fair means get out of him.

These considerations were of great pith and amount, and they had their full effect upon Mrs. Williams; so, instead of bursting out with any further reproaches, she sat down and commenced a softening process by a copious flood of tears which she had always at command.

"Oh," said the old admiral, "you may well cry over it, old girl. I suppose you really thought you had hooked the old man at last, eh? But never do you mind, you may make a good thing of it yet, if you get hold of that scoundrel, Pringle, and serve him out well. I'll pay for that job more willingly than for anything else I know of just at present."

"Don't speak to me of that brute, my dear sir," sobbed Mrs. Williams. "It's a very cruel thing, of course, to be used in this way, and, as it's all a mistake on my part, I hope you will excuse and look over what has happened. I am sure I should be the last person in the world to trouble anybody with visits who did not want to see me; and so, I dare say, we shall only meet once again in this world."

"Once again, madam! What is the use of our ever meeting again?"

"It would look decidedly disrespectful on my part, if I were not to hand you the bill myself for the little matters that you were kind enough to say you would pay for on account of what I had expended on Helen's projected marriage with the vampyre baron, you know, admiral."

"Oh, ah! I recollect now. Well, well; I don't want to go back from my word, and as I did promise you, why, I will pay you; but as I don't want, on any account, the pleasure of your company again, you will be so kind, ma'am, as to take this twenty-pounds note, and keep the change."

This the admiral thought liberal enough; for his idea of matrimonial preparations consisted of a new dress or two, or so, and which twenty pounds ought fairly enough to cover; and he thought he would do well enough by overpaying Mrs. Williams, as he believed, with that amount.

When Mrs. Williams recovered from her surprise, not unmingled with indignation, into which this most audacious and, to her, extraordinary offer threw her, she spoke with a kind of scream, that made the old admiral jump again, as she shouted in his ears,—

"What! twenty pounds? Are you in your senses? Twenty pounds! Why, my bill will be, at least, five hundred pounds."

"What?" roared the admiral. "Are you in your senses? D—n it, ma'am! you may swallow your bill; and you had better do so, for all the good it is likely to do you; for, if I pay a farthing more, may I be hung up at my own yard-arm. Why, you must think that a British admiral is another name for a fool."

"Then I tell you what," said Mrs. Williams—"I tell you what, you stupid, old, atrocious sinner—I tell you, I will

bring my action against you for breach of promise of marriage; and I'll swear that, before your gang of people here came in — who, of course, will swear black is white, and white is crimson for you, because, I believe, you are the father of them all — that you first asked me to live with you, and when I refused, you said you would marry me by special licence to-morrow."

"Madam," said Charles, "now that you think proper entirely to forget that you are a lady, allow me to beg of you to retire; because it is quite impossible, after what has happened, that I should hold any further conversation with you."

"Yes, Mrs. Williams," said Henry, "I hope you will perceive the propriety of at once leaving."

At this moment a note was handed to Henry, who, upon opening it, read aloud, —

"The Baron Stolmuyer, of Salzburgh, presents his compliments to Mr. Bannerworth, and begs to state that Mrs. Williams has received from him the sum of five hundred pounds for expenses to be incurred on account of the wedding of her daughter; and he hereby fully empowers Mr. Bannerworth to demand of Mrs. Williams that sum, and to devote it to the service and uses of Mr. James Anderson, of whose existence the baron was not aware when he made his proposal to Mrs. Williams for her daughter, whom she sold to him, the baron, for that sum."

"Hilloa!" cried the admiral; "what do you think of that, Mrs. Williams? I don't know what you will say to it; but I know very well that I should consider it a shot between wind and water."

"I trust," said Henry, "that you will now still further see the propriety of leaving here, and of letting this matter completely rest; because it strikes me that the more you investigate it, madam, the more it will turn out greatly to your disadvantage."

"I don't care a pin's head for any of you, nor half a farthing," cried Mrs. Williams. "The baron gave me the money, and he has no power to get it back again, as you know well enough. I'll bring my

action, and my principal witness shall be Mr. Pringle, who came to my house, and who, if put upon his oath, will be obliged to swear —"

"That it was all a lark," said Jack, popping his head just within the amazingly short distance that he opened the door, and then he disappeared before a word could be said to him.

Mrs. Williams who, notwithstanding all her threats, seemed to have a lingering impression that she was victimised in the transaction, had all the ire of her nature aroused at once by the sight of Jack, and she at once rushed after him, leaving the admiral and the Bannerworths not at all lamenting her loss.

Jack had no idea that he would be followed by anybody but the admiral, and to distance him he knew there was no occasion to run; so, when he had got down to the hall of the hotel, he subsided into a walk, until he heard a tremendous scuffling of feet behind him, and, upon looking round, saw Mrs. Williams in full chase, and with an expression upon her countenance which plainly enough indicated that her intentions were not at all of a jocular character.

"The devil!" said Jack; "if here ain't Mother Williams coming full sail, and at fourteen knots an hour, too, with a fair wind, I'll be bound. Never mind — a stern chase is a long chase, so here goes."

As Jack uttered these remarks, he dashed onwards at tremendous speed; but the sight of him again, had inflamed Mrs. Williams's wrath to madness, and she made the most incredible exertion to come up with him, so that it was really wonderful to see her.

But Jack, being less encumbered by

apparel than the lady, would have distanced her, but for an unlucky accident, that gave her a temporary mastery. The fates would have it, that a baker with a tray upon his head, containing sundry pies, was coming up the street, and as people do sometimes, when they are mutually anxious to pass each other without coming in contact, they dodged from side to side for a few seconds, and then, of course, ran against each other as if they really meant it, with such force, that down came Jack, and baker, and pies, in one grand smash.

In another moment the enraged Mrs. Williams reached the spot.

To snatch up the only whole pie there was left, was to the lady the work of a moment, and to reverse it upon Jack's face, was the work of another moment; and then, in the vindictiveness of her rage, she stamped upon the bottom of the dish until his head was embedded in damsons,* and he was nearly smothered.

From the window of the inn the Bannerworths and the admiral saw all this take place, and the delight of the old man was of the most extravagant character,

exceeding all bounds, while the Bannerworths, for the life of them, could not help laughing most heartily.

"Now, you wretch!" said Mrs. Williams, "I hope this will be a lesson to you. Take that — and that — and that, you sea-snake! you odious tar-barrel!"

As she spoke, she hammered on the dish till it broke, and that was for Jack the best thing that could have happened, for it gave him a little air, and by a frantic effort he scrambled to a sitting posture, and commenced dragging the damsons out of his eyes and mouth. Mrs. Williams then thought it was high time to leave, and so muttering threats, to the immense amusement of a crowd of persons who had assembled, she walked away, leaving Jack by no means delighted with the end of the adventure, and to settle with the infuriated baker as best he might.

It was no small additional mortification to Jack to look up and see the admiral and the Bannerworths at the window of the hotel, enjoying his discomfiture, and laughing most heartily at his expense.

---

* A type of plum.

*"Oh, God! that thing from the grave has been sucking my blood from my veins.
See — see yonder — he moves! Watch him — note him, father!" (see page 866)*

PART III:

The Colonel and his Intended.

CXXVII.

A CHANGE OF SCENE AND CIRCUMSTANCES. — AN EVENT IN LONDON.

THE RECENT EVENTS which followed each other so rapidly, were strangely concluded by the sudden and mysterious disappearance of Sir Francis Varney. That he should thus have eluded all, was aggravating to a very large class of people, who seemed to insist that he should have come to some notable catastrophe.

"Had he only been killed," they argued, "we should have known the last of him."

Of the truth of this there could be no doubt. When a man is dead and buried, you do, as far as human nature serves, know the end of him; but this great fact does not always come within the knowledge of men, who sometimes, contrary to expectation, drop off themselves, and instead of knowing the end of somebody else, why, somebody else knows the end of them.

It is a well known fact, that as some die before others, that it does sometimes happen that those who wish to see another out, may be seen out themselves; besides, taking the question of longevity aside, it does not follow, because we so wish to come to the conclusion of an affair, that its author may but change the scene, and transport it elsewhere, and the good and curious lieges become defrauded of their self-satisfying knowledge, *viz.*, the end of the affair.

Of course it was an aggravation, to know that there was an interesting and highly exciting affair gone off, and they were not allowed to peep into that mystery, the future; but so it was — they were not gratified.

Some were of the opinion that he had departed this life in a mysterious and unsatisfactory, because secret, manner, and that was why nobody could tell anything about it.

But there were other opinions afloat, and among others, that of the admiral, which was pretty general, which was, that he had very likely disappeared from that part of the world to seek in some other place the renovation his system required, by means that were natural to him, but hideous in others to contemplate or think of.

This was generally the received opinion, for it was universally admitted by the wise people thereabouts, that he must at certain times recruit himself.

The opinion thus entertained by all who lived thereabouts, became less and less absorbing; other matters began to be thought of, things began to flow into their usual channel, and a subsidence took place in the turmoil and excitement consequent upon the presence of the vampyre.

About this period, while these parts were regaining their original serenity and calmness, and while the vampyre was looked upon as an awful and fearful episode in the life of those who lived there, there happened in London a circumstance that it is necessary to relate to the reader, inasmuch as it is very important, and bears strongly on our story:

Not far from Bloomsbury-square, which, at the period of our story, was a very fashionable place, and in one of the first streets thereabout, was the house of a widow, whose name was Meredith. She had been the wife of a man in good circumstances, but at his death she was left with a house filled with furniture, some little loose cash, and several daughters, marriageable and unmarriageable, this being all Mr. Meredith had to leave.

There could be but one way of obtaining a living — at least, but one that suggested itself to her, which was to turn lodging-house keeper of the better sort. Her children had been well educated, that is, sufficiently so, to pass off in life, in decent society, without any particular remark.

As she was well calculated for the object she had in view, it was no wonder

that she succeeded in her undertaking, and appeared to do very well.

About this time an arrival occurred at an hotel not very far from this spot, which caused a communication to pass to Mrs. Meredith, who had been recommended lodgers from the hotel, when any of the inmates desired to be accommodated, and wished for a place with all the comforts of a home, and domestic attention.

"Mrs. Meredith," said the head waiter of the hotel, "I wish to have a word in private with you."

"With greatest pleasure, Mr. Jones," said Mrs. Meredith, who was extremely civil to the waiter; "will you be pleased to sit down."

"I have not the time, I thank you — I have not time; but I have run over to you to inform you we have an old invalid colonel at our place, who seems as if he did not know what he wanted; he wants some kind of lodging — he don't like the hotel — whether there is some genteel family, whose kind attentions would soothe his disorders, and, I suppose, his temper."

"Oh, poor gentleman," said Mrs. Meredith; "how unfortunate he should suffer — is he rich?"

"Yes, I believe so — very rich, he's a colonel in the India service; he's been a fine man, but he has had some hard knocks. I have seen more ricketty matters than he before to-day, and he will do very well. I told him I knew where there was a lady who occasionally admitted an inmate to her house, which was a large one, but she must be satisfied that her lodger is a gentleman.

"'Has she any family?' he inquired; 'because I hate to go where there's nobody but the lady of the house, because she can't always attend upon me, read to me, and the like of that.'"

"Goodness me, what an odd man!"

"Yes, but he pays well; a retired colonel — large fortune. You know that these East Indians expect I don't know what; they are even fed by beautiful young black virgins."

"The wretch!"

"Oh, dear, no; it's the custom of the country; so, you see, he's been humoured, and it will be necessary yet to humour him, if you mean to have him for your lodger. I expect he'll only be troublesome; but, when they pay for trouble, why, it's all profit."

"Very true," replied Mrs. Meredith; "is he a single man?"

"Yes, oh, yes; I believe he has never been married; has had so much to do in India, that he had nothing to do with marriages."

"Where does he come from?"

"India. I believe he had a very fine palace of his own, at Puttytherapore, so I'm told. Lord, he seems to think nothing of these parts — but he's an odd man; however, as he pays well, he'll make a good lodger anywhere."

"Well, you may tell him, Mr. Jones, that we have a fine suite of rooms for his accommodation on the first floor, and bed rooms — every attention he can wish. You know our terms, Mr. Jones, I think — but I may as well tell you — five guineas a-week."

"Five guineas a-week, eh?"

"Yes; that is moderate, when you come to consider what a trouble and an expense it will be to get such things as will please the palate of an Indian."

"It is a trouble, certainly."

"And, besides that, he will have such a place and furniture as he seldom meets with in London; besides, from what you say, there will be little trouble in attending to him by myself and daughters, and you know I have several."

"Exactly — exactly; that is the thing he seems to desire; you will, therefore, have a preference over any one else who may have anything that he wants — a kind of domestic hearth; he has none of his own, you see."

"Has he no friends?"

"None living, I dare say; besides, he would hardly like to trust himself along with relations, who would poison him for the sake of his money; and, if he have any living, he may know nothing of them, where they are, or anything else, and they would be as strangers to him, for he would not be able to recognize them — but I must go now. Five guineas — that includes all?"

"Yes; all, except wines and liquors, you know."

"Very well, I'll let him know; and, perhaps, you'll be in the way, in case he should come round this evening to examine the place."

"Do you think there is any chance of his coming in to-night."

"Really, I cannot tell; he may, or may not, just as he pleases — he is an odd fish; but, good Mrs. Meredith, I will talk to him."

The waiter left; and Mrs. Meredith sat in her parlour, which was her own private apartment, which she and her daughters usually retired to and received their own friends. Here they remained, in some degree kept in continual expectation;

nothing was said, for some time, by either mother or daughter, for there was but one at home at that time.

"Do you know, Margaret," she said, "we are likely to have a new lodger?"

"Indeed, ma?"

"Yes, my dear; he is a fidgetty old man, a colonel from India; he is vastly rich, I am given to understand, and will require all the attentions of a relative. He will pay very handsomely; in fact, my dear, he will keep us all with a little care and management."

"Well, ma, the men ought to do so, the creatures!—what are they for, if they don't. I'm sure, if ever I come to marry, which I am sure I sha'n't, and if I found that he didn't find me in all I wanted, wouldn't I lead him a life!—I rather think I would," said the amiable child; "I'd never let him know peace night nor day. It would be useless for him to tell me misfortune had deprived him of means; that would do for me. Oh, dear, no; a married man has no right to meet misfortunes; indeed, he deserves to be punished for having a wife at all under such circumstances."

"A very proper spirit, my dear; but you must never let such a thing as that pass your lips, because it would be very likely to cause you to lose a chance; the men are so fastidious now a-days, and they think they win us, when we angle for, and catch, *them*."

"And this lodger, ma?"

"Oh, he's, as I told you, a rich old East Indian."

At this moment, a coach drove up to the door, and a tremendous double rap was played off upon the door, as if it had been committed by a steam-engine; so loud and so long was the application for the admittance, that both mother and daughter started.

"Dear me, that must be him," said the mother; "yes, a coach and all—there—there, I declare."

"What, ma?"

"Why, look at that girl next door out in the balcony; there's Miss Smith—that girl is always trying to attract some person or other; and the men affect to believe that she is beautiful; for my part, I think a girl of seventeen ought to have more modesty."

"The hussy!" said the young lady, contemptuously.

The servant now entered to inform her that a gentleman had called about the apartments.

"Ask him up stairs," said Mrs. Meredith; and she prepared to follow the colonel so soon as she heard he was ascending the stairs, which was a slow job to him, as he walked lame, with a gold headed cane.

When Mrs. Meredith came to the room, she saw a tall gentleman; his height was lost, on account of him stooping; he wore a green shade over one eye, and he had one arm in a sling; besides which, as we have before related, he was rather lame.

"Not so bad as I thought for," muttered Mrs. Meredith, to herself, as she curtseyed to his salute.

"I have been recommended to seek here a lodging, ma'am. I do not know if I am correct in believing you have such as I want."

"This, sir, is the sitting-room; it is a very handsome one, and above what is usually offered at a lodging-house. The fact is, sir, the house was never furnished for letting, but for our own private occupation; therefore, it has all of the comforts of a private residence."

"That is what I chiefly want. You see, I do not care to undertake the trouble of setting up an establishment myself. I am alone, I may say; therefore it is I seek such a lodging as comes nearest to what I should myself choose if I were to make a home of my own."

"Precisely, sir. There is the back drawing-room, and a bed room up-stairs."

"Oh, very good; I need, I presume, make no inquiry as to what kind of table you keep; the best, I dare say. I was informed of the price you asked."

"Yes; we consider that quite moderate, sir."

"I dare say," said the Indian, looking about the place with an air of curiosity; "I dare say."

"Yes, sir; you see the advantages we offer are much above the usual run. Besides, you are an invalid, and will require extra attention."

"Yes; there is much truth in that; I have got used to it, and therefore you will see that I bargain for it; but, at the same time, you will not find me difficult to please, I flatter myself; but we shall know more of each other the longer we are together."

"Certainly, sir. I can assure you, that should you take the apartments, nothing on my part, or my daughters', will be wanting to make your stay agreeable."

The stranger examined the appearance of the room, and the others, and then, after much conversation with them, he agreed to take the lodgings, and to come into them on the morrow, as he was extremely particular as to well-aired beds,

and should require them all to be re-aired.

"And now, madam, before I finally agree to come in, will you show me the means of escape, if any, in case of fire. I am anxious about that; I have read so many calamities arising from that cause of late in London that I am somewhat nervous about it, though I am so much of an invalid that I should hardly be able to avail myself of it."

"You shall see, sir," said Mrs. Meredith; "we have ample and safe accommodation in that respect. You see, here is a pair of broad steps that lead up to that door — a trap-door; and here is another, that opens upon the leads at the top of the house."

The colonel made shift to walk up, and to look over the house-tops; there was a sea of chimneys and pantiles, at the same time they were all easy of access on this side of the street; so there was no danger from fire, and each house there was similarly provided.

"Well, madam, I think I may say that this affair is concluded. I will leave you my card, and, if you think proper, you can obtain what information you desire of me at the hotel."

"I am quite satisfied, sir," said the landlady, as she took the card that was proffered her, and also a bank-note which he offered her, in token of his taking possession of the lodgings.

Mrs. Meredith curtseyed, and the colonel left the apartment, and descended the staircase with great deliberation, for he could not go very swiftly; he was lame, and one arm was up in a sling, and therefore he had not the free use of his limbs.

As he came down the stairs, and when near the mat, Margaret, the eldest daughter, came out and passed into the back parlour, for no other ostensible purpose than that of seeing the stranger, whose eye was instantly, but only momentarily, fixed upon her; but it was enough; they both saw each other, and had a glance at the features, and Margaret disappeared.

The stranger stepped into the coach, and, as the door was being shut, he looked up to the windows of the next house, where the young lady, nothing daunted, still sat at the window; and so little was she interested with her neighbour's affairs, that she barely bestowed a momentary glance upon the coach or its occupant, whose solitary optic took notice of her, and then the Jehu* drove away with his rumbling vehicle.

"Well, I never saw such impudence, in my life!" said Mrs. Meredith, as she came to the parlour-windows, which happened to bow outwards, and gave her a better opportunity of watching her neighbours to the right and left of her.

"What is the matter, ma'?" inquired her daughter.

"Why, there's that minx still up yonder. I declare if she didn't stare at the colonel; he saw her, and noticed her, too. Well, I wouldn't have had her there to-day for a trifle; he will think he has got into a bad neighbourhood, seeing her so bold.† Really, now, she lays herself open to all kinds of imputations. I do not mean to say any evil of her; but, really, if she will do that now, what will she not do

bye-and-bye? I am sorry she has no one to advise her better."

"I am sure she is old enough to know better," rejoined the daughter. "I am quite sure she's no beauty, and, if she wants to catch any of the men, she won't be successful in that manner; unless, indeed, she doesn't care whom she picks up with."

"Oh, that is, I fear, too often the case with young girls with weak intellects. But did you see our new lodger, my dear?"

"Yes, ma'."

"And what did you think of him?" inquired Mrs. Meredith, with an amiable whine, and a gentle rubbing of hands.

"Think, ma', think — what can I think of a man whom I have hardly seen, ma'? He only passed me; I could not recollect him again if I tried."

"Ah, well, my dear, you know best. I can always recollect people whom I have once seen? He is a very fine man — at least, he has been; he has lost much of his height, for he is lame, and stoops much; but still he has been a handsome man."

"One eye, only, ma', I think."

"Yes, my dear, one eye, as you say; but I think a remarkably keen one, too. He's quite the gentleman, too; he's been used to command, you can see that. These military men have an air about them that you cannot mistake; and even this gentleman, though, you see, wounded and lame, yet he has the air of an officer about him."

"He may have, ma'; but, you know, if he have the air of a general, with nothing else, it would buy a very poor dinner."

"So it would, my dear. You certainly are an extraordinary girl, Margaret, a very extraordinary girl, and will be the making of your family. Only suppose you should marry this rich colonel, what then, eh? I

---

* *"Jehu," a reference to a ninth-century-BC king of Israel chronicled in the Bible, was 18th-century slang for a coachman, especially a reckless one.*

† *Meaning a neighborhood in which prostitutes live and work.*

only say, suppose you were to marry him? — because it isn't certain, yet — well, wouldn't that minx next door think you were lucky? She would bite her nails in anger."

"Yes, she would, ma'; but it may never happen. But, if she thinks to get a beau that way, she's much mistaken. I am sure she will get insulted."

"No wonder. But, Margaret, my dear, you must do your best to please this gentleman; he wants to have people about him just as if he had his own home. He has no friends or relatives; who knows what may happen yet?"

"No, ma'; we don't know what may happen, and I will do my best to please him; but I sha'n't court him, you know, ma'; he must do that."

"Yes, certainly, my child, he must. No; you mustn't appear anxious about it; but merely say you are pleased to have his good opinion, and you must be a little coy of everything else; for there are times when such old gentlemen are easily entrapped. But I must set about having things aired and put into order for his arrival to-morrow."

CXXVIII.

THE NEW LODGER. — A NIGHT ALARM. — A MYSTERIOUS CIRCUMSTANCE.

IT WAS NOT UNTIL LATE the next day that Mrs. Meredith heard anything of her new lodger. All she had heard was that he would be there during the day, but whether to breakfast, dinner, or tea, she could not tell which, and now she was waiting with expectation, if not anxiety; but, at the same time, she knew she was quite sure of her lodger, because she held his bank-note.

It had been a dull day; there are many such in London, and therefore that was no singular circumstance. It was one of those dull, leaden-coloured days of which you can predict nothing with certainty, or even a chance of being right; it was rather squally at times, and at others a west wind blew; not cold — at least, not particularly so; but, yet, notwithstanding the heavy appearance of the sky, there was a clear white light that made every object look more disagreeable than ordinary.

The landlady and her daughter were both on the *qui vive*, as it is called, looking out for their new lodger, whom they expected the more immediately as the evening drew on, for there was less likelihood of his coming in the middle of the day than towards the evening, and less after evening had set in than before, for he was an invalid.

It was, they thought, just about the time when he must arrive, when there could only be the uncertainty of a few minutes. The whole house was in order; nothing was left to chance; Mrs. Meredith herself had gone over the whole place, and took especial pains to find all sorts of fault with the unfortunate drudge who did the work, of course, aided by the mother and daughter; but such aid was distressing, because she had to wait upon both, and do her own work as well.

However, all was in readiness, and they were looking out at every coach from between the blinds. The sound of wheels was enough to cause them to start, when suddenly a coach drove up to the door, upon which had been carefully packed several leather boxes and portmanteaus.

"Here he is," said the daughter; "here he is."

"Yes; and, as I am alive," said Mrs. Meredith, as she cast her eye upwards towards the next house, "as I am alive, there is that girl again. I do believe that she does it on purpose. It is done to aggravate me, and to attract attention from the men. The hussy!"

There was now no time to lose, the knocker at the door giving pretty clear indication that instant attention upon their part was requisite, and up jumped Mrs. Meredith and her daughter Margaret. Immediately the servant opened the door into the passage, the coach door was opened, the steps let clattering down, and Colonel Deverill entered the house.

"Will you walk into the parlour, colonel," inquired Mrs. Meredith, "until your boxes are all in, and you see they are all correct? There is a good fire."

"Thank you, madam," said the colonel, with some difficulty walking along. "I am scarcely so well able to walk as I was yesterday."

"Ah! colonel, you must have suffered much. But I am glad the parlour is so handy — it will save you the walk up stairs at present, until you are quite recovered from your fatigue. Pray be seated, colonel, by the fire. The man shall bring them in, and lay them before the door."

"Thank you," said the colonel, and he sat down in a large easy chair, having first dropped his cloak, which was a large blue military cloak, lined with white, with a fur collar, and looked extremely rich and handsome; beneath which he wore an officer's undress frock, covered over with a profusion of braid.

The boxes and portmanteaus were brought in and laid down so that the colonel could see them; and, when that was done, the coachman made his demand, which excited an exclamation of horror from Mrs. Meredith, and a declaration that she thought hackney coachmen were the greatest impostors and extortioners under the sun. There never was such a set as hackney coachmen — never!

"Saving lodging-house keepers, ma'am — axing your pardon for saying so. Not that I means any offence, only I lived in one once, and ought to know summat."

The colonel, however, made no remark, but, pulling out an embroidered purse, which appeared to full of gold, he paid the man his demand.

"Thank you, your honour; you are one of the right sort, and no mistake." So saying, the coachman walked away, jinking the money as he walked along the passage, until he came to the door where the girl was standing, and then, giving her a knowing wink, and jerking his head backwards, he said, —

"They are a scaley lot here, ain't they, Mary?"

"Mary!" screamed Margaret.

"Yes, miss."

"Shut the door, and come away form that insolent fellow."

Slam went the door, and then the

servant went down stairs, and the parlour-door was immediately closed, and the colonel was given into the tender mercies of the lodging-house keeper; for, though she pretended that she merely offered a genteel and presentable house for such as desired it, and could afford to pay for it, she was, in every sense of the word, a lodging-house keeper.

The colonel, however, sat very composedly in his chair, and gazed at the fire in silence; and from time to time he gazed at the mother and daughter with his one eye; he had not lost the entire use of the other, but had a green silk shade over it. He watched what went on, and replied cautiously to what was said to him, but appeared inclined to silence, and occasionally abrupt in his conversation; but this they attributed to the habit he must have been in, when abroad, of commanding.

"Will you take tea at once, colonel, or at what hour do you choose to have it?"

"I will take it at once. I am tired."

"What will you take, sir?" inquired Margaret, at one end of the table; and, placing herself in an enticing posture, she awaited the answer, expecting to be looked at.

"Coffee," said the colonel, abruptly.

There was a pause; but Margaret said nothing more, and set about doing such little matters as appeared to be an employment. But it was a mere deception — it was all done; nothing had been left undone; they had taken care of that, as the servant knew full well.

However, there was little that passed of any peculiar character on that occasion, for the evening passed off very calmly and comfortable, the colonel giving his opinion somewhat dogmatically; but that, of course, was submitted to, as he was a military man and had much experience, and, moreover, he was a rich man — quite a nabob.

It is astonishing, as a general rule, what people will submit to when it comes from those who have riches at command. That fact alone seems to stamp all that is foolish and absurd, coming from such a quarter, with sense and worth.

It is in vain for any one not blessed with property to talk; his talking is nothing in comparison with what falls from the lips of the man who has property. You are talked down, and if you are obstinate, and won't be talked down, why, you are a disagreeable fellow, a dissatisfied man, and your neighbours ought to set their faces against you.

Thus, through life, he who does not submit to the wealthy, is always run down, and there is every disposition, if possible, of running him off the road altogether, no matter how great the injustice against him, and the enormity of the conduct of others; they are, as they think, justified, because he is not a genteel person; in fact, he is not evangelical.

The evening passed over, as we have said, in calmness and quiet, and Mrs. Meredith appeared to be well pleased with her lodger; and, at a moderately early hour, they separated and went to bed. The colonel retired, after taking leave of them, to his own room, complaining he was in great pain, and scarce able to walk, and so cold, he was nearly benumbed.

"This climate," he said, "is so cold, so moist, and altogether so uncomfortable, that I cannot understand how it is people ever endure it. Indeed," he continued to

Mrs. Meredith, "there must be some great difference between rich and poor in their conformation, else they couldn't stand it."

Of course, Mrs. Meredith assented to the proposition, as she would have done to any other, no matter what proposition, that had been so urged by such a person.

Thus it was with the colonel, who appeared very well satisfied with his lodgings; and all parties, for so short a time, were well pleased with each other.

The night was dark, that is to say, it was one of those nights in which neither moon nor stars showed themselves; no sound was heard through the streets, save the heavy step of the guardian of the night, or the midnight reveller, who might be finding his way homeward boisterously, and with scarce enough sense to enable him to take the right path.

There were clouds enough to have intercepted the moon, but there was a kind of light that was spread through them that you saw when you looked up, but which aided not the traveller below; but, then, there were countless lamps that illumined the streets.

At that time there was a man creeping over the house-tops. He had gained the housetop of Mr. Smith, the house in which resided Miss Smith, who had given so much offence to Mrs. Meredith by sitting so much out in the balcony. He stooped in the gutter, and looked cautiously around; no human being was within sight; he was alone, and no soul saw him.

Cautiously he crept towards the trap-door — it was bolted; but that was soon obviated — no sound, however, could be heard. The soft, but rotten, wood gave way under the steady pressure exerted upon the door, which at length opened.

He paused a moment or two, and listened carefully for several minutes. Then he entered the loft slowly and noiselessly, keeping as low as possible, so that he might run no risk of being observed by any one who might be passing the house, or who might be up by accident in any of the opposite houses, in consequence of illness, or any other cause.

There was a lower trap-door through which the figure passed. There could be no difficulty in passing, because that was always kept open, as it was considered to assist in ventilating the house; and then the intruder stood within the house.

He then drew himself up to his full height, and paused for some moments, as if considering the next step he would take; but then he descended to the second floor, on which were placed what are called the best bedrooms. He paused at one, gently tried the handle, and finding it turn, and the door open, he gave one look towards the stairs that he had just descended, and then he entered the apartment.

All was yet still; no sound met his ear, save the breathing of the sleeper within, who lay in a sweet sleep, and was as calm and unconscious as the blessed; perfect rest and forgetfulness had steeped the senses of the young girl, who lay in ambrosial sleep. One arm was thrown outside the clothes, and revealed, in all its symmetry, a snow-white bosom, heaving gently to the throbbing of the heart.

The intruder gazed at the young girl for some moments, and clasped his hands with trembling eagerness, and a ghastly smile played upon his terrible features, while a fearful fire shot from the eyes of one who thus disturbed the slumbers of the living.

He approached the bed, and took the hand within his own, and then the sleeper awoke.

It would be impossible to describe the look of terror and horror that sat on the young girl's face.

She could not scream, she could not utter a sound; her whole faculties appeared to have been bound up for a short time. She could not even shrink from the horrible being who approached her, she was so perfectly horror-stricken with that truly horrible countenance, the glance of which seemed as if it would destroy the power of speech for ever. She shrank now, but could not move.

The creature crept closer. It seized her hand, and held it within its own; but even that could not awake her from the trance she was in. She felt a horrible sinking feeling, as though she must sink through the very flooring of the house, and yet she could not stir.

It appeared as though, so long as the hideous face was opposed to hers, so long she was unable to move; it was a species of fascination; however great the horror felt, yet there was no help for it. She could not ever shut her eyes; that boon was denied her.

What she saw cannot be described. It is by far too horrible for pen to describe. The wild horrible insanity that appeared in the eyes of the creature, with their peculiar cast, was indescribable; the only light that entered the room, at that moment, came from a lamp below, and illumined only the upper part of the room above the window sills.

The creature then stood in relief against this light, a horrible dark object, whose glaring eyeballs were too terrible ever to be forgotten.

Then, again, while he with one hand held hers, he passed his other hand up her arm, and then felt along the soft, white flesh with its cold, clammy fingers, as if it were feeling for something, or greedy of the velvet-like substance.

Still keeping the eyes fixed upon the hapless and helpless girl, he drew the arm towards him, and, leaning upon the bed, suddenly plunged his face on the arm, and held and seized it near the middle with its teeth, and then it made an attempt to suck the wound.

This, however, broke the charm, horrible and complete as it was; for the creature's hideous countenance was lost to her sight, as he plunged his face to her arm.

Shriek followed shriek in quick and rapid succession. The whole house was alarmed by the terrible shrieks that came from the apartment. She struggled, and by a sudden effort, she disengaged herself from the grasp of the fiend, and rolled, wrapped up in the bed-clothes, to the other side of the floor.

The monster still pursued her with greedy thirst for blood, and had picked her up, and again placed her on the bed, with more than mere human strength, and again sought the arm he had been deprived of by the sudden effort of the young girl.

"Help! help! Mother! father! help! help!"

The shouts rang through the house,

awaking the affrighted sleepers from their repose, in a manner that may be called distressing.

It is distressing in the midst of a large city to be awoke, in the dead of the night, by loud and urgent cries of distress. It is such a contrast to the dead stillness that reigns around, and when the first cries are heard, it creates a terror and surprise that takes away all power of action.

It was not till the cries had been heard a second time that the inmates aroused themselves; the fact was, they were fearful of fire. The moment that idea floated across their minds, then, indeed, they started up, and the father of the young girl, hearing the fall, at once rushed to the room of his daughter. He arrived but in time; the hideous monster, being affrighted by the footsteps approaching him, turned from his blood-stained feast, and hid himself beneath the drapery, as the father entered the room.

"Mary," he said, "Mary! Mary! what means this — what can be the matter — are you hurt — how come you in this disorder?"

"Oh, God! that thing from the grave has been sucking my blood from my veins. See — see yonder — he moves! Watch him — note him, father!"

Believing she raved, her father paid no attention to what she did say, but continued to regard her with sorrow and regret, for he believed it to be a sudden attack of mania; but seeing the curtains move, he turned his head, and at once divined it to be the cause of his daughter's alarm.

The glance was but momentary; but he saw the figure of a man who was escaping from the apartment by the door by which he had at that moment entered.

"Help!" he shouted — "help — thieves — murder!"

And as he shouted, he rushed after the figure that was flying towards the top of the house. By this time the house was filled up with people, and the noise up stairs had caused the servants below to rise confused and thoroughly terrifed by the sounds they heard, and the cries of their master.

At that moment, one of those watchful guardians of the night passed by the house, and was immediately hailed by the unfortunate people below, who were afraid to go up stairs to offer any assistance, lest they might be knocked back again, which fear stopped all aid from below.

"Hilloa! what's the matter now?" inquired the worthy guardian of the night.

"Oh, I don't know — goodness knows. You had better go up and see. I'll come up after you. Don't be afraid; I'll come up after you, if you'll go first."

"Stop a moment while I spring my rattle," said the worthy functionary; who thereupon gave an alarming peal upon his instrument, and then he entered the house, with instructions to the servant to run down stairs and let any of his party in that might come up.

Then the guardian of the night hastened up stairs with all the haste he could, and came up just in time to pick Mr. Smith up, who was lying stunned at the foot of the stairs.

The fact was, Mr. Smith had pursued his adversary too quickly, and finding he could not get off, he turned round and felled him to the earth, like an ox. It was just at this juncture when the charley

came up stairs, and in another moment Mr. Smith recovered.

"What's the matter?" inquired the watchman; "is the house on fire."

"No, no; the vampyre — the vampyre!"

"Eh — what? Never heard on 'im afore — never seed him."

"Quick — quick! he has gone up stairs. Quick — after him!" said Mr. Smith, as he ran up the stairs, and was quickly followed by the watchman and some others who now crowded about, having had time to dress themselves and come to Mr. Smith's aid; and they now crowded to the house-top, for they saw the trap-door was unfastened, though it had been hastily pushed to. This they opened, and then looked on the house-top, first one way, and then another.

"He ain't here," said the watchman, "and we mustn't expect to find him here; he wouldn't wait for us, you may depend upon that. We had better search along the house-tops till we see him, or find some of the other traps open, and then you may guess where he has gone."

"The difficulty is, which way did he go?" said Mr. Smith.

"Oh, I saw him go that way," said another watchman, who came up stairs, having been first attracted by the sounds of the rattle, and then, looking up at the house, he saw the figure of a man stealing, with great rapidity of motion, across the house-tops.

"There I lost him, then," he said. "I didn't see him after that spot; but he may have gone further, for all I can say to the contrary. But we shall soon see."

"This trap-door is open," said the other watchman, as he pulled aside Mrs. Meredith's trap-door, which had only been pushed to. "We had better go in here, and see if he isn't gone somewhere into the house, and hiding himself until all is quiet, and then he will make off if left alone."

CXXIX.

THE UNSUCCESSFUL PURSUIT. — MR. SMITH'S DISAPPOINTMENT, AND THE TESTIMONY OF MRS. MEREDITH.

MRS. MEREDITH AND her daughters had long sunk into deep sleep before the events just narrated took place in her neighbour's house. There was a perfect stillness; the whole house appeared as though there were no living soul within it, all was so still and quiet.

Presently, however, there was a terrific sound; it was like that of a human being falling and bumping down stairs, and then there was a great deal of shouting and calling, and Mrs. Meredith opened her eyes and trembled in her bed, while her daughter Margaret, who upon the occasion slept with her, was likewise as frightened.

"What is th — that?" she stammered, with some difficulty.

"Oh, hear, I cannot think. Thieves — murderers, I dare say. Oh, merciful Heaven! what shall we do — where shall I go? We shall be murdered!"

Both females trembled in their beds, and were quite unable to move, breaking out in a profuse sweat from fear; and yet the noise came nearer and nearer, and there were many persons evidently in the house; their numbers were so numerous that they evidently didn't care to conceal themselves.

The fact was this: when Mr. Smith and his party found the trap-door open, they descended into the house, the watchman leading the way; but in going down the ladder, his foot slipped, and he came with a dreadful thump on the landing, and fortunately he rolled up against the servant girl's door, instead of down stairs. The door flew open, and the girl was too terrified to speak for some moments.

At length the watchman having got up, he made for the bed, upon which the girl jumped up, and began to scream out for help in piteous tones.

"Come, come — don't be frightened," said the watchman; "get up and show us over the house."

"Well, I'm sure!" said the girl, who had recovered some of her assurance, for the coat, stick, and lantern of the watchman at once assured her that she was in no immediate danger whatever. "Well, I'm sure! to think of coming in a female's room in this manner. You ought to be ashamed of yourself, you old wretch, you ought!"

"No names. If you don't get up and show us over, and call your master — "

"I ain't got a master."

"Well, your mistress, then — we will go ourselves, and we'll soon make short work of it. Come, come, no nonsense. We will dress you ourselves."

"You monster! Go out of the room, can't you? Have you no decency left you? I'll get up; but I'll lay a complaint before the lord mayor, and he shall tell you a different tale to this. I'm ashamed of you, and so you ought to be of yourselves."

However, during this energetic remonstrance, she contrived to shuffle on some things, and when she was ready, she came down to her mistress's door, and then began to hammer and kick at it, saying, —

"Oh, Mrs. Meredith, here's sich a lot of men in the house. Do come out, mem. I don't know what's the matter; but they'll break into your room, as they broke into mine."

"What do they want, Mary?"

"Don't know, mem."

"There is some one escaped into your house that has broken into the next house, and your trap-doors on the roof were open."

"Gracious me!" said Mrs. Meredith — "gracious me! Show them over the place, Mary. We will get up in a few moments, and come to you. Margaret, my dear, get up; some housebreakers have got into the house, and we shall all be murdered in our sleep if we don't find them. Oh, dear, dear! what will become of us? What will our new lodger say to this disturbance?"

Margaret made no reply, but began to dress herself, while the party began their search; and Mr. Smith hastened back to his daughter, to understand the nature of the attack that had been made upon her, and whether she were any better than she was when he left her.

However, when he came to hear what was the real cause of her terror, to find the marks on her arm, and the certainty that nothing had been lost or moved, he was perfectly staggered, and hastened back after the party he had left, to make some further attempt to follow the miscreant, and to discover, if possible, his retreat, and bring him to justice for the vile attack he had made.

When he returned, he met Mrs. Meredith coming out of her room, she having hastily dressed herself, followed by her daughter.

"Oh! Mr. Smith—Mr. Smith, what is the meaning of all this disturbance? Here are a number of strange men, who have forced themselves into my house, and whether their object is our property or our lives, we cannot tell. What can I do, Mr. Smith?"

"You have nothing to fear, ma'am."

"Nothing to fear, sir! Why, is not such an occurrence something to be feared for its own sake alone?"

"Yes, ma'am, it is very disagreeable, I am willing to admit; but I presume you would not give refuge to a vampyre?"

"A what, sir?"

"A vampyre, madam. I know not how to explain it to you, but I have to assure you my daughter has been attacked in her sleep by the midnight blood-sucker from the graves. Oh! God, that such a thing should happen in my family. I would not have believed it, had the same been related to me from anybody else."

"It must have been the night-mare," suggested Mrs. Meredith.

"Would to Heaven it had been so; but I came to her assistance, and saw him as he fled from my daughter's bedside, and I followed him to the roof, and he was lost on your house, and your trap-door was open, and we presumed he went in here."

"The door was bolted when we went to bed last night," said Margaret.

"Yes," responded her mother; "we always have that bolted every night, for it is our only protection from that side of the house; but no one can be here; we have no man in the house save our lodger, and invalid and quite a gentleman."

"Can we see him?"

"I should think not, because he is an invalid; he's a colonel in the East India service, and will, no doubt, be very angry at such a disturbance, and much more so when he finds he is wanted. I am really much shocked at this disturbance, which is the more unfortunate as it is the first night he has slept here."

"I must see him."

"Must, Mr. Smith—must! I cannot permit anything of the kind to be said in my house. I give you permission to look for him over the house, but I can't give any such permission with what my lodgers possess—it is not in my power to do so if I had the inclination."

While this was going on, the house had been rummaged over and over, and then a party of them, with Mr. Smith, came to the colonel's bedroom; a close travelling cap and a dressing-gown were found on the mat before the door.

"Oh!" said Mr. Smith, as he picked it up, "this appears very much like what I saw the figure was dressed up in—something like robes, and this would serve the purpose."

"Ah!" said the watchman, "we shall have him now."

"But the gentleman is an invalid; he can hardly walk up stairs, much less can he be scrambling over house-tops," said Mrs. Meredith. "You must surely all have been dreaming. Something has disagreed with you, and the result has been visions of which you can of course find no trace."

"Not quite that, either," said one of the watchmen, "for we saw him getting away, and he made for your trap-door, where I missed him. I could not see any more of him among the chimneys, or something of that sort, but I thought he came in here, and found your door open."

"And you saw him come in?" said Mrs. Meredith.

"I can't say I saw him come in," said the man; "I couldn't see through a brick-wall and a stack of chimneys which were in the way, but I felt certain he must have come in here."

"Well, this is very strange — very singular."

"The dressing-gown, too," said Mr. Smith, "is dusty and dirty all over — at least in places where it appears to have come in contact with anything dirty — possibly the roof of the house; certainly something of that sort has happened. It looks very much like it."

"And the cap sits close to the head; that is dirty."

"But it is dry dirt," said Mr. Smith, "and of the same character; we had better see this lodger of yours, Mrs. Meredith, and with your permission I will knock."

As Mr. Smith spoke he gave two or three loud knocks at the door, which were not answered for some time. But they were speedily repeated, and then a peremptory voice exclaimed, —

"In the name of goodness, what is the meaning of all this disturbance? Is the house broken into, or is it a resort for thieves? Be it as it may, if I am disturbed in this way, and you don't instantly get out of the way and make less noise, I'll fire through the door. I have loaded pistols by my side, and I will not submit to this shameful disturbance."

A the sound of these words, the two watchmen were much disturbed, and immediately stepped back so hastily as nearly to overthrow Mrs. Meredith and her daughter; but Mr. Smith, after a step or two backwards, resumed his place by the door, and exclaimed, — "I have not come here, sir, to be frightened; some strange circumstances have just happened, and I must beg you'll open your door to explain them."

"And who the devil are you?"

"My name is Smith, sir. I live next door, and my daughter has been attacked by a vampyre. I know not what nature the creature must possess, but it has shocking propensities — there are evidences at your door which make it appear he has got into your room."

"It would be very foolish in him to so anything of the sort," said the colonel, "for, in the first place, I will not suffer annoyance in any shape; and besides, I have loaded pistols for his reception. Wait till I am dressed, and then I will come out to you."

"I am sure the colonel will be very much offended by this conduct, which is very shameful; people's houses broken open and entered in this manner, and peoples's rest broken so. I am quite ashamed of my neighbours — quite."

"Really we have strong suspicions — strong grounds of suspicion, too, against that lodger of yours; look at that dressing-gown and cap, the open trap-door, and all — really I can't help thinking there is something very suspicious in all this."

"Yes, said the watchman; "I know there's nobody else in the house. I've been all over it, and it's very strange to me if he ain't the man."

"Well," said Margaret Meredith, "it seems as if you are most willing to accuse those who are quite incapable of doing what you accuse them of. This gentleman was barely able to get up stairs without assistance; besides, he could not have gone up stairs without some one being awoke by the noise. It's my opinion that it is a piece of impertinence altogether."

"So I think, my dear," said Mrs. Meredith.

"I am a father, Mrs. Meredith," said Mr. Smith, "and I have my daughter's safety and happiness at heart. I am sure there's much, too, very suspicious. You wouldn't like your daughter's blood sucked out of her arms. I am sure I don't, nor does she."

"Oh, botheration!" said Margaret; "who ever heard of such stuff? I'm sure I never did, except in some book of improbabilities, and nothing more; but here is Colonel Deverill."

At that moment Colonel Deverill opened the door, and then retired a little into his room, saying as he did so, in a very angry voice, but, at the same time, endeavouring to be courteous,—

"You can come in, now; but I am quite at a loss to understand the nature of this disturbance; the house don't appear to be on fire; and that is the only contingency in my mind that will justify such a disturbance. What is the matter, Mrs. Meredith?"

"I can hardly tell you, sir. I have been disturbed by finding a party of people in my house; it is most amazing to me how they came in."

"I will tell you, sir," said Mr. Smith. "My daughter has been terrified by the appearance of some one in her bed-room, who attempted to suck her blood from the veins of her arm. I don't know what to say about it."

"I am sure I don't," said Colonel Deverill; "but I must say it's a most unpleasant affair for those who have nothing to do with it. It is a pity your

domestic afflictions should call you out in this manner; take my advice, sir; go home, else you'll catch cold."

"You may repent making a jest of this—"

"I never repent anything, sir. I regret I am so unnecessarily disturbed; and it appears to me, your intrusion here is most unwarrantable."

"Is this your dressing-gown, sir?"

"Yes, it is."

"Well, then, how did it come here, and in this state?" inquired Mr. Smith, triumphantly.

"I don't know—I didn't put it there; but I suppose it must have fallen accidentally; it would not have been thrown there willingly," said the colonel, deliberately.

"Well, I don't know," said Mr. Smith, "but it strikes me you've been on the tiles this evening."

"My good sir, if you don't leave my apartment, it may happen I may forget my pains and lameness, and fling you out of the window. If this had happened in India instead of here, you would have had a particularly sharp knife inserted between your ribs, or have been thrown into a well. But I know nothing, of this matter, which appears so strange, as to be beyond all reason; neither experience nor common sense at all throw any light upon the matter; be advised, sir, and retire, and allow honest people and invalids to sleep the night out."

Mr. Smith looked very blank, and, unable to comprehend all that had passed, he could not tell what to think; he could not urge the matter further, for he was met by real contempt and perfect self-assurance on the part of the colonel, who moved about the room very lame, while his hand was in a sling, and a green shade was placed over his eyes.

"You see," said Mrs. Meredith, "you must be very entirely mistaken. Colonel Deverill, we are sure, is quite unable to run about over house-tops, even had he the inclination to do so, which is really absurd. It must be at least a great mistake on your part."

"Yes, I am sure, too, Colonel Deverill could not have left the house without our knowing it; indeed, it is a very silly affair, and has been a great nuisance, to say the least of it. I wonder Mr. Smith doesn't know better than to break into peaceable people's houses."

"But I did not do so."

"How came you here, then?"

"I followed some one else; the place was open; and yet you say it was shut at night, and you usually kept it so. How do you account for that?"

"I cannot do so, unless some neglect took place, or else you must have forced it open."

"Oh, no, ma'am," said the watchman; "I can swear Muster Smith didn't do that; it was open, and I found it so, so there's that to be accounted for; and then there's the togs a lying outside here, that's to be accounted for; so, you see, it's a werry suspicious case."

"You are a very stupid fellow," said the colonel, "a very idiot, if you imagine people are to be held responsible because a dressing-gown happens to fall down. I do not know but I shall proceed with this matter myself; it seems to me you have committed a trespass, to say the least of it. I can pledge my word, as a man of honour and a soldier, I have not left my room; indeed, these ladies know I could not do so; and their testimony would be ample in a court of justice, and to a gentleman."

"Yes, that is no more than the truth," said Mrs. Meredith, who was by no means pleased with the disturbance; and because she had no sympathy for the young lady who sat in the balcony to the annoyance of herself and daughter.

"And I can bear witness to the same," said Miss Meredith. "I think it is quite time Mr. Smith returned to his own place, and see what is the matter there; perhaps the person he saw may have passed him, and gone back again into his own house."

Mr. Smith lingered, looked wistfully, as if his doubts were not cleared off; but yet the testimony was so clear and so strong, that he could not dispute it; and, however unwillingly he was compelled to acknowledge, there were some matters that he could not dispute, though he was unable to solve them; and he and those with him returned from their unsatisfactory search.

CXXX.

A BREAKFAST SCENE. — A MATCH-MAKING MOTHER.

THE NEXT DAY THERE was some anxiety on the part of Mrs. Meredith, to ascertain how far her new lodger might have been disturbed by this event; and in what temper of mind he felt upon the occasion. It is usual in all lodgings, to have some little regard to the lodger's comforts for some days, perhaps a week or two, and then things are allowed to take their chance; and if the lodger complains, he gets for an answer, that they take a vast deal of pains to oblige him, and intimate that he is a peculiarly lucky man for having become a lodger at that place; and you would have been worse off if you had gone elsewhere, which, of course, you don't believe, though they tell you so.

It is an old and favourite saying, that a new broom sweeps clean; and, in time, an old one becomes very nearly useless. So it is with lodging-house keepers; the longer you remain, the more inattentive they become, until you get wearied, and are compelled to leave, and then you get some scurvy insolence, and your landlady eventually believes she is an ill-used woman.

But, in the present instance, Mrs. Meredith had other hopes and fears than those of a mere lodging-house keeper. Not that she had formed any plan in her own mind; but she had some floating idea that there was seldom such a chance turned up, because the colonel had evidently no relations; and who could tell

what, in the chapter of accidents, might happen?

"I am quite grieved," she said to her daughter, "it should have happened this night. What could be the meaning of the disturbance, I can't think. Now, it's very tiresome things will happen so cross as this, that I don't know what to think of it."

"It really appears as if it was done on purpose."

"It does; but I am sorry for it, because it would seem as though we were liable to some kind of interruption at all times, for they generally expect attention at the first, if at no other time; and he may think this is a bad beginning, at all events."

"But we shall convince him that we shall not treat him neglectfully, ma'."

"No, my dear; but these Indians are strange-tempered people, and when they once take a fancy, there is no knowing what they may do; and there is no knowing what a dislike taken at such an occurrence might produce, and likes and dislikes are taken without rhyme or reason."

"Yes, ma', so they are; and that is the reason why you took such a dislike to young Willis, for he was as nice a young man as I have seen."

"Nice, my dear — nice! I don't see why he was nice, unless it was because he was presumptuous, and had no money," said the amiable parent.

"He was not rich, ma'—"

"He was positively poor, Margaret," interrupted the mother, "and therefore it was absolutely necessary to discourage such persons; for, if they do no good, they are sure to be productive of mischief; for their hanging about, you know, deters others from coming forward who have means."

"He was very handsome."

"'Handsome is as handsome does,' my dear. You'll find that is a motto through life, that will carry weight at any time. All the good looks in the world would never put a gown on your back, or a sixpence in your purse, recollect; besides, he was not handsome."

"You are prejudiced against the young man. Not that I care anything about him, though he was a very agreeable and nice young man; so it's no use in saying that he wasn't."

"Well, my dear, it doesn't much matter; this is a matter of opinion. What do you think of our colonel? He is a fine man, and a rich one besides."

"He is tall, I admit, but stoops a great deal; is very lame; one eye much worse than the other, and one arm in a sling. Well, I can't see much beauty in all that; much out of repair, you must admit, ma'."

"Yes; Colonel Deverill has seen some service, and his misfortunes are so many points of honour; they are like so many medals which speak of his worth. Besides that, he is a most gentlemanly and pleasant man. I don't know that I ever spoke to a more fascinating man."

"That might be at times; but then that was evidently a constraint upon his natural temper, because he every now and then broke out abruptly about something or other, which proves that he has an abrupt and imperious temper, not to say savage and snappish."

"There you are clearly unjustifiable, my dear Margaret. The colonel, you see, is a military man, and used to command, and therefore it is a very usual occurrence, and not a matter of disposition at all; but what can that matter when you come to consider his wealth?"

"There is certainly room for congratulation there," said Margaret.

"Indeed, my child, there is room for congratulation; and I am convinced there is happiness where there is a fortune, for that will obtain all you want, and, when you obtain all you want, what can you be otherwise than entirely happy? — therefore, riches are happiness."

"Yes; there is much truth in all that, ma'," said Margaret; "and all I hope is, that I might obtain a fortune; then I would make you comfortable, ma'."

"I am sure you would, Margaret. My whole life has been spent in shifts to maintain you and bring you up in a manner that would enable you to become a fortune; which, thanks to my care, example, and precept, you are fully equal to at any moment it may become your lot."

"Yes, ma'; I feel that I was born to command, and the lady of a colonel would not be a bit too high in rank for my ambition or deserts."

"Indeed, it would not, my dear; but now listen to me. You know, my dear, I never plan anything but what is for your benefit. Now, I am given to understand that Colonel Deverill has no relatives at all, and I think hardly any friends, and we can make ourselves quite necessary to him — in fact, perfect friends to him. He will look upon us as his nearest relatives, and he may take a fancy to you, as you

may easily induce him. Old men like flattery, there is no doubt, and that kind of flattery which is called attention. Wait upon him most assiduously, and read to him, and all that kind of thing, my dear."

"Yes; I know, ma'."

"And then, dear, if you mind what you are about, the colonel and all his wealth may be yours before six months are over, or I am no witch."

"Hush! I hear him stirring."

"He's coming down stairs; there he is

in the drawing-room; I hear him over head. Go up stairs, my dear, and inquire when he will choose to have his breakfast."

"Yes, ma'," said the young lady, who betrayed an extraordinary desire to obey her parent, a matter not equally to be said of all young ladies, nor of this one upon many occasions; but, then, this was one that was quite agreeable to her own feelings, which explains the secret.

Colonel Deverill had, indeed, descended, and was seated in the drawing-room, with his feet on the fender and his head leaning on his hand, and his elbow on the table, when Margaret entered. He appeared to be thoughtful and unwell; he had, perhaps, passed a bad night, or the interruption had robbed him of his sleep, which to an invalid was the more severely felt.

"Good morning, colonel," said Margaret, advancing. "I hope the disturbance that so inopportunely took place, did not have the effect of destroying your night's rest."

"Indeed, it did do so to a very great extent," replied the colonel, "though not entirely; but still it makes one very poorly, gives one the headache, and causes a sense of lassitude and fatigue to oppress the body, which, added to the weariness incident to such cases, makes one very uncomfortable."

"I am sorry you have been so discomposed, and so is my ma'. She really is grieved; but you see, sir, it was a matter so entirely beyond any control, that she cannot be blamed for it, though it happened, most unfortunately, at a time when it was least wanted, or most to be avoided."

"True — very true. I can imagine all

that. I am not unjust enough to blame you for it. I could no more help it than you could, and I dare say you were none the better for such a disagreeable disturbance; I am not, I am very certain."

"No, sir, I am not. When would you please to breakfast?"

"As soon as I can have it," replied the colonel.

"You can have it at once."

"Then be pleased to let me have it. I have the use of but one arm entirely; may I beg your aid in making tea for me?"

"With pleasure, sir."

Margaret immediately left the room, and informed her mother of what had passed upon the occasion; and when the breakfast was laid, and all things ready, Margaret Meredith sat down with Colonel Deverill to breakfast. Before, however, they had gone far, he inquired if she had breakfasted.

"No, I have not."

"And your mother — has she breakfasted?"

"No, sir, she has not."

"Then give her my compliments, and I shall be glad to take breakfast in her company too; for I am very poorly this morning, and company is agreeable."

This was soon effected, and in a few minutes more they all sat down, the colonel being duly waited upon by Margaret and her mother; the latter being employed in aiding the former to pay great attention to their host; for they breakfasted at his expense, as a matter of course.

"It was really a most unfortunate occurrence, that of last night," said Mrs. Meredith; "very unfortunate; because some people have a difficulty in sleeping in a strange bed; and when once awake, they cannot easily, if at all, get asleep again, and that I had great fears might have been your case."

"Not precisely," said the colonel; "but the fact is, I have seen so much hard service, that I can sleep anywhere without any effort of mine; but when one has suffered from wounds, the heats of climate, and the terrors of imprisonments in Indian prisons, one's health becomes so shattered, that one's rest is not so good as it ought to be — but that is no one's fault."

"It is a grievous misfortune," said Mrs. Meredith.

"Yes," added Margaret; "and I think there is not enough gratitude in the country towards those who so nobly defend us in our homes; to do which they must not only brave danger and death in the field of battle, but all the evils that spring from climate, insidious diseases, brought on by the exposures and hardships of a soldier's life; and then when they see them return to their own country, with wounds that ought to bring honour, glory, and sure profit, they are omitted and neglected."

The colonel sighed deeply, but said nothing.

"My dear Miss Meredith, will you fetch me my keys? — I left them in the bureau."

"Yes, sir," said the amiable young lady, who arose, and left the room.

"Your daughter is an amiable girl, Mrs. Meredith," said Colonel Deverill. "She reminds me of one who is now dead, and at whose decease I left England for India; the country became insupportable to me at that time, but she now recalls all the feelings and aspirations of youth."

"Ah! she is an amiable and good girl — though I am her mother; yet I must not do her less than justice, because it it is usual to consider it partial or silly of a parent praising her own child; but she does deserve all that can be said of her."

"It is a blessing. There was the same class of beauty, and the same amiable and sensible deportment. Oh, dear! those days are gone by, indeed!"

"Who knows but they may return?"

"It is doubtful; more than doubtful — certain. I am an old man, now, Mrs. Meredith, — an old man. Yes; I have deserved some thanks at the hands of my country; and I am rich — yes, Mrs. Meredith, I am rich — very rich, I believe I may say."

"That is some reward."

"It is. But I cannot recall the past — I am no longer young — I have no young wife by my side — to soothe my pillow — to attend to my wants. No; I am an old man, as I said before, and cannot expect the attention of the young and beautiful."

"But, Colonel Deverill, you are not an old man; and as for your wounds, they are honourable."

"But my shattered constitution —"

"May be mended by care and attention, doubtless; and I am sure, while you are here, you shall want no attention we can possibly bestow."

"I thank you, Mrs. Meredith — I thank you," said the colonel.

"I only regret the disturbance you suffered last night," said Mrs. Meredith. "I am afraid want of proper rest has made you melancholy. I knew not of such a thing, neither was I at all aware of the fact of the trap-door being open — indeed, I can't understand it."

"Nor I, ma'am. I do not clearly understand what they said; they talked of some young lady being strangled or assaulted in her sleep."

"Yes, colonel. It was in her sleep, and I cannot help thinking it must have been a dream; however, if it were not, I do not know what to think of it."

"Nor I," said the colonel, thoughtfully.

"They talked about a vampyre, and said Miss Smith had been seized by the arm; and the creature had attempted to suck the blood from the veins."

"Dear me, what a strange affair."

"Very, sir; but I never heard of such things only in books; but, goodness help us from such strange unearthly beings — have you seen any in your travels, Colonel Deverill? You have travelled in hot countries, and have seen them, I should imagine."

"Not I, Mrs. Meredith; I have seen strange things, but I never saw a vampyre, though I have heard of such things; indeed, there are many disgusting things in creation, and that is one of them. But what could be the reason they should come to that young lady above any other, I cannot conceive."

"Nor I, sir."

At this moment Margaret returned, having recovered the keys, which were not wanted; only the watchful mamma thought there was an opportunity for a little tender gag relative to the amiability of the young lady, and, therefore, it ought not to be omitted.

Moreover, she saw there was no necessity for leaving them alone yet; there would be plenty of time yet for that, and she felt assured there would be ample opportunity for the progress of the suit she now confidently anticipated must take place; for she saw, however prompt and ready the colonel might be from habit, yet there was a good deal of the willing mood about him.

"His health and weakness," she thought, "causes that; and now, while his health lasts this way, he may be secured; or, at least, the foundation laid upon which we may build our hopes. He shall want no aid of mine to help him on that way."

"Have you been long in England, colonel?" she inquired.

"Not very long."

"The voyage homeward must have been very tedious."

"It would have been, but I did not come that way. I crossed into Egypt, and came to the Mediterranean, and thence to Italy; so I varied the scene, and travelled at leisure, and got here a month before the vessel I was to have come by."

"Oh, that was much more pleasant."

"Decidedly so; and then I came to the hotel; not that I had not all proper attention paid me — but then there is no sociality there; men only surround you with whom you can hold no converse whatever."

"Certainly not, they are menials."

"And of the lowest class. However, I sought out such a place as this, where I wished to have some of the domestic comforts around me, that I might have had, had I a home of my own; some one to whom I could speak more seriously; for I am debarred the affectionate regard of near and dear female relatives."

"You must look upon us in that light,

Colonel Deverill; as persons who are anxious and desirous of causing you to forget these wants by our assiduity and attention. I can speak for my daughter as myself; she will do all in her power to render your stay comfortable."

"She is young and beautiful."

"Ahem!"

"And doubtless will change such occupations to those of a more endearing character. Well, it is as it should be, and I am selfish to feel jealous. I wish I was young myself—but, enough of this. I have to express my obligation to you for the ready manner in which you came forward to speak of my being in my room last night, when that man was here and the watchmen."

"Mr. Smith?"

"Yes, that was the man; they would not have taken my word for it; however, I hope to be able to remain here until I find myself sinking to the grave; and those who act as you have began to act for me, I must and will remember at my death and afterwards."

"I do not act with such a motive, Colonel Deverill."

"No, no; I am well aware of that; but that renders it a duty in me. However, we will say no more now; I am even wearied out."

CXXXI.

MRS. MEREDITH'S FRIEND. — EXCHANGE OF SERVICES, AND COMPACT.

THERE COULD BE NO doubt in the minds of both mother and daughter that there was something much resembling a moral certainty concerning the fate of the retired colonel. That he must marry was evident—he was to all intents and purposes resolved to do so. He talked of a home and domestic comfort, and all that kind of thing; therefore it would be easy to entangle him in the meshes of love; the snares of passion might be successfully set, and they would be sure to be productive of some sport, and even a stray colonel might be caught, one who, having had enough of the wars of Mars, might now be considered to become a fair object of attack in those of Venus.

However, there appeared much in the colonel's circumstances and disposition that laid him open to the attacks of designing matrons and maidens. He seemed to appreciate female company—was particularly well pleased with female attentions; perhaps his health required their aid more than that of any other; and he had evidently been in love, and lost the object of his earliest affections.

One great thing in Margaret Meredith's favour was, the colonel had taken it into his head that she much resembled this lady, whoever she was; and this fact, no doubt, had opened his heart towards her; and he felt a kindly, and perhaps a warmer feeling, towards her. This, they calculated, would greatly assist them in their efforts to circumvent the colonel, and cause him to capitulate upon matrimonial conditions.

"There never was so good a chance," said Mrs. Meredith, in the course of a day or two after the above scene; "there never was such a chance as the one you now have."

"What, with the colonel, ma'?"

"Yes, my love, you may depend upon it, that is a very safe speculation. Why, he must be immensely rich. I am sure that some of the jewels I have seen on his fingers must be worth thousands of pounds. He is a very rich man, there can be no doubt."

"Yes, ma', he is very rich."

"And you will have many fine things that you have never dreamed of. Why, you will have a carriage; I should think he would never refuse you that trifle."

"He has not one now."

"Yes, that is true; he would never use it himself; and that accounts for it. But when he has a wife it is quite another matter; and one which you can easily manage when you are a wife; you can do more then than you can now. Besides, you'll see how the money is spent; and it must all go through your hands, you know; that can't be helped."

"No, I dare say not; but, ma', don't you think, when he dies, there will be a loss of the pension? and that would be a serious loss."

"It would; but then you will have a pension as an officer's widow, besides all his vast property, without any trouble whatever — with nobody to contradict you; that is, if he were to die; but I think he will not do that; he does not, at times, appear so old as one would think; and yet, he is very pale; but that, I suppose, is caused by his long residence abroad in hot climates, and being exposed to the weather of all kinds, attended by wounds and sicknesses."

"No doubt he has suffered much; but he has obtained a handsome fortune, which pays for a great deal, you know," said Margaret.

"Undoubtedly, my dear; by-the-bye, have you heard how that affair of Miss Smith was ended, and why they came in here in such a manner?"

"Oh, it was a very shocking affair; there were some marks in her arm, which I cannot understand; it does seem very extraordinary to me, but she says she was awoke in the night by some monster sucking her blood."

"Dear me! who ever heard of such nonsense?"

"I cannot but think there must have been something in it; and, yet, what could have been the reason for them all to utter a falsehood, I don't know. There was, you know, the father, then the watchmen, all of whom said they saw it; at all events, they appeared to have some idea that it must have been done by some one in our house; the dressing gown and that appeared to bewilder them."

"Did they say they thought so still?"

"No; they did not do that, we spoke so positive; and I saw when I went in to see her, she was much terrified at what had occurred, and could not get up; she had a physician to attend her, who will not hear of anything that she says."

"Well, I think he is right."

"But the whole family appear to side with her, and insist that it was no robber who made the attempt; for nothing was gone, nothing was attempted in the shape of robbery; nothing was touched nor moved; therefore, there could be no common motive, they said. Well, at all events, they have made somebody very disagreeable in the family, and they had better have been quiet, but they are a disagreeable set, and I shall not go in again."

"You are right; my dear; they would be glad to push that minx of theirs in here, and get an acquaintance with the colonel. No, it will be safest to keep them apart; we will have as few female visitors, my dear, as possible; not that I think you run any chance of rivalry, but, you know, men are such uncertain things."

"To be sure they are, ma'," replied Margaret.

"Well, then, if we have no female acquaintances, you see we cannot possibly run any risk, and the matter will not be so protracted, because everything depends upon things being smooth and uninterrupted; he will be the more ready to propose and push the matter to a point."

"Do you think him a likely man, ma', to marry?"

"Certain of it, my dear, quite certain of it. I know a marrying man as soon as I see him; the colonel is decidedly a marrying man, he talks of home, domestic comfort, and all that kind of thing; and when men do that, you may be sure, if you are cautious, to catch such an one."

"Well, I will try."

"Do, my dear; it will be worth your while, it will make all our fortunes. I wonder what his money is invested in."

"I should like to know that," said Margaret.

"And so should I. Do you know, I have been thinking of that myself more than once. It will be necessary to find it

out, and yet it is so delicate a matter, that I think you had better make no attempt to work it out of him. Let the affair take its own course at present."

"But I can hear all."

"Then you will act wisely, my dear, very wisely, prudently; but do no more—hear and see all, and say nothing—of course, I mean upon that subject alone. Now, if we proceed cautiously, we shall be sure to gain our object; I will take some method of obtaining the information I want at some future time, because it will be well to have him caught before we begin to pull tight the line; or, at least, before we begin to make any inquiries respecting his means he must give us some cause to do so."

"I dare say we shall know something by accident some of these days; perhaps, at the hotel where he comes from, something may be learned by inquiry."

"Possibly there may, my dear; but I do not like to go there. At all events, they can know but little, for he has not been long in England, and would hold but little communication with such people. We must have some better plan than that to go upon, else we shall never be successful, except at the cost of some cross in our hopes we would rather have avoided."

"Well, ma', you shall do as you like in this affair. I am sure you will do what is right and best for the occasion; besides, one plan is better than two."

"You are right, my dear. I am, however, resolved to have a visitor."

"A visitor, ma'?"

"Yes, my dear; only Mr. Twissel, the attorney."

"Oh, I know who you mean now; but why do you have him? He is a very funny sort of an acquaintance, especially if he is to meet the colonel."

"I wish him to meet him, my dear, for that reason. He will be able to get out of him, by some means, what he has got his money locked up in. A hint will serve him, and he can make inquiries, and learn it all, and then he will, if we are successful, have a good thing of marriage settlements, and so forth. Besides, I will make an agreement with him that he shall have a sum of money for his trouble."

"That will be a very good plan, certainly."

"Exactly, and you needn't be seen in it at all; so I think we shall be all very fairly put in the way of doing well. I shall go out this morning, and call upon Mr. Twissel, and have some conversation with him. He used to have some business of your father's to do, and has had much of his money, as well as a good word now and then."

"Dear me, who is that? There is a double knock at the door, ma'. How vexing it will be to have any one come here. I shall hate the sight of any one coming in now."

"Can't you see from the window who it is, my dear?"

"No, ma'."

"Then we must wait until the servant comes in."

The words had hardly been uttered, before the servant entered, and said that Mr. Twissel wanted to speak to Mrs. Meredith, if she was at home.

"God bless me! — send him in," said Mrs. Meredith, after the first surprise was over; and then, turning to her daughter, she said, "Talk of what's-his-name, and you are sure to see some of his friends. If I had wanted him to come, he would not have been here."

"Very likely, ma'; and yet you do, and he is here."

At this moment Mr. Twissel made his appearance, and entered the parlour. Having saluted the ladies, he proceeded to lay his hat and cane on the table, saying,—

"Mrs. Meredith, I dare say you are surprised to see me, after so long an absence."

"My surprise is not greater than my pleasure, Mr. Twissel. I am very glad to see an old friend of my husband's. Pray sit down, sir."

"Thank you, I will. I am glad to see you look so well. I need not ask how you are, and your amiable daughter too; she appears charming."

"Yes, Mr. Twissel, we are in tolerable good health; not often better."

"Do not let me disturb you, Miss Margaret," said Mr. Twissel, as she rose to leave the room.

"Oh, no, sir, not at all. I have something to attend to, if you will excuse me."

"Certainly, certainly. I hope I shall not be any cause of putting you to any constraint and inconvenience; at the same time, I shall not detain Mrs. Meredith long."

"Oh, we don't intend to lose you suddenly," said Mrs. Meredith. "Anything I can oblige you in I shall be very happy to do so, if you point out the how."

"Then I will proceed to do so at once," said Mr. Twissel; "I will do so at once. You see, when your late husband died, or before, he gave me several debts to collect."

"So I understood," said Mrs. Meredith.

"Exactly; I see you understand me.

Now, those debts I was to collect myself for my own benefit, he having, when he died, owed me a considerable sum of money. He assigned them to me, and I accepted them as payment of his debt due to me."

"I understood such to be the case, and at that point the matter was considered as settled; was it not, Mr. Twissel?" said Mrs. Meredith.

"It was so, and is so now, as far as I know now; but I want some few papers which it is possible may be somewhere in your possession, to enable me to secure the payment of them; and without those papers I shall not be able to enforce attention. Now, I want to know if you will oblige me with them if you have them by you?"

"I will certainly look and make any search I can for them, and if I find them you shall have them, certainly. But, now I have disposed of that, will you do me a favour?"

"Certainly, with pleasure."

"Well, then, Mr. Twissel, you see, there is a certain rich lodger of mine who pays certain attentions to my daughter Margaret," said Mrs. Meredith.

"I see," said Mr. Twissel.

"Well, then, he had made no positive offer yet; but we have certain expectations, you see, and in case those expectations become realized, I want to be in such a situation as to know at once what I shall do in such a case — what ought to be done."

"Very good, my dear madam; very good."

"Now, we only know from report, and from appearances, that he is rich; we feel quite convinced of that — he could not

well be otherwise," said Mrs. Meredith; "but we are anxious to know in what kind of stock or property he is likely to have invested it."

"Yes, I see. Well, then, all you have to do is to learn what you can from himself or his friends, and then make inquiries respecting the truth of what you hear. I should be very happy in assisting to make such inquiries, or in any way you may point out."

"I am very much obliged to you; but, Mr. Twissel, it is a very delicate subject for females to touch upon, and, moreover, it is worse, considering how my daughter is likely to be in connection with him."

"It is a delicate matter, certainly."

"Well, now, what I wanted was this; if you would on some occasion — I would let you know beforehand, — call in and take some tea, or whatever meal happened to be at hand, and get into conversation with the colonel, and get this matter from him —"

"Oh, he is a colonel in the army, then?"

"Yes; but returned, in bad health, from the Indies. He has come only recently."

"Aye, aye, I see; you have a nabob, I see. That will be a very handsome settlement for your daughter, my dear madam; a very handsome settlement."

"Yes, it will."

"Well, it is handsome; but there are drawbacks, you see."

"Oh, age, and ill health."

"Exactly; they are drawbacks, you see, that are not always to a young female's taste."

"No, no; but, then, my daughter is a reasonable young woman, Mr. Twissel, and would not object to a good fortune because there was a kind, though, perhaps, elderly, gentleman for a husband. Oh, dear, no, sir, I have no apprehensions of that character; she will be good and obedient, especially when she knows that it is all for her good; besides that, you see, the colonel, though an invalid, is not so very old, and is a most pleasant, and, I might say, fascinating gentleman to converse with; so that she can have no personal objection; and, besides, from what I can observe, I have reason to believe that the colonel is by no means disagreeable to her."

"Then I am sure it is a very handsome prospect for her, and one that might have been long in happening to one who had a better fortune to aid her."

"Yes, indeed, it might."

"Well, then, if I can aid you, command my services."

"In this respect you may do me much good, but I do not, as it will be some little loss of time to you, desire you should do so for nothing. If we succeed, and all is comfortable, you shall have a hundred pounds soon after the marriage — say three months."

"Very well. I am quite willing to accept the terms, and should I be wanted at any time, perhaps you will let me know as long before as possible."

"I will do so."

"And then, when I next come, perhaps you'll be able to hand me the papers, and be ready to sign some agreement which I will get ready for the purpose."

"Very well, I will do it."

"I am much obliged to you," said Mr. Twissel; "however, I suppose, when I am introduced to the colonel, I am only to come in as an old friend of the family?"

"Exactly so; that will be by far the best character to assume, because you may be anything; besides which, when matters come to a point proper for interference, you can do so the more easily, and with more effect, and he also will be less inclined to quarrel; and at the same time he can have less objection to do so, which, you see, is a little better."

"I see," said the attorney, rising; "and now, as we have settled this business so far, I will bid you good afternoon, as I have some business elsewhere this evening, which I must get finished."

After exchanging greetings, the attorney quitted the house of Mrs. Meredith without further remark.

CXXXII.

THE EXPLANATION, AND THE PROPOSAL. — A TETE-A-TETE.

A WEEK OR MORE had passed away since the visit of the attorney to Mrs. Meredith, and yet the latter saw not a sufficient reason why she should send for her friend. Things were not ripe yet; the colonel had, it was true, been melting gradually; but then to progress ever so little, was a great point in anything — no matter what it is — something gained.

Mrs. Meredith, however, by no means lost sight of her object; she had that steadily in view, and worked for it every day; and her daughter was no less assiduous — she was attentive and humble, waited upon Colonel Deverill with the affectionate assiduity of a daughter; while, on his part, he sighed and said, what a happy man he must be, who should have her for a wife.

It was arranged one day, when he appeared to be more than usually tender, that the mother should be out that evening, and see some of her friends, and break the news a little to some of them; a pardonable vanity in the lady, for it was not in accordance with her position in society that her daughter could expect such an offer as the one she daily expected.

The lady did as she had agreed, and left the house, while Margaret went to the colonel's sitting-room when his bell rang, and hoped he'd excuse the absence of her mother, as she had gone out to see some friends whom she had not seen for some time.

"I am happy having you attend to me, Miss Margaret. I cannot be attended to better. I am afraid, as it is, I am a terrible annoyance to you."

"Annoyance, colonel! far from it — very far from it; and I do hope you do not mean what you say, else I shall fear I have unwillingly given you some cause for your opinion, which I shall the more regret, as you are yourself so kind. I assure you it gives me great pleasure when I know I can do aught to alleviate the misfortunes, or satisfy the wishes of any of my friends."

"And do you reckon me one, Miss Margaret?"

"I hope Colonel Deverill will not consider me too presumptuous in looking upon him as something more than a mere casual friend or acquaintance."

"Casual acquaintance, Miss Margaret — casual acquaintance!"

"Well, friendship, if you allow me to say so."

"Friendship!" repeated the colonel, with a deep drawn sigh; "I would I could claim a yet warmer title than a friend. I could then hope for some of those pleasures which are denied a solitary man like me — I should then have those whom I loved to soothe my death-bed, and whom I could benefit by worldly wealth, could I, Margaret, think I could claim a feeling stronger than that of friendship."

"Oh! Colonel Deverill, how can you talk in this strain? Indeed, you — you are too good — dear me, I do not know what I was about to say."

"Miss Meredith," said the colonel, taking her hand with gentleness, and tenderly pressing it, "I am seen to a great disadvantage; I have been many years fighting for my country, and I have not had time to cultivate those sweet and tender emotions such as I feel at this moment."

"Yes, you must have suffered much," said Margaret.

"And now, when I return again, I am somewhat the worse in appearance; but my heart is as warm as ever it was, and I am more than ever alive to the charm of female society. It is that unreserved interchange of thought and good offices which attaches me to life, and makes me live even with hope. Do not dispel this day-dream of mine, Margaret."

The colonel paused and pressed her hand to his lips, while she appeared confused and irresolute, and was unable to withdraw her hand from his, but at length she sank trembling into a chair.

"My charming creature, may I suppose this emotion is caused by excess of feeling — that — that — in short, I am not wholly indifferent to you?"

"Oh, colonel! I'm really unable to speak!"

"My beloved girl, I am loved; yes, I see it — oh, happiness!"

Midst these broken sentences, the colonel contrived to slip his hand round the young lady's waist, and he pressed her close to him. For a moment she forgot his proximity, and remained passive; but suddenly and quietly disengaging herself, she said, —

"Pardon, me, Colonel Deverill; I had forgotten — I was unconscious — a weakness came over me, and —"

"You love me!"

"If you have become acquainted with that which was a secret, sir, you must use it as such; but you must not talk in this strain to me; promise me, colonel, and — and — I will see about the tea immediately."

"May I speak to your mother?"

"Colonel Deverill can do as he pleases. I have no secrets from my dear mamma."

"I will — I will, and Heaven bless you for saying so much. I may say you are not averse to me, and that, with her consent, I shall not despair."

"We will say no more, Colonel Deverill," said the cautious maiden.

"You shall command me — you are the arbitress of my fate," said the colonel, who had become warmer and eulogistic to a degree.

Much more, however, passed between them; the ice was broken, and they conversed more freely; for when they began the tea, much was said that did not partake of so warm a character as that which had already passed; but it, nevertheless, partook of the same purpose.

"When I am married," said the colonel, "I should like a carriage. I have no use for one now, as I could but very seldom ride; but when I had a wife, then I should wish for her accommodation as well as my own; but which do you prefer, country or town life?"

"There is much of comfort and quiet in a country life," said Margaret; "and yet I am not entirely wedded to country life — there is much of pleasure in London."

"So there is; and where you have no resources of your own, or in your own house, it is preferable; but when such is the case, London loses all its charms, or a great part of them."

"So it does," said Margaret.

"However, I am partial to both. I should like a partial town and country life."

"That, indeed, would be the very greatest delight one could experience; to live sometimes in one place, and sometimes in another."

"So it would."

"By the way, if we kept a carriage, which I would do," said the colonel, after a pause, "it would be a very excellent thing to enable us to travel about in."

"Perhaps you have been to some parts, and like them better than others."

"Yes, I have been to a good many parts; but I cannot at this moment speak of them; but we would look out for some place that would be more agreeable than others."

"Perhaps you have some place of your own you would like to live in?"

"No,—not exactly; these things are not of one's own choice, and not empty; and, therefore, are useless as residences."

"Certainly. Besides, you must be near enough to come to town for business purposes."

"Yes, I must, but that needn't be often," replied the colonel; "but where there is plenty of means, there is no fear of not getting what we want."

"No, indeed, there is not."

"And one thing alone would repay me for the hardships I have endured, the misery I have suffered, and the misfortunes I have experienced in all my marchings and counter-marchings; my sleeping in the open air by night, and scorched by the sun by day."

"And what may that be, colonel?"

"Why, the power it gives me of conferring happiness and wealth upon you; for, in the natural course of events, you will outlive me."

"Oh, for mercy's sake, don't talk of that, sir."

"But it is a matter that I can think of calmly enough; and, as a soldier, I have ample occasion, I can assure you."

"Indeed! I dare say you must have."

"I can remember, on one occasion, especially, which I will relate to you, if I do not weary," said Colonel Deverill.

"Oh, no—no! I cannot be weary," said Margaret.

"Then I will tell you. I was ordered to march some troops to attack the stockade of Puttythempoor, a very strong place."

"Was it a town?"

"No, merely a place of strength, where the enemy had gathered together in great numbers; and here we were determined to attack them. The stockade was a very strong place; and there were strong and high timber fences, with large mounds of earth and bags of sand, all tending to make the place one of great strength," said the colonel.

"What a place it must have been!"

"Yes; it was very strong. Well, my party did not amount to more than fifteen hundred men strong, while the enemy, with the advantages of the defence, were more than three thousand, giving them a vast superiority over us; but we were not to be daunted by that; we were determined to make a dash, and, from the character of the men I commanded, I had no fear of the result. We were sure to make our way among them, and then we were sure of the result."

"How dreadful!"

"Well, the men were divided into three bodies — five hundred each — and these into divisions of one hundred each, the one to support the other. We had no guns, and were therefore compelled to depend entirely upon our luck in the assault."

"Goodness me! I wonder how you could think of it with anything like ease or comfort. It would make me all of a freeze!"

"Oh, Margaret! when the soldier is in the field of battle, he must get the better of all feelings, save those of honour."

"It is too true!" said Margaret, with a sigh.

"And then," said Colonel Deverill, "we, having arranged our plans, and settled who was to take the command, if I had the mischance to fall —"

"Good Heavens!"

"Well, I say, having done all this, we were resolved to make a dash at the point, and take the place by assault. To do this the more effectually, we were resolved to make the attempt in three different places at once, so as to divert the enemy's attention, and to place them in a cross fire, and thus take them the more easily.

"This plan was carried out to the letter, and we made the attack; but the enemy defended their stockade so vigorously, and what with the strength of the place, and the determination of the enemy, we were for some time repulsed — at least, held at bay.

"This would never do, I thought. I must mount the breach myself; for, if my division was held at bay, I had fears of the rest; they might meet repulses also, which would occasion the loss of our whole party, which would have been sure destruction; not defeat alone, but imprisionment, and possibly death from ill-usage, or from malignant disorders."

"What fearful scenes!"

"I ordered my men to keep close and follow me. We made a dash at the stockade three abreast, and up we went. By Jove, it was fine work — a brave sight — a sight I can never forget while I have remembrance left me. We got up the stockade Heaven knows how, and were over it in the space of a minute; but the impetuosity of those who came first was not seconded by those who came after; it was easy enough to get down among the Indians, but it was very hard to get up; and while our friends were getting up, we were exposed to the strength of hundreds — only four men to as many hundreds for several minutes."

"Goodness, how dreadful! Were you not all killed?"

"Except for myself, they were all killed. Each received a dozen wounds, and I should have met with the same fate, but for an Indian officer, who, seeing me surrounded and thrown down, saved my life from the fury of his men; but, in a minute after, I was free — my own men came down by dozens, and the blacks were swept off by the hundred.

"At that moment, too, there were our other parties just appearing over the other parts of the stockade, so we had now plenty of assistance.

"The blacks now on all sides fell in numbers before the fire, and the place was our own; and a hearty cheer was given that made the woods re-echo again."

"Were you not glad the danger was over?"

"The danger was not over, though we thought it was; for suddenly the earth heaved up with a tremendous explosion, and many of our poor fellows were blown up into the air, and I myself was completely knocked over and smothered in dirt; however, it was dry, and we were soon put to rights again. I was picked up, and nothing more happened."

"What was the cause of your disaster?"

"Oh, a mine the scamps had sprung as they were retiring, hoping to do us more mischief than they did; however, we beat them off, and they lost many men on that occasion, and did not show themselves again, but made the best of their way through the woods and jungle by some paths that we did not know, and hence we did not follow them further."

"It must have been dreadfully dangerous."

"Yes, life was the game we played for, and it was won and lost often enough,

during that war; but we must expect it should be so."

"But you are now safe."

"Yes, I am now safe, and, I may say, happy. I have had some knocks, and am none the better for them bodily; but then I have had them well paid for, so I must not complain. I have now but one object to attain before I die."

"And what may that be, colonel, if it be no secret?"

"It is not to you, Miss Meredith," said the colonel; "it is an early day — a day on which I may claim you as my own; then, indeed, I shall have lived and accomplished something; an object worth living for, and, may I say so, worth dying for."

"Ah, I hope you may live many years yet, colonel — many years of life and happiness, to enjoy the fortune you have so gallantly won. Indeed, I think no fortune ought to give so much joy as the soldier's."

"And why, Miss Meredith?"

"Because there is none so arduously won; won often with bloodshed, and even life; it ought, indeed, to give great and lasting happiness."

"If I obtain my wishes, I shall be the happiest man in the universe; and I would go through all I have gone through over — aye, twice over, and that is no little — to have such a reward as the one I now seek — it is the crowning happiness of my life."

"You are very kind to say all this —"

"Aye, but I mean it. It is no common compliment," said the colonel; "I mean what I say, most earnestly. Do you believe what I say? I am not used to the pretty speeches of young men who make love — perhaps I ought; but I am an old soldier, and am but little used to these ways; however, I have spoken my mind, and I hope you will not allow any one else to injure my cause."

"Anything you have said, Colonel Deverill, has been of too serious a nature for me to think of anything save the object itself. Your conduct has been that of a gentleman, and I should be wanting in respect to myself, and courtesy to you, to think otherwise than seriously of it," was the wily reply of Margaret.

"You have my own thoughts," said the colonel.

"There is my ma'," said Margaret, as the knocker and bell sounded.

"You will do your utmost with Mrs. Meredith for me, and I will beseech her myself," said the colonel; "I hope she will take things in a favourable light."

CXXXIII.

MRS. MEREDITH'S CONSULTATION WITH MR. TWISSEL, AND HER RESOLVE.

MRS. MEREDITH'S arrival was very opportune, for it broke off the interview; and Margaret descended to the parlour, where her mother she knew would repair the moment she had freed herself from her dress. Margaret was now left alone for a few moments. She felt all the exultation of success in a strategy, and all the exhilaration of spirits that such a prospect of wealth and riches floating before her eyes, and all the natural consequents upon such possessions would give rise to.

"I shall be rich," she thought. "Aye, I shall not only be rich, but very rich — I know I shall. Well, he is old — no matter; better be an old man's darling, than a young man's slave. Yes; I shall know how to use wealth. I shall be able to spend a little of his countless hoards, and he will not thwart me, I am sure. He will be too fond — too doating, by far. I shall be indulged like a spoiled child, I am sure."

Margaret smiled at the thought of what length the colonel might not be induced to carry his fondness for her.

"He will not set any value upon what will give me pleasure. I am sure he will give me all I ask. I have but to ask him for what I want, and he must comply. I am sure he is too easy — too quiet and generous to make a moment's hesitation."

The colonel, too, was left to his reflections, but as to what they were we know not. He sat long, silently gazing at the fire.

Mrs. Meredith now entered the apartment, and, looking at her daughter, she said, —

"Eh! something been said, Margaret? I can see by your eye that the colonel has said something to you. Am I not right, my dear?"

"Yes, ma'; you are right."

"Well, my love, and what did he say? I am dying with curiosity."

"It will be quite impossible to do that; but he has been quite explicit enough, without any hesitation at all, or any reserve — quite candid and open."

"He has offered?"

"Yes; he wishes for your consent; for I told him I could not possibly decide without your consent and countenance. He did not disapprove of that, only he wished to propitiate you in his favour, and begged me to let him have the satisfaction of knowing that he had my good wishes, and that I could look upon him in a warmer light than a mere friend."

"Which I hope you did?"

"Yes, ma'. I let him imagine that I was not indifferent to his good opinion; but, at the same time, I would not commit myself,

but left him to infer a good deal. I think I know, ma', how to manage such an affair well — I may say, very well."

"Exactly, my love. I was sure you would."

"Yes, ma'; I should think I did. For when I found he had proceeded a certain distance, I was resolved that he should speak out plump at once; and when I found he paused, I paused too, and he was compelled to explain; but he betrayed no unwillingness, or anything like hesitation at all, but he has fairly proposed himself to me."

"And you have not committed yourself?"

"Not in the least."

"Very well. I must be cautious, too not to do so; because I must have some conversation with Mr. Twissel, so that we may proceed in a safe manner, and not commit ourselves in any way as we shall repent of afterwards."

"How do you mean?"

"Why, child, you would not marry the colonel if he was not a rich man."

"Not exactly; though I must admit, ma', he is a very nice man — a very nice man, and I should be entitled to a widow's pension, if nothing more, and that I might not have under some circumstances; even you yourself have been left worse off, you see."

"Yes, my child; but circumstances alter cases. I had a better prospect when I first married, else I would not have done so, you may depend upon it. However, we can always retrace our steps, and he cannot. But I will get Mr. Twissel to come and see into matters a bit for us."

"Well, ma', you shall do as you think fit — only, take care not to throw away a good chance because you have greater hopes."

"Has he said anything about his property?"

"Not a word, except it was to intimate it was large, and he had won it very hardly, with great danger; but he did not say what it consisted of. Of course I could not ask."

"Oh, dear, no."

"But he intimated he would keep a carriage, and a country house, as well as a town house, besides several other matters, which makes it plain enough he has been used to plenty; besides, as he spoke to me in describing some scenes in India, he appeared so much animated that I am sure he must be what he appears to be, and what he says he is."

"Ah, well, I think myself it is all quite right, and that we shall have nothing to repent there; but we will let all go on but the naming of the day — that must not be named, for, if we do, we shall not be able to retract."

"Oh, no, we shall not have any occasion to do that, I think; but I dare say he will speak to you to-night, as there is time at supper especially."

"No doubt. You may as well retire early, so that you may be absent, and that will give us greater liberty to talk than if you were present, my dear. I wish Mr. Twissel were here; but it can't be helped; and when he does come, I must have some conversation with him, and I must, in the meantime, learn what I can for him to inquire about afterwards."

Thus resolved, Margaret went to bed early, leaving her mother to attend upon the colonel, who sat looking at the fire without any change of posture since the last time he was seen by the girl; but Mrs. Meredith caused him to break the steady gaze and deep thought he was indulging in.

"I hope you have been quite well, colonel, since I left?"

"Yes, quite well, Mrs. Meredith."

"What would you choose for supper?"

"Margaret —"

"Eh?" said Mrs. Meredith, amazed.

"I beg your pardon; I did not know you were near — at least, I did not know I spoke at the moment; but, pray, what did you desire to know?"

"What you would have for supper, sir?"

"Oh, whatever you have at hand; some of what we had for dinner — I think I should like it as soon as you feel disposed to have it. I am ready — quite ready."

"Then it shall be had at once, sir," said Mrs. Meredith; "I will order it up immediately, for it is later than I intended to have stopped out; but the hours so soon ran away, and there were so many motives to forget the time that was flying so fast."

The supper was soon laid, and the colonel and Mrs. Meredith alone sat down to it, at his earnest request. Indeed, they used to have meals much in common; for the colonel professed to be very fond of female company, and was desirous of their company, which they translated into a desire for the presence of Margaret herself.

The supper was laid and over before the colonel said anything; but appeared to be absorbed in deep thought, from which it was difficult to arouse himself. But at length, after looking around once or twice, and not seeing Margaret at table, he said to Mrs. Meredith, —

"I hope I have not driven your daughter away."

"Oh, no, sir; she complains of headache, and has gone to bed somewhat earlier than usual."

"I fear I must lay the blame on myself."

"She did not say you were the cause," replied Mrs. Meredith, "of her ailment; and, therefore, I think you must be free from blame; for she would have said so, if it had so happened. She generally speaks the truth in such matters, at least, and, I believe, in every other."

"No doubt; but I have been speaking upon a subject that concerns my own happiness to her, and perhaps the excitement may have caused her some evil of that sort. She would not, perhaps, name it to you, Mrs. Meredith; but I will. You have been a wife yourself, and know that a few candid words are better, and more to the purpose, than a long desultory courtship."

"Yes, sir; it certainly is so."

"There is some difference, too, in our ages," said the colonel. "I have not overlooked that matter, at all events; but I hope that will be no cause of impediment or objection."

"It cannot be, sir, in such a case as your own, for instance."

"Well, then, I have proposed for her husband. I wish to make her my wife. I am yet hale and hearty, and have some few years yet which I could wish to pass in happiness, and which I will use to make her happy. And if I die early, I have ample means of providing for her—of leaving her a most handsome and ample fortune. Not more than she deserves; but possibly more than she might have thought of seeking."

"Certainly, sir."

"Then I wish for your consent to our future happiness."

"You may have my good wishes," said Mrs. Meredith.

"You are very good," said the colonel; "and I trust your daughter will live long to make you happy by making her own apparent to you."

"Of course," said Mrs. Meredith, "this is rather a sudden affair; you will not think of hurrying it to a conclusion, but permit her to become acquainted with you, and to know her own mind."

"Certainly, I do wish it pushed on to a conclusion; but not so much so as to cause any dissatisfaction. I am anxious to call her wife. My feelings are those of an ardent lover."

"I do not dispute it."

"Still you and she must be the best judges of all this. You will not, I hope, punish me by compelling me to a longer probation than you are compelled to put me to. I am not like a young man who has a fortune, or rather a living to earn; but I have one ready, a handsome one, and my wife will be a lady of fortune when I die."

"Do not think of dying at such a moment, sir."

"Why, it is not desirable," said the colonel, who did not deem it necessary to carry the conversation on any further that night; thinking, possibly, enough had been said for the first occasion of revealing his passion, and he, no doubt, considered his success signal.

The supper then passed off in the usual style, and Mrs. Meredith left the colonel, and wished him good night, with feelings somewhat akin to triumph, and returned to her own daughter's room, there to cogitate and sleep upon what had that evening taken place.

THE NEXT DAY she determined to send to Mr. Twissel, and arrange the meeting she desired; and, at the same time, she resolved that she would not push matters to the extremity, of making a point of knowing what his property were, for she might lose all; she was convinced that the colonel must be a man of large property; how could such a man live if he were not.

That was a speculation she could not help indulging in. She knew that a man in Colonel Deverill's line of life was quite able to support himself; besides, the jewels he had about him were worth a large sum of money; putting all things together, she considered it was not worth while to lose so good, so excellent an opportunity as the present for making a brilliant, at least, an excellent settlement for her daughter, and a home for herself.

"There can be no fear," she muttered; "there can be no fear; her widow's pension will be a better support to her than the livelihood of some."

Mr. Twissel was sent for; and, the papers she desired to find for him, she was fortunate enough to discover, and laid them by at once. The attorney came willingly enough, and was well pleased when he was informed of the success of the search after the papers, and produced the bond, by which she agreed to give him one hundred pounds for his assistance in the marriage affair.

However, he did not seem to agree with her, that she should not be over particular about the colonel's property; he thought that there must be some inquiries made respecting it, to ascertain if there were any or none.

"But," suggested Mrs. Meredith, "the colonel is a kind, but a proud man, and he would, probably, take great and deep offence at any inquiry being made into his pecuniary affairs."

"Hardly, my dear madam; don't you see, love would be strong enough to counter-balance that; he would make some allowance for paternal anxiety and love."

"There is much reason in all that; yet I have heard so much of these nabobs, that one is afraid to lose a good chance by inadvertently touching their weak points; for, the kind of society and company they have, theirs is so different to what they find here."

"Yes, that is very true; but we should like to know that it is true. What service has he been in — I think, though, you said in the East India Service?"

"Yes."

"Well, then, I will make some inquiries at the house; they will answer my inquiries, and no one will even be the wiser for it; they will, at least, tell me if there is such a person in the service, and, perhaps, I can learn something more."

"Very well, that may be done. Will you come round with me to tea this evening, as I will contrive to bring you in the presence of Colonel Deverill, whom you will then see and converse with? I am not sure of it, but I will try to do so."

"I will be here," said the attorney; and, in the mean time, I will make the necessary inquiries."

They parted upon this mutual good understanding; and the attorney, in high spirits, for the papers were of great value to him, and the promised reward was a stimulus to a greater exertion on behalf of Mrs. Meredith and her daughter, for he thought he could do business for the Colonel, after this affair was settled — such an opportunity of increasing his connection did not offer every day.

Mrs. Meredith redoubled her assiduity about the person of Colonel Deverill; and, at the same time, lost no opportunity of putting her daughter forward; nor was that daughter a bit disinclined to take such opportunity as was offered her, of making the most of herself on this occasion, to appear amiable, and in some new and languishing position, or to perform some new service for the colonel.

CXXXIV.

THE INTRODUCTION. — THE ATTORNEY'S FIRST FEELER.

WHEN THE ATTORNEY had left the house he proceeded upon some business of his own, and then he proceeded to the India House for the purpose of making inquiries after the colonel, for his friend Mrs. Meredith. In the course of the day he did go to the India House, and, upon making some inquiries, he was sent to a particular department of the house where he saw two gentlemen.

"Pray, sir," said one, "what do you want?"

"I wish to make some inquiries concerning a Colonel Deverill, who is employed, or was serving, in the Honourable East India service."

"In what part was he serving?"

"In India," said the attorney.

"But, to what presidency did he belong?"

"That I do not even know. He has been many years away from England, I understand, and some of his friends have not heard from him for many years, and they are desirous of finding out whether he is dead or alive; and if so, where he is."

"There is a Colonel Deverill returned this year from India."

"Indeed! Do you know anything of him?"

"Nothing more than he has retired from the service on his half pay, some time before he came home, on account of his wounds."

"Is he rich?"

"I can answer no such question."

"I am a solicitor, and do not ask the question from an improper motive."

"You may not, sir, but we cannot answer such a question. We have no inquisitorial knowledge of the private circumstances of those gentlemen who have served in the company's army;* but,

---

* At the time Varney, the Vampyre was written, the Honourable East India Company was a privately held joint stock corporation with a royal charter that handled all of England's colonial governance in India, basically ruling most of India in the name of the Crown. It

you put it to your own sagacity to consider how far it would be probable for a man so placed, as regards rank and opportunity, in India, without making money."

"I see; certainly — he must."

"And yet, you know, there are means of getting rid of money."

"To be sure. I see."

"Not that I have any idea that such can be the case; indeed, I should be disposed to believe the contrary, seeing the colonel must have been wounded long since, for the last engagement must have been some few years since."

"Thank you. I will report what I have learned. You do not know where he can be found at this time?"

"No, indeed; we have no information."

This being all he could learn, he left the India House, and as it was now about time to return to Mrs. Meredith, he at once went back, and having seen all his business transacted, he had now leisure to go there, and in a short time he arrived, and at once related to her all that he had heard respecting the colonel, from the first to the last word of it.

"Well," said Mrs. Meredith, "that, at all events, is very satisfactory."

"Yes, it is something," said the attorney, "to know your man; but, as the clerk said, he might have spent it, that is to say, dissipated it."

"Oh, it's impossible; he's been an invalid a long while now."

"Ah! there's no knowing what might be done in these cases. Who knows what he may have done — gambled and diced

---

maintained a private army of over 200,000 men, which was considerably larger than the British army itself. The government didn't take over direct control until 1858.

it away, and entered into extravagant speculations, which may have turned out ruinous bubbles."

"Well, well, Mr. Twissell, we won't say much about what might be," said Mrs. Meredith; "we won't care about them; but I am very much obliged to you for this trouble. It is, however, a very satisfactory thing to know he is what he represented himself to be."

"Yes, that is a very great point gained."

"His veracity having been found unimpeachable in one point, may be presumed to be so in another," said Margaret. "It appeared to me to be extremely probable, if not quite certain, he is what he appears to be, I am glad that all is so far good."

"Be that as it may, it will be more satisfactory to know what his property really consists of, and how much there is about it."

"No doubt; but it would not be worth while to risk anything on that account; he might imagine we were mercenary, and that would disgust him altogether."

"That's what I am fearful of," said the mother.

"We may not yet have occasion to ask him any question, or to make any inquiries of him at all, for we may be able to worm it all out of him."

"That is true," said Mrs. Meredith. "Dear me, there is the bell. Go, Margaret, and say we have an old friend come to to tea; perhaps he will excuse you — he may give the invitation we desire."

Margaret at once departed, and proceeded to the colonel's room, and began to wait upon him as usual; but he saw there was but one cup placed.

"Are you not going to take tea with

me, Margaret?" he said. "Am I to be a prisoner, and put in solitary confinement for the evening?"

"Why, colonel, Mr. Twissel has called to take tea with my mother, and as he was a very old and particular acquaintance of my father's, I do not like to put a slight upon him."

"He is a gentleman, I presume?"

"Oh, yes, colonel, he is a member of the profession of the law."

"Oh! Well, will you ask him to tea with me? As we shall be both united, I hope your friends will soon be mine; there can be no great objection to our acquaintance beginning earlier. I am not fond of being entirely alone."

"If we shall not be intruding upon you, sir," said Margaret, "I dare say my mother will. I will tell her of your kindness immediately."

In a few moments Margaret returned to her mother and the attorney, to whom she related the invitation she had received from the colonel, and instantly clutched at the idea of going to the colonel to tea, the thing, of all others, she most desired to do, and, at the same time, she had calculated upon it; for the colonel appeared to be wholly dependent upon them for society, which he appeared to be passionately fond of there, especially Margaret.

"That is just fortunate. Now, Mr. Twissel," said Mrs. Meredith, "you will be cautious, and do not make any open attempt to discover what may be the peculiar species of property he holds; it may do much mischief, you know."

"I am at your mercy," said the lawyer; "if you say so, I will not make any attempt, though I must tell you, Mrs. Meredith, that you will be to blame if you allow your

daughter to marry without some inquiry being made; and if he mean well, he will take no offence."

"You may do what you can without broaching the subject to him. Still I think we have heard enough to set all doubts at rest."

"I'm a professional man, my dear madam, and know what the world is, and have had much experience in these matters; however, as I think there is much probability in all he says, why, you shall see I will not do anything that will offend the nicest delicacy."

"That will be all we want, Mr. Twissel; and now come up stairs."

"MR. TWISSEL, Colonel Deverill — Colonel Deverill, Mr. Twissel, an old and dear friend of my late husband, sir, who has called to visit us."

"I am very happy to see the gentleman," said the colonel, but with the air of a man who is conscious of his own superiority, and that he is committing a condescending act. "Will you please to be seated. Excuse my rising, sir; I am an invalid, and am lame; but you are welcome."

"I am much obliged," returned the attorney, bowing. "My good friend Mrs. Meredith has made me intrude upon you, else I had not done so."

"You are welcome, sir," again repeated Colonel Deverill. "Pray be seated; I have seen but little company, and am glad now and then to converse with any one. Will you oblige me, Mrs. Meredith, with making tea for us? Your services are really invaluable."

"Ah, Colonel! you are really too good."

"Not at all. I'm afraid I'm too much in the rear of the march of courtesy since I left England, as our habits and manners in the East are very different to what they are here."

"Ah! I dare say they live in a style of regal magnificence and splendor," said the attorney.

"Yes; more so than you may at first imagine, and more so than in appearance; so much so that it is difficult for the law at all times to take its course. It becomes a mere dead letter, and the matter usually ends in some indignity being offered to its servants."

"Indeed, sir! that was dangerous."

"Not at all. It was an attorney, who having deputed some one to serve a process, and finding that he could not, imagined that it was the fault of the process server, and he determined to make the attempt himself, being well assured that he could succeed. However, he found himself mistaken, for, after several disasters, that he was led into purposely, he was well pumped upon by some slaves, and thought himself lucky in escaping with life."

"That would never have been permitted here," said the attorney.

"No, possibly not; but there are not the distinctions between classes here that there are there, and things are not on the same scale, either living or attendance."

"And yet, people who have passed their lives there, come to this country at last, they do not like it well enough to remain there. They come back to the land of their birth, where none of these things exist to fascinate them."

"Yes; they many live and die there — very many; but, at the same time, those who do return, do so because it is the land of their birth — because they love the country, and because they go there merely to make fortunes to come here and spend them."

"They don't like the kind of investments, perhaps?"

"They usually do so, and it fetches a high price — a very high price, and is considered equal to the stocks of the Bank of England."

"That is first-rate stock, and on dividend days the place is usually surrounded with strangers, who come to town for the purpose of receiving their incomes; indeed, it is quite an interesting sight to strangers. Have you ever witnessed it? It is well worth the while to go and see it."

"I never trouble myself anything about it," said the colonel; "but I must be going there, by the way, to-morrow. I must have a coach."

"Do you know the routine of the banking business? It is confusing to one not used to it."

"I know enough for my own purpose."

"Didn't you find London much altered," inquired Margaret, anxious to give a turn to the conversation, as she thought this attorney's conversation would appear as if it were much too pointed — "when you first returned to England, and came to live here again?"

"I cannot say much about that," said the colonel; "because I was not in a condition to twist about like many men; I am lame."

"Exactly; that must have deprived you of much of the pleasure one feels in surveying old places and well remembered spots."

"It was," replied the colonel; "but in a place like London, alterations and additions are not so extensive as to cause any alteration in general features, so as to make it perceivable at once. It is only when you come to examine localities that you notice it. You improve and alter parts, but the town is the same, and there is no doubt this appears the work of steady growth, and not any one of sudden effort; indeed, the very additions to it have a character which stamp it as being London."

"There is much truth about that," said the attorney.

"It is the same all over the world, and only in those places where the extent is but small, than any great alteration makes a conspicuous and general change, and gives a new character to the place."

As this conversation passed between them, the attorney making one or two delicate allusions to property, and asking his advice respecting some purchases he wished to make. To all which the colonel made but short and direct answers, and of such character, that it was difficult to carry on the conversation upon that topic, at least, and both mother and daughter looked beseechingly at him, so that he was compelled to desist, and found himself completely baffled by what appeared the colonel's pride.

"WELL, Mrs. Meredith," said Mr. Twissel; "I have done my utmost with this Colonel Deverill, and I can make nothing of him — nothing at all, I assure you."

"You cannot form a bad opinion of him?"

"No — no. He is at one moment one of the most agreeable men to converse with, and the next moment he is frigid and severe; perhaps pain, or perhaps contempt for any one else, may induce the alteration in his manner, and no allusion to himself does he make."

"Don't you think he is quite the gentleman, and a man used to good society?"

"Yes, I cannot doubt — he has the air of all that he says; but he is going to the bank to-morrow; now, I wonder if it is to receive dividends."

"I dare say it is," said Mrs. Meredith; "I have very little doubt of that, and yet I should very much like to know; it would settle one's mind — not that I would run any risk about the matter. I would not have him offended for the world; it would be wilfully destroying a chance that is so good, that we never can expect it to again occur, therefore we must not lose it."

"Certainly not; I will undertake the matter myself," said the attorney, "so that there shall not be any risk in a miscarriage, whatever. I will take care that nothing shall be done that will be at all likely to reach his ears, or that will be displeasing to him."

"We will trust to your prudence, Mr. Twissel."

"You may do so safely, and depend upon my caution in this matter. Now I will be at hand in the morning. If I am not here before he goes out, send for me, and let me know the hour; if there is not time to reach here send me the number of the coach; I will post off to the bank and there await until I see him come there."

"I will send to you, then," said Mrs. Meredith; "I think that a very good plan."

"But what will it do for you if you do see him enter the bank, that will tell you nothing, and I cannot see the utility of it," said Margaret; "many people go into the Bank of England, who do not go there to receive any money for themselves; so that would be inconclusive."

"It would," said the attorney; "but you must remember, I can enter too, and ascertain to what portion of the building he goes, and I can learn how much he received, if any—but I must bid you good-by, for the present; do not forget to send to me at the first blush of the affair, and then much subsequent trouble may be saved."

CXXXV.

MR. TWISSEL'S MISADVENTURES. — THE CONSEQUENCES OF BEING FOUND IN THE BANK WITHOUT GIVING A SATISFACTORY ACCOUNT OF YOUR BUSINESS THERE. — AN UNNPLEASANT DILEMMA..

THE PECULIAR POSITION of Mrs. Meredith and her daughter Margaret, in some measure, and to a great degree, tied their hands, and caused a corresponding desire to know more than was told them; at the same time, they were fearful of giving any offence to their new and wealthy lodger. They were both avaricious and designing. To make a good settlement was the grand object of their lives, and to that object they would sacrifice themselves — at least, sacrifice Margaret, who, by-the-bye, would consider it no sacrifice at all, but a great stroke of good luck.

However, they could do nothing of themselves; they saw there was a great, and glorious chance for the future; they felt they had entangled the colonel; they felt he had become a victim to their snares, and they were unwilling that they should run any risk of a failure of their plans.

"If we offend him, he may consider us avaricious and designing," they argued; "and that might prove too strong an antidote to even an old man's love, and the prize might be snatched out of our hands, and we might not only lose a rich husband, but a good lodger also."

These considerations induced them to act more warily and cautious than the attorney, Mr. Twissel, who was anxious at once to seize the bull by the horns, and come to an explanation, and thus save himself much labour and time, for the sooner there was an explanation the better; and he did not apprehend the result that they did; he believed it would only appear proper caution on the part of a mother.

They had different opinions; and, between the two, there was an indecisive policy adopted, which occasioned delay and uncertainty.

There was no doubt but the colonel meant matrimony; his infirmities were of no consequence. It was not the man, but the money, that was wanted, and which was sought with perseverance and constancy. They appeared negligent of money matters before the colonel; and, when he paid them, which he did regularly, he always appeared to have money about him, which, of course, increased their respect, and gave them increased confidence in him.

"It is all very well, ma," said Margaret, "but Mr. Twissel must not offend Colonel Deverill; he is evidently a man much above him; his actions and manner are such, that at once stamp him immeasurably his superior; now, as regards this property, there can be no doubt but he must have enough."

"I think so, too, my dear; but it would be a dreadful thing if it should turn out otherwise in the end; it would really be very dreadful; I should never survive it."

"Nor I, mother."

"What is to be done? — I declare I am at my wits' end."

"There is no fear, ma; do you not remember that Mr. Twissel himself has found out that he is Colonel Deverill, and that he has retired from the army of the Company?"

"Indeed, my dear, that is correct; I had forgotten that — quite forgotten it; but it may so happen he has no money at all; he may have spent it."

"He does not appear to be extravagant," said Margaret; "he has retired upon his half-pay, which you know must be a very good living, and I am sure of a widow's pension, if nothing more; and, besides, I am sure, from what he has said, there must be money."

"Well, I think so, too, my dear," said Mrs. Meredith; "and I think it will be better that things should go on as the colonel desires; to lose him would be horribly aggravating."

"So it will, ma, because I am sure he will do justice. It is not like as if we had money, too, and were as willing to have our affairs investigated, as we are to investigate his."

"That is very true, my dear, very true; and Mr. Twissel does not seem to know that; that I will tell him when I see him; by the way, I must send to him, to tell him the colonel is going out in about an hour. If he can find out anything, without compromising us in the affair, why, he may do so, and welcome; for, you must acknowledge, it will be all the more satisfactory."

"Yes, yes, I admit that; but I would not wilfully lose a good opportunity."

"I must now send off to him. Mary must go, and that, too, as quickly as she can; for I shall want her back again very soon, so she must run."

"Then, the sooner she goes the better," said Margaret.

Mary was sent to Mr. Twissel, who happened to be at home at the time, and judging that Mary had been a good time on the road, that there would be no time to go to Mrs. Meredith's house, and then follow the coach, so he determined to go to the bank at once, so that he would be there in time to see the colonel descend and enter the bank, into which he would follow him.

He sent word back to Mrs. Meredith that he would go on, and see her as soon after as he could; and then he made the best of his way towards the bank, where he arrived in good time — indeed, half-an-hour before the colonel, who did not set out so soon as he intended.

"Now," thought Twissel, "if he were to turn out all right, why, I shall be in good fortune; but if bad, it would be laid upon my shoulders. They shall not say that I have not given them attention enough for their money; and if I don't do something, they will say I haven't earned my money; and though I can enforce payment of the bond, yet it may hurt my future prospects with regard to my future connection with the family, which I hope to make a profitable one in the long run."

Filled with these thoughts, he determined to watch with due caution for the arrival of the colonel, on the other side of the way.

It was some time before the coach drove up, which it did after a considerable lapse of time, and then Mr. Twissel crossed over, and placed himself in a position by the lamp-post where he could obtain a good view of any one passing in and out of the coach.

"'Tis he," he muttered, as he saw the colonel step out of the carriage, and walk into the bank very leisurely and quietly, leaning upon his stick, and walking lame. He watched him into the bank — he saw him go some distance down the passage, and then he muttered,—

"Now, I will follow him up closely."

And, after a moment's pause to permit some one to pass him, he then darted down the passage into a kind of yard; but no, he could not see him; he was not there; and yet he was so lame, he could not have got out of sight so soon as all that.

"He's gone to the dividend-office," he muttered; "I shall find him there," and away he posted to that department; but he could not find him, he was — he was not there. Then what could have become of him? That was a point he could not solve.

"Well, this is very odd," he muttered; "very odd."

He paused to think over the matter; but that did not aid him. He was in the dark but thought it was no use in waiting in any one place, so wandered about from office to office, until he came to the body of the place, when he waited until some one came up to him, and touched him on the shoulder. He turned round, and at once perceived it was an officer.

"What do you want with me?" inquired Twissel.

"What is your business here?" returned the officer, by way of reply.

"I am here upon my own business. I am at a loss to understand what you mean by asking me such a question in a public place. What can you mean by it? I was never asked such a question before, and cannot see why you should do so now."

"Excuse me, sir, I have ample warrant for what I am doing."

"Have you? Then state it."

"Easily. I have followed you about this last half-hour, and you have been wandering about the place for some time, and looking about you in a manner that has excited a good deal of suspicion, to say the least of it; and I must have some satifactory explanation."

"You can have that," replied Mr. Twissel, very much annoyed; "you can have any explanation you can require. I am very sure I came here on my own affairs; what other explanation can you require?"

"Your affairs may be ours also, and the explanation you have given will be just enough to justify my taking you into custody — so if you have no more to say, I must request the favour of your company;

that's my card of invitation; do you hear, sir?"

"Yes, I do; I am an attorney-at-law, and you may depend upon it I will not be content without punishing you for this indignity — I came in here because I saw a friend call, to whom I wanted to speak."

"Where is he?"

"I don't know," said Twissel; "I have missed him."

"Very likely, and your friend will miss you for a short time; for you must come with me; — you have been found here without being able to give any account of yourself."

"I tell you I came in here to see Colonel Deverill."

"Well, what do we know of Colonel Deverill? We don't know anything about him, nor you either; you must come with me. We are obligated to be very particular when we see strangers walking about with no object whatever in view — it is very suspicious."

"But I tell you I am a respectable attorney — a professional man. I had no bad object in view."

"That may be as you say; but you must come with me."

Seeing there no help for it, Mr. Twissel resigned himself into the officer's hands, and followed him to the station-house, where he was examined by the inspector, at the place where he was taken.

"Well, sir," said the inspector, "this may be all very true, but we must have some proof of what you assert; then we can let you go."

"I'll have a complaint against you."

"You may; but you must prove not only that what you say is true, but that there was no cause for suspicion, and that you were not loitering about the bank, as the officer asserts you were."

The attorney thought that it would be quite unnecessary to get into the public prints, because it would not do for him to make use of Colonel Deverill's name; and that he had already done. What was he do do? he had got into a very disagreeable scrape, out of which he must now get in the best manner possible, and which he could not see his way clear to do.

"What do you want me to do?"

"Give us some proof that you are the person whom you represent yourself to be," he replied, "and then we can let you go at once."

"Then I will give you my card," said Twissel, producing his card-case.

"That is no proof," said the constable. "A man might have robbed you of your card-case, and you would have some one passing himself off for yourself."

"What shall I do, then?" inquired Twissel.

"Send for some one who knows you, or send for your own clerk — that will do."

"That I can do at once," replied Twissel; and he at once wrote a note to his clerk, and gave it unsealed into the hands of the constable, and asked if there was any one who would go with it.

"You can send a messenger; there are many who will do that if you pay them for it," replied the constable; and in another minute, for the sum of half-a-crown, a messenger agreed to take the letter to his office, and deliver it to his clerk, and wait for him.

This was done, and until that time he was locked up in a cell, where he had a light certainly, but in which he had no other comfort at all; but in about an hour and a half there was the prospect of a relief; for he saw his clerk come into the station-house, and with him the messenger, who came to the constable and said that was Mr. Twissel's clerk.

"Do you know Mr. Twissel?" inquired the constable.

"Yes, I do; he is my employer."

"Then point him out," said the constable.

At that moment, Mr. Twissel was brought in, and he at once pointed him out to the satisfaction of the constable, who, with an admonition, consented to the enlargement of Mr. Twissel, and in answer to his threat of future investigation, said to him, —

"You see, sir, the bank is such a place, that we are compelled to keep all persons out who have no business there, and it must not be a place where people meet who have no particular bank business to transact; do not wait about, then, for the future, sir, else you may run the same danger."

Mr. Twissel left the station-house with a feeling very much akin to anger, and he walked home with a very disagreeable feeling. He felt that he had been baffled, and had been also much ill-used, and very much affronted.

"Where could he have got to?" he murmured. "He must have turned in some of the offices — confound him! I wish he had taken it into his head to tumble. I am sure he ain't no good; if he were, I should not have been placed in such an unpleasant position."

Suddenly he recollected that there was no necessity for his going home, unless there had been anything happened since his departure; and upon being informed that such was not the case, he determined to alter his course, and proceed to Mrs. Meredith, and relate the misfortunes that had befallen him.

"And if that don't satisfy her I have her interest at heart, why, nothing will."

And he left his clerk, after giving him some directions, and then turned off towards Bloomsbury-square, where he arrived just before tea time.

CXXXVI.

AN EVENING WITH COLONEL DEVERILL. — THE STRATEGEM OF MRS. MEREDITH.

MR. TWISSEL SEATED himself by Mrs. Meredith's fire, not at all pleased with what he had anticipated and expected on that day, and yet well pleased that there was an end to it; but, at the same time, he had conceived a dislike for the colonel, of which the reader can easily guess the reason. The colonel had received him rather haughtily, and he was annoyed at it, and he was resolved that he would do him no service; and now, the indignity he had received was so vexing, that he knew not on whom to wreak his anger — at all events, it gave him a great dislike to the colonel, which would require a considerable time to overcome.

He sat there, waiting for Mrs. Meredith, who was then engaged somewhere else; but it was not long before she entered the apartment in which Mr. Twissel sat meditating upon his misadventure, and considering in his own mind what would be the best course to pursue.

"Oh, Mr. Twissel!" she said, "I hope you have not been waiting long for me."

"Not long, ma'am."

"And how have you got on to-day, Mr. Twissel?"

"Rather indifferently indeed," said Twissel, with a groan; "I may say very indifferently indeed. I have had plenty of incident—I may say of adventure—I ought to say misadventure, which appears to have dogged me step by step in this affair."

"Indeed! I am amazed at that," said Mrs. Meredith.

"You would be more so if you knew all."

"Tell me what has happened, Mr. Twissel," said Mrs. Meredith. "I am anxious to hear to hear what can have happened to you of this character. I hope it did not happen in consequence of your doing anything in this affair of Colonel Deverill's."

"Indeed it did, Mrs. Meredith," said the attorney, solemnly. "I have been sedulously engaged in this affair, and I have been seriously inconvenienced by it."

"I regret it very much."

"But you could not have helped it, Mrs. Meredith," said Twissel. "You could not have helped it at all. I know that very well, therefore there is no blame attached to you. You are free; but I have suffered, nevertheless. I have suffered."

"Dear me, how sorry I am, to be sure."

"Yes, ma'am, but it can't be helped. I was taken into custody as a suspicious person, and had some difficulty in getting my release from custody."

Mrs. Meredith lifted her hands and her eyes to express the amount of astonishment she felt.

"Yes, Mrs. Meredith. I followed the colonel into the Bank of England, and there I saw him enter, but by some wonderful means he suddenly disappeared. I missed him, and could not again obtain the slightest clue to him. I did not again set eye upon him, and while endeavouring to regain the track, I was taken into custody for loitering about."

"Indeed. Then you have learned nothing about the colonel?"

"Nothing at all. I missed him. I saw him going into the bank, and that was all."

"Well, he has come back, and appears to have received money. I should think there could be doubt as to where he got it from."

"It is a mystery."

"Indeed. I should hardly think it possible, as you saw him go in. What would he go there for but for money matters? It seems clear enough to me. I have no doubt in my own mind—everything appears to be straightforward and plain."

"Indeed," muttered the attorney; "there is much truth in that. I have had a straightforward intimation that I have been considered a suspicious person."

"I regret it very much; but here's Margaret."

At that moment Margaret entered the apartment in which her mother and Mr. Twissel were seated. There was an air of triumph in her eye when she entered, and her mother at once divined the cause; but she said nothing, and waited until Margaret spoke.

"Ma," she said, "it is tea-time, and the colonel expects you up stairs; and if you had any friends, he hoped you would not deprive him of your company on that account, but bring them up stairs to tea. He is particularly good-humoured to-night."

"Curse him," involuntarily exclaimed the attorney, as he heard of the good-humour the colonel was in, and he had so much cause to be vexed himself.

"Will you come with us, Mr. Twissel?"

"I will, thank you, ma'am. I am very tired," said Twissel, as he thought it would afford him some opportunity of discovering something that would enable him to be revenged, and at the same time do a seeming service to the other party.

"At all events," he muttered, "it will give me a change of making a more intimate and useful acquaintance with him. I must do something or other, and I may as well make a good thing of it as well as a bad one. That wouldn't be bad policy."

"Then you had better come up at once," said Margaret, "for the tea is waiting."

Thus urged, Mrs. Meredith and Mr. Twissel followed Margaret, and walked up to the drawing-room, where the colonel was, as before, seated in an easy chair, with the green shade still over one eye, and his arm carried in a sling, though he did not appear to have lost the entire use of it, and by his side was his stick, a valuable Malacca cane, with which he walked, and his lame foot was supported by an ottoman.

"Well, sir," said the colonel, "I have the extreme felicity of meeting you again; be seated. It is a very charming day, the most comfortable that I recollect since I have returned to England."

"It is remarkably fine," said the attorney, shrugging his shoulders, and giving a suspicious glance towards the colonel, as if he thought there was a latent smile lurking upon the colonel's countenance; but he could not detect it, and yet he felt very much aggravated.

"There is, even in this climate," continued the colonel, "some decent weather; but then, when matters go on happily and cheerfully, then the climate appears more genial and kind."

"Strange that it should be so," said Mr. Twissel; "but I can't help thinking he looks more provoking than ever I saw in my life."

As he muttered, the colonel said,—

"What did you say, sir?"

"I merely said that we, who are used to it, look upon it in some other light than that of a merely negative character; that is, we look upon some of it as positively good — nay, we are apt to call it beautiful, especially when it continues fine."

"Continues fine!" said the colonel; "does it really continue fine in this climate?"

"Why, one would think, colonel, you have never been in this country before, to hear you talk; and yet you are a native of this country."

"Yes, I am; that is, I believe so; but I have spent so many years in Asia, that I am more a native of India than this country. However, I believe what you say to be correct; but, you see, the slightest change of weather affects my wounds, when you could not believe any change that had taken place; or, at all events, the change would be so slight as to cause no difference to you, and yet, even before that comes, I feel the approaching change."

"I day say you do, sir; but it must be unpleasant in the extreme."

"It certainly is; and I have found it so. Mrs. Meredith, I hope you enjoyed your walk; did you go far?"

"No, Colonel, I did not; else I had not been back so soon. By the way, how do you feel after your walk, or, rather, ride? I had not time to ask you before."

"Oh, I am very well; I enjoyed it much; but I must take another the day after tomorrow," said the colonel. "That is, another ride; for I cannot walk far."

"Do you intend going far?"

"To the South Sea House," replied the colonel.

"To the South Sea house," repeated the attorney to himself, as he sipped his tea; "he has some of the stock on his hands. Well, I dare say that is likely; people belonging to these companies generally prefer them to any other stock. However, I will follow him there, and see if I can't do better. I will tread upon his heels but what I will find out something this time, at all events."

"Are you acquainted with that stock?" he inquired, after a pause.

"What, the South Sea stock?" inquired the colonel.

"Yes."

"Not much; but I believe it to be a good, steady stock — a very good investment; it will pay you a better interest than the funds." *

"But is it as secure?"

"Well, that is a very difficult thing to answer," said the colonel; "but I think is safe enough. I have that opinion of it that I do not object to hold it."

"That, of course, is the best answer one can have to its presumed security."

"Yes, I have a good opinion of it, and do not object holding it, as I said before; and that is the best opinion that can well be offered. Have you any?"

"None, sir; but I have a friend, who wanted to purchase stock of some kind, or to place money out to advantage, and I wished to learn a little more concerning it."

"I do not mean to say there is no better; but when you have once invested your money, you do not like to change the stock."

"Certainly not; it is inadvisable," said the attorney, "unless you have some specific reason for so doing at the best of times. You are the loser by the expenses."

"Well," said Mrs. Meredith, "I am very glad to see you are so well after your journey."

"Journey, do you call it? Why ma'am, I cannot call anything less than some few hundred miles a journey; anything less is a mere bagatelle."

"Dear me, colonel; what journeys you must have travelled."

---

* *An inside joke. The South Sea Company was another private corporation founded in 1711 to monopolize trade in enslaved Black people to supply labour for tropical plantations. As readers in the 1840s would have been aware, in 1720 its share prices, having risen to nearly £1,000 apiece, collapsed to under £100, ruining thousands of investors; it was known as the "South Sea Bubble." The events of this part of the story take place in the 1730s, so anyone describing South Sea stock as "good, steady stock" would be either a fool or a trickster.*

"Indeed I have, madam; some of them beautiful and romantic, and some of them dreary, and some terrible, from the obstacles that opposed us, and others, from the nature of the ground that we had to go over, and the dangers attendant from fatigue, climate, and the enemy."

"It must be a terrible thing; females in those parts are out of the question."

"Oh! dear, no; there are ladies, and English ladies, too, who live there for years, and who follow their husbands' movements with the camp, and who undergo all the dangers and fatigues merrily and cheerfully, and even put some of the best of us to the blush for fortitude."

"Well, I am glad we have a good character, even so far off as India."

"It cannot but be expected but the mothers of such men can bear fatigue and hardship, else their sons could never be what they are. However, we have many examples of heroism in India, not of men only, but women also."

"Then there are many interesting points for us to hear explanation about India," said Margaret; "I love to hear such things, especially from those who have been there, and mixed up among the people who live here, and who have had much experience with them."

"I hope we shall have ample time to talk over many such matters," returned the colonel, "for to me it is pleasant to speak of the past, and relate all I have seen, known, and taken part in, in a place so distant from us all, as our Eastern empire."

"Indeed, I love to hear them," said Margaret.

"I am afraid she will keep you pretty constantly employed in relating all that you have ever seen, colonel," said Mrs. Meredith; "she's a strange girl, and has many fancies that way; she is fond of the wild, irregular life that you describe; she would have made an excellent soldier's wife, I am sure; she's so fond of that kind of thing."

"I hope she will do so now, madam: and that she will have less of the fatigue and danger that fall to the lot of a good many, for I candidly tell you it is one thing to hear these things talked of, and another to bear with them. Plains of burning sand, and want of water, mountainous regions covered with snow, and no means to obtain warmth and shelter,—these are things exciting enough in a narrative, and yet heartbreaking to experience."

'Oh!" said the attorney; "there can be no doubt it's much better in perspective, than it is to experience. I can easily imagine when you hear of battles and sieges, how they wish they had been there; and how much would have been done by our individual exertions. But, dear me, that's as different from being shot in the beginning, and so seeing none of the fun that was to follow. Lord bless my heart, being put out of the way in that manner, positively makes me nervous, I do believe. I could be hanged before I marched up to the breach."

"Fortunately, all men are not of that opinion, else we might all of us be murdered in our beds, and no one to protect us," said Margaret, contemptuously.

"It is necessary," said the colonel, "that some men should be born for one purpose, and some another. Some are poltroons from their birth, and require better men to take care of them, while others win honour and profit on the field of death and danger, and snatch triumph from the hands of death."

'Exactly," said the attorney; "half a loaf is better than no bread; and half a man is better than no man at all; and I believe that many of them leave the field of battle, leave it in a very little better state. Now, I should not care for life upon such terms; it must be such as is worth living for, and such I do not consider life, when one is rendered a cripple all one's life."

"Well," said the colonel, "we all have our different ideas upon that subject; but I rather think the state would be nothing without the profession of arms, and the lawyers would grace the lamp-posts, if I might judge from popular opinion."

"Popular opinion is nothing in this country upon such matters," said Twissel, contemptuously.

"It amounts to something," retorted the colonel; "and you would say so, I imagine, if you felt it clinging to your throat in the shape of a halter, administered by the *canaille*."

"Why," said Mrs. Meredith, "I dare say it isn't always expressed so forcibly, and Mr. Twissel does not hold it of any importance, so long as it is not expressed so loudly as that."

"Certainly, Mrs. Meredith; that is my meaning; for an illegal act committed by a contemptible portion of the population becomes of importance."

"So it does," said the colonel; "that is easily verified."

"But still we may be thankful to those who bravely fight and die, that we may be here in ease and quiet, and free from danger, and able to enjoy our lives and homes in peace."

"That is true," said the attorney; "the one part of a nation cannot do without another; all are necessary, and produce a powerful kingdom, and not only powerful, but rich and intelligent."

"No doubt of that," said the colonel.

Tea was now cleared away, and some wine was placed upon the table, and the colonel took a few glasses of some rare wine, of which he offered the attorney to drink, and the latter willingly accepted, and found it some of the best he had tasted; and he continued to taste it until he got quite talkative, and, to the pain and mortification of Mrs. Meredith, began to talk in a strain that would in a short time have done them much discredit and mischief.

Mrs. Meredith, however, always full of expedient, soon devised on that had the effect of putting an end to a scene she feared would come to an unpleasant act, if continued in; and therefore, left the room for a few minutes, and then when she returned, she said,—

"Mr. Twissel, you have been sent for; you are wanted immediately."

"I—I sent for?"

"Yes, sir, you are wanted."

"Nobody knew I was here. Oh, yes, I told my clerk as I came along, confound him! Just as I was so comfortable, too."

"We can finish this another time," said the colonel, pointing to the bottle.

"Yes, thank you. Good night, Colonel Deverill."

"Good evening, Mr. Twissel."

Mr. Twissel quitted the drawing-room, vowing vengeance to himself against the brute of a clerk of his, who should dare to come and interrupt such an agreeable evening. It was most horribly provoking. He could have called down the vengeance of the universe upon the head of the offending mortal who had come for him, and in this mood of mind he entered the parlour.

"Where is he — where is he?"

"Where is who?" inquired Mrs. Meredith.

"My clerk — the man who came for me."

"Listen, Mr. Twissel," said Mrs. Meredith; "I have called you out. No one has been for you; but I had no other means of calling you out, as I wanted to speak to you."

"Well," said Mr. Twissel, half surprised and half vexed, "what do you want to say to me now I am here."

"I want to impress upon you the fact, that the habits of the colonel lead him to retire about this time, and I feared you, not knowing this, might stop beyond the proper moment, and so took this method of telling you what I am sure you would like to know."

Mr. Twissel could not object; there was something reasonable in it, and yet he was at heart vexed, and could not help saying, — "I should have thought the colonel would not have been so pleasant and so talkative; if he had not been comfortable, he would have said so."

"Oh, dear, no, he would not have done that, even if you had remained till daylight; he has too much courtesy towards a stranger to do so."

"Very well," said Twissel, "I will be gone. However, I will take care and not forget the South Sea House the day after to-morrow. You must make the best of it you can, and let me know when he is likely to go, so that I may not lose any chance."

"Certainly not. I'll do as I did before," said the lady.

"Do so."

"And I hope you will meet with better luck than you met with before."

"I hope so too," said the attorney, gravely. "However, here I am, and I'll do all that I can do for you. Good by, Mrs. Meredith — good day — good night."

"Good night," said Mrs. Meredith, and the attorney left the house, to their inexpressible relief, for he was growing very talkative and very troublesome too, for the misfortune was, he more than once touched upon forbidden topics.

CXXXVII.

THE DIFFICULTIES TO BE ENCOUNTERED IN THE CHOICE OF A BRIDESMAID.

"WELL, Margaret," said Mrs. Meredith, when they were alone in their own apartment — "well, and how have you got on with the colonel?"

"Oh, very well indeed, ma'."

"I am glad of it. Has he proposed anything new to you, my dear, or has he said anything more to you of a particular character? Has he said anything respecting property? That is what we want to know pretty well, and that is the only point that can be more than usually interesting to us."

"No, ma', nothing about property. I could not expect he would say anything to me, and I hardly expect he would to any one at all. You see, he is no doubt a rich man."

"Well, and he would not consider it at all necessary to say anything about it to any one; that it is so peculiarly private, and has nothing to do with any one; and he does not imagine that we require anything of the kind. I am sure if the thought entered his mind, he would at once satisfy us upon the subject. I cannot speak to him about it, because, having none, I am really not entitled to do so. That's my opinion upon the subject, though Mr. Twissel, I dare say, has a different one to me; indeed, he generally has one of his own."

"Yes, you may depend upon that; but I have been thinking the matter over, and I am sure he is what he says he is. But what did he say, my dear?"

"Why, he insists that I shall name an early day."

"Insists! my child. What does he mean?"

"Merely in a good-natured, though urgent manner. Indeed, he wishes me to make up my mind and have him at once. If I'll consent to have him, he'll obtain a special licence to solemnize the marriage here in this house, or at church, which I like best. Which shall I consent to, ma'?"

"Well, my dear, I think you may as well be married at home; it will be so much more fashionable than going to church."

"It will be much more trouble, and will hardly seem like a marriage, I think, if it is not done at a church. What do you think?"

"It will make more noise," said Mrs. Meredith, "if it is done at home; and yet nobody can say a word about it if it takes place at church."

"So I think, now; so I think."

"Well, what did you decide?"

"I did not decide upon anything," said Margaret; "I declined to do so upon the moment, but said I would think about it, and after a few words, I promised I would let him know the next time he spoke to me about it, which should not be before tomorrow afternoon."

"Very well, my dear. A becoming reluctance will never hurt your cause; you have done quite right, and I have no doubt but he will feel more pleased with you than if you had at once consented upon his first asking."

"So I thought, ma," sad Margaret.

"But you must not carry that too far, or it may defeat its own object, when next he asked you, you must affect a great deal of emotion — trembling and blushing, and all that kind of thing, which you can do very well; or if you should distrust yourself, you can practice it a bit before a glass. I did it when I was your age, and I did it well."

"Yes, ma', I can manage all that well enough; but what time shall I name?"

"Well, that must in some measure depend upon the humour you find him in. If he be very pressing, you may shorten the period; if he appear distant, lengthen it; but if there is any danger, take him at his word at once, and have no delay. It will not do to lose a chance; he must not be allowed to get off in that manner; and you must declare your confusion to be so great that you hardly know what you say, but, as he is so very pressing, you will give in to his wishes, and you may name any day you like best; and then he is caught, you see."

"I understand that clearly; but what time would you, as a medium time, give, which I out to lengthen or shorten as occasion may seem to require?"

"Well, my dear, about a fortnight."

"Ah, that was on my own tongue, too. Well, then, I should not have done wrong in naming three weeks or a month, which I felt disposed to say at first."

"No, no, but you need not make it more than three weeks, unless you see any fitting occasion, or any necessity for so doing," said Mrs. Meredith.

AFTER AN AMIABLE council the mother and daughter held, having for its object the entanglement and speedy marrying of the unfortunate East Indian colonel, they both indulged in balmy sleep, and slept till morn. The colonel himself said no more about the object of the previous day's conversation, when the amiable mother left the daughter alone with the colonel, who appeared as if actuated by clock-work; when the hour of his forbearance had passed, he again spoke of the matter.

"Miss Meredith," he said, "my impatience will, I hope, be excused, on the score that my love is ardent; and I have already waited as long as I promised. You know to what I allude."

"I am afraid I must say I do, Colonel Deverill," said Margaret; "but will you not grant me more time to consider this matter over? Remember, it is a serious matter."

"Of that there is no doubt," said the colonel; "but I do not feel the same doubts you do, for I only feel how much I can do for your happiness, and how willingly I will do it."

"Of that I can have no fear."

"Then why not consent at once? Consent to have the man who loves you, who doates upon you, and who will do all that an ample fortune can enable him to do for your welfare, and your future prosperity and comfort. Consider all that."

"I have considered much; I don't know that I need consider more than my present happiness; the future will take care of itself; at all events, we can do no more than to deserve to do well, and to succeed in all our undertakings — to deserve to be happy."

"And do more you cannot; and who is there that can do as much?"

"We all endeavour to do so."

"I hope we do so, though I am sure there are many who might do better; but, to return to my hopes, when will you consent to become mine — say the day on which I am to be made happy; and, if you really love me, make it as short as you can."

Margaret appeared to hesitate, and hung her head, trembled, and the blushes mounted her cheek; the colonel caught her in his arms — and pressing her to his bosom, he said, —

"Come, come, my own Margaret say when shall I be made happy."

"Oh! Deverill," she sighed, as she hid her face; "what shall I say — you are so urgent; shall I say a — a fortnight; and yet that is, — too — too soon."

"No — no, not at all — not at all; thank you, dear Margaret, thank you."

"I — I — I fear I have said too much; forgive me —"

"Nay, nay, no more about it; I will be content; to-morrow I will go to the city, and   then   I   will   purchase   the wedding-ring. I will obtain a licence, and then we shall be ready against any contingencies; and on our wedding morning, I will have some jewels ready for you. I have given them some orders, but they take a long while in getting ready."

"Oh, you are too good."

"Not a bit—only just," said the colonel; and he appeared as though he were quite satisfied with his conquest, and looked very well pleased with the success he had met with in the prosecution of his suit. It was a settled thing now, and he was, or professed to be, in ecstacies.

"MOTHER," said Margaret as she entered the room, "it is all settled at last; I have given my consent, and the day is named."

"Indeed! I am glad of it. When will the day arrive—what day is it?"

"This day fortnight."

"This day fortnight! well—well, that will be a very good time—very good time, indeed; we shall have a very busy time of it, for we must make the most of our arrangements between this and then; for we must get you in a fit-out; but if you have a dress to appear in, that is as much as I shall be able to afford you, for my means are so short."

"I know all that; but he has promised me jewels, which he has ordered, but which will take some time in making; but he expects them to be ready by our wedding-day. Come, now, this seems to me to be a very handsome provision."

"Very, my dear; very fortunate, too, because you see the furniture was becoming somewhat less new and fine that it was; that would have compelled me

to lessen my terms; so we should have gone gradually back, and, perhaps, been obliged to seek some other mode of living."

"But you have some money by you?"

"That was reserved in case of extreme misfortunes, and I cannot realize that immediately; however, it would only put off the evil day; but we are saved that, now—we have caught a rare good fish—we have only to land him, that is, get some little to be done before we pull him ashore. We must keep up the farce; but, I tell you, we must not be guided by Mr. Twissel, though he is of great use."

"No, ma', we must not; I have thought on that."

"And yet I do not like to give up the idea of finding out first what he may have in the shape of property, though I am sure it would do no good; yet, to have one's curiosity satisfied is something gained. Still, I am not so curious that I must be satisfied at the expense of our prospects."

"No, ma'; I am sure I want badly enough to know all about it, but I will restrain my curiosity until I find out by means and at a time when no offence can be taken; or, if it be, why it's of no consequence, and I don't care anything about it, because I shall have a right to speak for myself."

"Certainly, my dear, that is a very proper spirit—a very proper spirit, indeed; but then he won't interfere with you much, except it is to want you to be always at his elbow."

"Ah, I won't mind that, because, you see, he may make a will; but I'll take pretty good care that nobody comes in between him and me."

"Exactly; you have no relatives on his

side to tease you, or give you any trouble; therefore you have all plain sailing before you."

"I have; and now, I suppose, it will not be too much to speak to one's bridesmaids?"

"Ah! my dear," said Mrs. Meredith, with a shake of the head.

"What's the matter, ma'?"

"Ah! my dear, there is the difficulty; you know how easy the colonel has fallen in love with you; how sudden that has all come about, and how short a time the courtship has continued."

"So much the better, ma'."

"Certainly, my love; but it should make you cautious — very cautious, how you act with bridesmaids, because you don't know what may happen with such old people as the colonel — they are dreadful sometimes, and you don't know what they will do. They will fall in love with anybody; it is quite shocking to think of it; but it don't so much matter, only you see he may take a violent fancy to some one, and then you may lose by the whole affair."

"How so, ma'?"

"Why, suppose he takes a fancy to one of the bridesmaids? — you don't know what may pass between them."

"Certainly not."

"Very well; then he may make a will to reward her, as he would call it, and then you lose so much, which is a clear robbery, as I call it."

"So it would be, ma'; and yet, after all's said and done, I cannot tell what else we are to do; some female friends we must have; and the only precaution we can take will be to get some one as ugly as I can, and then keep her away as much as possible."

"The latter is the only effectual method, for ugliness is not always a safeguard, for men have got such tastes, and what we think extremely plain, they, by a perversity of taste, will persist in believing to be interesting, at least, if not pretty. I have known so many instances; besides, I do know that even ugliness itself is no safeguard."

"Indeed, ma'!"

"No; I had an instance of that — I may say two — even with your father, who took a fancy to two of the servants, one after the other. I am sure there was nothing in the hussies to attract any attention; but then men will be men, and you can't help it."

"We must get rid of them."

"Yes, that is all you can do; but whom did you think of having?"

"There are the two Miss Stewards —"

"They are called pretty. I heard a gentleman say so at the last party we went to, so that I think decidedly bad policy. I know the men's taste very well, my dear, but it is different to what we call taste; I don't know why, but it is so."

"Well, ma', if the Misses Steward won't do, what do you say to the Misses Brown? They are anything but even passable; besides, they are pitted with the small-pox, and very light hair, almost carroty — they are anything but fascinating."

"That may be all very true, my dear, but you know the Misses Brown sing, they are called good figures, and dashing young women, and they are very bold, which might tempt many people, especially when they are looking about for sweethearts."

"Yes, that is very true; then there are

the Misses Smith — they are very young — much too young to be at all likely to cause men to have any fancy for them."

"There, my dear innocent girl, you are entirely wrong — most entirely wrong."

"Indeed, ma'?"

"Yes, my dear, you are innocence itself, because you have been brought up at home; but, look here, men are the nastiest creatures alive — why, some of them would fall in love with a girl sixteen or seventeen years old. Aye, more than that, — I have seen some of them married at that age."

"Oh! I am shocked," said Margaret, as she lifted up her hands in amazement at this description of the vices of men. "Ah! well they may say at church, 'And there is no good in us.'"

"Indeed, my dear, you are quite right, and so is the Prayer-book — but it is as I tell you; beside, men never forget these things; they will remember faces they have seen for a year or two, and then they will begin their games."

"Dear me, ma', what shall I do?"

"That is the difficulty, my dear. I would not have unfolded this book of vice before you, had it not been necessary for your happiness."

"Oh! fiddle de dee, ma' — it's the money that I care for; it ain't the colonel, poor old cripple. He may do as he pleases, as long as I get the gold."

"Well, my dear," said the careful mother, who felt the sedative effects of this speech, "well, my dear, but you know they do waste their means in these affairs, and that most outrageously, sometimes, to cause a ruinous effect upon their home."

"Oh! but he's too much of an invalid."

"Do you know, Margaret, I think the colonel is more of an invalid from habit than reality. Sometimes, when nobody's looking, he can walk and use both feet alike, and even use his left hand without any trouble at all."

"Do you really think so?"

"Yes, but I don't mean to say it is all sham. Oh, dear, no, but long habit, and the laziness of these rich Indians is so great, that there is no knowing its extent. I don't believe they would eat, if it wasn't for their being hungry."

"What is to be done?"

"I will tell you, my dear. Have Miss Twissel and her friend."

"Miss Twissel and Martha Briggs," exclaimed Miss Meredith with a giggle. "What a fright!"

"So much the better, my dear — so much the better. It is just what you want — the very thing above all others. Have a fool and a fright, and you can drop their acquaintance whenever you like, and I think there can be no danger of the colonel's falling in love with them. At least," added Mrs. Meredith, with emphasis, — "at least, upon such an occasion."

"Very well, ma'. Let it be Miss Twissel and Martha Briggs. Goodness me, how I shall be attended upon this occasion — it will be quite laughable. I mustn't let the colonel see them before the morning arrives, else he will be sure to laugh at them."

"Ha! ha! ha!" laughed both mother and daughter at the idea of the two frights, as they called them, being bridesmaids; and in high good humour they both retired to rest for the night, to dream of the forthcoming occasion.

CXXXVIII.

MR. TWISSEL'S MISFORTUNES, AND HIS RESOLUTION TO NEVER GIVE IN.

THE NEXT DAY AFTER that on which the conversation respecting the choice of a bridesmaid took place, was the day on which the colonel was to visit the South Sea House.

Early that morning he ordered a coach to be in attendance, and left the house, saying that he would be back in time for tea; that he had to make several purchases, and transact some necessary business that would occupy him until that time. He kissed Margaret, and whispered in her ear that he should call and see about the jewels, and urge the jeweller to get them ready.

"These people are so dilatory," he said, "that, unless I worry them, they will disappoint me of them; and I would not be without them on the occasion of our marriage for a trifle."

"We must not set our happiness upon such things," said Margaret.

"Ah, what self-denial you can exert!" said the colonel, playfully.

"No; my happiness is not fixed upon such objects as those, and, therefore, it is no trouble to renounce them when it is necessary to do so."

"I hope there will be no need. I believe there will be none; but good-bye till tea-time, and then we shall pass a pleasant evening together."

The colonel left the house, and no sooner had he done so, than Mrs. Meredith wrote a short note to Mr. Twissel, informing him of the colonel's departure at a much earlier hour than she had anticipated.

"Here, Mary," she said to the drudge.

"Yes, ma'am," replied the domestic.

"Just run as fast as you can to Mr. Twissel with this note, and don't let the grass grow under your feet. Do you hear?"

"Yes, ma'am."

Away went the drudge as fast as she could to the man of law, and arrived there out of breath; and having gone there fast, according to orders, she thought herself at liberty to take her own time in going back, which she performed to perfection.

Mr. Twissel cursed himself for this unexpected departure; but there was no time for deliberation. He crushed on his hat, took a coach, and drove as hard as the mysteriously-kept-up cattle could carry it, and was fortunate enough to see the colonel go by in another. He jumped out, paid the jarvey, and then made a rush after the colonel, whom he saw going up the steps.

Determined that he would not be outdone this time, he rushed through a crowd of men who were near at hand, and jostled them so, that they gave him more oaths than was consistent with courtesy, and one of them desired to know if he were running after himself or anybody else.

Heedless of this, he pushed on, and trod upon a bricklayer's foot so hard, that the man gave a great shout, and, by way of retaliation, brought his heavy hand down so hard upon the attorney's hat, that the article of wearing apparel was forced below his chin, much to the detriment of his vision, which was totally eclipsed.

In an instant he was struggling with his hat, and yet was unable to release himself from the durance in which his head was held; but he found this was not all he had to contend with, for he felt himself pushed and hustled about in a strange manner, till he was thrown on a door step, and then he was suddenly left to himself, with no soul near him.

"Upon my word, this must be done on purpose, I do verily believe," said Mr. Twissel, as he at length succeeded in wrenching his hat off his head, after many violent efforts; but even then it was at the expense of the lining and skin off his nose, which was a very disagreeable affair, after all.

Mr. Twissel, for a moment or two, stared round him, and wondered where he was, until, at length, upon some examination, he found himself round the corner.

"Oh, I must have got hustled round the corner—yes, yes, I see how it is; it's a down-right conspiracy of theirs—there can't be two minds."

But then, again, he thought what conspiracy could there be necessary to marry a girl without money? If she had money, he could have understood it, but not as the matter stood—that was quite impossible. It was an impenetrable mystery.

As these thoughts passed through his mind, he was sitting on the step of a door, and, seeing the blood trickle off his nose in vermillion drops upon the pavement, he felt for his handkerchief to wipe the injured feature, and stop the bleeding.

But, alas! it was not in this pocket, nor in that; it was not in his hat—he never carried it there; if he had, his head would never have reached the crown of his hat—that was quite certain; it would have been better had he done so.

But, as it was not about him, where could it be? He knew that he had had it before he left home on this errand.

The truth, however, was not long before it came across his mind like a flash of light. He had got among a gang of London thieves, who had hustled and robbed him of his handkerchief.

This was suggestive of other matters, and he, in consequence, put his hand to his watch-fob, but also that was gone, too. He gasped—felt his breeches pocket, and then he sank back, for he found his garments had been slit open by some sharp instrument, and his purse had fled.

"D—n!" said the attorney, in a fury; but this subsided in a moment. The loss he had felt, and the pushing about he had experienced, was too much; he felt weakened and disheartened, and paused to think upon what he should do, and which way he should go.

"It's no use giving in," he muttered; "no use at all. I must go on. And yet, I had better go and see if the coach is gone, for if it is still there—and it can't have gone away yet—I'll yet go in and see if I can find him."

He walked round the corner, much shaken with what he had received in the way of knocks and kicks, but when he did get round, he saw the coach was gone. There was, however, a ticket-porter at hand, and he determined to go and ask him a few questions.

"My friend," he said, feeling in his pocket; "do you know a Colonel Deverill?"

"No," said the man; "never heard of him — where does he live?"

"He came in here just now."

"Ah, did he?" replied the man, kicking a piece of orange peel off the pavement; "I don't know him."

"Do you recollect a hackney-coach coming up to the door just now, with a lame gentleman, who got out?"

"Yes; with a green shade over his eye."

"Yes — that was the man."

"Oh, well, I never seed him afore — I don't know him — he didn't stop a minute."

"Oh!" said Mr. Twissel, and then he turned away, and walked towards his own house. However, he felt in his pocket for some money; a small sum in silver was loose in his pockets, and this he had saved, and he determined to treat himself to some brandy-and-water, for he was really much knocked about, and terrified and nervous, so he went into the first public-house he came to.

This was a low house, the parlour of which was situated a long way back, and he walked in and threw himself into a seat.

"Well, well; here I am. This is disaster the second. Well, who would have believed I should have met with such misadventures as those I have just gone through? There's a fate in it. I am sure this is an unlucky business altogether — of that I am certain. I got into the watchhouse on the first occasion, but now I am worse than that; I have been knocked about and robbed of money and goods — fifteen pounds in my purse — confound Colonel Deverill, I say."

"What will you take, sir?"

"Eh?" inquired the bewildered attorney, who forgot that he had entered a public-house, and the waiter was desiring to know what he wished to have.

"What will you like to take, sir?" inquired the waiter, again.

"A glass of brandy-and-water, and a biscuit."

The man left the room, and Twissel retired within himself to contemplate the evils he had suffered, and those he was likely to endure.

"Well, I never thought I was in such a thing as this. Who would ever have believed it? None, I am sure — no one could. Confound them! I'll give it up as a bad job, and a bad job it has been for me, I am quite confident of that."

"Brandy-and-water, and a biscuit," said the waiter, laying down the articles enumerated, and Twissel gave the necessary cash, accompanied by the customary gratuity, which ranges from ten to twenty-five per cent upon the money paid for the articles purchased.

We have often thought this a most exorbitant tax upon those who require accommodation. If people cannot pay their own servants, they ought not to keep them; to be sure, you are told you need not pay anything — it is entirely voluntary, and that they do not wish it; but you only obtain a flippant answer, so as to attract every one's eyes in the place, and the end of it is, if there is much business, you don't get any attention at all.

"Well, I won't give in," said Mr. Twissel, with a thump on the table; but he had drank nearly two-thirds of the brandy-and-water.

"No, I won't give in."

He swallowed down the remainder, finished the biscuit, and leaned back in his seat, and then he began to talk to himself.

"I will not give in; after all that has passed, it would be a shame to be done, robbed, beaten, and kicked; and then give in — nonsense! I will go through the whole affair, and that shall repay me in the end. I'll lay it on the thicker for this."

This was a comfortable resolution on

the part of Mr. Twissel, and which appeared to please him well, for he smiled quietly, and then rose much refreshed and left the house.

This last allusion of Twissel's was consolatory, and had an intimate connection with certain imaginary charges he would make to the Deverill family when he got the business; but as that was a matter buried in the womb of futurity, we will not follow him in his speculations.

"I won't give in," he said, as he walked on, and thrust his hand into the slit that had been cut in his trousers to extract his purse; but this only confirmed him in his resolution, and he uttered again and again, "I won't give in."

"I won't give in," he murmured, as he sought the knocker of Mrs. Meredith's door. "I won't give in—I'm not a man whose resolution is easily shaken. Oh, dear, no; I'll tell my good friend, Mrs. Meredith, all my troubles, and then ask her what she thinks of me—if I ain't an indefatigable friend, one who will never sink under difficulties."

CXXXIX.

MRS. MEREDITH HAS A CONVERSATION WITH MR. TWISSEL. — THE ANNOUNCEMENT,
AND THE INVITATION.

WHEN THE SERVANT answered the knock, Mr. Twissel learned, to his severe disappointment, that Mrs. Meredith was from home; and he was about to turn from the door, after leaving his name, when the girl said that her mistress had left a message, the purport of which was, that if he, Mr. Twissel, was to call, she would feel obliged by his awaiting her return, as her absence would be but short, and the subject upon which she wished to see him was one of particular importance.

Mr. Twissel was shewn into the parlour much about the same as usual; but he himself was somewhat of a different state. He himself was considerably disgusted with his share of the business; but, as we have before stated, he was resolved never to give in; no, he was resolved to carry it on to the end.

"It must come to a wind-up somehow or other, and at some time or other; but, at the same time, as I have taken so much interest in that I am resolved to see it out, I won't lose all I have lost for nothing; it shall be with me a neck or nothing affair; and, however aggravating it may be, you will have a greater chance in the long run of coming off victorious."

Several minutes passed away, and still Mrs. Meredith came not. At length the attorney began to grow somewhat impatient, and he looked around the apartment, as if to find some object to pass away the time until her arrival. On a table in the centre of the room lay several books, and he opened one or two of them for the purpose of ascertaining the nature of the contents. The title of one of them attracted his attention; it consisted of a collection of tales of the supernatural, and he opened it upon a legend called "The Dead Not Dead." It possessed considerable interest, and Twissel was soon lost in its details. It ran as follows: —

THE MOON, WITH HER train of glittering satellites following with silent grandeur in her wake, is sailing, in lustrous glory, through the heavens, and shedding such a flood of light over the face of nature, that the mountains and trees look as if some mighty hand had tinted them with silver.

Our scene is a rocky pass amidst the stupendous Appenines — one of the wildest, and yet most beautiful of that romantic region.

At the foot of a tree, and on a spot on which the rays of the moon fall with all their power, sits a young man, who is evidently watching over what appears to be a dead body that lies prostrate at his feet. His head is resting on his hand, and he is regarding the form before him with mingled fear and determination.

Hark! he speaks! What are his words?

"For full an hour have the rays of yonder luminary poured their radiance upon the ghastly features of my dead master, and yet there is no effect visible. Surely he must have been labouring under some fearful delusion of mind, and the dreadful compact of which he has spoken had existence but in his imagination. I certainly had some little faith in the existence of those scourges to mankind — vampyres; but now, I am inclined to think, my faith will be terribly shaken. In God's name, I hope it may."

The moon rose higher and higher, until, as she reached her zenith, everything was so bathed in her gentle light, that

scarcely a shadow was thrown around, save by the tall pines that were scattered here and there upon the face of the rocks.

Suddenly there was a movement in the form of the dead man — a spasmodic jerk of the whole muscles of the frame, as if a galvanic battery had been applied to it; and then the eyes slowly opened, though at first there was but little or no expression in them.

The young man started to his feet with an exclamation of horror, and stood glaring upon the form with fixed and protruding eyes, his limbs trembling, and every feature distorted with mental agony.

"Holy mother of God!" he murmured, in a low tone, "he moves! he moves! The terrible compact is too true."

At this moment, though there was not the slightest appearance of a cloud in the whole heavens, mutterings of thunder were heard, and the lightning was seen playing around the tree-tops with a pale and sickly glare. The young man, so intensely was his attention fixed upon the corpse at the foot of the tree, did not notice this phenomenon; and he was at length horrified at beholding a ball of blue fire dart from the air, and glide into the ground immediately at the head of him whom he had named as his master. Then there was a loud explosion, and a glare of light so broad and strong that the watcher of the dead was obliged to veil his eyes with his hands, and he could scarcely tell for some moments whether he were deprived of his sight or not.

When he opened his eyes again, it was with a start of surprise, for, before him, with his arms folded on his breast, and regarding him with a calm and untroubled countenance, stood his master;

while the moonlight streamed out upon the landscape, and as great a silence as when he lay in death upon the ground reigned around.

"Oh, signor," he at length stammered, in broken tones — "my vigil has been one of the most terrible —"

"Silence, Spalatro," said the resuscitated one, in a deep and hollow voice — "silence. Not a word, now or henceforth, must pass your lips respecting what you have seen to-night. Breathe but a syllable of what I am to a human being, and naught on earth shall hide you from my vengeance."

Spalatro bowed before his master in obedience, while his frame gave a shudder of horror, as he regarded the deathly appearance that still lingered in the signor's features.

"Spalatro," resumed the signor, after a slight pause, "you have rendered me great and faithful service, and your reward has been proportionate; but there is yet another service which I would seek at your hands. The Lady Oriana, for the possession of whom the Signor Fracati and I have fought, and for whose sake I received the wound which deprived me for a time of life, is at Florence, and at present ignorant of the mishap that befell me. The Signor Fracati and yourself are the only persons who are aware of it. He will carry to Florence the news of my death; and, on my re-appearance before the Lady Oriana, what tale can I invent to satisfy her? No, no — he must not reach Florence — he must never look upon the Lady Oriana again. You, Spalatro, wear a poniard, you have a powerful hand — and you know well where to strike. Rid me of this hated rival, and wealth shall be yours."

Spalatro stood rooted to the spot while the signor spoke, and an expression of mingled horror and disgust crossed his countenance as the latter proceeded. When the signor had concluded, he stepped a pace or two back, and in a tone full of indignation, said, —

"Signor Waldeberg, I am no assassin; my poniard is yet guiltless of shedding human blood. I saw you receive what was thought to be a mortal wound in honourable combat with the Signor Fracati, and in these arms I beheld you sink in death. You had extorted from me a promise that after a certain lapse of time I would convey your body to this vast solitude, and lay it where the moonbeams should fall upon it; for that then life should once more revisit you. All this I have done, and faithfully; I feared to fail in my promise, for I knew the penalty you would pay if I failed to fulfill the conditions of your compact. But, signor, I am now no longer bound to you; you have commenced a fresh existence, which you would baptise with blood; you have passed the portals of death, and I will no longer serve you. I will seek another service and another master, who will require less at my hands, though his pay may be lighter. Farewell, signor, and better thoughts to you."

Spalatro turned upon his heel as he spoke, and with a hasty wave of his hand was leaving the spot, when the signor drew a pistol from a belt that was fastened round his waist, and, exclaiming, "He knows too much respecting me to be suffered to live," fired it full at the head of the young man. The latter uttered a yell of agony which echoed loudly amid the awful silence, and fell lifeless on the earth. When the smoke from the pistol had

cleared away, that lonely spot was deserted save by the body of Spalatro, whose blood, streaming upon the ground, reflected the moonbeams with a dull red glare.

WHEN THE MORNING SUN broke over the mountain tops, its rays fell upon the form of the still insensible Spalatro. It was but seldom that any footsteps, save those of the wolf or the goat, left their impress on those rocks, and it was almost a miracle that the body of the unfortunate man was not left a prey to the former.

About an hour after daybreak, the bells of a string of mules were heard in the distance, accompanied by the cheerful song of the muleteer. A short time sufficed to bring the cavalcade to the spot, where lay the body of Spalatro, and the muleteer, with a cry of alarm, brought his train to a stop. Finding that life still remained, the humane mountaineer raised him from the ground, placed him across one of the mules, and then hastened forward to the next inn, which, however, was at some miles distance.

On arriving there, he found that the only apartment was occupied by a signor and his daughter, who, however, when the condition of the wounded man was made known to them, instantly relinquished it to him, and, after seeing his wounds looked to, ascertained that no mortal result was to be feared, and giving orders that he should want for no attention that money could procure, they pursued their journey.

It was many weeks before Spalatro recovered, and when he did regain his strength, he learned, with a feeling of deep gratitude, that the lady who had been so instrumental in his recovery was no other than the Signora Oriana. In an instant a vow was upon his lips that he would save her from the power of the fearful monster, whose only mission now on earth seemed but to destroy the most beautiful of nature's creation. With this purpose fixed in his mind, he one morning bid adieu to the residents of the little inn, and set off on his self-imposed errand.

SOME DAYS AFTER the scene we have described as occurring on that lonely mountain pass, a report reached Florence, where the Signora Oriana was then staying with her father, that the Signor Fracati had met his death at the hands of a bravo, and that his body had been discovered stabbed in innumerable places. The grief of Oriana was intense, for she held the signor in great estimation, and she would have had but little hesitation in bestowing upon him her hand, if her father's consent could but have been gained to the union. Signor Vivaldi, however, had been captivated by the great wealth, personal appearance, and captivating manners of the Signor Waldeberg, and he had fixed his mind upon him becoming the husband of his daughter.

Weeks passed away, and the memory of the murdered Fracati was gradually fading from the mind of Oriana. The respectful yet warm attentions of Waldeberg won upon a young and innocent heart that had always felt a slight esteem for him, and as she knew that her father's happiness in a great measure depended upon her consent to the union, it was at length given with a freedom that brought joy to the old man's heart.

It was arranged that the ceremony should take place at a chateau belonging to Waldeberg, in the neighbourhood of Lucca, whither it was resolved at once to proceed; and for this purpose Signor Vivaldi and his daughter, accompanied by Waldeberg, left Florence for that city.

As they were passing through the gates, a monk, with his cowl drawing carefully over his face, stepped hastily up to the carriage window, and, thrusting a letter into the hands of Oriana, as hastily disappeared.

With some surprise, she opened it and read it, and then a paleness overspread her countenance, and she sank back in her seat almost insensible. Her father snatched the paper from her trembling hand, and hastily glancing over its contents, with a look of anger, handed it to the Signor Waldeberg.

"See, signor, what some meddling fool, envious of your happiness, has done to alarm my daughter's fears. Does he deem us so grossly superstitious as to believe in such children's tales?"

The signor took the paper, which he found to run thus: —

SIGNORINA, —

A grateful heart warns you. Wed not the murderer of Fracati — wed not him who, once returned from death to life, seeks but your hand to provide a victim for the purpose of prolonging a hateful existence. If you despise this warning, at any rate, postpone the ceremony but for seven days from hence, and then his power of injuring you will have departed from him."

"Do you know the writer, signor?" asked Vivaldi.

"It is evidently the handwriting of a servant of mine, whom I dismissed for insolence some few weeks since," returned Waldeberg, a shade of vexation evidently passing across his brow; "and he now takes this means of endeavouring to obtain his revenge. But I will take means of having him punished."

They now endeavoured to soothe the agitation of Oriana, but the incident seemed to have taken a firm hold upon her imagination, and, in spite of all their efforts, she found it impossible to shake off the effect it had upon her.

The chateau, the place of their destination, was at length reached; preparations were instantly commenced for the celebration of the marriage, which was to take place, by the Signor Waldeberg's express desire, on the sixth day from that on which they had left Florence. As the day drew near, the spirits of Oriana grew gradually depressed, and a slight feeling of dread seemed to steal over her, whenever she found herself in the presence of her lover. Her father questioned her as to its cause, and then she confessed that the mysterious warning she had received preyed deeply on her mind. It might be a superstitious weakness, but she could not repress it; and she requested her father, however reluctant he might be, to consent to put it off for at least another day.

The entreaties of his daughter, though he laughed at her fears, prevailed upon the old man, and he gave his consent to her request; but when he mentioned the alteration in the time to Waldeberg, the countenance of the latter underwent a complete change to the hue of death. No prayer, however, could prevail upon the old man to recall his consent to his daughter's wish, and the signor departed evidently in a state of the greatest despair.

That night the Signora Oriana was missing from her chamber, and though the strictest search was made for her, not the least trace of her presence could be found. The grief of the father and the lover knew no bounds, and there seemed to be no hope of consolation for them.

IT IS THE NIGHT of the sixth day — that day against which Oriana had been so mysteriously warned. In a large vault, far beneath the chateau, and lighted by innumerable torches, that threw a red and smoky glare around, stood the beautiful Oriana and the Signor Waldeberg. The former was pale as marble, and an expression of the most intense despair was upon her countenance.

The signor, resolved that she should become his wife before the expiration of the six days, had torn her from her chamber, and immured her in that fearful place, with the hope of forcing her to become his bride; but Oriana revolted at such usage, and feeling more convinced than ever that the warning she had received had its foundation in truth, had resisted alike his persuasions and his threats.

The hour of midnight was fast approaching, and before an altar that stood at one end of the vault, was an old and venerable priest, with an open book in his hand. Waldeberg drew Oriana towards him, and forced her to kneel at the foot of the altar. She entreated — she supplicated — she appealed to the priest; his only answer was a solemn shake of the head, and then he proceeded to read the marriage ceremony. Waldeberg took her hand — but she suddenly flung it from her, and uttered the most piercing screams that echoed fearfully amidst those cavernous places. Still the priest read on, and despite her emotion and her agony of terror, Waldeberg regarded her with a cold and determined gaze.

"Faster! faster!" he muttered to the priest, "or all will be lost!" and he glanced anxiously around the vault.

At the moment, striking fearfully on the silence, came the sound of the turret clock telling the hour of midnight. On the first stroke, the most fearful sounds the human ear ever listened to filled the place — strange indefinite shadows flitted around, filling the air with a rushing sound, as if of mighty wings — the altar changed to a heap of human bones — the priest to a ghastly skeleton. Then came darkness, terrible and distinct; and Oriana swooned upon the damp floor.

When she recovered, she found the day had broken, and the sunlight was streaming upon her face; while her father and the young man whom she had seen wounded at the inn on the mountains were stooping over her in alarm.

The inhabitants of the chateau had been alarmed in the dead of the night by a terrific storm, which had thrown into ruins a part of the castle, and a vast chasm had been made in the foundations, disclosing the vaults, the existence of which had been until then unknown.

Beneath the rich vestments of Waldeberg, and lying in a heap on the ground, were the remains of a human skeleton — all that was now left of the guilty being who had thus paid the penalty for failing in complying with the conditions of the fearful compact into which he had entered with the unholy powers of darkness.

It was many months before the mind of Oriana recovered its strength, and when it did, she entered a convent of Ursuline nuns, and endeavoured to forget, in the consolations of religion, the fearful trial she had undergone.

MR. TWISSEL LAID DOWN the book which he had been reading, and fell into a strange kind of musing, in which the vampyre, Waldeberg, and the East India colonel were strangely mixed up together. From this reverie he was awakened by a rap at the street-door, and then, in a few minutes afterwards, Mrs. Meredith entered the room, exclaiming, —

"Well, Mr. Twissel, you always come in luck's way."

"Indeed!" said Mr. Twissel,

involuntarily thinking of what he had that morning undergone, as well as what he went through a day or two before; and, for the life of him, he saw not what might be called luck, unless it was that species known as ill-luck.

"Yes, Mr. Twissel, you are; you've just come in time to hear the news."

"What news, ma'am — what news? If you'll be pleased to enlighten me upon that subject, I shall be better able to understand what you allude to."

"Why, you see, the colonel has been so pressing, that my daughter has been induced to name the day. Yes, Mr. Twissel, she has named the day — not a distant day either. He begged and entreated you don't know how hard, which, at least, shows how much he meant it."

"Well, truly, it is news, Mrs. Meredith," said the attorney; "but, at the same time, it is what I expected, though not just at this juncture. The fact is, there is but little can be said against Colonel Deverill; but, at the same time, there will be but little said for him. I am by no means sure that there will be any property found. If he were a man of money, he would not hesitate to lay his circumstances open."

"He is too proud a man for that."

"Well, it may be all very well to attribute it to that cause. However that may be, there can be no doubt you have a right to do as you please, and I bow to you decision; but, still, I do so, having expressed my opinion to the contrary, being very suspicious of him. But, as I said before, you are entitled to do what you please in the affair; I have no right to do more."

"My daughter and I have been considering the matter over and over again, and we have come to the conclusion that it should take place, and she has consented that it should take place in about ten days' time, when we shall expect to have your company, Mr. Twissel."

"I am obliged to you, and assure you my opinions upon this matter are not at all personal. I will meet the colonel, and I will be present with you all on that happy occasion with much pleasure; and I hope it will be a fortunate and happy marriage."

"I hope so, too," said Mrs. Meredith; "and I have every reason to believe so."

"That is good," said the attorney.

"And now, Mr. Twissel," said Mrs. Meredith, "what did you do this morning at the South Sea House? I could not send to you so early as I could have wished, as I did not know he was going till the coach was ordered, and he went away almost immediately. I then sent Mary to you; I don't know at what time she came to you, but at all events she was not back here until late."

"She must have got to my place in good time, if she only started after the colonel had left this house," said the attorney.

"I am very glad of that, at all events; but what success did you have?"

"Success, indeed," said Mr. Twissel, with a shrug of mortification. "I have only succeeded in getting myself into a very serious difficulty, and the colonel has eluded me again. I can't understand it all. I don't know what to think; but I am sure of this, that I have been in a series of disasters ever since I undertook to follow him about, and I have discovered nothing concerning him."

"What has happened to you to-day, then?" inquired Mrs. Meredith.

"Oh! as for that, what seems to be but

natural in itself; and, therefore, it may be said not to be connected with him; indeed, though that were really the case, yet there is so much concurrent action, I cannot divest myself of the idea that it is a fatal affair, as far as regards looking after him."

"Then don't do so any more, Mr. Twissel."

"I'll never give in," said Twissel.

"Well, but what need you trouble yourself more about the affair? I assure you we're all well satisfied that Colonel Deverill is Colonel Deverill, and that he had property; that being the case, I am sure you have nothing to trouble yourself about, or to blame yourself for."

"I am conscious of that," said the attorney, rubbing his knee. "I have done all I can; and I have given my advice — I hope I have done my part."

"Yes, you have," said Mrs. Meredith. "I am quite satisfied; but what has happened to you?"

"I will tell you, my dear madam — I will tell you. I have been assaulted, knocked about, robbed, and my faculties all confused, and no use to me. I have lost my handkerchief, watch, and purse; and I have had my trowsers ripped open; and I can't tell what besides. I am safe, however."

"Well, that is right, at all events; but it is most annoying to me that you should be subject to those terrible accidents. I can't understand the meaning of it."

"I can't," said the attorney.

"But why should you, more than any one else, be subject to these misfortunes? I can't understand it at all, Mr. Twissel. Perhaps you do something or other unusual on such occasions, which had been the cause of such terrible trouble."

"Not that I am aware of," said Twissel;

"but the fact is, I don't know of anything peculiar in my appearance or behaviour, that should cause this disaster. But I am sure of this, that there is nothing more singular about me, than what there usually is; and why it should only attract notice on these occasions and no other, I cannot tell."

"Nor I. Well, I suppose it must have been there was some other circumstance, independent alike of him and you, that had caused this disagreeable affair."

"Perhaps there might be."

"Well, now, Mr. Twissel, there's another affair I wish to speak to you about; or, rather, it's a thing my daughter Margaret should speak to your daughter Elizabeth and Miss Martha about. You see, as they are not very often together, I thought it right to speak to you first."

"Yes, ma'am — go on, pray."

"Well, my Margaret is to be married in a few days. Now, we don't want relatives at all; and I was advising her to beg your permission to have the two young ladies whom I have named, as bridesmaids, and who will be of essential service to my daughter."

"I have no doubt but they will feel very much gratified with the proposal; and one could not have been better devised than this one to please them."

"Then, will you invite them to come here, and spend the evening with Margaret and yourself, Mr. Twissel, the first evening you find leisure and inclination?"

"Well, I have destroyed to-day, so far as a business day, by drinking brandy-and-water early, and I may as well finish it in an agreeable manner."

"That is very good; we shall expect you to tea this evening."

"You may," said Mr. Twissel; "if you are not otherwise engaged. I may as well do all that is necessary, so as to have as little to do, by-and-bye, as possible. Has the colonel come home?"

"No, not yet; I did not expect him to come home so soon as this, but he will be back in a very short time, now, I dare say."

"Then I will bid you good bye, for it will be unnecessary to meet him in this plight; indeed, he might think I paid him no respect to do so; and besides it will be better, altogether, that he should not see me so soon, lest he should have caught sight of me in the city; which, indeed, I think wholly impossible, for I only had a distant glimpse of him."

"Then, good-bye, sir; I shall see you and the young ladies."

"Both — my daughter, and her young friend, Martha."

Mr. Twissel arose, and left the house to return to his own house, and get his daughter prepared for the visit, and her friend also, while Mrs. Meredith and her daughter, Margaret, consulted together, as to what would be the best method of doing honour to the occasion of the forthcoming marriage.

"You see, my dear," said Mrs. Meredith, "we cannot very well invite our own friends, because they are such a greedy, rapacious set; they would sooner spoil a good chance for us than let us have it unmolested; they are by far too greedy — no, no, they must not come — they will think themselves injured if they cannot share the harvest."

"And all will be lost."

"To be sure; and, moreover, we could not shake them off when we wanted, and which we must do very soon, for the colonel will never abide them."

"No, ma' I think not, indeed — they are decidedly low people, who are genteel only of a Sunday; it will never do to have such people about us."

"Oh, dear, no."

"Here is the colonel come back; see if that girl has got the water hot, he will like his tea early; I am quite sure she hasn't got it ready — what a provoking girl that is, to be sure. She does nothing all day; I must get rid of her."

"Yes; but she is very ugly."

"That is one great recommendation in her favour," said Mrs. Meredith; "one very great recommendation; it ensures domestic peace, to say the least of it, and there's not so many followers usually. Now, however, we must do the best until we have money; but here he is."

At that moment the colonel entered the house, and proceeded at once to the drawing-room, having first divested himself of his hat and cloak in the passage. Upstairs was a good fire and an easy chair, with ottomans for his feet, and a comfortable well furnished apartment it was.

Mrs. Meredith followed him up and entered the room after him, to inquire what he would like done next; and with her assistance, he took his boots off and put on a pair of splendid slippers, and reposed with a groan of satisfaction on the chair.

"I think, Mrs. Meredith," he said, "that the best thing I can have will be some tea. Where is Margaret? when she is at liberty, I wish to see and speak to her."

"She will be here in a few moments, colonel," said Mrs. Meredith; "I will send her to you."

"No hurry for a few moments," said the colonel.

"Something about the jewels, I'll be sworn," said Mrs. Meredith, to herself; "I wonder what he has in that parcel; a present, I dare say."

Mrs. Meredith sought Margaret, and related what the colonel said, with his desire to see her, and that young lady at once proceeded to the drawing-room.

"Oh, my dear Margaret," said Colonel Deverill, "I see you are pleased to see I have returned; your very eyes tell me so. Come here to me, dearest."

"Ah, my looks, I am afraid, say too much."

"Not at all—not at all," said the colonel; "I love to see them, especially when I know they are sincere, when they come from the heart, you know; I love to see innocent and heartfelt satisfaction beaming from such a face as yours."

"Oh, colonel, you are really too complimentary; not that I think you don't mean what you say, but your partiality is too great to allow you to judge as a stranger would."

"I do not desire to judge as a stranger would; it does not give me any satisfaction. To look upon you with the eyes of a lover, is a privilege I most desire, and very soon with those of a husband; then my happiness will be complete. How I long for the days and the hours to fly by—they cannot go too fast now; bye and bye they may pass as slowly as you please—that done, then I am quite content, because I shall pass them happily, rapturously."

"Ah, you are so kind-hearted, so good, that I can never repay you."

"Do not seek to do so, you will only make me the heavier in debt; but come,

there is a small parcel, with a few trinkets I have purchased; the jewels I spoke of are in hand, and they will be ready in time for our marriage."

"Nay, do not think about them — not to disturb yourself, colonel; I am quite content if I am dressed as befits the occasion; but I am really obliged to you for your present, whatever it may be; and I may as well tell you I have thought — indeed, I have said as much — I should like to have a couple of female friends to visit me on that occasion."

"Yes, my dear, you may depend upon it, I shall be the more happy when I know you are so too; but no matter, ask whom you please; as far as I am able, I will make them welcome and happy. I suppose, however, you are alluding to your bridesmaids."

"I am," said Margaret.

"I shall be most happy to see them, or any friend you may desire," added the colonel.

"And will you have no one on the occasion?" inquired Margaret; "won't you have somebody to keep you in countenance upon the occasion?"

"No," said the colonel, "I shall not; I have no friends with whom I am intimate enough, that I know of, at this present moment; there may be people in London, with whom I have been, in India, intimate with, but I do not know for certain; but time and accident will turn up old friends, and I have not the desire to seek for them; but if we must have some one, I do not know whether Mr. Twissel would not do quite as well, if he would come, and your mother had no objection."

"I am sure she would not. Mr. Twissel was an old friend of my father's, and, consequently, he would be no stranger at all to the family; besides, it is daughter, and her friend, Martha, that I have invited upon this occasion; have I done wrong?"

"Not at all, it could not have happened better; I am sure they must be very worthy people, and any one whom you please, or they know, that you feel disposed to invite, do so, with the confidence that whatever pleases you on the occasion, will please me."

At that moment there was an alarming rapping at the door, which caused them to pause a few moments; then they continued their conversation until the servant announced to Miss Meredith, that Miss Twissel, her papa, and her friend, Martha, were come.

CXL.

A PLEASANT EVENING. — THE BRIDESMAIDS.

"I KNOW HOW that is," said Margaret, before she left the drawing-room; "that was through my ma'. I dare say she has invited them to take tea with her to-night. I should not at all wonder about that. I have not seen them for some time. They keep a great deal at home, and visit but little. They are playful, homely girls, but good-hearted, and that is why I prefer them to more fashionable friends, whose goodness of heart I cannot rely upon. They are insincere."

"You are very right; but you will, I hope, let me see your friends, and unless you have family matters to speak of, perhaps you will take tea up here with me. I shall be all alone if you do not; so, you see, I am speaking from selfish motives; but do not think I shall be at all hurt if you do not see fit to accept the invitation for them."

"I will accept it for them cheerfully, and shall be much surprised if they do not do so too," said Margaret, as she walked towards the door, and then left the apartment, to proceed first to her own room, and there to examine her present, before she sought the visitors to give them their invitation.

The parcel contained some handsome laces and other matters, beautiful and expensive, such things as she could wear, and excite the envy of others; which was, of all things, and usually is of women in general, the most enchanting thing in all the world, and gives intense gratification.

After admiring for a moment or two the beauties of the laces, she could not help involuntarily exclaiming,—

"This will be beautiful, so very becoming, and so much above anything else that can be brought by my bridesmaids. I shall be a queen amongst them; indeed, they will but set me off to the utmost advantage. I shall be the glory of the occasion."

Having secured her new acquisition from inquisitive eyes, by locking it up in her drawers, she returned down stairs, and then entered the parlour, where, truly enough, as she had imagined, there was Mr. Twissel, Miss Twissel, and Miss

Martha, all of whom were dressed out for the occasion.

There was some truth in what Margaret had said to her mother, that the two intended bridesmaids were not likely to induce any one to fall in love with them. They were oddities of the first water. Miss Twissel had light brown hair, bushy eyebrows, a straight masculine nose, a mouth that turned up on one side, and one of her eyes had a gentle inclination to gaze at her nose, while her complexion was increased by a vast quantity of sun-freckles.

Then, as for Miss Martha, she was another beauty of a similar class; hooked nose, with one eye paying undue attention to the auricular organ, while the other was somewhat injured by a blank appearance; her hair was red, and she was pitted by the small-pox to a fearful extent.

Such were the two friends whom Miss Meredith had chosen for bridesmaids, with the laudable view of putting no temptation in the way of the colonel, which Mrs. Meredith, her mother, most strenuously advised, as she had experience of the men.

"My dear Miss Twissel, and you, Martha!"

"Ah! Margaret, God bless me, who could have imagined, above all things, what I have come about. What can you be thinking and doing? here you've no friends to help you. I see you have done it all yourself. What can you think of people? you have no mercy."

"Aye," said Martha, "there's no doing anything while you are about. No one else has a chance, but you must tell us all about it."

"Yes, yes, I will tell you all about it; and more than that, you shall see the colonel if you please."

"That is what we should like, above all things."

"Oh! it is a colonel, then — a rich Indian colonel. Upon my word, you will have to be presented at court next."

"He! he! you are joking me now. Well, never mind, I shall joke you some of these days. You may depend upon that; my turn will come next, and then I won't forget you. But seriously, there are more unlikely things may come to pass than that."

"Well, now; I dare say. Who would have thought of that, now? But then you are so lucky, you see; only think what might have been the case if the colonel had been a young man! why he might become as great a man as the Marquis of Granby. Why, you'd have been a marchioness then. Well, bless my heart, how things do come about!"

"Well, you had better come up to the drawing-room," said Margaret, "and see the colonel, who is waiting tea for us all. Come, ma'."

"Yes, my dear, I am ready. Mr. Twissel, will you come?"

"If you please," said Mr. Twissel, "if you please. We shall now soon have the pleasure of seeing an end to this affair; for, as it is to come off, why, when it is over, it will be all the better. Expectation is always a time of uncertainty and anxiety — at least, to most people."

"So it is, Mr. Twissel, so it is; and I am not without my share of it; for, in the first place, human life is short, and circumstances may alter cases; so I am anxious to see it over, and offer no impediment in the way of the completion of the marriage."

"Certainly, you are quite right; having made up your mind to permit the marriage to take place, why, the sooner the better."

They were all now introduced to the colonel, who was very polite and courtly, which in some degree embarrassed the young ladies, who were compelled to put on, as they expressed it, their best behaviour, and so did not become quite so familiar. However, that did not spoil the harmony of the meeting, for the young ladies considered there was more respect paid to them, and the less they were able to appreciate the politeness with which they were treated, the more they believed themselves honoured.

They were well enough pleased, and the conversation turned upon various matters, while Mr. Twissel was uncommonly attentive to the colonel; indeed, he watched him most narrowly, every turn and every expression, as if he were resolved to ascertain, by constant surveillance, whether there was any foundation for his half-inspired doubts respecting him; and also as to whether it were possible that he could have had any hand in the disasters which he had on two several occasions suffered.

But yet he could see nothing — nothing at all that gave him the slightest pretext for persisting in his suspicion. He appeared the same easy, careless individual, who would not trouble himself to consider whether he was watched or not, or whether his actions were the subject of other people's thoughts, or whether they were unnoticed, it mattered nothing to him.

"It is singular," he muttered to himself, "very singular, how it could all happen by accident, and only at moments when I was watching him. I can't tell; and yet the occurrences were of that character, to another they would seem wholly unconnected, and I am unable to connect them, save by fancy; but he looks not a very old man, but rather like one who has the full use of his faculties. He is singularly pale, to be sure, and yet, at times, he does not appear so old, nor does his arm and leg seem quite so bad at others; perhaps it varies, according to circumstance, weather, the moon, or unforeseen changes."

He remained cogitating very quietly by himself; he was thoughtful, and could by no means divest himself of the idea that there was something more than common about the colonel.

"He don't seem so blind with that eye as he might be," he muttered; "but there is no use calculating about an Indian; they have got such luxurious habits and fancies, that if he fancies one of his eyes is in any degree weak, he will wear a shade for its preservation. Well, he is entitled to do so, but he ain't so old as they imagine. And that will be no detriment to him or to them; so much the better, unless they reckon upon the colonel's death, which would hardly be an object to them, seeing that it could bring them no more; indeed, it would diminish their income. But he is a tall man now, and, if he did not stoop so much, would yet be a fine man."

These thoughts passed through his mind, time after time, during the whole evening; while the colonel himself was at times conversing in the most refined and courtly language, and doing much towards amusing them with anecdotes of the places he had seen, and the battles he had fought.

"You would be surprised," he said, "to

hear that, in India, there are places so cold that they more resemble the Polar regions than central Asia, of which we only used to think of as being one of the hottest regions in the world, filled with wild animals and numerous serpents."

"Certainly, we hear more of that than anything else — the yellow fever, the cholera, and all these kinds of things, caused by exposure to the heat."

"So they are; but it is only in the plains, and not on the high table lands and mountains, where you gradually meet with more temperate climates, many of which equal northern Europe for salubrity; and, further up, you come to frozen regions."

"Indeed! that is a phenomenon."

"Oh, dear, no; the altitude of the plain, and the exposure, make the sole difference. I remember once, I was sent with some other regiments to chastise some of the hill tribes."

"Under whom was that?" inquired the attorney.

"General Walker," returned the colonel; "he was a very able general, and we performed some extraordinary marches under him, as well as some service."

"Oh, indeed!" said the attorney; "what might have taken place?"

"I will tell you an incident that did take place; and not relate more scenes of carnage that we passed through in the execution of our duty than shall be actually necessary. We had, on one occasion, to storm a city; on another, a fortified town; it was strong, and well protected by nature and art.

"Well, we arrived there, and the gates were closed against us; guns were brought to bear, and men appeared on the walls.

"We expected, of course, a sharp time of it, and being only the advance guard, we halted for the main body to come up with us; and, after having summoned the garrison to surrender, we put posts and watchers for the night, not expecting to do anything upon that occasion; nor did we expect the main body up with us till the middle of the next day, they having sent word on to me that they would not be up in consequence of some accident to some part of the train, which would have to be repaired; but a portion of the troops would advance a stage nearer to me, in case of an accident, upon which I could retire for support, or send to them to come up as the exigencies of the moment should most require; but they did not anticipate any movement at all. Nor did we; the fact was, we had made a forced march of it; and had got over more ground than we had expected, and our main body did not think we should have been so near the scene of action as we were.

"However, a counsel of war was held amongst the officers; and it was resolved that we should attempt nothing without the assistance of our comrades, as the place was very strong, as I have before told you.

"Well, sir, half the night was over, and we lay fast asleep, having had a hard — very hard day's work of it, — so hard that we could sleep sound on the bare earth; we were all suddenly awakened by a loud explosion, which shook the very earth under us; and, upon starting up, and rushing out of our tents, we saw the earth and air illumined by the explosion of, as we afterwards learned, and guessed at the moment, one of the enemy's powder magazines.

"In another minute we found there were plenty of falling missiles, with the debris of the magazine, and the mangled corpses of the men who were near it.

"There was an instant order to muster the men; everybody knew what was meant. They were all ready in a few moments — indeed, we slept by our arms — fully accoutered, so it did not take long to be ready for action.

"We were ordered to form in divisions and bodies, and as there was ample breach made by the explosion there, I was ordered to mount the breach, and enter the town for the purpose of assault.

"We did this. We marched down upon the breach after some difficulties, and were fairly in it; but had our commanding officer known any of the difficulties; he would not have incurred the responsibility of ordering us to advance, for the ruins we had to scramble over were dreadful, and, had there been light, we could every one have been picked off by the enemy.

"Darkness was our friend, and we got into the town with a comparatively trifling loss, and when our men got together they began to tell a tale, for their volleys were well directed upon the enemy, who were drawn up in masses, and whose fire directed ours. We were not completely exposed to their fire, for the same objects that exposed our men, as they were surmounted before reaching the enemy, protected them from immense volleys of musketry.

"However, we carried the point, and at that moment another explosion took place in some other part of the town, which illumined all around for a moment or two, and then came masses of bricks, and stones, and timber, killing friend and foe.

"For a while we were staggered; we did not know what to think of this affair. We knew not whether we had an enemy to fight, or even where he was. We were completely at a standstill.

"But this did not last long. The defenders fled, and left us masters of the field. We remained under arms all that night, till daylight.

"Glad were we, indeed, when daylight came; we were fatigued, so much so that our men could scarcely stand in the ranks. Then parties were sent out to look after the wounded, who had been left in all imaginable situations. It was at such a moment that I was discovered; my leg was shattered by a musket bullet."

"And you lay bleeding all night?"

"Yes. Not exactly bleeding, for I had sense left me to bind a ligature over the wound to stop the effusion of blood, which would have killed me in a very short time. However, there was no necessity to lose my leg, but it has made me permanently lame."

"I see you are so, sir," said Twissel; "but do you never feel it worse at some times than at others?"

"Yes, I do. There are times when I do not know that I have received a hurt at all; but sometimes I suffer a little, and am a little more lame in consequence."

"It was fortunate," said Twissel, "it was your leg, for it might have been your head, you know, and that would have been a death-blow to your fortune."

"Yes," said the colonel, mildly; "I might have been killed, as you observe;

but at the same time I should have done my duty, which in these cases is all we looked to. I might have saved a better man, who had a wife and family — I had none."

Conversation now ran on the forthcoming event, and Mr. Twissel was invited by the colonel, and the whole party were well satisfied with each other, and parted very good friends, with the promise of meeting again before the propitious morning which was to unite the fates of Margaret Meredith and Colonel Deverill.

CXLI.

A NEW CHARACTER. — MISS TWISSEL'S VISITOR. — THE INVITATIONS.

NOTHING COULD EXCEED the smoothness and easiness of the course of things in the wooing of Margaret Meredith; all things appeared so well ordered. People were all of one mind; and it is needless to say that the young lady was elated. She was elated, and we might not be out of the way in saying she was elated overmuch, and knew not how to keep the exhibition of her joy within proper bounds; she could not help showing she was to be the lady of a colonel.

Mrs. Meredith, too, was well pleased. What could she do but feel proud at the change that was about to take place? She would go to watering places in the summer, and remain in town during the winter; they would lead a very fashionable life — they would be of the elite, and all their acquaintances they would be compelled to cut, or, at the most, only speak to them when they were unseen by any others.

It is astonishing how a change of circumstances produces a change in our habits and feelings; how it happens that those who were considered respectable acquaintances suddenly become the objects of our aversion, and we begin to devise all sorts of methods for evading recognition, or of speaking to them when we can avoid it.

This arises merely from the change in one's circumstances, which causes us to look for something much beyond what we have been used to; but, unfortunately, it brings ingratitude often in the train of its consequents.

"My dear," said Mrs. Meredith to her daughter Margaret, "we really cannot know the people at the corner house over the way, who invited us to their parties."

"Oh, dear, no, we cannot think of it; but we must get rid of them the best way we can. You see they will not be quite the thing for us when we come to have our change of circumstances, you may depend upon it; it will become necessary to weed one's acquaintance."

"Yes, that must be done," said Mrs. Meredith.

"And the sooner we set about it the better; for the more intimate we continue now, the more trouble will there be of getting rid of them afterwards."

"Certainly; we need not accept of their invitation for to-night."

"Oh, dear, no; I have dismissed the whole affair from my mind, and there is no need even of thinking of it any more. I shall not even think of sending them an answer; the consequence will be, they will be angry, and expect we shall go and apologise, and when they find we don't, but that we try to get rid of them, they will be baffled, and the whole affair is settled."

"That is a very good plan, my dear. Then, you know, there are the Morgans; we must positively get rid of them. It will never do to have those young men hanging about; the colonel would do something dreadful, to say the least of it. Why, he would shoot them, and perhaps have a separation, who knows?"

"But then I should be entitled to a maintenance."

"You would, my dear; but unfortunately you well know you have no property, and that, added to an early separation, would put it in his power to offer you and compel your acceptance of a very small sum, which he may pay as he pleases — weekly, monthly, or quarterly."

"I see, ma; but we will run no risk of that kind of thing. Moreover, there would be those girls, they would be a nuisance hanging about the colonel."

"No doubt, and the cause of unhappiness in the extreme. Better to leave all such people; you are a great deal better without them. Why, I tell you what, you will be at no loss of company or acquaintances, you will find they will be sure to spring up; property is sure to enable you to choose those whom you will have, and whom you will not — the reason is obvious enough. Moreover, like loves like, you know, and people with means soon find out people who have none."

"Yes, ma, and those who have plenty; besides, a colonel, and a man of rank and standing — and everybody knows that a colonel in the India service is a rich man — and that would bring us all into the best of society. Only think of my going to Bath, Bristol, and Brighton, in their seasons. Of course we couldn't keep company with people who can't afford to go to some fashionable place at least once in a year."

"Oh, dear, no; certainly not, my dear; but there is no need of our troubling ourselves about that matter; we shall only go when the colonel goes, and we shan't be seen without him, and he'll be a constraint upon them; and, therefore, where they find themselves uncomfortable, they will not come again."

"That will be a very good plan, for it will appear as their own faults; but, at the same time, I do not trust to that upon all occasions; it might fail, and then we should have to take some unpleasant steps to get rid of them, which is certainly easily done, but unpleasant."

"Yes, yes, certainly," replied the mother; and then suddenly, as a knock and ring came upon the door, Margaret said, "Dear me, who is that? — I hope none of these people whom I have been speaking about — it will be a dreadful nuisance to all; especially when I am to be married in three days more."

"You needn't be seen, Margaret; I'll see them."

"Do, ma; and I'll go up stairs. But let's hear who it is first, who comes today."

At that moment she heard the door

open, and her own name pronounced, and at once knew the speaker, and she said to her mother, —

"Oh, ma, 'tis Miss Twissel, my bridesmaid; what an infliction! but, then, I must see her. She has come, I suppose, to consult me about some new gown, or the way in which she and her friend will have their hair done up on the occasion — nothing more important, I dare say."

"Very well, my dear; they had better come in — send them in pray," she added to the servant. "Oh, Miss Twissel, how glad we are to see you."

"Now, really," said Miss Twissel; "how kind you are, for I am sure you speak the truth. Oh, Margaret, don't you feel all of a flutter?"

"I don't, indeed; I am very comfortable. I hope you are all quite well — don't put yourself out of the way on this occasion; you need not, I assure you."

"Oh, I have got my pa to give us new gowns, and some lace; but I did not mean to tell you that — I and Martha had agreed that that should be a secret between us; that we should not say anything about it to any one; but surprise you on your wedding morning."

"Ah, you have been at a great deal of trouble and expense about this affair, I am sure. You really must not think I wish you to do all this; I really don't know how to scold you enough, for I shall be dressed very plainly indeed."

"Oh, but then you are the bride — we ain't, you know, and that makes the difference; besides which, we have a visitor come up to London to see us."

"Indeed! some young gentleman, I suppose, whose heart you want to run away with, and so have another wedding, and upon your own account this time; and, perhaps, you are helping Miss Martha to a husband. What is he — a physician or a divine?"

"Neither — but, I will tell you, he is only an old man."

"An old man! What a sweetheart you have chosen, to be sure! but, I dare say you have your reason as well as other people. But have you know him long?"

"No, we haven't done so; but, the fact is, pa' and he have had some business together, and they are very much in each others company. He's a man, however, of great rank, though a very odd man to talk to, I assure you, but a man of rank and property."

"Indeed! Oh, tell me what he is — a lord?"

"Well, he is not much short of it; and he is higher than a great many lords, I assure you. Why, he's no less than an admiral — only, I wasn't to say anything about it."

"Oh, will he be with you when my marriage takes place?"

"Yes, he will; and I wanted to know, as he will be much with my father, and as a visitor, shall we be intruding to bring him here to grace your wedding?"

"Oh, yes; by all means," said Margaret, who thought he presence of an old man could in no way interfere with any of her schemes; besides, a man of rank, such as an admiral, would greatly increase the noise of her marriage. Indeed, here was probably a new acquaintance with whom she could be intimate; besides, it was some one of consequence on her side that the great man was to come, and would, she thought, add some lustre to herself.

"Well, then, I would not ask him until I had seen you, because it might turn out you would be displeased; and, as I have not done so, I cannot tell you whether he will come or not. He's a strange man, and I won't ask him until the night before."

"Very well; we shall be quite happy to see him. I dare say he'll come, if you tell him who's going to be married. Indeed, if he's likely to come, I'll invite a few friends to meet him; but I won't say anything to anybody about it."

"No; let it be a surprise to them all; and let nobody know whom they are going to meet."

"That will be delightful, certainly — very delightful. What a surprise it will be to them to be introduced to Colonel This and Admiral That. I declare I long for the day on account of the confusion that some persons will be in."

"I must now bid you good-bye; for I've got to call upon my dressmaker, to give her some orders."

"You will stop and take tea with us? Surely you won't run away."

"Oh, but I must," said Miss Twissel, and so said Miss Martha, and after much pressing and refusing, they parted, and left Margaret filled by other thoughts than those she had so recently held.

"Ma'," said she, after a long pause, "do you know what I have been thinking of?"

"No, my dear, I do not."

"Well, then, it is this, that after all, we may as well make a bit of a figure for the last time. That we will have some friends who will figure upon that occasion and no other."

"What makes you think so, my dear Margaret?"

"Why, you see, ma', we are likely to have a distinguished visitor, and we may as well have as many as we can; their number and dresses will look well, and as we shall leave town immediately, I don't see that we shall be at any future time annoyed by their visits. Indeed, it will be retiring from their society after giving them a feast."

"Well, to be sure, I never thought of that," said her mother — "I never thought of it. What shall we do now — how can we provide for so many?"

"Send an order to a pastry cook to provide breakfast for so many, whether they come or not, and then we need trouble ourselves very little about giving them time. If we tell them about the day before, they will have all in readiness for us."

"Well, well — and as for the expense, it will be of no consequence."

"None," said Margaret. "I shall be able to pay that and others, if we owe any. But now comes the job of inviting visitors, and we must only invite those who will make up a show, dress well, and pass off on the occasion for fashionable people."

"Oh, as for that, there are many people who never had a penny in their lives to call their own, may be very fashionable-looking people, and pass for men of a thousand a year, to say nothing of a lord looking like a workman, and the like, which is common enough."

"Then we'll settle it at that point, ma', and you had better superintend the invitations and the other affair — the breakfast, I mean."

"Very well, my dear; you know that I have no objection. I have seen such occasions before, and I well know what they ought to be; therefore you may safely rely upon my judgment in such an affair as that at least."

"And about the selection of friends — visitors, I mean."

"That you may also leave to me," said Mrs. Meredith; "and, depend upon it, I will not invite one party whom we shall have cause to say we are sorry they came; though, you know, every allowance would be made for them by the colonel or admiral, if he come. By the way, I would not tell the colonel a word about it, for sometimes the land service hates the sea service, and the latter often laugh at the former; so it will be safest to say nothing."

"No, ma, I won't — I didn't intend to do so."

Thus both mother and daughter had suddenly changed their views of what was to take place on the day of the intended marriage. They were now resolved they would have as many of their old friends as they could get together upon the occasion, to cause the affair to go off with all the *éclat* that it was possible; it would be the last ball of the season — that is, it would be the last she ever intended to give them, and that would be the last occasion upon which they would meet.

Her respect for Miss Twissel was augmented by the knowledge that she had an admiral for a friend or a visitor, it didn't matter which. Who could tell what might happen? Mightn't Miss Twissel marry an admiral, as ugly as she was, as well as she should a colonel? but there were many reasons why she should. She, too, might have had some means of entangling his heart; perhaps, after all, she only came there with him for the purpose of showing him off.

"At all events," said Margaret, to herself; "at all events, he is one that we can keep on terms with; and it will look well to be acquainted with some person of rank. I am, at all events, well pleased it has happened as it has."

Mrs. Meredith, on the other hand, appeared to think her daughter's marriage with a colonel, ought to be celebrated by no common rejoicings; that, indeed, the marriage ought to go off with as much disturbance to the whole neighbourhood, as it was possible to make.

This could not be better effected than in the manner we have referred to; namely, inviting a number of persons to come and be present at the ceremony, and to take a late breakfast, and to wish the bride joy, to see her depart, and then to lose sight of her, as she hoped, for ever.

This purpose Mrs. Meredith ably carried out, and she succeeded in inviting about two- or three-and-twenty persons together; and any person who had a carriage and would come in it, was sure of an invitation — that was a passport to the marriage feast.

"Well," she muttered to herself, as she reckoned up the number of persons whom she expected to be present upon the occasion — "well, I don't think I have omitted any one who ought to be present, nor have I invited any one who ought not to be here. I shall have a busy day of it — very busy day; but the result is everything; so long as the marriage takes place, and we are really married to an East Indian colonel, why we shall do, there can be no doubt of it."

This was a consolatory reflection. There was but little else, indeed, that could be done — little, indeed. The cook had the orders for the entertainment the next day; they had but little to do in the household with that; indeed, they had extra hands, lest there should be any need of them, as she would not have anything go wrong upon such an occasion, for worlds.

But there was one thing that gave her some satisfaction, and that was, Mr. Twissel had not been to them lately to give any doubtful counsels; ever since she had announced her intention of permitting the marriage to take place, he had not been to express any doubts about the matter; but had been a mere spectator, doing all that was necessary. He had forgotten all objection, and never made one. He was perfectly quiescent; but would now and then look very hard at the colonel, but that was all; he never discovered anything, and all was smooth and pleasant.

CXLII.

THE WEDDING MORNING. — DISRUPTION OF HARMONY, AND THE NEW ACQUAINTANCE. — THE CONCLUSION.

ACCIDENT, STRANGE TO SAY, had taken our old acquaintance, Admiral Bell, to the house of a lawyer, there to transact some business, as well as to lodge at his house. The fact was, the old admiral hearing that a brother officer was in trouble — one who had shared with him the dangers of the sea and the fight — he came to town to see, himself, what could be done; and finding the affair beyond his comprehension, or, at least beyond his power of personal interference; that, in fact, it required the aid of a third party, and that third person must, of necessity, be a lawyer, he determined to employ the man who happened to be conversant with the circumstances of the case, and this was no other than Mrs. Meredith's friend, Twissel.

However, the admiral's good will towards the race who follow the law, not being so great as his philanthropy, he determined to watch every stage of the proceedings, and to permit nothing to be done without his knowledge, and to see that nothing was neglected.

Hearing from Mr. Twissel the affair that was to take place, a sudden crotchet entered his head, that he should like to be present at the ceremony, and he broached it to Mr. Twissel, who turned to his daughter to ascertain if it were at all possible.

That young lady was desirous of shining among her acquaintances, as one who could introduce an admiral, and who did not like the idea of Margaret Meredith being so fine a lady as she now attempted to make herself appear; indeed, she would have been willing to have assisted in raising her some species of mortification; she felt more than true pleasure in the disaster that would be the cause of such feelings. There was a very general dislike to Miss Margaret Meredith, and the truth was, she was much more than usually arrogant and proud, and took all imaginable methods of vexing and mortifying those around her.

But there is little to be said about that; the consent was brought back to the attorney, who felt somewhat elated at it, and communicated it to the admiral, with some remarks upon the kindness and condescension of the persons who had done him so much honour.

This, however, only had the effect of drawing from the admiral, the word, "swab," and then he became silent and did not appear to be at all taken aback by the knowledge that an East India colonel was the bridegroom on the occasion, and one of very large property and singular behaviour.

THE EVENING BEFORE the marriage was a busy one. The young ladies had to arrange and to re-arrange all their finery; and the bride herself had the task of seeing how she became her bridal dress, to do an infinity of other little matters, and to contemplate the change that was about to take place in so short a period. A few hours more, and she would become a wife.

The colonel, himself, did not in the least fall off in his ardour; he was particularly anxious it should, on no account, be delayed after the day fixed. A later day he appeared to have the utmost objection to; indeed, he declared he would do anything if it came but a day or two earlier.

However, this was considered impossible, and the young lady was permitted to have her way, though it was expressly stipulated that it should not be an hour after the appointed time, for he declared himself dying with impatience to call her his own.

"Now, ma," said Margaret, as she sat talking to her mother the night before; "now, ma, I hope you will not give any of these people countenance when I am gone, and throw off their acquaintance; you will be firm on this point for my sake."

"I will, my dear," said Mrs. Meredith, "I will."

"Then, when I come back, I shall know more of the colonel's mind about where we shall live, and how we shall live. He must let me have something handsome; I have no doubt but what he will; he does not appear to be a close-handed man, quite the reverse; and, all things considered, we shall be able to make a very agreeable living out of it."

"Why, yes, my dear, I cannot doubt it; he is, no doubt, a man of property and can well afford us enough, and some sum as pin-money; indeed, he is too liberal now to be otherwise bye-and-bye; perhaps he will keep on this house, and pay for proper domestics, and keep a carriage. What a change it will be for us all, and how the neighbourhood will stare!"

"Yes, ma, they will; but suppose we were to reside out of town, we should have our carriage driving into town, as a matter of course, and now and then sleep in town when we made up a party, or went to the theatre."

"Yes, my dear. What time shall you see the colonel in the morning?"

"Not before I am ready to go."

"To church? Well, but you will have some breakfast with him?"

"No, he will be in his own room, I dare say, till late; he will scarce present himself before the time has come to start;

you know his habits, he does not get up very early, and I do not expect to see much alteration. At eleven o'clock we are to be at church. We breakfast at nine, you know, so we shall have time."

"Oh, he is sure to be down to breakfast, there can be no doubt about that; indeed, he must be called for the purpose; of course, there must be some deviation from a regular rule upon extraordinary occasions like the present."

"Well, well, there may be; but have you given all the invitations you intended to give? — and have you got any answers to them so as to ensure their attendance?"

"Oh, yes, that is all safe and fixed; we shall have a good many here by half-past eight in the morning, at the latest; but you must contrive to let me have money very soon, or to send me some up, as I am getting very short, for I have laid out a great deal of money lately, and much more than I could, under other circumstances, spare or afford."

"Of course, ma, you will not lose anything by this; I shall take care of you; not a penny that you have laid out but what shall be repaid, and with a handsome return; but do not think about this, it grows late and I must to sleep."

"Do, my dear, and I'll wake you in time in the morning."

THE MORNING CAME, and some of them were about early. Mrs. Meredith was up, and so was Margaret. She could not lie so late as usual. She had done much, and yet she had so much to do still. It was really astonishing to see what there was to do — no one would have believed it, and even Margaret became surprised.

The morning was now fairly come; the servants were about in the house, and the neighbours were up and about; she could hear her mother chiding and scolding; she could hear the sound of her voice, and she began to believe there was now no time to lose.

The hour of nine was now gone. The knocker and the guests had been heard for the last half hour at the door, and she could hear the voices of the guests below, some of whom spoke audibly enough; then they soon after descended to the breakfast-room, which, by the way, was the drawing-room, as there was not enough room below.

The colonel, at the same moment, entered the room, and a vast number of congratulations were given and received, from side to side, with the utmost urbanity and good will. The colonel, for the first time, had thrown on one side the green shade which he usually wore, but he looked remarkably pale, though he had still the looks of a hearty and healthy man.

The paleness, which seemed to be constitutional, was very extraordinary; but that was explained by the colonel saying, that he had been so ever since he had the yellow fever, which had had that effect upon his complexion.

There was much rejoicing at the occurrences that were now in progress; everybody praised the viands; everything was of the best and first-rate quality, and there were many attendants, which made it so much the better and the more comfortable, as everybody had an abundance of everything.

Mrs. Meredith now shone in the greatest triumph; there was none so great and grand. She patronized everybody, and appeared remarkably condescending, considering she was the mother of a daughter who was about to marry a retired East India service colonel. There were few who did not understand fully the nature of the condescension of the lady herself; besides, she was the presiding goddess of the feast.

Among those who had been invited was Miss Smith and Mr. Smith. This was the young lady who had been so terrifed at the attack that had been made upon her the first night that Colonel Deverill lodged there, and on that night he was so terribly vexed and disturbed.

Mrs. Meredith had invited them, because they were people of means, and Miss Smith could not now do any mischief, because the colonel was pledged to Margaret too far to retract; and as there were several young females, why, the more the better, because it would divert his attention.

Miss Smith, however, came out of curiosity, and because it was a wedding party, which is the delight and admiration of all young females, and Miss Smith was no exception. Mr. Smith was civil and polite, and hid his internal dislike to the colonel, which he felt and could not account for it; neither did his daughter — she had a great aversion to him, but at the same time suppressed it.

The colonel was courtly and complimentary, and made civil speeches to such as spoke to him; indeed, he never for a moment lost his self-possession; he stood in a less stooping posture than usual, and he was considered a tall, handsome man — a fine man.

"Mr. Twissel," said the colonel, "I am happy to see you — especially gratified to see you — you will be witness of my happiness to-day — you will mark my progress in this affair, and learn what lesson it may teach. That is the way we should pass through life, Mr. Twissel, is it not? Gain knowledge by experience, and become, in old age, a wise man."

"Why, yes; oh, yes," said Twissel, who felt there was something in the remark that touched him to the quick, and he winced under the smart; but he thought it might have been accidentally given, and the colonel was quite ignorant of his disasters; and yet it was a very home thrust, without any previous introduction to it, that made it all the more uncomfortable, and he merely replied, —

"I am happy to see you, Colonel Deverill, and to see you so happy, and the young lady, who, I am sure, deserves to be happy; in fact, I think you both deserve happiness; I am sure, I wish you every imaginable joy, and it gives me great pleasure in seeing it."

"I am sure you do, sir; but you do not seem to eat and enjoy yourself."

"I am so occupied in witnessing the felicity of others, that I had forgotten it; moreover, I expect a friend to be present who happens to be late; he is quite a stranger to all present, and therefore I wished to countenance him as much as I could on that account."

"Then I will not press you now; perhaps you'll do me the favour of introducing your friend to me when he comes, yourself, and I shall be most happy to receive him."

"Thank you, colonel, you do me much honour; I will accept of your great kindness, and do myself the pleasure of presenting him to you, and to Miss Meredith, whom I hope to see soon changed in name."

"I hope the time will now be very short. What hour is it?"

"Half-past nine," said the attorney, consulting his watch.

"At eleven we must be at the church. Well, if we leave at half-past ten, then we shall be there in ample time; I would it were over and that we were on our journey."

"Ah! you are impatient, colonel," said Margaret, as she came up to him.

"My dear angel!" replied Deverill, bowing, "how could I be otherwise when you are the object of my affections? It is not impatience to leave this good company — quite the reverse. But it is because the change of scene, travelling, and change of air will do you much good, and is, I can see, quite necessary for you."

"I think it will do me no harm," said Margaret; "but here comes ma, who really looks tired."

"Well, my dear, I am a little fatigued, but you know I shall have ample time to recover myself. I shall have nothing to disturb my repose."

"Indeed, Mrs. Meredith!" said the colonel; "I am sure we must alter that; we must find some other kind of employment for you, and not suffer you to remain hidden at home. You have catered so well for us this morning, that I am sure you are a most valuable acquisition to a household; with such a superintendence as yours, we should have everything in the utmost plenty, and at the proper moment."

"Ah, colonel! you are flattering — you are."

"We shall soon show that we are not flattering, I hope," said the colonel. "My dear madam, you are the life and soul of the whole company. What should we have done without you? I hope all our friends here are happy and comfortable. I do not know them well enough to pay them all that attention and respect they deserve."

"Exactly, colonel; they all know that well enough, and are fully alive to the honour you do them in being present in the midst of them."

"Who is that young lady who was looking here just now?" inquired the colonel.

"Who? the young lady with the elderly gentleman by her side?"

"Yes; I should like to be introduced to her," said the colonel.

"Oh! certainly," said Mrs. Meredith, vexed in her own heart that she had invited her and her father, now, for she had no wish that any one present should be future acquaintances; but there was no help for it; she must introduce them, and accordingly she went up, with the best grace she could put on, to them both, to request they would be introduced to the colonel, who desired the honour of their acquaintance.

There was no hesitation, of course, and they at once advance to meet him, and were introduced to the colonel as Miss and Mr. Smith.

"I am most happy to see you, sir," said the colonel; "and the young lady here is your daughter, I can see, by the family likeness she bears to you."

Miss Smith, however, could not repress a convulsive shudder as she looked upon the colonel. It might have been his complexion, or it might have been that his features brought some terrible

recollections to her mind; but she could not, for a moment or so, speak.

"The young lady is ill!" said the colonel, who noticed the emotion.

"What is the matter, Clara, my dear?" said Mr. Smith; "what's the matter — you are ill?"

"No, no," said Miss Smith; "it was a — a — sudden — sudden dizziness that came across me. I dare say I shall be better bye and bye. I am sorry it should have come upon me now."

"Ah! my dear young lady," said Colonel Deverill, drawing himself up to his full height, and looking gravely, but speaking with the utmost courtesy, "you have nothing to regret respecting the occasion; the illness itself is a matter of regret to us all, I am sure; however, let us hope it will be but temporary, and that you will be able to wish me joy, and my beautiful bride."

"You see, Colonel Deverill, ever since the night she was disturbed by the strange attack of what she believes to have been a vampyre, or something that had the form of a man, and a taste for blood, she has been affected thus."

"Dear me!" said the colonel; "what a shocking thing — a very shocking affair! I think perhaps, the young lady is subject to illness," and he touched his forehead, as much as to intimate an insinuation that the young lady might be somewhat affected in her intellects.

"No, sir; quite the reverse," said her father. "I myself saw a tall, gaunt figure gliding away, which felled me in an instant, and I lay half a minute stunned."

"God bless me!" said the colonel; "this affair is quite romantic! If a German writer had such material by him, what would he not make of it?"

There had been a loud knocking at the door, and some one announced; but nobody took any notice of it. Colonel Deverill did not hear it, but stood talking to Mr. Smith; while Admiral Bell was introduced by Mr. Twissel, who led him towards the group, explaining what had happened.

"By G-d!" said the admiral; "d'ye see how they are crowding about the poor girl? Why, they'd extinguish a fire — if there was one! Why don't you give the young woman air? If you don't stand on one side, I'll put a whole broadside into you, as I would into a Frenchman!"

This singular address produced an immediate sensation, and many moved away.

"Colonel Deverill," said Mr. Twissel, "allow me to introduce my friend Admiral Bell to you. Admiral Bell, this is Colonel Deverill. — Eh? — oh! — eh?"

These latter exclamations were uttered in consequence of the extreme surprise depicted on the countenances of both parties. Admiral Bell's surprise was nothing out of the way; but that of Colonel Deverill was a matter of consternation to many of them. He stepped back a pace or two, and then his lips parted, as though he would speak, but he could not; he panted — his eye glared, and his nostrils dilated.

"Shatter my mainmast — upset the cabouse — turn my state-cabin into a cockpit, and the quarter-deck to a gambling-booth to the whole ship's company!"

"What's all this about?" exclaimed Mrs. Meredith. "Oh, that odious man! — who is he? — what is —"

"Why, ma'am, I'm old Admiral Bell; very well known for having beaten the French, and the terror of all vampyres. Why, look at the swab — but you ain't going to get off this time!"

"What is the matter, dear colonel?" said Margaret. "You are ill — speak — what is the matter?"

"Ah!" said the admiral; "let him speak, and he'll tell you he's no colonel, and his name ain't Deverill, or, if it be, it ain't his only name; he is Varney the vampyre!"

"A vampyre!" said Miss Smith, starting up with a shriek; "a vampyre! Good heavens! I was not mistaken, then; that must be the man!" and she sank back in her father's arms.

"What! has he been at any of his tricks again!" exclaimed the admiral, and he made a stride towards him; but Varney—for it was he—avoided him by stepping aside, and placing some other person between himself and the admiral, and then he said,—

"What this madman will say you will not listen to—you—"

"Madman! well, I'm hanged; call me madman!" said the admiral. "I wish I had my sword by my side, and I would teach you how a madman can fight; but you are not going; I have something to say to you first. If he's going to marry that young lady, all I can say is, she will be food for him—she'll never live till to-morrow; her blood will make his pale face ruddy!"

Varney stood no longer; but seeing many around him who appeared to have an inclination to stop his passage, he suddenly made to the door, which he secured for a moment on the outside, and then in another he was clear of the house.

This was no sooner done, than all present, who were staring at each other in mute amazement, and unable to account for what had happened, looked at the new comer, the admiral, who immediately began to relate enough of Varney that made it apparent to all present that he was not what he represented himself to be.

AMID THE COMMISERATIONS of their friends, and their jeers, Mrs. Meredith sold all her furniture, and, with her daughter, retired to some little place, where they opened a small shop, to eke out a living by such means. They were unable even to pay many debts they had contracted on account of this marriage, and they were, moreover, ashamed to be seen by their former acquaintances.

Presently the corpse opened his eyes and glared full at them. Oh, such glistening, lead-like orbs, that froze the very current of their blood ... (see page 963)

PART IV:

THE VAMPYRE ESSAYS TO DIE OF STARVATION.

CXLIII.

A SCENE IN WINCHESTER CATHEDRAL. — THE CATHEDRAL-ROBBERS. — A STORM. — THE VAULTS BENEATH THE AISLE. — THE FLIGHT OF THE ROBBERS, AND THE RESUSCITATED CORPSE.

THE SUN HAD LONG deserted the horizon, and the good city of Winchester had been buried in darkness many hours; while the moon, though high in her course, was obscured by the hazy clouds that drifted from the south-west. The gusty winds whistled round the walls of the cathedral church, producing an unpleasant sensation, with a foreboding of a coming storm.

The inhabitants of the quiet, orderly town were steeped in repose, and a stranger who might by chance have wandered at such an untoward hour abroad, would not have found one single ray from any window; save, perhaps, at one or two hotels, which merely keep open till the London mail passed through, lest any passengers should make their stay at Winchester.

Save at these places, all were reposing peaceably in their beds; and the tower of the cathedral frowned majestically upon the tombstones below, and upon the surrounding buildings, which appeared to peep upon the limits of the grave-yard; while the fir trees that were yet standing bent beneath the blast, as it swept across the low walls, by which the cathedral on one side is bounded.

But the solitary churchyard was not without its occupants, living or dead; for its sanctity is invaded by the presence of three men, who emerge from the narrow streets and courts situated between it and the cross, and then crossing beneath the shade of some object, they stood beneath the low wall which surrounded the churchyard.

They paused for several moments, and gazed around them in every direction, and up at the houses that were nearest to them; but there was no sign of light or anything stirring in any of the houses adjacent.

"I think all is right to-night," said one of the men to his companions.

"Ay, right enough; there will be nobody near us to-night."

"No," replied a third; "and if the signs of the weather are good for anything, why, we shall have a rough night; and though that is unpleasant, yet it makes interruptions less likely, and success more certain."

"You are right, Josh; we shall have a good job this time."

"There, then, that will do until we are safe; it's no use talking here; if the old watchman comes round, we may have to book it, and then we may not have a chance."

"Ha, ha, ha! as for the old watchman, he is not the fool you take him to be, if you imagine him at all likely to disturb himself on such a night as this; he'll sleep in his box till he wakes and finds it is fine."

"Well, be that as it may, " said the other, impatiently, "it is all right now."

"Yes, all right."

"Then just help me over, and I'll get down on the other side, while one of you can get up on the wall and hand the tools down to me."

"Can't you throw them over?"

"I could, but it is not worth while to make any noise, even though we felt sure that it will not be heard. There have been most strange things done in our time, you know, and there is no telling what may happen."

"Ah, the dead may come to life, Josh."

"So they might; and a pig might fly, but, as they say, it is a very unlikely bird."

"Well, then, up with you."

As he spoke, one of the men gave one of his companions a lift up, and with this aid he got on the wall, and then quietly slipping down into the burial-ground, he awaited his companions, one of whom immediately mounted the wall in the same manner, and who received a bag, which he handed down to his comrade, who was in the graveyard belonging to the cathedral.

"Well, is all right?" he said.

"Yes, all right; don't stay up there like a cat on a wall; come down, or you may by chance be seen."

The other two men immediately came over the wall, and they all three collected round a monument that stood up, and here a short consultation took place.

"Now, how shall we proceed?"

"We must get into the vaults somehow or other, if we dig our way in, which I think is much the most easily done."

"What! undermine the building?"

"Scarcely so much as that."

"Well, but we can get into the body of the cathedral, and then into the vaults that way. There is a door."

"Yes, there is a door, but it is so close to the verger's door, that you are sure to awake him."

"I have opened more than one door in my time, and yet I never awoke anybody in doing so; he must sleep wonderfully light."

"Aye, so he may; but in this case the door is so strong that there is no chance of breaking it open, without great inconvenience and noise; there is no room to work in, and, moreover, the verger keeps a little cur always sleeping on the mat close to his door, so that no one can approach without his giving alarm."

"What a brute!"

"Yes; but there is a means of entering besides that."

"Where — and how?"

"In the back of the cathedral there is a large marble slab, on which is carved some letters, that I never could make out; but I'm told it says that somebody lies buried underneath that stone, but I know immediately below are the vaults."

"Well, but the marble you speak of would weigh fourteen or fifteen hundredweight, which would be no joke."

"No, by Jove," said his companion; "we had better by far dig our way in, since we shall have so much difficulty in getting in; we can soon dig out soil enough to let us get down into the vaults."

"Well, we had better set to work at once, lest we lose all chance. If we have a long job, we had better set to work early, as well as stop here, for if we are surprised we shall have to run."

"And the yard will be watched ever afterwards, as sure as we shall have a storm presently."

"So we shall. Work away, Josh; where are the tools?"

"Here they are," said the man, throwing the bag down and opening it; and then he pulled out some tools, consisting of pickaxe and shovels, and a crowbar or two, and several other little materials, which were useful upon such occasions.

"Well, now, where shall we commence?"

"Just at the side here; we are safe to get in somewhere where the wall is weakest, for I believe the vaults are all walled in."

"They must be, to have a secure foundation for such a weight as there must be about it; and, to my mind, we have got a decent job. It's very much like a fortress, and if it was easy to get in this way, we should hear of such things being done much oftener than they are, that is my opinion."

"And a very good opinion it is, too, until another is heard; but it is no use being faint-hearted; the harder the job, the harder we ought to set at it, that's all; but there are some few things not thought of by others, you know, and it is sometimes the hardest thing in the world to think of the most simple."

"There's some truth in that."

The men having found the spot they most desired, they set about digging and picking it up in good earnest; but it was difficult work, and the soil about the cathedral was very hard, owing to the quantity of rubbish that had been driven or trodden into the earth for centuries, either through accident or design, to harden and secure the permanency of the work around. There were many heavy and large stones, as well as small broken stones; also, flint in no small quantity, that every now and then resisted the blows of the pick.

"Well, I'm thinking we have all three worked half an hour, and have not got a foot deep yet."

"We have not got much deeper, certainly."

"Do you think we shall get in to-night?"

"To-night or never," said the third man.

"You are right, comrade; shoulder your picks and then we shall see what way we can make in another half hour. Who can tell? we may come to a softer soil below; this is only the filling-up."

The men again set to work heartily, but they seemed to have no success — they could not make anything of it; it appeared to resist all their efforts; and the sparks often flew from the blows they made with their tools.

The perspiration ran down their faces, and as they paused to wipe their foreheads, they gazed upwards at the clouds. It was heavy, and the wind was blowing fresh, and now and then a heavy spot of rain.

"By St. Peter," said one of them, "I expect we shall have a storm presently. I already feel the heavy drops that fall occasionally; and if one may judge by them of what we may expect, we shall have it heavily."

"So much the better; we shall have less interruption."

"Well, I don't know what you call interruption, but this is a complete stopper; I can't make any impression with the pick, it is as hard as rock; and then comes some of those old walls that are rather harder than granite — you may as well pick at a cart-load of pig iron."

As this was said, the clouds suddenly appeared to open, and such a deluge of rain descended, that the earth seemed to smoke. The drops appeared to be continuous small spouts of water — a shower is too mild a word — it was a deluging, as if some waterspout had burst.

The men stood a moment or two, but it was useless to work; they could not do it, and they rushed to a part of the wall which sheltered them from the fury of the storm that was raging.

"Well, I never saw anything like this before."

"Nor I. Hark at the thunder! There's a flash! Who would have expected that at this season of the year?"

"Not I."

"Nor any one else; but it seems to me as if we were to be defeated to-night. I am sorry we made the attempt, since we are sure to find the yard watched after this, for they will see what we have been up to."

"Yes, it is vexing, but we cannot help this; it is quite impossible to do anything in such weather as this. I do not care about a wet jacket, but I cannot see, and hardly breathe, with so much falling water about me."

"Nor I; but yet I am loath to give it up; consider the jewellery and money he had about him — it will pay us handsomely."

"Well, it was a strange start of him, at all events. I wonder how he came to be buried in such a manner — how was it?"

"I don't know. All I know is, that the thing was kept secret because it was considered that it would be a temptation to disturb any grave when it was known that he was buried in his clothes and jewellery, and that his money was buried also with him. It was certainly a temptation I could not resist."

"Are you sure?"

"Yes; I will tell you, another time, how I came to know all about it; indeed, I saw him screwed down, and the consequence is, I know that he has the money and valuables about him."

"Then I am sure we had better get into the church itself; we can do more with your slab of marble than on the outside of the wall. And besides that, I do not think that this rain will give over; the hole we have already made is fast filling up with water, and we shall find it impossible to work."

"So we shall. What do you say to getting inside the cathedral?"

"Agreed, my lads; as quickly as you like; for, if we stay here much longer, we shall certainly be drowned. I'm wet through as it is."

"So am I; but never mind, my boys, bright gold and jewels will warm your hearts, and that will keep your outsides dry, or at least you will not feel it. I am sure that I should not if I can but get it."

"Aye, that is all I care about; but, if you get foiled, you may depend upon it you don't feel any the better — you are rather worse, and feel everything more; but what do you say to yon window?"

"That will do if we can reach it: that is my only difficulty."

"That is one that is easily overcome," said his companion, "for I know where the ladder is, and that is just over our heads; all you have to do is to put the point of the crow-bar under the staple to which the chain is fastened that secures it, and then you have the means at once of entering."

"But if we get in and are detected, how shall we get out again?"

"Are we not three to one? If the old verger should come, I think we could make a dead body of him in a very short while; and I cannot tell where you will be if you can't get the better of the old man."

"Well, say no more about it; up with the ladder, and we will get in and chance it. Such a night as this, it would be strange, indeed, if anybody heard us; but, as there is much to be got, why, we can't grumble at the risk."

The three men set to work about wrenching the staple out to which was attached a chain which secured the ladder. That was soon effected, and the ladder placed against one of the lowermost windows, and then one of the men went up, and forcing the window open said, after he had looked in, —

"All right — come up. We have got to a right place."

They all three came up one after another, when the first up crept in at the open aperture, and by means of ornamental work, and a monument that there projected from the wall in a manner that enabled them to descend with ease, and in a few moments more the whole three stood in the old cathedral of Winchester.

At that moment the bell tolled heavily the hour of twelve. The sound was solemn, and it made a deep impression upon the robbers.

"What a dismal, hollow sound that has, to be sure," said one.

"Yea; it sounded like tolling."

"Pshaw!" said one of them; "'tis no matter — if it be tolling, it is not for us, nor for the man we come to visit, so no more old women's fears; if you don't like stopping in this place, you had better set to work and be quick, when we shall have no further need of staying. Of what use is it for you to stare and gape about with white faces, and swelled eyeballs, like so many cats; be men — be active, and use your arms."

"Well, where are we to use them? What are we to do? You brought us here, and yet you do not tell us what we are to do. You know all about this matter, and you cannot, or do not point out where we are to commence."

"Here, then; on the very stone you are standing; set to work to raise this, and then we shall soon find our way into the vaults below, and we shall then satisfy ourselves for our trouble, and be well paid too, I hope."

"I hope so, too, Josh; for, to tell you the truth, I don't ever recollect so uncomfortable a job as that which I am in to-night."

"Well, you ain't got paid all, I'll warrant."

"I haven't got paid at all, yet; but we waste time; lend me a pick. I don't see how I am to get a tool in here. The chinks are all so small, that you can hardly put in the blade of a penknife."

"There is a hole somewhere near the head. There is a small piece of black marble."

"Yes; here it is."

"Well, chip that out, and then you may insert a crow-bar, or pick, beneath the stone, when you will find that it will lift up, and then, by main strength, lift it back, and we may go down."

These instructions were followed out. The black marble was discovered, and then knocked out, when a large crevice was discovered, into which a powerful crow-bar was immediately thrust; and then, by one united effort, they contrived to lift the marble slab up out of its place, though not above a foot, which required a great effort, when it is considered that it was imbedded in cement.

"Well, we shall be able to get it up now, I think."

"Don't be too sure, for we have not got it far — it is enormously heavy, and the lever has done all as yet."

"Well, then, are you all ready? A long pull, you know, comrades, and a strong pull, does the business. Now, then, altogether."

"Heave, ho!" whispered another, and they all three made a prodigious effort. It was not only a strong pull, but a very long pull, for the stone was so heavy, it came slowly and unwillingly upwards, and it was nearly three minutes before the enormous mass stood upright in the aisle.

"Well, I didn't think it would have been done. That's the hardest job that ever I had a hand in, and don't desire to have such another, but yet, hard as it is, it is easier than what we had to do outside."

"Yes, much, and you will soon find it is so. Lend a hand to clear away the rubbish that lies here; there's a trap-door underneath that leads into the vaults; it belonged to the monks of old, of whom it is said it served either for the same purpose of burial, or for a cellar for wine."

"Well, well, there are some things better than wine, I trow, in the cellar, now, if we can find the coffin; there has been no other burial in the vaults since he was buried, so we shall not have much trouble."

"But what are we to do with the stone? If we let it down again, we shall do some mischief."

"We must turn it corner by corner until we get it against the pillars, and there leave it; for if we let it down, it will go down like the report of a gun, and smash all that comes in the way."

This was agreed to, and it was not long before they propped the heavy mass of stone against one of the pillars, and then returned to the place where it had been raised, and began to clear away the rubbish, when a trap-door was plainly observable; and after much labour and force, they contrived to open the door, when there appeared a dark aperture, into which they could not look without some misgivings, for nothing could be seen.

"Well, who's to go down?"

This was a question that no one liked to answer. And certainly no one would volunteer to go below. It was too dark to be inviting, and the men looked at one another as well as they could, for it was total darkness, or nearly so, in the aisle; and below, it was so utterly dark, that it was impossible to make out anything.

"What is to be done now? Have you got the lantern?"

"I have, and matches, but did not think we ought to use them before, lest we attract attention; however, we will have a light now, and should anybody look down, they will think there is a general meeting among the dead."

So saying, he lit the lantern, which threw a light into the vault, and rendered visible a flight of steps that ran up to the opening, but which were invisible in the darkness that had reigned in the place.

"Now, then, jump down, and see where the last coffin is placed; it is easily known from all the others, for I don't think there has been a burial here for many months — the old cathedral is not often disturbed for the reception of the dead, and only when some rich man dies and fancies he may lie more comfortable here."

"Ay, rich men can afford to be buried in a good suit of clothes, and money in their pocket, to bribe St. Peter to open the gate."

"Ha! ha! ha! well said; Peter has the keys."

"Yes, and here we have the coffin."

"Have we? Is this it?"

"Yes; don't you see that it has all the signs of newness about it? There is hardly any dust collected upon it; here we shall find our treasure; the coffin is a strong one, and will, I think, take some trouble to break open."

"Indeed! We shall be choked with the horrible stench which we have below. I can't stand it another minute — I shall be sick."

"Ay, and I too."

"Here, then, I have the lantern. Lay hold of the coffin and bring it up stairs;

we can carry it amongst us."

"Ay, anything but remain here — that I cannot do."

"Be quick, for confound me, but such a mass of putrid flesh as there must be here, is horribly sickly. I would sooner be hanged than pass an hour here."

"I'm not so afraid of death as all that. I could manage to live through a night."

"You might, but you would soon find out the ill effects, and die of some fever or other; and that is what we shall have, if we remain here much longer."*

The three men then shifted the coffin from its place, and then on to their shoulders, one at either end, and one under the centre.

The coffin was heavy — very heavy, and the men were tottering under their burden. They were strong men, but hardly equal to the task of carrying so dead a weight; but yet they never shrank from it, but, with slow and unsteady steps, they gradually neared the stairs that led upwards. They paused. If it was a task before, it was worse now. What more exertion could they make?

"Do you think the steps will hold us?" said one.

"I'm sure I cannot say; and perhaps not."

"I think they are rotten, or partially so; what do you say? How shall we get the body up?"

"There is a rope, is there not?"

"Yes."

"That will do then. I will get that; by its means we may hoist the coffin up to

---

* *In the 1840s when this book was written, the germ theory of disease was still decades in the future, and the mainstream theory of how disease spread was through miasma, or "bad air."*

the stone pavement above. I'm almost sick."

"And I too. This place is enough to breed a pestilence in a town."

The smell in the vaults was certainly very strong and very pernicious. The foetid odour that rose from the vaults was especially disagreeable; the smell that comes from the accumulated and putrefying remains of human bodies, is of all odours the most noisome, and, to our tastes, the worst.

Right glad were the men, who had propped the coffin up against the ladder, to get up into the aisle above, to breathe a less impure atmosphere. They gasped again; and one of them climbed up the monument, to get to the open window, at which they had entered, to inhale some of the pure moistened air; and then, after a few inspirations, he returned, at the call of his comrades to aid them.

The rope was procured and secured round the coffin, and one man remained below to guide it, while the two others remained above to haul up the rope, which would bring the body, coffin and all, to the top.

"Well, Josh, how goes the storm?"

"It is blowing over, I think; it does not rain, and it is breaking. I shouldn't wonder if we don't have moonlight after all, and, if we should, we shall have a trouble to get away unperceived."

"You forget what hour it is."

"Hark! there are the chimes."

The four quarters now chimed from the great clock, and sounded solemnly and mournfully in the dead of the night. The iron tongue struck one, and the last sounds of the clock died away before any of the men moved or spoke.

"Well, we have been here an hour, and nearly two hours since our first commencement. It's nearly time, I'm thinking."

"Yes," said the man below.

"Heave ho!" called out the leader of the gang, in a low voice.

The two men at the top hauled at the rope, while he below pushed the coffin up with all his strength, and after a time they succeeded in causing it to rise about a foot, or something less, at each haul, and as it got higher, the man below could the better apply his strength to it, and at length it came up to the top.

Here, however, they experienced another difficulty. It was hard to pull up so high as to enable them to throw its weight on the pavement, and the rope was almost useless as a means of pulling it up higher, and the only one who had it in his power effectually to apply his strength, was the man below. However, after a while, to their great relief, the coffin lay fairly upon the stone pavement.

"A good job done!"

"So say I, Josh; and such another would completely finish me for the night. I might lie down and defy the world."

"How about the coffin — there is no time to rest. I have a small flask of rum in my pocket, which we will discuss as soon as we have broken open the coffin, which I expect is the last hard job we shall have."

"And a hard job it would have been, had I not come provided with a screwdriver — one that is used by undertakers in such work."

"Set to work — good luck to you. I am quite dry, and quite tired too, and the sooner this is over the better. There, the screws come out easily enough, though they are long and hold firm."

"Yes, they go deep; but they have a wide worm, that carries them down or brings them up so quickly."

In a few minutes more the whole of the screws were drawn, and the lid of the coffin was thrown on one side, and the corpse was at once discovered to them. It lay calm and quiet; but yet it was terrible to look at. The living man had been tall — remarkably tall, as well as remarkable-looking.

He was dressed as if for walking. It was strange, the corpse was apparelled as if were in life; and this, perhaps, caused the extreme paleness — even extreme for a corpse — to be so apparent that they spoke not, but gazed in silence upon it, until at length one of them said, —

"Put out the light. We have the moon's rays — at least there is enough to enable us to see what we want, and the light is dangerous."

The light was put out, and the subdued light of the moon rendered all apparent enough to the robbers.

The storm had lulled and altogether ceased, while they had been busy in the vaults and getting up the body, and now it was a perfect calm. The moon, though obscured at the moment, promised to shed her rays upon the earth; and as it was at the full, and the clouds clearing off, the probability was that the town would become as light as day.

"There he is," said one of the men.

"Yes; and about as ugly a chap as ever I saw."

"He is no beauty: but he's been a fine man."

"If you mean tall, I dare say you are right; but he's not fine as I take it. He's not quite full enough about the chest and shoulders."

"He's got some fine rings, and a gold watch and chain. Well, there is a good ten or fifteen pounds each, and if his pockets are well lined, why, he will afford us a tolerable good booty."

"Yes; we must not complain. Shall we replace all?"

"It is not possible to do so, either in time to enable us to escape, or to do it so as to escape detection. Besides, there would be no use in it. See how bright the moon is getting. We shall have as much to do as we shall get through to escape being seen. I am sure we shall run a great risk."

"I think so too."

"Well, then, commence proceedings. Ha!"

The moonbeams had fallen upon the corpse just as he was speaking, and he thought he observed a motion in the body.

"What is the matter, Josh?"

"Didn't you think he moved."

"Ha! ha! ha! dead! ha! ha! ha! dead moved — buried moved — ha! ha! ha! Eh? why — oh — it's all fancy; you'll see me believe it, presently. I do declare — well, a man dead and buried — I suppose a week."

"No."

"I think so —"

"Well, it does not matter much how long he has been buried; but he can't move unless you move him. — D — n!"

As he spoke he started to his feet, and his hair began to straighten, and his limbs quiver, and yet he appeared to think he might be mistaken; for he endeavoured to speak to his companions; pointing to the corpse, he contrived to say,

"I —'ll —'ll take the j — j — jewels;

he — he — he moves."

"Eh? Well, I told you I thought so, but you said no, and only laughed at me for doing so; but stand on one side, and let the moonlight come upon him, we can tell better then if he really does move; though, notwithstanding all I saw, I am inclined to believe it is quite an impossibility; but the more light we have the better we shall be able to tell how the mistake arose."

"I thought I saw his eyes move."

As he spoke he moved on the side, as

he had been standing between the corpse and the moon's rays, and for the most part intercepted them; but the moment that he did move away, and the rays came full upon the corpse, a shivering motion appeared to pervade it, to the intense horror of the robbers, who could not believe what they saw, but believed they were yet mistaken, though they were too much terrified to speak or even move. They stood gazing upon the body with bursting eyes and gaping mouth, as if they had suddenly become spell-bound by the wand of some magician.

Presently the corpse opened his eyes and glared full at them. Oh, such glistening, lead-like orbs, that froze the very current of their blood; they knew not what to think, but when the body turned on one side, towards the moon's rays, all doubt vanished and the spell was broken.

"The devil, by —!" exclaimed Josh.

Not another word was uttered by either of the other two; but they sprang like emancipated madmen up the slippery sides of the monument, and out at the windows, as easily as a fly can run up a wall. It did not occupy more than a few seconds to enable them to clear the place. Half a minute had not elapsed before they stood shivering by the beautiful old cross, at Winchester.

THE CORPSE in the cathedral, which mysteriously became animated when exposed to the moonlight, turned towards the moon's rays and gazed upon the flying and terrified robbers, who had just exhumed him.

No word passed his lips, and he looked around him for some time in silence, upon the scene before him.

The moon came in at the tall windows of the cathedral, throwing long streams of silvery light upon the stone flooring, and upon some of the monuments that were erected by the pillars, or columns that rise to the roof.

All was silent, all was still — no movement was discernible, save in the form that now sat up, and leaned on his elbow in his coffin; and he but turned his head slowly from side to side, as though he were meditating upon the lovely and solemn beauty of the place.

At length he arose, but he appeared to move with extreme difficulty, and once or twice he placed his hand in the region of the heart, as if he felt something there that pained him, and tottered about; but seemed to recover himself a little after a time, and muttered to himself, in low but distinct tones, —

"I must have another victim; I am weak, the vital action is languid, and my veins are empty; I must satisfy the instinct of my nature, and another victim must restore me to life and the world for a season."

He looked up towards the window, gave one look around him and on the coffin, while a shudder passed though him; and then, gazing on himself and feeling for his valuables, he slowly clambered up the monument, and carefully got through the window, and thence into the open air, and he finally disappeared from Winchester churchyard.

CXLIV.

THE STAR HOTEL, AND THE STRANGER'S ARRIVAL. — A REMARKABLE
COUNTENANCE. — THE ILLNESS AND DEATH OF THE STRANGER. — A STRANGE
REQUEST COMPLIED WITH.

SOME DAYS PREVIOUS to the scene related in the previous chapter, the London coach drove up opposite to the Star Hotel, and, as usual, out came a couple of waiters to see what there was from the metropolis, in the shape of a passenger, who might become an inmate of the hotel, and a customer, of course.

"Now, then, Billy," said the guard, a stout, good-humoured fellow, to a very stiff and punctilious waiter, dressed in black, with a white neckerchief.

"My good friend, my name is William, if you must be familiar, though I am sure I don't number you among my acquaintances."

"Very good, Billy. I declare you are one of the politest waiters that is to be found between Portsmouth and London; aye, and more than that, you are *the* politest. Didn't you say you were edicated among a lot of gals — young ladies, I mean?"

"I never held any discourse, relative to my early days, with you, my friend; I am not, just this moment, aware of it."

"Ah! I see you are too polite to pass an east wind without taking your hat off to it; how do they when they have none?"

"Have you anybody for us?" said William, mildly.

"Yes, my pink, I have."

"Who is he, and where is he? I must not waste my master's time; it is an impropriety I am especially anxious to avoid."

"You needn't be in a hurry, nevertheless, especially as I see he is fumbling about for small change; but what will you say if I introduce a customer to you, a good six foot high, and perhaps a little to spare; and the colour of a well-scraped horse-radish? Eh? what do you say to that, my promrose?"

William did not know what to say, but, after a moment's hesitation, he said,

"We don't charge our customers by the room they take, or by their personal appearance. A gentleman is a gentleman, Mr. Guard, all the same, whether he have a red face or a white one."

"Well, that's good, Billy; but the chief thing is, after all, of what colour is his money, and how he parts with it; eh?"

The guard winked and William's impassive features were lit up with a spark of intelligence and vivacity, which, however, was only transient, and he relapsed into his old state of extreme and unimpeachable gentility.

"Hold your tongue, Billy; here he comes."

At that moment the gentleman pulled down the window, and said to the guard,

"Open the door, if you please; I shall get out here."

"Yes, sir," said the guard, who immediately obeyed the injunction; and a tall, but awfully pale, individual descended the steps, wrapped up in a huge cloak, so that but little of his person was seen, or features either; what little there was visible was not prepossessing by any means by the colour.

"This is the Star?" said the stranger, inquiringly.

"Yes," said the guard.

"I'll stop here. Are you the waiter?" said he, addressing William.

"I am, sir," said William. "Will you walk this way, sir?"

"Yes; show me into a private apartment — let me have a good fire, for I am exceedingly cold."

William immediately took him into a room where there was a fire, saying, —

"If you please to remain here, sir, we will make you a fire and warm the room; and, as you are cold, perhaps you will prefer this to going into a room without a fire there already lighted for your reception."

"Certainly, I much prefer it."

"Would you like to take any refreshment, sir?" inquired William.

"Not now," replied the stranger, in mild accents.

William left the room, muttering to himself, —

"Well, he deserves to be a prince; he is as mild and gentlemanly as a prince. I vow I never heard any one speak in such a tone, and with so much amiable condescension. What a pity he is so white — at least, that he is so, I only infer from the nose, and part of the forehead and cheeks around the eyes — these being the only parts that I have noticed; he is, indeed, not much unlike, in colour, to the guard's vulgar simile — a well scraped horse-radish. I

never saw white so opaque and dead before."

While those thoughts passed through the mind of William, he saw that the apartment was placed in readiness for the stranger's reception, and placed himself in communication with the proprietor, and obtained his orders; he then returned to the stranger, and conducted him to his proper apartment, and then awaited his commands.

The stranger gave him some orders, which were at once executed, and then he said, —

"I shall sleep here, of course."

"Yes, sir," said William.

"I am very particular about my beds — I must have my bed well and thoroughly aired."

"Oh, yes, sir," said William; "we always —"

"Never mind, never mind all that," said the stranger, blandly. "Never mind all that; I know what you would say. All your beds are always aired. Well, be it so — I have no desire to dispute it — but I once slept in a damp bed — I fell ill, and have never entirely recovered from it."

"Oh, that makes him look so horrible pale," thought William.

"So you perceive, my friend, that I have cause to be particular, and, therefore, you will excuse me when I inquire minutely into the character of the beds."

"Oh, certainly, sir — certainly, sir."

"Then you will see that my bed is aired, will you not?"

"Yes, sir, I will take care that it is especially aired; and, if you approve of my doing so, sir, I will have a fire lit in your bed-room."

"If you please. If you will do all this,

you will greatly oblige me. Are there any females in the family?"

"Yes, sir; the servants," said William, fearing some impropriety was meant.

"Oh, the servants; and no others?"

"None," said William, quite suddenly.

"Oh, yes, that is right — none but the servants. Then my requests will not put you to any serious inconvenience?"

"Not in the least, sir," said William, pleased to find that the females had only been inquired about for fear of annoying them.

The stranger sat up in his room, and appeared to be very ill, and ate and drank but little, though he ordered whatever was requisite for a liberal individual; and, though taken away untouched, yet it was clearly understood he would have to pay for it.

The bed was used and approved of, and the tall, remarkable-looking stranger expressed himself satisfied to the proprietor of the hotel, who came to inquire if he should desire anything more or different from what was already done.

This was at once answered in the negative, and the proprietor retreated by no means prepossessed in the stranger's personal appearance, which was remarkable to a degree — that was noticed by every one in the hotel.

"Winchester is an old town — a city — sir," said the proprietor, by way of entering into a conversation with his guest.

"Yes, very old," said his guest.

"And the cathedral, sir, has been built in part ever since the Saxon times, and then increased by the Normans."

"Aye, it is very beautiful; one could

wish to lie there, it is so calm and beautiful," said the stranger, with a shudder, which he endeavoured to suppress; and then he added, "The grave-yard is quiet and retired."

"Yes, sir. You have been in Winchester before?"

"I have," replied the stranger.

Finding any further attempt at conversation likely to appear intrusive, the landlord quitted the apartment with a bow, which was condescendingly returned by the guest, who folded his hands one over the other, and turned towards the fire, upon which he gazed thoughtfully for some time in silence.

The strange and ghastly-looking countenance of the stranger had created quite a sensation among the individuals at the hotel, all of them declaring they never heard of, or saw anything equal to it in all their lives. But what was it? How did it happen so? They had seen dead men, but they had never seen any so ghastly and so fearfully pale.

"He doesn't seem long for this world," said one of them.

"If you had said he didn't belong to this world," said another, "I should almost have been inclined to believe you."

"He does look like a corpse," added an old woman.

"Yes, and what a tooth he has projecting out in front. Upon my word I never saw his like."

"And I," said another, "never beheld such eyes. Why, he is scarcely human. Such eyes as those I scarcely wish to look at again."

"He always appears to me to be in some dreadful agony," said the cook; "he really looks as if he had a perpetual pain in his stomach, and had eaten something that had disagreed with him."

There was some truth in this last assertion, for the stranger always did appear as if suffering from some internal pain — mental or physical, or both — and it was soon seen that he was rapidly losing strength, and could scarcely walk abroad.

The cause of all this none could tell; possibly, it was only a sudden illness, or perhaps it was a long affliction, to which he was used to, and hence the terrible expression upon his countenance, which appeared as if it had never been otherwise, so deep and so settled was the expression of pain.

THE STRANGER APPEARED anxious to get out, but was unable to do so; he could just walk across the room several times in the day, but was unable to get down stairs; and whenever he attempted to do so, he sunk down, his limbs losing the power of sustaining his weight.

"I can go no further," he muttered to himself, as he endeavoured to walk down stairs; "I am lost."

As he spoke, a truly horrible expression came across his countenance, that made William, who came to his aid, step back terrified.

"You — you are ill, sir," he said, in somewhat uncertain accents.

"I am ill," he replied, "very ill."

"Will you allow me to help you up, sir, to your room?"

"If you please," said the stranger, who was endeavouring to rise by the aid of the bannisters; and by these, and with William's assistance, he got up; and then,

with some difficulty, he reached up stairs — his own bed-room.

"I will send master immediately, sir."

"You need not be in any hurry," said the stranger. "I do not desire his presence."

However, William left the stranger to seek his master; and when he found him, he said, —

"Oh, sir, the strange-looking gentleman in No. 5 is very ill."

"Is he, William? What is the matter with him?"

"I am sure I don't know, sir; he sank down on the stairs just now, and could only get up to his room again by my help."

"Something serious I think, then. I thought he appeared ill when first I saw him, from the expression of his countenance."

"Yes, sir; 'tis very strange."

"Very," said the landlord, thoughtfully. "I'll go and see him; but, in the mean time, you had better send for Doctor Linton, who knows me, and will come at once."

"Yes, sir," said William.

The landlord immediately sought the stranger's apartment, which he entered without any ceremony, and advanced to the bed in which the stranger lay; and, upon his first glance at the occupant, the landlord stepped back in affright, so truly terrible did the countenance of the stranger appear.

"Ah," said the stranger, as he turned his glassy eyes upon him.

"I — I — I have come to see you," stammered the landlord. "I have come to see you; my servant informed me you were ill, sir."

"I am very ill."

"I feared so, and I have sent for Doctor Linton, who will be here immediately."

"It is of no consequence; I believe, I am too far gone to recover." Another horrible spasm passed across his countenance.

"What does your illness arise from?"

"Decay of the system. I want renovating," said the stranger.

The landlord paused; he didn't understand this at all, for the stranger did not bear the appearance of decay about him. He was tall, and seemingly of the middle age, he thought, and nothing about him to savour of decay, save, indeed, the terrible and remarkable paleness which his flesh appeared to bear; and his system generally, in other respects, bore nothing of the appearance of general decay.

"Shall I send for any one, sir? Have you any friends I could write to for you?"

"None, sir, thank you," replied the stranger, who, however, bated nothing of his politeness, even in his present position.

"Have you any desire to see any one in particular?"

"No one, I thank you."

At that moment Doctor Linton was announced, and the proprietor having introduced him, left the apartment, leaving the doctor and his patient together; the former at once perceived, and wondered at his extraordinary paleness. After a few preliminary questions, he appeared quite puzzled, and said to him,—

"May I inquire what is the cause of this extraordinary complexion?"

"Certainly," said the stranger; "it was caused by damp beds."

"Damp beds," muttered the doctor, amazed, and hardly comprehending what was said, or the nature of the reply; he was at a loss, but did not say so, what was the connexion between cause and effect.

"Yes, damp beds," said the stranger.

"Have you ever suffered in this way before?" inquired the surgeon.

"Yes, more than once."

"And you have recovered?" said the doctor, abstractedly.

"I am here," said the stranger, mildly.

"Truly, you are," said the the surgeon. "I had almost forgotten that, your case is so singular. Your pulse is very low and irregular."

"It is," coolly replied the stranger; but immediately a kind of spasm shot across him, as he had before exhibited to the landlord.

"Do you feel much pain?—does that often happen?"

"No, only occasionally. I don't think you are at all likely to benefit me, sir," said the stranger, with much courtesy in his manner. "I do not mean any disrespect to you; but my complaint is a fatal one in our family."

"Are you all afflicted in this manner?"

"Yes, all before me died," replied the stranger; "and when it does come on, we have no means of avoiding the end that approaches; there is no medical aid that can be rendered, ever did us any good."

"You are quite an exception to nature, sir," said the medical man, "quite an exception. Your case cannot be beyond the assistance of medicine—if not to cure, to ameliorate—though its nature may not be ascertained; but if we could do so, we could tell you what we might be able to do."

"That has been attempted before," said the stranger, mildly; "and hence it is I am loath to give you needless trouble."

"Well, I will call upon you, and see you again; but you ought to take some medicine. I am persuaded that it is some great and extraordinary derangement of the system — a complete sinking of the whole system."

"Most undoubtedly it is a sinking in the whole system — a sinking which has never yet been stopped by human aid. But you can pursue what course you may deem proper."

"Will you take medicines if I send any?"

"Yes," replied the patient; "I will take them when you choose to send them."

"I will endeavour to send you something that shall infuse something like vitality into the system, that will indeed help you to rally."

"That will, indeed, be doing something more than was ever yet done by any one who attended any individual of our family. I feel I am very weak, and am sinking fast, and do not expect that I shall again have the honour of seeing you."

As he again spoke, the same spasm seized upon him; his frame was convulsed for more than an minute, and his pallid features appeared to give forth expressions which it was impossible to describe.

The doctor paused, and gazed with something like fear and awe upon him. He had never before seen such a case so destitute of facts, nor yet such a man; it was quite beyond his experience; there was nothing like it in all his previous experience; there was no apparent cause for all that he saw. It might be some severe chronic disorder which did not manifest itself outwardly. If this were the case, it was most extraordinary.

But more extraordinary than all was, apart from the medical question, the strange and terrible appearance of the stranger; his paleness — the terrible expression of his features — the strange, and even revolting cast of his eyes, that completely baffled all his attempts to understand them, or to remember anything he had ever heard of, or seen.

The stranger languidly turned in his bed, and then closed his eyes, leaving his medical attendant to his reflections.

"Well," muttered Doctor Linton, as he looked at his incomprehensible patient. "I never met with so fearful a human puzzle before. I never saw such an expression of countenance in all my life; nor did ever I meet with such a case. Had he been one of the fabled monsters of old, the creation of the German mind, he could not have been more unlike a human being, to wear a human form."

As he spoke, he quitted the room, and made his way to the proprietor of the hotel, who was as anxiously waiting to see him, as he was to meet him.

"Well, doctor, what do you think of the patient?"

"Why, I don't know what to think. I never saw such a man before in all my life — I cannot make him out."

"Nor I. I can't understand what he means or what he is."

"Nor anybody else. But he is quite a gentleman; and yet there is something very frightful to be seen in him. I don't know why it is, I don't care about going oftener to him than I am obliged."

"I don't doubt it. There was something in the feel of his hand more like a corpse than anything I ever felt before."

"Indeed — it is a queer affair."

"Do you know him?"

"No, I do not," replied the proprietor. "He has not been here more than two days; and when he entered he had that deadly paleness which he has now."

"Did he indeed. It is, I dare say, natural to him, though it must create an unpleasant sensation, go where he would."

"He must feel it to be so, no doubt; but, at the same time, he could not avoid it. Have you come to any conclusion respecting his complaint?"

"I have not indeed; I will send him some medicine; though, to tell you the truth, I can hardly tell what is the matter with him. His disorder seems to consist of a rapid sinking of the whole system, accompanied by a few minor symptoms, and a spasm, which must be very painful; for it produces an extraordinary effect upon his visage, and his eyes glisten like a piece of tin."

"That's it, doctor. Do you know, I have been thinking for something to which I could liken those eyes to, but could not do it. When do you see him again?"

"To-morrow, some time; in the mean time I must bid you good day, for my presence is wanted in the Dundrum family."

"Oh, have you any of them for a patient?"

"Yes, two. Good day — good day."

"Good day, doctor," said the proprietor of the hotel, as he bowed the doctor out and then, returning to his own apartment, he wondered, in his own mind, at all that had been said by that learned individual, when William entered his room with a hastiness of manner quite unusual to him.

"What is the matter, Willam?"

"Oh, sir — I beg your pardon — but the strange gentleman —"

"Eh! — Well! — What?"

"Why, he's dying, and wants to see you, sir."

"To see me, William — and dying!"

"Yes, sir — it's very sudden — but good Lord, how dreadful he looks. He clasped his hands and shook — it made the bed shake and the windows rattle, just as if an earthquake were taking place."

"Goodness me!" muttered the proprietor, who immediately quitted the apartment, and followed William to that of the stranger, who lay in the same attitude as that described by William; but he was evidently endeavouring to repress all nervous emotion, and by the time he was spoken to, he succeeded in this endeavour completely, and lay apparently calm and collected for the landlord's appearance.

"I believe you sent for me," said that worthy, in a subdued tone.

"Yes; I wish to speak a word to you before I die."

"Die!" said the landlord, with a start. "No, no, you cannot mean that — you will get better — you are deceived."

"No, no; do not endeavour to persuade me from believing what I know is the truth. I shall die, and that, too, before many hours."

"If the case is so urgent, let me send to Mr. Linton; he cannot have gone far, and he will return."

"Nay, do not do that; his aid is utterly useless — utterly."

"He is a clever man; but still, if your own feelings tell you that you can't live, allow me to send for a clergyman."

"My friend," said the stranger, "I have settled all that in my own mind. My affairs are all made up, my account is cast, and I shall learn the balance where I am going to. I wish, while I have breath, to beg a favour of you."

"Anything on earth that I can do, I will," said the landlord.

"Nay, I do not desire — all — that — I — I only want you to — to — to — promise me you'll — attend to my funeral."

"All shall be done as you desire."

"My breath — I feel it going. I have money enough about me; you will find in my pocket-book and purse, a certain sum."

"Yes, sir — yes."

"And with that you will have the goodness to liquidate my debt to yourself, my funeral expenses, and place the residue of that sum about my person."

"When you are dead!" exclaimed the landlord.

"Yes; will you promise me — will you swear to see it done?"

"Yes, I will — I do swear."

"See you keep the oath; my breath is going fast — my strength is leaving me — and — and —"

"I will do all." said the landlord again. "Will you have any friend attend your funeral obsequies? It's melancholy, but I am obliged to speak of it to you, because I cannot otherwise know your wishes."

"Do not mind that," said the stranger, turning towards the landlord; "but when I am dead, dress me in my clothes, just as if I were about to walk; let me have all my property and my money — such of it as remains after paying all charges — the remainder cause to be placed about my person — in fact, all that belongs to me; and place — me — and place me — me — me —"

"Where — where would you be buried?" said the landlord.

"Place me," gasped the dying man; "place me in the — the —"

A gurgling noise, succeeded by a sharp rattle in the throat, was all the sound that escaped him, while his glazed eyes were fixed, with a truly horrifying expression, upon the features of the landlord, whose presence of mind appeared to forsake him, and he exclaimed, falling on his knees in affright, —

"Lord, have mercy upon us, what a dreadful affair!"

"Horrible, sir," said William.

"Oh! are you here, William?" inquired the landlord.

"Yes, sir," replied that individual.

"Oh, I'm glad of that; did you see him die?"

"I did, sir. How dreadful!"

"Very; but I am glad you were here because he has made some singular requests about burying him, and in a certain manner, with all his clothes on and his jewels and money about him. Now I should be considered foolish if I did anything of the kind; but I have promised, and as he has no friends, I will do what I have promised."

"It is very good of you, sir; though I think he has been very silly in making such a request; yet you cannot be so considered for performing the wish of a dying man; it is the duty of any one so promising to perform it."

"Quite right, William, quite right; but did you understand what he meant by his last words? I mean, where he wished to be buried."

"I don't know positively, sir, but I think he meant the cathedral — I thought so, at least. I am not sure he said so, but I believe he meant to do so."

"Well, I think so myself; and in the cathedral he shall be buried; but it is a terrible-looking corpse. I'm sure I could not sleep in the same room with him. Poor fellow! What he'll come to at last there is no telling."

"Yes, sir; he does look dreadful."

"You needn't tell anybody we have a dead customer in the hotel, William."

"No, sir."

"Because people might be curious, and wish to see him, and if they were to do so, I am sure they would leave the house."

"So they would, sir. He's a dreadful-looking corpse. I never heard of such a one. What can be the cause of it? — and to be buried in his clothes, too!"

"Aye, and his money and his jewels; that is very strange!"

"Very strange, sir, indeed; and the fewer persons who know of it the better, else the body will not lie very long in its grave. There will be those who would not mind turning resurrection-men* for the value of what he had about him."

"So there would be, William; and now I think of it, the authorities of the cathedral shall know nothing about it; for who can tell what fancy they may take concerning it being an unchristian burial?"

"And yet, sir, he paid all his debts like a Christian."

"Yes; and left a remembrance for the waiter."

"There could not be a more Christian act than that, for who could be more

Christian-like than to remember the waiter?"

And William at once admitted the truth of the assertion, and they both left the room, and instructions were given to William to obtain the proper aid respecting the funeral, and an order was given to the undertaker to come and measure the corpse for its last garment.

All these things were duly attended to, and kept secret, so that a very few persons were aware of the fact that so strange an occurrence had taken place in the good city of Winchester, much less were they acquainted with the precise locality of the very house in which the occurrence took place.

When the morning arrived on which the funeral was to take place, some persons were surprised to behold a couple of mutes standing side by side at the door of the Star hotel, and there had been no previous signs of mourning.

The hearse and one mourning coach, however, were all that attended, into which one solitary mourner entered. There were several others made up for the occasion, to give the cavalcade an uniform appearance.

The body was carried down by eight men. It was very heavy, and the men bent beneath the load they bore, and when it was placed in the hearse, the one mourner got in, and they proceeded towards the cathedral, which was quite close at hand.

A few — very few minutes served to bring them to the goal, and before the entrance of the cathedral they stopped, and out came the undertakers, who contrived, with much exertion, to carry the body into the church; and then, after some preliminary ceremonies, it was

* A "resurrection-man" was a slang reference to the grave robbers who dug up freshly buried corpses and sold them to medical schools as cadavers.

conducted into the vaults, where it was deposited, and the burial service was said over it most duly and solemnly, and then left, it was presumed, safe and secure, to abide its final doom at the day of judgment.

But many thoughts prove but the shadow of our wishes, and this seemed but as a mocking shadow; as our readers are aware by this time of what actually took place in the dead of the night.

"In what name was the deceased registered — the burial, I mean?" inquired the clergyman, whose memory, like some of his other faculties, was obscured by age.

"His name was Francis Varney," replied the chief-mourner, who was no other than the proprietor of the Star hotel.

In a small cupboard were packed a heap of human bones — more than bones, for they had yet the flesh dried and sticking to them — the skull was brown and bare, save here and there remained some hair. ... (see page 1017)

PART V:

The Vampyre Woos a Bride on Holiday.

CXLV.

A RURAL SCENE BY MOONLIGHT. — THE STORM. — AN ACCIDENT ON THE ROAD. — A NEW AND STRANGE ACQUAINTANCE ACQUIRED. — A DISAPPOINTMENT.

IT WAS ONE OF THOSE pleasant, moonlight evenings that are frequently felt, as well as seen, towards the end of August, that a party of individuals sat in a travelling-carriage, and were proceeding at an easy pace on one of the cross-roads that run from Winchester to Bath, and also from Southampton, the Isle of Wight, between Salisbury — more properly speaking — and Bath.

The evening was lovely: the day had been sultry, and the sun had not been gone down so long but that the heat of his rays yet remained. Indeed, though the moon gave light, yet the radiated heat from the earth, first received from the sun, was so great, that the light evening breeze barely tempered the air.

The party thus proceeding had been spending a few weeks in rambling about Southampton, Portsmouth, and Salisbury, and were now wending their way to the city of Bath. They consisted of but four individuals, — Captain Fraser, his wife, her sister, and younger brother. The latter did not count more than twelve years, while the sister, Miss Stevens, was just seventeen years of age.

Captain Fraser had scarce been married six months, and was upon one of the early matrimonial jaunts which often take place in the earlier part of the married life, when all is sunshine, and the matrimonial barometer might always have the index nailed to "set fair" at such periods.

The lady's sister and brother were residing with her; for their parents were dead, and hence they, the captain and his lady, were their natural protectors.

They were riding in an open carriage, the head parted, and thrown back; and even in this manner they felt the evening air was scarcely, though riding, cool.

"I don't think," said Mrs. Fraser to her husband, "that ever I beheld so beautiful a scene. The time — the warmth of the air — the occasional delicious feel of the light evening breeze — the serene light of the moon; altogether, I never felt so comfortable, or, I may add, so happy as I do at this moment."

"I am glad to hear you say so," said the

captain; "it gives me an additional pleasure to find I can please you."

"Now, Fraser, that is too bad of you."

"What is too bad, my dear?" said the captain, inquiringly.

"Why, to say you are glad you can please. That is as bad as to say that it is a very difficult matter; and you know I am very easily pleased, especially when you make the attempt," said Mrs. Fraser.

"Well, we will not quarrel about that, my dear. But I must say, with you, this hour, time, and place are all one could desire, and such as we seldom meet: the scene across the country is truly beautiful!"

"Yes," said Miss Stevens; "it is beautiful, as far as we can see."

"What river is that yonder?" inquired the brother.

"That is the Willey; the same that we saw at Salisbury," said Captain Fraser.

"Indeed! I thought that came from another direction more northerly."

"That was another arm of the same river, and joined this about there, and all the low grounds on this side of yon hills are called the Valley of the Willey; and a beautiful little vale it is, too, fruitful and picturesque."

"How beautiful the moonbeams glisten on yonder water!"

"They do; but not so strongly as they did."

"No. What is the reason of that? The air appears to darken. I have noticed it for some minutes past. Why is that?"

"I suppose it is caused by the evaporation from the grounds and heavy dews, to compensate for the want of rain that usually takes place at this time of the year."

"Then we shall be obliged to shut up

the carriage, for the dew is more likely to cause cold than anything else."

"It is so; but we are upon comparatively high ground here; and, moreover, they will not reach us yet; but, here are shawls; you can wrap up if you feel chilly, or you can put on your veils."

"It is yet so warm," said Miss Stevens, "that I should be reluctant to put on any more clothing yet-awhile."

"Do as you please, but do not take cold," said Captain Fraser. "How indistinct the scene becomes around; the river, which we just now saw so plain, is quite obscured, and you can scarcely tell where it is, save here and there, where the doddered willows appear, and which mark out the course of the stream."

"It is so," said the youth. "I can just see the green tops of the trees appear above the thick mist that rises from the river below."

"Exactly; that is the fact."

"And see how it spreads itself over the cornfields and meadows."

"Was that not a flash of light?" said Mrs. Fraser, suddenly.

"Light! I saw no light," said the captain.

"Nor I," said the youth; "did you, sister?"

"No, I did not do so; but it is very sultry, and therefore it is very likely just at this time of the year. How much farther have we to travel before we stop for the night?"

"I suppose seven or eight miles, not more."

"There, that was no mistake, however," said Mrs. Fraser, as a flash of light shot across the heavens, and left not a trace behind it.

"No, there was no mistake about it; nor did I think so before," said Captain Fraser, "only I have not noticed it; but it is harmless — it is what is called summer lightning, and has none of the the ordinary results of lightning."

"It will possibly make the air cool," suggested Mrs. Fraser, "and, in that case, we shall have a more agreeable temperature; to tell the truth, the extreme warmth and dryness of the air gives a strange uneasiness to the body."

"Another flash — ah, that's a change in its character."

"Yes; that is the blue-forked lightning, and I am much mistaken if we do not have a sudden change — hark!"

At that moment, a sullen and deep rumbling was heard in the heavens, followed by another flash, and then such a peal of thunder that boomed and rattled through the air in a manner that startled the dull echoes of the night, and made the welkin resound with the fearful sounds that filled the heavens.

"We shall have a fall of rain in another moment," said Captain Fraser; "push on, drive on, and let us get out of this as soon as we can."

"Aye, aye, sir," said the driver, and crack went his whip — the horses increased their speed, and they rattled on at a good pace.

"Had we better not stop and have the hood closed?"

"No," said the captain; "I can manage that very well, with the assistance of your brother, and we shall not lose time."

Captain Fraser, and the young gentleman alluded to, brought the coach-top up and secured it, just as a heavy shower descended in such torrents that they could scarcely hear themselves speak, so heavily did it rattle upon the leathern covering of the vehicle, and they sat for some time in silence.

Soon, however, the thunder and lightning filled the air with sounds and flashes in a manner that began to create a feeling of alarm in the minds of the ladies, and some uneasiness in the mind of the captain; not upon their account only, but because the cattle might take flight under the circumstances, especially as they were fresh, and had now scarcely run three or four miles; for their stage was a long one before they reached their destination, which was now about two days' easy journeys.

The thunder and lightning appeared to become more and more terrible; the storm, indeed, appeared to increase rather than diminish in intensity; the very centre of the storm appeared to be fast approaching, and making the spot upon which they stood the pivot on which it turned; its fury increased, and with it the horses were each moment becoming more and more unmanageable. Though in some measure aware of the fact, Captain Fraser kept his place, fearful lest he should alarm his wife, and at the same time distract the coachman.

Suddenly there was a bright and vivid flash of light, such as they had not seen before, but which illumined the whole place around them, and made everything as visible as if placed in the strongest light imaginable, followed by such a crashing peal of thunder that the living earth appeared to rock again.

It wanted but this to make the horses perfectly ungovernable, and they dashed away at a furious speed along the road.

"Good heavens! the horses have taken fright," said Mrs. Fraser, as she became aware of the speed they were going at.

"They have merely taken fright, my dear," said the captain, unwilling to increase their alarm by informing them of his own; "he will keep them in the middle of the road, and we shall be at our journey's end the sooner, and the more so the better."

They were upon the point of being satisfied, when the jolts of the carriage, added to its eccentric course from one side of the road to the other, attracted so much of their attention that Miss Stevens said,—"See, captain, how the carriage sways from side to side; we shall all be over in another minute or two—we shall all be killed!"

"There goes the thunder again, worse than your kettle drums," said young Stevens, who appeared to think it rather a joke; "the lightning flashes, too, as if we had got into an electrical machine."

"Do not talk in that way, Charles, for goodness sake," exclaimed his younger sister. "We shall all be killed presently."

"I hope not," said Captain Fraser, "though I admit it looks serious; but all you can do, and the best under all the circumstances, is to remain calm and quiet, and see what happens."

"See what happens! Dear me, captain, what do you think we are all made of that we should sit calm," said Miss Stevens, "and see what will happen, when there may be broken limbs, at the least, if not death?"

"It is the best advice I can give you."

"Had we better not get out—I don't mind trying?"

"Aye, if you wish to run imminent risk of instant and violent death, you will make the attempt; if you remain in here shut up, you have every probability that, if we do have an upset, which is not yet certain, we may all escape with but a little fright, or at most a few bruises."

"Yes, sister; you had better wait for the worst, if the worst must happen, rather than rush into it."

This was sensible advice, and the whole party fell into a deep silence, which was unbroken save by the sounds of wheels, the rattling of the carriage, the rain, and the roar of thunder, enough to employ their minds, and at the same time to keep them in momentary dread of the fearful catastrophe.

Suddenly there was a crash and dreadful jolt; they knew not what had happened, except they felt that the vehicle was turned over.

In a moment more the door was opened, and a stranger lent assistance in getting out the unfortunate travellers.

"Do not be alarmed, ladies," said a strange, but courteous voice. "No further mischief can happen now, beyond inconvenience."

As the stranger spoke, he lifted the two ladies out of the carriage, and placed them in a sheltered position by the body.

"Are you hurt?" inquired the stranger, as he assisted Captain Fraser and young Stevens out of the fallen carriage.

"No, sir, I am not; I thank you for your timely aid. Where are the ladies?"

"There they are; I hope, uninjured."

Captain Fraser immediately ran up to them, and, seeing them in safety, said,—

"I am glad to see you are safe. I was stunned at first by a blow on the side of my head."

"Yes, we are safe; but we have to thank this gentleman that we have been so speedily and so easily extricated from our unpleasant prison."

"I am much indebted, sir, for your aid to the ladies. May I trespass upon your kindness to lend me a little further assistance?"

"I shall be happy to assist you under these unpleasant circumstances; but, allow me to suggest as the first thing, that the cushions be placed under the hedge for the use of the ladies, and what cloaks or coats you have should be thrown over them."

"Right, sir; I thank you."

"If you are deficient in them, my cloak is at their service, though I am afraid that it is almost saturated."

"I have enough here," said Captain Fraser, as he pulled out several articles of that nature; and then he, with the assistance of the stranger, placed them so that Mrs. Fraser and sister were almost, if not entirely, sheltered from the storm.

"Now," said the stranger, "the first thing that can be done will be to right the carriage, and place it in a position where it will receive no further damage."

"But the driver and horses," said Captain Fraser, "I must look after them. Had we better not look after them? He may be dying."

"By no means," said the stranger; "he will do very well; if we place the carriage upright, we shall be able to replace the ladies."

"We can," said the captain, who appeared to be divided between the duties of humanity and the tender anxiety he felt for his wife.

"Exactly," said the stranger; "and permit me to suggest that he has either gone on beyond our aid, or does not require it."

"It is possible."

"And very probable," said the stranger; "but if you prefer it, and think the ladies will not suffer, we can walk on ahead till we come up with them, if they stop before the end of the stage."

"No, no, sir; you are quite right; I will get the carriage up if you can so far assist me; we shall then place the ladies in comparative safety."

"We shall so."

They immediately walked round the carriage, and examined its position, as well as they were able, when, to the captain's great relief, he found that it was still on its wheels, though the body was thrown over on its side.

"How can it have happened?" inquired the captain.

"I cannot well see," replied the stranger; "but you will perceive something must have caught the off-side wheel, and turned the whole of the fore carriage that way, which has left this corner of the body without support; added to which, the speed or momentum it must have acquired in its course, has thrown it over."

"Precisely. I see now how it is; but if we get the body up, it will fall again over on this side, since it has no support."

"Oh, yes, it will remain up, since it has lost all force, all moving power; unless, indeed, any of the straps are broken. We can try."

"Here, Charles," said Captain Fraser, "we shall want your aid."

"Oh," said the stranger, "the slightest assistance is valuable; it is the last strain or effort that may complete the removal. Now, if we can lift it up from this side, we shall soon right it, and then the fore carriage can be forced round, and the ladies replaced, until we can better dispose of them."

The stranger placed his shoulder to the carriage, as well as the captain and his brother-in-law, young Stevens, and thus aided, he soon lifted it up into its old position, and there it remained very quietly.

"Now we had better pull the wheels round."

This was done, and the carriage assumed its former state.

"Well, how could they have got away?" inquired Captain Fraser, examining the axles and the bars; "all appears right."

"They have broken the splinter-bar, and here are the remains of the traces. The splinter-bar, I find, has only lost its hooks, so it will do again. Come, sir, you have less damage to regret than I at first thought it possible you could have escaped with; I am truly glad it is so."

"Thank you, sir; your kindness and assistance has been truly great and efficient; but I have yet to find the poor fellow who drove us."

"We will seek after him; or, I had better ride on to the next town or house where I can obtain assistance, while you will be better able to protect the ladies by remaining with them, and my horse will carry me quickly enough."

"Oh! you are mounted."

"I am; but the ladies wait."

Thus admonished, the captain turned to the ladies, and, with the stranger's assistance, he conducted them back to the carriage, where they were replaced, without any material damage or misfortune of any kind, save what might arise from fright.

"Some one is coming this way," said the stranger. "If I mistake not, they are your runaways, by the sounds."

They listened, and distinctly heard the sounds of horses' feet coming along, with the jingling of harness, that made it pretty certain that what the stranger said was correct, and that it was most probable that this was indeed the man who drove

them coming back with the same cattle, or some fresh.

A few moments more decided the speculation, and the man himself rode up, and looked at the carriage, saying,—

"Well, I thought it was upset."

"So it was, but we have righted it now. Has no accident happened to you? But these are the same horses!"

"Yes, sir. When they got loose, or broke away, they went as if they were shot out of a gun, and away they went for some miles, until I contrived to stop them, which was a hard job; however, I thought then, as there was nothing the matter with them or with me, I had better return and see what was become of you, sir, and the ladies."

"Quite right. Do you think they will go quietly in the harness again?"

"Oh, yes — oh, yes, sir."

"Then we will harness them, and go on to the end of the next stage, when we can see exactly what mischief, if any, has been done."

This was immediately put in practice, and they were soon harnessed, the broken straps and traces being mended in the best way time and circumstances admitted, but effectually enough for the present purpose.

"Now, sir," said Captain Fraser, "do you continue this road, or the one we have come? I suppose we must have overtaken you, as you were coming this way."

"No; I was a traveller going in the same direction. I saw your speed from a distance, and, believing your horses to have taken fright, I rode on, and, being well mounted, I overtook you just as the accident happened."

"Then we may have the pleasure of your company on the road for some distance to come, I hope, sir?"

"As far as the next place to stop at, at all events; for I do not desire to travel further than I can avoid to-night."

"Then I shall be able to thank you more at leisure, and at a better opportunity than at present," said the captain.

"Do not name it; I am too happy to have had it in my power to render you any assistance. Shall I ride on and secure you proper accommodation when you do arrive there?"

"You kindness is very great," said the captain again. "I am much beholden to you; but if we can get as far as we hoped to do, we shall not require it; there will be sufficient for travellers under the ordinary course of events. We shall do very well; and if we should not be able to get so far, we must make ourselves content with whatever chance accommodation we get on the road."

"Then we will journey for that distance in company," said the stranger, as he mounted his horse, which had stood quietly by while the tall stranger rendered the timely assistance he had to them.

They proceeded along now at a cautious pace. The weather had abated, and the rain was now less severe; the thunder only heard in the distance; while the lightning could only be seen in occasional flashes in the distance, in a direction away from them. The clouds began to lighten, and then the diffused light of the moon came and shed a gentle light upon the scene, though it was very scarce, and of comparative little use save it enabled them to see their way all the better.

The roads were good, and they travelled onwards with some increase of speed; and finding none of their amended horse-tackle had given way, they still kept journeying onwards at the same pace.

Time brought them to their destination, and when they arrived at the inn at which they were to stop for the night, they found it had not made much more than an hour or an hour and a half's difference.

When they were fairly housed, the stranger took an apartment to himself. It was while he sat before the fire that Captain Fraser entered his room.

"I must apologise for my intrusion," began the captain.

"Do not say a word on that head, sir," said the stranger; "it is no intrusion — you are welcome. Be seated, if you please; I am alone, and perfectly at leisure."

"I have come to thank you for the service you have done us, and to beg that you will sup with us, and permit the ladies to have an opportunity of thanking their preserver in person. You will oblige us all by accepting the invitation."

"I am much obliged for your courteous offer," said the stranger, who was a tall, dignified man. "I will come after supper, if you please, and shall feel it a great honour, I assure you; but I am so truly sensible that my efforts were more owing to accident than to anything else, that I do not wish to hear anything more of it."

"You must not be so self-denying, sir. We do not wish to put any more merit on your act than we think it deserves; but that much you must accept, if you will permit me to use such a word. Shall we have the pleasure of your company?"

"After supper."

"I will not press you against your feelings; but you will come in after supper, sir? I hope I may have the pleasure of drinking a bottle of wine with you. Will you come?"

"I will, sir, and thank you for the honour."

"May I have the pleasure of being able to introduce you to the ladies by name?" said the captain, with a little hesitation.

"Certainly — certainly. I beg your pardon. I am somewhat forgetful; I forgot I had not passed through an introduction," said the stranger. "Permit me to give you my card."

As he spoke, he handed Captain Fraser a beautifully-embossed card, upon which was printed, in Italian characters, — "Sir Francis Varney."

Captain Fraser took the card and read the name, and then, passing a compliment, he said, that since he could not have his company to supper, then he should expect him when he felt at leisure and disposed to do so.

"MY DEAR," SAID Captain Fraser to his wife, when he returned to his apartment, "our new friend will not come to supper but will take a glass of wine with me afterwards."

"I am sorry he will not come; though, under other circumstances, I should have been glad of it; but I am sorry on this occasion."

"And why would you have been glad?"

"Because, after the flurry and upset we had, I am hardly fit to see any one, much less a stranger; but he so kindly and promptly rescued us from our danger, that I cannot feel reluctance at any time."

"Yes," said her sister; "and I must say I never heard a voice that sounded so really like a gentleman's — indeed, I could fancy

that any one could positively assert that he was a gentleman, only from hearing him speak, without seeing him at all; but, be that as it may, I felt convinced he was such."

"He is very courteous, I must say," said Mrs. Fraser.

"And who do you think he is?"

"I have no means of forming any judgment."

"Well, then, he is Sir Francis Varney."

"Sir Francis Varney! Well, I do not know the name; I never heard the name before that time; but I think there was some one of that name in the time of Queen Elizabeth — an attendant on the Earl of Leicester."

"Are you not joking?"

"Indeed I am not; I have read so."

"And you think this gentleman may be a descendant of his?"

"There is no impossibility nor improbability about it, that I see," said Mrs. Fraser; "but I am the more obliged to him for his timely assistance. I am sure it was fortunate that he was so close at hand."

"Yes, it was very fortunate. Mary, my dear, we shall be introduced to a baronet. It is quite a prophecy of yours in saying he was a gentleman when you only heard him speak. By the way, Fraser, what sort of a man is he?"

"Very singular indeed."

"Singular! Aye — he is very tall."

"Yes, he is tall; but very pale; more remarkable and dignified than handsome; extremely courteous and polite."

"What age is he?"

"Well, I cannot tell; perhaps forty, perhaps not so old by ten years; it is quite impossible to say."

"Dear me, how strange! I think I could guess anybody's age better than that."

"You shall have an opportunity of doing so, then, in an hour or so, when he will come; and I think I may venture upon saying you will be pleased with his dignified politeness, and say he is much superior to most men."

THE SUPPER ENDED, and the wine was produced, and Captain Fraser, his lady, and two young relatives, were seated round a good fire — for the storm had chilled the air; besides, the damp they had stood in rendered such a precaution necessary and pleasant, notwithstanding the day had been sultry; but the change in the temperature was sudden and great — awaiting, with something like impatience, the stranger's arrival.

"He does not appear to come," said Charles Stevens.

"He is not here, certainly; but he will come, no doubt, the moment he is quite sure that we had done our supper, and he had finished his own; perhaps he takes longer than we."

"Perhaps so; but I am strongly tempted to go to him again."

"It might be construed into undue urgency, or something of the sort," said Mrs. Fraser; "and yet he might be waiting for something of the sort."

"So he might," said the captain. "At all events, I will go and see; if he were inclined to do so under other circumstances, he would not take offence under the present."

"Perhaps not."

At that moment the door was opened, and the waiter presented a note.

"A note for me?" said Captain Fraser.

"Yes, sir."

"Who can it be from?"

"From the gentleman up stairs, sir, who came with you an hour back."

"Oh!" exclaimed Captain Fraser.

"He was taken ill, and obliged to go to bed, sir."

Captain Fraser immediately tore open the note, and read as follows: —

SIR, —

I deeply regret I cannot keep my promise to take a glass of wine with you, and have the honour of being introduced to the ladies. Favour me so far as to make my excuses to them. It is a great pleasure lost to me on the occasion; permit me to say deferred, rather than lost; and if I might venture to make an appointment, under the circumstances, I can only say that, if convenient, I should be happy to breakfast with you, and then have the honour and happiness I have now the misfortune to lose.

Sudden and severe indisposition alone have caused me to retire before I had the honour of seeing you, and expressing my inability to attend you. —

Yours, obliged,
FRANCIS VARNEY.

There was a blank upon the countenances of all present. Evidently a deep disappointment was felt by all; but the captain was especially surprised, and, turning to the waiter, he said, —

"Did you see this gentleman?"

"Yes, sir."

"Was he unwell?"

"Yes, sir."

"I mean, was he, or is he, dangerously ill?"

"He was very ill, sir; but I don't know that he is dangerously ill. He suffered much pain, and he was obliged to have aid to go up stairs."

"Did he say what it was that ailed him?" pursued Captain Fraser.

"Not that I heard; though some said he had got the cramp and cold by being too long in the wet."

"Perhaps so — very likely — very likely — that will do. Let me know how he is the first thing in the morning; do you hear?"

"Yes, sir, I will take care."

"Well," said Mrs. Fraser, when they were alone, "I did not expect such a disappointment this evening. However, he makes up for it by appointing the breakfast hour for our meeting; it is the more agreeable, as we shall have had a good night's repose, and shall be the better able to appear to advantage."

CXLVI.

THE ALARM AT THE INN. — BED-CHAMBER TERRORS. — A NIGHT SCENE. — A MORNING SUCCEEDING TO A NIGHT OF ADVENTURE.

THE INMATES OF THE INN are all fast bound in sleep. The senses of all seem steeped in deep forgetfulness; even the hour of dreams was passed. The storm, which had raged so violently in the early part of the evening, and which had appeared to have gone and a calm succeeded, had returned, and the fury of the blast was only equalled by the deluging rain and the fearful rumbling of the thunder.

But calmly slept the beautiful and innocent Mary Stevens. She was young, and her mind bore no weight of care; when she slept no dreams disturbed her rest, but a calm, death-like sleep sat upon her soul, and steeped it in forgetfulness.

The storm raged around, but she heard it not; she was unconscious of it. Perhaps the disturbance and fatigues of the previous day caused a greater degree of depth to her insensibility, and rendered her mind less liable to slight interruptions. But she slept soundly, and even did not hear the intruder who walked across the floor of her bedroom, and stood gazing on her fair arms as she lay sleeping.

The intruder was a tall man, enveloped in some strange mantle, all white. He stooped over her, as if he listened to the beating of her heart, while his strangely bright eyes, which shone fearfully, appeared to express a horrible kind of joy, too terrible for human nature to contemplate.

He stooped — he placed his hand upon her heart, and felt its pulsations, and a terrible and ghastly smile passed over his features, while a movement of the lips and mouth generally, appeared as if anticipatory of a coming meal.

Then he took the white arm in his hands, and cast a longing look at the features of the maiden, who appeared disturbed by the rude action, and moved in her sleep, and was suddenly aroused from her slumber by a severe pang in her arm, as though some creature had plunged its fangs into her flesh.

She started up, and found herself flung upon the bed with gigantic strength. She screamed, and uttered scream upon scream.

The old inn was filled with sounds of terror and pain. There was a loud knocking heard at the door. Then, indeed, the assailant left his prey to provide for his own safety; but it was almost too late, for the door was burst open violently, as he made for another means of exit, which was the means by which he had entered the apartment; but he was prevented, and, as the first person entered the apartment, he threw him down by placing something in his way. The light was thrown against some furniture, which immediately rose up into a flame.

"Help! help! Fire! fire!"

These were fearful sounds, such as had never before been heard in that place, and the inmates, woke up by the screams from deep slumber, were startled and terrified at these sounds, and springing at once from their beds, echoed the sounds as they run wildly about from place to place.

"Where is the fire? What's the matter?"

"Fire in the young lady's room."

All eyes were directed to that quarter, and in another instant there were several persons rushing to the room, the glare of the fire in which at once attracted their observation, and they rushed to the rescue; among the foremost of whom was Sir Francis Varney, whose bedchamber was not far distant from Mary Steven's. He rushed to the bed, and wrapping the bedclothes round her, he carried her out of the room and the scene of danger, and, as he came out of the room, he inquired, —

"Where is Captain Fraser?"

"Here — here I am, Sir Francis," said the captain, coming hastily forward.

"Then, Captain Fraser, I resign my charge up to you — you are her proper protector; but I must apologize for my hasty intrusion into her apartment."

"Do not think of speaking in that manner, Sir Francis; we are already indebted to you for our lives, and now we are again your debtor. Your ready aid has twice saved the young lady."

Captain Fraser took Miss Stevens form Sir Francis, and then carried her, as she was quite insensible, to his own room to his wife, her sister, where she was laid upon the bed, and found to be quite insensible.

There was much confusion in the inn — people were running about from place to place, and tumbling over each other in the confusion of thought; and the moments were precious, for many were running about, yet none did effective service, though all were willing enough to do all that could be done by them under the circumstances.

"You had better get some water," said Varney, "as quickly as you can. It is useless to run about and stare at each other. Get all the buckets you can. Be quick about it. There may yet be time enough to save the inn, and keep the fire to the room where it is; but that time will soon be at an end."

Instantly two or three of the men ran down and got a plentiful supply of water, and then, under the direction of Sir

Francis Varney, the fire was very soon got under, and the flames were extinguished.

Then came an inquiry how the fire had first appeared.

"Do you know how it happened?" inquired Sir Francis Varney, of the innkeeper, who stood quite mute with astonishment at the scene before him.

"Know, sir!" said the the innkeeper. "I don't know anything. I don't know myself. I don't even know where I am, or what's the matter."

"Then I beg to tell you, sir," said Varney, with much sauvity of manner, "then I beg to tell you, sir, that there has been a fire in your inn — a young lady frightened out of her senses, and I know not the cause."

"No more don't I," said the landlord, with a short grunt, indicative of wonderment and alarm. "I wish I did. I wonder who set the place a-fire; that's what I wants to know, and why he did it."

"The motive was not a bad one, I believe."

"Not a bad motive, that which causes one man to set fire to and destroy another man's property!"

"Not when it is not only not done with any evil intention, but it was not even done wilfully," said Sir Francis.

"Perhaps you saw it done," said the landlord, with another grunt.

"I did," replied Varney; "hearing the disturbance, I hastily threw on some of my clothes, and ran out of my apartment to ascertain what was the matter, and found several others had got here before me, and had burst open the door. The first who entered, had a light in his hand, and fell with it, setting the place on fire, which burned furiously for a minute or more, the hangings being dry and old. I took the young lady out, else I am sure she must have perished."

"Well, I saw you come out with her in your arms, like a salamander; but what I most want to know is, what was it that disturbed my customer? That is of the greatest consequence to me."

"You are perfectly right, my friend," said Sir Francis, with much composure, "to make that inquiry, that being the origin of all that subsequently took place. You are a man of discernment, and must see that the young lady herself can alone give us any account of that."

"True, sir; but I am much obliged to you for the trouble you have taken, not only for the young lady's sake, but for the property you have prevented being destroyed. You have, no doubt, saved the inn, and all it contains."

"That is enough, sir," said Varney, waving his hand, "you have said enough. I am glad I have rendered you a service, and that it has been effectual."

"It has been just the thing," said the landlord.

"Then take my advice. See the place is secure, and send all persons to bed, save, perhaps, a single individual, who might be set to watch the room which has been on fire, and which may have some slumbering spark in it, though I think not; but the quieter the place is, the sooner the young lady's alarm will be over, and then all will be well."

"Certainly, certainly," said the landlord, "it will be better to do so; but here is the only gentleman who can tell us how the young lady is."

Sir Francis Varney turned round, and beheld Captain Fraser coming towards them with a very grave aspect.

"Captain Fraser," said Sir Francis, "perhaps you can tell us what we are so very anxious to learn, and what we have been inquiring about."

"What may that be, Sir Francis?"

"We have been trying to learn what it is that caused the young lady to scream out in such a fearful manner. We have settled the cause of the fire — that has been manifest enough to us all."

"Indeed! I am not acquainted with it."

"It arose from the first person who entered her apartment after the door was burst open, falling over something, and setting fire to the curtains, which blazed up in an instant, and set the whole room on fire."

"Indeed!" said Captain Fraser, almost incredulously.

"Yes, I saw that myself," said Varney, "and I stepped over him as he lay on the ground, and therefore know it; but how is the young lady? Has she recovered from the extreme fright into which she has been thrown?"

"It is a much more serious affair than I had any notion of, Sir Francis."

"I am concerned to hear you say so."

"Shall I send for the doctor?" inquired the landlord.

"Do — that is what I came to ask you to do; she has recovered once, and has fainted again. I know not what to think. She has a singular wound in her arm. I can't understand that, at all events."

"I did not see it when I took hold of her; though, to be sure, what I did, was done in smoke and flame, and I could not be supposed to scrutinize very closely, had I been so inclined; but what kind of wound is it?"

"I can hardly describe it to you, save it is a bite; and there are teeth-marks plain enough to be seen; though we have no means of telling what kind of creature it was that inflicted the wounds."

"Indeed! I am concerned, for the effect upon the imagination will be very bad; but did she not see, or fancy she saw the object that injured her?"

"It was dark, and the storm raged without; moreover, she was held down by a powerful grasp; and when she attempted to rise, she was flung down, and she could feel the blunted teeth enter her flesh, and the creature appeared to suck her blood."

"Dear me," said Sir Francis, "what a very strange affair! It is fortunate I was obliged to retire early, and I slept the lighter, and was therefore easily aroused from my sleep; but I am proverbially a light sleeper."

"Are you, sir? But what has caused the wound in her arm I cannot tell; it is quite a mystery. She has got a fancy into her mind that it was a human being; but that could not have been the fact."

"I should imagine not," said Sir Francis.

"And then, I know of no animal who could commit such an act: a cat or a dog could not have done it, though a dog might have made the teeth-marks; but a dog would hardly have attempted to suck blood."

"They will do it," said Sir Francis, "that I know to be a fact; and I believe it to be one that is generally admitted by all persons, especially that breed of animals mostly kept, and which have something of the bull-dog in them."

"It may be so; but how could she be held down by one of them? She could not be struck down when she attempted to rise."

"It is not for me to combat the young lady's opinions; but, remember, my dear sir, how terrified, not to say how horrified, she must have been at such an unusual, and, I may add, unheard-of an attack; if you consider such things, and the improbability — not to say what appears to me, the impossibility — you will see plenty of room for mistakes to arise, and give her notions a wrong turn."

"That is very true."

"And besides, I would, if I were

convinced of the contrary, endeavour to persuade her of her mistake, unless you can discover the perpetrator of the outrage, when justice demands that such a savage should be severely punished."

"By G—d! Sir Francis," said the captain, "if I could see him, I would shoot the scoundrel! But, then, I am getting angry without a cause; it may not be what she thinks, and then, you know, all one's anger goes for nothing."

"So it does; but, in the meantime, great care and attention is requisite to regain her confidence and serenity of mind."

"Oh, a day or two will make a great difference in these matters, when we come to change the scene."

"Are you travelling far, Captain Fraser?"

"As far as Bath," said the captain.

At this moment the landlord returned, saying to Captain Fraser,—"I have sent to Mr. Carter, who will be here, no doubt; he is close at hand, and will come in a moment. He's a very clever gentleman, is Mr. Carter. I saw him perform four operations on coach accidents."

"Operations on coach accidents!" said Sir Francis Varney; "a curious matter, that. How did they succeed upon such materials?"

"Oh, they were two broken arms, and three broken legs."

"Indeed! Did they all recover?"

"No; only one got over it."

"Upon my word, a promising member of the faculty to entrust so tender a charge to, under such delicate circumstances. But, landlord, have you any bad characters about your house, or in the neighbourhood?"

"I can't say anything about the neighbourhood, though I believe it is as quiet and orderly as can be, or usually is. I never hear anything against it, and know nothing against it; and as for them in the house, I can answer they would not hurt a fly, unless provoked to do so; but what I mean is, they are all honest and tried servants."

"Well, that is saying a good deal," said Captain Fraser; "but, have you any dogs about the house—I mean, any large dogs?"

"Ah! dogs! Yes, I have several dogs, and good dogs they are, too."

"Could any of them get into the rooms—the sleeping-rooms? I mean, could any of them get into the room that has taken fire?"

"No, unless the door was opened," said the landlord. "They are not allowed to run about loose here, lest any one should get up in the night and be mistaken for intruders; for my dogs, gentlemen, would take any one they saw moving about outside of a night; but, otherwise, they are quiet, well-conducted dogs."

"Well, you mean to say they could not have got into Miss Stevens's room."

"I do; I am sure of it. They could not, because there were none of them about the house when we went to bed—when the house was shut up at night. However, here is the doctor."

The medical man now arrived, and was forthwith introduced to Captain Fraser, who conducted him to the apartment in which Mrs. Fraser and Miss Stevens were awaiting the coming of the doctor. Captain Fraser, after having introduced him to the invalid, returned to the landlord and Sir Francis.

"Well, I cannot make it out at all," said Sir Francis. "There must be some mystery in it, I am persuaded; and if that could only be discovered, the matter would lose half its terrors to the mind of the young lady."

"No doubt it would do so," said the captain. "The fire and her wound together, have made a deep impression upon her."

"The wound!" said the landlord. "Is the young lady hurt, then?"

"Hurt, indeed! she is seriously hurt. She has received a severe wound in the arm, by some one, or some dog having seized and bitten her seriously."

"God bless me!" said the landlord; "I never heard of such a thing. Somebody began to eat her, I suppose. Upon my word, it would almost make one believe we are in the Cannibal Islands, to say the least of it."

"Here is the surgeon," said Sir Francis, who noticed that gentleman's approach.

"Well, sir," said Captain Fraser, "how is your patient?"

"I fear she is much terrified; and if she were to remain here long, I should hardly like to answer for her health. She has received a very severe shock."

"Her wound—what think you of that, sir?"

"I really can't say anything about it, save that is is a bite; but how inflicted I cannot say. It is very mysterious, indeed; very strange! But, what I look upon as most important in the affair, is the impression it has produced upon her mind; that, you see, may last her all her life, and produce very unfortunate consequences. I do not know that it will be so, but I state what there is a possibility of—or, I may, more correctly speaking, add,—of what there is a great probability."

"I regret to hear you say so," said Sir Francis Varney. "Do you really imagine the young lady has been bitten by any animal?"

"Yes, I do; there are evidences enough to prove that. There is the wound in her arm, and the marks of the teeth quite plain; and she suffers from the anguish of it much; but I shall be better able to say more about it early in the morning, when I call again to see her."

"She will be able to travel, I hope?"

"Oh, yes, she will be able to do that; indeed, I would recommend she should try to do so, as the best means of throwing off all the unpleasant feelings and thoughts upon the occasion."

"Will you call early to-morrow?"

"I will," said the doctor; and then he bade them good evening, and left.

"Well," said the landlord, "I'm amazed at what the doctor says about the young lady. I'm sorry it should have happened in my house; but I hope something will turn up to make it turn out different."

"That I'm afraid is not possible, seeing you have a clear demonstration of what it is now; the mischief has been done."

"I am the more sorry," said the landlord, "that it is likely to prey upon the young lady's feelings, which are to be considered in the case."

"Certainly, certainly; there is where the mischief is likely to spring from."

"However, it is of no use to stand here all night—it is cold. I must get an hour or two's sleep before I get to business in the morning."

"I think so too," said Captain Fraser; "well, I will bid you good night, Sir

Francis, and shall expect you in the morning to breakfast."

"With pleasure," replied Varney; and they all parted, each going to his own dormitory, to sleep or to think over the events of the night, as best they might.

CXLVII.

THE NEXT MORNING CAME, and with it came also the usual bustle of a country inn, when strangers are stopping there, especially carriage strangers; as well as the usual coach stoppages, when they change horses, which they did more than once that morning. It was at a later hour than usual when the party breakfasted, and it was somewhat late when Sir Francis Varney entered the room.

"Good morning," said Sir Francis, with great suavity of manner, and in a most courtly tone; "I trust I see you somewhat recovered from the fright you were put to last night."

"Oh, Sir Francis," said Mrs. Fraser; "it was a dreadful fright, indeed; but we have so much to thank you for. To you we owe much, and my sister owes to you a double obligation — you have rescued her twice."

"I am happy to think I have been a fortunate instrument in serving you. I trust Miss Stevens is better than she was."

"I think she is better, Sir Francis; but she desires to remain in her apartment until we are ready to start. Though I thought it somewhat unreasonable, because, if she is to travel, she had better have come out."

"But her rest was disturbed by the accident, and it might have been early before she slept; and an hour's rest and repose might do much towards recovering her," said Sir Francis; "her own feelings are a good guide under those circumstances."

"I think so, too," said Captain Fraser.

"I," said young Stevens, "was awoke by a desperate riot caused by people running about; I did not hear anything of the scream."

"I was awoke by it," said Captain Fraser. "How did you hear of it — how were you awoke?"

"By a loud scream," said Sir Francis; "I was asleep, and when it awoke me, I knew not what it was. I remained for a moment or two in doubt as to whether I had not dreamt, but a repetition assured me that I was not dreaming — and knowing from the sound it was a female's voice, I jumped up, and dressed myself as well as I could; but, before I could do that, I heard people running about, and when I got into the gallery, I heard the door burst in."

"Did any one come out?"

"I cannot say — I saw no one; but the man who first entered the apartment fell down, from some cause or other, and set the bed-curtains on fire — accidentally, of course, but it was the same in effect."

"Did you see any one in the room, Sir Francis?"

"No one at all; I did not even know who slept there; but seeing the form of a human being lying there, and wrapping the bed-clothes, or rather seizing her and the bed-clothes, by grasping with both arms, I carried her out. I used but little ceremony, and the urgency of the case must be my excuse."

"And it is, Sir Francis, though I know not in what way we can manifest our feelings of gratitude to you."

"You may, madam, by saying no more about it; but I shall be delighted to think you have such a good opinion of my services; and the knowledge that they have been useful, that is a gratification to me."

"And one you are well entitled to, Sir Francis," said Captain Fraser.

"How far are you travelling?" inquired Mrs. Fraser.

"As far as Bath, madam, for the benefit of my health."

"We are going to Bath, Sir Francis, as well. I am sure it will be a great pleasure to Captain Fraser, to find that we are to have such a travelling companion — that is, if you can accommodate yourself to travelling in a carriage."

"I can travel as you please. I am mounted, and am used to such travelling, for months at a time."

"Do you travel much at a time, Sir Francis?"

"Yes, I have been a great traveller, for years; not so much as regards distance as to the constancy of my perambulations; for I continue for months together out, riding from one town to another."

"Without an attendant?"

"Always; I never carry a servant about with me; it cannot be done with comfort by any one. You have always proper attendance if you stop at a respectable inn, or hotel; or, if not, if the road you have to travel be a cross route, you cannot expect any additional comfort from a servant, but you are troubled at his not being comfortably lodged; at least, I am, for I have tried it."

"I dare say there is much wisdom in that. I know from experience that a single traveller, who has leisure, and is willing, may enjoy himself better than he could if he were attended by his servant. You are somewhat restrained in your motions, and cannot do as you would please under all circumstances."

"I am fully persuaded of that, from experience; but I shall travel on horseback till I get to Bath, and then I hardly know whether I shall remain at an hotel, or take lodgings for the season — or what."

"What we intend is, to take lodgings," said Captain Fraser, "for a time — as long as we feel inclined — and then to enjoy ourselves."

"Quite right," said Sir Francis; "quite right. I am glad to hear you say so, and I hope it may be of advantage to Miss Stevens."

"I hope so too. Shall we have the advantage of your company *en route?*"

"I shall have great pleasure in having your company so far. It will give me great gratification, indeed; I shall be most happy to bear your company as far as the city of Bath, and shall consider myself the gainer by your society."

"No, we shall be the only party that will benefit by it; but we shall feel greatly your kindness, and I, for one, anticipate much pleasure on the road from your society, and also when we arrive in Bath."

"I feel such will be the case."

At this moment Mr. Carter was announced also. In a few moments more this individual was introduced to them; he was a plain gentlemanly man, who really was a clever man, notwithstanding the fearful account of his prowess and skill which the landlord had descanted on the previous night.

"Well, Mr. Carter," said Captain Fraser, "how do you find my sister — do you think she is any better than she was?"

"I think she is calmer, and much of the first violence of terror is gone; but I cannot say any more — she is still much disturbed."

"Do you think there is anything dangerous in her state?"

"No, sir, I do not; though I cannot hide from you the possibility that there is of her being permanently affected by it — I mean mentally; it may take a deep hold of her, and there will be no getting her free from it, save by judicious treatment."

"You do not consider much, then, of her wound?"

"The arm? Oh, yes; that looks very angry, and has been a very severe bite, and has caused her arm to swell; though I have no doubt about its getting well, still it will be very painful for some days; and, had it been a little more severe, it is possible that some of the tendons might have been injured, or an artery wounded."

"Upon my word," said Sir Francis Varney, "this had very nigh turned out a very bad and serious affair, if not a dangerous one."

"Of that there can be no doubt," said the doctor.

"Well, but, after all, what was it that has caused all this disturbance? What was it, a man or brute?"

"Decidedly the latter," said Sir Francis Varney, "decidedly the latter, be the form of the creature what it may."

"Indeed, you are right, Sir Francis," said Mrs. Fraser; "but she insists it was a human being who made this abominable attack upon her — why or wherefore, no one knows; but she insists it was a man."

"What do you say, doctor?"

"I only know, sir, what the young lady says."

"Do you think it probable?"

"I cannot say I do. I think it most unlikely; though, to be sure, there is nothing in it that is impossible. Had any one felt maliciously towards the young lady, they might have perpetrated the crime; but, in the absence of all malice, I cannot think so bad of human nature as to believe it."

"You discredit it, then?" said Sir Francis Varney.

"I do," said the doctor, "with all due respect to the young lady; but the probability of mistake is so great, and when you consider the terror so natural to the occasion, her powers of observation were limited and liable to error, that I cannot myself believe otherwise than there is a great mistake."

"And what do you consider of the wounds? I mean, do you think it possible they were inflicted by human teeth? Are they of that shape and character that could be inflicted by human teeth?"

"Yes, decidedly; that is, so far as I am able to judge, while the wound is swelled and angry, I should consider them just such as might be inflicted by the teeth of a man or woman."

"That corroborates the young lady's own belief."

"It does, so far," said Mr. Carter.

"Then comes the question of how could it have been done, and by whom?"

"These seem to be questions which cannot be answered. I asked the landlord all that could tend to elicit that information, but with no success; he knew nothing that could throw any light upon the subject."

"Perhaps he knew nothing," suggested Mrs. Fraser.

"Most probably he did not," was the reply.

"I know the landlord to be a respectable, though somewhat eccentric man; and I think him quite incapable of being a party to such an outrage upon any person, much less upon a lady who was stopping at his house."

"Well; however true that may be, yet it is undeniable that this outrage has been committed, though by whom we cannot say, for we do not even suspect anybody. I can't understand it at all."

"Nor I; but, as you observed, sir, the outrage has been committed, and here, too; but, unfortunately, no one is suspected, and justice cannot be done, which, in such a case, ought to be fully and clearly made out, for there can be no palliation."

"None at all."

"I wish," said Captain Fraser, "I had been first in the room."

"Why, sir," inquired Sir Francis Varney, "do you wish that?"

"Because you see, sir, I should have felt that inward satisfaction arising from the fact, that I fancy I might have ascertained whether any one was, or had been, in the room."

"The young lady said there was," said Sir Francis.

"Yes — yes; but then you saw the door opened, and saw no one come out."

"I did not, though, after I had Miss Stevens in my arms, I came away, and then it was possible any one might have got out, though there were others who would have seen them; but still, in the bustle and confusion of the moment, there might have been somebody."

"Yes, there is that possibility," said Captain Fraser; "and I don't see why I should trouble myself about this affair — I mean, by wishing myself there; but I should have done nothing but carry out the body — that would have been my first act."

"No doubt," said Sir Francis; "and what made such an act the more necessary is, the fact that she was in instant danger of death from burning, or suffocation."

"True — true; who would have coolly gazed around him, when there, on the bed, lay the unfortunate victim of God knows what."

"Well, sir, I must bid you good day. I have some patients to visit."

"Not before we square accounts, which is easily done. Let me know how we may stand, sir, and I will pay you at once."

This little affair was soon settled; and the doctor was about to depart, when he said, before he left the room, —

"I have given the young lady directions what to do relative to her arm. She must not use it much; but any medical man who may chance to see it, will be able to prescribe for it; though what I have given I deem almost enough to effect her complete restoration, as far as regards the arm. The shock, the mind and nervous system have sustained, will only be eradicated by time and change."

"Thank you for your advice; that shall be attended to."

The doctor now quitted the hotel; and the landlord entered the apartment with a very serious aspect; and, after making his bow, proceeded to say,—

"I am very sorry, sir, for the occurrence of last night—very sorry, indeed. Indeed, sir, I cannot make it out at all. I have inquired all over the house, and nobody at all knows anything about it, nor can't think how it could be. A good many of them won't believe it at all, though I told them there could be no doubt of it, for the young lady was burnt, and the bed set on fire."

"You may be sure of that, landlord; the young lady has been bitten on the arm most severely."

"And, as for the fire," said Sir Francis, "I saw how that occurred."

"So you said, sir," replied the landlord; "if that fellow as fell down had stood up, why, it wouldn't have set the curtains a fire."

"No, that is true."

"Well, then, he would have been able to have seen what was the matter, instead of his filling the room full of smoke and fire as he did; he hadn't no excuse to tumble down—nobody knocked him down."

"But didn't he hurt himself very badly?"

"Oh, only about two or three square inches, or perhaps a patch as big as your hand, off his chin—that's nothing to such as he."

"Very good. But have you examined the place, to see if anybody could have got in and concealed himself? Was there any possibility of a man's getting into your house, and secreting himself in any part of the bed-room, which would thus afford

him an opportunity of doing what has been done?"

"Why, sir, I don't think it likely; and yet these people are so cunning, that you could not, by any possibility, guard against them in any way, especially in an inn. But there is no house free from intrusion of that character; but in this instance they could have had no notion the young lady was to sleep there."

"That is very true," said Captain Fraser, "and tends to show she was not singled out for outrage; but what seems very singular, is, that any one should secret themselves, and that with a view to commit such an outrage."

"That is very true," said the landlord; "but people do very strange things sometimes, and I think the object of any one hiding himself in the house in such a manner as this rascal must have done, was robbery."

"But he met with no resistance, and there could have been no excuse for so cowardly an assault as this complained of."

"There is much truth in that, and yet we don't know what human nature is capable of," said the landlord. "I have known a few things in my time; but the man, or whatever he might be, might have been tempted to make the assault complained of."

"What? Then, landlord, you imagine that a thief who had got into the house, would make an attempt to eat a young lady?"

"Why, as to eating her, sir," said the landlord, scratching his head, "I cannot say that he would. I don't know what his intentions might be, nor do I profess to understand it all. I can't, however, see what can be the motive, save malice and spite; they mightn't care whom they injured, so long as somebody was hurt."

"They must have been very bad."

"Yes, sir; and I wish I had seen them; if I had, I would no more mind chopping them in two than I would cleave a marrow-bone. I truly hope, sir, you won't consider that, however unfortunate the circumstances are, that I am blameable in this affair. I took all the usual precautions in this affair — that is, my house was secured as usual, and the place watched during the day; for we are particular in that respect, knowing that we are very liable to be robbed."

"Exactly," said Captain Fraser; "and though I much regret the occurrence, yet, I tell you, I do not see anything in which I say you are to blame. It is simply a great misfortune, and there ends the matter."

"Thank you. I regret it as much, I am sure, as anybody, because I am very likely to be injured by it."

"You are not to blame. Allow my carriage to be at the door in half an hour, as we shall leave almost immediately."

"And my horse, too, landlord, as I bear this gentleman company."

The landlord departed, and went towards the stables, and gave the necessary orders; while the guests remained conversing on the extraordinary occurrence that had taken place, and much pleased with the courtesy of their new friend.

Many were the speculations that were indulged in respecting the attack upon Miss Stevens; many of them wild, but all wide of the mark, fortunately, for her frame of mind; and then, before they had at all come to any conclusion, or any satisfactory probability, the carriage was announced.

"Well, Sir Francis, I presume you will ride with us?"

"Yes, on horseback."

"I understand so; we shall be much indebted to you for your goodness; but here is Miss Stevens."

At that moment the young lady entered the room, ready attired for travelling, but looking very pale and timid. Sir Francis advanced, and, taking her hand, said, —

"May I have the pleasure of hearing you say the occurrence of last night has done you only a temporary mischief?"

"I hope not," said Miss Stevens; "but, to you, Sir Francis, I owe everything. I am grateful to you for your ready and effectual aid under such trying circumstances. I am sure I never can repay you for your goodness."

"Nay, the task is easier than you imagine," said Sir Francis; "to know that I have saved you, and to see it has been effectual, is repayment enough. I am sure we never feel so much satisfaction and pleasure as when we find our endeavours, however important or unimportant they are, have proved effectual — that we have done what we desired to do — that is ample reward."

"You are so good, Sir Francis."

"We will say nothing about that. None are so perfect but we may see room for amendment; but we will have a truce, I hope, upon this subject, and now converse upon the pleasures of our journey."

"They, I hope, will be very many," said Mrs. Fraser.

"I have every expectation of it myself,"

said Sir Francis; "the day appears fine, and the sun is high. The storm of last evening has cleared the air of much of its heat; it is cool and pleasant. The country will look refreshed, the fields will be quite gay and pleasant, and the face of nature renewed."

"Well, I am certain it will be a pleasant journey under such a change, for I must say it was very sultry yesterday."

"It was," said Captain Fraser; "the appearance of the earth alone will tell that. But are you all ready?"

"Yes, all," replied Mrs. Fraser.

"Now, my dear Charles, what are you about?"

"I'm looking for my gloves," said the youth; "but I can't find them."

"Never mind them; we shall be off without you."

"I'll come before you have all got into the carriage, so don't wait."

"Permit me, Miss Stevens," said Sir Francis, as he offered his arm, "to have the pleasure of seeing you safe into the carriage."

They young lady accepted of the proffered arm of Sir Francis, though not without something like reluctance, though, why, she could not tell; but yet she did not like to appear to hesitate, and forced herself to do what common courtesy, if not gratitude, demanded she should do. She took his arm, and the whole party were shortly seated in the carriage, and with Sir Francis Varney mounted beside them, they all quitted the inn, where they had experienced such strange vicissitudes of fortune during one night, that it would never be erased from their memories.

CXLVIII.

THE ROAD, AND THE TRAVELLERS. — THE PLEASURES OF DOING GOOD. — THE
BEGGAR-WOMAN. — SIR FRANCIS VARNEY, A PHILANTHROPIST.

THE ROAD WAS PLEASANTLY bounded on either side by hill-and-dale scenery, while it was itself of a very diversified character; and at one moment they passed through long avenues of trees, at other times a bare heath, without so much as a dwarf hedge; and then well-cultivated country would succeed, studded with handsome villas, and country seats, old half-castellated mansions and halls, where gentlemen lived in the abodes of their ancestors, and felt pride in doing so.

The air was balmy and beautiful — every object appeared fresh, and every tree and shrub looked as though new life had been infused into it; the birds sang merrily, and the whole party were in high spirits.

"Such scenes as these," said Sir Francis Varney, "please me better than the gaieties and follies of the town. I am sure there is much more happiness to be found by a contented mind, than there is in the feverish pleasures of a city."

"There is much truth in that, Sir Francis," said the captain; "but, in my own case, connected as I am with my professional friends, I cannot follow what is the natural bent of my taste; but I find pleasure wherever I go, for I am determined to make the best of all that passes beneath my observation."

"Sweets can be extracted from every bitter, and therefore it is good philosophy to take the bright side of a picture, in all the ordinary relations of life; we are better men and better subjects by so doing."

Thus the distance was soon passed over, and a stage was but the same as a pleasant morning ride; and then an hour or two spent of the heat of the day in quiet in some small, but respectable, inn, with wine and pleasing conversation, gave them a relish for the life they led.

The style of the conversation of the stranger, Sir Francis Varney, was pleasing in the extreme; he was evidently a man of great and varied talents and attainments, and one of great experience, and who had seen much of life.

TWO DAYS PASSED this way, and they had not reached Bath; they were tempted to stop longer by the way than they would have done.

"To-morrow," observed Sir Francis, "we must reach Bath. About three short stages will place us within its precincts, and then I presume the assembly-room, as well as the pump-room, will occupy much of your attention."*

"We shall certainly go there."

"Have you been in Bath before?"

---

*   *The Grand Pump Room was (and still is) a large, ornate building next to the old Roman baths, at which visitors to Bath "take the waters." The assembly-rooms at Bath were like dance halls on a grand scale, where high-society balls were held regularly.*

"Yes, but many years ago, when we were quite children, so that I have no recollection of the place."

"And you, Captain Fraser?"

"No, I have not, I am quite a stranger there; but for the kindness of your offer, I should have to trust to strangers, or my own good fortune, to find out those things which strangers usually seek, and those places they usually visit."

"I shall have great pleasure in showing you that which is worthy of your attention. It is now some years since I was there; but I believe, though there may be improvements, yet the place is essentially the same."

"No doubt; cities seldom alter much, unless it be in their suburbs. If the alteration be great, it will point itself out."

"Exactly so."

The party were seated beneath a large cedar tree, which stood in the inn garden, with a table, upon which were spread some wine and biscuits, walnuts, and a few things besides, of a character agreeing much with the place.

Into this garden crept an unfortunate beggar woman, who, espying the party from the road, escaped the vigilance of the waiters and menials who hung about the inn, and entered. She crept timidly towards the party, looking wistfully, but yet fearful of the consequences of the intrusion; for there was a notice in the village, which gave forth fearful threats to them, should they dare to beg for the bread for which they were starving.

Presently, finding the captain's eye fixed upon her, with a beseeching look, she dropped her curtsey.

"Who is that woman, and what does she want?"

All turned to look upon the unfortunate creature, who began her petition by saying,—

"Kind ladies and gentlemen, pity a poor woman who is starving. I am very weary, and am weak with travelling—"

"Eh! what do you do here?" exclaimed the waiter. "Come, come, we don't allow beggars in this place. The high roads, or the Bridewell, are the only places we have in these here parts."

"Do not be in a hurry," said Sir Francis, to the officious waiter. "It might have been right enough to prevent her entering; but now we have seen her, I cannot, if she deserve it, refuse to aid her in her affliction."

The woman dropped a very low curtsey.

"My good woman, where have you come from?"

"From Bath, sir," said the unfortunate creature.

"From Bath, eh? And what took you there?"

"I lived there."

"You lived there; if that were the case, why should you leave a place where you did live, to wander about where you cannot live? That is a bad policy, methinks. What do you say, captain?"

"I think so too, Sir Francis," said the captain; "but that may be only a verbal blunder of the woman; we can't expect propriety in speaking from such people; it would be expecting too much."

"So it would," said Mrs. Fraser.

"I have left Bath for two reasons, sir," said the woman; "one is, I was too unwell to work, and then my rent got into arrears. While I could work, I did pay my way, though living very hard."

"And what was the other reason?"

"Why, sir, I was turned out of my lodging, and having nowhere to go to, and finding nobody would assist me, was compelled to beg."

"What induced you to take this road, my good woman?"

"Because, sir, it will, if I live long enough, carry me to Portsmouth."

"Are you known there?"

"No, sir."

"What induces you to go so far? Speak out and do not be afraid; we have no object in asking you questions, save with the view of assisting you if we find you a worthy object."

"I am going to Portsmouth," replied the poor creature, "in the hope that I may hear from my son, whom I have not seen these many years, and who went to sea about seven years ago."

"You have a son then?"

"Yes, sir, I had one. God knows if I have one now."

The poor woman uttered these words with such sorrowing, that all were convinced of the truthfulness of them.

"Speak out and tell us your story. Bring the poor woman some refreshment," said Sir Francis; "her tale may interest us, and give us food for reflection. I am sure one cannot hear the misfortunes of others, without feeling grateful for the luxuries and blessings one enjoys over and above the common lot of mankind."

"That is very true, Sir Francis," said Mrs. Fraser; "and I am sure we ought not to pass those whom we can assist by a trifle, when our means will permit our doing so."

"You are perfectly correct, ma'am."

"Have you no husband?" inquired Mrs. Fraser.

"None, ma'am, none. When I had one, I had a good home over my head. I would not wish for happier or better days to come again."

"What was your husband?"

"A respectable tradesman, who kept a good house and his own servants. We spent such a life as that for nearly fifteen years."

"And how came it to a close?"

"His death, sir, which was brought on by a sudden cold; in a few days he was a corpse. I can never forget that dreadful day. We were living very comfortably and happy. My husband had just at that time entered into some speculations that promised to make a handsome fortune in a few years; and all promised success and happiness, complete and continued."

"How great a change!" said Miss Stevens.

"Yes, miss, great indeed. My husband hearing some news that caused him to be anxious to ascertain its truth, he left home one wet night, and got drenched through; and where he went to, he was obliged to remain in damp clothes, and not being a strong man, he took a violent cold, and inflammation followed.

"After this he had medical advice; but he soon sank, and was pronounced beyond recovery; he died a very few hours after that, and I was left a widow. A few short hours caused a great change in my circumstances."

"What became of the business?"

"Why, that was carried on for a time; but an accident deprived me of that."

"What was that?"

"I will tell you, sir. My son was about fourteen years of age when his father died, and was just able to carry on the business; and I believe we should have done pretty well, because he was a steady youth, and I could trust him; and he looked after the men employed, and I was not robbed.

"However, a severe misfortune awaited me. I thought the loss of my husband a dreadful misfortune; and I believe it was; but in his case he left one behind who could help to maintain me. His loss I mourned; but it did not produce the same disastrous results that the loss of my son produced."

"How came you to lose him?" inquired the captain.

"Why, sir, I had occasion to have some business transacted at Bristol. I could send no one else, though I could ill spare him; but then I was compelled to send him, and did send him. It was to accommodate some terms of sale; and he only knew the affair. He, therefore, went to Bristol. He was pleased enough, being his first journey; and I could hardly have resisted his importunity, if I had been so inclined.

"He left me, and arrived safely in Bristol, and was there a day or two, when, walking about one evening by the water-side, he was seized by a press-gang, and carried out to sea. It was useless for him to complain or to entreat; they would take him, and forced him on board a man-of-war."

"He served his king and country, then?" said the captain. "I honour him, upon my soul; and you are going to learn something of him — if he be dead or alive?"

"Yes, sir; I know this much, he was alive about two years ago, and expected to reach Portsmouth in a couple of years."

"Well, proceed."

"When I heard my fate — the detention of my son — I was thrown on a bed of illness, in which I lay for nearly three months, during which time I was completely robbed, and run into debt; and when I recovered, I had but a few pounds in the world, for an execution had been put into the house, and all was sold.

"Thus was I left without a friend or a soul to comfort me, or any relative upon whom I could call for aid and assistance. I had no right to do so to any one; and after my misfortunes, I found that my former friends deserted me. I found that it was necessary to have the means of purchasing friends, just the same as anything else. I could obtain them for money; but without money I had no friends."

"I was by far too independent to ask for what I felt I was capable of earning. I could live upon little, and I at once left all who had formerly known me, before I attempted anything. I was determined that I would not even ask work at their hands, but get it among strangers.

"Of course this caused me to seek a subsistence in the lowest capacity, and I cared not for it, because it put a still greater barrier between me and my late acquaintances. It was a long time before I obtained any employment, because I was unknown to any one who could recommend me, or who wanted my services.

"This was to be expected; but the first place I obtained work at was through the interest of my landlady; and then I obtained more afterwards, and one led to another, till I obtained a hard-earned but honest living.

"I had a little money by me — some

two or three pounds; in case of being out of work, or in case illness overtook me, then I had something to fly to, the workhouse being a place of all others I most dreaded; sooner than go there I would consent to die by the roadside, and I have put my resolution to the test." *

"You lost your work?"

"I fell ill for some months; all my little store of money was gone, and my rent grew in arrear. I became more and more deeply indebted, and what food I obtained was given me by others out of charity; but this could not last long, and as soon as I was able to walk, my landlady asked me for my rent.

"I then told her that I had no money, but that, in a few weeks, if I could find food to enable me to get up my strength, I should then be able to work, and I would then pay her off by degrees, until I was out of debt.

"She knew what I had been, and had some thought that I had money, or if I pleased I could obtain it from my former friends, and expected me to make the attempt; but this I refused, and upon my doing so, she, after the first expressions of astonishment and anger, gave me the alternative of doing so or leaving the house.

"I was turned out, and had no refuge. I wandered about, and knew not where to go, or what to do; indeed, I was houseless and friendless — a wanderer without a

---

* *The woman's reluctance to apply for admission to the workhouse would have met with a ready nod of understanding and approval from readers of this story in the 1840s. Workhouses were widely regarded with horror and dread. Readers who have read the novels of Charles Dickens, and especially* Oliver Twist, *will understand why.*

penny. I could not now obtain work — I could not do it; and my appearance caused people to shut their doors against me, and I wandered about begging.

"This was the first time I ever took what I had not earned, save what was voluntarily given me when I was ill.

"One evening, as I was creeping about, I heard some men conversing about the different vessels that were out at sea, and one of them named the one in which my son was. I instantly listened, and heard one of them say that she was on her voyage homewards, and would be home in a month.

"I had no sooner heard this than I had some hope.

"'I will go,' I said, 'to Portsmouth. I will meet my son, and he will not refuse to support his unfortunate mother. I know his disposition too well to dream of it; and should he be unable to do so, I will beg for him.'

"I slept in Bath that night, and then began to consider how I should get to Portsmouth. It was a long road; many weary miles must be walked over ere I could get there; and as for the means, I must trust to the charity of the passengers. It would not be much more than what I was doing. I could sit on a doorstep and beg; but to walk on the road where there were few or no passengers, I might starve.

"However, I resolved to make the attempt, because I loved my son; and if I could see him I should see an end to my misery.

"I started out about four days ago, and I have got this far; but I have had only bread on the road, and almost despair of being able to reach there; and the charity of people is not enough to support life upon."

"And where have you slept as you came along?"

"Wherever I could, sir; beneath the haystack, or even a hedge."

"Where did you sleep last night?"

"Beneath a haystack about seven miles from this place."

"And is that all you have got through to-day?"

"Yes, sir, every step; and considering my weak state, I consider it good travelling, and shall feel thankful for even that rate of travelling. You do not know how intensely I wish to get to see my son."

"I have no doubt of it, my good woman, and if I can, I will help you on the road. I think yours is a case that deserves some attention. If you choose to remain here all night and rest, you may. You shall have food till you go, and some food shall be placed in your hands before you go."

"Got bless you, sir," said the poor woman, in tears; "you will, indeed, do an act of kindness to me."

"You will stop?"

"And be be grateful to you for your kindness."

"Here, waiter," said Sir Francis.

"Yes, sir," said that worthy, running up.

"Just take this person, and see that she wants for nothing — let her have a bed here and breakfast in the morning, and let me know what the charges are, and I will pay for it — do you hear what I say to you."

"Yes, sir," exclaimed the waiter, who considered the charge as one beneath his dignity; but he was forced to obey, and the woman was desired to follow him, which she did, after thanking Sir Francis Varney for his humanity and generosity.

"**U**PON MY WORD, Sir Francis," said Mrs. Fraser, "you do those things as if they were common occurrences to you."

"Why, madam, I am — and perhaps I ought to abstain from making the confession — one who does not love to come in contact with misery; but then one does not feel justified in turning away from it."

"You must have a deep purse to be able to satisfy all such claimants."

"I cannot do that, if I were inclined, or they were deserving, which many are not, as you no doubt must be well aware."

"Indeed, that is a fact. Very few of the claimants possess the same strength of right to our pity and commiseration. I am certainly struck with the woman's manners, and her artless mode of telling her story."

"Exactly. It bears the impress of genuineness about it."

"So it does."

"And when that is the case, I cannot resist the sense of my duty, which impels me to aid the distressed. But then I injure no one. I have ample means; and, therefore, others may do less, and yet deserve more credit. I have no heirs to come into my property, and I cannot, therefore, injure any one; if I were to give it all away, I should be entitled to do so."

"You are as good, Sir Francis, as you are courageous and fortunate," said Miss Stevens; "I am sure I have every reason to be thankful to you for two preservations."

"Nay, say no more about the past; you say things at which I ought to blush to hear, for my modesty is greater than you imagine; but, seriously, I take more pleasure in it than most people, and that may be a set-off against my disinterestedness, for I am only laying out my money in pleasure and amusement."

"No, no, that will not pass."

"It will, I hope; but permit me to return and see how they have disposed of this temporary *protegée* of mine."

"Certainly, Sir Francis; don't let us detain you; we shall remain here some time longer, and then we shall leave the shelter of this house."

CXLIX.

THE ENTRANCE INTO BATH. — A NEW SCENE. — THE HOTEL AND THE LODGINGS. — THE ATTENTIONS OF SIR FRANCIS VARNEY.

AFTER SIR FRANCIS Varney had left the place where the Frasers were sitting, there was a long silence, in which each of the party appeared to be engaged in meditating deeply upon something or other, and yet each shrunk from expressing them. The first who broke the silence was Captain Fraser, who said, —

"Well, my dear, what do you think of our new acquaintance?"

"I think he is a most amiable man."

"Very courtly," observed his his sister.

"Yes; a sure sign of good breeding — of good company."

"He is that," said Captain Fraser. "I never met with one in whom dignity, ease, and complete and unceremonious courtesy were so blended."

"And he appears to be a very kind and amiable man."

"But," said Miss Stevens, "he is also a very strange and a very singular man — a very singular man indeed! I never saw such a man before, or any one approaching him. What a strange complexion!"

"He has a singular complexion, and it strikes me he is well aware of it, and that is the reason why he prefers a country to a town life; and his solitariness, together with his manners, all indicate that his peculiarity in this respect causes him much annoyance."

"I dare say it may," said Captain Fraser.

"I never saw anything so truly terrible!" said Charles.

"Hush! do not speak in that way, Charles; it is ungrateful."

"I hope not; it is merely the truth. I never saw a corpse so pale! Indeed he is just such an one as you might imagine to have started out of a grave with an unwholesome life, and whoever had resuscitated him had forgotten to warm his blood, or to put blood into his veins."

"How very absurd you are, Charles! I am sure Sir Frances Varney deserves better of you than that. You are under a great obligation to him. I feel assured he feels the peculiarity of his complexion — I mean it has an effect upon his mind; and, if we knew the cause of it, it is possible some disinterested action, terminating in evil to himself, has been the cause of it."

"Well, sister, I do not mean to say that you can admire such a visage; but you ought not to say I am ungrateful, for I am not; and, moreover, I never saw any gentleman whom I liked better — his conversation is quite superior; but then, gratitude, surely, does not prevent one noticing so glaring a circumstance."

"Certainly not," said Captain Fraser; "though I fancy it would be better to remain silent upon such topics, if we cannot commiserate them."

"I think you are quite right, Fraser,"

said Mrs. Fraser; "he deserves respect at our hands, and the less that is said in regard to his misfortunes the better."

"I think the evening is getting very cool," said Miss Stevens; "will you remain here any longer? — I shall return to the house."

"We may as well all go — especially if you feel chilly."

"I do."

"Then come along; to-morrow we shall be in Bath. Come, sister, you must be quite well to share in the gaieties of the place. You know you said you should have the greatest pleasure there — you have been anticipating it all along."

"I did," said her sister.

"Well, but you will do so now. Why should your expectations not be fulfilled? I can see no reason why they should not. Bath is a gay place, and a city apparently made solely for the amusement of those who can pay for them."

"I have been so alarmed and terrified, sister."

"I know that, my dear; but you have had now two days' constant change of scene, and lived, I may say, almost wholly in the open air, so that you ought not now to be very nervous, sister."

"I might have been worse under other treatment," replied Miss Stevens; "but at the same time you can have no idea of what it is to suffer from such an outrage; you cannot conceive anything like it."

"I dare say not; I am sure it must have been dreadful."

"It must," said the captain; "but we will not say anything about a matter so disagreeable and so inexplicable."

"Suppose we go in."

"With all my heart; we shall be in Bath to-morrow, and you will have nothing to fear; how does your arm feel now?"

"Sore, but much of the inflammation has gone down; that I think will soon be well, and then I shall be able to use it as I used to do; I don't think it will leave any permanent injury of evil behind."

"I am glad of it," said the captain.

They now all returned to the inn, while the whole of the party passed the remainder of the evening in company, retiring at an early hour with the view of rising early for the purpose of getting into Bath in the afternoon, or before the evening set in, at all events.

THE NEXT MORNING came, and with it a cloudless sky. They were all in high health and spirits, and sat down to a breakfast that was especially prepared for them.

"What has become of your *protegée*?" said Mrs. Fraser to Sir Francis.

"I have not seen her this morning. I have not risen long, and I have had no time to spare, but intend to see her before I go, and see that she has means to reach Portsmouth in safety."

"Will you send for her here, Sir Francis?"

"Certainly, if you wish it," said Sir Francis; "I will tell the waiter to inquire if she be ready, and, before she goes, to send her up."

"That will be the best."

This accordingly was done, and in about a quarter of an hour the poor woman came up to the room; there were several alterations for the better in her appearance, and she did not look so careworn and cast down as she had done;

she appeared thankful, and refreshed with rest and food.

"You are now ready to start, my good woman?" said Sir Francis.

"I am, sir, thanks to you."

"I wish you all possible success in your mission, and I hope your son may be living, and prove grateful to you, as his mother."

"If living, I am sure he will, sir; and I do not doubt now but I shall be able to meet with him, thanks to your bounty."

"I hope you may. Have they treated you well in the house, below?"

"Yes, very well, sir, and kindly."

"I am glad of it. Have you any food given you to carry you on your road?"

"I have, thank you, sir."

"Then there remains now nothing to be done, but to give you some silver to enable you to provide lodgings, and now and then a lift on the road."

"Thank you, sir," said the unfortunate widow, as she took the silver which Sir Francis held out to her. She could only shed tears of gratitude; and Miss Stevens added some to it from her own pocket.

"You have our best wishes," said Sir Francis Varney. "Go now; we have done all we can for you — good day."

"God bless you," said the woman; "may you never experience misfortune, or ever know the want of even luxuries; you who can give, deserve to have. The poor and unfortunate have few such as you, sir, for benefactors."

"That will do," said Sir Francis. "Good day to you."

"Good day, ladies and gentlemen," said the woman, curtseying low, and then turning round, she left the apartment.

"Poor thing," said Sir Francis, "she has a long journey before her. A temporary aid given to poor people, often lifts them above want, and places them in a decent position in society."

"So it does," said Mrs. Fraser.

"Yet, you see, people disclaim charity, and say private charity is pernicious in its effects. But are there not two sides to any picture? An individual might as well say it was pernicious to take medicine because people sometimes poison themselves with some of the ingredients. Besides that, it does good to the state; for it often prevents such a one from coming to the state, and being a burthen upon society at large. I am really of opinion that much temporary distress might by aid be avoided; while, without that aid, it would, in all probability, become permanent."

"There is much wisdom in what you have said, Sir Francis; though you must be aware that it opens a door to much abuse and reliance upon the charity of others, which can scarcely be credible."

"Oh, yes; I expect there is an abuse of everything; but we do not, from that, argue its total cessation."

At that moment the landlord entered the room, saying the carriage was ready, as it had been ordered.

"Then we may as well at once proceed to the carriage, which is waiting, and we are ready to depart."

"And," added Sir Francis, "I am ready too."

They once more left the house they had slept in, and the carriage again bore them onwards towards the city of Bath, which was now only three short stages from them; and where they could arrive at almost any hour they pleased, if they chose rapid travelling; but this they did not, because it deprived them of much of the pleasure of travelling — the views and beauties on the road.

There were many gentlemen's seats on the road, which called forth comment and admiration; as well as many smaller estates and houses, that were often picturesquely situated, as well as lonely.

At length they came within sight of the famed city; and, each moment they neared it, saw fresh evidences of a large and populous place. However, they stopped not; but the closer they came to the town the faster they went, until they were really within the city.

"Here we are in Bath at length," said Sir Francis. "It is a fine city, and much of fashion and talent may be found here."

"I am glad we have arrived here at last," said Captain Fraser.

"And so am I," said Mrs. Fraser; "for I am almost tired of riding every day. I begin to want rest; I want to stop for a time in one place."

"We get fatigued, even with a change," said the captain, "after a time; and yet our lives are a complete round of change."

"Yes; if you consider the character of time."

They now stopped at one of the principal hotels, into which they all entered, and ordered their dinner; and, while the ladies arranged themselves for the occasion, Sir Francis Varney and Charles walked out into the town, where they amused themselves with looking at the different objects which were presented to the gaze of the stranger. In all these things Sir Francis appeared to be well versed — knew what was now, and what had been formerly.

TWO DAYS HAD passed by, and there had been but little time lost, so far as the visiting of one part of the city and another was concerned, and they gradually became acquainted with and visited the different places of amusement — at least, so many of them as could be visited by them in the time.

Sir Francis Varney was the chaperon; and, as he obtained attention and consideration wherever he went, he was a valuable aid and assistance, and the family had now got quite used to him, and he to the family.

The peculiarity of his countenance or complexion wore off, his pleasing manners producing an effect that acted as an antidote to that, which was likely to cause some peculiar feeling in all who looked at him; but his courtly manners completely took from any one with whom he came in contact the power and the desire to exhibit any dislike or aversion.

However, there was not one among all those who looked upon him who did not look upon him with various emotions; but they were only such as result from a source that acted upon their feelings and tastes, without producing any deep or permanent emotion in any one.

Great care was taken by Sir Francis in dress, and his display was altogether good, but there was no ostentation; his manners were those of a man who was used to the position and sphere above what he even then moved in.

There was no mistake in the matter at all, and the Frasers were well convinced that he was what he appeared to be; and there was, moreover, an evident partiality for Miss Stevens manifested by him, which had already been more than once remarked by the captain and his lady, who tacitly approved of the honour, though nothing was broached on either side.

"Sir Francis appears to be a very gentlemanly man," said the captain.

"Very," said the lady — "very. I never saw one whom I could find so little fault with; indeed, I may say he had none."

"That is a very extensive compliment, at all events," said the captain. "No fault is a thing you can say of but very few people indeed."

"I mean, as far as personal behaviour is concerned. Of course I know nothing more; his demeanour appears perfectly unexceptionable. I am sure I never saw any one at all his equal in that respect."

"Perhaps not. He appears to be very attentive to your sister; indeed, I should say he appears to be very partial."

"I think so too. What do you say to Sir Francis Varney, Mary," inquired Mrs. Fraser, "as a lover, eh?"

"I cannot think of him in such a light," said Miss Stevens.

"And wherefore not?" inquired the captain.

"Because I could not bear the idea. I don't know why — I can't tell you; but I could not do so — it would be against my nature to accept of such a lover. It would much pain me to refuse one who had done so much for me; but I could not accept of him."

"Upon my word you appear to feel strangely upon this matter," said the captain; "but I think you might think twice before you answered thus."

"No; think how much I might, it could make no alteration in my mind; for the more gratefully I think, and the more

I endeavour to be, yet the stronger would be my repugnance to have such a man for a lover."

"Dear me, Mary! how can you say so?"

"I do indeed."

"Ah, well! girls will be girls; but he has not done you the distinguished honour to ask you, so you must not refuse in anticipation. You may consider the grapes are sour because they hang so high."

"You ask me a question, to which I have given you the best answer I can upon the moment. Besides, we know nothing of Sir Francis."

"We know enough of him, I think, to speak and think with the utmost gratitude of him. Not that that should make any of us overlook the precautions that are usual on such occasions.

"And as for your opinion, why, that might be amended by time; and I am sure that what we do know of him is enough to cause us to respect him, and to have confidence in him. He has not sought our acquaintance, and that is one guarantee in his favour."

"So it is."

"But all this is useless. Sir Francis appears very sensitive. He is of retired habits and tastes, and, perhaps, something of that may result from the disadvantage under which he lies, which he may feel severely."

"So he might; and, therefore, I would never, if I could help it, make any personal allusion of any character before him, even though I were speaking of some one else, and it had no reference to him, as he might apply it to himself."

"That is quite right, and just what it ought to be."

CL.

SIR FRANCIS VARNEY IN BATH. — THE OLD WOMAN AND HER FANCIES. — THE MURDER IN BATH. — THE TREASURE.

SIR FRANCIS VARNEY, when he walked out into the city of Bath, appeared to be lost in deep thought, and walked along as if he saw nothing that was going on around him; he was lost in meditation — something weighed heavy upon his mind, and he now and then muttered inaudibly to himself.

Whatever might have been his purpose, he merely wandered about without going to any one place, as if he were in the search for an adventure, rather than having any specific and determinate object. But, after much wandering about, he came near the corner of a street, where he saw two persons conversing together. A stray word appeared to rivet his attention, and he paused, and then stepped into the shadow of a doorway and listened.

"You see, Matthew, Aunt Martha is an old miser. She would sooner see all the world at the last gasp, before she would dream of parting with a shilling. I am sure it is much too bad."

"What is too bad?"

"Why, that she, and such as she, should have so much money, and others, who would work hard, should have none, or even the means of procuring it."

"Yes, it is hard; and yet if those who have it did not keep it, there would be no one who would be worth money."

"That is all very well; but the more money circulates, the more hands it gets

into; and that, of course, enriches every one who has for a time the possession of it, for they do not part with it unless they have value for it."

"Well, well, that may do very well; but it does not appear to me to be any business of mine that such an one should beg anything of anybody else; but no matter, she has money enough."

"She is single, is she not?"

"Yes," replied the other.

"Then you may, after all, possess all she has."

"I may, but she is fat and forty; she may live for years, and in the meantime I may be a beggar all my life."

"No, no, not so bad as that."

"And what is worse than all, while she is living, she is decreasing the money she has, and it will yearly get less and less, till, if any comes to me, it will be so small a portion of it, that I am sure there will be but little good come of it."

"Indeed. If she be such a miser as you speak of, I should have imagined that the property, personal or real, would increase under such management as that."

"It would, if she were not living on the principal."

"On the principal — what do you mean?"

"That she lives on the principal, as I told you. She has got some strange fancies in her head, and one of them is, that the banks will break, all and every one of them, from one end of the kingdom to the other."

"What a notion."

"Yes, and that is not all; she believes that all banks will break, so all the public securities will be of no use, but only so much waste paper; and real property will all be seized, and there will be I don't know what universal ruin, desolation, and disorganization."

"What does she do?"

"Why, keeps all her cash at home; and then goes to her strong box and takes out her bright gold guineas, which appear in such abundance, that it would seem as if it could never sensibly diminish; and thus she has been going on for a matter of two years or more."

"Upon my word, what can she dream of? If she go on in that manner, I am sure, too, that she will be a beggar."

"That is certain; but she thinks not, and you can't argue her into any other belief whatever that is contrary to this matter. However, I have no favour in her eyes, because I am her relative."

"And why should that be?"

"Because, being her relative, she thinks I may be wishing her dead every day she lives; so, you see, if she go on with this feeling about her, she may take a complete dislike to me, and I should never have a farthing left me, even if she died before all was gone, and dissipated."

"Very true. Where do you live?"

"I have been living with my aunt.

"Indeed! And where may that be?" inquired her companion.

"Where — why, don't you know number one hundred and nine, Chapel-street? but I have left there — that is, I shall do so to-night."

"Will you? You are wrong."

"I doubt it, very much — very much indeed."

"What motive can you assert there is, to make it good policy in doing this?"

"She will think I do not care about waiting for her money; and that motive being observed, I am sure it will influence her in my favour."

"Then, you will not go back to-night?"

"No, not at all."

"Well, you know best; but I should. However, I must now leave you, and bid you good day. I must go."

"Good day," said the other, and they quitted the place.

When the two speakers had left the spot, Sir Francis Varney came forth from his hiding-place, and gazed after them for some moments in silence; but when they were no longer in sight, he muttered, —

"Could anything be more fortunate! I am reduced to the last guinea. I have not another pound to pay my way with. Just at a moment, too, when I think I may be successful at last in securing a victim."

He then walked onwards until he came to the neighbourhood of the street he had heard the stranger name, and then he paused and approached the house with some curiosity, but passed by it without stopping.

It was a corner house, and a blank wall ran a short way down the street, being the side of the house, and a small portion of ground called a yard; here the wall was lower — here there was a chance of getting over, and here Sir Francis Varney paused a moment, as if examining the place with care and scrutiny.

He looked all around, and saw no one approaching; he heard no sound, and he saw no face in any window that was within sight. It was, moreover, too dark to be seen, and he, without a moment's hesitation, ran a few paces towards the wall, and by a violent effort succeeded in placing one hand upon the summit, and then the other soon followed.

Sir Francis Varney was a man of great agility and strength, and he was not long in drawing himself up to the top, and then he dropped down.

It was fortunate he dropped heavy, and also fortunate, from that circumstance, he fell upon something soft. The good fortune of the occurrences was dependent upon each other. We say it was fortunate he fell heavy, because he fell upon the old lady's yard-dog, an unamiable cur, and prevented an alarm, for the dog was crushed, and unable to utter a single howl before the animal died.

There was now nothing to do but enter the house if the back door was open; but upon trial this proved not to be the case.

This was a matter that required some consideration; the door was not to be forced, and he hoped to get in by that means, but he was foiled; but yet it was something to have possession of the yard, he could hide here; but yet that increased his danger, for if he remained there, he was liable to a discovery, and that, too, before any attempt had been made upon the coffers of the old woman, and no good effected by him.

What to do he could scarcely tell; but after some thought, he determined to attempt the back windows in the parlour, or room above the ground; and to effect this purpose, he would have to get upon a water-butt, and thence to the railings facing the window of the room, and which appeared to have no shutters.

Having once made up his mind, he set about it at once, and was soon on the top of the water-butt, and made good his hold upon the small balcony, and then he drew himself up.

This was a work of some difficulty, because the balcony was very close to the window, and left him no room to lean over; but yet he succeeded, and found to his great joy that the window was only closed without being fastened; he had only cautiously and noiselessly to lift it up, and he could enter it.

This he did at once, and then stood in the room; but all was dark, and he could not hear a sound throughout the house, for he listened many minutes, lest he might be suddenly intruded on by some one, and then there would be no escape from there, and he would possibly lose all.

Caution, therefore, was the order of the day, and he gently closed the window, lest the draught might be felt in some of the other parts of the house.

That was very fortunate, for there was every possibility of a discovery resulting from such a course; for any one, feeling a greater than usual draught, would soon inquire into the cause.

Having got thus far, he opened the door and walked into the passage, and then he heard the sound of conversation being carried on in an undertone; he listened at the door, and heard two female voices.

"Betty," said one.

"Yes, ma'am," replied the other.

"Have you shut the shutters, and locked up all the doors?"

"Yes, ma'am.

"The kitchen-door?"

"Yes, ma'am — all right as can be; nobody can get in, I'll warrant."

"You don't say so?"

"Oh, but I do; the dog's out in the yard, too."

"When you have had tea, I'll have him brought in; he mustn't lay out there, poor creature, to spoil his coat, and catch cold. I'm almost thinking I ought not to let him stay out to this hour."

"He's well enough — he'll not hurt — he's got the kennel to sleep in, and he's plenty of straw; there's many a one about these parts as would be glad of such a bed. I've taken care of him."

"Very well, Betty; sit down to tea, and, when it is over, I'll bet you anything that old Martha Bell will be here."

"Lord bless me, ma'am, you don't say so!"

"Yes, I do; but I won't be at home; she and I have fallen out of late, and I'm not inclined to make up the quarrel, for she won't believe the banks will break, and you know they will, Betty."

"To be sure, ma'am, they will — I know very well they will; it's quite certain — as certain as the almanac."

"Yes; and, what's worse, she wanted to borrow ten pounds, and that, you know, will never do at any price; she would break, too, and then I should have loss number one, and no one can tell how soon number two might follow."

"He! he! he!" said Betty; "oh, lawks, I shall split."

"What's the matter now — what are you laughing at, silly?"

"Oh, you are so funny, ma'am; I'm sure you'd make anybody laugh — you do joke so, it makes one laugh."

"Laugh! — what is there funny in losing ten pounds, I should like to know? Nobody would laugh at that, I should imagine; I am sure I should laugh at nothing of that sort. If you were to lose ten shillings, I am sure that I should not laugh at you, nor do I think you would, either."

"No, ma'am, I'm sure you would not, and I am sure I should not; but you do say such things that make me forget all about the money."

"Well, then, go down stairs and fetch some more coals."

"Yes, ma'am," said Betty; and, before Sir Francis Varney had time to slip back and open the door of the other room, the door of the one he was listening at was suddenly opened, and Betty stood before him.

She came out plump, before he had time to step back; and she ran against him before she was aware any one was there; for coming from a room where there was light, she could not see at all in the dark passage.

"Oh, my —"

She had got thus far in her exclamation, when she received a heavy blow from the intruder, which felled her senseless to the floor, and, as quick as thought, he drew his dress sword, and plunged the point through her heart. Not a groan followed — she was dead, and might be said to have died while bereft of sense or motion.

"What is the matter, Betty?" said the woman — her mistress.

No answer was returned, and Varney paused, as if uncertain what to do. He was in some doubt if he should or not go in, or await the woman's approach to where he

stood. He had not been seen, or she would have screamed out; and if he went to her she would see him, and have time to alarm people.

He paused, and awaited her coming; but she appeared to defer doing so, and merely said,—"Betty—Betty, what has ailed you? What can be the matter? You don't mean to say that the tea has got into your head? No, no," she muttered, after a pause; "that can't be the case. She must have been to my medicine bottle, and that has been too strong for her. I shall discharge her. She'll be breaking something or other, and then who knows where that will end — begin by breaking a basin, and end by breaking a bank."

So saying, she muttered something unintelligible to Varney, and then began to rise and walk along the room towards the door.

This was a moment of suspense — the door opened suddenly, and then she stood before Varney, who made a rapid thrust with his sword. This would have been as fatal as that which he had dealt Betty, but the mistress was more fortunate, at the moment, for a steel busk was the means of preventing its taking effect.

"Murder! What do you want! Oh, you wretch — I know you now! Depend upon it you shall be hanged! Murder — murder!"

"One word, and you are a corpse," said Varney.

"Mercy — mercy! Will you spare me — will you spare my life?"

"I will."

"Oh, thank you — thank you! I never hurt you, and I don't think you would me. I am very sorry that I made any noise — but you will spare me?"

"Yes, upon one condition."

"On a condition?" said the woman, tremblingly.

"Yes, upon a condition."

"Tell me what it is you require of me, and I will comply."

"Then," said Varney, after a moment's pause, "show me where you keep your money. I must have money, so give me plenty."

"Plenty of money, did you say?"

"Yes, plenty. I want some. You have money I know — gold — gold in quantity."

"Ha, ha, ha! gold! Oh, yes — gold! Ha, ha! how funny!"

"Funny! Is my sword funny?" asked Varney; "because, if you think so, you may have a small portion of it, which you may consider funnier still."

"No, no; but I have no money — none at all, save a little money I have for immediate expenses. I have but little; for nobody now-a-days keeps money in houses, if they can get any at any time."

"But you have plenty of money."

"I haven't any, upon my —"

"You have. You keep it in the house, you know, because the banks might break, and you would lose all. Now give me some at once, or you are dead as any nail in your house — mark that!"

"Oh, dear! — oh, yes! What would you have of me?"

"Money," said Varney, pressing the point of his sword against her side.

"Oh, mercy! I'll tell you all; but — but you must be satisfied with what I have got, and not leave me a beggar, or kill me because I have no more."

"I will be satisfied with what you have got; but that I know to be much more than I can carry away with me."

"Oh, good lord, you don't know me, or else you would know the reverse of that. A poor lodging-housekeeper is not the person to have much money in the house; but if the truth must be told, I have up stairs my quarter's rent, which I ought to give my landlord. I can give you that, but God knows how he will believe me when I tell him I have lost it."

"You have all your property about you. You have gold in quantities."

"I have not."

"Then take the fruits of your obstinacy," said Varney, in a fury; and, making a savage and sudden lunge at her, he passed his sword through her breast, and with a smothered scream she fell to the earth, where she lay gasping and writhing for several seconds, when a rapid gurgling sound came from her throat, and she died.

"'Tis done;" said Varney to himself; "'tis done, and it would have been as well if I had done it as first; but no matter, 'tis done quietly."

There lay the two bodies upon the flooring, the one in the passage by the door, and the other in the parlour. There was a long pool of black blood, extending from one to the other of the two corpses — they mingled their blood in death, though they held different positions in life. What could be done? there they were, and even Varney could not pick his way without treading in the blood.

He at once entered the apartment, and began to examine the whole place, but he did not find much there — a few odd pounds, and yet he turned everything upside down, to use a common phrase; but yet there was nothing of the sort which he hoped for, and expected to find.

"Can I have mistaken the place?" was his first thought.

Upon consideration, he saw reason enough to make his mind easy upon the score of mistakes in that matter. There was the number and the street, and the old woman, and her conversation answered exactly to what he had heard; and after a few moments' consideration, he muttered, —

"It must be right; there are more rooms than one in the house. I will go and search through the rooms, and if I don't find any, I will set the house on fire. Indeed, I think that will be better done, it

will prevent the deed taking light, and as little suspicion may be as well incurred as can be."

This was a thing only thought of to be resolved on; but he cast that aside, and proceeded with his search, and having finished that room, he splashed through the blood, and once more stood in the passage.

"And now for the bedrooms," he muttered.

The candle he held was the only one he could obtain, and he was compelled to walk steadily, lest he should lose its aid by going out; however, he soon got up stairs, and walked into the best bedroom, where he again began to search about for the hidden treasure, but found it not.

"Curses upon the stupidity of the old fool, where does she hide her money? I am sure she has it here, and I wanted to get back without delay. I did not want to be away long, and here I have been, I dare say, an hour."

This was true, and he turned things over and about in great haste; but his endeavours had liked to have been useless, as regarded the discovery, only his eye chanced to light upon a panel.

He started up and pulled away a part the bed-curtains, behind which it was partially concealed.

"Ha! ha! what have we here? What I have been wishing to find, no doubt. This is the secret hiding-place of her gold — the treasury."

However, whatever it might be, it did not appear to be in his power to determine, for he could not open it.

This was, of course, a provoking state of things; and Varney seized hold of each implement that came to his hands, but threw each down again, being unable to effect his object by any means whatever.

He started up suddenly, after making many desperate attempts to break the door open, which, however, were futile, and exclaimed,—

"There are keys to these places, and I am sure the old woman must have them about her, if this place be really the receptacle of her wealth, as I have every reason to believe it is. I will find out, if I can; no doubt, however, I shall find it upon her somewhere—I'll try."

He immediately went down stairs and found the body of the old woman; it was fast stiffening; but the clothes were all sopping in blood, and he turned her over hastily until he found out the pocket; and from that he drew a bunch of keys. They were all bloody, but he did not hesitate about seizing them.

"These will, no doubt, let me into the secret. I shall find my way in, now, and then the house will no longer hold me."

He turned, and quitted the corpse; and, in going upstairs, he saw for the first time that the stairs all bore the imprint of his own foot; he saw they were stained in blood, and were clear, distinct, and well defined.

"It matters not," he muttered; "fire will, and shall efface that; and, besides, if it did not, what care I?"

He ran up the stairs, and again entered the bedroom, and was once more kneeling before the door of the cupboard. The bunch of keys was composed of many, and he tried one after the other, until, after many trials, he came to one, which was of a peculiar make and shape, and which convinced him he was now in possession of the right key.

"I think I have succeeded, now," he muttered, as he put the key into the lock. It fitted very closely into the lock, and then it slowly turned, and he saw the door open; but it only disclosed another door.

"What is the meaning of this?" muttered Varney; "what, is there another door to be found? I suppose some of these keys will fit this as well."

However, he was not compelled to make the search, for the key of this inner door hung up by one corner, on a little hook, in a niche which had been apparently cut out on purpose.

This was soon opened, and then came rather a startling sight.

In a small cupboard were packed a heap of human bones — more than bones, for they had yet the flesh dried and sticking to them — the skull was brown and bare, save here and there remained some hair.

"What is the meaning of this?" he muttered, angrily — "and have I troubled myself in this manner for only these few bones?"

It was, however, an apparent fact. There was the place, and it was now opened, and the contents were plain enough — bones! — bones! — human bones! There could be no mistake; and Varney rested his hand on his knee, and gazed intently into the cupboard at the bones, and everywhere else.

He was about to rise, when, somehow or other, he was induced to push the bottom shelf — why, he could not tell; but, when he had done so, he found it give downwards. Yes, the whole cupboard went down; he pushed, and pushed, until the roof was no higher than the floor; then,

indeed, he saw a sight that caused him to feel a satisfaction.

"Ah!" he exclaimed, "ah! this is what I have sought, and I will have it — gold! — gold! — aye, here is gold in heaps, more than I can carry."

He stretched forth his arm, and leaned into the cupboard, and then examined the contents, and felt assured that there were several thousands of pounds; the glittering heap before him was what he wanted, and for which he had remorselessly committed such fearful crimes.

"But I must make haste — I must make haste. I shall lose what I have such a certainty of possessing."

So muttering to himself, he put as much gold into his pockets as he could, and carrying a bag under his arm, he re-locked the cupboard. Having retraced his steps below, he replaced everything; while at the same time he carefully examined his person, to see that there were no traces of his deeds upon him; and then, wrapping himself up in his cloak, he left the house, and proceeded towards his hotel.

CLI.

THE SCENE AT THE HOTEL. — THE RELATION OF THE CAUSE OF SIR FRANCIS VARNEY'S PALENESS.

WHEN SIR FRANCIS Varney reached his hotel, he hurried to his own apartment, and then he called for his luggage; and when that was brought to him, and he was alone, he unlocked a portmanteau, and placed his gold in it; and then, having taken care to dress himself, he again met the Frasers below, at the evening meal.

"I have been strolling the streets for an odd hour," he said, "and find things pretty much as they used to be; I don't see many alterations worth speaking of."

"And yet they say they are improving daily."

"They may be; but only in parts and places; and it does not alter the general plan of the place, though appearances may be benefitted."

"Exactly; that, I dare say, may be the case; as, indeed, it is most likely to be the fact, especially when we see that, save in the case of entire new streets, all improvements are effected by individual exertions."

"Exactly; but life and happiness is the result of individual exertions," said Sir Francis; "but yet many shrink from prosecuting a scheme of happiness, lest barriers be placed in their path that would be as injurious to all as they are effectual."

"Indeed, that is often the case."

"I have met with many instances of blighted devotion since I have wandered about over the green vales of England."

"I dare say you have met with some adventures?"

"I have, sir. I have met with many that, perhaps, few men would have ventured into, and ever expect to come out alive; but I have not done so without paying dearly for my temerity."

"Indeed; have you incurred much danger?"

"I have, sir."

"But still it must be pleasant to fall back upon the remembrances of the past, and recall scenes and events that possess interest to your mind."

"It is so. I remember well that, some years ago, when I was in the north, that an occurrence took place that has left a lasting memorial upon me, and one I can never forget as long as I live."

"It must have been a serious affair."

"It was a serious affair—a very serious affair. I was going to Scotland, when, by some accident, the carriage in which I was travelling broke down, and it was unable to proceed, and I took up my abode at the nearest inn; where I determined to remain until the carriage was repaired, which would, it was said, take a couple of days, at the least.

"Well, in the evening of the first day, I walked about visiting the different places where I could hope for any pleasure; in doing so, I was wandering slowly down a lane, when I heard voices on before me. The wind blew from them to me, and I heard all they said.

"'Then this evening,' said one.

"'Yes, yes; I consider this the most favorable opportunity than can be taken advantage of.'

"'Well, then, we had better go at once.'

"'Yes; now we are on our road there, you see, and we shall be soon there; there will just be light enough to reconnoitre.'

"'Very well. We can secret ourselves somewhere about the place, where we shall not be discovered, and then we can get into the house at our leisure.'

"'But we may have to meet with opposition.'

"'Then, we must resist, too. You don't intend to be taken, I suppose?'

"'No, not I.'

"What did you intend to do if you were caught?'

"'Fight my way out, or, if need be, I can push my knife into the ribs of any one who may be in my way.'

"'Right. I shall be inclined to do for any one who wants to keep me against my will—you may reckon upon that for a certainty; and if the old man but as much as moves or utters a single cry, I will do for him.'

"'You don't mean that, do you?'

"'I do, and will do it.'

"'Then I know, and I will do the same. I like to have a pal that will stick by me, and have no nonsense. However, we need not be in a hurry, and just do what is necessary—go to work steadily and determinedly.'

"'Agreed. We will now go on—strike off to the left here, and we come then to the house. There's only one manservant, but he can be dealt with; and as for the old man himself, he cannot do much.'

"Then they both proceeded across the fields until they came to some thick wood, when I lost sight of them.

"Well, I knew the house they were both going to, and I determined to proceed by another route to the same place.

"I followed the lane as far as it would go, and found it led up to the very house which I had heard the men declare their intention of robbing, and possibly of murdering the owners—the inhabitants, I must say, for master or servant alike they would not hesitate in destroying.

"I entered the house—the door was open,—after having walked up a broad and stately avenue of linden trees which lined the way up to the hall door. I was for some moments unable to make any one hear, but soon after I heard some one approaching the hall. I paused, therefore, and presently there came an elderly gentleman, with a grave but pleasant countenance, upon whose shoulders fell a profusion of snow-white locks; he was venerable, yet pleasing in the expression of countenance.

"He bowed when he saw me, but looked rather surprised.

"'I dare say, sir, you appear surprised at my intrusion; but I do not come without a motive.'

"'I dare say not, sir. But you are welcome; will you walk in?'

"'Thank you,' I said, 'but I have come to put you on your guard against an attempt at robbery, and possibly murder, that is to be made upon your house to-night.'

"'Indeed, sir. I can hardly believe any one would be so wicked as to do anything of the kind; and yet, I am sure you would not say so if you had not some grounds for such a belief.'

"'I have,' I replied, 'and I will relate them.'

"I then related to him distinctly all that I had overheard in the lane, and the direction the men had taken. He appeared very thoughtful for some moments, and then he said to me, as he led the way upstairs,—

"'Will you walk up stairs with me?'

"I did as he desired, and followed him up stairs, until he came to a small observatory erected in the top part of the house.

"'You say you saw them enter the copse between here and the lane yonder.'

"'Yes, I did; and I imagine they may be seen if watch is kept in such a place as this; for I am sure they intend to examine the house, as to the means of approaching it, and they expect to find only yourself and a man-servant.'

"'They would have met but little more, indeed; however, I am fore-warned, and I will take care to be fore-armed.'

"'That is my object in coming to you; to effect this is all I seek; and now I will bid you good evening, for I have got some distance to walk before I can get back to the hotel where I am staying.'

"'Are you staying at an hotel?'

"'Yes,' I replied; and I named the place where I was stopping, when he said,—

"'You are welcome, if you are pleased to do so, to remain here; I shall be most happy with your company.'

"'Thank you," I said; "and frankly I must say, I should like to see the issue of this affair, and will accept of your invitation, though, perhaps, I have accepted of your invitation too readily.'

"'Not at all—not at all, you are heartily welcome; we will sit up and wait for these fellows; when we have beaten them off, we can retire in security to rest, without fear of disturbance.'

"'Do you see them?' I inquired, as he was looking through a telescope towards the point I had named.

"'No, I do not see them yet,' he said; 'no, no; and yet I—I think I see something now through a portion of the copse—it's difficult to tell what they are about; if they go much further in that direction, they will be plain enough; there—there they are; I can see them both plainly enough.'

"'Two of them?' said I.

"'Yes,' he replied, 'I see two; they appear to be looking this way; what are they doing now? Oh, I see, they are making for a place of concealment nearer the house. Well, sir, I am much obliged to you—very much, indeed; for you have evidently saved my house from being robbed, and myself from murder — I owe you my life.'

"'Nay, sir, not so bad as that; the villains might not have been successful enough to have effected an entrance before you were alarmed.'"

"'And if they had, what could I have done? Why, truly, I have fire-arms, but I should have been loath to have used them, and my hesitating might have cost me my life; so I have to thank you for life and property.'

"'As you please,' I said; 'but what steps do you intend to take towards your own and your property's preservation?'

"'I shall obtain the aid of another, and quietly await their coming; but as I think, from their appearance, they are not mere country people who come about robbing from distress, but men who make a kind of profession of housebreaking, I will have both taken and dealt with according to law.'

"'It is their deserts,' I said, 'for a more deliberately planned affair I never yet heard of; and what makes it so very black, is the fact of their early making up their minds to murder any one.'

"'No doubt,' he replied; 'but that is an inducement to take them in the fact. I will send for one man, and, what with ourselves, we can secure the villains; we are enough to do that.'

"'They are desperate,' I said.

"'But they will yield to numbers,' he said.

"'No doubt; but there must be a yet greater number; the odds, in my opinion, are not great enough to secure victory. These are desperate men, for they will not be taken, and two to one will not deter them — one, or even two lives may be sacrificed before they are secured, if they do not get off.'

"'Well, then, you appear to think that we had better obtain more aid?'

"'I do,' I replied. 'At least, a couple of men, if not, three, over the number you first spoke of, if you wish it to be perfectly harmless in its results.'

"'I should so desire it,' he replied.

"'Then you'll find that requisite,' I answered.

"Then I was invited down stairs, and great hospitality shown me by the old gentleman, who was an exceedingly pleasant companion. He was well informed, and a well-read man, and was the only inhabitant of that large mansion.

"He had been many years a widower, and had but one child, a son, a young man of great promise; he was abroad on a tour, and he was awaiting his return with great anxiety, as he was somewhat longer than he had anticipated.

"We sat conversing for some hours. We had a handsome supper, and afterwards some choice wine, and then in came three stout countrymen.

"'My friends,' he said, 'I want you to keep watch and ward to-night in my house, to protect it from robbers.'

"They agreed to do so, but expressed some surprise at what had occurred, and appeared to believe it hardly possible that any one could have been wicked enough to compass such an object.

"However, he told them all I had said, and they were sent below, where they were served with a very good supper, and promised reward, with injunctions not to speak after a certain hour.

"This all arranged, I and my host

seated before a fire, and with some wine, we passed the time agreeably enough."

"'THE TIME PASSES,' said my host, as the clock chimed the hours. 'I wonder if anybody is about now?'

"'I should think,' I replied, 'they must be about thinking of what they have in contemplation. I am sure it is a quiet hour in this part of the world, and I should imagine that no human being can be awake about here.'

"'None, I dare say, save ourselves, and our assailants, if they have not altered their minds, and given up their intentions, or altered the night they intended for the attempt. Who can tell? they may have done so.'

"'I hope not.'

"'No; it will be very uncomfortable to be in constant dread, never knowing any night I lay down what I may come to before morning; I may lose my life, and never again see my son.'

"'Yes," I replied; "but had we better not put out the lights?'

"'I will order it to be done.'

"As he spoke, he rang a bell, and when a servant appeared, he said to him,—

"'William, you had better put out all lights, and be quite silent; and if you hear any noise, get out of the way, and remain silent, unless they try to get away and elude us.'

"'Very well, sir.'

"'And as soon as you hear them at work, you had better steal up and let me know, as I intend to be present when they are taken into custody, as I have a particular desire to see it done.'

"'Very well, sir; but you don't know the danger you run. These men are desperate men, and they care not what they do.'

"'I know all that, William; but hasten down, and see my orders executed.'

"'Very well, sir,' said the servant, who at once left the room.

"'These people,' said my host, 'are not willing that I should run any risk; perhaps they think they will not have so indulgent a master in the next. Perhaps they are right; for I give but little trouble, and my servants are mostly out visiting some of their relatives.'

"'Indeed. I thought you were somewhat slenderly attended.'

"'I am. I have two very ill away at this moment, and I have another away on a visit to some relative.'

"'Indeed; they have an easy life under you.'

"'It is much the same as not having them at all; and yet, I must say, I have nothing to complain of; my wishes are complied with, and I have all my work done well, and punctually to a minute; and, if they have extra work to do, they never complain, but set about it cheerfully.'

"At that moment we heard William creeping up the stairs, and my thoughts soon reverted from the contemplation of the calm contentment in which all here appeared to dwell, to the confusion and bustle that was now likely to ensue.

"'Hilloa, William!'

"'Yes, sir, they are come,' said William, in a low voice.

"'Where are they getting in at?'

"'In at the pantry window, sir. I can hear them unbolting the shutters. They have cut a hole out of it, and they will be clear in in another minute.'

"'Very good. Now do you all keep together, and, at the appointed signal, rush upon them, and bind them hand and foot.'

"'It shall be done, sir, as soon as they get into the kitchen.'

"'Very well. I will come down and watch the operations; but don't let them get back again.'

"'Oh, we'll take care of that.'

"'Make haste,' he said, 'and station some of them under the stairs, so that they cannot escape. They must both be taken.'

"'And they shall."

"'Go on. Will you come down with me,' he said, turning to me, 'or will you remain here till we have secured them? You, sir, are a stranger, and, perhaps, you had better remain here.'

"'No, not I,' said I. 'I will go down with you, by all means, and we will see how these fellows behave themselves under these circumstances. Let me see them. I was the first to discover them, and I hope you will not refuse me permission to be present at a *dénouement* which I have, in some measure, been instrumental in bringing about. I wish to be present.'

"'Then follow me,' said my host; 'we shall not be too soon, for several minutes have elapsed.'

"I waited not a moment, but hurried down stairs, and found that, as I was going down the kitchen stairs, the robbers were well aware of the fact that they were entrapped; and, in their rage, they fought with desperation, and forced their way out of the kitchen, and through the barrier placed below; and, seeing they would effect an escape, I jumped over the rails, and stood between them and the way out.

"I had but my sword, and I drew that, and placed myself in a position, threatening destruction to the first who should attempt to pass.

"This, however, was disregarded; and the two men rushed at me, hoping to bear me down, but my weapon ran through the first, when a pistol bullet laid me low, and the man rushed over me."

"Good Heavens! and were you shot, Sir Francis?"

"Oh, yes, and was severely injured; and it was some months before I was cured, the bullet having wounded an artery."

"That was dangerous."

"Yes, so much so, that two surgeons declared that, had I bled another half-second, I must have been dead — that I must in fact have bled to death, and I should never have recovered; for I had, they thought, scarcely half an ounce of blood in my whole body — scarcely sufficient to cause the heart to beat."

"It was a fearful state — where did you remain?"

"I remained at this gentleman's house the whole of the time; he was very liberal, and very generous; I wanted for nothing. He said that, but for the immediate attention of the surgeons, he thought I must have bled to death; he saw me fall, and one of the men, without waiting for orders to do so, ran for a surgeon, and hence the rapidity with which the medical man was in attendance. And, what was worse, I had, in about two months afterwards, to undergo an operation to have the bullet extracted."

"Good Heavens! you had a severe time of it?"

"I had; and I had nearly lost my life a second time, for I lost a vast quantity of blood again; and, ever since that, I have been of the extraordinary pale complexion which you now see."

"I thought it was natural," said Mrs. Fraser, suddenly; but a look from Mr. Fraser told her she had done wrong.

"No, ma'am, it is not, indeed, natural."

"It was not until the loss of blood occasioned it, I presume?"

"No, captain, it was not; it resulted partly from the dreadful loss of the vital fluid which I sustained, and partly from a most violent virulent typhus, which I took in consequence of my looseness of system — that, I believe, did more than anything else towards bringing me to my present position — for, before, I was considered fair and florid in complexion, but my friends hardly knew me, or professed they did not, and I have not seen them from that day to this."

"Upon my word, Sir Francis Varney, you have had some extraordinary occurrences in your life. I am amazed at them; indeed I could scarcely believe one person, especially a gentleman of your property and standing —"

"Why, as for that, I can only say that my position and rank here have given me the means to enable me to go through them without any inconvenience, for I have no home or place dedicated to domestic delights; such a life I should be proud and happy to possess, but which I can never accomplish; indeed, I may say, I fear to make the attempt; but, no matter. The prime of life will, in a few years, pass away, and then I shall be past the desire for a home; and yet Varney-hall in the north, is an ancient, palace-like abode, that would grace a duchess."

"Is that your ancestral hall?"

"It is," said Varney, with emotion.

"And now uninhabited?"

"Oh, dear, no. When I determined to lead the life I do, I could not permit the old place to become ruinous and deserted and, therefore, let it, and those who now live there, are well able and willing to keep the place in repair."

"That is fortunate."

"Well, sir, I hardly know what is fortunate or unfortunate as regards myself; but I have one of my old fits of melancholy come over me."

"Nay, you must battle against them, Sir Francis."

"I have ever endeavoured to do so, but I don't know how it is — I cannot, somehow or other, bear up — I feel a terrible depression of spirits."

"I am truly sorry to hear it; but let us hope that the gaieties of Bath will restore you to your wonted serenity."

"I am sure I wish it," said Mrs. Fraser; "but where are we to go to-morrow? — can you tell me that, Sir Francis?"

"To the pump-room in the morning — the library and the assembly in the evening, if you are inclined to do all at once."

"Yes; well, then, suppose we make the attempt; we can but give in if we find it too much exertion, though I am inclined to believe we shall not find it beyond our strength," said Mrs. Fraser.

"Then that is our agreement," said Sir Francis.

"Yes; it is."

CLI.

THE SCENE OF THE MURDER. — THE VISIT TO THE HOUSE. — THE MYSTERIOUS
DISAPPEARANCE OF THE TREASURE.

THE NEXT DAY CAME; there was much excitement in the family of the Frasers; each one could see the partiality of Sir Francis Varney for Miss Stevens. She herself could not pretend that it was not so, or that she was unable to see it. It was quite plain and evident, and yet it gave her great pain, because she had an unconquerable aversion to him, who was her benefactor, and to whom she owed so much.

This, however, was a strong and inexplicable feeling in her own mind, and she felt that if death or Sir Francis were her only alternatives, she must choose the former. This was from some feeling, from what source it sprung she could not tell you, that appeared to forbid her permitting the approach of such a lover.

It might have been instinct, or it might have been that she had taken a personal dislike to him on account of his complexion; and yet she could not admit so much even to herself as that, and yet it must have had an origin.

She looked at him much more and more each hour, and more and more did she dislike him. At length she felt so much repugnance to him, that, if it were not for the deep gratitude she owed him, she would fly from and not even endure his society, good as that she was compelled to admit really was.

When he offered her his arm in their walk to the assembly-rooms and the pump-room, they were much pleased with the appearance of everything, and with the attentions of Sir Francis, who certainly did all he could to make the party comfortable and amused, he was so well acquainted with every object.

As they returned to the hotel, at which they all remained, they passed the house of the old woman who had been so cruelly murdered the night before. Sir Francis cast a cursory glance at it as they passed, but there was no sign of the door having been opened, and the murder had not yet been discovered; and this arose from the fact that the old woman was an eccentric, and her shutters had remained in that way before; and, therefore, no one took any particular notice of it.

When the party had reached the hotel, Sir Francis said, —

"You will, I presume, attend the ball this evening at the assembly-rooms?"

"We should wish to do so," replied the captain. "Do you intend to go, Sir Francis?"

"I will, captain. It is now some time since I went to such a place, and I think the change will be so great and agreeable, that I will go."

"Then we shall have the advantage of your guidance," said Captain Fraser; "and I hope we shall long have the pleasure of doing so."

"You are very good in saying so, captain; and, if agreeable to yourself and the ladies, I am willing, and shall be happy to bear you company."

"I am sure," replied Mrs. Fraser, "we shall always be happy with Sir Francis Varney's company, and thank him for his condescension — shall we not, sister?"

"Yes. I am sure I shall be much obliged to Sir Francis for this, as well as many other services he has done us."

"Do not talk in this manner," said Sir Francis, — "do not speak of the past, Miss Stevens; it is the present I would wish you to think of; at the same time, I desire only to be accepted, because I may not be thought intruding."

"Dear me, Sir Francis, how you talk! Really, I am afraid we have said something to give you displeasure, or my sister, here, has misbehaved herself; if so, I shall really take her to task for so doing."

"You will be acting unjustly if you do. But permit me to leave you for a short time. I have some matters to transact. I expect a remittance of money to this place, for I usually appoint some particular town or city, for I do not consider it safe to carry any great amount of money about me; it gives such temptations to robbery and violence that, travelling as I do, from place to place, I am especially liable to such attempts."

"Certainly, you are."

"Then I will bid you good evening, for the present," said the baronet, and he left the room.

WHEN SIR FRANCIS left the apartment in which he had been with the Frasers, he walked to his own apartment, and taking a large cloak and a small portmanteau he had purchased, he made his way to the very house where he had the night before committed such a double murder.

Before he reached there, however, he put the cloak on, and when he approached the house, he found the street entirely deserted; then hastily stepping up, he put the key into the key-hole, and at once opened the door and walked in.

He paused a moment or two, and then went down the passage a few feet, until he came to the body, for which he felt with his foot.

"Ah!" he muttered; "I see all is right — quite right; here is the body — nobody has been here to disturb it."

He took out materials for obtaining a light, and then he pushed past, and walked up stairs, until he came to the bed-room, where he again opened the strange receptacle of gold and bones; but, as he did so, what was his amazement to find a small packet of paper lying down, but all the gold gone!

He started up in an instant, and laid his hand upon his sword, but at the same time he appeared rivetted to the spot, and paused in this attitude for more than a minute.

Then, recovering himself, he gazed round slowly and carefully from side to side, as if to assure himself he was not trapped. But hearing no sound — nothing stirring from any quarter whatever, he began to think there might be some mistake in his vision.

"Surely — surely," he muttered, "no one could have come in, and, seeing the bodies, possessed themselves of the money, and then walked out. They would surely have given the alarm; besides, any one who had entered would never have gone further than the bodies.

"It is impossible," he muttered, and he again stooped down to examine the cupboard from which the treasure appeared to be abstracted. But there was nothing to be seen, save the bare boards; no signs of the treasure remained. This was a strange and mysterious disappearance of what could not have gone without human means.

"How did they get at it?" he muttered; "the place was locked, and in the same order as I left it; there is no getting into such a place without unlocking or forcing open the cupboard, or, I may say, chest, for this is a strong place; it is not broken open, and I have the key."

Varney paused for several moments, and then he picked up some paper, which was folded up, and seeing it was written upon, he thrust it into his pocket, and again looked into the treasure coffer, but all was gone.

"D — n!" muttered Varney, furiously stamping his foot, as if at that moment only he had become perfectly aware of his disappointment. "What can be the meaning of this? But this is no place for me; some one has been here, and the murder is known. I must quit it — eh?"

At that moment there came such a peal at the door with the knocker, that made the house appear as if it were a pandemonium of noises and echoes, which followed the first stunning sounds that filled the place.

Varney started and listened.

"Ah," he said, "they have tracked me here. What can that mean? Have they, indeed, laid a trap for me? Do they think I am caught? But, no — no, I am too fast; they know me not, nor can any one have traced me here, for they know not where I came from, and — but there, it is useless speculating; they may have laid a trap to catch whom they could, or they — ah, they have seen the light, and the house being shut all day, they now want to see if anything is the matter; but I'll warrant all is safe and clear; there is nothing known, and all I have to do, is to get away."

That was very true; all Sir Francis had to do was to get away; but it was somewhat more difficult to perform than he had any notion; for, as he came out into the landing, he found there was an unexpected obstacle in his path. As soon as he attempted to descend to the back parlour for the purpose of getting out of the back window, he found the door had been burst open by the impatience of the mob who stood below, and the door not being very strong, the shoulders of those who were nearest were sufficient to force it open.

In a moment the passage was filled with the crowd, the foremost of whom tumbled over the body, and were up in a moment.

"Good God!" exclaimed one, "here is somebody lying down in the passage."

"It is a corpse," said another.

"The woman's murdered," said another, "Get a light — get a light, and let us see what is the matter. Here is a dead body — a light — get a light, can't some of you?"

"Well, I suppose we can; but what of it? I expect it can't be done without giving anybody time to do it in; if you think it can, you had better do it yourself, and perhaps you'll begin now."

However, there was a light produced, and that put an end to the altercation, and silence was immediately restored, when

they saw the congealed blood, and the body lying in it; and then one, on pushing his way into the parlour, exclaimed,—

"And here's the old woman, she's dead and cold."

"She's murdered!"

"Yes, there's no doubt about that, poor creatures; and no one at hand to lend them any assistance. What a horrible affair!"

"Yes, horrible; but who's done it? There are rooms up stairs; they had better be searched; let's go up at once."

"Aye — aye."

Sir Francis waited not a moment more; he had heard enough to convince him his only chance was to escape while he could, for if they once seized him under such circumstances, he would not be able to escape again, and he immediately rushed to the back window; but there was no balcony there; he could not get out there, so came to the landing, and just reached the short steps that led to the roof, and there, had scarcely got the trap-door unbolted, when the heard a voice say,—

"Up stairs, lad—up stairs. I hear somebody there trying to get out—up stairs, lads, and follow him—up stairs."

There was a shout, and then all rushed up stairs, and Varney had scarcely got into the loft, when some one called out,—

"I see his legs—he's got into the loft. Up the steps."

"Hurrah! hurrah! up the steps, my boys; follow me," said one man, as he got on the landing, and ran to seize the ladder; but Varney saw the necessity of preventing immediate and hot pursuit, lest he should be recognised and followed to the hotel, when that would be death to his hopes.

Just as the man had reached the ladder, Varney lifted it off the hooks upon which it hung, and flung it back against the man, who fell back, and he, with the fallen ladder, created a dreadful confusion amongst those who were coming up stairs, many being knocked down, and the remainder retreated, thinking that at least there were a battalion of murderers.

This gave Varney time to get to the roof, and he then crept along several house-tops, without being discovered, though he could hear the shouts and hum of the mob, as they gathered round the house he had left.

Then how to get out of his present position was a question he was not well able to tell. He must let himself out through some of the houses, and to do that without raising a hue-and-cry, was a question he was not able to solve. Once or twice he thought of letting himself down from the outside; but this he gave up as being impossible, for destruction to himself would be the instant result.

"I must get into one of these houses, and remain concealed," he thought, "till the dead of the night, and then I could get through the house without any trouble, or fear of detection—but then the Frasers. I must not disappoint them."

This last consideration appeared to determine him, for he immediately crawled to one house that appeared to be the best calculated for his purpose, and he at once entered it by means of a small window that belonged to an attic. In this room was to be seen only a bed, and a few chairs, and a table.

All was silent, no one was moving; he stepped up to the bed, but was somewhat startled to find it occupied by some odd-looking human form, wrapped up in a curious and uninviting manner.

"Ah!" thought Varney, "I didn't think to have found any one in possession of this place so early; but they sleep, and that is enough."

He had scarce said so, when a voice said,

"Nurse, nurse—confound you, why don't you bring my posset?* Do you hear, cuss you? here have I been kept here for

---

* *A drink made with hot milk curdled with wine or, in this case, rum, commonly taken as a remedy for colds and sniffles.*

two hours without my supper, and what you gave me last night had no rum in it. How's a man to get well, and kept upon short allowance? I tell you it cannot be done, not at any price. Will you bring me my grog posset, or won't you? You inhuman wretch, to keep an old sailor upon short allowance of grog and won't give him any except in the shape of a posset!"

This was pathetic, but Varney paid no attention to it, and gently glided out of the room. When he quitted the apartment, he descended the stairs, and then he came to the passage or hall, when he was met by a stout female.

"Whom do you want?" exclaimed the fat female.

"Madam," said Varney, "are you aware of the calamity that has befallen you?"

"No, sir. What — what is it?"

"The lunatic in the top room has in a fit of malignity set the upper part of your house in flames. You had better take care of yourself."

"Oh, my God! the house is on fire!" said the fat woman. "Oh, mercy, mercy! Fire! fire! fire! The house is a-fire."

Varney turned round and opened the door, just as several people were rushing out of their rooms at hearing these alarming exclamations.

"That will do," muttered Varney, as he closed the door behind him, and then walked hastily towards the hotel, to which, however, he did not go quite straight; he went a little on one side to avoid meeting the crowd, as being an unpleasant mass of human creatures which are singularly unpleasant to meet with, leaving them to secure themselves and find the murderer, if they were able to do so.

CLIII.

THE ASSEMBLY. — SIR FRANCIS'S FIRST OVERTURES TO MARY STEVENS. — THE BREAKFAST SCENE. — AND THE HONOUR DECLINED.

SIR FRANCIS VARNEY, as soon as he reached his hotel, changed his habiliments, and sought the Frasers, whom he found ready for the assembly, and somewhat fearful he was not coming; but he easily excused himself on the score of illness, and then they persuaded him to remain at their abode, and they would all do so too; but at the same time Sir Francis insisted that his indisposition was but temporary, and he would rather visit the place, as it was a ball night.

Thus persuaded, they agreed, and the five of them proceeded to the assembly rooms, where they amused themselves as fashionable people usually do. They danced, and were highly delighted with the place, which was certainly of a very superior description, contained the very

élite of the Bath visitors, and appeared to advantage.

The wealth and beauty to be found in the room would have caused many a heart to bound with rapture, whether it was the miser's or the lover's; for both could there find that which gladdened them most, gold and beauty — wealth and youth; each could gloat his eyes on that he held dearest.

"Did you ever witness a scene like this?" said Sir Francis Varney, as he led Miss Stevens to a seat, and handed her refreshments. "Did you ever behold one in which was collected so much beauty and youth?"

"There are many happy faces," said Mary Stevens.

"And hearts, too, I hope," said Varney.

"I hope so, too," replied Mary.

"There are several here who have never been to a ball before; 'tis their *debut* in life, and a fine and lovely commencement it is; and if all their future years should be such a round of pleasure and gaiety as this, they needs must be happy."

"I am sure they must. People here seem to wish to make each other happy."

"And if they strive in heart, they must succeed in doing so, and in making themselves happy too."

"No doubt they do."

"And you, Miss Stevens, would you not make yourself happy when you make others happy?" inquired Sir Francis Varney.

"I certainly do feel happy when I am an instrument in the hands of another doing good, and seeing it really gives others happiness."

"That is one of the noblest ends of life."

"And one which you, Sir Francis, have pursued to some purpose. You ought to be happy, if any man can claim happiness."

"I am, in one respect; but when there is a great void in life, which has to be filled — when that void is in the affections, can it be surprising that sorrow and grief are there?"

"I cannot give you an answer, because I have no knowledge of such an existence; had I, it would be otherwise; but I cannot say yea, or nay."

"Well," said Sir Francis, "it is so; that void is in my heart; and, before I saw you, I felt it not; but now," he paused, "but now I feel it — feel it deeply, and I shall ever do so unless — but I hardly dare say more — my heart will never again know sorrow, and never again feel tranquil. Wants and wishes have sprung up which, until now, have never presented themselves in the shape of possibilities, much less probabilities, and which now are realities."

"This is a strange conversation, Sir Francis."

"It is, Miss Stevens, and I feel it to be so; but, unfortunately, I have a certain difficulty to overcome, which, perhaps, accident, more than courage, will enable me to break through. But, to speak plainly, before I saw you, the whole world was alike to me; I cared not for one more than another; but, now the world has new charms, I have new hopes and wishes. God knows if they are to be dissipated, like the morning mist before the glories of the rising sun. Love has made sad havoc in my heart; and to love and despair is the bitterest lot humanity can fall into. Man can bear all that adverse fate may entail upon him; but that saps at the foundation of the superstructure, our love of life, without which, society could not hold together; and, with disappointed love, there is no love of existence."

"Indeed, Sir Francis, I regret to hear it."

"Will you prevent it?"

"I cannot now answer you any such question, if I were inclined to do so — I have not the power. See, Sir Francis, there is another set."

"Will you dance?"

"No; I do not think I will dance any more to-night; but I shall be glad to rejoin my sister and brother."

"I will lead you to them, with pleasure; but will you allow me to name this matter to Captain Fraser?"

"I have no right to dictate to you, Sir Francis," said Mary, with evident embarrassment, "much less would I do so, or endeavour to do so to one to whom I owe so much; and yet I fear it will be fruitless."

"There, yonder, are your friends."

As Sir Francis spoke, he pointed to another end of the room, to which he was leading her, and which was occupied by many of the most fashionable and beautiful; they also had to pass down a lane of fashionables who were occupying seats, having been fatigued by dancing — many not having danced at all, but come to keep watchful and Argus eyes upon the sons and daughters whom they brought with them.

These, at least, noticed them — all eyes were fixed upon them, and Sir Francis, certainly with an air of triumph, led the beautiful Mary Stevens towards her friends, who were gazing at them with attention.

Mary thought herself somewhat awkwardly situated, and knew not how to release herself; and also felt that any attempt of the kind would really be as ungracious as it would be ungrateful, and so resigned herself.

A few yards more, and then she was once again in the company of her friends, but not released from Sir Francis, for he seated himself by her side with the ease of one who was well accustomed to their society, and of those around him.

"Well, Sir Francis," said Mrs. Fraser, "you have not been unnoticed in the ball-room. You have created quite a sensation; your dancing is superior, and your tall figure has set you off."

"You mistake, Mrs. Fraser; the object of such general attention was no other than your beautiful sister — my fair partner."

"Don't make her vain."

"That, indeed, would be a misfortune; but she has such an excellent capacity of mind, that she runs no danger of such a misfortune; but even were it not so, there would be much excuse."

"You are flattering, Sir Francis."

"Not I, I assure you. How do you find yourself?"

"I am getting fatigued. My recent journeys must plead an excuse for my weariness at such a time and in such a place as this."

"I am not surprised at this, considering how you have been riding about for many days past. Would you choose to retire to-night, and remain later on another occasion?"

"I think," said Captain Fraser, "it may be as well. What do you say, my dear?"

"I am quite willing."

"And so am I," said Mary. "Indeed I would much sooner we left early — if midnight can be called early."

"It is much past that hour now."

"Then I think we are decided upon going."

"Very well," said Sir Francis; "then I will obtain a carriage for our use, and then we shall retire to our homes."

"If you please, Sir Francis."

Varney then rose, and went out for the purpose of procuring what was wanted, and, by the aid of a little silver, he soon obtained what he desired, and then returned to inform his friends of the success of his mission.

They then left the ball-room, and proceeded at once to enter the carriage, which was so placed that they could at once enter without any inconvenience; and they soon gained their hotel, and, after a slight repast, they separated.

IT WAS LATE NEXT MORNING when Sir Francis Varney entered the room in which he usually took breakfast with the Frasers; but, though late, he only met Captain Fraser.

"I am afraid, Captain Fraser," said Varney, "I have kept you all. Perhaps the ladies are gone out?"

"No, no; they have not yet come down. Indeed, had you been in five minutes earlier than this, you would not have found me here."

"Well, I know not the reason, but I slept well myself. To be sure," said Sir Francis, "I did not fall readily to sleep, and that may account for it."

"Indeed! and do you not sleep sound?"

"Usually — I may say, generally; but sometimes some reflections keep the mind actively employed against one's own wishes."

"They do so, Sir Francis. I have myself found that to be the case; but I am sorry my female folks do not come down."

"Nay, nay, Captain Fraser, do no wish that on my account. I am rather pleased they are not down than otherwise."

"Indeed, Sir Francis!"

"Yes," replied Sir Francis, " as it leaves me an opportunity of saying a few words to you, Captain Fraser, upon a subject that concerns myself nearly and deeply."

"You amaze me, Sir Francis."

"I had hoped you might have had some guess at it, Captain Fraser, as it would have helped me through my task; for my heart almost fails me when I think of the possibility of want of success — my want of nerve is not habitual."

"I can depose to so much, Sir Francis; you showed courage, and nerve, where courage and nerve were most wanted."

"Ah, well, Captain Fraser, If I had been brought up to your noble profession, I should have been better able to make an impression; but I will do my best; but the subject is a grave one, as it relates to my feelings toward your sister-in-law, Miss Mary Stevens."

"Indeed, Sir Francis!"

"Yes, Captain Fraser. I, who have passed through so many ordeals of beauty, have at last been compelled to bow before the shrine of beauty. I am a devoted and humble admirer of Miss Stevens's charms and virtues."

"Well, Sir Francis?"

"I now beg your permission to visit her, and be accepted in your family in the character of one who ardently wishes and desires to become a member of it by means of an union between myself and that young lady."

"Personally, Sir Francis, I have the greatest pleasure in hearing you say so much."

"Then I am likely to be fortunate."

"So far as my approbation, and my consent are concerned, Sir Francis, you certainly are successful; but, according to the vulgar proverb, as one swallow makes no summer, so one individual's consent is not decisive where two are required to concur."

"Certainly, Captain Fraser. I was not wishing to put the young lady aside; but having your consent, I may go on to endeavour to obtain the happiness I so much look forward to — but I may count upon your good offices?"

"You may, most certainly."

"And your amiable lady?"

"Yes, I think I may say she will unite with me in using all due means of aiding you in your wishes — but here she is."

At that moment, Mrs. Fraser entered the apartment, and advancing to Sir Francis, offering him her hand and saying, —

"Sir Francis, how do you do this morning? I am afraid I have kept you — ah, I see you are alone with Captain Fraser — where is my sister?"

"Mary has not yet come down," said Fraser.

"Ah, we are both late, I think."

"I am, madam; but you have come at a right moment."

"Have I? Why do you reckon it so?"

"Because I was just at that moment speaking of you, and here you are; so that I can speak to you, which is much better."

"Well, so it is — but what is it about?"

"Your amiable and lovely sister."

"Ah, that is what you men always say — it is just what Captain Fraser said to me."

"Then may I hope for a like success?"

"I don't understand," said Mrs. Fraser, doubtfully.

"Why, I was saying to Captain Fraser, if he could obtain your aid in my behalf in an attack upon your sister's heart. I have been unable to hold out any longer — I am deeply and desperately in love."

"Well, that is a very dangerous disorder, and I must see what Mary can do to console you in your affliction."

"You will indeed deserve my best thanks if you will do so; and, should success crown our efforts, how deep a debt of gratitude will mine be to you."

"How much are we not yours already?"

"But my whole happiness will be through your efforts."

"Oh, no, no; remember, you said but just now it was my sister you meant to wed, and not me."

"Good God! how could you imagine I had any such profane thought?"

"Ha! ha! Sir Francis, I must see what I can do with Mary; but, she comes — another of the *dramatis personae*."

Mary Stevens at that moment entered the room, and felt most abashed at finding all eyes rivetted upon her without speaking, and she advanced towards the fire, having made an inclination to Sir Francis, saying, as she came down, —

"I fear I have been the means of keeping you waiting. I am sorry you did so; but I was really not aware of the hour."

"Nor were we," said Mrs. Fraser; "and it appears we have all been late, save Sir Francis, who, like a true knight, has been at his post, I don't know how long before I came down myself."

"Nay, don't you listen to any charges, Miss Stevens. I have been here but a very short time, though I ought to have been here earlier."

"It is fortunate then you did, Sir Francis, and I am relieved of the charge of detaining breakfast to an unusual hour."

"It matters but little when it is had, so long as it is to be had when it is wanted. What say you, Sir Francis?"

"I believe that the grand object of all our wishes and wants, is to have what we want when we want it. An eastern potentate could not be better served, or more powerful, or richer, than to be able to say so much."

"You are his equal."

"I am in some things certainly," replied Sir Francis; "but I want an empress, and thus, you see, I am dethroned and rendered powerless by a few words."

"You can obtain even that."

"Not exactly; for she whom I might choose might refuse to become mine; then, I am a weary wanderer upon earth's surface — I am no longer one among men; but a mere existence, moving about without filling any allotted position."

"This is very doleful, Sir Francis," said Mary; "if you say much more, you will spoil your appetite for breakfast."

"Mary, that is a cruel cut, you did not mean it, I dare say; but it is a sufficient rebuke. I must come to plain speaking, and at once hope you recollect the subject upon which I spoke to you in the ballroom last night."

"I do, Sir Francis; it would be affectation to say I did not."

"Well, I have sought Captain and Mrs. Fraser's permission to endeavour to win those smiles and good wishes, that I so much desire should be mine."

"You can never deserve less than good wishes from me," said Mary Stevens; "you cannot have less, I am too deeply indebted—"

"There, now, pray permit me to interrupt you. I must not hear any more of that; I did my duty on that occasion—"

"Occasions!"

"Well, occasions; and I hope no gentleman, having the power, would have done otherwise; and if so, I have only done what others would have done under the same circumstances—a very ordinary act indeed."

"You are making less of it than it deserves, were it only for our sakes."

"I see you won't entertain my wishes seriously; but, recollect, what is sport to you is death to me—the affections of a blighted heart cannot weigh lightly when the evil is consummated."

"Do not think, Sir Francis, I wish to evade or to slight any wishes you may form; as far as I am concerned, they are a great honour to me; but I am yet too young, and averse to anything of the kind yet to feel justified in seriously entertaining such matters as those you allude to."

"That, indeed, must be a mistake; you are not too young. Let me hope that you will not refuse to allow me the satisfaction and pleasure of your company; that would indeed be a greater misfortune than could otherwise happen to me to be deprived suddenly of that, I assure you."

"Certainly I cannot feel otherwise than gratitude to you, Sir Francis, and derive that pleasure in your society which others feel, and which all your friends must experience; but we will say no more upon this subject, except that I have given as serious and positive an answer as I can."

There were many other observations made during breakfast-time to much the same effect, but it is unnecessary to record them, and the breakfast passed off as pleasantly as possible, under the circumstances.

CLIV.

THE TWO SISTERS. — MARY STEVENS'S DISLIKE OF SIR FRANCIS VARNEY. — AN
USELESS SUIT. — DISUNION.

THERE WAS MUCH STIR in Bath next day on account of the murder that had occurred, and everybody spoke of it. The papers were filled with it, and it was thought to have been the most barbarous murder that had ever been committed, and most active exertions were being made to discover the perpetrators of this horrid deed. All sorts of conjectures were being made as to who the murderer might be, and his object in becoming one. Gold, of course, was assigned as that.

There was something terrible in the fact that this should have occurred just as the Frasers had arrived in Bath—it was startling, they thought, though they could of course have no connexion with it whatever.

While the examinations were being proceeded with, Sir Francis Varney appeared out in the streets as seldom as possible; not that he had any fear of recognition, for that was impossible; but, at the same time, he would not run unnecessary risk, while so much was to be won.

The days passed, and many very pleasant hours were spent, and the gaieties of Bath were enjoyed to their fullest; while Sir Francis was their great friend everywhere, for, somehow or other, Sir Francis obtained the precedence go where he would, and they shared it with him.

He pressed his suit with much ardour, and Mary Stevens appeared each day less and less inclined to accept of Sir Francis Varney for a lover. She felt a greater and greater repugnance to Sir Francis, who, however, pressed her more hardly and more assiduously than ever.

However, Captain Fraser and his lady were sensible of the advantages of such a match to themselves and to Mary, for they could not believe that one so courteous and brave could do otherwise than make any lady happy; the first objection would wear away in the person of such a man as Varney; they therefore espoused his cause warmly when they found that Mary was averse to the match.

"What can be your objection, Mary?" inquired Mrs. Fraser.

"I cannot tell."

"Surely it cannot be an insurmountable objection," said Captain Fraser, "since you do not know what it consists of. You cannot have a very definite idea; and possibly a little explanation may set the matter to rights."

"I know well enough what it means."

"Do you, dear? Why not tell us?"

"I will. It consists of a strong dislike to Sir Francis. I cannot tell you why; but it is a very strong and yet distinct feeling."

"What can it arise from?"

"That I cannot explain."

"If you could, we should be able to come to some conclusion respecting it; but at present it appears like a blind, causeless antipathy, and, against one so well calculated to make any female happy as Sir Francis Varney, is so extraordinary that it really exceeds belief. I cannot express my regret and astonishment. I cannot understand it."

"I am sorry for it."

"And more like ingratitude, Mary, than I though you capable of. There are two occasions upon which you stand indebted to him for your life. He risked his own greatly on the last occasion."

"I am truly sorry it should happen so, sister."

"Well, then, Mary, amend the error; for if it were an ordinary affair, common dislike might pass very well; but towards such a man as Sir Francis Varney it is decidedly wrong. Indeed, when I recollect the horrors of that night—when I remember the flames and smoke, and saw you wrapped up safely from the effects of the fire, while he was exposed to every breath of hot air —"

"Hush! I recollect it all; but it makes me shudder."

"Can you, then, regard such a man with cold dislike? Upon my word, I am shocked at your baseness."

"Sister, sister, you are too severe — too severe."

"Only just, Mary — only just."

"More than just. Do not turn persecutor."

"I would not; but this conduct of yours make me feel strongly — very strongly, and I can hardly face Sir Francis Varney and tell him that one who belongs to me can treat him in such a manner."

"Does love always spring from gratitude?"

"It is useless to ask such questions, Mary, or I might retort by asking if such services as his always produced dislike. But Sir Francis is no ordinary man. Suppose you do not love him, which might be explicable; but then you have no other love; you are fancy free, are you not?"

"Yes, yes."

"Well, then, you have no motive for dislike, though you might be indifferent. In such a case, I should not have thought it possible that there could have been less than gratitude, and the warmest esteem for his services and his own good qualities; for he has as good qualities as a man can have."

"Yes, sister; but that dreadful night has left such an impression upon my mind, that I cannot, dearest, do what you desire — I mean I cannot love Sir Francis Varney."

"What! not love him because of the remembrance of his services?"

"You quite misunderstood my feelings upon that occasion. I can never feel grateful enough for the rescue from the horrible monster who attacked me while I slept at the inn. I can never forget that moment of horror and terror. I cannot even to this day make out the object of the intruder. It was not robbery, and it could not have been any ordinary attack, for it was not carried on in the usual manner. To seize any one by the arm, and suck the blood from their veins, appears to me to be a proceeding quite unaccountable in the ordinary course of things."

"It was very strange."

"Yes; and, stranger than all, it has given me a perfect horror of man in general. I cannot abide the thought of being married at all; indeed, I won't, and I hope that is enough."

"Upon my word, my good sister," said Captain Fraser, half angry and half jestingly, "you would almost make me believe you were desirous of taking the veil; but you cannot have any reason for taking such a strong antipathy to male creatures. You must know very well that, because you have got a fright in a country inn, that all the abodes of men in the world are not filled with goblins, spirits, and the like, and wicked ogres, who are only waiting to eat up young maidens."

"It was no jesting matter to me."

"I do not say but what it was a frightful reality; but, at the same time, such terrible occurrences as these cannot be supposed to happen every day in one's life; indeed, one in a long life would be a terrible frequency which is never known, and I think you might dismiss the subject from your mind, as an inexplicable event, unpleasant and unprofitable to recall."

"But it has been too terrible and too mysterious for me to ever forget; and, least of all, could I do it in so short a time."

"Well, I do not expect you could forget it immediately; but, at the same time, I cannot see how it could affect your opinion of your preserver. Indeed, it is a strange perversion of intellect, not to say a degree of ingratitude, that it is difficult, if not impossible, to understand or believe."

"Well, I can say no more," said Mary.

"That is very resigned and easy on your part; but what we are to say to Sir Francis Varney I am sure I cannot tell. It appears to me that you have a childish dislike to him — one for which you can allege no reason, and, therefore, improper. I wonder what he, or any impartial person, could think of it, if they had all fully and carefully explained to them."

"I am sure I do not know; but it is usually sufficient, in a case of this kind, to say one cannot love the party, and to escape from what becomes an infliction, or, in time, a persecution."

"But this is not such a case as you would appear to imagine. There is no persecution, and Sir Francis only desires that you will permit him to attempt to obtain your good will."

"But knowing he cannot obtain that — speaking in the light you mean — it becomes a serious annoyance to me to think I should always be attended by a person who, on the score of having done me some services, expects me to listen to his addresses, and to accept him as a lover. It is becoming a slave, indeed, when one must not exercise one's discretion in a matter that so nearly concerns the happiness of my future life."

"You are making mountains out of mole-hills, Mary."

"I have not taken the same view of this matter that you have," replied Miss Stevens, "and therefore you quarrel with me. I think that a great deal too bad; I did not believe you would have quarrelled with me upon such a subject — one that concerns me so much, too, as this."

"Exactly; it does concern you, and it concerns us also, and that is the reason why we feel warmly upon the subject. Your want of motive is so apparent that it quite concerns us — we are completely staggered. What it can all end in I am sure I cannot tell; but Sir Francis must think us an ungrateful set, or at, least, he must believe you are actuated by the worst and most ungracious caprice, and capable of great ingratitude."

"I am sorry for it; but for all that, I cannot consent to marry Sir Francis Varney. I know not why, but I do."

"You really ought to be ashamed of such an admission, for I am sure he does not deserve such treatment."

"I am compelled to admit that to be true."

"Then why, in the name of Heaven, should you let prejudice surmount reason — and reason that you acknowledge ought to be paramount? You know your folly, and yet you persist in it. Was there ever such folly? Come, Mary, come, you must give up this kind of nonsense; you must act as I have always believed you would; you must meet Sir Francis in a proper spirit, and the result will no doubt be that you will banish all these idle fancies."

"I should be glad to do so, for they make me very unhappy."

"Well, well, they are calculated to do so, and when you have cast them aside, your own happiness and that of your friends will be much increased."

THERE WAS MUCH STIR in Bath on account of the murder, and the papers were filled with terrific descriptions of the scene, which some even went to the trouble and expense of producing sketches of, which, what with being badly drawn, badly copied, blotted, and printed, and being as unlike the original as possible, gave the inhabitants and strangers not a very vivid idea of the place.

When, however, the details were adverted to they were terrible enough; and when Sir Francis Varney entered the apartment in which he usually dined, he found his friends were full of the discussion.

"Have you seen anything of the murder, Sir Francis?"

"No, sir," replied Sir Francis.

"Well, there is a dreadful affair happened. How horrible to think — they might not have been discovered at all, but for the neighbours breaking the doors in."

"What is it all about, captain?"

"Why, two old women were murdered a few nights ago, and they have but just been discovered; the papers are full of it."

"What, the murderers? Well, that was a quick discovery."

"No, no; I mean it was not discovered at all, as it is supposed, till at least four-and-twenty hours after the deed."

"Dear me; how was that?"

"I cannot tell, except the old woman was an eccentric, and her shutters had been closed before for a whole day; but there were no other signs of life about the house the whole day, which alarmed the neighbours much, and they began to take precautions towards the evening to force the door, when a tall, peculiar-looking man was observed entering the house by means of a key."

"They observed that, did they?"

"Yes; he was seen quite plain."

"It will be fortunate, if he should have been the murderer, because they can identify him."

"Undoubtedly they can."

"I am glad of it," said Varney.

"Well; he was seen to go in, and then to go over the house, because there was a light seen to travel up stairs, and stop there some time; and then they knocked for admission, but not being answered, they at once forced open the door, and they all rushed in, but were horrified to find themselves tumbling over the dead bodies of the old woman who kept the house, and her servant."

"Ah! it must have been a startling thing, certainly."

"Well; they stopped a moment or two — as was most probable at such a sight — and then they ran up stairs, believing the murderer was there."

"And was he there?"

"He must have been so, because they heard him get up to the roof, and they followed, but were baffled, because he threw the ladder down, which caused them some confusion, and during that the murderer contrived to escape."

"Well; it was quite a field of adventure; but it is to be lamented," said Varney, "they were not successful in their endeavours to catch the murderer; but what is the alleged motive for the deed?"

"They say that she had some strange fancies, and that, among others, she had all her money in the house — her capital, upon which she lived, without any fear of exhausting it. That was known to some one or other, and got whispered about, and it is presumed that for this purpose the poor woman was murdered."

"How horribly barbarous! but ain't there any suspicion upon any one, because it is usually the case?"

"There is, I believe."

"And upon whom does it fall?"

"Upon a relation of her own, who has not been seen for some days, and who had been known to have spoken with impatience at the old woman's life, and the mode in which she spent her money."

"That speaks for itself," said Varney.

"So it does; but they have not taken him yet."

"I hope they will, I am sure; because the whole affair is so truly horrible!"

"So it is. Will you go to the theatre to-night; there is no ball — we can have an excellent box?"

"What do you say, my dear?" said Captain Fraser to his lady.

"I am willing. Are you agreeable Mary?"

"Yes; I am quite content with your decision."

"Then we are all agreed to the proposal. There will be a celebrated actress from London there, and I hope we shall find the entertainment well worthy of our patronage — indeed, I have little doubt of it."

CLV.

THE EFFECTS OF PERSEVERANCE. — SIR FRANCIS VARNEY AND MARY STEVENS. — AN EVENING PARTY AND CONVERSATION.

THE EVENING WAS SPENT agreeably enough at the Bath theatre; Sir Francis Varney having taken the greatest pains to ingratiate himself with Mary Stevens so much and so delicately, that she could not but feel ashamed at her antipathy towards him, and certainly did all she could to get the better of it, and succeeded in some measure in doing so.

They all returned home in very good humour with themselves and everything. Captain Fraser and his lady were completely predisposed to look upon Sir Francis Varney as one of the first men in England for rank and breeding; even Mary Stevens was compelled to admit she never saw any one whose demeanour was to be more admired more than his.

The next morning they all assembled at the breakfast-table, and were all full of lively images and thoughts of the preceding evening.

There was much more of cordiality and intimacy than had been felt among them before; for Sir Francis Varney's courtliness gave way, and he became almost as one of the family. Mary looked upon him with something like wonder, to see how agreeable a man could be whom she disliked.

One or two days more passed in this manner; and the dislike of Mary Stevens to Sir Francis, if not less, was at least not so active or violent; but she received him as an old friend.

That much emboldened Sir Francis, who again resolved he would speak to her, and that in the presence of her brother and sister, hoping by such a proceeding he should be able to overcome her dislike or fears by his own efforts, aided by Captain and Mrs. Fraser, who would create a diversion in his favour.

"I wish not," he said, "to be importunate; but, in a matter that concerns one's future hopes and wishes — one cannot well slumber over them — I wish to become one of such a family as that into which I find myself so strangely and accidentally introduced, though I fear I have failed to make myself as acceptable as I could wish."

"No one could think Sir Francis Varney otherwise than acceptable," said Captain Fraser; "your services to us alone would be enough to endow us all with the most lively gratitude and admiration, were you only to appear amongst us with no other qualification; but you add those which evidently make any gentleman an ornament to the circle he may grace with his acquaintance and friendship."

"You take a favorable view of all that you see, Captain Fraser."

"No, no; I merely speak what I think upon a subject which I have had, I may say, some experience. I have myself had some dealings in the world; my profession puts me forward, and I may repeat what I said."

"No, no, I will not suffer you to do that; what I wish to do is, to impress, if possible, my fair friend here with favourable sentiments towards myself. I am not as some of the young men of these times, who win by the violence of their suit, which they urge with all the haste of violence to attack and storm the citadel."

"That is a very good plan, Sir Francis; why don't you yourself pursue such a system? It must carry the citadel by assault."

"No, no," said Mary, "you will not do anything of the kind. Was that the way in which you yourself acted? If so, I am sure I pity my sister; for what can she hope for when she was taken in such a violent manner?"

"Oh, no, no; Fraser was the unfortunate victor, who was taken prisoner in the moment of victory."

"Yes, that is the fact; I was taken prisoner; but I have since been appointed governor in the enemy's country."

"Ha! ha! ha! well, that is a fortunate issue to your adventure. I would that mine were as fortunate — I love, and yet fear to say so."

"Fear never won a fair lady," said Fraser; "so don't be afraid."

"What does my fair enemy say her?"

"I have said so much upon the subject, sir, before, that I was in hopes I should not have had any occasion to say more."

"I am sorry to hear you say so."

"Why, it is a pity to render a matter that is settled uncertain, without the prospect of anything being gained by it."

"So it is; but I hope that is not the present case, Miss Stevens. My petition, I hope, is not rejected merely because it has suffered so before. I cannot but hope, though despair for ever stare me in the face for it; but perhaps devotion and heartfelt love may make some impression upon you, and soften the rigours of a heart that cannot, I am sure, feel any pleasure in the distress of another."

"No, no, Sir Francis; you only do me justice in saying so much. I can, indeed, feel no pleasure in such things. You may rely upon it, gratitude alone would prompt me to comply with any request you might make at once and cheerfully; but you must admit that this is a question that alters the complexion of other matters, and what might be proper under other circumstances, cannot be expected under this."

"Nor am I so unreasonable as to expect anything of the kind. Now, Miss Stevens, you much mistake Sir Francis Varney if you think him capable of such meanness. I wish you to act from your own unbiassed judgment, and, however painful the result, yet I would in silence put up with your decision. But still I hope you will not act imperatively — that you will look upon my suit with, at least, not a harsh and averse spirit. Have some compassion upon one who is entirely at your mercy."

"Come, Mary, do not act unkindly."

"I — I do not know what to say. I — I cannot give any other answer."

"Nay, I won't hear of such a thing, Mary," said Mrs. Fraser; "now or never. I will not say that you must not be mindful of the past; but you were never ungrateful, that I know. You cannot be otherwise than happy."

"You embarrass me."

"Miss Stevens, let nothing weigh with you, save your own happiness; that is my object, and my own at the same time."

"Say yes, Mary."

"I — I cannot."

"Will not! What objection? What on earth could you wish for more?"

"Do not press me."

"I should be sorry to do so at such a moment, were it decidedly your desire not to give an answer now; but I do beg you will not let me linger longer than necessary. Indeed, I find I cannot exist in your society and be deprived of the hope that I may call you one day mine own."

"Do, Mary, say yes — say yes!"

"Will Miss Stevens give me leave to suppose that there may be a time when I may be rewarded for my patience? I will not press you for a plain answer now, but give me some token that I am not to remain unhappy."

"Come, Mary, come — Sir Francis gives you every indulgence."

But Mary was obstinate some time longer, until Sir Francis, in a transport, pressed her hand, and placed it to his lips; at the same time she suffered her silence to be construed into a consent to his wishes.

"WELL, SIR FRANCIS," said Captain Fraser, "let me congratulate you in having subdued the enemy, and you, Mary, in having such a conqueror. I protest it was a hard fought battle, and one that I could not tell who would prove triumphant."

"I feel well assured you may congratulate me, Captain Fraser. I congratulate myself, I assure you; therefore you may do so to me."

"I do heartily."

"Thank you; I shall be happy. But

what are the tactics for the night?"

"What are we to do?"

"Yes, precisely."

"Oh, suppose we have a nice party among ourselves. We can amuse ourselves, I dare say. I am fatigued myself, and care not to go out to-night. We have all gone out so lately that it will be a change and a rest."

"So it will," said Miss Stevens. "I am really glad that we shall have one night, on which we can retire at early hours."

"Are you willing, Sir Francis, to spend a dull evening?"

"It cannot be dull, at all events, in such company. I shall be happy to remain with you, indeed. I feel that a quiet, happy evening is a thing that would be very acceptable to me, at least; but still I can do as you please."

"Then we'll have a quiet evening among ourselves."

"Have you heard anything more about the murder that took place the other day?"

"No," replied Sir Francis. "Have you?"

"I have," said Mrs. Fraser.

"What have you heard?" inquired Sir Francis.

"I will tell you," replied Mrs. Fraser. "You recollect that the nephew had been suspected of having murdered the two women, and committed a robbery afterwards."

"Yes, yes; I heard so much."

"Well, they have taken the nephew now, and he has been examined before a police-constable, and will be again examined in another day or two."

"Indeed! they have made quick work of it. How can they suspect he had any hand in the affair?"

"I believe they knew he had been very

poor, and had been very impatient for the old woman's death, that he might have it all. Now, such a line of conduct was bad, and has caused persons to suspect him; and, also, the fact, that he has got a quantity of gold about him, for the possession of which he cannot account."

"Ay, that seems bad; but what kind of excuse can he give for the possession of such treasure — he is surely not silent?"

"Oh, dear, no, he is not silent. All he says, however, is, that his aunt gave it him to leave the country with."

"That is strange — very singular."

"It is, and that is why they disbelieve it; besides; he had made no preparations for his departure, that have yet been discovered — besides, his shoes were evidently soiled with human blood, and the footsteps in the passage and on the stairs — at least, some of them, were exactly of the same size."

"That is a strong proof."

"So it is; but there appears to have been an accomplice, for there are other footmarks of a different size, much larger and longer."

"Dear me," said Varney; "didn't you say there were many people who ran up stairs after the man, who got away?"

"Yes; to be sure."

"Well, some of them might have left a foot-print."

"Well, I suppose they might, and yet they must have reasons for saying that these footsteps were those of an accomplice; perhaps they were fresher than the others, or it may be they have a different appearance from the more recent ones."

"It may be so."

"However it may be; it is quite certain

that he has done the deed; whether he had any help or not, he, at least, will be punished."

"No doubt he ought to suffer for such a deed; it is that which gives security to the rest of society."

"But it was a dreadful thing. A murder committed by a friend or relation is, I think, more heinous, if possible, than when committed casually, by ordinary murderers, whose sole crimes are murder and robbery."

"To be sure; when any tie that can bind one individual to another is broken, who would have taken precautions against such as those whom we value; but he was ungrateful, and killed his benefactress — for such she had been."

CLVI.

THE WEDDING MORNING. — THE PROGRESS OF JUSTICE, AND THE DISCOVERY OF THE MURDERER. — THE DISSIPATION OF A SCENE.

THE DAYS FLEW BY, and the aspect of affairs insensibly changed. Sir Francis Varney gradually drew over the scene such an appearance of candour and disinterestedness, that the Frasers were delighted with the prospect of such an alliance, and they left no means of propitiating and influencing Miss Stevens in his favour; and they succeeded to a certain extent in stifling all expressions of dissent, and brought her to a state of passive obedience.

She had nothing to allege against Sir Francis but her dislike to him, and even that she felt was weaker, and the more she exerted her mind, the weaker such impressions appeared to be; a convincing proof to her that it was a mere blind, reasonless prejudice which it was her duty to throw off, and she exerted herself to do so.

Thus it was she became passive in the hands of her friends; and Sir Francis Varney had the satisfaction of seeing that he was about to pick up a bride at length.

His pleasure knew no bounds, and his eyes glistened in a manner, that once or twice Mary recoiled from him in terror, and she had nearly revived her first feelings against him.

However that might have been, he saw his error, and he conducted himself differently afterwards; for he too well knew the effect it must have upon the artless and beautiful young girl, whose affections he cared not to win, so that he stifled her objections, and obtained her hand — her heart was not with him an object.

"I think now," said Captain Fraser to Sir Francis, when they were alone — "I think, now, Sir Francis, that we ought to come to some understanding."

"I shall be but too happy, Captain Fraser, to do so, in every sense of the word, and upon every subject we can have in common."

"Then we shall have no difficulty in this affair."

"I hope not, I assure you."

"Well, then, Sir Francis, you desire to marry into our family?"

"Most unquestionably; my heart and fortune are at the disposal of Miss Stevens. I care for nothing else but her — fortune, Captain Fraser, is no object to me; I do not care for a single penny piece. I have enough for myself."

"Money is not happiness itself," pursued the captain.

"I believe it — I feel it."

"And yet Mary is not penniless; she has her dower, though by no means a large one; yet she has one."

"Then let the whole, whatever it may be, be safely, securely made over for her own use, and that of her children."

"It is generous — very generous of you, Sir Francis; and your generosity much embarrasses me, and I hardly know how to proceed with a little matter which I deem a part of my duty to perform."

"Do not let me be an hindrance to you; I am sure I should regret it much; besides, the more we know of each other, the greater confidence we have in each other, provided our knowledge is of that character that will increase our respect."

"You are quite right, Sir Francis."

"Well, captain, I hope what you are going to say, will not give me cause to feel myself less happy than I am."

"I hope not; I believe not; but what I was about to say is a very ordinary and common occurrence on an occasion like the present."

"Well, let me know all about it, and then the murder will be out."

"Good. We have but little more than personal communication with each other, apart from our respective homes; and we do not know much of each other in the ordinary acceptation of the word. I wish to know something relative to your private affairs."

"I really cannot do so, unless you travel northward with me."

"Indeed — indeed —"

"Stop. I can give you corroborative proof; I have none direct about me; but I can do that much; but perhaps it will not do."

"Quite enough. I am satisfied — if you can give me corroborative proof of what you say, and that without premeditation, it will be still stronger and more valuable."

"If you think so, what do you say to those two letters, Captain Fraser?"

"Two letters."

"The one is from my gamekeeper, and the other is from my bailiff, who has to overlook my property, and advise me of what was being done on the estate, and the state of my financial affairs."

"They will do, sir, I believe."

As Captain Fraser took the two letters, he looked at the post-marks, and saw that they were plain and readable, and the date: they had been correctly described by Sir Francis Varney — they came from the north, and one was a business-like letter from the bailiff, and one quite in keeping from the head gamekeeper, both of whom mentioned many local and petty matters, that fully bore out all that was to be expected from them.

"And do you keep up an establishment of this character, Sir Francis?"

"I do. I can afford it, and I do not like to turn the knaves adrift on the world, who have, ever since they have been born, looked for abundance from the soil that produced them; and I don't think I shall be justified in having the hardness of heart to turn them off."

"You are a kind and good master."

"I wish to be so."

"And when, Sir Francis, do you intend to return there?"

"I am glad you ask the question. I should like to take my bride there to spend the honeymoon. I wish now to leave other objects, and to get back as soon as the ceremony is over. There I should like to take her; it would be a rare and splendid life to lead in the old Gothic mansion — as much like a castle as anything I can describe; but an ornamented castle, of course, for I don't mean high walls, and no windows."

"Certainly not."

"But will you assist me in obtaining her consent to a speedy union; and, that effected, we will whirl off for the mansion, and you can follow us at leisure. The union will, I hope and believe, be most happy."

"I hope so. I trust and believe it will."

"In the meantime, any more information or proof you can desire shall be obtained for you. Do not be backward upon this head."

"I am quite satisfied, Sir Francis."

THUS SIR FRANCIS VARNEY had succeeded in hoodwinking Captain Fraser and his wife, and had now entirely subdued all shew of objection, and had so far succeeded as to obtain a quiet and tacit consent to all he desired.

The interview described was reported to Mrs. Fraser and her sister, and was considered liberal and satisfactory, and the marriage was spoken of as likely to be immediate, which brought forth no remark from Mary, and the matter was considered as nearly settled; the day only was to be appointed, and that could not be very distant.

One morning as they were seated at breakfast, and that after the day had been fixed at a greater distance of time than Sir Francis Varney liked, the subject of the murder was again brought up, and Mrs. Fraser said, —

"There is nothing more about the murder now — is there?"

"No," replied Sir Francis; "not that I have heard of. I believe the unfortunate man will be tried one of these days — he stands committed."

"Stop," said Captain Fraser, "here is something in the paper."

"What is in it?"

"Something more about the murder."

"What is it?" inquired Sir Francis. "I am anxious to learn if they have done anything more, for I was sick of it, and wish to know when such a horrible tragedy will end — the sooner it is past and forgotten, the better."

"That is true; for knowing a man is lying waiting for the hour to arrive when he shall die a violent death, is truly terrible."

"So it is. They seem to say there is some clue to another person, of a most remarkable appearance, who escaped through another house, and deceived the inmates by describing a fire that was up stairs."

"Indeed! How strange," said Sir Francis.

"Yes; they say they will not publish more, lest it defeat the ends of justice."

"Something else sprung up, I suppose?"

"No doubt. But here is something more: the prisoner will be tried in a few days, and, if condemned, executed in a very short time."

"Then I wish that one happy marriage would come off before that time. I am sure Mary will be wretched, and I cannot be so happy as I could wish to be."

"Then postpone it for a few weeks."

"No, no, no; that would never do; hasten it. Besides, we should have to pass through all the wretchedness consequent upon knowing a man — a murderer, it is true, and perhaps two of them — that is waiting to die."

"I think myself," said Captain Fraser, "that we might, with advantage, leave Bath before the trial takes place. It would certainly be more comfortable."

"So it would," said Mrs. Fraser; "and, to tell the truth, I begin to get tired of this place, beautiful as it is. In fact, I want to get to your mansion in the north."

"Not more than I do, madam," said Sir Francis. "Will Miss Stevens permit me to persuade her to shorten my period of probation, to escape some of the disagreeables we have mentioned relative to this unhappy affair?"

THE WEDDING MORNING was arrived. Sir Francis Varney had not been sparing of his ill-gotten gains. He willingly made some handsome presents to Mrs. Fraser and Mary Stevens; jewels were the form he gave them in; and Sir Francis himself took care to display no small degree of ornament, and yet he appeared to be a man, who, though wearing and having the best of all, still wore but little ornament. But the occasion made the change in his habit.

And now the post horses are ready at the door — ready to bear them northwards. They are at the church. Sir Francis, and Mary Stevens leaning upon his arm, come before the altar, and the friends of the bride were on either side of them. The clergyman was about to read, but asked first, if any knew any causes or impediment, &c., to the marriage.

No answer was returned; when there was some bustle at the other end of the church, and the clergy man paused to ascertain its character.

In a moment more there was a motley group of persons making towards the altar; and foremost among these were two or three peace officers, and after them a woman, dressed in many clothes, which added to her natural obesity.

"Ah, that's him — that's the wagabone that said my house was on fire when it warn't; that's him as frightened me so, that I'm quite thin through it."

"Shiver my timbers, and they begin to creak a bit now — d — n the gout! — but that's Varney, the vampyre! Who'd a thought he would always be turning up in this way, like an old mop as nobody can use?"

Varney turned to the clergyman, and begged that these mad people might be turned out, and, after the ceremony, he would meet any proper accusation at a proper time and place; but he showed his anger so strongly, that Mary shrank from him; while the two officers demanded him as a prisoner.

The clergyman yielded; and Sir Francis, striking the officer near him down, made a rush at a side door, and escaped.

The fact was, there had been more than one doubt about the murder; and Sir Francis had been followed to the hotel the night of the murder by one of the waiters, who came up behind him. They took his shoes, and found they were bloody; and all things being traced home to him, it was agreed to capture him at home; but he had left for the church, when the officers followed him. Old Admiral Bell, who was gouty, happened to see him pass, and determined to unmask him, which he did.

The stranger spoke not, but furiously threw himself upon him, and endeavoured to beat down his guard, which his great strength and height almost enabled him to do ... (see page 1056)

PART VI:

The Vampyre Goes a-Courting in a Convent.

CLVII.

The Murder in the Wood Del Notti. — A Neopolitan Scene.

THERE HAD BEEN A GREAT HEAT during the day, even for the sunny shore of Naples. Not a cloud had been seen all day, not a breath of air had been stirring; all was golden sunshine — all was fair; the very sea glittered like molten gold, and the heat was oppressive in the extreme — so much so that even the Neapolitans themselves stirred not out of doors, but sank listless and sleepy on the couch, fanning themselves, and endeavouring to create an air that would give some slight refreshment.

Even the sea was calm — the very waves lashed the shore lazily, and appeared to partake of the general weariness that came over all nature — all things that moved.

There was no soul stirring in the villas that were seen dotted about the environs of Naples, most of them like palaces, surrounded on every side by gardens and fountains, walled in, and secure from the intrusion of a stranger.

There was one of great magnificence adjoining the small wood Del Notti, that reared its stately structure on a slope looking towards the sea, though at a mile or two's distance, but close adjoining the wood.

The gardens were extensive, and abutted on the wood, which was a cool and shady spot at most times, and if such a one were now to be found, it would certainly be found in the wood Del Notti.

The trees grew tall, and spread their branches out until they interlaced each other so completely, that when the foliage was on them the light rarely found its way to the earth, save in a dim and diluted form.

Here there might now and then be found some of those who had been overtaken by the heat of the day, or who from choice preferred the coolness of the woods to the walls of their houses. Here, then, reposing beneath the great trees, might occasionally be found a few individuals who slept in coolness and shade.

Near the wall of the villa where the wood ran were some tall black trees, mostly fir and cedar; there beneath one of the latter lay a tall, gaunt-looking man, who, notwithstanding the weather, was wrapped up in a cloak of large dimensions, and sable colour.

There was something strange in that man's appearance; above all, the cloak which he wore was a thing so much out of place, that none other than himself could or would have worn it. What was his motive none could divine, were it not for the concealment of his person, which seemed likely enough.

His slouched hat was bent over his eyes; his face was scarcely distinguishable between the collar of the cloak and the hat, though he lay on his back motionless, and without heeding aught that neared him.

It was true, there did not exist any reason why he should take any heed, seeing that at that point no one ever came. It was a spot that was not frequented, having a bad name, which usually deters people from trusting themselves in such a place.

However, the stranger lay motionless, and apparently without fear. Perhaps it was the long two-edged sword he wore, that gave him his security; at all events, he lay there in silence, and almost motionless — quite and entirely so, save the motion in breathing; and his eye now and then turned in a particular direction.

The hours rolled by, and no one approached, till the sun sunk towards the ocean, there to bury himself till another morrow appeared.

The heat of the high noon was past, and the shadows of the trees reduced the light in the wood to a twilight; and the stranger arose and stood beneath the shadow of a tall one, while he appeared to be listening for some sound which he appeared to expect from some particular quarter of the wood.

The hour of noon is some hours past; and with it a gentle sea breeze begins to fan the heated shores, and here and there might be seen some of the inhabitants creeping about in the shady places.

The stranger listened, and from the quarter to which he appeared most to direct his attention, he heard sounds proceed. These were those made by persons walking over the dried leaves and sticks which lay scattered about from the effects of the storms that sometimes visit even these pleasant shores.

"She comes!" he muttered, and his eye glanced round, and he grasped the hilt of his sword. "She comes! but does she come alone?"

He paused, and again listened.

"She comes not alone — another is with her; but no matter; she shall come. I have the means of security here. But, above all, I need *her*."

He paused again, and listened, but quietly drew his sword, which was long and sharp, and stood beneath the tree, while the voices and sounds slowly approached, until they came quite distinct and audible.

"And so," said a man's voice, but in a low key, "the marchese is not well."

"She is quite indisposed."

"I was about to say I could hardly feel it in my heart to regret it."

"And why could you be so unfeeling?"

"Because, my dear Fiametta, had she been well, you would scarce have got away from her this evening, and I should have had but little of your sweet company."

"I admit that; but were you not selfish in desiring it?"

"Yes, I was."

"And are you not ashamed to say so?"

"No, I am not, Fiametta. I can acknowledge anything that concerns myself and you; for I must admit a great deal of selfishness in this matter. I love you tenderly, and that puts all the world beside us. I think nothing of any one save you, and for you I would sacrifice the whole world."

"I am fearful of you."

"And wherefore should you be fearful of me, fair one? Am I not willing and ready to fight and die for you? I would not fear the summons of death this moment, if I knew that I could save you but one hour's pang."

"I hope," said Fiametta, leaning on her lover's arm, "I hope that you will never be called upon for so sad a a sacrifice. I am sure I should never know an hour's happiness if I thought there was a possibility of it."

"I do not think there is any possibility of that happening. But, Fiametta, when do you hope for an end to this slavery? Can't you leave the old marchese? — she is anything but kind to you, and would marry you to one of her poor relatives; and unless you marry with her consent, you will never be rewarded for the many listless hours you have passed, night after night, at her bedside."

"But she will reward me when she dies."

"What an age to wait!"

"Surely you cannot grudge her life!"

"I do not, only so long as it is a term of imprisonment for you. If you would leave her, and come back with me, I will make you happy. You shall have a happy home, and form new ties, and new affections."

"I have not got so tired of the old, that it is necessary to change them; but I cannot leave the marchese. She is almost alone — no one goes near her to do her a good office, and I am her only friend."

"And yet she won't give you liberty."

"She says I am too young, and, if you must know all, she says I am too pretty to be trusted in everybody's company."

"I must admit there is much of truth in that, and yet I cannot see its application in this instance, as far as I am concerned."

"No; that is not to be expected from you, you know; but this must be admitted, that she speaks of men in general. Besides, she says, if I have patience to await her death, she will handsomely endow me."

"Upon my word, I think the old woman only wants to lease her life a few years longer, or, I should say, wishes to live forever."

"How can you make that appear?"

"Thus — when you are waiting for people's deaths, you never do succeed in hearing of their dying within any reasonable space. It gives them new life, and the spirit of opposition and obstinacy is created within them, and they won't die."

"For shame."

"Nay, you will find, Fiametta, that we shall both grow grey-headed in waiting for the happy moment when you and I are man and wife. Do not stay, then, any longer, leave here, and come with me; we shall be happy, and defy the world."

"But look what a dowry I shall lose."

"Never mind about that. Such a dowry would not make you young again, nor would it recall many years of past service and attendance upon her. You must know how very precarious such a life must be. It may so happen that you may forfeit all you have deserved through some fancy of this old woman. She may take it into her head to insist upon your marrying her poor cousin there. You know, if you were to displease her, she might very easily leave you nothing for your pains."

"I admit all that; but it amounts to nothing, because she has said as much that she would never force me, only she wished me to marry him, as being a worthy man and one who would act justly to me through life."

"Justly through life! What a sound! It sounds but little of love. Justly, indeed! I would I could act no otherwise to others, but to you, Fiametta, I should as soon think of forgetting you as merely acting justly. I love you; I would, at this moment, lay down my life for you."

At that moment they neared the stranger, who was standing silently and motionless, with his sword concealed beneath his cloak, but eagerly watching them, and devouring every word they uttered; and, by degrees, they drew nearer and nearer.

"I am sure it will be wise to wait awhile. I am sure the poor old marchese will not live long. She cannot eat and drink, save with great difficulty. I am sure we shall not have long to wait."

"I am willing to abide by your wishes, Fiametta; but it cannot be well to wait for an age — it cannot be well to wait till we are old."

"I know that; but —"

Fiametta screamed, as her eye fell upon the stranger, who rushed out upon them, with his sword drawn. This gave her male companion time to defend himself, by, in the first instance, jumping aside.

"Mercy! mercy!" screamed Fiametta.

Her lover drew his sword, and put himself upon his defence, saying, as he parried the first thrust of his enemy, — "Villain! what mean you? Is it robbery you would attempt, or murder alone? Will nothing but shedding blood satisfy you?"

The stranger made no reply, but pressed on furiously, and with great strength and skill, for two or three minutes, when Fiametta's lover, by changing his ground, contrived to elude so desperate an assault upon his life.

Fiametta, however, believed her lover was getting the worst of it. She screamed out for help several times, but none came. However, it caused the stranger to press his adversary more quickly, and to hasten his own movements, for he was quite desperate and furious; but this laid him open to the assaults of the other. But, so fierce the attack, and such was the strength exhibited, that Fiametta's lover was compelled to give ground.

"What is your object, villain? — speak!"

But the stranger spoke not, but furiously threw himself upon him, and endeavoured to beat down his guard, which his great strength and height almost enabled him to do; but as the other gave ground he was obliged to follow him, and then his foot caught against some of the tangled roots that grew out of the earth, and threw him forward; and his adversary, not slow to profit by it, and rid himself of so dangerous an enemy, stepped forward and received him upon the point of his sword.

"A good deliverance," said the lover, drawing his sword out of the body as it fell to the earth — "a timely deliverance, truly."

He wiped his forehead, for the perspiration streamed down his face; the day was warm, and his exertion great.

"Oh, Jose," exclaimed Fiametta, "what a horrid man!"

"A brigand, I suppose."

"But he said nothing — he asked nothing."

"No, he meant murder; there is no doubt of it, now, in the world; but I never saw such an ill-looking wretch before."

As Jose spoke, he kicked the hat and cloak off which the brigand wore, and which remained partially on. There was a ghastly wound in his breast where Jose's sword entered and let out the life of the the stranger.

He was very tall, but thin and emaciated; his features remarkable, and he wore some straight, straggling hair, that was disordered, and fell over his forehead and face of more than marble paleness.

"Well, I never met with such an encounter before, and I never met with such an ill-looking villain," said Jose. "Come away, Fiametta; we need not say anything to any one about the affair. I will not come here again, though it may be needless to take the precaution, seeing that none could be brought to match this fellow in villany and ugliness; at least, it is so to my mind. Come away."

Wiping his sword on the cloak of the fallen man, and sheathing it, he took the hand of Fiametta, and drawing it through his arm, left the spot.

CLVIII.

A MAIDEN'S MIND DISTURBED. — AN EASY WAY OF PROMOTING COMFORT OF
CONSCIENCE. — THE MONK.

THE SPOT WAS DESERTED, and no soul came near; but the body lay, with its ghastly wound, all sopping in its gore. It was a fitting place for such a scene as this; no sound was heard, and the lazy hours turned slowly over, till the shades of evening came on apace; the light grew dim, and darkness increased; but there the dead body of the tall, remarkable-looking stranger lay, without motion. It was cold and bloodless — death had long since deprived it of its last spark of animation.

Jose and Fiametta quitted the neighbourhood of the deed of darkness as quickly as they could, and it was many minutes before either of them spoke, so filled were their minds with the reflections natural to, and consequent upon, the strange occurrence that had just before fallen upon them.

At length Fiametta broke silence, by saying, — "Oh, Jose, what a dreadful thing has happened!"

"Truly, it had like to have been a dreadful affair; but it don't matter now, he's settled, I believe."

"Yes; but you have killed a man."

"Truly, my dear Fiametta, I have killed a man, or devil, I don't yet know which; but that man would have killed me if I had not done so."

"Yes, he would; but how dreadful."

"So that being the case, it is, in my opinon, a very good job he is dead; a very good job, indeed; he will be safe where he is."

"But still," said Fiametta, crossing herself, "how dreadful it must be to be slain thus; with all one's sins upon one's head."

"What would have been my fate?"

"As bad, and to me it would have been worse by far; but still it is really dreadful to think that there should be a soul thus sent to heaven without so much as the good offices of a priest."

"He would have killed me without giving me time for repentance. He would have forced me to leave a world in which I have all happiness yet to know; a world which I am by no means prepared to quit."

"Truly no, Jose, nor I; but what a state for this man to be in; he is so much the worse prepared than even you, because his end was bad; now, you had no evil intention."

"None — none."

"You did not know even that you were in danger from him."

"I did not, Fiametta, else I had never brought you there. I cannot understand what brought him there — what he wanted, or why it was he made such a desperate attack upon me; my life was aimed at."

"It was, Jose; but have you no private enemy, whom you believe capable of such a deed as this? Surely — surely it cannot be done, save from some motive."

"That is the thing that most puzzles me; I cannot understand the motive. I know him not; I have no enemy who would hire an assassin; but there let him and his deed lie buried in oblivion."

"He has no burial."

"He deserves none," said Jose.

"But, dear Jose, do you not think we ought to give him one."

"Are we his executors or heirs?"

"God forbid! — but we saw him die, and not for his sake, but for the sake of human nature, do not let us leave him unburied like a dog. He may not deserve it, but he has answered all his offence."

"Yes, yes; I admit he has been punished — he paid to the uttermost all he owed me, and I gave him a receipt in full. He will never make another demand upon me; we have quite done with each other, I believe."

"I shall never forget the horrible sight; it will haunt me day and night; I shall not be able to banish the terrible features from my mind. I shall, in truth, pass a sad life; I wish this had never happened."

"Why, so do I, dear Fiametta; but, surely, you do not accuse me of wrong, in having, to save my life, killed this man. I was compelled, forced to do it; it was either his life or mine; and, the truth to tell, I never was in such peril, from any single sword, in all my life, and but for the lucky accident that laid him open, I had not been here with you, but where he now is."

"Thank God for your deliverance, Jose; but — but what a revolting thing to remember, that in the wood Del Notti, there lies a corrupting mass of humanity, over which loathsome insects crawl; a

thing that had once been a living soul like ourselves; but now, alas! what is he?"

"But, Fiametta, your grief appears misplaced; you mourn this stranger as if he was near and dear to you. Do you know him?"

"Not I," said Fiametta, sorrowfully.

"Then what have you to grieve about, Fiametta? Tell me truly. You have nothing to blame yourself with. I do not feel I have acted wrongly. Say what it is that causes you so much sorrow."

"I grieve to think that the body of that sinful and wicked man lies unburied, and that no masses have been said for the repose of his soul."

"If that be all you require to set your mind at rest — though the villain deserves it not — I will see that he is buried and masses said for him."

"Will you, indeed, Jose?"

"Upon my conscience, I will see your desire executed."

"Well, then, Jose, yonder lives a holy monk. He is a pious and good man, and will, I am sure, do all that is required — watch and pray by the body till midnight, and continue there until the sun shall illumine the wood."

"Be it so, my dear Fiametta — be it so. We will go to the holy man and tell him of our distress, and will reward him; and then I will see you in safety, and return to conduct him to the spot where you know we left the body. I would the villain had come by a less noble death than falling by the sword."

"It will be a danger that will never be forgotten by me," said Fiametta.

"Nor by me," replied Jose. "What that man meant I cannot conceive. But then there can be but one answer to the question — he meant robbery; nothing else could have tempted him to draw his sword upon me."

"But why did he not demand your money at once?"

"Because he might meet with what he has met; and he took me at a disadvantage, and, of course, gave him a better chance of killing me, and running less danger in doing so. I am not, therefore, surprised at it."

"Here is the holy father's residence. He is poor — very poor; but, withal, he is very good. He is a holy man."

"Then he will serve our turn the better; for it would, in my opinion, take something more than a saint to pray out of purgatory such a soul as his must be. It must wing its way through space very much like a bat."

"Hush, Jose — hush! Not a word about that. Here is the holy man's abode. Shall I enter with you?"

"If you will, Fiametta — if you will."

Fiametta stood by her lover's side while he knocked at the holy man's door, and, after a pause of about a minute, a deep voice said, —

"Who is it that knocks at my door?"

"'Tis one who needs your service, good father."

"Enter," said the monk, and a bolt was withdrawn. The door opened, and Fiametta followed her lover into a hovel, or rather a bare room, in which was nothing, save some straw in one corner, and some few clothes; besides which there were one or two articles of necessary use and convenience, but they were very few indeed.

"Well, my son, what wouldst thou? Dost thou require mine aid to bind thee to this maiden, and she to thee?"

"I do indeed wish so much, but she is not willing."

"Not willing! Then wherefore dost thou come to me?"

"You see, holy father, as we were walking in the wood Del Notti, which I dare say you well enough know —"

"I do, my son."

"Well, I was talking to my companion, heedless of danger, nor dreaming any could be at hand, when my attention was attracted to a spot on the right of me whence a man rushed out upon me, with a drawn sword, and attacked me.

"I should not have had time to see him, much less time to draw and defend myself, but for the scream of her who was by my side. I looked where I saw her look, and saw him advancing, and had time to spring back and draw."

"Did you kill your opponent?"

"As it fell out, good father, I did. He rushed on and pressed me so hard, that I had no alternative. My life was in great danger, and I could not rid myself of my enemy, or preserve my own life, except at the expense of his."

"Did you slay him?"

"I did."

"Another soul ushered into eternity," said the monk, gloomily. "How long will it be before the wickedness of men shall cease to bear such fruits?"

"But, holy father, I did but act lawfully in saving my life. It was only the law that nature has implanted in us, and can hardly be called wickedness, since Heaven itself gives us the power and impulse."

"Hold thy peace, my son, thou knowest nothing of these matters; therefore I say hold thy peace, and let me know what it is you desire of me."

"That you will say masses for the repose of his soul, and give him Christian burial. I do not like — we do not like such a portion of humanity to remain where it is; we would it were not entirely neglected, or deprived of burial rites."

"It is but just of thee, my son; but I have known many who would have neglected it altogether, and permitted the body of one of God's creatures to lie and rot like a dog. My son, you have done well, and I will, for your sake, do mine office."

"Nay, holy father, I cannot permit thee to do it wholly without giving the church some due, and here in this purse you will find all I have."

"I take it, my son, not for my own sake, but for that of the church, to whom belongs all that is offered her."

"And this, too, holy father," said Fiametta, giving a small purse; "take that, and for my sake do what may be done by those on earth for those who have departed from it by a violent and sudden death."

"I will, daughter."

"And now, holy father," said Jose, "if you will, I am ready to take you to the spot where fell this man."

"I will follow, my son," said the monk, concealing his two gifts beneath his garments, but rising at the same time — "I'll follow thee."

They all left the place, but went a circuitous route, to enable Jose to leave Fiametta in safety at the marquese's villa, where she resided in half dependence, being a distant relative of hers.

Jose led on the monk until he came to the spot where the stranger fell, and where he yet lay just as he had fallen — a ghastly corpse.

"Here, holy father, you see the caitiff, a treacherous villain, who has now been paid for his villany — for, perhaps, a life of villany."

"Perhaps so, my son. He does not appear to have been formed by nature when in one of her most kindly moods; but yet it might have been she impressed his character upon his features as a warning to the rest of mankind."

"It was so, most likely; but you see he

is slain. Fiametta would never have known peace again unless the body was watched through the night by some holy man, and prayed for. That is what is desired, holy father; and now I will leave you to your task, bidding you adieu, and wishing your office a prosperous one, and a pleasant night to watch by."

CLIX.

THE WATCH BY THE DEAD MAN'S SIDE. — THE DEAD ALIVE. — THE DEATH-STRUGGLE, AND THE MURDER OF THE MONK.

THE MONK GAZED AFTER Jose for some moments, until he had vanished from his sight; even then he continued gazing upon the vacant space that he lately filled, as if meditating in his own mind, and quite unmindful of the present. At length he turned and gazed upon the clay-cold corpse before him.

There it lay in all its hideousness — all its horrible reality. The slouched hat was knocked off in the fall, and the face was exposed to view.

"Ave Maria!" muttered the monk, telling his beads. "I never before saw so unfavourable a -looking creature. I pray Heaven he may have been better favoured in grace than in features — that he may make a better appearance spiritually than bodily. I would I had had time to speak with him before his spirit fled, for I misdoubt me much of his salvation — but I will not charge him with unknown sin."

"That," he muttered, after a pause, "might, indeed, be quite unnecessary, seeing his appearance and his deeds — at least the only one I know of is of a like character; were it otherwise, I would be loath to doubt him; but two such proofs are enough to damn the best spoken-of being in all Christendom."

He paused again; examined the features of the dead man, but could not appear at all satisfied with the success of his ministry.

"I would sooner have had some poor, but honest corpse to watch by," he said as he gazed upon the long white visage of the dead man, whose leaden eye appeared fixed upon him; "I would," he continued, "much sooner have had some early flower cut down before its prime — I could have wept and prayed for him, then; but this, alas! was but full-grown iniquity, I strongly fear — it cannot be otherwise."

The monk sank down upon a tree.

"Alas! what a sinner I am, for uttering such a thought — nay, I am worse for conceiving such a thought, and expressing it must be heinous. To have such a one would be to cut off the most worthy, instead of looking at the destruction of the full grown sinner in all his pride and moral deformity, as being the full extent of the length he was permitted to go by Divine wisdom and intelligence. He has filled his measure of iniquity, and the Lord hath cut him off in the midst of his sins."

The monk now devoutly crossed himself, and muttered several of his Ave

Marias and paternosters, and prayed in bad Latin for some time, nearly an hour, when he appeared to think he might be indulged in a rest from his theological labour, and that his mind might refresh itself.

The monk arose and paced about the body for some minutes in solemn and deep wonder at the place chosen for such a deed.

A number of fresh thoughts now rushed through his mind, as he assigned all possible motives for the deed that had been done, or attempted to be done; and, also, for the choice of spot; but this speculation was more curious than useful.

Time passed by, and the hours rolled on, and darkness came on apace. A heavy atmosphere seemed to hang over him, and the light gradually faded away, and the moon showed no light on that night.

"It is dark," muttered the monk, "but the Lord is my light, and darkness has no fears for me. I am in the discharge of my ministry, and am safe. The dead man lies quiet and still — no sound comes thence."

He listened, but no sound; not the rustle of a leaf could be heard; not a breath of air stirred. All was silent and still; no one sound disturbed the stillness of the night — all was quiet.

"It is a night of death," said the monk to himself — "a night such as might be supposed to exist if the last man had ceased to live."

There was a weight in the air that appeared stronger, and had an effect upon the monk, and made a gloomy feeling come over him.

"What ails me?" he said to himself. "I am not strong and confident as I am wont to be — the reverse; I am doubting, and

very sad. Yet why should I be sad — I, a minister of religion? I, at all times, am prepared to die, or ought to be.

"And yet there is the clinging after life, as in all; but I am mortal, as other men are. I have not all the motives for life they have. I am alone in the world. I am but a pilgrim, whose stay is short, and who leaves behind him nothing to remember, and no one to remember me. It is better it is so than otherwise."

The monk paused again, and approached the trunk of the tree, upon which he sat in deep meditation for more than an hour, without altering his posture, or uttering a single word. A whole hour passed thus.

"Now," muttered the monk, as if waking up from a profound meditation, "man is here but in a state of probation. If he were not, what would be the explanation of the chequered course he runs, what the use of all the various stages he goes through during a long life, and then to drop into rottenness at last?"

"Why are we educated and improved, if for any other purpose? Why should we spend years in improving ourselves, only to be deprived of the jewel at last, and to have it not only taken, but destroyed.

"No — no; it is for better use."

The monk's mind was evidently disturbed in regard to some speculation which had been suggested by the solitary moments of his watch. At such times, all the strange and inquiring thoughts that could be devised by man usually arise and enter his mind, and strange doubts and fancies will supervene, when all other thoughts have been banished, and they take their place.

Man's mind is always liable to these

fanciful intrusions, and will remain so, while there is a single important assertion or circumstances existing, incapable of positive and mathematical demonstration.

When all shall be clear, and when there shall be no longer any play for the mind — any room for imagination — any possibility of conception left, then doubt may be cleared up, and an unanimity might be raised upon such a structure that never would be raised under any other circumstances whatever.

But, as this is not likely to happen, human doubt will exist, more or less, to all; we shall none of us be freed from that great cause of all the calamities of races.

But to proceed with our narrative:

The monk looked around him. He could, however, see nothing, save the few trees near him, but beyond that he was unable to see. There was a strong mist up — one that limited vision, and left no room for any other object to shine through, and diversify the scene.

"I would," muttered the monk, "that the morning would come. There is no light; the moon is hidden; no rays penetrate the dense air; and all the while the air is close and muggy. Not a star out, or luminary visible."

He looked upwards, and found he could see the spot where the moon was striving to force its rays through some thinner stratum of the clouds; but it was doubtful, and the monk, of very weariness, began to count his beads and to repeat his paternosters, between whiles and alternately, until he grew weary.

It wanted yet an hour of midnight, and the night would not be passed for many hours, and the monk thought that the nights were long.

"It is cold," he muttered; "but yet 'tis not midnight. 'Tis the moisture with which the air is loaded, and thus it is cool more rapidly than it could have otherwise happened; but it matters not to me — if I were to lose my life, I shall only be called home in my ministry; therefore it matters not. I am in the discharge of my duty, and shall have the reward appropriate to the service."

A slight breeze sprung up, and in a short time the mist was cleared off, and not a cloud was to be seen on the horizon.

There might be seen the moon rising slowly and majestically, while a gentle and diffused light shed its influence throughout the wood. Of course its direct rays could not enter until it had risen to its full height.

"Ha!" said the monk, "now I shall be relieved of some of the terrors of my watch; it will cease to be so tedious and so long; but, no matter, I am content, quite content. Soon I shall be able to see the body, and then I will close its eyes. I had forgotten to do so before; but it is time enough."

"Pater noster," again began the monk, until he came to the last word, by which time the light was enough to enable him to discover the body plainly; then he knelt down by its side to pray, and gazed on its features.

"I see its eyes are glaring wildly — aye, no wonder! no wonder! he met with a sudden, painful, and violent death.

"Poor erring mortality! what an end to come to; but, alas! what can men expect? He who lives by the sword will die by the sword."

The monk closed the eyes of the dead man, and pulled the cloak, which lay open, over him, and then leaned back against a tree, and shut his eyes for a moment; but they did not remain long shut, for some fancied noise drew him out of a train of speculation he was indulging in.

"He moves not!" he muttered.

However, he knelt down by the side of the body, and began to repeat his paternoster again, and for a few moments shut his eyes, as if he had no service for them, and continued his prayers without intermission.

The moon's rays now came with their full effulgence, and the forest appeared like some enormous piece of lattice work; for the moon's rays were able to penetrate the leaves and branches of many of the trees.

The moonbeams at length fell upon the body of the dead man, and he got slowly up until he rested on his elbow with his face towards the moon; and the monk, who yet remained kneeling, was still praying with his eyes wholly shut.

"Ha!" groaned the stranger.

The monk stopped in his prayer, started, and opened his eyes, which were fixed, in an extremity of terror and horror, upon the apparition before him — he was entranced, and had no power to remove his eyes.

"Ha!" said the figure, slowly rising to a sitting posture, but, at the same time, immediately facing the unfortunate and wretched monk, who was prostrated by fear.

"Ha!" groaned the figure, by a strange effort.

"My God — my God!" exclaimed the monk, "save me — save me!"

He endeavoured to rise, but shook so much he could not do it, for the figure kept its horrible eye fixed upon him, and he shook violently; but after a while he contrived to say, scarcely audible though,

"Avaunt, Satan, I command thee."

The figure heeded it not, but took some ominous proceedings, by laying its hands upon the monk's shoulder; but this had the effect of releasing him from his spell, and he sprang to his feet, exclaiming, —

"The Lord of Hosts aid me!"

The figure replied not, but rising without taking his hand off, a deadly struggle ensued between the two, which lasted some minutes. The monk, being driven desperate, resisted with great strength; but he had one to deal with, whose strength was far beyond his, and he felt himself gradually sinking, till, after another effort, which ended in a wild shriek, he was forced on his knees.

In this posture the strange man seized him by the throat, which he compressed, and thrust his knees into his chest, until the unfortunate and wretched man was quite dead and senseless.

CLX.

THE DEVIL A MONK WOULD BE. — THE DEMAND FOR ADMISSION INTO THE
CONVENT OF ST. MARY MAGDALEN. — THE FORTRESS AND THE MONK.

IT WAS SOME MINUTES before the stranger, who had so newly risen from the dead, let go of the grasp he had of the monk's throat. He held him firmly by the throat by both hands; but as he stood grasping him, his face was turned upwards towards the moon's rays, which fell upon his breast and features, insomuch that he appeared to gain strength at every breath he drew.

But what a ghastly face he wore; what a death-like paleness spread over his forehead; the horrible-looking eyes appeared to throw back the light of the moon, much the same as its rays are reflected by glass.

The unfortunate monk was partially kneeling, his back forced against the trunk of the tree, upon which he had been sitting, his face turned upwards, and his eyes almost bursting from their sockets, while his hands convulsively grasped those of his enemy; but his strength decreased as that of the other increased; his cowl fell off, and his bare head was exposed to the moonlight.

There was a death-like pause, and the figure slowly released its hold upon the throat of the monk and stepped back a pace or two to look upon his work. The monk's body retained the posture given to it by the efforts to extinguish his life, and appeared as though his muscles had rigidly set in death, but the trunk of the tree itself was a sufficient support.

"Dead!" muttered the figure; "dead!"

Again he moved about, and went into an open space, where the moonlight came uninterruptedly, without any barrier, and from this spot he surveyed the hideous work of his hands.

"Dead — dead!" muttered the figure.

This was undoubtedly true; and yet there remained the body of the monk, which, but for the turn of the head backwards, and its face upwards, it might be easily supposed that he had died in the attitude of devotion or supplication; but, as it was, it was evident by what means he had come by his death.

"I must have a victim," muttered the stranger; "am I always to meet with the pangs of death but to renew such a life on such term! Never to obtain a renewal without the pangs of death; and why? because I have not been able to obtain the voluntary consent of one that is young, beautiful and a virgin; I might then for a season escape the dreaded alternative."

He walked round and round the body of the monk for some time, and then he came and sat down by its side upon the trunk of the tree, and appeared lost in contemplation; but at length he looked at the body, saying, —

"Aye, aye — I have a plan. The church has furnished many a victim — let it furnish me with one. The church will furnish the sacrifice, and will give me the means of obtaining the offering.

"Well and good; it shall be done."

He arose, and walked about the body once more, and then approached it; having apparently made up his mind, he came to it, saying,—

"I will become a monk, too, of the most holy order of St. Francis; yes, that will serve me well enough. I will take his cassock, it will serve my turn, and be a ready introduction to the religious world. I am the good monk Francis myself. My learning and sanctity is great; it will carry all before it, and I shall be in great request. It will indeed be strange if there be no fruit upon such a tree. I am sure I shall deserve it."

He seized the body, and pulled off the monk's clothing, and quickly apparelled himself in it, leaving the body as if fell by the side of the tree; and, having thrown his own clothes on one side, he drew the cowl over his head, and, seizing the staff he brought with him, he was about to leave the spot; but a sudden thought occurred to him, and he turned back, and began to rummage among the pockets of the monk.

"These churchmen, I have heard, never travel without something of value about them, and his gold, if he have any, may as well be mine as any one else's who may be passing this way."

He found the two purses that had been given him by Fiametta and Jose, and some that he had beside; moreover, there were some letters and papers, which he put into his pocket, merely observing,—

"These will enable me to pass for the character I assume successfully. I am and will be a monk. I will shrive and confess poor deluded souls, and send them on their eternal journeys."

A ghastly and hideous smile crossed his face; and having burthened himself with what he thought necessary, or worth while, he quitted the spot.

THERE WERE TWO CONVENTS, or nunneries, near the city of Naples, at some short distance apart from each other.

One was the convent of St. Mary Magdalen, and the other was the convent of St. Cecilia, about a mile and a half apart, or perhaps more—some said a league; and so it was by the road, but not in a direct line.

It was late one evening, when the great bell of the convent of St. Mary Magdalen gave warning from without that some one demanded admission. The superior of the convent, a woman far advanced in age, and somewhat proud of her character, and not a little disposed to personal comfort, was much annoyed at the sound which gave some promise of trouble.

"Well," muttered the portress, as she rose from before a fire, and tottered towards the gate, looking through the iron grating for the object that disturbed her in her meditations and her devotion to the good things that Providence had furnished her with,—"well, what do you want?"

"I am a poor travelling brother of the order of St. Francis; I am benighted, and I wish for a lodging and food."

"Friend, brother of St. Francis, this is at a later hour than that at which we open our gates to strangers."

"They little think at Rome," said the monk, "that, to obtain a shelter, we have to get to the gates of a holy house before a certain time; and those who most need shelter, because it is less to be had, must wait and perish in the cold."

"The gates are shut."

"I see it."

"And the abbess has got the keys."

"Will she not give me shelter and food?"

"I may not ask her."

"I must, then, remain here outside the walls until the morning, and then I will wend my way back to the holy city, where I will say their messenger could not obtain rest and shelter at the convent here."

"Do you come from Rome?"

"I do; and do you refuse to tell your abbess an unworthy brother of holy St. Francis is here, and waiting for admission?"

The portress made no reply; she was by far to indignant to make any answer, and yet too fearful to refuse to do his bidding; for he spoke in a peremptory tone, that indicated an authority beyond what was usual in his appearance.

She, therefore, found her way to the lady abbess, to whom she began with every expression of submission and respect.

"My lady," said the portress, "there is one without who wants to come in."

"Well," said the abbess, "we can't let him in."

"I told him so," replied the portress; "but you would hardly credit it what he said about a holy pilgrim from Rome, stopping outside the gate all night, and returning to the holy city and speaking of our inhospitality."

"Did he," said the abbess, "say so much?"

"He did."

"Then let him in," said the abbess.

"Let him in!" said the portress, in an ecstacy of surprise, opening her eyes very wide, and repeating the words "Let him in."

"Yes; do as we bid you," said the abbess.

"Yes," replied the portress, "certainly; whatever our holy superior orders, it is for me to obey. I do your bidding."

Away went the holy portress to discharge her spleen in privacy; and, at the same time, unable to account for the orders given her, she returned to the portal, and having unbarred the gate, she drew the bolts and turned the lock, and opening the door, stood for the monk to enter.

"Come in," she said. "What do you mean? — do you not want to come in?"

"Am I free to enter?"

"Wherefore do I hold the gate open — for pleasure?"

"No, sister," said the monk, "through anger, I believe; but if you can find it in your conscience to be angry because I am at the door and give you this trouble, what will be the feelings of St. Peter, who keeps the gates of Heaven, when you present yourself thereat a hungry being and erring sinner; but peace be upon this place."

"Amen," said the portress.

At that moment one of the nuns came from the superior of the convent, saying, —

"Holy father, when you have rested and refreshed yourself, our worthy abbess will be glad to converse with you."

"I am even now at her commands," said the holy man.

"Will you not taste food, and rest yourself?"

"I never tire or need food, when I have aught to do that in any way concerns our religion."

"But, holy father, the body needs refreshment."

"It can be supported upon spiritual food alone, if the Lord wills," said the monk, crossing himself most devoutly.

"You must have great gifts, holy father!"

"Not I, but he that sent me," said the monk, solemnly.

"Will you follow me, holy man, and I will lead you to the abbess, who will be right glad to speak with you? She wishes to speak to one lately come from the holy city; you can tell her news of the holy father."

"I can, my sister."

"Then, come this way," said the nun, who immediately led the way to the abbess, and the monk followed her closely, till he was lost sight of by those in the waiting-room.

CLX.

FATHER FRANCIS'S INTERVIEW WITH THE ABBESS OF ST. MARY MAGDALEN. — THE
OBJECTS AND WISHES OF THE HOLY FATHER.

AFTER PASSING THROUGH a few passages, they entered into a room which had the appearance of a waiting-room, in which were placed chairs and seats; but they did not stop here, for the sister approached a door, at which she knocked, and paused a moment; but a voice from within desired her to enter; and, beckoning the monk to follow her, which he did, they both entered a comfortable room in which the abbess was seated.

"Here is the holy father," said the sister, "who demands lodging and refreshment; but he will take nothing until he has done all that may be required of him."

"Holy brother," said the abbess, "the traveller needs rest, and he that is hungered requires food. Will you partake of our hospitality?"

"I was told you desired to converse with me, and I could not let my ministry wait while I, like a glutton, ate and drank."

"No, brother, it was not for such a purpose I sent for thee, but to hear what news thou hadst from Rome, whence I heard you have come."

"I have come thence."

"But will you not take some refreshment here — it shall be brought thee, if thou wilt have it, or in the buttery, which you please."

"Whichsoever you please, sister," said the member of St. Francis.

"Then let some of the best be brought, sister, for the good man; and stay, I ate none at the last meal, which I may amend now; let me have a small moiety of a pasty, and a small trifle of cold venison."

The sister departed, and the abbess opened a small cupboard, from which she took a bottle and two glasses, of goodly dimensions, considering the fact that the place was inhabited only by females.

"Pronounce a blessing upon us, holy

father," said the abbess. "This has been tasted by no unhallowed lips; it was a present from a holy lady to me, to take myself, and to offer to such as I deemed worthy of it—and you, holy father, I believe are worthy."

The worthy monk pronounced the required benediction, and drank as fine a glass of real Burgundy as ever went down consecrated lips.

"Thanks, worthy sister, thanks."

"Brother, I am glad to be able to give it thee; it gives me more pleasure to do so than thee to drink. I'll warrant me, that never has such wine passed through the merchants' hands, because he would never have parted with it at a price that would have made it procurable in a place like this, for we are, holy brother, poor, very poor."

"The people who live in these parts are, I fear, not so godly as they should be, to let a house like this want."

"There are many nobles."

"And they ought to pay handsomely."

"They do, I am thankful; but I should like to be able to offer the poor, diseased, and helpless men, better sort of diet than I do."

"It ought to be in your power when the rich and great are so close around you here. You ought to have rich penitents."

"But few of the rich are penitent, brother."

"Naples I was told was a sink of iniquity. I did not expect to find it in reality such as I have heard it described. But, sister, we must be thankful that we have what the times will afford; but, at the same time, when he enemy is thus about, we must be up and doing, and preach salvation to them."

"But they only answer by sending invitations for Sabbath balls," said the unfortunate abbess, in great dolour.

"That must be looked to. They must be chidden."

"And then they withhold their hands from works of charity—from doing any good deed to us—and we have no gifts and offerings."

"But that ought not to be any motive. When they see you in earnest, they will not resist any longer; they will, as they must, give in."

"Ah, holy father! you don't know the Neapolitans; they are the most sinful set of men that you ever met with."

"The holy father must know of this; he must be informed of the character of these bad people—of these facts. It is a melancholy state of things, which is a disgrace to a Christian country, and must be amended."

At that moment the nun returned with the refection for the monk and the abbess, who cast a longing glance towards it.

When this was laid on the table, the abbess gave a signal that there was no need of the further attendance of the servitor, who quitted the room, leaving the abbess and the monk to enjoy each other's society at leisure.

Some minutes elapsed before either spoke, which time was spent in mastication of no ordinary morsels, being some of the most delicious meats that could be obtained for a religious house of this character, and they were usually supplied with the best of everything that could be had.

"Holy father," said the abbess, "the fare is poor; but I hope it will relieve those calls which imperious nature demands you to satisfy."

"Yes," said the monk; "I am well satisfied."

"Permit me to press upon your notice those venison pasties; they are made by Sister Bridget, who never made an indifferent one in all her life."

"I decidedly approve of Sister Bridget's skill," said the monk. "She is no doubt a worthy woman, and a woman fit for her station."

"I would not have another to do her duties for a trifle, save as a penance," said the abbess. "I will, at all events, retain her while the convent will give her a place of shelter."

"Very right, sister — very right."

"But what news from Rome, brother?"

"Little, save the holy pontiff has been very ill."

"I heard as much; and by many it is presumed that his holiness will be translated, if he should not be better soon."

"No: his holiness is safe, as far as it is possible for any human being to be. God preserve him long!"

"Amen!" said the abbess, devoutly.

"But have you no penitents, holy sister?"

"I have several, but they are all in the way of performing their penances, save one, who is somewhat refractory, holy father, and I know not what to do with her. She has no respect for those in authority."

"Is she one of the order?"

"No, a neophite."

"How is it, then — what brings her here?"

"She is sent by relatives who are afraid of a disgrace, and will not give her any chance of committing their family to such a disgraceful marriage. She at one time pledged herself to take the vows, but now has some objection to do so."

"On what grounds does she refuse?"

"Because she thinks she shall not be happy."

"Absurd! Where is she?"

"We must have been compelled to secure her, for she has made more than one attempt to escape, and I have reasons to believe that these efforts have been aided from without."

"'Tis a serious offence — a very serious offence to those concerned, and would inevitably lead to a terrible example, if they were detected."

"No doubt; and we should feel it our duty to make every exertion to punish any one who makes an attempt to violate the sanctity of our house."

"It must be so, sister."

"Yes, certainly; and I have secured the maiden, who, if she be brought to their mind, will largely endow the convent."

"That ought to be seen to."

"I am, as you may imagine, holy father, anxious that the young maiden should become a member of our house. Who can tell," muttered the abbess, half aloud, "but she may become a chosen vessel by which much good may be effected?"

"She may," said the monk. "I am from Rome; you may examine the these credentials which I have with me. I will take the charge of this refractory sister of yours, and will pursue such a course as will bring her round to your way of thinking."

"And the endowment?"

"Will still belong to your house, to which it will be given. I have no object, sister, save the welfare of the church; reward I seek not, save what may be given in the good words of the wise and good."

"You are deserving of all praise, holy father. I was not thinking about the endowment, holy father, because, you see, it will not belong to me, but to the church, and this house in particular, for the use of the poor lambs here, over whom I am appointed shepherdess; so I have no feeling in the matter beyond what I ought to have in the spiritual welfare of our fellow sinners."

"I have no authority to interfere in aught else."

"I see, holy father," said the abbess, "you are a wonderful man, and such a one as will do much good."

"I will make an attempt to do good, sister."

"And I will make bold, holy brother, to say you will be successful; though, I venture to say, with humility, that I have tried everything with the unfortunate young woman, which appears to aggravate the evil, rather than give any promise of the future."

"So I might expect."

"You will pursue a different course?"

"I may; but it must depend upon circumstances. If I find it necessary, I must have some place of security, where no one can have any communication with her, save when I shall order it, or deem it proper she should be so confined."

"Certainly; very right."

"Moreover, if I find she needs such severe measures, I shall not let any food be given, save what is given by me, or in my presence, which, of course, amounts to the same thing."

"Exactly, holy father."

"And," continued the monk, "I will not permit this holy house to be insulted by a recusant, for I am quite resolved that no heretick shall baffle the ministers of religion."

"Oh, very improper; it would be indeed, not only an aggravation, but a decided loss to the church, which would damnify it to that extent."

"Undoubtedly," replied the holy man, "undoubtedly; and with your aid I hope to be able to make one good effort, and I pray heaven it may be attended with grace."

"I trust so; and now, holy brother, what may I call you?"

"You will see by these presents I am called Father Francis, of the order of St. Francis; an unworthy brother, who has, perhaps, beyond his gifts, obtained the praise and good wishes of his holiness the Pope, who has been pleased specially to send me forth on a travelling commission, to report to him and to stay where I thought my services might be required."

"Holy father, we may have you stay here some time, I hope, and your favourable report of our poor endeavours; they are in the right direction, and carried on with the right spirit; but we are all weak and erring mortals, we cannot always be as successful as we would wish, and in this matter we have been unsuccessful."

"You have done all that could be expected; there are some matters that will not yield to the weaker vessel, but which would yield to the stronger; therefore you have nothing to blame yourself with; but you are to be commended for what you have done."

"Thanks, holy father; I would not be willingly found wanting."

"Nor are you, sister, according to my poor judgment."

"And when will you see this neophite?"

"I will see her on the morrow; and in the meantime I must be chargeable to you for board and lodging, if you will so far grace me."

"Name it not, holy father; I have nothing here but what is yours; and when you choose to retire, there will be the best traveller's bed ready for you."

"Straw and sackcloth are good enough for me," said the monk, ostentatiously.

"But it concerns our housekeeping, holy father, and our hospitality too. We must not let you lodge thus. I pray you, for our sakes, permit us to do what the credit of the place will permit us to do in the way of entertainment."

"Be it even as you will, sister; it does not beseem me that I should contend for matters like these — be it so; I will retire."

"It grows late. I will summon Sister Agatha to show you your dormitory."

Accordingly, Sister Agatha was summoned, and the monk was, after another delicate libation of rich Burgundy, led to his room.

CLXII.

THE CELL OF THE NEOPHITE. — THE INTERVIEW. — THE UNEXPECTED TURN GIVEN TO THE AFFAIRS AT THE CONVENT OF MARY MAGDALEN.

THE MORNING BROKE, and the matins were duly performed at St. Mary Magdalen.

This was what happened every day in the week included, for the convent was always alive to the performance of its duties from the dawn of day until sunset and after; but it was their business — a business from the toil of which they rested not on the Sabbath.

But then it happened that there was no labour; it was all easy-going, straight-forward work, and was a mere pastime, that only occupied the lips and ears; for not half of it was understood, and the other half had long since ceased to produce any impression upon the stagnant minds of the mewed-up sisterhood.

However, there was not lack of comfort, especially for those who held any of the good offices in the convent. The holy Father Francis was met at table by the abbess, who was great and gracious to him.

"Will you inform the sisterhood, holy sister, of my stay here, lest it bring any scandal upon your house, the well-being of which is to me of importance."

"I have already done so. I anticipated your wishes on that point, holy father — in fact, I did it on my own account, too, for we live in evil times — in very evil times."

"We do, sister."

"So that being done, you have but to express your wishes; for of course they are the wishes deputed of the pope."

"Certainly — certainly; it could not be otherwise."

"I knew," said the abbess; "and now I wait for your wishes; let me know them, and I will answer for it, that nothing that is desired by his holiness through you shall meet with any other than the most profound attention and willing obedience."

"You are a worthy superior, and if Heaven please to permit me, I will not fail to let his holiness know of all this devotion and obedience; and, not less, your regularity and religious observances; he will be well pleased, I am sure."

"Thanks, holy father."

"Nay, 'tis justice. But I would now see your unworthy guest."

"The probationist? Yes, she can be seen. She has had her food given her for breakfast, and will be ready to receive you."

"I am ready, then. In the meantime, what is her name and designation?"

"Her name is Juliet, and of a noble house—that of the famous Di Napotoloni."

"Indeed! 'tis very strange."

"She desired to marry against her friends' wish, who would not hear of the iniquity that was desired to be perpetrated."

"I will see her, then. I may be able to do some good."

"You cannot fail."

"I do not know. The race is not always with the swift, nor the battle with the strong; but I will essay to try."

"If you will come this way, holy father, you shall be admitted into her cell. Shall I remain, or shall I return?"

"I will be alone, for I will confess her, and bring her mind to a calm state. Then, when I have her confidence, I will begin the object in view, and then we shall find whether there is any probability of that system being successful."

"Certainly; but if not?"

"Why, we must adopt more energetic means, and these we must continue to pursue until there is an end of hope, or life; for when coercion is once begun we must continue it on without intermission."

"No doubt—no doubt, holy father."

"Have you any others who are in a very similar state to this unhappy being?"

"None, holy father, none; but this is her door. She will be sulky, or spiteful, as the humour may be; but, at the same time, she will not spare me, because I have, as you see, thus confined her to this place as a punishment."

"You have done right, sister, quite right—there is no blame."

The abbess opened the door, and at the same moment they both entered the dungeon in which the unfortunate young female was thrust by the aid of paternal authority, sanctioned by religious usage, and a presumed right they had over her actions.

"This, holy father," said the abbess, "is the unfortunate female whose case I told you of as being so desperate, that there is no remedy left but that to which we never resort, save in an extremity, and upon no other occasion whatever."

"I see, sister—I see; but I hope one so young has not been entirely won over to the enemy. I trust she will not strive against those who strive for her."

"This holy man," said the abbess to Juliet; "this holy man has travelled from St. Peter's, at Rome, and has come to examine, with the sanction of his holiness the Pope, the state of our spiritual existence. See that you give good account of yourself."

"What the lady abbess has stated to you," said Father Francis, "is no more than the truth. I am so come, and for such a purpose. Prepare, therefore, to confess, and tell me freely what it is that troublest your soul. Confess, daughter."

The monk drew a stool towards him, and having sat down, he waved his hand towards the abbess, who stood by, saying,—

"I will hear her confess; we must be alone."

There was an instant movement on the part of the abbess, and she quitted the cell of the lady, placed the key of the door on the inside, and left them alone.

"Daughter," said the monk, after awhile, "daughter, what is this I hear of you?"

The unfortunate young woman fixed her eyes upon her questioner, and took them not off him during some minutes; and a shudder seemed to pass through her mind.

"I have spoke to thee," said the monk.

"You have," answered Juliet.

"Then answer me."

"I cannot. I know not what has been said."

"Could you not guess?"

"I might, holy father; but what can that be to such as you? You must know that I have been put here according to the abbess's orders."

"I do know so much, daughter. What more have you to say?"

"Simply, that I know not what I am thus confined here for."

"Since you know it not, I will tell you. You have disobeyed the abbess's orders—that is what you are now punished for—'tis a heinous offence."

"I am not yet one of the order, holy father; and, therefore, the abbess has no right to do this; and if she did not know

that my friends were her abettors, she dare not do it; 'tis a grievous injury, and a deep and shameful wrong. Instead of religion being, as it ought to be, the safeguard of the poor and weak against the rich and powerful, it is a means of oppression against those who have no power."

"These are hard accusations, daughter."

"They will bear the proof, however, and that fairly. Where have I taken the vows?—where am I the sworn sister?—tell me that, holy father."

"I have come for another purpose, daughter; you have been undutiful to those whom nature and God gave control over you; and you have desired to live disgracefully; surely, these are things that deserve punishment, for they are great moral crimes."

"I cannot see any such, holy father."

"I am afraid your soul is in an unclean state, daughter. There is no hope for you until this is amended; depend upon it, you can never prosper while you set at naught the desires of those who rule you."

"But they have no right to force me to an alternative that my soul revolts at."

"You cannot mean you revolt at becoming one of the holy and chaste sisterhood here?—that must be a libel upon your chastity."

"Holy father, it is not the age, nor under the circumstances, at which such a proposal can be made with any chance of success; for I am quite confident that I am born with better prospects than those which now threaten me. My father and mother had no right to send me here; they led me to believe I should inherit a fortune, and now they desire I should enter a cloister."

"And you have given them cause to change the original intention they had concerning you; you are disobedient, that is enough."

"But, holy father, there is a power stronger than a father's or a mother's — a power of which the church approves. What would you more?"

"What power?"

"The divine command which says, we shall leave a parent and fly to the arms of him whom we have chosen to become our husband."

"The devil can quote scripture when he has any object in view. But, Juliet, you are carried away by the strength of your own passion. This is a disgraceful marriage, and one you should not contract — one that would never be sanctioned by them."

"It might be so — that is, unsanctioned by them; but there is no disgrace in being married to a young officer who loved me."

"And whom you mean really to marry?"

"Yes."

"And you would, in fact, marry any one who would offer himself, instead of being a nun?"

"I would sooner die — and I will, by slow starvation — sooner than become one of this or any other order."

"I see — but who was this young man?"

"Jules di Maestro."

"How strange — how passing strange!" said the monk, changing his tone from one of severity to one of sadness and sorrow.

"Why, what ails you, holy father? Has anything happened?"

"I know not, my daughter, whether to feel most sorrow or most anger; but your case is one that requires some care. Whether to tell you all, or whether to conceal a part, or — or — in fact, to tell the whole and trust to your goodness."

"What do you mean — what do you mean? Your manner distresses me. I cannot understand you at all — speak, for the love of Heaven!"

"I can hardly do so, unless, by a solemn vow, you promise secrecy."

"I swear," said the hasty and impatient Juliet.

"Then listen."

"I do — I do. For Heaven's sake, keep me no longer in suspense!"

"Well, then, Jules di Maestro and I concocted a plan together, which we were to execute with the view of getting you out of this convent, so that you might both quit the kingdom of Naples, and get into some of the free states."

"Oh, dear Jules! and did he really take so much trouble about me — did he really mean to do so much? I can never be grateful enough to him."

"Why, you remember his last attempt?"

"I heard of it; but it did not succeed, But it must be two months ago."

"It was. We both were present."

"Both! You?"

"Yes; I was present, and wounded in the affray, though not so bad as poor Maestro."

"Hurt! but he has got over that, else you would not come here from him to plan another escape, which I see you have. I am truly sorry for his hurts; but he is, no doubt, well again."

"Stay — stay — you are much too sanguine."

"He has not forgotten me?"

"No; but you must permit me to speak. I am quite sure that had you heard the whole of the affair, you would not speak in this strain; for had I known that I had to tell you unwelcome news, I would not have undertaken this affair, even urged as I have been by him and your beauty."

"What mean you?"

"Why, that Jules is dead. He died within a few days after the last attempt that he made to rescue you from your captivity."

"What, do I hear aright! Jules dead! Great God, impossible — quite impossible! Nothing so dreadful can be real."

"I am sorry to say it is so," said the monk; "very sorry."

"But how did it fall out?" asked Juliet, who appeared to be too much stunned to feel anything acutely; "tell me how."

"When we made our last attempt to get you out, it failed; for we were both compelled to defend ourselves, and to fly before a numerous body of men. I should have got clear of them, but I saw that Jules was made prisoner, so I charged and rescued him from their hands."

"It was nobly done of you."

"Then, you see, I got some marks that I could not help; there were too many; but poor Jules got mortally wounded."

"Heaven be merciful to him!"

"I hope so; but he was not killed immediately. I got him quite away without any one being able to tell who he was, but that was an effort that cost me much. I took him away, as I said, and I sat by his side when he breathed his last breath."

"And what said Jules?" inquired Juliet, as she shed many bitter tears. "What said he? did he not curse her who had caused him such an end?"

"No, no; Jules did not; he wept when he knew his wounds were mortal, not because he was to die, but because he must leave you here, and you would be for ever ignorant of his fate; that is what most affected him, I assure you."

"Ah! he was of a noble, generous nature."

"I, however, promised him that I would see you, and let you know how the matter had stood with him; and he gave you his last blessing, and desired me not to tell your family that he was dead, as it would be a triumph for them; at the same time he wished, if possible, I could supply his place to you in his stead."

"No, no," said Juliet; "no, no; that can never be. I loved Jules, and can never love any one else, and will never try. No, no; Jules and Jules only, will I live for!"

"But he is dead."

"Then for him will I die, too; he died for me, and I will for him."

"But his last words were to me — 'Go and see Juliet, tell her truly how I died, and what my last wishes were. Those I have formed with the full belief that they are for her benefit. I know how she is placed — without a friend, and in danger.'"

"Yes, yes; now I have no one to help me."

"You have me, if you choose."

"Not at the price you spoke of."

"But you know not how clearly he expressed himself upon the matter; he knew the life you lead then — what it will be by and by — you know the starvation which you will have to feel, and, perhaps, be built up in a wall after all."

"Oh, God!"

"He said, 'See, and tell her you have nearly lost your life in serving me, and in serving her; that I am under an obligation to you for saving my life more than once. Thus, Juliet is the last word I pronounced, and the last I thought of — but if I had a legacy to leave you,' he said, 'I would leave her, and die happy if I thought you would enable her to escape. Marry her, and keep all the world at defiance — then, indeed, I could be happy — almost as happy as if I lived to be in your happy position.'

"'I will,' I replied; 'I will endeavour to obtain her escape.'

"'Will you swear?'

"'I do swear,' I replied; 'and at the same time I will risk my life, and lose it, if she will accept of me for a husband; but I cannot for less.'

"'You have said enough,' he replied; 'I am satisfied.'"

"And he died?" said Juliet.

"Yes; he died; but I have been long enough. I will see you again before another day is past, and then I will learn your determination. Do not let my cause be rejected because I have not urged it forward as I could have done; but the truth is, it is an honest one, and it will speak for itself. Farewell for the present; be secret and silent. They think me monk, for I have assumed this disguise, at the peril of my life, which will be taken with cruel tortures if I am discovered."

There was a pause, when the monk resumed again, —

"If you can consent to become my wife by this time to-morrow, I will endeavour to free you from bondage."

"Why purchase the motive to a good action?"

"I do not do so. I only purchase a right which, if risk of life, and all that man hold dear, be anything, why, you will not think me a Jew in the bargain. Think, lady, think upon what I have offered you."

"I do think; but 'tis a hard bargain for me to lose my liberty either way."

"Nay, you gain it, for you would be my mistress. But, hark! here comes the abbess. I must bid you adieu."

"How fares the penitent?" inquired the abbess, entering.

"I cannot gain either a satisfactory or an unsatisfactory answer to your inquiry. I will, however, see her to-morrow again, and if I find she is obdurate, perhaps the shortest way will be an application to the inquisition."

"Think of that, daughter," said the abbess, leaving the cell.

"Think of that," added the monk, "as your means of leaving the cell — of escaping. Farewell, daughter. Benedicite."

CLXIII.

THE NUN'S ATTEMPTED ESCAPE FROM THE CONVENT OF ST. MARY MAGDALEN. —
THE PURSUIT AND THE DISCLOSURE. — THE ESCAPE OF THE PRETENDED MONK.

THE NEXT DAY ALL NAPLES was alive to the fact that a holy man had been murdered in the wood Del Notti — a holy brother of the order of St. Francis, who was much respected by the good people of Naples.

Jose and Fiametta both attended before the municipal authorities to give the required information that they had given the monk gold to remain by the side of the dead man whom Jose had killed.

There was a general terror throughout Naples, for no one was aware of how the matter had fallen out, nor how the enormity would be punished, and who would be the sufferers in the present case.

The officers of the state were in active search after the perpetrator of so wicked a deed — as well as the officers of the Inquisition.

THE NEXT TIME FATHER FRANCIS called at the convent, he went straight to the lady abbess, and said to her with some earnestness, —

"I am sorry to tell you, the more I reflect upon the conversation I had with your neophite Juliet, I have some strong doubts about the course I originally thought of pursuing towards the young person."

"In what respect, holy father?"

"I thought of pursuing a mild course towards her."

"I have done it, and failed."

"The reason I think is not that she is hardened, but that she simply does not believe we will proceed to the extremity that we have threatened."

"I think she is hardened, holy father."

"Time alone will show; but I have altered my plans respecting her."

"In what respect, holy father?"

"I think I will begin to strike terror into her soul, and at once shew her the reality of my intentions, with respect to what I shall subject her by way of punishment for her resistance to her religious superiors."

"Very good, holy brother; I think it the plan that will most likely succeed the best; if she be terrified, she will be obedient."

"And to that end," said the monk, "I have ordered the alguazils of the Inquisition* to be here in half an hour's time, when she will be carried there, and subjected to the first process of torture."

"You will not hurt her?"

"Not much."

"Just enough to teach what powers you can exert."

"Yes, just so. Now, when they come, let me know, and, if she consents to go, all well and good; and, if she do not, we must use force."

---

* *Apparently an error. An "alguazil" was an officer of the Spanish Inquisition, not the Roman one.*

"And how long will you keep her at the inquisition?" inquired the abbess; "because, eventually, the parents will claim her of me."

"About three weeks, at the farthest; but, if the parents are troublesome, name the inquisition, and say holy brother Francis, from Rome, will come and confess them, and make some inquiries concerning their belief and faith in the church."

"I will, holy father."

The monk now returned to the cell where the unfortunate Juliet was confined, and, on opening the door, he found her in tears.

"Juliet," he said, "I come again."

"You are here;" she replied, "I see."

"And I am here with all the means of escape; you have but to say the word, and you are free and at liberty."

"I cannot — I cannot."

"You cannot. Do you love life — do you love liberty?"

"I do."

"And yet you choose the cold, bare walls of a cloister, to a life of happiness and love; to a life that is made for such as you."

"I cannot love you."

"I love you; that I have risked my life for you more than once, is true; my persecution is another proof of that."

"It may be so."

"Then why not consent? you have no alternative that can interest you more, or that will offer you more happiness."

"I cannot so soon forget Jules."

"Nay, we will not quarrel about that; I cannot expect you. I am not unreasonable, because I know so well the circumstances of the case. All is haste and confusion; there is no time for thought or preparation — all lies in self-preservation; say at once you will have me; I will endeavour to gain your love and esteem afterwards; our happiest days, our courting-time will come after our wedding."

"It cannot come."

"But will you choose the horrors of the inquisition rather than wed one who would give life and fortune to you?"

"Who speaks of the inquisition?" inquired Juliet, terrified.

"The abbess spoke to me about it when I came here last time, and said she had your father's commands to deliver you over to them."

"I'll not believe it."

"I entreated her not to do so, but to leave it in my hands, and I would undertake to communicate with the inquisition, and bring their officers here to-day."

"And have you?"

"I have brought those who will counterfeit them, and carry you off. The plan is matured. Will you leave this place, wed me, and be a happy woman, or remain here to be tortured and disfigured by the tortures of the inquisition — perhaps to die in their hands?"

"Horrible!" said Juliet, with a shudder.

"Think on this and on that."

At that moment a tremendous uproar occurred in the convent, and a ringing of bells. The pretended monk started, and listened attentively.

"They come," he muttered — "they come!"

"Have they discovered you?" inquired Juliet.

"I know not — I care not if they have.

Will you quit the convent, and leave Naples with me? Will you become my wife? You see what I have risked for you. I wait but your answer: they are coming."

Before any answer could be given, the door was thrown open, and the abbess, followed by a troop of soldiers, entered the cell, and, among them, the vampire monk saw his late adversary, Jose, and his love, Fiametta.

"There is the murderer," said Jose, pointing to the monk, whose cowl had fallen off; "and he is the man whom I believed I had killed."

"Oh, yes, it is the same horrid face!" said Fiametta.

"The murderer of Father Francis?" said the abbess.

"I know not how it was done; but I told Father Francis to watch and pray by the dead body, and see it decently buried, and he said he would do so. I gave him gold, and left him at his watch and his devotions."

"And he is dead now — his cassock and papers torn from him."

"Seize him, comrades!" said the officer.

At the sound of the officer's voice, Juliet looked up, and beheld her lover, Jules di Maestro, whom she was told had been killed. She sprang up, saying, —

"It is all false, then. You are not slain — you are still living — and you did not send this man to marry me?"

"I — who — Oh! Juliet, have I found you?"

"I am here, dear Jules. Take me hence — take me hence!"

"I will not do so now; but I have their majesties' favour, and will take care you shall be released from this vile durance."

"And that man —"

"Ay, look to your prisoner," said the officer.

But there was no prisoner to look to. He had slipped off his cowl and cassock, and left the convent, leaving all present immersed in their own affairs.

The abbess was indignant at the imposture, and would not risk Jules's appeal, on behalf of Juliet, to the king, and at once consented to her release and immediate marriage; and at the same time Fiametta consented to wed Jose, so that all was forgotten, save the murder of the holy Father Francis, and the resurrection of the vampire monk, who was, in reality, no other than Sir Francis Varney, who was no more heard of in Naples, but supposed to roam about the world at large.

In a moment afterwards they were lifted up, vessel and all, and carried a few yards further onwards and then left, with a report that seemed like that of a cannon to them; but they felt the shock, and when the wave left them, the vessel was no more; a mere mass of boards and other matters floated about ... (see page 1089)

PART VII:

The Sea Will Not Hold Him.

CLXIV.

THE STORM. — A SHIPWRECK AT SEA. — THE HAPLESS FATE OF THE MARINERS.

THE MORNING WAS USHERED in with wind and rain; a tempest was howling over the main; the seas lashed the shores with a fury that made it dangerous for even such vessels as were moored; and great fears were entertained that many wrecks would be seen before the night set in.

The roar of the ocean and the bellowing of the wind was almost deafening; and the few fishermen and sailors that now and then showed themselves, as they came towards the shore to ascertain the safety of their little barques, could scarcely make themselves heard.

The sky was too heavy, and the rain too incessant, to permit them to see very clearly or very far; they could not see any ships in the offing.

"Neighbour," said one, "did you hear the wind in the night?"

"Hear it!" replied the man spoken to; "could I help it? Who is there that could sleep, while such a tempest was blowing great guns. I never heard anything like it in all my life. God help those poor fellows who are at sea such a night as this."

"So say I, neighbour, so say I; if there be any upon this coast—if any awake with the morning dawn and find themselves upon a lee shore, they will never get off again, depend upon it; they are all lost men."

"So they are; there's no hope for them on this shore; every vessel must, indeed, come upon it, and no aid could be rendered to them."

"You are right, neighbour. I am glad our boats are high and dry; for, if they were not, they would never be on the sea again, except as fragments; every timber in them would be broken to pieces, and scattered about the beach."

"Aye, aye, 'tis an awful day. I propose, neighbour, we should make an attempt to get our boats still higher on the beach; see, the sea comes now within a few boat-lengths of them; a few more waves heaving one upon the other will at last reach them, and, if so, we are, indeed, poor men, neighbour."

"With all my heart; we have no time to lose, neighbour—see, the waves have got nearer yet — come on, come on."

The two fishermen hurried down to
the beach; and, with the aid of one or two
more, who had hurried onwards with the
same object as themselves, that of putting
the boats out of danger from the waves,
they succeeded; and then they returned,
leaving their boats, their only wealth, high
above the reach of the most tempestuous
sea.

"There, neighbour, I never heard such
a sea. I will go and see what can be done
in-doors by the fire-side; this is not a day
to be out in; you are wet through in about
ten minutes, and nothing to do but to
look on the black clouds."

"No, neighbour; though I don't think
in-doors much better, for I expect our roof
to come off, or the chimney to fall over;
and must consider myself very fortunate if
I do not have the whole house blown
down."

"Aye, aye; but I expect to hear of a few
accidents. I don't see any vessel coming in
the horizon at all — do you see any?"

"None."

"Well, I hope there may be none. I'm
for the house; too much of this may be
hurtful to a fisherman; so, good day."

"Good day, for the present. I dare say
we shall see each other before the day's
out, if anything may happen in the shape
of wreck."

"Safe and sure to be out."

"If you hear a gun, let me know, if I
should not be out; for the wind blows and
the sea roars so loudly that I can scarcely
hear at all."

"I'll be with you; and do you the same
for me, if I should happen to miss it;
though I can't tell how that can be, as the
wind blows dead in shore."

"It's a bargain — I'll do it."

The two fishermen parted from each
other, and entered their own dwellings to
escape the fury of the elements; for there
was nothing to keep them outside, but
there was everything to induce them to
stay in-doors — a warm fire and freedom
from the wind and rain, though that
howled and roared in the chimneys in a
frightful manner.

I F THE ASPECT OF THE AFFAIRS was
bad on the land, it was much worse at
sea; for there a vessel rode out the fury
of the storm gallantly enough, and resisted
the force of the winds and waves for some
time; but she could not resist the
impetuosity of the elements, though she
strove hard and resisted long.

She strained, and timber after timber
started, masts were gone, and the rudder
became damaged, and at length no hope
was left.

The crew was not a large one, and the
pumps had become completely choked
and useless; while the vessel was drifted
hither and thither without any means of
guidance whatever; she was at the mercy
of wind and waves.

"We are drifting towards the shore,"
said the mate to the master; "we cannot
keep her head out to sea at all."

"I know it," answered the master,
gloomily — "I know it; she has been
making land for some time now, and as we
have neither rudder, nor sails, nor masts,
we may as well make our peace, for the
worst must soon come."

"I expected that some time ago, when
I found that the wind was set dead on
shore, and the rudder was gone."

"Surely, we haven't much time to lose;

let the guns be fired, as a signal of distress; it may give warning to those on shore."

"We cannot expect assistance."

"Not here, I know."

"Certainly not; no boat would live for a moment in a sea like this."

"No, I know it would not; but it may put them upon the look out, and some of our poor fellows may get picked up; for we don't exactly know how far we may be driven towards the land, and we may be sent right on to the beach, for aught we can tell."

"So we might."

"I hope we may."

"Are the guns ready?"

"Yes, sir, they are loaded; but there is only one barrel of powder dry."

"Let it be cared for; fire the guns."

The order was promptly obeyed, for the men had left off pumping, conceiving it useless to continue it any longer; indeed; they could not, for the pumps were no longer serviceable, and they saw the land ahead, and each man made up his mind that the struggle for life was about to commence; while the firing of the guns was a measure of precaution which might, or might not, be of use; and as every one clung to hope to the last, the order was obeyed with alacrity.

The guns were fired in minute intervals, and at length every half minute while the powder lasted, and then they ceased.

There was not more than from fifteen to twenty souls on board; but there were several passengers among them; one in particular was remarkable for his height, and the singular pallid hue of his features.

He was reserved, but of gentlemanly deportment; he was well aware of his danger, but it did not appear to render him incapable of seeing and understanding what was going on; but he was grave and melancholy.

"How long, captain, do you think it will be," he said, approaching the master, "before the vessel will break up; for I see that we shall be wrecked, that is no secret at all to any of us, and certainly not to me."

"I don't know, replied the captain; "it is impossible to say."

"Cannot you form an opinion upon the subject?" inquired the stranger.

"I can; but it is only an opinion. I can give you no information," replied the captain, who did not wish to give an opinion upon such a subject.

"Certainly, I am aware of that. I asked for an opinion; if you have one, perhaps you may be good enough to favour me with it, if it be not too great a favour to expect from you, sir. I thought you had experience enough to enable you to form an opinion, and it was for that reason I asked you."

"Well, sir, we strike in five minutes, perhaps in twenty; it depends upon wind and waves, our course, and how far we may go ashore."

"I understand you; if we are forced in upon the shore in a direct line, we may expect the shortest time."

"We may."

"And if we should not meet with any obstruction, we may be thrown far on shore."

"Yes; if we had but the means of guiding the vessel, I could steer her within fifty or a hundred yards of the shore, where she would strike, and a better chance would then be had of some reaching the shore."

"Which is now rather more than uncertain."

"It is so," said the master.

At the moment there was such a shock from the vessel striking upon a sunken rock, that they were all thrown down on the deck, and the sea made a clear breach over her, and swept away several of the crew.

The master contrived for a moment

or two to secure himself to a spar, with the hope that he would be able to float off; but this was a vain hope, for a moment after he was lifted up by a sea, and dashed against the stump of the mast, and crushed in a horrible manner, his blood dying the deck for a minute, and then it was washed away, as he himself was by the same wave, and was not seen again.

The master no doubt had been killed, and there was nearly all of the crew swept away; but among those who yet survived, was to be seen the tall stranger, who stood in the storm, and held on by a portion of the vessel; he still braved the fury of the waves as they broke over the deck clearing all before them.

Each breach of the sea made away with some one of the unhappy mariners who yet clung with hopeless desperation; but yet they feared to quit their last hold, and to throw themselves into the foam that was boiling around them.

In the meantime the vessel heeled about, and every now and then, being in shallow water, a great wave would come and lift her up, and then leave her higher on the rocks, but giving her each time dreadful shocks, and breaking her keel up.

The only hope the unfortunate men had, was that some portion of the wreck upon which they might chance to be, would be floated to the shore before life was extinct; but this was more and more hopeless, for the breakers over which they would have to float would probably be their destruction, for they would be dashed to pieces.

The wind and the waves howled and roared, and drowned all noise — nothing could be heard, and nothing seen, for the waves broke over them so furiously, and raged so high above them, that they neither could do so, nor even see the shore. Nothing but a white sea of foam and spray met their eyes, whenever they cold raise them, and free them from salt water.

At length an immense wave came rolling towards them; the men shrieked as the flood came onwards. In a moment afterwards they were lifted up, vessel and all, and carried a few yards further onwards and then left, with a report that seemed like that of a cannon to them; but they felt the shock, and when the wave left them, the vessel was no more; a mere mass of boards and other matters floated about; she had been utterly and entirely destroyed; no vestige of her was left, and nothing but a confused mass of planks was to be seen, with here and there a human being clinging to them for life.

But, alas! their efforts were vain — they sank — they could not sustain the battle with the waves and the breakers; they were dashed to mummies, and every limb broken on the foaming, raging breakers.

CLXV.

THE FISHERMEN. — THE DESPAIRING CRY OF THE MARINERS. — THE BREAKERS
FROM THE SHORE.

ON SHORE THE DAY wore away; the wind blew furiously, and the oceans roared to such an extent, that no other sound was audible; and the fishermen who lived upon the coast kept within doors, knowing that nothing could be done out of doors on such a day; and each one seated by the fire, began to recount some wonderful tale of death and shipwreck, or of happy escapes from the boiling sea, until noon had long since passed, and the turn of the day showed a decided approach towards evening; but no abatement of the tempest.

The principal fisherman on the coast, a man whose poverty was less, rather than his wealth was greater than his fellows, sat by his fireside, with one or two others of his class seated with him.

"I never saw a worse storm," said one of them.

"I have," said Massallo, the fisherman.

"You have?" said one of his comrades, in his turn.

"I have, I can promise you — one that blew me upon this coast, where I have ever since remained, and intend to remain."

"I have heard you say so; but I never heard the particulars of that story; it must have been many years ago, I fancy."

"Yes, it must have been fifteen years ago," said Massallo, speaking; "fifteen years ago at the very least, if not more than that."

"Well, I think it must be quite that time; for my old man has been dead these fourteen years, and he remembered you very well, and used to speak of you; and, as I thought, you must have known him more than a year."

"Aye, two."

"Well, it must, then, have been more than sixteen years ago since you came here."

"I dare say it was; very nearly seventeen years ago, now I come to think of it. The storm, if possible, blew harder, and the waves beat higher than they do now; the rain was heavier than it rains now; and, in addition to all, the thunder and lightning were tremendous, not a sound could be distinguished. The speaking-trumpet was useless — no sound issued from it — all was confusion and danger."

"It must have been a rare time, certainly."

"It was a time for devils to be abroad, and not for men; but we were compelled to pump, and cut away the wreck. Why, you see, we had been chased by the Algerines, and we had got nearer to the land than we would have gone, but for the fact that we desired to escape from a superior and formidable enemy, who knew no mercy. *

"Yes, the Algerines, if they had spared

---

* *"Algerines" were Barbary Coast pirates and slave-raiders, mostly of Moorish descent but including also a number of European renegades.*

us, would have made slaves of us for our lives, and there would have been little wisdom in being caught by them, if we could help it."

"I should imagine no one would ever do it."

"Well, that was the cause of our being in shore nearer than we ought; but we noticed that the Algerine sheered off at a moment when there was but little chance of our escaping him; but we could not tell the reason; but we concluded that he saw some danger, of which we were at that moment ignorant.

"Well, we had not time to haul out a little before we were surprised by a tremendous clap of thunder and lightning, as vivid as if it had been brought from all quarters of the world, and loosened at one and the same moment."

"It must have added to your terrors."

"It was the main thing that wrecked us on this coast."

"What, the lightning! why, I suppose it struck you, then?"

"Yes; we could have held off, or run the vessel bump ashore — almost dry — but we lost all command over her, when the lighting shivered our mast to atoms and left the stump burning in the vessel; then, more than that, it killed two of our best hands at that moment, and most of us were knocked up and unable to work at the pumps; but it was of no use; we came ashore, crash went the vessel, and we were all in the boiling sea in an instant, and a wave or two more threw me on the beach, without any fatal injury, and I scrambled up out of their reach."

"And then you remained by us."

"Yes; I did not find means to return whence I came for some years."

"Perhaps you had reason."

"I had; I was a rival for a girl; I was then endeavouring to win money; I had entrusted some money in the vessel — all I had; and with her I lost all, and with that all I lost even hope, and never returned to my native home."

"Did the girl love you?"

"She liked me well enough to have me, if her relations would consent, but they would not, unless they saw I had more money than I could obtain; and, in default of that, they would marry her to another, who had more money than I; and I only obtained time to get money by the girl's intercession; but I was baulked."

"Well, that was bad; but I suppose you were well assured that you would be rejected if you had not money."

"I was, by her family."

"And herself —"

"That was not so sure; and yet they had great influence upon her; but I could not have the courage to go back and ask her to wed poverty; a man without even the means of purchasing a wedding garment."

"You did right, neighbour."

"I did, and I knew it," replied the fisherman, bitterly.

"But you have prospered since; and you have been happy, if I mistake not."

"Yes, I have been prosperous, and tolerably happy; it is wonderful how men adapt themselves to the circumstances around them."

"They do; if they did not, how insupportable would life be."

"You are right; I should have been miserable for ever; I should never have recovered my feelings, and should never have been what I am now."

"The storm seems as furious as ever, neighbour," observed one of the fishermen, after a long pause, for they were meditating upon what they had heard, "and I think we shall have but a very rough night of it."

"Good; we shall have a night of it."

"I think," said another, "I must be getting near my own fireside by this time; they will expect me home, or think some accident has happened."

"And I will step out to see how the weather looks before it grows dark; there appears no change."

"Hark! what is that?"

There was a moment's pause, and in about a minute, in one of the lulls of the wind, they thought they heard a gun; but the storm increased so as to leave them in great doubt of what it was.

"It was a gun, I think," said the fisherman. "Such sounds as those I have heard before; but 'tis hard to tell them from the sounds of the elements."

"We can tell when we get outside, I dare say; but the wind sweeps all sounds past so rapidly that it is scarcely possible to tell even there; but there is yet light to see, and as the sun sets in the horizon, we have a chance of seeing a sail if there be one."

"We have, but not of helping her."

"True; there is no help for those on board."

"May Heaven have mercy upon the poor mariners," said the fisherman's wife. "It is hard times with them now. Life is dear to all, and they will cling to it. Do what you can for the poor beings."

"There's no doing anything," said the fisherman, gloomily. "Neither boat nor ship can ride through such a sea, on the ocean or at anchor."

"But they may be cast ashore, and they may not be quite dead, you know; instant aid might avail much, when even they had ceased to feel."

"We will not fail in that particular. We are going down to the beach now, and shall not neglect any means that are in our power, at all events; more we cannot do, but that much shall be done, and I hope it may be of some service."

"Hark! the same sound again," said his companion.

"I did not hear it."

"Nor I."

"Come on; we shall now know better in the open air," said the fisherman, as he wrapped himself up in a large rough coat, and pulled his hat over his eyes. "The rain is as heavy as ever, and I think it will soon fill the sea to overflowing."

The fisherman left the hut and proceeded towards the beach; at least, they did not go down, for the waves ran so high that they beat a long way inland — more so than they had ever done before.

"What do you think of our storm?"

"It is a complete tempest — furious; and the wind blows the waves towards the shore, and that is the cause why we have the sea so high; and should the wind continue in that quarter for a day or two, even our cottages will be in some danger."

"I dare say they would; but it would be without example if the winds were to continue in that quarter for so long a time, blowing a complete hurricane without any intermission. I should almost think the world about to end."

"Do you see any vessel out in the horizon?" inquired one of the fishermen.

"Not I."

"But I can hear the gun."

There came booming across the waters the sound of a piece of artillery. There was no mistaking it — it was plain and evident to all that there was a vessel in distress somewhere, but they could not exactly tell where.

Again the sound reached them on the wind, accompanied by the roar of the elements; but it was enough to distinguish it by from the rest of those awful sounds, which spoke plainly to them of the dreadful fate of the unfortunate men who were on board the vessel in distress.

"Can you make them out?" inquired one of the fishermen of his companion. "I cannot see her, though I hear the guns, and can almost imagine her whereabouts."

"No, I can't see her," replied the man spoken to.

"I can, though," replied the first fisherman; "she lies close in shore, not a mile out, nor yet that. I think she's dismasted."

"I see her now, myself. I looked about in the horizon, above her there. She labours much, and the sea breaks over her."

"She has lost her rudder, I have no doubt, and is drifting right in shore. What will become of them, I cannot well think."

"It is too easy to think."

"Do you imagine that one man among the whole crew can be saved?"

"Hardly, on such a shore as this, with rocks on all sides; every man that is swept overboard will be dashed to pieces, and disabled, even if lashed to spars."

"You are right; for if one man survives this wreck, it will be a miracle, and I can hardly believe it to be possible."

They now watched the course of the vessel. The guns had ceased to fire, and daylight was fast departing; and though she came nearer, yet she became less distinct; but still they could see her, and note her progress well through the surf that rose up around her as it dashed against the labouring vessel's side.

"She strikes," cried one of the men; "that shivering action is her first shock."

"Yes," said a companion. "Poor wretches, they have but a short time now. She will go to pieces on those rocks as sure as they are there."

"May she not hold together?"

"No; see, she heaves up again! No; as there are but bare rocks under her, and she will not settle into any place, but continue beating and bumping upon them until she will break and split to shivers, not a timber can hold."

"Too true — too true," said his companion.

The fishermen now bent their eyes upon the ocean, where this exciting scene was going on, but they spoke not. It was growing yet darker, and yet they gazed steadfastly, heedless of the beating and overwhelming rain; but they could hardly see the vessel, until at length a loud shriek came to them, borne to them upon the hoarse winds, and heard distinctly above the roaring of the ocean.

The fisherman knit his brows, and compressed his lips, as he heard the sounds, and then, clasping his hands, he said, —

"Heaven have mercy on them! for I fear the sea will have none. It's all over, and they are dead and dying. Follow me!"

CLXVI.

THE ONE BODY WASHED ASHORE. — THE FIRST REQUEST. — THE SHIPWRECKED
STRANGER.

THE FISHERMEN FOLLOWED down towards the beach, for they had been standing upon some cliffs which commanded the sea below, which now was one dark boiling mass, in which nothing at all was distinguishable; and, therefore, they could not tell what went on below.

They soon arrived at the little bay, in which their fishing-boats used to ride; but they had been drawn up beyond the reach of the sea, though the sea now ran quite up into the land, and they stood watching the waves as they rolled upwards.

"Had we not drawn our boats higher," said one "they would have been wrecks by this time, and we should have been beggars."

"Aye; so we should, neighbour."

"Don't you see the waves beating over the very spot were they lay?"

"I do; and they ain't far from them even now, and I am in some fear lest they reach them; but they have been moored as well."

"They are doubly secured."

"Do you see anything upon the water yet?" inquired the first fisherman.

"Nothing."

"Nor I, and I have strained my eyes to their utmost. They are most likely all dashed to pieces, and they are not likely to live through such a sea."

"No, no; they must be overwhelmed with water. God help them, poor fellows! and if they are not to be saved, may they soon have an end to their tortures, for the strife after life must be dreadful."

"It is dreadful," said the other; "but you must know that the sufferings are endured under excitement, and therefore not so much felt as when they have been saved. To have passed the barrier of life, and to become insensible to all, and then to be recalled to life, is an agony not to be described. I have seen men who have been restored to life, and who have solemnly declared that the pangs of death they could encounter, and not those of a return to life."

The fisherman made no reply, but stood listening to the howlings of the storm, and watching the waves; but this was productive of nothing — they watched for more than two hours, and yet nothing came ashore.

"I don't see we can do any good here," said one.

"Nor I. Those who were alive, must now have been dead some time."

"Yes; the sea don't wash them this way."

"Most likely," added another, "they are washed among the breakers, and dashed against the cliffs, and therefore cannot reach this place, where they can reach the land."

"It usually happens so."

"It does; but we may as well return. There is a wreck, no doubt."

"That is quite settled."

"Quite, as you say; but there are no signs of it."

"Save such as you saw."

"Yes; we have evidence enough of the fact. We saw her go to pieces, and we have heard the death-shriek of the mariners, and more we cannot have seen. When we come down here in the morning, we may indeed see the bodies, and the broken and severed planks of the unfortunate vessel, strewn over the sands."

"I shall return again after I have had an hour or two's turn-in," said the fisherman.

"Give me a call," said his companion, "and I will go with you."

"And I."

"Agreed. Then about midnight we will again visit the beach, and see if any of the men are ashore."

THERE WAS NO ONE now by the shore, and nought save the sounds of the turmoil of the elements could be heard. What other sounds can be any possibility be distinguishable at such a time? There was nothing that could be done there that would sound. The loud roar of the breakers was tremendous; the dash of the waves against the cliffs, and the steady bellowing of the wind, which sounded not much unlike a steady and continued report of great guns fired at a distance, were as but one sound and that sound of a strange, awful, and furious character — perfectly dreadful.

There was one body, however thrown up by the waves, as if they would yield that one alone, and no other, or as if that one was the only one they refused to swallow; it floated about for some time, and was thrown hither and thither, now thrown on shore by one wave, and withdrawn by another.

At last a high wave came rolling onwards, and falling upon the shore, it lifted the body up, and carried it further upon the beach and there left it, and no subsequent wave came so far as that, and it was left unmolested.

That body was the carcase of the stranger, who of all the rest had been swept towards the little bay, and deposited there alone.

THE FISHERMAN LEFT his hut to call his companions, and having done so, they came towards the beach, while they conversed together.

"Well," said one, "I did not expect to see the storm abate so soon."

"I did not," replied his companion, "though, I dare say, it was much too violent to last much longer; and yet I can scarcely credit my senses that it is really gone, and that the deluging rain has ceased altogether."

"Yes; and there comes the moon peeping behind that mass of clouds."

"The wind blows stiffly yet; but it has greatly moderated, and I think it will continue to do so."

"I hope it may; but the sea does not abate a bit, and will not for many hours, even if the wind was to go down."

"Oh, dear, no; the waves will keep on in this fashion for some hours; and I dare say it will be useless to get our boats out; we shall not have any more fish for some days to come."

"Most likely not; but I would not venture to go out while the sea is heaving, after such a storm as this; there would be but little use in doing so, I am quite persuaded; but what is that yonder?"

"Where — I see nothing?"

"There, lying a few yards from the reach of the waves; to me it looks like a human body. It is quite quiet and still — no motion — it is, I fear, dead; there is no motion, and the attitude is that of one who has not moved after he was thrown there — I think not, however; but let us see what it is."

The fishermen now went down onto the beach, where the body lay, for such it really was; and, when they reached it, at once saw it was a human body, and they all paused before it.

"Bring it higher up on the beach; the waves may come upon you presently — they are high enough. Bring him up higher on the beach, and you will then see what state he is in; for if his limbs are broken, and his body otherwise injured to any extent, you may spare much useless labour."

The fishermen drew the body up higher; they then carried him to a dry and sheltered spot, and examined him, but found no particular injuries to speak of, but that he was apparently drowned.

"What course to pursue," said one, "I don't know; no doubt but he is quite dead; he must have been in the water several hours, besides being knocked about on the breakers, which is enough to destroy life itself."

"I should imagine so; and yet, we had better take it up to the cottage, and place it under cover; indeed, we cannot tell how long it has been thus; therefore, I say we had better make some attempt to recover him; he may yet come round, though there may be but little hope in it."

"We will try; stand out of the moonlight — we shall be able to see presently better what he is, than we can now."

The moon was now freed from the mass of deep heavy clouds that hung over it, like a curtain before that luminary, and which now shed a brilliant light upon the earth. The fishermen stood round gazing upon the body of the stranger.

"Ha! it moves," said one.

The body did move, and no sooner did the moonlight fall full and fair upon its form, than it slowly raised itself upon its elbow, and gazed around. A deep inspiration took place, almost a groan, and some sea water was vomited.

"He lives — he lives!" exclaimed the fisherman.

"Take him to the hut," said another.

They all stooped down to aid him, and began to lift him up.

"He lives — he lives!"

"Away with him to the hut," said several of the fishermen. "Before a warm fire, and with some warm drinks, he will get better."

"A little more light — a little more light, if you please," said the stranger, in a bland but broken voice, as he attempted to move his hand.

"He speaks!" exclaimed the fishermen in a breath, and at the same time they removed a pace or two, and looked at each other with amazement, and then again at the stranger, who gradually rose up, and sat upright in the light of the moon.

"Are you any better?" inquired one of the men who had looked on in silent amazement, not unmixed with awe, as they gazed.

"Yes; much better. What a vile thing

is sea water," said the stranger, turning such a ghastly face upon the men that they shrunk in horror, and yet they were not men used to fear or any like passion.

However, they soon approached him, muttering to each other,—

"What manner of man is this?"

They did not long consider what was to be done, for one of their number replied,—

"Poor fellow! he is not used to the rough usage of the waves, and therefore does not improve upon their acquaintance. But let us lend him a hand."

"With all my heart," replied his comrades.

"Will you come with me to my cottage?" said the fisherman. "You will benefit more by a good fire than by the cold moonlight, I'll warrant. I never throve upon night air and wet clothes, and I cannot believe you will."

"We all know our constitutions best," said the stranger; "but if you will grant me the accommodation you speak of, it will be welcome."

"Come, lean upon me; never mind your clothes being wet."

The stranger rose, and, to the amazement of all, he appeared to walk as well as any of those present; and the only difference was, he was ghastly pale, and he was dripping with sea water, which left a track after him.

"Had you been long on the beach?" inquired one.

"I don't know," replied the stranger. "I was insensible."

"Can you form any idea how long you have been in the water?"

"I really cannot tell even that; for I was insensible immediately after the ship went to pieces, which she did about the close of the day; and I only remember receiving a hard blow by being struck against a rock, or a piece of timber, I cannot say which."

"You must have been insensible for some hours."

"I dare say I was."

"I never heard of such a miraculous preservation."

"Nor I."

"To come to life, too, without any aid to recover you, that is what entirely bothers me."

"Well, they do say, those that are born to be hanged will never be drowned," added one of the fishermen, in an under tone, to his companion.

They soon arrived at the hut of the fisherman, in which there was a good fire, and the wife and daughter were ready to do all that could be done for the unfortunate stranger.

"You have saved a mariner, then?" said the wife.

"We have picked up one from the wreck, wife; but we cannot call him a mariner. This gentleman was, no doubt, a passenger."

"Welcome, sir! I did not expect to see any one alive from the wreck, much less in condition to walk an speak."

The stranger paid them some compliments; but contented himself with sitting by the fire, and being entirely passive in their hands, and eventually retired to rest well wrapped up and warm.

CLXVII.

THE FISHERMAN'S COTTAGE. — THE FIRESIDE, AND THE TRAVELLER'S BED.

THE FISHERMAN'S HUT was large and roomy. There was no choice furniture, though there was enough of the homely conveniences that were to be found in such habitations — much more so than is usual. There was a large fire-place, upon which some faggots had been newly laid, and which now blazed away most cheerfully.

"Our home is humble, sir," said the fisherman; "but such as it is, you are welcome to it, and may it serve you instead of a better."

"I am much beholden to you," replied the stranger; "much beholden to you, and cannot thank you enough. This change is most valuable. I do not know in what state I should have been, had you not come forward and offered the shelter of your house to me. I am very cold, indeed, and the warmth of your fire is grateful to me."

"I am glad of it, sir. You are the only one, I fear, as far as I know, that is saved. Was there many on board?"

"About twenty, I think."

"Poor fellows! they have met with a watery grave."

"Yes, they have, I fear. They have had a fearful struggle, for many were lashed to spars, hoping they might be washed, or floated, ashore. I hope I am not disturbing, though I fear I am, your wife and daughter — that is your daughter, I presume, if I may judge from her likeness to yourself."

"Yes, sir, that is my daughter; she's a good girl, sir, though I say so, that am her father; and if a secret must be told, in another month she will exchange a father's for a husband's control and care, which will I hope, be a happy change."

"They have long loved each other," said the mother, "and, to my mind, it is cruel to keep them apart. Times will never be better, and I don't see but they may begin the world as well as others, with little more than a will to work."

"You are right," said the stranger; "you are right; it was never intended that mankind should wait till circumstances were propitious, or it would have made the desire dependent upon circumstances, too."

"You have hit the right nail, sir — you have spoken the truth; but still we must recommend caution."

"Very right. I wish them joy and prosperity," said the stranger.

There was now a bustle in the cottage. Some of those who had accompanied the stranger into the hut, now departed, while the remainder left a few moments after, in company, leaving the fisherman and his family with their guest.

"Well," said one, "of all the odd looking fish that ever I saw come out of the sea, I think he beats all; not but what I make every allowance, but I cannot make any in such a case, because he has not been drowned."

"He was quite insensible, and had been so for a long time. Don't you remember what he said about his becoming insensible immediately after the ship struck."

"Yes; I heard it all, but hang me if I can understand it. He is as if he had been bled to death, and then came to life."

"He ain't got much of a colour."

"No; but more than that, the dreadful deathly, or ashy paleness is fearful; and then his peculiar features, his long hair, flattened to his head by the water, and the teeth in his head, which appear as if they had been set with the express intention of enabling him to catch otters."

"That would be no easy task, either; but I must say, as you say, that there have been better looking men than he, at all events."

IN THE FISHERMAN'S HUT the stranger was willingly attended to by the fisherman and his family, without any invidious attention; and when he had changed his habiliments, he seated himself again by the fire, when some warm drinks and other refreshment were given him.

"I did not think to find any one alive when I went down to the beach," said the fisherman. "I thought all were lost."

"And I doubt not but they are all lost, save myself," said the stranger, blandly; "and though I do not appear much hurt by the occurrence, yet I feel as if the whole mass of my blood was changed, and that I should never again be what I was; that, in fact, I shall always carry about me the appearance, and certainly the feeling, of a man torn from the arms of death, and made to live."

"It does affect some people strangely," said the fisherman. "I know what shipwreck is myself, and, therefore, can easily guess what it is to those who are unused to the sea. I was the only one saved out of a whole crew."

"Indeed! then your case is identical with mine."

"In that respect it is," replied the fisherman; "but I was used to the dangers of the sea; and, though that makes no difference when you find yourself in the boiling waters, yet a man who has the fear of wreck constantly before his eyes, can see the danger — take more precaution, and is not so likely to lose that presence of mind which at such times is so valuable."

"So it is; though I took it very quietly, and stood still until I was thrown down by the first shock of the vessel."

"She struck more than once?"

"She did; four or five times; she was thrown upon the rocks in shallow water, I believe, as I understand these matters."

"Yes, it was so," said the fisherman — "it was so."

"Well, it was only when the waves left us that we came down with a dreadful crashing shock, which caused the vessel to shiver as if she had been but a leaf. Well, every time a wave swept towards us, it lifted the vessel off the rock, and carried her a few yards further, sometimes scraping and scratching her keel as she went along; at other times, she was lifted clear of the rocks, and then suddenly thrown upon them with great force, and then every timber separated."

"Just what might be expected."

"And just as it occurred," said the stranger.

"And, of course, the crew were carried into the sea, and drowned."

"Yes; but what became of them — I mean where they were carried to — I cannot tell; but I suppose among the tall rocks that I saw before the wreck. But why was I not carried there and left?"

"It is something that neither you nor I can tell," said the fisherman.

"Perhaps so; but I am safe, and only so to tell the disaster to others, not for a warning; for it can be none, but I am saved."

"You are. Perhaps you would like to lie down for an hour or two before daylight comes, and then we will take a walk down to the shore in the morning, and see if there is anything washed ashore."

"I am tired, and think that it would be of some service, if I can sleep; though I dare say I shall be dreaming of what I have seen and felt, and hardly dare to sleep, so great is the disturbance in my mind."

"Sit up, and welcome, by the fire," said the fisherman; "you can do so; it may be as well, perhaps, too — you may be able to sleep that way."

"No, no, I'll lie down on the boards — I am not particular upon such an occasion; and, as it has turned out, I shall be too much in need of rest to sit up. The warmth of the fire, too, draws me off, I can find, and I dare say you feel it too."

"It has that effect, as much as I am used to it," replied the fisherman; "but do what you please; I shall turn in till daylight, unless you want anything more."

"Nothing, thank you, my good friend, but a place to lie down on, and then I am quite content for the remainder of the night."

"There is a settle up in yon corner where you can sleep; it is rough and homely, but we have nothing otherwise here."

"No apology; I am too thankful for what I have escaped from, and for what I have received, to look hard at the mercies afforded me."

The stranger said no more, but took the fisherman's advice and walked to the settle, and then lay down with his face towards the fire.

"Good night," said the fisherman; "pleasant slumbers."

"The same to you, my friend; I hope I have not dispossessed any of your family of their means of rest. I have, perhaps, deprived them of their bed."

"No, no; sleep in peace; we are all provided for. I sleep here," he said, as he was about to open the door; "and my daughter sleeps there," he added, pointing to a small door. "So, you see, we have our appointed places, and that on which you now sleep is retained for the use of any strange traveller or friend that may need it."

"Then good night," said the stranger, which was returned again by the fisherman, who entered his own room, leaving his guest lying on his bed, and looking around him by the light of the fire, which burned yet for some time.

CLXVIII.

THE NIGHT IN THE FISHERMAN'S HUT. — THE MIDNIGHT FEAST OF BLOOD. — THE CHASE, AND THE GUN-SHOT.

THE STRANGER, AS HE LAY, listened to the sounds that were emitted by, and occasionally opened his eyes to gaze upon, the flames, as they ran upwards; he watched the forked tongues as they played about the faggots, and then turned his eyes towards the various parts of the apartment as it was now and then illuminated with its warm glare.

What might have been his feelings after his escape it is difficult to conjecture, for he appeared not inclined to sleep, but to gaze about him and keep watch over the fire, which every now and then blazed up afresh; and his mind appeared to be intent upon something else than merely thinking of the past — there was too much of inquiry and curiosity about it.

"The time has come round again," he muttered; "my blood requires renewal, my strength renovation, and no aliment will do that but maiden's blood."

A horrible expression of countenance came over him that must have caused a feeling of horror to have crept through the veins of any one who might have been near to see him; but, as it was, he was alone, and there was no one to be terrified.

"Yes, yes; I must have that supply, else though the sea may give up its dead, and the earth refuse to cover me, yet I may sink into that sleep I would so willingly escape from; then, indeed, I should suffer what I cannot bear to think of.

"Yet how near have I been to that death from which I have believed it impossible to return; but yet the moonbeams have found me, and I have again been re-animated, and the horrible appetite has returned which must have its periodical meal — its terrible and disgusting repast. It must be done, aye, it must be done."

As he muttered, his lips met, and his long tongue was occasionally thrust out, as if he were anticipating the pleasures of the feast.

"Yes, yes; this very night must renew the life that has been this night restored to me. I must make a fresh attempt. I think he said his daughter lay in yonder chamber; in another hour I will adventure upon this scheme."

His eyes were fixed upon the door, which he appeared to watch and examine with the utmost care and avidity.

He watched, however, for some time, and the flames appeared to subside, and the embers gave out a dull, red glare, and some warmth.

"Now is the moment," he muttered, as he rose softly from his bed; "now is the moment — all are asleep, and stillness reigns around me. I will go and ascertain if all be quiet, and then to my midnight orgies — a feast that shall restore me to my life — my former self."

He crawled out of the bed, and stood upright for a moment, and listened, and then, with a noiseless step, he crept to the

door of the fisherman's bedroom, and then listened for some seconds, and muttered as if he were satisfied,—

"Yes, yes; they sleep sound enough, and will not readily awaken."

He then took a small cord, and tied the handle of the door to a nail on the post, so as to offer an impediment to egress from the sleeping-room, and then he went towards the other which the fisherman had told him belonged to his daughter. He paused, and listened at the door for a few moments, and then he said,—

"Yes, yes; that is the maiden's chamber—that is sure to be her chamber—her father said so, and I have no reason to doubt he told the truth, since he had no cause to lie; here, then, is the casket that contains all my treasure—the *elixir vitae* of my life—the undefiled blood of a maiden's veins."

He tried the door, but it was secured on the inside.

This, for a moment, disconcerted him, and he took a moment or two to consider what best could be done; and at length he saw a small chink in the wall, which he approached; then, peeping in, he saw that if he could enlarge the hole, he might push his hand in, and open the door by undoing the fastenings.

This was effected by means of a chisel which happened to be lying near at hand; then he opened it, and thrust in his hand and withdrew the bolt that held the door, and quietly opened it.

With cat-like caution he approached the bed where the fisherman's daughter lay. She was a beautiful girl, scarce eighteen, and, by a consent of all, the queen of the place, in respect of beauty.

With greedy eyes the vampyre approached the bed on which lay the form of the sleeping maiden, and gazed upon her fair white neck and bosom—heaving with the sleeper's breath; and then, as if he could contain himself no longer, he eagerly bent down over her, and then, as her face was turned on one side, his lips and teeth approached the side exposed.

A SCREAM RAN THROUGH the fisherman's hut that awoke its inmates in an instant, and which, though it banished sleep, yet it gave not the power of thought.

"Help! help! help!" screamed the maiden.

"'Tis Mary!" said the fisherman; "surely—"

"Hasten, and see what 'tis that ails her. She never would scream so, unless in utmost peril; hasten, and see."

"Help! help!" again screamed the maiden, as she struggled in the arms of the monster, who kept her in his powerful grasp while he sought the life current that crimsoned her veins with horrible desire.

"The door is secured; d—n!" muttered the fisherman. "What does this mean? Give me my gun down, while I force the door."

The old woman handed down the gun, while the fisherman put his strength to the door, which quickly gave way and flew open.

"Here is your gun. Be quick; but do not be too hasty in its use. See to Mary and the shipwrecked voyager."

"Who secured my door, dame, but he?"

"The door! Ay, I remember—hasten!"

"Help—help!" again shouted or screamed Mary, but not in so loud a voice as before; she was getting weaker, and just as the fisherman emerged into the large room, the faggots fell together and gave forth a sudden blaze, and in an instant the whole place was lighted up, and the fisherman's eye sought the couch of the stranger whom he had lodged, but the bed was empty.

"Gone!" he muttered—"gone!"

He turned his head in the direction of his daughter's bedchamber, and saw the door was open, and he heard a struggle and a sucking noise.

"Ha!" he muttered, and rushed in exclaiming—"What means this noise? Who calls for help?"

The appearance of the fisherman was so opportune and so sudden, and so intent was the vampyre upon the hideous meal, that he did not hear the approach of the fisherman, and it was not until the latter shouted that he turned and saw him.

"Treacherous and ungrateful villain!" said the fisherman, who was almost powerless from terror and astonishment.

The vampyre turned and dropped his victim on the bed, while he endeavoured to pass the fisherman; but the act recalled him to himself, and he made a blow at him with the butt-end of the gun; but the vampyre jumped back, and the blow missed its intended object, and they both closed for a struggle.

The fisherman, however, found that he had one to do with whose strength was even greater than his own, however great that might be; and in a moment more he was thrown down, and the monster rushed across the outer room, oversetting the fisherman's wife; and forcing open the outer door, he fled.

"I am thrown," said the fisherman, rising; "but not done for. Mary, are you hurt?"

"Oh, my God—my God!" exclaimed the poor girl. "He had begun to eat me and suck my blood! I have the marks of his teeth in me."

"I'll have revenge upon him yet."

"Nay, father. He is some monster—do not go!"

"No, no," said his wife—"no, husband, do not attempt it! Strong he is; he may do you a mischief."

"I know," said the fisherman. "He has thrown me, and he has abused my hospitality; he is not fit to live. He has not, however, any means of fighting against the contents of my gun. I have got that loaded, and will punish him. Be he man or devil, I will make the experiment of following him."

All this took place in less time than it takes to relate it, and the fisherman rushed out of his hut to follow the stranger who had acted so badly.

It was now early dawn; and, though the waves still lashed the shore in angry violence, and kept up a ceaseless roar, yet the sky betrayed none of the the signs of yesterday's storm, but was serene and calm, and not a cloud was to be seen—nothing but a dim, grey night pervaded all space.

There was just light enough to see objects moving about, and when the fisherman got outside the hut, he saw, about a hundred yards or better before him, the form of the stranger, making for the woodland at the height of his speed.

The fisherman hastened to intercept him which, however, was unnecessary, for another, coming from that quarter, turned him, and he fled towards the sea, whither he was followed, and, when upon the cliffs, the fisherman fired, and the vampyre fell over and was supposed to have been drowned.

"Call out some of my people," said the wounded man, "call them out. I am very stiff, and not able to get out." In a few minutes more several men, all in livery, ran down the steps to the gondola, and lifted their master out, who appeared to be unable to do so of himself. ... (see page 1112)

PART VIII:

The Vampyre's Florentine Bride.

CLXIX.

THE ASSASSINS ON THE RIALTO. — THE ATTACK AND DEFEAT. — THE STRANGER.

ON THE RIALTO, one evening, as the sun was sinking in the golden west, a stranger was seen walking to and fro in deep musing, apparently unmindful of what was passing around him, or of the approach of evening, an hour when the remorseless assassin is known to stalk abroad in the streets of Venice, and there the dagger finds its victim.

Several individuals looked hard at the stranger in the cloak, but no one approached him, save those who passed him, and in doing so bestowed a passing gaze upon him, which was not returned, for he heeded no one. But he was not much open to recognition even if he were known, for the cloak with which he had enveloped himself was of such ample dimensions that it completely concealed him from the curiosity of the many; indeed, his face was hardly visible, for the fur collar he wore hid all save the bridge of a prominent nose, and his eyes, which had a peculiar lustre.

The evening still grew darker and later, and the passengers were fewer and fewer, but still the tall stranger walked slowly up and down; but no one ventured to say anything, though more than one had the inclination to speak; but the tallness of the man, and the point of the long rapier which appeared beneath the cloak, checked any inclination to familiarity, and induced a more voluntary courtesy than might at all times have been accorded.

There were, indeed, a small knot of three individuals, who kept near the same place, and whose eyes every now and then directed their glances towards the stranger, as if they regarded him with impatience.

These men were of a suspicious character; they all wore cloaks and slouched hats, but they had all seen some service, and were somewhat the worse for it. They conversed together, and walked away for a short space, but they returned presently, and still found the stranger as before at the same spot.

"Well," said one of the three, as they again met at a certain spot, "what think you now — is he a spy or not?"

"I don't know what to think, Rubino.

Spy or no spy, he will interfere with our duty to-night. I wonder what is best."

"What do you mean?"

"Why, would it be better to chance his presence, or shall we put him away? He evidently intends remaining there, the devil only knows how long."

"I believe you; but it appears to me that both plans are objectionable to the last degree, though I confess I can see no alternative whatever."

"Which do you consider the least objectionable plan? — that is what we have to consider, for there are but two plans, and we cannot fail to do our business; should we do so, we should lose something, and we should never get any more employment."

"Good. If we attack him, we shall lose our chance with our better customer. We shall lose our man, at the least, if we get clear."

"He wears a long sword, and is a tall man. If he has any skill, and I dare be sworn he has, he will prove an ugly customer."

"We are three."

"That is very true; but an encounter only makes it the worse, and even if he be killed, which, if we are true to ourselves, he must be, we shall be obliged to quit the spot, and our main object defeated."

"That is most true; but shall we risk the attempt when there are two? It will make it too many odds; we shall not be so sure of success as we ought to be."

"We have the advantage of striking when we are not seen. A blow is sure when no hand is raised to ward it off."

"Aye, we should dispose of one before he has made any resistance, and before the other can offer any opposition or attempt any assistance, should the first have life enough to call out. Come, come, let's have no fear of the result; it is all in our own hands."

"Shall we not run more danger during the encounter of being taken by others who may come up, attracted by the fray? There is much to be said about making an alarm, because numbers will then be drawn upon us, and you know we have little sympathy among the multitude."

"No, no; we must make all possible haste, and then we may elude all possible chance. Strike the blow home, and then we may baffle all; for if he cry, he will fall, and those who help him, will raise him, and we shall have time to make our escape."

"No doubt — no doubt; 'tis a good plan — a very good plan, and one that I think will succeed; at all events, it only wants a good trial to make it succeed; you see, a strong arm, quick eye, and swift foot, is all that are necessary."

"I see; and one more quality."

"What is it?"

"Good luck."

"Granted; but that often comes from the manner in which a thing is done, and sometimes from the want of skill in those who should make it the reverse. Confusion for a moment gives us our luck, and then we are safe."

"So we are."

"How goes the time, Rubino?" inquired one of the assassins, for such they were.

"Oh, it yet wants one hour of the time in which we are to meet him."

"Well, then, we have more than a chance yet of our being undisturbed here, and the stranger may leave for some other part of the city; but our plan is fixed whether or no. Shall we turn into a vintner's?"

"No; we have no time for that, as yet."

"No time! What mean you Rubino?"

"That we have no time," replied Rubino, "to quit this neighbourhood, because you will perceive he may come any time these next two hours, which is a matter of some importance; for if he reach home alive, we have miscarried, and incur great displeasure, if not vengeance."

"We care but little for the vengeance of another."

"We may not individually; but you must know, this one knows too much of us and our haunts to be a safe and pleasant enemy; besides, we shall lose a liberal patron — one who has given us some gold and promised us more."

"Aye, aye; he's the man to serve, and we will not disoblige him; we'll deal fairly by him, and he cannot expect more."

"And he will reward us liberally."

"Amen, say I. Now we have waited long enough, let us walk down the Rialto, and when we get to the other end, we can plant ourselves in such a position to watch his advance towards us, and then we can walk to him."

"Had we better not remain somewhere nearer at hand, because we can then start on him unawares, and thus have a blow without alarming him; and, if that be a deadly one, why, then we are safe. No one will know the mischief is done."

"So much the better; but come, we will continue our walk; it will lull suspicion, and when we come again, one of our number can creep into one of these alcoves, and there wait against his coming."

"And you will be at hand?"

"Of course; we shall keep upon the look out, so as to be near at the moment you commence the attack."

"But suppose I should fall?"

"Then you must continue the attack in a sharp and rapid manner, engaging all his attention to defend himself."

"Aye; and leave me to myself to the attack of that man yonder, should he be at hand at that moment."

"Oh, no, no. Do not hurt yourself. You need be under no fear of that sort, for you see it will only be man to man, and a fair encounter."

"It has never yet been fairly done, and will not be with me in this matter, don't you see. If help arrives, I'm lost; and, if I be lost without help, it will be the worse for you. I'll take my share of danger and mishap, but I won't be imposed upon by a comrade, and so you will understand it first."

"Who was desirous you should? Shall we not be at hand?"

"At your heels, I expect; but don't you see that, by giving a minute's time, you endanger all; for, if my first attack fail, he ought not to be allowed rallying time; he ought not to be permitted to recover himself, and attempt defence, indeed, because that gives time, and we may be beat by others coming from whatever quarter we may go."

"We do not intend it. We only are desirous that one of us should be prepared to make the attack, while we are walking to and fro, and perhaps attracting his attention, and drawing it from you. Then we aid you; but, should you be foiled, why we will hasten as if we were coming to help him."

"I see; well, let it be so."

"Good. We can then act effectively, and we are the gainers by this stratagem. Now then, Roberto, do thou hide thyself in yonder alcove."

"I will. My dagger is sharp, and you know my arm is not usually a weak one, and that I have done some service with it ere now."

"Thou hast."

"And it will again do more."

"Hush! hasten in. I hear footsteps yonder. 'Tis he, I think. We will not go far, but within the reach of your eye; fifty yards, at most, will be the distance. We will take and come towards you the moment we find he has reached you."

"Good. Begone — he comes."

The assassin stole into an alcove, and then paused in the deep shade of the place where he had concealed himself, and the other two walked down a short distance — about a hundred and fifty yards or so — and then paused and looked back.

"Do you see anything of them?"

"No; I don't at this moment. It is getting very dark."

"We had better return and see what happens. We shall get up in the very nick of time, and be able to take part in the fray."

"Well, be it so," replied the other. "I'll go with you; but we run some risk in encountering the stranger in the rapier and long cloak."

"Most true; but we shall not have taken any part in the affair; that will clear us of anything that may tend to inculpate us. We are right; and, if we find our comrade hardly pressed, we can aid him, and that at a time when it is unexpected by the other party. Hark! they are at it already."

"Come on."

They both hastened towards the scene of combat, towards which they both ran, for they knew their comrade's voice.

The other villain awaited the coming of the stranger, whom he was waiting to assassinate, as soon as his comrades had left him.

The unconscious stranger walked down the Rialto with a slow and steady gait, humming an air from some opera as he walked along, well pleased in his own mind. He wore his cloak open in front, and his sword dangling at his side, and altogether most unsuspicious of an attack.

Scarcely, however, had he passed the assassin's hiding-place, than the fellow rushed out and made a desperate blow at him with his dagger, which, however, miscarried, on account of the loose manner in which he wore his cloak; the blow was foiled by the folds of the garment, and the wearer turned round.

"Villain!" he exclaimed, "thou shalt have thy deserts;" and, as he spoke, he drew his sword, and became the assailant in his turn.

"Help! help!" shouted the villain, who found himself beset by one who would quickly make him repent his temerity.

At that moment the rest of the assassins came up, and commenced a furious attack upon the single stranger, who, of course, from being almost a victor, was immediately compelled to give ground to the three.

"Help! help!" shouted the stranger, as he was forced on one knee, and that with a wound; but at that moment help was at hand, and the tall stranger stepped up to his side, and casting his cloak on one side, and drawing his rapier, he ran one of the assailants through the body and he fell backwards dead.

A furious combat ensued between the stranger and the other two assassins, who were compelled to fight, so closely were they pressed by the stranger; however,

after a few moments, they turned and fled.

The stranger then turned towards the wounded man, who was rising from the ground by the help of the pillar that was supporting the sides of the alcove, and then endeavoured to stanch the wound he had received.

CLXX.

COUNT POLIDORI'S PALACE. — SIGNORA ISABELLA, THE COUNT'S DAUGHTER. — THE INTRODUCTION.

THE STRANGER WALKED UP to him and offered his services, saying, — "Are you hurt, signor? — you bleed!"

"But slightly hurt, signor, thank you for that; you have saved my life. I had been cold meat, indeed — a bloody corpse for all Venice to look upon to-morrow, but for your valour and stout assistance."

"Name it not, signor; but the rascals have been well paid. There lies one of them — the others have escaped; but permit me, signor, to say, that the sooner you get away from this spot the better, for the knaves may return in greater force than before, or they will wait till you leave; by that time they will have rallied, and dart out upon you as you pass along."

"I do not fear that, signor, much; but the fact is, I am almost too weak to walk unaided."

"Permit me to render you the assistance you require. I am a stranger in this place, and therefore unused to your ways; but — "

"Say no more, signor; I will accept of your services if you will accept of a lodging

at my poor home. I have that which shall make you welcome — heartily welcome; and the signora, my daughter, shall make you welcome, too."

"Signor, if I can be of service to you I will do so with pleasure. Lend me your arm, signor; but your wound is not stanched — let me bind it more carefully and securely; you ought not to bleed from such a wound when bandaged."

"Perhaps, signor, you have had more to do with these matters than I. I am a peaceable Venetian of rank, and neither afraid nor unwilling to draw a sword in a good quarrel, shrinking not from some odds, but I have had no practice in these matters; times and circumstances have not been propitious."

"It matters not," replied the stranger; "you shewed what you were when you had nearly defeated one, and afterwards kept at bay three. He must be a man who can behave thus, sir; he must have the heart and conduct of a soldier — you would be one did occasion serve — no man can be more; but I have seen many climes, and have therefore some knowledge in these matters beyond the mere inward power and courage. I have, from sheer necessity, been compelled to mix in *mêlées*, and not from inclination."

"I thank you for your skill as a surgeon, for truly you have stopped the bleeding, which I had not been able to do myself."

"Lean on my shoulder, signor; it will enable you to walk better. Have you far to go?" inquired the stranger.

"No, signor; but we will take a gondola, it will be the easier travelling, and, moreover, it will land us at my house, where you shall be most heartily welcome. If we turn down here, we shall soon obtain the aid of a gondolier. I had intended walking, but I have enough of that for one night, even if I were able to walk, which I am not."

"As you please, signor."

As the stranger spoke he walked towards the place indicated by the wounded man, and in a few moments more they reached the grand canal, and finding a gondolier sleeping in his gondola, the stranger left his wounded companion to wake the sleeper to his duty, by shaking him.

"Hilloa!" said the stranger, "will nothing wake you — get up instantly, and about your duty. Do you always sleep here?"

"No, signor," said the man, sleepily.

"Well, then, are you engaged?"

"Yes, signor, if you engage me."

"Well, then, I do."

"Where to, signor?"

"Come with me to bring a wounded gentleman into the gondola, and he will tell you where to. Come, quick — have you not yet awakened?"

"I'm awake, signor, and willing," said the gondolier, following the stranger to the spot where the wounded man was standing, and, by direction of the stranger, he aided the wounded signor into the gondola.

"Now, signors, I have but to know where you desire to go to."

"Row on until I tell you where to stop. Follow the course of the grand canal, and you will go right enough."

There was some time spent in silence, while the gondolier rowed as desired up the grand canal, until they came to a large mansion, which the wounded man gazed upon, and, after a moment's pause, as if he had a difficulty in speaking, he said, as he pointed to the building, —

"There, row up to yonder steps; there I will land — that is my house."

The gondolier immediately obeyed the injunction, and pulled for the stairs, and when they reached the place, the gondolier stepped out and secured the gondola.

"Call out some of my people," said the wounded man, "call them out. I am very stiff, and not able to get out."

The gondolier obeyed, and in a few minutes more several men, all in livery, ran down the steps to the gondola, and lifted their master out, who appeared to be unable to do so of himself.

The gondolier was rewarded according to his deserts, and the stranger followed the wounded man into his own house, which was a most extensive building, and filled with servants, and furnished in the richest manner, displaying magnificence and wealth to a degree that was scarce to be surpassed in Venice.

They were shown into an apartment replete with every appointment that

wealth or luxury could suggest, and the wounded man was placed on a sofa, and his attendants stood round him as if waiting his orders.

"Signor and stranger," he said, "welcome to my house, as the preserver of my life. All I have here is at your service."

"I am obliged," replied the stranger, with a dignified acknowledgement of the courtesy—"I am obliged; but I cannot recognise on my part any such right. If I have done you service — as I will not affect to believe I have not — still you overrate the amount of it. But I will accept of your hospitality for this night; for I am a stranger in Venice, and have little or no knowledge of the best course to pursue."

"Remain here."

"But you had better dispatch some one for aid," interrupted the stranger. "You are in pain, at this very instant; send for some assistance. You require the aid of a leech immediately."

"I am faint — very faint," he replied.

"Hasten," said the stranger — "hasten some of you to fetch a leech, instead of losing your wits in silent astonishment."

The servants immediately bustled about, and seemed to have awakened from a trance, and were seen running in different directions. The room was soon cleared, and the tall stranger seated himself by his wounded host.

"In me you see the Count Polidori." The stranger bowed. "I am not a native of this city, though now one of her favoured citizens. I have left the land of my birth because I and my rulers could not agree, and I ran some danger in staying against their will, and I have settled and married here."

"Our adopted country is that which demands our care and preference," replied the stranger. "That, at least, is my opinion."

"No doubt. I am now," he continued, "a widower."

"Your lady is dead?"

"Yes; I am sorry to say so. I have, however, one child living at home, and one who is serving his country in her fleets, an honour to our house; but my greatest comfort is the dear image of my lost wife — my daughter."

"Is she here now?"

"Yes; in this palace. Signora Isabella is devoted to her father, and would not for the world do aught that would give me a moment's pain; indeed, she would die for me rather than I should feel displeasure."

"Such a daughter must be a treasure."

"She is a treasure."

"And what an inestimable jewel would she be as a wife."

"She will be when the day comes when she will mate, which I hope will be before I die; for I should be too anxious respecting the worth of the man who was to be her husband, to permit me to die happy, unless I saw and approved of the choice, or chose the individual myself."

"I see you are more anxious," said the stranger, mildly, "in providing future happiness for your daughter, rather than in hoarding wealth or titles for her."

"I am," said the count.

"And a most laudable ambition, too; an ambition that few parents do not neglect in the pursuit of one of a different character — either some young love, or some one who is endowed largely with worldly goods or titles."

"My Isabella will have enough of both; and, therefore, she will not need to seek for them; but she will not throw herself away upon any nameless adventurer who may love her fortune better than herself."

"That would be as cruel a neglect as the other," replied the stranger; "and, in my opinion, more culpable of the two."

"So it would."

At that moment the door opened hastily, and a light step was heard, and before the stranger could turn round, a lovely young female rushed to the side of the count, throwing herself on her knees, saying, —

"Oh, heavens! my dear father, what has happened? Are you hurt? For Heaven's sake, my dear father, what is the matter?"

"Little or nothing, my dear Isabella."

"But you are wounded. Ah! there is blood! My God! my God!"

"Hush, Isabella. I am wounded, but not hurt seriously."

"I pray Heaven it may be so. But what sacrilegious hand could be raised against you? You have wronged no one."

"I am not aware of having done so, certainly," said the count; "but that does not always give any security to the wealthy. They will sometimes destroy them from motives apart from individual revenge."

"The monsters! But have the villains been secured?"

"One has paid the forfeit of his life for his temerity and villany; the rest fled."

"Ah! what will these assassins not risk?"

"Well, my dear Isabella, I have answered your inquiries, and now, perhaps, you will see if you be alone with me."

"Alone with you!" repeated Isabella, not quite comprehending the words; but she looked up, and her eyes encountered those of the stranger, who was gazing earnestly upon her, and she started, as she rose and said, —

"Excuse me, signor, excuse me — I knew not any one was present."

"Nay," said the stranger, "filial love and respect need no excuse, signora. Do not think so badly of me as to imagine I can think otherwise than you were actuated by the tenderest impulses."

"Your kindness, sir —"

"Isabella," said the count, interrupting her, "but for this gentleman's timely and efficient aid, I should at this moment have been a corpse in the streets of Venice."

"You, my father?"

"Yes, my child. This signor came up just as I was wounded and beaten down, and saved me from death. He killed one of my assailants, while he put to flight the other two, who left their dead companion in the streets. Thank him, my child, for he is my preserver, and he deserves thanks for the deed as well as for the bravery with which it was done, for he ran great risks in such odds."

"He must. Signor, I know not how to thank you or what to say; the greatness of the obligation paralyzes me, and I have not words to tell you how grateful I feel for your goodness and courage; but 'tis an obligation that can never be forgotten or ever repaid — it is impossible."

"My dear signora, permit me to say you rate my services too highly."

"Nay, that is quite impossible; for my father's life I prize far before my own — before anybody in the world; and to save that is to lay me under the heaviest obligation it is possible to impose upon me."

"Say no more, signora; I will not underrate it after what you have said; but you must say as little about it as you will. I am happy, however, to have done any act worthy of your thanks."

CLXXI.

THE OPINIONS OF DR. PILLETTO. — THE STRANGER'S ACCOUNT OF HIMSELF. —
THE WELCOME OF THE SIGNORA.

A T THAT MOMENT the door opened, and a servant announced the arrival of a leech, the famous Doctor Pilletto, who forthwith entered the apartment, and advanced towards the couch on which the wounded man lay.

"Oh, doctor, do what you can for my father," said Signora Isabella.

"I will, signora," replied the doctor. "I will; but what are his hurts or his disease? for I see he has been taken very badly; but why this paleness? You appear to have lost blood."

"I have bled, doctor, and I want you to dress my wound. I am hurt in the side here, and but for my friend here I should have been hurt mortally."

"It was not a duel then?" said the doctor.

"No, no, doctor, no, no; it was an attempt at assassination, and I have escaped the death some one with more enmity than courage had doomed me to; but, at the same time, I am free, and one of his agents has perished."

"'Tis but just," said the doctor; "but I must now see the wound; with your good leave, we'll strip the wounded part and apply bandages to it, so as to secure it; after which something else must be done."

The wounded Polidori was stripped, and, after some exertion, the wound was dressed, and all bleeding stopped.

"What is your candid opinion concerning my wound, doctor?" inquired the count, "What do you think will be the result? I would be truly informed of whatever probability of danger there may be remote or immediate, as the case may be; tell me, I beseech you, doctor."

"I will, count."

"I have those things to do which are important, and the execution of them depends upon your answer; so do not mislead me."

"I will not; I cannot form so clear a judgment of your case as I can in a few days hence, when I may see the progress of the wound towards healing; though at present I see no signs of danger, yet some may come."

"You do not consider the wound dangerous of itself?" said the stranger.

"No, not of itself; but it is so close to a mortal part that it cannot be considered free from danger; indeed, it may become so. A little more on one side would have made it quickly fatal; but, as it is, if it heal well, there will be no danger. You must keep your couch for some days."

"That will be a lighter evil than any other," replied the count.

"You have lost much blood, and that alone will make you very weak, and it will take some time before you will be entirely recovered from your present state, and then your wound will probably be healed."

"And what you appear to think may be dangerous, is only any possible interruption from the wound itself."

"It does so happen sometimes from bodily infirmity, it shews itself in healing, and the wound, which now appears healthy, may turn to gangrene, and then the worst may be apprehended."

"It may," said the stranger; "but these things are only the worst that may happen in extreme cases."

"Exactly," said the leech.

"And you have seen nothing in this case to induce you to anticipate any such result as this — it is only what may happen."

"That is all. It appears to me that all is well at present."

"Then I think the count had better be left to himself in quiet, and he may have a good mind upon his recovery."

"It will be best," said the doctor.

"I am fatigued and sleepy," said the count; "I would be alone. Daughter, you must entertain this gentleman as I would do were I able to do so. Signor, the signora will do the office of hostess — excuse so cold a welcome."

"Name it not," said the stranger. "I am well cared for. A welcome from such a one is well worth the acceptance of a prince, much less that of a stranger unknown in Venice. I thank you for it."

"Say no more on that head," said the count. "I came here almost a refugee, and quite a stranger myself."

"Will you come this way, signor," said Signora Isabella; "we will leave my poor father to himself, he will sleep."

The stranger rose, and Doctor Pilletto also, both following the signora, who led them into a separate, but splendid apartment, and entreated them to sit down, and apologised for her own want of spirits to entertain them suitably.

"For that matter," said the doctor, "I am by no means surprised; for such a mishap can never be heard of without producing lowness of spirits."

"And such a misfortune is always productive of grief," said the stranger. "Signora, say no more, I would not interfere with your grief. I do not wish to stop it, and shall feel myself a bar to your own feelings if you say any more. I am made welcome, and feel myself so."

"You are, sir — your kindness deserves no less; but I pray you tell me how this affair occurred, in which you have been of such signal service to my father, in saving his life?"

"To tell you that, signora, I must first tell you who and what I am."

"I do not wish to be thought unduly curious," replied signora.

"Not at all. I am bound to acknowledge you have a right to it, for you have no introduction with me which usually supplies the place of an account of who and what we are; therefore I'll tell you, though I cannot boast of being more than a simple chevalier of now no fortune, having left my country because I raised my voice against the abuses of state; therefore I am but a nameless and fortuneless stranger."

"Many a worthy gentleman has been in such a plight before now," observed the doctor. "I have known many such."

"And I am one. Not that I am without means," added the stranger; "I have been lucky enough to provide against such a calamity as that which has befallen me, though not to the extent I could have wished."

"You are fortunate, chevalier."

"I am so far. I came but this morning

to Venice; I landed here, and agreed to meet the captain of the vessel, who promised to meet me on the Rialto, to conduct me to some quiet and respectable changehouse where I could lodge."

"And he met you not?"

"No. While I was waiting for him, I heard a cry for help, and found, upon running up, the Count Polidori beaten to the earth, beset by three villains, who had already wounded him in the manner you have seen; and I at that time stepped up, and, being unexpected, the men were confused, and one of them fell, mortally wounded; and, after a little further desperate fighting, they all fled."

"It was fortunate you yourself were not beaten down too with such odds; for these men are usually desperate."

"True; but, you see, one was gone, and they could not tell how it might be with the count—they did not know how far he might be able to join in the fray again, and if he were to do so, there would immediately be an equality between us, and such men do not seek such a fight."

"Truly not, chevalier," replied the signora—"truly not. When they are safe and secure in their deeds of blood, they will perpetrate them; but in fair contest such men never shine—their deeds are of darkness."

"Most true—most true."

"But they have a deal of ferocity," said the stranger; "and, when they can, will pour out blood like water; but what amazes me is, that one like the count, your father, should have been beset by such villains. They must have had some object to accomplish in getting rid of him by such means."

"Private enmity."

"Indeed! It must be a bad state of things."

"It is, chevalier. It is a sign of great degeneracy in the state; but it is so. For gold you can procure the death of any man in Venice."

"Horrible!" said the stranger. "I have heard of such things; but I deemed them fabulous, or, at least, overrated."

"No, no—I fear not; and yet, who could have an enmity so deep as only to be healed by blood? and yet, the good and great have as many enemies as the wicked, for they are always opposed to each other."

"Undoubtedly," said the doctor; "good and bad are always antagonists."

"Exactly. What, however, is the worst in these cases is, the bad very often get the better of the good, which is the reverse of what ought to be done; because, you see, if we are to suppose that there is a power above that rules men's actions, surely we might expect to see goodness manifest in the majority of cases; whereas, we usually see, to a much greater extent, the success of evil."

"Not always."

"Not always, certainly," said the doctor; "but the exception proves the rule. Goodness ought to be the great object of men's lives; but it is not; yet it ought to rule, and we must endeavour to be ruled by it, despite the way of the world, which is often, as we daily see, the reverse of what it ought to be."

"But," added the chevalier, "when ambition rules the minds of men, you will find that all other principles give way."

"It is so; but why, I cannot see."

"Because 'tis the master emotion of the mind," said the stranger.

"And ambition appears to possess the souls of those who govern, whether for good or for evil," said the signora. "Some are ambitious of being rulers — some of being conquers, and some of politicians; but they are all moved to it by ambition."

"Aye," said the stranger, "the lover is ambitious of the smiles of his mistress, though ill fortune will, now and then, deny him the good luck to win them."

CLXXII.

THE COUNT POLIDORI'S RECOVERY. — THE INTERVIEW WITH THE SIGNORA ISABELLA. — THE CONSENT..

A FEW DAYS' CONFINEMENT placed the count beyond the reach of danger. His wound healed rapidly and favourably, but which was more than anticipated by the cautious leech, who abstained from saying so, but took his daily seat beside his patient's bed, and, with his prosy and imperturbable gravity, he continued to give his advice.

"Count," he said, " your wound is healing."

"I feel it is so," said the count.

"But you must be cautious. I would not have you be too sanguine, or trust your feelings too much."

"I do not; but I may take wine?"

"Indeed, I would recommend you not to do so; for wine is inflammatory, and you are likely to suffer for it."

"And yet I took a bottle last evening."

"Last evening, count?" said the physician.

"Yes; I speak truly."

"I doubt it not; but it was very imprudent — very imprudent, indeed; for, though half a bottle may do no hurt to a man in full health, yet a whole can do him no good, even if it do him no harm; but, in your case, it is dangerous."

"It might be; but surely the danger is past now?"

"If you have taken it over twelve hours — though four-and-twenty would be better."

"It is over twelve hours."

"'Tis well; but it was hazardous; you are fast getting well, and, as it happens, you have no fever, or other evil changes about you; therefore, you may continue your wine, but not in such quantities."

"I will be more cautious; but, Pilletto, what is your opinion of my guest?"

"Your preserver?"

"Yes; the same."

"He is one of the most learned men I ever met with; even professed scholars have not been found so full of knowledge."

"That speaks something for his youth."

"Most undoubtedly."

"But what think you of him as a man of the world?"

"I think he has a vast fund of information; he has had an enlarged experience of society, and has visited, I think, all the continent of Europe; he understands their languages and manners, too, and has the appearance of a traveller, and a man used to the best and most distinguished society."

"That is just my opinion of him."

"I understand he is from France."

"Yes."

"A refugee, in point of fact, I suppose, without means."

"No, he appears to have means, and hopes that times my so alter to permit his return, and the resumption of his former fortune."

"I understand as much, and he has spoken of people whom I know well in France, that would not associate with any beneath their degree; and he has told me things they would have divulged to none, save their equals and families."

"It is my opinion of him."

THE DOCTOR TOOK HIS LEAVE, and the count was again left to himself, and he began evidently to ponder over something in his mind, which appeared to demand his attention, and he, for some time, sat immoveable.

"My daughter," he murmured, "is a rich reward even for such a deed. I do not pit my life against hers; no, no; she is by far the most valuable; she I love more than life, and would provide for her in a manner that shall procure her future happiness, rather than her immediate approval.

"The dear girl does not well understand these matters; she does not know that present pleasure may be followed by future pain. She knows not that we should forgo the present, to ensure future happiness."

He paused a moment, and then he continued,—

"But I cannot be mistaken in this man. No, he has done a deed, which,

though I value it not at so high a price, yet gratitude impose upon me the necessity of showing the highest consideration. She is fancy-free; and I do not see there will be any difficulty in the way whatever."

At that moment the door opened, and Signora Isabella entered, and advanced towards the couch on which he lay.

"My father!"

"Ah, Isabella, I was but then thinking of you."

"Of me, father? I come to see how you are. Our good guest and preserver had been telling me he is quite sure you are much better than Doctor Pilletto will admit; for he is slow and cautious to a degree."

"My dear, he is quite right — I feel it."

"Oh, how joyful I am!"

"What think you of our guest, Isabella? Do you not think him a man well worthy of our warmest esteem and gratitude?"

"Indeed he is, father — he is noble."

"I think so — the true nobility of soul can be seen in him; to such a man as the chevalier, would I see my Isabella united; to such a man could I confide my daughter's happiness, for he would secure it."

"What mean you, father?"

"That the stranger, of whom you speak so highly, is to be your future husband; the preserver of the father will not act unkindly by the child."

"My father, I am stunned."

"Yes, my dear daughter, I have fully settled this matter in my own mind; he has asked your hand — go see him — you have my blessing. I am sure he will be happy. Isabella, you never disobeyed your father; such an act would be the cruelest stab that ever was planted in my bosom."

"But when," said Isabella, almost trembling; "but when will this be? When am I to be given away, father, as you would a present of flowers?"

"Isabella, when have I deserved, when have I had such an answer from thee? Let me have no more of this."

"But when have you fixed as a time upon which I am to be sent away from home to strangers?"

"You will not leave this palace, Isabella; you and your husband will always be here, and I shall have the satisfaction of seeing the happiness I have planned and made. He will be a father to the child, as well as a husband."

"I do not wish for any such change. I am happy, but shall be otherwise, if I am compelled to wed."

"Compelled, Isabella, compelled! Do you speak of being forced, when I wish it? Now that I have settled it in my own mind, love and duty to me, and gratitude to this gentleman, all conspire to point out how you should act."

"But when, father, when?"

"To-morrow."

"To-morrow!" repeated Isabella, in mournful accents.

"Yes, my child; 'tis better done at once — 'twill, at all events, save any of those unnecessary thoughts that might disturb you."

"My father! my father!" said the young lady, as she sunk upon her knees before him.

"Well, my child?"

"Pardon me for once begging a favour of you."

"What mean you by such words?"

"I wish a longer interval to be allowed me before I am — I am —"

"Married," said her father.

"Yes, father; that is the dreadful word."

"Isabella, mind, my love, what my wishes are."

"I have heard them, father; but give me a week — indeed, you cannot decently bring this matter to a conclusion before the end of that time. I have had no previous warning from you, or this stranger, that such a thing was in contemplation."

"If I grant it you, my Isabella, I must be obeyed."

"You shall be obeyed, father," said Isabella, with an effort, "if it cost me my life, and it will be near it; but let me keep my room until that period is up, and then do with me what you will."

"Be it so, Isabella; though it will look ungracious to our guest, yet I will endeavour to excuse you with the best grace I can."

The Lady Isabella was deathly pale, and, as she rose, she staggered, and could scarce support herself out of the apartment.

CLXXIII.

THE WEDDING MORNING. — THE NEW ARRIVAL. — THE DISAPPEARANCE OF THE VAMPYRE BRIDEGROOM.

THE SIGNORA RETIRED to her own chamber, and remained there for many hours; but during that time two messengers had left the mansion secretly, and then all was still. The lovely and beautiful Isabella, however, was not to be seen in her usual walks, or at her father's board, as was her wont. She was only seen within the precincts of her own apartments, pallid, sad, and sorrowful.

"Your daughter, count," said the stranger, one morning, "does not appear as usual. I trust she is quite well?"

"Yes; quite well."

"I hope I have given no cause of offence if so, I hope I may be informed of my error, that I may speedily amend it."

"There is none, chevalier; but my daughter, Isabella, has asked a week's preparation for the nuptials — which week she will pass in her own apartments secluded, and at the end of which time, she leaves them for your protection, and which will, I trust, be to her happiness."

"It shall be my business to make her happy, and, for want of good will and hearty endeavour, she shall never lack content and bliss. I have every presage of a most happy and felicitous life in the future. I am sure she will be happy."

"It is my great hope, chevalier; it is the one object of my life. I would it were settled, and the affair over. I should die unhappy if I thought poor Isabella in the hands of any one who would not use her as she deserved to be. She is of herself a treasure."

"She is — she is."

"And when she is once a wife, she will not look for a father's protection, neither will she need it. My death, when it does happen, will be a great and heavy blow; but it will be less when she has the comfort and consolation of a husband to console her for what would otherwise be irreparable."

"Yes, it would have the effect of deadening the blow, and of shortening the duration of its intensity, though it will be by no means prevented."

"I cannot say I should desire it."

"No, certainly not; and Signora Isabella never could forget such a parent."

"I have done my duty, I hope."

"And may congratulate yourself, count; but then, with regard to Isabella, she will meet me as usual here on the day of the ceremonial."

"Most assuredly."

"And I am to be denied her company till then?"

"Yes; she will meet you on the morning at the altar."

"Be it so — but I could have been happy in her society. At any rate I must be so, by reflecting that I shall soon be the favoured, happy husband of Isabella, for with her my happiness will be complete."

"And my happiness will be complete, in knowing hers is so."

"I could have wished that some of those who have known me in France had been here to see my happiness; but that cannot be."

"Could you not send to them?"

"There would not be time for their return. And, moreover, if there had been, I question whether I ought to hold any communication with them, lest I bring them under the ban of the government, and I may not do that."

"Truly, you have the same feelings as I used to have; but I have long since ceased to feel any of that kind of interest."

"Time cures that."

"It does; and you will find it will heal all those wounds which such a separation from your country causes you."

"I hope so. My offences there they will never forgive."

THUS CONVERSED the stranger and the count, and thus six days passed, during which time the Signora Isabella was seen by none save her attendants, who were few, and most of her time was spent in tears and prayers.

She had a heart full of grief, but whe dared not disobey her father, he whom she loved so well, and whom she had never thought for one moment as being opposed to her own ideas of propriety and her own wishes. She had always been taught to suppress her own, and submit to his.

Thus it was now, at the eleventh hour, she had no means of fortifying herself in any preconceived liking she may have had.

Submission was all she had learned — a blind and willing submission to a fond and doating parent. She knew no other course of action.

Her heart, however, had other yearnings. She had loved another; but she knew not how to act. She dared not even entertain the thought of throwing herself at her father's feet, and imploring him to save her from perpetual sorrow — much less did she think of opposing him; but she had done this much.

In the first moment of her terror and anguish, she had written off to her brother, informing him of her danger; but, at the same time, she had advised nothing, and expressed no wish — only told him the fact and her fears.

THE WEDDING MORNING arrived, and the house of the count gave indications of the festivity; and, with the day, came guests richly dressed, and the bells rang a merry peal upon the occasion, and the count was in high spirits; but the bride was not seen.

"How is Signora Isabella, your daughter?" inquired one of the guests.

"She is as well as maiden modesty will permit."

"I have not seen her."

"Nor I."

"Nor you!" replied the guest, astonished.

"No; she has secluded herself, but will appear presently, when the bell rings for the service. The fact is, she cannot leave her father, even for the arms of a husband, without feeling a grief for the change."

"I hope she will be happy."

"I have no doubt of it; the man is worthy of her."

"And capable of making her happy, I hope."

"I have no doubt of that."

"Hark! the bell sounds; is that the signal?"

"Yes; follow on. I will bring my daughter forth;" and, as he spoke, he left the guests, who hurried to the chapel, and found the stranger awaiting his bride with some impatience.

He acknowledged the courtesy of those who came to him, and looked towards a small door, which presently opened, and the count and his daughter appeared. She was of marble paleness, and no signs of happiness were seen in her face. She trembled, and her whole soul seemed to be intent on something afar from her presence.

She lifted her eyes and gazed upon the throng; but apparently saw none — or not those whom she wished. Her father spoke to her; she heaved a deep sigh, and appeared to be resigned to her fate.

THE CEREMONY COMMENCED, and Isabella stood; but her eyes occasionally sought the chapel door; and in a few moments more, before the important part was concluded, a bustle took place near the door, and, immediately afterwards, some officers, in the Venetian uniform, entered the chapel, among whom was the young count, Isabella's brother, and with him a young officer, into whose arms she instantly threw herself, and fainted.

"Father," said the young count — "father, this must not be."

"Why not, my son?" said the count.

"Because my sister loves another, and yon man is a monster."

"What mean you, sir?" said the chevalier. "If you were other than what you are, your words would beget a different answer."

"You are a vampyre," replied a young Neapolitan, who stepped forward. "I knew you before. Know you not the holy father whom you murdered?"

"'Tis false. I'll bring one to prove it."

As the chevalier spoke, he crossed the chapel, and left the place; but he did not appear again; and, upon inquiry, he had quitted the palace in a gondola, and never reappeared.

The expression of horror in the grazier's face, and the swelling of his eyes almost out of his head, at once showed them there was something extraordinary, and they both mutually turned round, and to their extreme terror they perceived the very man, or his double, they had left dead upon the spot where the grazier had seen him ... (see page 1139)

PART IX:

The Vampyre and the Highwaymen.

CLXXIV.

THE TWO HIGHWAYMEN. — THE MURDER AT THE GIBBET'S FOOT. — THE RIDE TO THE GOLDEN PIPPIN.

THE EVENING SET in a stormy mood; sudden, gusty showers rattled against the traveller; whilst the wind swept over the country, bending the tall trees, and whistling round the peasant's cot, and making the chimneys appear as if they were the residences of imprisoned spirits, which moaned and groaned most dismally to hear.

The clouds came rapidly across the sky; now darkening the earth, and now they had fled past, leaving the moonbeams pouring a flood of light upon the fields and roadways; but this was soon followed by another darkness, a cold rain, and rushing wind, the night being inclement and very boisterous — not to say a night too bad to permit travelling.

It was late on such a night, when down a lone cross-road a single horseman might be seen to ride slowly and carefully. He was wrapped up in a large cloak, and rode a powerful horse, and appeared to be somewhat tired. There was much difficulty in travelling over a bad road, that was loose and shifty, with here and there a slough of some magnitude.

In a very wild and desolate spot stood a mound of stones that had been heaped at the foot of a gibbet, and had been collected there in consequence of the unpopularity of the occupant of the instrument of punishment.

On the gibbet, swinging to and fro, was the body of a malefactor, hung in chains — an awful and disgusting spectacle — whose death no one regretted, inasmuch as he was the terror of the whole neighbourhood.

It was the body of a highwayman, or of a robber, who had committed all kinds of depredations, and several murders. He was the son of a person of property, but addicted to vicious courses, and, to support them, he had recourse to robbery and murder.

Several of his former friends were robbed, and at length his own father fell by his hands, when he refused to give up his purse in the road at this spot. His own son shot him through the heart.

This was the last crime he ever committed; for he was taken and tried, when enough was proved that would have

hung a hundred men; and there was not one man who could, or who would, speak one word in his favour. He was executed; and so detested was he by all, that every one who came by this spot threw a stone, until it grew, by these means, a goodly heap, which remained a memento of their hate.

It was this spot the stranger was nearing, and to which he appeared to look up with some degree of either curiosity, or interest; but, before he got there, there was another horseman riding along the country lane, and who would arrive there about the same time as the first; but when he came there, it was easy to perceive that he was not alone, but another horseman was in waiting beneath some trees, and hidden from the traveller.

In a few moments more, the traveller reached the spot, and, looking up at the dead body that was swinging to and fro in the night air, the other horseman rode up; upon which the traveller was about to push his horse forward at an increased speed, when he found that there was not space enough.

"Which side do you take?" he inquired of the stranger.

"Stand and deliver!" was the reply.

"That is uncivil," replied the stranger, "and a request that I do not feel at all disposed to consent to."

"Deliver your money and a pocket-book, or you are a dead man."

"Nay," said the stranger; "I have means of defence, too."

And, as he spoke, he pulled out a bright, double-barrelled pistol, which he levelled and cocked, saying, as he very leisurely did so,—

"Beware! you are playing with a determined man. I am not disposed to play. Get out of my way, or you are a dead man!"

"Ha, ha, ha!" laughed the other, and made way at the same moment, thus bringing himself alongside the traveller, leaving him room to go on. "You are not to be frightened—well, well, go on."

The traveller put his spurs to his horse, but at the same moment received a bullet from the treacherous highway-man.

"Ha!" cried the traveller, putting his hand to his side, and in a moment more he staggered and fell over the side of the horse on to the ground.

"Ha, ha, ha!" said the highwayman, who immediately dismounted; but before he could search the body, the other horseman came up at a gallop.

"Well, Fred, have you quieted him?"

"I have."

"Resisted, then?"

"Yes. Have you got your lantern?"

"Yes; but it is not yet lighted. But that is soon done."

"Then let us have it as quick as you can; for he has fallen down here in a slough, and I should like to get the money without more mire than I am obliged to put up with."

"Here it is," said the other, handing the lantern—a small one, which he had lighted by means of some chemical matches.

The highwayman took the lantern, and, after some examination, he secured the pocketbook and the purse, and having done this, he examined the fingers, but saw no rings and no watch, and he said to his companion,—

"Just come here. Did you ever see such a set of features as these? They are truly strange and singular; I could never forget them."

"Indeed! I must have a look at them," said his companion, dismounting and bending over the body; and when he looked at them, he said,—

"I saw that man to-day where I dined, and thought he took the other road, and there waited for him."

"Did you, though?"

"Yes, till I was tired; and then I came across the country in search of you, but did not expect you to have any quarry."

"Did you ever see such a countenance? it is most strange and ghastly."

"Yes, it is; but he has died a violent death, you see, and therefore there is much to be done by way of allowance."

"Yes, yes, I know all that; but the nose, mouth, and teeth—"

"They are not the most agreeable in the world, certainly. Well, well, it don't matter; you have done all your business with him, have you not?"

"I have got all, I believe," said the other. "He has no watch or chain—not even a ring has he got on his finger."

"Perhaps you'll find enough in his purse and pocket-book to console you; though I must say, Ned, that he dined very sparingly. But no matter the amount; ride on, for you know it is not a good plan to stand longer here than necessary; for we may have other riders down upon us."

"Not very likely, on this road, and as this hour; but 'tis bad. I'm off, and he will remain behind till found by some frightened peasant or other, who will go to the nearest market town, with a frightful account."

"Ride away; I hear horses' feet, I think."

"I am ready; forward! ho!"

The two highwaymen rode off at a rapid rate, conversing as they went; but yet it was in suppressed tones for some distance; and after some riding, one of them pulled up his horse, partially, saying,—"Well, I don't think it wise we should thus wear our steeds out; there is no need of our riding for life; our horses never ought to be put to their mettle, unless there be plenty of occasion, which there is not."

"No — all is right, to-night."

"Have you done much lately, Ned?"

"No; I have been rather upon the seek than find; I have been looking out brightly, but have not been successful."

"I have myself only done moderately; but I have done better than I should have done, because I was fortunate enough to come across a fat grazier who had more money than any three or four persons I have met lately."

"Your fortune is somewhat like mine."

"You have met with little good then, Ned."

"Indeed, I have not; but it is a long lane that has no turning,"

"Yes; indeed, it is."

"However, I hope this queer-looking customer will reward one for one's pains; if you can but keep the game a going, you are sure to succeed in the end; 'tis only two years or better since I first began to ride."

"That is, put a period to other people's riding."

"Exactly."

"Well, then, where do you intend to put up for the night? for I suppose you do not intend to stay out all night any more than myself."

"No; I think of going on until I come to the Golden Pippin, where I intend to stay for the night. The landlord can wink hard at his friends, and not know they are in the house, or he can tell them a thing if they want to know anything at all to their interest."

"He's the sort of man; I know him. I was thinking of going there; I don't know better or snugger quarters than are to be had at his hostel."

"Then we'll have a good supper and a bottle at the Golden Pippin."

"With all my heart; but you don't think there'll be any danger of our being pursued for this matter."

"Oh, dear, no; the direct road lies another way, and we shall be quite fifteen miles from the spot where the body lies."

"So far."

"Yes; we have come over the ground very rapidly, and have gone more than two-thirds of that distance. When we get there we shall be safe, easy, and comfortable; and right good wines are there to be had at the Golden Pippin."

CLXXV.

THE HORRORS OF THE NIGHT. — THE DISCOVERY IN THE ROAD. — CONTENTION BETWEEN MAN AND HORSE. — COMFORTABLE QUARTERS IN THE GOLDEN PIPPIN.

THE MALEFACTOR'S BODY swung to and fro on the gibbet, and the chains squeaked and groaned as the wind impelled the body's motions. The wind itself whistled heedlessly by, and the transient but heavy shower passed on, heedless of the deed of blood that had been perpetrated beneath its monitory shadow.

Now and then there was a little light, and then the body might be seen heaped up, and lying in the mud and mire, which was all discoloured with the blood of the fallen man — he was motionless. The rain fell on him, but it mattered not — the body felt it not. The wind blew the cloak about, but the body remained quiet, and nothing appeared to spare the body.

There was no one nigh; that was a lonely spot, and that was tenanted by two dismal gipsys. The body of the malefactor swung to and fro while the body of the murdered traveller lay quiet enough.

The clouds travelled across the face of the moon, and intercepted her light from the earth; but yet it was light enough at intervals to enable the traveller to see his way on foot, or on horseback.

ABOUT TWO HOURS after that in which the traveller had been stopped and murdered, there came another individual riding towards the scene.

This was a countryman — a grazier, who was well-mounted, and came along at a rapid rate, having a stout trotting nag under him.

When he neared the spot where the murder had been committed, he gave a look up at the disagreeable object — the gibbet — and when he had done so, he put the spur to his horse's side, with the intention of going by at a quickened pace, exclaiming as he did so, —

"This is no pleasant place at nine o'clock at night. I wish I were at the Golden Pippin, instead of here."

As he spoke, he pushed his horse, as he manifested a design to stop; but the animal, instead of going past, reared up.

"Hilloa! brute. What art after now, eh?"

The spur was again applied, but the animal only became more and more unmanageable, and the rider near losing his seat; but he was, nevertheless, the more anxious to get onward, for the neighbourhood was not pleasant; added to which, it was a wet and dismal night, and late for a cross-road.

"Curse you!" muttered the grazier; "what the deuce is the matter with you? — did you never see the gibbet before? If thee hadn't, I should not have been surprised at thee shying at the man swinging on the gibbet; but thee hast done so, and now thee art frightened. Whoa! d — n thee."

He made another attempt to force the

horse by, but it was fruitless, and he was at length unseated into the mire.

"D — n!" muttered the man; "the first time I have been thrown these ten years, drunk or sober, and now I am sober."

This was apparently the first reflection that came to his mind after the first effect of the concussion; he then scratched his head, adjusted his hat, and was getting up, when for a moment his eyes rested on something dark lying in the middle of the road, and at which his horse had in reality shyed.

"Oh!" he exclaimed, with a visible alteration in his demeanour; "that's what Peg shied at, eh? What the devil is it?"

As he muttered these words, his hair began to stand on end; and the more he looked, the greater his apprehension; for he began to think what he wished was further from the fact, though his notions were far from being definite, and he did all he could to dispel the rising terror.

"Why — it ain't — no, it can't be — and yet it must be! What makes 'un lay there — he must be dead, surely!"

Thrice he scrambled to his feet, and then walked a little towards the object against which his horse stood smelling and snorting with evident signs of fear.

"Whoa, brute! What's the matter with thee? — confound thee! But I suppose thee wast frightened."

As the man spoke, he walked up to the animal, and, taking the bridle, he passed it over his arms, and then approached the body.

"Aye, sure enough, he's insensible — if not dead, poor fellow! What can be done — there's no one near at hand to lend assistance?"

He paused to consider what was to be done, when it occurred to him as being the most likely thing that could be done was to probe the unfortunate man; he could not say whether he was dead or alive, from his position in the middle of the road.

"If 'un ain't dead," he argued, "he would come to no harm; for it wasn't every horse that cared as much for a man as Peg did; they might get run over, or cause some desperate accident."

Having made up his mind what to do, he secured Peg, and turned his attention to the body of the stranger, which had been left on its back, with its face upwards, but the wind had blown the cloak over it, and it was not seen by the grazier, who now essayed to move the body.

After some trouble, he succeeded in dragging him there, and propping him up against the bank, upon which grew a stunted hedge, and, when there, he opened the cloak, and looked upon the features of the dead man.

"Well," he muttered; "I never yet saw such a face! I am sure I can never forget that. Of all the ill-looking thieves, he is the worst! but much, I suppose, must be set off on the fact that he is a dead man, and a murdered one, to boot."

There was a strange markedness in the style of features in the dead man, that gave no pleasing impression to the mind; it was one that could not easily be forgotten, especially accompanied by all the horrors of their place and circumstances.

"He has been shot, no doubt," he muttered. "This must be all blood. Aye! in the breast, or thereabouts. Oh! he is dead. Well, I'll ride to the Golden Pippin, and then I'll give them notice of it."

He was just about to turn and mount his horse, when the clouds parted, and the moonbeams, for a few moments, came upon the body, without any hindrance, and the grazier thought he saw a movement.

"It must have been gammon," he muttered. "I'll be off — I'm quite cold and shivery here. I'll go to the Golden Pippin, and get some good cheer, for I'm terribly shaken. Eh! what was that? The devil!"

The latter exclamations were uttered in consequence of the figure turning towards the moon's rays, and then opening its eyes, which had such an effect upon the unfortunate man, that he staggered back terrified.

"Lord have mercy!" he ejaculated. "What's — what's that? He — he's coming to — hilloa, friend! — how are you?"

The figure turned his large motionless eyes upon the terrified man, and they had such an effect upon him, that, despite all he could do to rally himself, he sprang involuntarily to his horse's back, and galloped off furiously.

IT WAS SCARCE AN HOUR before this occurred, when the two highwaymen rode up to the Golden Pippin.

"Hilloa! hilloa! ostler — here!" shouted one of them, and in a few moments more the ostler came out, willing enough.

"Hilloa, Jem! you are sharp to-night. How is it you are not asleep?"

"I was just going to roost, master; but I shall have a job instead, I can see."

"You will; but not an empty handed affair, this time; take care of the nags, and there's a crown for you."

"Thank you, master — you are always generous."

"When I can, Jem; but what company have you in the house?"

"Little to speak of," said the ostler; "about three or four people, as lives about here; but nobody that I know — anybody or anything — only people that have to earn their own living; they are in the kitchen."

"Good fire?"

"Yes."

"Then we will go there, too," said the highwayman; "it's a raw cold night, and one in which a good supper and a good fire will do one good."

The two highwaymen then entered the house, and walked into the kitchen, which was a large room, with beams across the top, and a variety of utensils proper to the place; but the grand feature was the large fire-place, in which burned brightly some good logs, and threw a glowing warmth and bright light over the whole apartment, in which, however, was one candle, as if to be mocked by the light of the fire. The use of this solitary wick was to enable the smokers to light their pipes without stirring, and also to be taken away at a moment's notice for any purpose that might be needed.

The three guests turned their attention to the new comers, without, however, exchanging one word, and the landlord himself arose.

"Oh, landlord," said one of the highwaymen, "I'm glad you have a good fire; 'tis one of the best things, after a cold ride, a man can have met with."

"Except a good hot supper, and a cup afterwards," said his companion.

"All these are very good things in

their way, gentlemen," said the landlord, emptying the ashes of his pipe out into the fireplace by tapping the pipe on the toe of his shoe, and thus dropped the ashes out of danger.

"You are right, landlord," said the other.

"But I always, think, gentlemen," said the landlord gravely, "that they are always a great deal better when they can be had together — they are better for their company's sake — the one helps the other."

"So they do."

"Well, then, let us have them all, old cock, as soon as you please, for we are both cold, tired, and hungry."

"And they are the best accompaniments you can have as a preparatory for all that is to follow."

"Amen! and about it," said the highwayman.

The two new guests sat themselves down in one quarter of the kitchen, and near to a table facing the fire, where they could enjoy its genial warmth, which they appeared to do with much gusto.

Having opened their coats, and taken off their shawls, removed their hats, and sat down in a comfortable manner, they began to look about them.

"Well, Ned, we have made a good exchange."

"How do you mean?"

"Why, we have exchanged the road to comfortable quarters, which, you will, at least, admit, is all the better."

"Yes, much better; though I have ridden many a long and weary a night before now, with the runners at my heels."[*]

"Aye — aye, so have I; but hush — say no more of that there. I have no idea of letting these blacks suspect anything; they are what you call honest men, and men who would give a clue in a moment, if they thought it was wanted."

"I dare say it is so, Ned; but what are you going to have for supper?"

"I don't know. Landlord, what can we have for supper — anything hot?"

"Why," said the landlord, "I can kill a couple of chickens and brander them, or there is some chicken pie, and a cold ham."

"Well, what do you say, Ned?"

"Can't you make the chicken pie warm?"

"It is warm now," said the landlord. "I can't make it quite hot without doing too much; 'tis uncommon good, and has not long been put by from supper; it was made for supper, but there's a good half left."

"Eh? What do you say to chicken pie, Ned?"

"With all my heart; chicken pie let it be, then," replied Ned.

"Well, then, landlord, put the chicken pie on, flanked by the ham — some of your foaming October, you know." [†]

"Aye-aye, sir; some with a head on, that would take a blacksmith's bellows to blow off, it is so strong."

"Ha — ha — ha! that's the strike for us."

The landlord now arose, and set about getting the necessary articles, and spreading them upon a table before the

---

[*] *A reference to the "Bow Street Runners," England's first professional police force, established in 1749 to pursue and arrest highway robbers.*

[†] *October ale was the strong, malty kind brewed just after the barley harvest was in, with a flavour along the lines of what we know today as barley-wine.*

two guests, who were nothing loath to see the expedition that he had made to please them.

"I think," said the landlord, "you will say you never eat such chickens; they are my hatching, and have been well fed; they have been well killed, cooked, and I hope, will be well eaten."

"That is our part of the business, landlord; and if they are such as you speak of, why, you may depend upon our doing our duty by them."

"And the ham is my own breeding and curing."

"Better and better,—and the October?"

"Why, I am just going to get that. What say you to a tankard?"

"Yes, a foaming tankard."

"Yes, gentlemen, I will obtain what you want; it is in beautiful condition, and when chilled, will give you a cream as thick as new cheese; and as mild as new milk."

CLXXVI.

THE GRAZIER'S RELATION, AND HIS FIRST TERRORS. — THE EFFECTS OF GOOD CHEER AND THE SUDDEN INTERRUPTION TO A PLEASANT PARTY.

THE LANDLORD WAS NOT long gone for the October; he came back with a placid smile and a smacking of his lips, when he shut the door behind him, and then deliberately placing the candlestick down, he said, handing them the tankard,—

"There, gentlemen, if you find any better brewed than that in the three adjoining counties, why, you may take measure for my coffin, for I won't live after I am told there is any so good anywhere else."

"We will not take your word, landlord," said one of the highwaymen, putting the tankard to his lips, which act produced an approving nod from the jolly landlord, who said, with much encouragement,—

"That's right; never trust nobody; that's my motto, and I chalks it up over the fire-place, and acts upon it — try for

yourself, and then you won't be deceived. What's your opinion upon that now, sir?"

"Never drank its equal, ever here."

"I thought you'd say so; it comes out of a particular cask — one as I puts by for myself; but you have ridden hard, and I thought a brew of an extra strike would be an acceptable drink."

"You are right. It is cold and very wet. I'm as tired as if I had ridden far — the wind has blown me about so."

"Ah, don't you hear how it roars in the chimney?"

"So it does. What do you think of the brew, Ned — ain't it first rate?"

"Indeed it is: I never had any equal to it. I tell you what, landlord, it will make an excellent night-cap, for a man who has taken a glass or two of this, would not be better able to keep his saddle."

"No; it's lucky we intend putting up for the night here; you have beds."

"Yes, good, and well aired."

"That is capital. Well, your chicken-pie is good, landlord, your ham good, and the October excellent; and now — what's that?"

At that moment there was a sound of horses' feet galloping furiously towards the houses; and they had not listened long before they came close to the door, and then there was evidently a sudden pull-up.

"Hilloa! what is that?" said his companion.

"I think it is somebody pulled up at the door," said the landlord; "whoever they are they have come in haste."

The two highwaymen half rose, but a look at each other caused them to resume their seats, and in another moment there was a loud shouting, and a call for the ostler; but there was no one at hand.

"Where is that Jim got to — I must go and see after him, at all events — he won't come if I don't."

So saying, he walked away whilst the guests remained silent watching the actions of the two highwaymen.

"It is but a single horseman," said the first.

"No," said the other; "but still he may be mischievous; and yet I can hardly think he would venture here at such a time; besides, it can't be known; we are much better here than anywhere else."

"I think so; we have nothing to fear."

"Nothing."

At that moment the landlord retired; and, at the same time, the door was suddenly opened, and the grazier entered the kitchen. He glanced around him, much confused. The fire and light, no doubt, had some share in that; but he stared, and appeared terrified, and all splashed over.

"Where's the ostler?" he cried out.

"Here I be," said the worthy behind.

"Look after my horse; he is very hardly ridden. See to him, that's a good fellow," said the grazier.

"Yes; I'll see to 'un," said Jem, who departed with the animal.

"Landlord — landlord!"

"Yes; here I am, Master Green — here am I!"

"Give me something strong; I'm half dead. I'm cold, and I'm frightened, and that is the truth. Where's the fire?"

"Why, Master Green, I never saw you in this state before. Give me your hand, Master Green. I'll show you the fire," said the landlord, holding out his hand to Green. "Why, you are cold — what has happened?"

"You shall hear — you shall hear," said the half-terrified Green. "Only give me a toss of brandy, and get me a supper, and then I shall be able to tell you more about it. At present I can say nothing."

"Well, that is pretty well for a man that can't speak," said the landlord. "You are getting better, Mr. Green."

"I hope I shall; the fire is comfortable."

"Here's some good brandy; take a gill, man. It won't hurt you on such an occasion as this. I have seen you do as much before; but, as for supper, why I can't say much. These two gentlemen have had the only thing I had in the house, and, save the ham, I doubt much if there will be any left."

"If the gentlemen will join us, he is welcome to take a share of what we have," said one of the highwaymen. "Here will be enough for us all, I dare say, sir, if you do not object to our company."

"Thank you — thank you," said Green. "I will accept of your offer gladly; for I have had a long ride, and have had much that is uncomfortable to put up with, to see and to fear. Lord have mercy on me, say I!"

"Well, what is the matter, Mr. Green?"

"Why," said Mr. Green, as he, between his words, poked in large mouthfuls of food, and now and then washed it down by the aid of the October. "You all of you know the highwayman's corner, about fifteen miles from here?"

"Yes," said the landlord, "I know it well; there's a chap hanging up in chains there, now, at this present day, that is, if nobody hasn't run away with it, or it hasn't been blown down."

"Exactly. Well, that's the spot; there's been another dreadful murder been done there. Oh! it was dreadful."

"Well, did you see it?"

"Yes; I did."

"What! the murder!" said both highwaymen at once.

"No; the body — I only saw the body."

"Where was it lying?"

"Stop, stop a bit — not so fast," said Mr. Green, who was eating very fast indeed, but paused a moment. "You must not ask too many questions at once, because I have one way of telling a tale, and you'll spoil it."

"Well, go on your own way."

"Well, then, listen. I was coming along at a rattling pace, I can tell you, for I was late, and tired, as it was. When I had reached the gallows, I looked up at the body swinging in the wind, and creaking and screaming on its rusty swivels; but I had scarcely done so, when my horse

shyed, and very nearly landed me in the mud, but I contrived to keep my seat, though not without trouble."

"What! at the dead man?" inquired one of the highwaymen.

"Aye," replied his companion. "I am sure they ought not to put men up there like scarecrows, to frighten horses with; for my part, I never pass it but my horse snorts and bolts, and I am obliged to be wary."

"I don't know much about that. I have come by without my nag being any the worse. At all events, I thought there was something in his shying at the gallows, and I tried to push him by, but he would not go."

"What did you do?"

"Why, I was obliged to get down," said the grazier.

"Thrown?"

"No, no."

"Forced to get down, you mean," said the highwayman.

"Why, in some sort of way I did feel myself compelled to get down, because the brute wouldn't go a-head, and I saw something on the ground as the clouds cleared away a little, and showed me that there was something suspicious in the middle of the road, very much like a bundle of clothes."

"Indeed!" said the landlord, "what was it?"

"I'll tell you, in course. Now, you see, I saw the animal would not move, so I got off to see what was the matter."

"Forced off," added the highwayman.

"D — n it, man, what can it matter; then I got off," said the grazier, getting into a passion, and then, after a pause, which he employed in taking a long pull at the October, and then wiping his lips, he continued,—

"What is the matter now?" thought I; "so I went to the object, and found it was a man rolled up in a cloak in the middle of the road, dead."

"Dead?"

"Aye, dead as a door nail."

"Lor!" said the highwayman. "Why, then he must have been murdered, I suppose?"

"You may take your davy of that," said the grazier; "but I tried to wake him up, but he was not to be disturbed, so I dragged him to the bank, where I left him."

"Where was he hurt?"

"Shot right in the side, or stabbed, I don't know which, but that's where the blood came from, so I was sure he was dead; but when I removed the cloak from his face, I saw he had as ugly a set of features as a man can desire—a long, peculiar face, large, but thin nose, an awkward set of teeth, with one or two projecting in front, and oh! such eyes, that is when he opened them."

"Opened them," said the highwayman; "both?"

"Opened them," repeated the landlord; "why, did you not tell me he was dead?"

"Aye; but when the moonlight came upon him, he opened his eyes. Oh! what eyes—why, they were like a pair of enormous great fish eyes—cod's eyes, that had become suddenly lighted up, or the moonlight reflected back from the bottom of a new tin saucepan, and then you have 'em."

"The devil," said the highwayman; "and what did you do?"

"Why, I came away as fast as I could. I wasn't to be done by a dead man. I didn't wait to see more than that. He turned round and stared at me. He was so horrible, that I got upon my horse the best way I could, and came on here as fast as the animal would come."

"The body, I dare say, rolled over, and you thought it moved of itself."

"I know better; besides, it opened its eyes."

"The moon shone on them, and you thought he looked at you. You were terror-stricken, and that is the truth of it."

"Then I know better," said the grazier, doggedly; "it ain't anything of the kind. I know it ain't a matter that happens every day, and that's why you don't believe it, and don't understand it, but I know I'm right."

"House, here, house! ostler!" shouted a loud, authoritative voice without the door of the inn, which caused them all to start and listen for a repetition of the same sounds to prove that they were not illusory.

CLXXVII.

THE MYSTERIOUS STRANGER'S ARRIVAL. — THE CONSTERNATION OF THE GUESTS. — THE GRAZIER'S TERRORS, AND POWERS OF IDENTITY. — THE LANDLORD'S DAUGHTER.

"HILLOA! HOUSE! HOUSE!" shouted the strange voice on the outside, but in a tone that seemed unearthly; whether it were merely a fancy, or reality, yet it had its effect, and the landlord sat staring vacantly with his two hands resting on either knee, leaning forward as if he was staring some imaginary object out of countenance.

"Well," said one of the the highwaymen, "ain't anybody going to the door."

No one answered, but Jem the ostler was hastening by another passage to the door, and then they heard some confused speaking, as if the stranger was giving some directions for the care of his horse.

The grazier was fixed in his attention to what was going on, and appeared petrified, and held a morsel on the end of his fork, halfway between his mouth and the plate, with his eyes directed towards the door.

In a few moments more they heard the steps of some one approaching the door, and one of the highwaymen said to his companion, —

"Ned, there are people late on the roads to-night."

"Yes; it appears so, but it is very uncomfortable travelling; the night is bad, and the roads no better. Who's this, I wonder?"

"We shall now see," said the other, but their backs were turned towards the door, and they could not see who entered the door so well as the grazier, who sat in the same attitude, without a motion or movement, even to wink his eye, when the door opened, and in walked a tall man, wrapped in a horseman's cloak.

The expression of horror in the grazier's face, and the swelling of his eyes almost out of his head, at once showed them there was something extraordinary, and they both mutually turned round, and to their extreme terror they perceived the very man, or his double, they had left dead upon the spot where the grazier had seen him.

Neither were they alone surprised, for all present were able at once to recognise the same man without any difficulty.

"It's the same man — I'm d — d!" said the grazier, as if he had made an effort to speak, and when he had so, he couldn't help himself. "Oh, Lord! — who would have thought it? — it's — it's the — the — what do ye call it?"

"The devil," suggested the landlord.

"No," said the stranger, "no. I am merely a traveller, somewhat weary and tired — do not disturb yourselves. I am cold — very cold — the fire will do me good; it is a very cold night — the roads are bad, very unsafe."

"Very," said one of the highwaymen, involuntarily.

"The same as you," replied the highwayman.

The stranger made no reply to the highwayman, whose natural effrontery, and the necessity he always had or presence of mind in circumstances of peril, gave him a greater superiority than most men possessed under such circumstances.

"I'm not well," said the stranger.

"Perhaps you've ridden far."

"I have," replied the stranger. "Landlord, will you have the goodness to let me have some supper; I am weary."

"I have only the remains of the chicken-pie and some ham," said the landlord, looking black at the already referred-to chicken-pie, which, thanks to its being made of great size, had already supped three hungry men,—"and there is but little of that."

"It is not much that I want—a small

"Did you speak?" inquired the stranger, suddenly turning to the highwayman who had spoken with a look of such a peculiar character, that he caused the bold roadster involuntarily to start; but he suddenly recovered himself, and said,—

"I did."

"What did you say, sir?"

matter will suffice — a little ham, and something warm, and then I will to-bed — 'tis late."

"Very well, sir," said the landlord; "here's some good October; will you like that? or is there anything else? I have French spirits."

"Then let me have some brandy."

"Yes, sir, I'll fetch my daughter down stairs," said the landlord; "she's young, and her hand is steadier than mine. I shall upset the bottle; my — my hand, you see, is always unsteady after I've drawn the October; somehow or other I always get out of order."

"What is the reason of that?" inquired the highwayman.

"Why, it's so strong; I believe it's nothing else whatever."

As the landlord turned to go, he give another look at the guest, and appeared greatly disturbed, and certainly thought him a strange and unaccountable man; for he believed that he was in truth the very man spoken of, who had been left for dead on the bank, near the foot of the gallows.

"Mary," said the landlord, when he had ascended half a dozen stairs, which led out of the kitchen, "Mary."

"Yes, father," was the ready answer, in a clear, pleasing voice.

"I want you, my dear. Bring the brandy down — the French — the sealed bottle; the other's out; I took the last this morning before breakfast."

"Ho! ho!" said the highwayman; "hark at our landlord, how early he must begin — no wonder his hand shakes."

"Ah!" said the landlord, as he came back with a wink; "when you have been a father and an innkeeper as long as I have,

you'll do many things you don't now dream of; but, no matter, I ain't as young as I used to be."

At that moment a very pretty and genteel girl, about eighteen, descended the stairs with a spirit bottle in her hand, and advanced to the table.

"How will you take it, sir?" inquired the landlord.

"Mixed."

"Make a glass, my dear," said the landlord.

"Is that your daughter?" inquired the stranger, fixing his eyes upon her, — and they were such leaden eyes, that the girl shrank from him in dismay.

"Yes," said the landlord.

"Any more?"

"None," replied the landlord, and then there was a pause of some moments, during which the stranger watched the young girl's motions with a greedy jealousy, as if he feared to lose one movement, and in a manner that especially annoyed the old landlord, who, however, could say nothing, he having been quite cowed by the stranger's superiority in station and demeanour; besides which, there was something very strange and peculiar, not to say superhuman, about him that gave weight, and caused a kind of awe to pervade all present, and they looked upon him as something fearful or terrible.

It was not long before the stranger ate his supper — it was soon done; he ate but little, and, when that was done, he turned to the brandy and water; but there appeared an air of compulsion, upon his part, as if everything he took was taken under the feeling that it was absolutely necessary to take something, which did not escape the discerning eyes of all present, especially the landlord, who felt it a slight upon himself and his cheer.

"If I had known you were coming here," said the landlord, "I would have got something ready for you, but, as it was, I had nothing but 'pot-luck' for you."

"What is that?" inquired the stranger.—"What is that?—I never heard of such a dish before. I am a stranger in these parts."

"Oh, it only means you could have anything what is in the house."

"It will do," said the stranger, quietly.

"Will you have anything more that we have in the house?"

"Nothing. I came by the gibbet, not far from this place; and I met with an accident there that has left me but little stomach."

"By gosh, I should think not," muttered the grazier; "it would have settled my stomach altogether, and anybody else's."

"Well," muttered one of the highwaymen, "It would have left me no stomach, save what would be in a fair way to become food for the worms."

"What kind of accident was it, sir?"

"A terrible blow in the side; it seemed to go through me."

"Well, well, I imagine there would be but little comfort in a man's bowels after he had anything go through his side."

"It depends upon the constitution," said the stranger quietly.

"The what?" inquired one of the highwaymen, incredulously.

"The constitution," replied the stranger, quietly.

There was a pause for some minutes, during which the strangers exchanged glances at each other, when one of the highwaymen said,—

"Perhaps a bullet put in your side might be no hindrance to your animal economy, and would in the course of nature become digested."

"Why, I dare say it would not hurt me so much as many; but it would take me some little while to recover the shock, which would be great; but I am unwell, and perhaps had better retire. Will the young female, your daughter, act as my chambermaid and show me my room?"

"Yes," said the landlord, mechanically; "here, Mary, show the gentleman into No. 6, and leave the light."

"Good night," said the stranger, rising, and walking away erect, but slowly, from the group, who gazed after him with amazement.

"Good night, sir," said the landlord, which was echoed by those present; and, when the stranger was gone, there was a general release in their conversation from the constraint which the presence of the last comer occasioned.

"Well, what do you think of him, Mr. Green?" inquired the landlord.

"The very same man I saw on the bank at the gallows corner."

"Are you sure?"

"Quite."

There was a general pause, as if there was something for them all to think over; and their thoughts appeared to be so unsatisfactory, that those who lived close at hand left the house, and those that remained there went to their respective beds, and in half an hour the house was quite silent.

CLXXVIII.

THE MIDNIGHT CRY OF ALARM. — THE VAMPYRE'S MEAL. — THE CHASE ACROSS
THE FIELDS. — THE DEATH OF THE LANDLORD'S DAUGHTER.

THE OLD INN WAS in a state of repose; its various parts were no longer vexed by the busy tramp of men, the noisy voice of the toper, or the untiring hands of the housewife, who does not spare any part of its edifice from her ablutions. The brush and the broom are sad intruders and disturbers, and yet they are in perpetual requisition. However, the inhabitants were all steeped in slumber.

Among those who lay in that house, there was not one, except one, indeed, who did not lie down to rest, and fall into a deep sleep; but that one exception was the stranger, who appeared to have other views.

He threw himself into a chair, and there appeared to meditate upon the clouds which passed across the sky, in endless variety of shape and form. He sat motionless, and still his large, lustreless eyes were fully opened, and he was gazing earnestly for nearly an hour without motion.

At length, as if his attention was of itself wearying to continue so long, he moved, then sighed deeply, or rather groaned.

"How long is this hated life to last?" he muttered. "When shall I cease to be the loathsome creature I am?"

There was some reflection in this that was very bitter to him. He shuddered, and buried his face in his hands, and remained in that state for some minutes; but then he lifted his head up again, and turned towards the moon's rays, muttering, —

"But I am faint; I feel the want of my natural slumbers. Blood alone will restore me my strength. There is no resisting the dreadful appetite that goads me on. I must — I must — I will satisfy it."

He arose suddenly, and drew himself up to his full height, and threw aloft his arms, as he growled out these words with frantic energy; but in a few seconds he became more calm, and said, —

"I saw the maiden enter the room next to mine. I can enter it by the same door, for I have the key, and that will place her at my mercy. Good fortune for once avail me, and then my wants will be satisfied."

He walked softly to his own door, and undid it stealthily, and listened for some minutes.

"They are all asleep," he said — "all, save one. I alone walk through the place. All are in peaceful slumbers, while I, like the creatures of prey, seek those whom I may devour. I must on."

He crept into the passage, and advanced to the door of the young girl, who lay soundly sleeping in innocence and peace, little dreaming of the fate that awaited her — much less did she think that the destroyer was so close at hand.

She might, indeed, have dreamed that there was some one in the house who was scarcely of her nature—one that was loathsome and dreadful—one who, in fact, lived upon the blood of the innocent and fairest.

"She sleeps," he muttered—"she sleeps!"

He listened again, and then he gently put the key into the door, and found that it was not locked, and then, turning the handle, he found there was some impediment to its opening; but of what character he could not tell.

"'Tis unlucky; but this must be moved."

He place his hand and foot close to the door, and pressed it gradually and hardly against it, and he found that it gradually gave way, and that the impediment gave by degrees, and that, too, with hardly any noise.

"Fortune favours me," he muttered; "she does not hear me. I shall win the chamber, and shall, before she can wake up, sieze upon the dear life-stream that is no less precious to me than to herself."

He now had succeeded in effecting an entrance into the room, and found that it was only an easy chair that had been placed against the door, because there was no other means of securing it, the key having unaccountably disappeared, and left her without any other means of securing her door.

"I will lock it," he muttered; "if I be disturbed, I shall be better able to escape, and I shall be safe. My meal will be undisturbed; at least not before so much has been taken as will revive my strength."

He now approached the bed, and with eager eyes devoured the fair form of the youthful and innocent sleeper.

"How calm, and how unsuspicious she lies," he muttered; "'twere a pity, but I must, I must—there is no help."

He leaned over her. He bent his head till his ear almost touched the lips of the sleeper, as though he were listening to the breathing of the young girl.

Something caused her to start. She opened her eyes, and endeavoured to rise up, but she was immediately thrust back, and the vampire seized her fair flesh with his fanged teeth, and having fleshed them, he was drawing that life current from her which ensanguined them both.

Horror and fright for a moment deprived her of strength, or the power of uttering a sound of any kind; but when she did do so, it was one wild unearthly shriek, that was heard throughout the whole house, and awakened every human being within it in a moment.

"Help! murder, murder!" she shrieked out, as soon as the first scream subsided, and she regained breath.

These cries she uttered rapidly, as well as attempting a desperate resistance to her persecutor; but she was growing gradually more and more faint.

THE LANDLORD HAD JUST got out of an uncomfortable dream about some strange adventure he was having with some excisemen when he was young, when the heart-piercing shriek of Mary came upon him.

"God bless me," he muttered, "what's that? I never heard anything so horrible in all my life. What can it be?"

He sat up in bed, and pulled his nightcap off, while he listened, when he heard the cries of help issuing from his daughter's room.

"Good God! it's Mary," he muttered, "What can be the matter?"

He did not pause a moment, but huddled on his clothes, and then rushed out of his room with a light, to his daughter's bedroom.

"What is the matter?" inquired one of the highwaymen, who had been disturbed by the dreadful shriek.

"I don't know; but — but help me."

"Help you to what?"

"To burst open this door; 'tis my daughter's room, and the noise comes from that place. Hark!"

"Help, help!" said a faint voice.

"Damnation!" said the highwayman, "something's wrong there; somebody's sucking; surely the stranger is not there?"

"Burst the door open."

"Then lend a hand; it must give," said Ned; and they all three made a rush at the door, and in it went, for their weight carried it all before them, and they all three went into the apartment without any hindrance, for the frail lock gave immediately, and the other impediment only served to add to the noise.

Though they went in easily, yet they did not do so quickly enough, for they all rolled over each other, and before they could rise they distinctly saw the figure of the stranger start up and rush out of the room with Mary in his arms.

"Help! help! mercy!" she shrieked out.

" 'Tis she," said the landlord.

"Mary—"

"Yes, after her boys — after her; for Heaven's sake, after her."

"We will not leave her," said the highwaymen in concert, and at the same moment all three rushed after her.

"The stranger has made his way down into the kitchen, and I think he has her with him," said the landlord.

"I will after him," said Ned; "I saw her in his arms. She was all over blood. Good Heavens! what can he mean? does he want to murder her?"

"Help! help! murder!" shouted the girl, and at that moment they heard the stranger attempting the kitchen door below. In a moment they all three ran down stairs as fast as they could, to seize the villain before he could escape; but they had hardly got into the kitchen before they saw the door swing to after him.

"He's gone," said the landlord; "he's gone."

"We'll after them; come on, never mind a chase; she's in white, and the moon's up, so we shall have them in sight."

"Away after them, lads; save my girl — save my Mary!"

Away they went with great speed, but the stranger somehow or other kept ahead of them; his great height gave him an advantage in length of stride; but then he bore the landlord's daughter in his arms, which was more than enough to balance their powers; for though she was not heavy, comparatively speaking, yet she was heavy to be borne along in this manner; but the stranger appeared to possess superhuman strength, and moved along safely until they lost sight of him among some hay-stacks, for which they made.

"There, he's gone into Jackson's rick-yard," said the landlord; "get up; push on; we may be yet in time to prevent mischief."

The highwaymen ran hard; they had been out of breath for some time, and cold hardly move their feet, but they made a sudden effort, or spirt, and away they ran, and, in less than a minute, came up to the rick-yard.

They rushed into the yard, and then beheld the stranger seated upon some partially cut hay with the helpless maiden on his lap, but his fanged teeth were fleshed in her fair neck, and he was exerting himself in drawing the life stream from her veins.

As soon as he saw the highwaymen he arose, and the unfortunate girl rolled to the earth, and he started up and fled, the highwaymen firing a parting shot after him, with pretty good aim, yet it took no effect.

The landlord's daughter was picked up warm, but lifeless. Whether it was in consequence of her wound and loss of blood, which was doubted, or from sheer fright, is not known, but the latter was considered most probable.

The corpse stood up in the coffin, and the moonlight fell full upon him.

"Vampyre arise," said he who had just spoken to Varney. "Vampyre arise, and do your work in the world until your doom shall be accomplished. Vampyre arise — arise. Pursue your victims in the mansion and in the cottage. Be a terror and a desolation, go you where you may, and if the hand of death strike you down, the cold beams of the moon shall restore you to new life. Vampyre arise, arise!"

"I come, I come!" shrieked the corpse. *(see page 1179)*

PART X:

The Vampyre and the Heiress.

CLXXIX.

THE HOTEL. — THE FASHIONABLE ARRIVAL. — THE YOUNG HEIRESS.

CAN IT BE TRUE, and if so, how horribly strange, that a being half belonging to a world of spirits, should thus wander beneath the cold moon and the earth, bringing dismay to the hearts of all upon whom his strange malign influence is cast!

How frightful an existence is that of Varney the Vampyre!

There were some good points about the — man, we were going to say, and yet we can hardly feel justified in bestowing upon him that title, considering the strange gift of renewable existence which was his. If it were, as, indeed, it seemed to be the case, that bodily decay in him was not the result of death, and that the rays "of the cold chaste moon"* were sufficient to revivify him, who shall say when that process is to end? and who shall say that, walking the streets of giant London at this day, there may not be some such existences? Horrible thought that, perhaps seduced by the polished exterior of one who seems a citizen of the world in the

most extended signification of the words, we should bring into our domestic circle a vampyre!

But yet it might be so. We have seen, however, that Varney was a man of dignified courtesy and polished manners; that he had the rare and beautiful gift of eloquence; and that, probably, gathering such vast experience from his long intercourse with society — an intercourse which had extended over so many years, he was able to adapt himself to the tastes and the feelings of all persons, and so exercise over them that charm of mind which caused him to have so dangerous a power.

At times, too, it would seem as if he regretted that fatal gift of immortality, as if he would gladly have been more human, and lived and died as those lived and died whom he saw around him. But being compelled to fulfill the order of his being, he never had the courage absolutely to take measures for his own destruction, a destruction which should be final in consequence of depriving himself of all opportunity of resuscitation.

---

* *A line from* Epipsychidion, *an 1821 poem by Percy Bysshe Shelley.*

Certainly the ingenunity of such a man might have devised some means of putting such an end to his life, that, in the perishable fragments of his body there should linger not one spark of that vitality which had been so often again and again fanned into existence.

Probably some effort of that kind may yet be his end, and we shall see that Varney the Vampyre will not, like the common run of the world's inhabitants, be changed into that dust of which is all humanity, but will undergo some violent disruption, and be for ever blotted out from the muster-roll of the living creatures that inhabit the great world.

But to cease speculating on such things, and to come to actual facts, we will now turn over another leaf in the strange eventful history of Varney the Vampyre.

ONE STORMY, INCLEMENT evening in November, a travelling carriage, draggled with mud, and dripping with moisture, was driven up to the door of the London Hotel, which was an establishment not of the very first fashion, but of great respectability, situated then in Burlington-street, close to Old Bond-street, then the parade of fashion, and, as some thought, elegance; although we of the present day would look with risibility upon the costumes that were the vogue, although the period were but fifty years ago; but fifty years effect strange mutations and revolutions in dress, manners, and even in modes of thought.

The equipage, if not of the most dashing character, was still of sufficiently aristocratic pretensions to produce a considerable bustle in the hotel; and the landlord, after seeing that there was a coronet upon of the panels of the carriage door, thought it worth his while personally to welcome the guests who had done him the honour of selecting his house.

These guests consisted of an oldish man and woman, a young man of frivolous and foppish exterior, of about twenty-two years of age, and a young lady, who was so covered up in a multitude of shawls, that but little of her face could be seen; but that little was sufficient to stamp her at once as most beautiful.

The whole party evidently paid great court to this young lady, but whether they did so from affection, or from some more interested motive, it would not be proper just now to say, as those facts will come out before we have proceeded far in this little episode.

"Mind how you step, Annette," said the old gentleman, as the young lady descended the carriage. "Mind how you step, my dear."

"Oh! yes, yes," said the old lady, who was not so very old either, although entering upon the shady side of fifty. "Yes. Oh! mind my dear, how you get out."

The young lady made no reply to all these kind injunctions, but pushing aside the proffered arm of the younger gentleman, she tripped into the hotel unaided.

The old lady instantly followed her.

"Now, Francis," said the old gentleman to the servant, who got down from the rumble of the travelling carriage. "Now, Francis, you perfectly recollect, I hope, what my brother, Lord Lake, said to you?"

"Yes, sir," said Francis, but there was not the most respectful intonation in the world in the voice with which he returned the affirmative.

"You remember," continued the old gentleman; "you remember, Francis, that my brother told you, you were to wait upon us just the same as upon himself, with the carriage."

"Oh, yes."

"Oh, yes! what do you mean by saying 'oh, yes!' to me?"

"Do you want me to say, 'oh, no?'"

"Francis, this won't do. You are discharged."

"That for you, and the discharge, too," said Francis, as he snapped his fingers in the face of the old gentleman. "I never meant to serve you, Mister Lake; I'm Lord Lake's groom, but I ain't a going to be turned over to a canting fellow like you, so you have only took the words out of my mouth, for I meant to discharge myself, and so will George. I say, George."

"Yes," replied the coachman; "what is it?"

"Are we going to be at the beck and call of Jonathan Lake?"

"See him d—d first," was the laconic reply of the coachman.

"Now, Mister Lake, added Francis, "you knows what we thinks of you. You is a humbug. We only came so far, because we wouldn't put Miss Annette, our young lady, to the inconvenience of a post-chaise, while my lord, her father's carriage here, was so much more comfortable. We shall take that to the coachmaker's, where my lord's other carriages are standing, till he comes to England, and then you won't see us no more."

"You rascals!"

"Oh, go on. You're a humbug; ain't he, George?"

"Oh, a *riglar* one—a *numbug* he is," aid the coachman; "and what's more, we don't believe a word of all what's been a going on. Lady Annette is Lady Annette, bless her sweet eyes. Come on, Francis, I'm wet."

"And I'm damp," said Francis, as he shook himself, and made as much splashing round him as a great Newfoundland dog, who has just had a bath. "I'm ready now, mister, and you knows our minds, and we ain't the sort of folks to alter 'em. We serves our master; but we doesn't serve a humbug."

Some of the waiters at the hotel had come to the door to hear this rather curious colloquy, and not a little surprised were they at it. At all events, whatever other effect it had upon them, it did not increase their respect for the new arrivals, and one of them, named Slop, ran after the carriage, and called out to Francis,—

"I say—I say!"

"Well, what?"

"I say, young fellow, just tell me where you will be staying, and I'll come and see you, and stand a glass."

Francis leant over the roof of the carriage, and said,—

"George—George!"

"Here ye *air*," said George.

"Here's one o' the waiters at the hotel wants to make an acquaintance. It won't be a bad thing to know him, as you see he can tell us all about Lady Annette, and what the ladies are doing. What do you say to it, George?"

"A good idea, Francis."

"Very well. Hilloa! what's your name, old fellow?"

"Slop—Solomon Slop, they calls me."

"Well, if you come any evening to the King's Head, in Welbeck-street, you'll find either me or George; and we always likes good company, and shall be very glad to see you whenever you like. Supppose you say to-morrow?"

"I will,—I will; to-morrow I can come easily at eight o'clock, so you may expect me. Good night."

"Good night, Slop. Pleasant evening, ain't it? Drive on, George; I shall be in a ague presently; drive on, good luck to you, and let's get a change of things, whatever you do I never was so wet, I do think, in all my life."

"Nor me, nor me," said George, who it will be perceived was not very particular about his grammar; but that didn't matter much. He was paid for a knowledge of horses, not of moods, tenses, and cases.

Leaving the servants, then, of Lord Lake, as they had announced themselves to be, let us return to the hotel, where the family party had by this time got into comfortable enough quarters.

As far as the landlord of that establishment was concerned, Mr. Lake had won him over completely, by ordering the best rooms, a supper, as good as the house could afford, regardless of the price; the best wines, and altogether showed a right royal disposition as regarded expenditure.

But the waiters, who had often found by experience that the most extravagant people were not the most liberal to them, did not forget what had passed at the door, and many a whispered surmise passed from one to the other regarding the circumstances that had induced the coachman and groom to treat the family so very cavalierly, and so obstinately to decline serving them.

When Slop returned, he got some of his companions round him in the hall.

"I shall know all about it," he said; "I'm to go and take a glass with them to-morrow night, at the King's Head, in Welbeck-street, and you see if they don't tell me what it's all about. I wouldn't miss knowing for a trifle."

"Nor me — nor me."

"Well, I'll of course tell you all when I come back. You may depend upon it it's something worth knowing. Have you seen the young lady any of you. I caught just a look of one eye, and the end of her nose, and I should say she's a out-and-outer, and no mistake."

CLXXX.

THE SECOND ARRIVAL AT THE LONDON HOTEL. — THE MYSTERIOUS GUEST.

SCARCELY HAD THE BUSTLE of the arrival we have noticed subsided at the London Hotel, when another travelling chariot dashed up to the door, and the landlord made a rush out to welcome his new arrival, considering himself quite in luck to have two such customers in one evening.

A gentleman, on whose head was a fur travelling cap, was at one of the windows of this carriage, and he called to the landlord, saying, —

"Are your best rooms occupied?"

"Not the best, sir," was the reply, "for we have several suites of apartments in all respects equal to each other; but we have a family just arrived in one suite. The Lake family, sir."

"Well, it don't matter to me who you have; I will get out if you can accommodate me."

"Oh, certainly, sir; you will find here accommodation of the very first character, I can assure you, sir. Pray, sir, alight. Allow me, sir, to hold an umbrella over you. It's a bad night, sir; I'm afraid the winter is setting in very strangely, sir, and prophetically of—"

"Silence. I don't want your opinion of the matter. If there's one thing I dislike more than another, it's a chattering man."

This rebuff silenced the landlord, who said not another word, although probably he thought the more; and those thoughts were not of a very kindly character as regarded the stranger, who had so very unceremoniously stopped his amiable remarks.

Indeed, when he got into the hall, he consigned the new comer to the care of the head waiter, and retired to his own apartment in great dudgeon.

"I hope everything is quiet here," said the stranger to the head waiter.

"Oh, dear, yes, sir; the house is as quiet as a lamb, sir, I can assure you. We have only three inmates at present, sir. There's the Lakes, — highly respectable people, sir. A brother of Lord Lake's, sir, I believe, and the—"

"I don't want to hear who you have. What the devil is it to me? If there's anything I dislike more than another, it's a d—d magpie of a waiter."

The head waiter was terribly offended, and said not another word, so that the gentleman was left in the sole occupation of his apartments, and then to fling himself upon a couch.

"Ah, ah! God knows how it will all end. Well, well, we shall see, we shall see. They have arrived, and that's one comfort; I am now, then, I think, so well made up, that they will not readily know me. Oh, no, no, I should hardly know myself, now, shaven clean as I am, after being accustomed on the continent, to wear beard and moustache. Well, well, we shall see, how it will all end. Thank the fates, they have not gone somewhere where I could not find them."

He rang the bell.

"Waiter, let me have the best the house affords, will you? and remember my name is Blue."

"Sir! Bl—Blue, sir?"

"Yes, Diggory Blue."

"Yes, sir,—yes sir. Certainly.—What an odd name," soliloquised the waiter, as he went down stairs to tell his master. "I say sir, the gent in No. 10 and 11 says his name is Diggory Blue."

"Blue, Blue," said the landlord, "it is an odd name for a Christian."

"Perhaps he ain't a Christian," said the very identical Mr. Blue himself, popping his head over the bar in which the little discourse was going on, between the landlord and the waiter. "How do you know he's a Christian?"

"I beg your pardon, sir, really I—I—a-hem! a thousand pardons, sir."

"Pshaw!"

The strange gentleman went to the door, and gave some directions to the servants belonging to his carriage, which sent them away, and then Mr. Blue started up into his rooms again, without saying another word to the landlord, who was terribly annoyed at being caught canvassing the name of one of his guests, with one of his waiters.

"Confound him," he muttered, "he has no business to have such a name as Blue and good God! if his surname was Blue, what the devil made his godfathers and godmothers call him Diggory? Sam, Sam!"

"Yes, sir."

"Put down in the book, Diggory Blue."

"Yes, sir."

"Bless us! why there's somebody else as I'm a sinner."

The landlord could not have sworn by a better oath.

He ran to the door, and there beheld another travelling carriage, out of which stepped a gentlemanly looking man enveloped in a rich travelling cloak lined with fur.

"Can you accommodate us?" he said.

"Yes, sir, with pleasure."

"Who have you here, landlord?"

"A family named Lake, sir, and a Mr.—a—Blue, sir."

"Quiet people I dare say, I shall most likely remain with you a week or two. Let me have the best apartments you have unoccupied at present."

"Yes, sir. This way if you please, sir—this way."

The last arrival seemed to be in bad health, for he walked very slowly, like a man suffering from great bodily exhaustion, and more than once he paused as he followed the landlord up the principal staircase of the hotel, as if it were absolutely necessary he should do so to recover breath, and moreover the landlord heard him sigh deeply, but whether that was from mental or physical distress he had no means of knowing. His curiosity, however, was much excited by the gentleman, and his sympathies likewise, for he was the reverse of Mr. Blue, and listened with a refined and gentlemanly courtesy to whatever was said to him by any one apparently, although it was evidently an effort to speak, so weak and ill did he seem to be.

"I am sorry, sir," said the landlord, when he had shewn the gentleman into his rooms, "I am sorry sir, you don't seem well."

"I am rather an invalid, but I dare say

I shall soon be better, thank you — thank you. One candle only, I dislike too much light: charge for as many as you please, but never let me have but one, landlord."

"As you please, sir, as you please; I hope you will make yourself comfortable here, and I can assure you, sir, that nothing shall be wanting on my part to make you so."

"I am sure of that, landlord; you are very good, thank you."

"What name shall I say, sir, in case any gentleman should call to see you, sir?"

"Black."

"Black, sir!"

"Black."

"Oh, Mr. Black! — Yes, sir, certainly, why not? Oh, of course. I — only thought it a little odd, you see, sir, because we have a gentleman already in the house called Blue. That was all, sir. Mr. Black, thank you, sir."

The landlord bowed himself out, and Mr. Black inclined his head with the look of a condescending emperor, so that when the landlord got down stairs, he said to his wife, —

"Now that *is* a gentleman. he listens to all you have got to say, like a gentleman, and don't snap you up as that Mr. Blue did. Mr. Black, it is quite clear to me, is a man of the world, and a perfect gentleman. Hilloa, what's that? Eh? What! why it's Mr. Black's bell, and he must have almost broken the wire. Sam, Sam! run up to 8, and see what's wanted."

Sam did run up to 8, and when he got there, he found Mr. Black lying upon the floor in a fainting fit, and wholly insensible.

The alarmed waiter ran down stairs to his master with the news, and the nearest medical man was sent for, but with as

little parade as possible, for the hotel-keeper did not wish to alarm all his other guests with the news of the fact that there was a sick person in the house, which he knew was not pleasing to many persons, and might induce them to change their quarters.

When the medical man came, he was shown up stairs at once, when Mr. Black had been lifted on to a sofa, where he lay without any signs of consciousness at all, much to the horror of the landlord, who began to think he was dead, and that there would be all the disagreeableness of having a corpse in his house.

The surgeon felt the pulse and the heart, and then he said, —

"He is in a swoon, but he must be in a desperately weak state."

"He looks it, don't he, sir?"

"He does indeed. How dreadfully emaciated he is!"

By dint of great exertion and the use of stimulants, the surgeon succeeded in restoring Mr. Black to consciousness, and when he was so restored, he looked around him with that strange vacant expression which a man wears who has newly come out of a trance and whose memory is in a state of abeyance.

"Well, sir, how are you now?" said the surgeon.

He made no reply.

"I should advise that he be put to bed, landlord," added the medical man, "and something of a warm nourishing quality given to him. I will send him some medicine."

Mr. Black now made an effort to speak, and his memory seemed to have come back to him as he said,

"I fear I have been a deal of trouble,

but the fatigue of travelling fast — it is that has unnerved me — I shall be much better to-morrow. Thank you all."

"I will call to-morrow" said the surgeon, "and see how you get on, if you please."

"I shall be much obliged; I feel myself quite strong enough to retire for the night without assistance, thank you."

He made no opposition to the landlord sending him up by Sam some spiced wine, and when it came, he said, —

"I hope no one sleeps near me who will come in late and disturb me, as I require a full and clear night's repose."

"Oh no, sir," said Sam, "it's a young lady sir, as belongs to the Lake family sleeps in the next room but one to you, that is to say, No. 9. The very next room ain't occupied at all, sir, to night, so you will be as quiet as if you was in a church, sir."

"Thank you, thank you; good night, Samuel."

CLXXXI.

THE NIGHT ALARM. — A SCENE OF CONFUSION. — MR. BLUE SUSPECTED.

IT IS MIDNIGHT, and the landlord of the hotel suddenly springs out of bed on to the floor as if he had been galvanised, carrying with him all the bed-clothes and leaving his wife shivering.

"Good gracious! what was that?" he cried.

And well he might, for the repose of the whole house was broken in upon by two loud shrieks, such as had never before sounded within those walls, and then all was still as the grave.

"Murder! murder!" shouted the landlady, "somebody has stolen all the bed-clothes."

"Bother the bed-clothes!" cried the landlord, as he hurried on his apparel by the dim light of a night lamp that was burning on the dressing table. "There's something wrong in the house, or else I have had one of the strangest dreams that ever anybody had, and one of the most

likely reality too. Did you hear them?"

"Oh, those horrid screams!"

"It's not a dream then, for two people don't dream the same thing at the same moment of time, that's quite clear. Hark — hark! what's that, what a banging of doors to be sure. Who's there? Who's there? Wait a bit."

The landlord lifted the night bolt of his bed room, and then there dashed into the room in only one garment, which fluttered in the breeze, no other than the young man who had come with the ladies. He made but one spring into the landlord's bed, crying, —

"Oh! take care of me. Oh, save me! There's thieves or something and I shall be hurt. Oh, save me, save me, I can't fight, I never did, spare my life, oh, spare my life."

"Oh, the wretch!" shrieked the landlady, and the landlord, justly enough enraged at that intrusion, seized upon the intruder and shot him out of the room *vi et armis*, and that with such force too that he rolled all the way down the stairs, upsetting Sam who was rushing up with a lantern, it having been his turn to sit up all night, as one of the establishment always did, in case of fire or anything happening which might make it necessary to arouse the inmates of the house.

The landlord, however, had completed enough of his toilette to enable him to make a decent appearance; so out he sallied, having lit a candle, and the first person he met upon the landing was Mr. Blue, fully dressed and with a pistol in his hand.

"Good God, sir," cried the landlord, "what is it all about, what has happened sir?"

"I cannot tell you, and am as anxious as you can be to know. This way, this way. It was the young lady who screamed. For God's sake, lend me a light!"

The landlord resigned his light mechanically, and he saw to his surprise, that there was a black patch now over one of Mr. Blue's eyes, and he thought his face was painted. At all events, he was so much disguised that it was only by his voice that the landlord knew him.

Before however, they either of them got across the corridor to the door of the young lady's room, Mr. and Mrs. Lake half-dressed, made their appearance, both eagerly inquiring what was the matter.

"I don't know," said the landlord, "I only heard a scream."

"Which came from the apartment of that young lady," said Mr. Blue.

"What young lady?" said Mr. Lake sharply. "It's rather odd that you, a stranger, should know so precisely which was the apartment of that young lady. Mrs. Lake, go in and see if anything be the matter with Annetta; I hope to Heaven, nothing is amiss with her."

Mr. Lake looked suspiciously at Mr. Blue, and so did the landlord, for when Mr. Blue had spoken in the presence of the Lakes, his voice was completely altered, so that the landlord no longer could have recognized him by it, and he was more puzzled than ever.

"Oh! come in, come in, Mr. Lake," cried Mrs. Lake, appearing at the door of Annetta's room, "she is dead."

"Dead!" cried Mr. Blue with a shout, "Oh! no, no, no!"

He dashed past Mr. Lake, the landlord, and Mrs. Lake, and was in the room in a moment. They went after him as soon as they had recovered sufficiently from their surprise to do so, and they saw him with his hands clasped, and bending over the form of the beautiful young girl as she lay in bed.

"No, no, no," he said, "she is not dead. She has fainted. God knows what the cause may be, but she is not dead. Thank Heaven!"

He turned from the bedside, and without saying another word to the parties present, he walked away to his own room, and left them staring at each other in surprise. The young lady now opened her eyes, and looked wildly about her for a few moments, and then she spoke quickly,

"Oh, help! help! help! away, away. Oh, horror — horror — horror!"

"Annetta, my dear Annetta," said Mrs. Lake, "what is this? — Pray, sir, retire," to the landlord. "My dear Annetta, what has alarmed you? My dear, go away, Mr. Lake.

I will let you know all about it. It's a mystery to me at present. Go away, I'll be back soon."

Mr. Lake left the room, and in the corridor he found the landlord, who was looking as bewildered as any mortal man could well look, for he could make neither head nor tail of the whole affair.

"Landlord," said Mr. Lake, "who is that party who behaved so strangely just now?"

"His name is Blue, sir."

"Blue — Blue. An odd name, and an odd man. Where can I have seen him before. Just as he cried out, and went into the room, I thought there was a something in his voice that came familiarily to my ears, and yet I don't know him; I suspect landlord, that he has had more to do with this midnight disturbance than he would care to own."

"Well, sir, I don't know," said the landlord, whose interest it was not to disoblige, or throw suspicion upon any of his guests. "It really ain't very likely, sir. I should say the young lady has had a bad dream, sir, and that's almost all that can be said about it."

"It may be so."

"You may depend that's what it will turn out to be, sir."

"I hope so, I hope so. These things are not at all pleasant, and if anything of the kind should happen again we should have to quit directly, you know, but I can say nothing now about it until I have heard from Mrs. Lake what account Annetta gives of the affair. That alone must guide us in the whole business. In the morning we will talk about it, sir."

There was a great deal of austerity in the manner of Mr. Lake; indeed he might well enough be excused for not being over pleased at what had taken place, and as for Mr. Blue there certainly was sufficient in his behaviour to induce a large amount of suspicion, that he was in some way connected with the affair. Moreover the efforts he evidently made in the way of disguise were extremely suspicious in themselves. He evidently had a something to conceal, and when the landlord was now left alone in the corridor, he was strongly induced to make one of his first acts in the morning a notice to Mr. Blue, that he would much prefer his room to his company at the London Hotel.

And then it all of a sudden came into the landlord's head, how poor Mr. Black must have been distressed at what had taken place; for Sam had told him what Mr. Black had said about wishing to sleep quietly, so that he felt quite a pang at the idea of so civil a gentleman having been so awfully disturbed, as he must have been, and he had no doubt but that in the morning he would go away.

"I wonder if he is awake?" thought the landlord; "if I could but make some sort of apology to him to-night, and soothe him, all might be well. I'll first go and listen at his door; it may be that he really wants something, and if so perhaps it would look attentive to knock and see him; I think I will. It's quite out of the question that he should have slept in the middle of all this riot."

He approached Mr. Black's door, and listened.

All was still as the very grave.

"What a horrid thing it would be if the shock, in his weak state, has been the death of him!" thought the landlord, and the very idea made him quake again.

After a few moments passed in this state of painful thought, he found that it would be quite out of the question for him to go to his own room again, without ascertaining how Mr. Black was, and accordingly he knocked at the door, first gently and then louder, and then louder still, but received no answer.

"Oh, this won't do, I must get in somehow," thought the landlord.

He tried the handle, and found in a moment that the door was not fast; a light was burning on the side of the table which was close to the bed, and there lay Mr. Black fast asleep, and looking so calm and serene, although he was an ugly man, that the landlord was truly astonished to see him.

"Well," he said, "that's what I call sound sleeping, at all events. It's a mercy however." Oh lor! he' going to awake."

Mr. Black opened his eyes, and looked up.

"I beg your pardon, sir," said the landlord, "I earnestly beg your pardon, but as there had been a little noise in the house I came to see, first, if you had been disturbed, an then if you wanted anything, sir."

"No, no, thank you. Has there been a noise, do you say."

"A — a little, sir."

"Well, I was fast asleep and did not hear it. However, I do sleep so sound that I think a cannon going off at my ear would hardly awaken me. I am much obliged however for your attention, landlord."

"Can't I get you anything, sir?"

"Nothing until the morning, thank you."

"Thank you sir, good night sir, good night."

"Well," said the landlord, as, finding all quiet, he took his way now back to his own room, "well, he is a gentleman, every inch of him, that he is. How very mild and polite. — He hasn't been disturbed, well, that's a comfort."

CLXXXII.

THE WAITER TELLS THE STORY OF THE LAKES' DISTURBANCE TO GEORGE AND FRANCIS.

NOTHING FURTHER OCCURRED during the night to cause any alarm to the inmates of the London Hotel, but we may as well give Miss Annetta'a account of the night's transaction; an account which she gave to Mrs. Lake at the time, and which soon spread all over the hotel, with, no doubt, many additions and embellishments as it was carried.

She said, that having retired to rest, she, being fatigued by her journey, soon dropped off asleep. That she, to the best of her belief, fastened her room door, although she certainly could not absolutely swear to having done so, she was so very weary. She did not know how long she had slept, but she had a frightful dream, in which she thought she was pursued by wolves who ran after her through a large tract of country until she took shelter in a wood, and then all the wolves left her and abandoned the pursuit, except one, and that one caught her and fastened his fangs in her throat just as she sunk down exhausted upon a great heap of dried leaves that came in her way in the forest.

She then went on to say that in the agony of her dream she actually awoke at that moment, and saw a human face close to her, and that *a man had his mouth close to her neck, and was sucking her blood.*

It was then that she uttered the two screams which had so alarmed the whole house; and then she stated that the vampire, for such she named the apparition, left her and she fainted away.

Now this story so far as it went, might all be very well accounted for by being called a dream, and the change from a wolf to a man might be but one of those fantastic changes that our sleeping visions so frequently undergo, but — and in this case this was a serious "but" — but *she showed upon her neck the marks of two teeth,* and there was a small wound on which even in the morning was a little portion of coagulated blood.

This staggered everybody, as well it might, and the whole hotel was in a state of confusion. Mr. Blue kept his room. Mr. Black got up and declared that he was much better than the day before, attributing his indisposition to bodily fatigue; and the Lakes were in a state of consternation difficult to describe.

The landlord, too, was nearly out of his senses at the idea of a vampire being in his house, and a grand consultation was held in the bar parlour between him, Mr. and Mrs. Lake, and Mr. Black, who was asked if he would step down and give his opinion, which compliment was paid to him on account of his being such a gentlemanly and quiet man.

They took it in turns to speak, and the landlord had the first say.

"Gentlemen," he said, "and you madam, you can easily conceive how grieved I am about what has taken place, and I can only say that anything in the world that I can do to find out all about it, I will do with the greatest possible pleasure. Command me in any way, but — but if I have a suspicion of anybody in this house, it is of that Mr. Blue."

"And I too," said Mrs. Lake.

"I don't know what to say further," remarked Mr. Lake, "than that my suspicions of some foul play on the part of Mr. Blue, are so strong, that if he is not turned out of the Hotel, we will leave to-night."

"That's conclusive," said the landlord. "But if you, Mr. Black, would favor us with your opinion, I'm sure, sir, we should be all much obliged."

"I am afraid," said Mr. Black in his quiet, gentlemanly way, "that my opinion will be of very little importance, as I know nothing of the whole affair, but just what I have heard from one and another; I slept all the while it appears. But there is one circumstance that certainly to me is an unpleasant and a suspicious one, and that is that Mr. Blue, as he calls himself, was up and dressed, and that, with the exception of your night-watchman, he was the only person in the hotel who was so."

"That's a fact," said the landlord, "I met him."

"Then that settles the business," said Mr. Lake, "send him away. God knows if there be such things as vampires or not, but at all events, the suspicion is horrid, so you had better get rid of him at once."

"I will — I will."

"Stop," said Mr. Black. "Before you do so, is it not worth while to make some effort to come at the precise truth, and that in my opinion, would be very desirable indeed."

"It would — it would," said Mr. Lake, "you must understand, sir, that the young lady is especially under my care, and in fact I esteem her greatly — very greatly I may say, for a variety of reasons, and therefore anything that I can do, which may have the effect of securing her peace of mind and happiness will be to me a sacred purpose."

"Then I should recommend," said Mr. Black, "that this lady and your wife, landlord, keep watch in the young lady's chamber to-night."

"Oh, I couldn't — I couldn't," said the landlady.

"Nor I," replied Mrs. Lake, "nor I, I'm sure, I cannot think of such a thing, I could not do it, I should faint away from terror."

"And so should I," cried the landlady. "I feel quite ill even now at the thought of the thing."

"Then I can say no more, ladies. Of course, gentlemen cannot very well, unless they are very near relatives, undertake such a job. I tell you what we can do, though; suppose we watch in the corridor, you and I, Mr. Lake, and leaving the door of the young lady's chamber just closed we shall hear if there be any alarm given from within and effectually secure her from intrusion without. What say you to this, as a plan of proceedings? There is your son too, might keep watch with us."

"I'm afraid he is too nervous."

"Yes," said the landlord, "and he might pop into my bed again, as he did last night in his fright. Oh don't have him gentlemen, I beg of you. I would go myself, but I am so sleepy always, that I never can keep my eyes open after twelve o'clock. Not that I am at all afraid of anything, but it's downright sleepiness you see, gentlemen. I am on my feet all day, and — and so you see I'd rather not on the whole."

"I am willing," said Mr. Black.

"Sir," said Mr. Lake, "I am quite ashamed of giving you so much trouble, but I can only say that I shall be very much obliged indeed, by your company, and I do hope that we shall have the pleasure of catching Mr. Blue if he be guilty."

"Or acquitting him if innocent," added Mr. Black. "Let us be just even in the midst of our suspicions. It would be a terrible thing to stigmatise this gentleman as a vampire, when perhaps he may have as great a horror of such gentry as we possibly can."

At this moment young Lake made his appearance. He looked rather pale as he apologised to the landlord for his unintentional intrusion into his room over night.

"The fact is," said he, "I am as constitutionally brave as a lion, and so whenever anything occurs I run away."

"Indeed, sir, an odd way of showing courage," said Mr. Black. "Why do you run away?"

"For fear, sir, of doing something rash."

"Well, I certainly never heard a better excuse for an undignified retreat in one's shirt, before in my life. But you will not be called upon to do anything to-night. You had better shut yourself up, and let you hear what you will, you need not come out of your room, you know."

"Well, do you know, sir, I think that it would be the best way, for if I came out I might do something rash, such as kill somebody, which I should afterwards be sorry for, you know."

"Certainly."

"Then that's understood, father, that let what will happen I won't come out. I have been speaking to Annetta, but I can't somehow or another get her to be pleasant."

"Hush!" said old Lake, and he bent his brows upon his son reprovingly, as if he fancied that he was letting out more of the family secrets than he ought to have done. The young man was silent accordingly, for he seemed to be in great dread of his father, who certainly if not a better man, was a man of much more intellect and courage than the son, who was but a very few degrees removed from absolute silliness. He was fool enough to be wicked, and the father was cunning enough to be so. How strange that vice should usually belong to the two extremes of intellect, that folly and talent should lead to similar results, a disregard of the ordinary moral obligations; but it is so.

WE MAY PASS OVER the rest of the day, and we do so the more willingly, because we are anxious that the reader should be possessed of some particulars which George and Francis, the servants of Lord Lake, communicated without any reserve at all to Slop, the waiter.

Indeed, far from having anything like a wish to conceal anything, they seemed to glory in saying as much as they could with respect to those matters that were uppermost in their mind.

This was just the frame of mind that Slop would have wished in his prayers, had he prayed at all upon the subject, to find them in; for although Slop was quite remarkable for neglecting his own affairs, he never neglected anybody else's and curiosity had been the bane of his existence.

Upon arriving at the King's Head, in Chiswell-street, he found that the servants of Lord Lake were there, according as they had said they should be, and glasses of something uncommonly hot and strong having been ordered, they and Slop soon grew quite happy and familiar together.

First, though, before they would commence a history of anything they had to tell of the Lake family, they resolved upon hearing from Slop all that had passed at the London Hotel, and you may be quite sure, that it lost nothing in the telling, but was duly made as much of as the circumstances would permit. No doubt the fumes of the something hot materially assisted Mr. Slop's invention and general talents upon the interesting occasion.

CLXXXIII.

THE THE COMMUNICATION OF THE SERVANTS RESPECTING THE LAKE FAMILY.

THE COACHMAN AND groom evidently listened with great interest to what Slop had to relate. For a wonder, they were completely silent while he spoke; and when he had concluded, they looked at each other, and nodded, as much to say,—Ah! we can draw some conclusion from all that, that you Mr. Slop, really know nothing at all about.

"Is that all?" said George.

"Yes," said the waiter, "and sufficient I think."

"More, a good deal," remarked Francis. "But howsomdever, as you seem a proper sort of fellow, we don't mind telling you what we think of the matter."

"No, no," interposed George, "not exactly that."

"And why not?"

"Because you see, Francis, we have never known yet, my boy, what to think about it."

"Well there's some truth in that at all events. But we will tell Mr. Slop what happened once before that wasn't much unlike what has taken place at the London Hotel."

"Well, but tell him first who she is," said George. "Then he'll understand all the rest better, as well as taking more interest in it."

"Very good. Then listen, Mr. Slop."

"With all my ears," said Slop.

At this moment a bell rung sharply, and Slop on the impulse of the moment, sprung up,—

"Coming—coming—coming."

Both George and Francis burst into a great laugh, and Slop was quite disconcerted.

"Really, gentlemen," he said, "I'm sorry, very sorry, but I'm so used to cry, coming, when a bell rings, that, for the moment, I forgot there was no sort of occasion to do so here. I begs you won't think no more of it, but tell me all as you have got to tell."

"Don't mention it," said Francis, and then after taking another draught of the something-strong, and settling himself in his seat, commenced.

"Lord Lake, you know, is our master, and a very good sort of a man he is, only he's a—a—a; what did the doctor call him George?"

"Oh, I know, a—a—a, what was it Frank?"

"Well, I asked you. It was a *wallytoddyhairyhun*, I think."

"Something like it. Odd wasn't it?"

"Wery."

"I beg your pardon, gentlemen," said a gentlemanly looking man who was seated in an obscure corner of the room, and who was desperately ugly—at least so much as could be seen of his face, for it was much muffled up. "I beg your pardon, but the word you mean I suppose is valetudinarian."

"That's it, that's it! I knows it when I hears it. That's it; well they say that in consequence of being that 'ere he was rather cross-grained a little when there wasn't no sort of occasion for it, and barring that, which, poor man, I suppose he could not help, he was about as decent a master as ever stepped in shoe leather, wasn't he, George?"

"I believe you, my boy."

"Well, the Countess of Bhackbighte was his mother-in-law, you see, a wicious old woman as ever lived, and when Lady Lake died it was she as brought the news to Lord Lake that his wife was dead, and the wirtuous baby as she had just brought into the world was dead too, wasn't that it, George?"

"I believe you my boy, rather."

"Well, Lord Lake was *inconsolotable* as they says, for ever so long, and he made friends with his brother who would come next into the property; they all went abroad together."

"All who?" said Slop.

"Wery good, I'll tell you, Lord Lake, his brother, his brother's wife and son. Them as is now at the London Hotel. Now you knows, don't you?"

"Go on, I knows."

"Well they hadn't been there above a matter o' fourteen years when the old Countess of Bhackbighte dies, and then there comes a letter to my lord as says that the precious baby as his wife had brought into the world just afore she went out of it herself, wasn't dead at all, but had been smugged away by the old Countess, nobody knows what for, and that she was alive and kicking then, and ready to come to her papa whenever he said the word, and so come she did, you see, and that's our young lady Annetta, you see, as is at the London Hotel."

"Well, but I don't understand," said Slop.

"Of course you don't."

"Oh."

"But you will if you goes on a-listening; you can't expect to understand all at once you know. Just attend to the remainder and you'll soon know all about it; but George is the man to tell you, that he is."

"Oh, no, no," said George.

"Why, you heard it, and told it to me. Come, don't be foolish, but tell it at once, old fellow."

"Well, if I must, I must," said George, "so here goes; though when I has to tell anything, I always feels as if I was being *druv* with a curb half-a-dozen links too tight. But here goes."

"I am very much amused," said Slop, "and should certainly like to hear it all. Pray go on?"

"Well, you must know we was at an old tumble-down place in Italy, as they calls Rome. Horridly out o' repair, but that's neither here nor there. In course we had stables and riding-out; and there was a nice sort o' terrace where Lord Lake used to walk sometimes, as well as his brother, while the carriage was being got out, so that I could hear what they said if I chose to do so.

"Well, one day the brother, Mr. Lake, or the Honourable Dick Lake as he was sometimes called, was walking there alone, and I seed as he was all of a tremble like, you understand! but I could not have any idea of what it was about. Once or twice I heard him say, — 'It will do — and it will do.'

"Presently, then out comes Lord Lake, and he says, giving the other a letter, 'Good God, read that!' — Give us a trifle more sugar?"

"What?"

"Why, what do you mean," said Francis. "Is that the way to tell a story, to run into what people says what you happens to want yourself? Here's the sugar, and now go on."

"Well, the brother reads it, and then he says; 'Gracious Providence,' says he 'this here says as the Lady Annetta, ain't your daughter, but a *himposter.*'

"'Yes,' says Lord Lake, 'oh, what will become of me now?'

"'Calm yourself,' says the brother, 'and leave this affair to me. Let her go with me to England, and we will clear up the mystery. I love her as I would a child of my own; but still this here letter,' says he, 'seems to contain such a statement;' says he —"

"Well? Well?"

"That's all! After that, they walked off the terrace and I didn't hear no more at all. After that, in a day or two Lord Lake comes to me; and says, 'George, my brother and his family, with Lady Annetta, are going to England. I wish you and Francis to accompany them and to attend upon them, just the same as you would on myself,' says he, and in course I didn't like to say anything; so we came, but as our idea of the brother is that he's a humbug, we wouldn't have no more to do with him, after we got to London, you see; and so off we went as you heard."

"Well, but," said Slop; "there was a something else you was to tell me."

"So there was," said Francis "and this was it. While we were staying at a place called Florence, and sleeping all of us in an old palace, there was an alarm in the middle of the night, and we found it came from the chamber of the Lady Annetta; who said that a man had got in by the window, and she just woke in time to see him; and when she screamed out away he went again, but nothing could be seen of him; the oddest thing was that the window was so high from the ground, that it seemed to be quite out of the question that he could have got at it without a ladder; yet the deuce of a ladder was there to be seen."

"And who was it?"

"Nobody ever knew, but the night after it was said that a vampire had visited a cottage near at hand, and fastened on the throat of a little girl of about seven, and sucked half the blood out of her, so that she was lying at the point of death; and the description the child gave of him was so like what the Lady Annetta said of the man that had got in at the window of her bedroom, that my lord got very uneasy about it, and moved away from Florence as quick as he could, and no wonder, either, you will say."

"It was odd."

"It was, and what you have told me of last night, put me in mind of it, you see."

"No doubt; Lord, I'm all of a twitter myself."

"Why, what need you care? those who know about vampires say that there are two sorts, one sort always attacks its own relations as was, and nobody else, and the other always selects the most charming young girls, and nobody else, and if they can't get either, they starve to death, waste away and die, for they take no food or drink of any sort, unless they are downright forced."

"But who told you?"

"Oh, an old Italian priest, who spoke English."

CLXXXIV.

THE MYSTERIOUS STRANGER. — THE NIGHT-WATCH.

AT THIS MOMENT, the stranger who had put the coachman and groom right about the word valetudinarian, rose from the seat he had occupied in the corner of the room, and uttering a deep, hollow groan, walked towards the door.

The party looked at him with awe and astonishment. He was of great height but frightfully thin, and the slight glance they could get of his face, showed how perfectly ugly he was. In another moment he had left the place, and there was a silence of several minutes' duration after he had done so, but it was at length broken by the coachman, who said, —

"I say, Frank, my boy."

"Here you is," said Francis.

"Don't you think if you never seed anybody as looked like a vampire before, you have seed one now?"

"The devil," said Francis, "you don't mean that?"

"Yes, I do though, and it strikes me wonderful as we have been a telling all we had to tell afore the very indiwidual, of all others, as we ought'nt to a-told it to, that's a vampire. If a *hoss* is a *hoss*, that's a vampire, Frank! I knows it — I feels it."

Frank looked aghast.

"Why, why," then he said, "we have just told him where to find the Lady Lake if he wants her. Lor'— what — suppose it's the same one as got in at the window at Florence! I'll have him, he can't have got far, I should say, by this time, and hang me if I don't stop him and know what he is, afore he goes any further. I shan't sleep if I don't."

Without waiting for any reply, although the coachman, and Mr. Slop both seemed to be upon the point of saying something, out rushed the valorous Francis into the street. But in about three minutes he came back, and sat down with a disappointed look.

"He's off," he said.

"In course," said the coachman, "through the air like a sky rocket, you might a know'd that; but arter all, Frank, he mayden't be a vampire. Do vampires come into public houses, eh? Answer me that will you; I rather think that's a settler, Frank."

"Do you?" said Frank. "It might be, old fellow, if you could prove it. It would be an odd thing for a vampire to come into a public house and drink, but I don't see, if he has anything again by it, anything to prevent him coming and ordering and paying for something, and then leaving it. Look there!"

Frank pointed to the brimming glass of something which was on the table just where the mysterious man had sat, and this to the coachman and to Slop was such proof positive that they both looked at each other with the most rueful expression of their countenances.

"I think you are convinced now, you old ump," added Frank.

"Rather, rather."

"I'm all over of a cold *inspiration*," said Slop.

"Well," added Frank, "it's not never of no use, you know, putting yourself out of the way about it, and that's the fact, and all I've got to say is that I've got nothing to say."

"Wery good, wery good."

"But if you, Mr. Slop, will give us a call to-morrow and let us know if anything wrong has took place at the London Hotel, we shall be very much obliged to you; for it's natural for us that we feel an interest in what's going on there on account of our young lady, who we won't and don't think is anything else but our young lady, and if she was not, she ought to be; and I tell you what, just keep an eye on the spooney, young Lake."

"I will."

"He wants to be be quite sweet with the Lady Annetta, but she can't abide him. But you tell us if he tries to pitch it too strong, and we shall perhaps hit on some scheme of operations."

All this Slop promised faithfully, and with his own nerves rather startled at the idea of having been in the same room for the better part of an hour with a vampire, he walked back to the hotel, and as he had not been enjoined to any secrecy he gave the landlord a full and particular account of all that had taken place.

This was listened to with no small degree of interest, but as mine host of the London Hotel could make nothing of it, he could do nothing with it.

"Slop," he said, "I don't like the state of things at all, I assure you, Slop, and I rather shake than otherwise about what's to occur to-night. You know there's to be a watch kept in the corridor by the young lady's room, or else poor thing no doubt she wouldn't get a wink of sleep, and I'm quite sure that I sha'nt at all events, let what will happen or what won't; I'm all in a twitter now as it is, I've broke nine wine glasses already; and all I can say is, I wish they would all go away."

The landlord did not like to give good guests notice to quit his house, but he had a consultation with Mr. Black, whom he considered to be quite his sheet-anchor in this affair, for if that gentleman had not offered to sit up and watch for the vampire, he, the landlord, certainly would, despite all profitable considerations, have requested guests who brought with them such questionable connexions to leave.

THE NIGHT HAD NOW come on, and as hour after hour passed away, the anxiety of all concerned in the affairs that were taking place at the London hotel increased. But we need not occupy the time and attention of the reader with surmises and reflections while facts of an interesting and strange nature remain to be detailed.

Suffice it that at eleven o'clock the Lady Annetta retired to rest.

Two chairs, and a table on which burnt two candles, were placed in the corridor just outside the room in which the fair girl who had the previous night had such a visitor reposed, and there sat Mr. Black and Mr. Lake, both determined to do their utmost to discover the mystery of the vampire's appearance, and to capture him should he again show himself.

During the first half hour's watch, Mr. Lake related to his companion the particulars of the affair at Florence, which, as it has already been told by Francis, we need not again recapitulate; suffice it to say that the narration was listened to by Mr. Black with great interest.

"And did you," he said, "make no discovery of who this midnight visitor was?"

"None whatever."

"'Tis awfully strange."

"It is, and has given her abundance of uneasiness."

"And well it may, sir, I shall be very happy if through my means any elucidation of these mysteries and truly terrific visitations should take place."

"You are very good, sir. What is that?"

"Twelve o'clock, I think, striking by some neighbouring church time-keeper. Hush! is it not so? Yes, twelve."

"It is. How still the house is. I was told this was a very quiet hotel, and so indeed I find it, but yet, I suppose upon this occasion there is more stillness than usual."

"Doubtless. Hush, hush! what was that? I thought I heard something like a window opening slowly and cautiously. Hark! There again. Do you not hear it. Hush, hush. Listen now."

"On my life I can hear nothing."

"Indeed your sense of hearing then is not so sharp as mine. Look there."

He pointed as he spoke to the door of Mr. Blue' chamber, which was opened a very short distance, not above a couple of inches, and then he added in a whisper, "What do you think of that?"

"By heaven! I suspected him before."

"And I — and — be still, whatever you do. But yet perhaps it would be better. Go down stairs and bring up the hall porter;

we may as well be in force, you know. The door at the head of the stairs is open. You can depend upon my keeping a good watch while you are gone. Now, now, quick, or we may be pounced upon and murdered before we are aware."

Thus urged Mr. Lake ran down stairs for the purpose of rousing up the night-porter, and he found that that individual did indeed require rousing up.

"Hilloa, my man," he said, "get up!"

"Eh? eh? what? fire!"

"No, no, they want you up stairs, that's all. You are a pretty fellow to consider yourself a night-watch here and to be fast asleep. Why, with the exception that you have your clothes on you, you are no more ready than anybody else in the house."

"I beg your pardon sir, I always sleeps with one eye open."

"Well well, come up stairs!"

A loud scream at this moment came upon their ears, and the night-porter staggered back again into his great leathern chair, from whence he had just risen, and looked aghast, while Mr. Lake turned pale and trembled fearfully.

"Good God!" he said, "what's that?"

A bell was run furiously, and then ceased, with a sudden jar, as if the wire had broken, which was indeed the fact. Then Mr. Lake, mustering all the courage he possessed, ran up stairs again, leaving the night-porter to follow him or not, as he felt inclined; but when he reached the door at the top of the staircase, he found that it was fast, nor could he with all his strength force it open.

"Help! help! help!" he heard a voice cry.

CLXXXV.

THE VAMPYRE'S FEAST. — THE ALARM AND THE PURSUIT.

A GENERAL RINGING of bells now ensued in the hotel, from all the bedrooms that were occupied, and the din in the house was quite terrific.

Mr. Lake hammered away at the door leading to the corridor, and he was soon joined by the hall-porter, who having now recovered from the first shock which the scream had given him, showed more courage and determination than any one would have given him credit for. He was rather a bulky man, and without any more ado, he flung himself bodily against the door with such force that he dashed it open and rolled into the corridor.

All was darkness.

"Lights! lights! lights!" shouted Mr. Lake. "Lights! — Mr. Black, where are you? Mr. Black! Mr. Black!

A door, it was that of Mr. Blue, was now dashed open, and that gentleman appeared with a candle in his hand, and a pistol firmly grasped in the other. It was very strange but he wore an artificial masquerade nose of an enormous size, and had on a red wig.

"Who locked my door?" he cried, "who locked my room door on the outside and forced me to break it open — who did it?"

"Where is the vampire?" said Mr. Lake.

"Lights! lights! Lights!" shouted the night-watchman, and in another minute the landlord and several waiters, half-dressed but carrying lights, and each armed with the first weapon of offence he could lay his hands on at the moment, made their appearance on the scene of action.

"What is it? What is it?" cried the landlord. "Oh what is it?"

"God knows," cried Mr. Lake, and he darted into the apartment of the young lady. In another moment he emerged, and tottered towards one of the seats.

"She is covered with blood," he said.

Mr. Blue and the landlady of the Hotel both made a rush then into the room, and the former came out in a minute, and going to his own apartment shut the door. They thought that they then heard him fall at full length upon the floor. All was mystery.

"I'm bewildered," said the landlord, "What *is* it all about?"

"And where is Mr. Black?" asked Mr. Lake.

"Here," cried a waiter as he pointed to an insensible form lying so close to the table, that nobody had as yet noticed it. "Here he is. He looks as if he was dead."

Poor Mr. Black was lifted up, his eyes were closed as well as his mouth, and he seemed to breathe with difficulty. He was placed in a chair, and then held, while water was dashed in his face to recover him, and after a time, just as one of the waiters who had been sent for the surgeon again who had before attended the young lady, made his appearance with that gentleman, he slowly opened his eyes.

"Oh! mercy, mercy! Where am I now?"

"What is all this about?" inquired the medical man.

"Nobody knows sir," said the landlord, "that's the beauty of it. But the young lady is very bad again; will you, wife, show the doctor into her room. Good God, I shall go out of my wits, and my hotel that has a character forming one of the quietest in all London — yes, the quietest I may say. I'm a ruined man."

"Mr. Black," said Mr. Lake, "I implore you if you can to tell the meaning of all this."

"All — all I know," said Mr. Black faintly. "All I know —"

Everybody gathered round him to listen, and with looks of fright and apprehension, and a trembling voice, he said: —

"I — I was sitting here waiting for Mr. Lake to come back with the night porter, for we had some cause to wish for further help, when somebody came suddenly up to me, and struck me down. The blow was on the top of my head, and so severe, that I fell as if shot."

"And then? and then?"

"Nothing. I don't know anything else till you recovered me, and then, I seemed as if all the place was scouring round me; and then —"

"But, Mr. Black, cannot you tell us who struck you? What was he like? Could you identify him again?"

"I fear not. Indeed I hardly saw more of him than that he was tall."

"Well," cried Mr. Lake, "all I can say is that I have had my suspicions since last night, and now I am certain, that is to say circumstantially certain. What say you,

landlord? Is there not one person in the house who may not fairly enough be suspected."

He looked towards the door of Mr. Blue's room, as he spoke, and indeed all eyes were turned in that direction, and the landlord mustering up courage advanced to the door and said, as he did so, "We will have him out. He shall not stay another hour on my premises. We will have him out, I say. This sort of thing won't do, and it shall not do. We will have him out. I say gentlemen we will have him out."

One thing was quite clear, and that was that the landlord wanted somebody to come forward, and assist him in having out Mr. Blue; but when he found that nobody stirred he turned round at the door, and looked rather foolish.

Under any other circumstances, perhaps, this conduct might have excited the risible faculties of all who were present; but the affair, take it all in all, was of too mysterious and serious a character to indulge in any laughter about.

"I," said Mr. Lake, advancing, "will have him out, if nobody else will!"

It would appear as if Mr. Blue had been listening to what was going on; for on the instant, he flung open his door, and said, —

"Who will have me out, and what for?"

"Vampire, vampire," cried a chorus of voices.

"Idiots!" said Mr. Blue.

"Detain him!" sad Mr. Lake; "detain him, we shall never be satisfied until this affair is thoroughly and judicially enquired into. Detain him I say."

"Let him who sets no value on his life," said Mr. Blue, "lay but a hand upon me, and he shall have to admire the consequences of his rashness. I am not one to be trifled with; it is my fancy to leave this hotel this moment; let any one dare to stand in my way."

"Your name is not Blue," said the landlord, "you are not what you seem."

"Granted."

"Ah! you admit it," said Lake. "Lay hold of him, I will give ten pounds for him dead or alive; I have often heard of vampires, and by Heaven, I now believe in them. Seize him, I say, seize him."

He dashed forward himself, as he spoke, and was on the point of seizing hold of Mr. Blue, when one well-directed blow from that individual sent him sprawling.

After this nobody showed any very marked disposition to attack him, but he was allowed to walk calmly and slowly down the staircase of the hotel; while Lake gathered himself up, looking rather confused at the tumble he had had. But his passion was not subdued, for he made a rush still after the supposed vampire, but he was too late. The hotel door was closed with a bang, that reverberated through the house, and Mr. Blue was gone, vampire, or no vampire.

"Landlord, I shall leave your house," said Lake.

"I'm ruined," said the landlord. "This affair will get into some Sunday paper. Mr. Black, what is to be done?"

"Really, the top of my head is so hurt," replied Mr. Black, "that I can think of nothing else."

"A plague upon the top of your head," muttered the landlord.

The Lakes now, that is Mr. and Mrs. Lake, found their way to the young lady's chamber, when they found her in a state of great alarm. The story she told amounted to this: —

She was asleep, she said, having perfect confidence that no harm could come to her, while the door of her room was watched in the way it was. She had a light burning in her room, but it was one that gave a very faint light, as she had usually an objection to sleeping otherwise than in profound darkness; but she had no notion of how long she had been asleep, when she was awakened by a hand being placed over her mouth, which prevented her from breathing.

She struggled to free herself but it was in vain. The monster attacked her on the neck with his teeth, and all she remembered was getting sufficiently free to utter one scream, and then she fainted away.

"My dear," said Mrs. Lake, "I must have some serious talk with you upon a subject which I have before urged. Go away, Lake."

Lake left the room, and then, Mrs. Lake continued.

"This is a very dreadful affair, Annetta. You know that it is fancied you are not the child of Lord Lake, and that we have the care of you. Now we so much love and admire you, —"

"Stop madam, stop," said the young lady, "I know what you are about to say, you are going to urge me again to marry your son, which I will never do, for I have the greatest aversion to him."

"You will not? who will protect you from a vampire better than a husband?"

"Probably no one, but at least I reserve to myself the right to choose to whom I give that task. I am ill now and weak, I pray you not to weary me further upon a subject concerning which it is quite impossible we can ever agree. I only wish I were dead."

"And that you may very well soon be

if your blood is all sucked away by a vampire."

"So be it. Heaven help me!"

"Pshaw! — you may die as soon as you like."

CLXXXVI.

THE MEETING IN ST. JAMES'S PARK.

ANOTHER DAY PASSED over at the London Hotel, and as Mr. Blue had been kind enough to take his departure, and that departure seemed to be final, for he did not show himself again, Mr. Lake rescinded the resolution he had made to leave.

Probably it was much more convenient for him to stay, although he pretended that he did so out of consideration for the landlord, who ought not to be punished for innocently harbouring so suspicious a character as Mr. Blue, whether he were a vampire, or not.

But the day, as we say, has passed away, and it is about half-past eight o'clock in the evening, and quite dark, for the moon did not rise for an hour afterwards, when Mr. Lake might have been seen making his way towards Saint James's Park.

He entered it by the narrow mode of ingress by Spring Gardens, and made his way towards the palace of Saint James, that is to say, the wall of its private gardens that look upon the park; and then, under some shady trees, he paused and looked inquiringly about him.

"He was to have been here a little before nine," he muttered. "Hush!"

The Horse Guards clock chimed three-quarters past eight.

Mr. Lake draw back, as two men came at a slow pace towards where he stood, and then he muttered, —

"It is Miller, but confound him, who is that he has brought with him? Hang the fellow! I did not give him leave to make a confidant in this ticklish piece of business."

One of the men only now advanced, leaving the other about twelve paces from him.

"Mr. L —, I think," he said.

"Yes, Miller, it is I; but who in the name of all that's infernal have you brought with you? Are you mad to trust to anybody but yourself?"

"Oh, don't trouble yourself about that, sir. The fact is, he has been with me for a number of years; he is my managing clerk, and as great a rogue as you would wish him to be. I cannot keep anything wholly from him, so the best way, I find, is to make a confidant of him at once."

"I don't half like it."

"You may thoroughly depend upon Lee, that is his name, and you never knew such a rogue as he is, sir; besides, somebody, you know, must have been trusted to personate the father, and he will do that, and then, you know likewise, sir, that —"

"Hush, hush! speak lower! will you? bring this accomplished rogue this way, since I must do business, it seems, with him! Call him here, Miller, and we will talk as we walk on, that is always safer than holding a conference in one spot, near which any one may hide; but it is a much more difficult thing for a spy to follow and overhear you at the same time."

"You have a genius, Mr. Lake."

"Bah! I don't want any compliments from you, Miller; we want downright business."

By this time, Mr. Miller had made a sign to his clerk, Lee, to come up, which that individual did, and at once saluted Mr. Lake, and made some trivial remark about the weather, in an off-hand way.

Mr Lake made rather a distant reply and then he said, —

"I presume, sir, that Mr. Miller has made you acquainted with the affair in which, it seems, I am to purchase your kind co-operation?"

"Oh no," said Miller, "I have certainly given him a brief outline, but I always prefer that the principal himself should give all the directions possible to every one, and tell his own story."

"Well, sir, I think you might as well have told him, and not given me the trouble. But, however, if I must, I must; so pray attend to me sir."

"I will," said Lee.

"My brother then, is Lord Lake. It's a new title rather, as our father was the first who had it, and he left large estates to my brother, and to his son if he had one, or his daughter, if he had one. The title descending to heir males, I must have the

title by outliving my brother, if I do, but hang it all, he has a daughter, and she will have the estates."

"I comprehend."

"The old countess of Bhackbighte smuggled the child away at its birth, and took care of it for a consideration that used up two-thirds of my income, but the old cat on her death confessed that the child was Lord Lakes's, but luckily, you see, without criminating me. Now Mr. Miller was her solicitor, and so between us we have forged a letter supposed to be found among the old countess's papers, in which she states that she intends to palm off a child as the Lord Lake's when she is dying, but that his child really did die, you see."

"Oh yes."

"Now this has had an effect upon Lord Lake, who to some extent had repudiated the girl, and what I want is to clinch the matter, by providing some one who will actually own her."

"I understand," said Lee, "but it will be an awkward affair if found out."

"I want to provide against any consequences of a disagreeable nature, by getting her to marry my son, but I don't think she will. Absolute distress, to which I am determined to bring her, if I can, may move her to that step, and then all's right. The secret is in my hands to play with, as I think proper."

"A very good plan."

"You see, there's a lover of hers too, a young officer in the Guards, but he will be off as soon as he finds that she's the daughter of a lawyer's clerk instead of a lord — ha! ha! ha!"

"Likely enough. I'll father her."

"Thank you; and now about money

matters. Miller gets a thousand pounds — what do you want? Be moderate."

"I ought to have five hundred pounds to pay me."

"The deuce! Well, I don't want to stint you. But you will bear in mind that that is very good pay; and now we must get up a first rate story, so complete in all its parts that there shall be no sort of doubt about it, you see — a story that will stand the test of examination and criticism."

"That can be better done in my chambers," said the attorney; "I think now we understand each other perfectly well, and that we need hardly say any more just at present. Money matters are settled, and as Mr. Lee has once undertaken the business, I am quite satisfied, for one, that it will be well done."

"I am glad to hear you say that, Miller, and I am quite reconciled, which I must own I was not at first, to Mr. Lee having a finger in the pie."

"Thank you," said Lee, "thank you; we shall manage it all right, no doubt. Indeed now that you have fully explained it to me, it seems quite an easy and straightforward affair."

"You think so."

"I certainly do think so."

"Then you take off my mind a load of anxiety, for I thought it would be a difficult thing to arrange, and require no end of chicanery and trouble, but you quite reassure — you quite reassure me, Mr. Lee."

"Oh, these things are done every day, my dear sir."

They had walked to and fro as they spoke till now, by the time they had settled their affairs thus far, they stood by the centre of the principal mall. The park was very quiet, and had quite a deserted aspect. Indeed, it was near the time when there would be more difficulty in traversing it in consequence of the extra vigilance of the night sentinels.

The moon faded gradually away, or seemed to fade away as the light fleecy clouds swept over its face, and the parties who had held this interesting dialogue separated. Mr. Lake walked hurriedly towards his hotel, and the attorney and his accomplice stood for a few moments conversing in whispers. They then turned towards the Green Park, and as they did so, they were crossed by a tall, spectral-looking figure wrapped up in an immense cloak, but who did not seem to observe them, for his eyes were fixed upon the moon, which at that moment again began to emerge from the clouds.

He stretched forth his arms as if he would have held the beautiful satellite to his heart.

"An odd fish," whispered the attorney.

"Very," said his companion. "I should like now to know who he is."

The attorney shrugged his shoulders, as he said, "Some harmless lunatic most likely. They say that such often wander all night about the parks."

"That's strange; only look at him now. he seems to be worshipping the moon, and now how he strides along; and see, there is another man meets him, and they both hold up their arms in that strange way to the moon. What on earth can be the meaning of it?"

"I really don't know."

"Some religious fanatics, perhaps."

"Ah! that's as likely as not. We have all sorts of them, jumpers and screamers and tearers, and why not a few who may call themselves Lunarians. For my part I would rather worship the moon than I would, as most church and chapel going women do, worship some canting evangelical thief of a parson, who has — oh dear! such elegant hands, and such whiskers, and speaks so soft and impressive. Of all the rogues on earth, I do detest those in surplices!"

CLXXXVII.

THE CHURCHYARD AT HAMPSTEAD. — THE RESUSCITATION OF A VAMPYRE.

IT WANTS HALF AN HOUR to midnight. The sky is still cloudy, but glimpses of the moon can be got as occasionally the clouds slip on before her disc, and then what a glorious flood of silver light spreads itself over the landscape!

And a landscape in every respect more calculated to look beautiful and romantic under the chaste moon's ray, than that to which we would now invite attention, certainly could not have been found elsewhere, within many a mile of London. It is Hampstead Heath, that favoured spot where upon a small scale are collected some of the rarest landscape beauties that the most romantic mountainous counties of England can present to the gratified eye of the tourist. *

Those who are familiar with London and its environs, of course, are well acquainted with every nook, glade, tree, and dell in that beautiful heath, where, at all and every time and season, there is much to recommend that semi-wild spot to notice. Indeed, if it were, as it ought to be, divested of its donkey-drivers and laundresses, a more delightful place of residence could scarcely be found than some one of those suburban villas, that are dotted round the margin of this picturesque waste.

But it is midnight, nearly. That time is forthcoming, at which popular superstition trembles — that time, at which the voice of ignorance and of cant lowers to whispers, and when the poor of heart and timid of spirit imagine worlds of unknown terrors. On this occasion, though, it will be seen that there would have been some excuses if even the most bold had shrunk back appalled at what was taking place.

But we will not anticipate, for truly in this instance might we say sufficient for the time are the horrors thereof.

If any one had stood on that portion of the high road which leads right over the heath and so on to Hendon or to Highgate, according as the left hand or the right hand route is taken, and after reaching the Castle Tavern, had looked across the wide expanse of heath to the west, they would have seen nothing for a while but the clustering bushes of heath blossom, and the picturesque fir trees, that there are to be beheld in great luxuriance. But, after a time, something of a more

---

* Hampstead Heath was, and is, a 790-acre heath in London, mainly given over to commons and parklands.

noticeable character would have presented itself.

At a quarter to twelve there rose up from a tangled mass of brushwood, which had partially concealed a deep cavernous place where sand had been dug, a human form, and there it stood in the calm still hour of night so motionless that it scarcely seemed to possess life, but presently another rose at a short distance.

And then there was a third, so that these three strange-looking beings stood like landmarks against the sky, and when the moon shone out from some clouds which had for a short time obscured her rays, they looked strange and tall, and superhuman.

One spoke.

"'Tis time," he said, in a deep, hollow voice, that sounded as if it came from the tomb.

"Yes, time," said another.

"Time has come," said the third.

Then they moved, and by the gestures they used, it seemed as if an animated discussion was taking place among them, after which they moved along in perfect silence, and in a most stately manner, towards the village of Hampstead.

Before reaching it, however, they turned down some narrow shaded walks among garden walls, and the backs of stables, until they emerged close to the old churchyard, which stands on high ground, and which was not then — at least, the western portion of it — overlooked by any buildings. Those villas which now skirt it, are of recent elevation.

A dense mass of clouds has now been brought up by a south wind, and had swept over the face of the moon, so that at this juncture, and as twelve o'clock might be expected every moment to strike, the night was darker than it had yet been since sunset. The circumstance was probably considered by the mysterious beings who sought the churchyard as favourable to them, and they got without difficulty within those sacred precincts devoted to the dead.

Scarcely had they found the way a dozen feet among the old tomb-stones, when from behind a large square monument, there appeared two more persons; and if the attorney, Mr. Miller, had been there, he would probably have thought they bore such a strong resemblance to those whom he had seen in the park, he would have had but little hesitation in declaring that they were the same.

These two persons joined the other three, who manifested no surprise at seeing them, and then the whole five stood close to the wall of the church, so that they were quite secure from observation, and one of them spoke.

"Brothers," he said, "you who prey upon human nature by the law of your being, we have work to do to-night — that work which we never leave undone, and which we dare not neglect when we know that it is to be done. One of our fraternity lies here."

"Yes," said the others, with the exception of one, and he spoke passionately.

"Why," he said, "when there were enough, and more than enough, to do the work, summon me?"

"Not more than enough, there are but five."

"And why should you not be summoned," said another, "you are one of us. You ought to do your part with us in setting a brother free from the clay that presses on his breast."

"I was engaged in my vocation. If the moon shine out in all her lustre again, you will see that I am wan and wasted, and have need of—"

"Blood," said one.

"Blood, blood, blood," repeated the others. And then the first speaker said, to him who complained,—"You are one whom we are glad to have with us on a service of danger. You are strong and bold, your deeds are known, you have lived long, and are not yet crushed."

"I do not know our brother's name," said one of the others with an air of curiosity.

"I go by many."

"So do we all. But by what name may we know you best."

"Slieghton, I was named in the reign of the third Edward. But many have known me as Varney, the Vampyre!"

There was a visible sensation among those wretched beings as these words were uttered, and one was about to say something, when Varney interrupted him.

"Come," he said, "I have been summoned here, and I have come to assist in the exhumation of a brother. It is one of the conditions of our being that we do so. Let the work be proceeded with then, at once, I have no time to spare. Let it be done with. Where lies the vampyre? Who was he?"

"A man of good repute, Varney," said the first speaker. "A smooth, fair-spoken man, a religious man, so far as cant went, a proud, cowardly, haughty, worldly follower of religion. Ha, ha, ha!"

"And what made him one of us?"

"He dipped his hands in blood. There was a poor boy, a brother's only child, 'twas left an orphan. He slew the boy, and he is one of us."

"With a weapon."

"Yes, and a sharp one; the weapon of unkindness. The child was young and gentle, and harsh words, blows, and revilings placed him in his grave. He is in heaven, while the man will be a vampyre."

"'Tis well—dig him up."

They each produced from under the dark cloaks they wore, a short double-edged, broad, flat-bladed weapon, not unlike the swords worn by the Romans, and he who assumed the office of guide, led the way to a newly-made grave, and dillegently, and with amazing rapidity and power, they commenced removing the earth.

It was something amazing to see the systematic manner in which they worked, and in ten minutes one of them struck the blade of his weapon upon the lid of a coffin, and said,

"It is here."

The lid was then partially raised in the direction of the moon, which, although now hidden, they could see would in a very short time show itself in some gaps of the clouds, that were rapidly approaching at great speed across the heavens.

They then desisted from their labour, and stood around the grave in silence for a time, until, as the moon was longer showing her fair face, they began to discourse in whispers.

"What shall become of him," said one, pointing to the grave. "Shall we aid him."

"No," said Varney, "I have heard that of him which shall not induce me to lift hand or voice in his behalf. Let him fly, shrieking like a frightened ghost where he lists."

"Did you not once know some people named Bannerworth."

"I did. You came to see me, I think, at an inn. They are all dead." *

---

*   *This story takes place roughly 60 years after the events of Parts I through V, as evidenced by references to the Vale of Health (which was not so named until 1801).*

"Hush," said another, "look, the moon will soon be free from the vapours that sail between it and the green earth. Behold, she shines out fresh once more; there will be life in the coffin soon, and our work will be done."

It was so. The dark clouds passed over the face of the moon, and with a sudden burst of splendour, it shone out again as before.

CLXXXVIII.

THE VAMPYRE. — THE FLIGHT. — THE WATCHMAN IN THE VALE OF HEALTH.

A DEATH-LIKE STILLNESS now was over the whole scene, and those who had partially exhumed the body stood as still as statues, waiting the event which they looked forward to as certain to ensue.

The clear beauty and intensity of the moonbeams increased each moment, and the whole surrounding landscape was lit up with a perfect flood of soft, silvery light. The old church stood out in fine relief, and every tree, and every wild flower, and every blade of grass in the churchyard, could be seen in its finest and most delicate proportions and construction.

The lid of the coffin was wrenched up on one side to about six inches in height, and that side faced the moon, so that some rays, it was quite clearly to be seen, found their way into that sad receptacle for the dead. A quarter of an hour,

however, passed away, and nothing happened.

"Are you certain he is one of us?" whispered Varney.

"Quite. I have known it years past. He had the mark upon him."

"Enough. Behold."

A deep and dreadful groan came from the grave, and yet it could hardly be called a groan; it was more like a howl, and the lid which was partially open, was visibly agitated.

"He comes," whispered one.

"Hush," said another, "hush; our duty will be done when he stands upon the level ground. Hush, let him hear nothing, let him know nothing, since we will not aid him. Behold, behold."

They all looked down into the grave, but they betrayed no signs of emotion, and the sight they saw there was such as one would have supposed would have created emotion in the breast of any one at all capable of feeling. But then we must not reason upon these strange frightful existences as we reason upon human nature such as we usually know it.

The coffin lid was each moment more and more agitated. The deep frightful groans increased in number and sound, and then the corpse stretched out one ghastly hand from the open crevice and grasped despairingly and frantically at the damp earth that was around.

There was still towards one side of the coffin sufficient weight of mould that it would require some strength to turn it off, but as the dead man struggled within his narrow house it kept falling aside in lumps, so that his task of exhumation became each moment an easier one.

At length he uttered a strange wailing shriek, and by a great effort succeeded in throwing the coffin lid quite open, and then he sat up, looking so horrible and ghastly in the grave clothes, that even the vampyres that were around that grave recoiled a little.

"Is it done?" said Varney.

"Not yet," said he who had summoned them to the fearful rite, and so assumed a sort of direction over them, "not yet; we will not assist him, but we may not leave him before telling him who and what he is."

"Do so now."

The corpse stood up in the coffin, and the moonlight fell full upon him.

"Vampyre arise," said he who had just spoken to Varney. "Vampyre arise, and do your work in the world until your doom shall be accomplished. Vampyre arise — arise. Pursue your victims in the mansion and in the cottage. Be a terror and a desolation, go you where you may, and if the hand of death strike you down, the cold beams of the moon shall restore you to new life. Vampyre arise, arise!"

"I come, I come!" shrieked the corpse.

In another moment the five vampyres who had dug him from the grave were gone.

Moaning, shrieking, and groaning he made some further attempts to get out of the deep grave. He clutched at it in vain, the earth crumbled beneath him, and it was only at last by dint of reaching up and dragging in the displaced material that lay in a heap at the sides, so that in a few minutes it formed a mound for him to stand upon in the grave, and he was at length able to get out.

Then, although he sighed, and now and then uttered a wailing shriek as he went about his work, he with a strange kind of instinct, began to carefully fill up the grave from which he had but just emerged, nor did he cease from his occupation until he had finished it, and so carefully shaped the mound of mould and turf over it that no one would have thought it had been disturbed.

When this work was done a kind of madness seemed to seize him, and he walked to the gate of the grave yard, which opens upon Church-street, and placing his hands upon the sides of his mouth he produced such an appalling shriek that it must have awakened everybody in Hampstead.

Then, turning, he fled like a hunted hare in the other direction, and taking the first turning to the right ran up a lane called Frognal-lane, and which is parallel to the town, for a town Hampstead may

be fairly called now, although it was not then.

By pursuing this lane, he got upon the outskirts of the heath, and then turning to the right again, for, with a strange pertinacity he always kept, as far as he could, his face towards the light of the moon, he rushed down a deep hollow, where there was a cluster of little cottages, enjoying such repose that one would have thought the flutter of an awakened bird upon the wing would have been heard.

It was quite clear that the new vampyre had as yet no notion of what he was about, or where he was going, and that he was with mere frantic haste speeding along, from the first impulse of his frightful nature.

The place into which he had now plunged, is called the Vale of Health: now a place of very favourite resort, but then a mere collection of white-faced cottages, with a couple of places that might be called villas. A watchman went his nightly rounds in that place. And it so happened that the guardian of the Vale had just roused himself up at this juncture, and made up his mind to make his walk of observation, when he saw the terrific figure of a man attired in grave clothes coming along with dreadful speed towards him, as if to take the Vale of Health by storm.

The watchman was so paralysed by fear that he could not find strength enough to spring his rattle, although he made the attempt, and held it out at arm's length, while his eyes glared with perfect ferocity, and his mouth was wide enough open to nourish the idea, that after all he had a hope of being able to swallow the spectre.

But, nothing heeding him, the vampyre came wildly on.

Fain now would the petrified watchman have got out of the way, but he could not, and in another moment he was dashed down to the earth, and trodden on by the horrible existence that knew not what it did.

A cloud came over the moon, and the vampyre sunk down, exhausted, by a garden-wall, and there lay as if dead, while the watchman, who had fairly fainted away, lay in a picturesque attitude on his back, not very far off.

Half an hour passed, and a slight mist-like rain began to fall.

The vampyre slowly rose to his feet, and commenced wringing his hands and moaning, but his former violence of demeanour had passed away. That was but the first flush of new life, and now he seemed to be more fully aware of who and what he was.

He shivered as he tottered slowly on, until he came to where the watchman lay, and then he divested that guardian of the Vale of his greatcoat, his hat, and some other portions of his apparel, all of which he put on himself, still slightly moaning as he did so, and ever and anon stopping to make a gesture of despair.

When this operation was completed, he slunk off into a narrow path which led on to the heath again, and there he seemed to waver a little, whether he would go towards London, or the country. At length it seemed that he decided upon the former course, and he walked on at a rapid pace right through Hampstead, and down the hill towards London, the lights of which would be seen gleaming in the distance.

When the watchman did recover himself, the first thing he did was, to be kind enough to rouse every body up from their sleep in the Vale of Health, by springing his rattle at a prodigious rate, and by the time he had roused up the whole neighbourhood, he felt almost ready to faint again at the bare recollection of the terrible apparition that had knocked him down.

The story in the morning was told all over the place, with many additions to it of course, and it was long afterwards before the inhabitants of the Vale could induce another watchman, for that one gave up the post, to run the risk of such a visitation.

And the oddest thing of all was, that the watchman declared that he caught a glance at the countenance, and that it was like that of a Mr. Brooks, who had only been buried the day previous, that if he had not known that gentleman to be dead and buried, he should have thought it was he himself gone mad.

But there was the grave of Mr. Brooks,

with its circular mound of earth, all right enough; and then Mr. B. was known to have been such a respectable man. He went to the city every day, and used to do so just for the purpose of granting audiences to ladies and gentlemen who might be labouring under any little pecuniary difficulties, and accommodating them. Kind Mr. Brooks. He only took one hundred pounds per cent. Why should he be a Vampyre? Bless him! Too severe, really!

There were people who called him a bloodsucker while he lived, and now he was one practically, and yet he had his own pew at the church, and subscribed a whole guinea a year to a hospital — he did, although people did say it was in order that he might pack off any of his servants at once to it in case of illness. But then, the world is so censorious.

To this day the watchman's story of the apparition that visited the Vale of Health is talked of by the old women who make what they call tea for Sunday parties at nine pence a head.

But it is time now that we go back to London, and see what is taking place at the hotel where the Lakes are staying, and how the villany of the uncle thrives — that villany of which he actually had the face to give such an exposition to Mr. Lee the clerk of the attorney.

Let us hope that the right will still overcome the injustice that is armed against it, and that Lord Lake and his beautiful child may not fall victims to the machinations that are brought into play against them, by those who ought to have been their best friends.

CLXXXIX.

MISS LAKE PASSES A FEARFUL NIGHT. — THE IMPOSTOR PUNISHED.

THE LANDLORD OF THE London Hotel made every possible exertion to keep a profound secret the events of the night, but people will talk when even they have not anything particular to say, so that we cannot wonder at their doing so when they have.

In fact the story of the vampyre at the London Hotel got known pretty well half over London in the course of the day succeeding that second attempt upon the life blood of the young lady, who had become the object of attack from the monster.

Mr. Lake was in a strange frame of mind as regarded the whole affair. He did not yet know whether to really believe it or not — whether to ascribe it, after all, to a dream, or, as Mrs. Lake hinted, for she was a woman fond of scheming herself, so always ready to suggest its existence in others — a mere plan upon the part of the young girl to get rid of the projected alliance with young Master Lake, and possibly evoke the sympathy of all who heard her story.

This view of the matter, however, although it did not make much impression upon Mr. Lake, suggested a something to him, that he thought would chime in well with his other plans and projects.

"If," he said "I could but instill a little courage into my son he might now, at all events, make a favourable impression upon his cousin."

Full of this idea, he summoned the young gentleman to a conference with him, and having carefully closed the door, he said in a low confidential tone,—

"Of course you have heard all about this — this vampyre business?"

"Yes, govenor, to be sure I have. Who could fail of hearing all about it? Why, nobody in the house will talk about anything else. I'm afraid to go to bed, I can tell you; that is to say, for fear I should do anything rash, you know, that's all."

"I understand you, and it's no use blinking the fact to me, that you are a coward."

"I am a coward, I — oh, you are very much mistaken. I'm a long way off that. I'm only always desirous of getting out of the way when anything happens, for fear of doing a rash act; it's excess of courage you know — that's what alarms me."

"Well, there are cases in which there would be no harm resulting, were you ever so rash."

"Ah! only show me one, and then you'll see."

"Very well, your cousin, you know — and you know she is your cousin — won't have you. Now, unless you are married to her, all our nicely got up plans are liable to be blasted by any accident, or by any breath of treachery that may come across them. But if you were the husband of your cousin, policy, habit, and, indeed, everything would combine to induce Lord Lake and her to smother up the affair. You comprehend."

"But what am I to do, if she won't have me?"

"I will tell you. You must awaken her gratitude by rescuing her from all these foolish terrors about vampyres, and when once a woman feels and knows that a man has done a brave act in her behalf, the principal entrance to her heart is open to him."

"Oh, but — I — I — the vampyre; that's rather unpleasant."

"Come, now, you are not such a fool as really to believe that it's, after all, anything but a mere dream. Don't tell me. Vampyres, indeed! At all events you can vapour as much as you like upon that subject without any danger occurring."

"Yes, yes — you may think so."

"I know so. Listen to me."

The son did listen, and the father added:

"You must volunteer to watch alone by your cousin's door for this vampyre, and of course nothing will think of coming. It's too ridiculous altogether, that it is; so, you see, you run no risk at all. You comprehend that?"

"Well, but if I run no risk, I don't see what's the use of doing it, you know; for if all is quiet, how can she be grateful to me for having rescued her from nothing at all?"

"Very well put, very well indeed. But as there will be nothing really to rescue her from, suppose we make something that will just suit our own purposes."

"What do you mean?"

"Why, you know my great grey travelling cloak — what is to hinder you having that with you, and whenever you are quite certain that your cousin is fast asleep, you can put that on over your face partially, and go into the room, and pretend to be the vampyre, and when she is in a paroxysm of terror do you dash out the light, and then in your natural voice, cry out, 'Ah, wretch, I have you, I have you. How dare you invade the sanctity of this chamber?' and all that sort of thing, you know, and you can knock about the chairs as much as you like, so as to induce the belief that you are engaged in a deadly struggle, and then you call for lights, and you are there, and the vampyre gone."

"Well, I rather like that, and if I were quite sure —"

"Of what?"

"That there was no real vampyre, you know, why I wouldn't mind it."

"Pshaw!"

"Well, well, I'll do it, I'll do it, I tell you. I see all the importance of getting her for my wife. Ahem! — and if I do," he added to himself aside, "I'll take deuced good care *you* don't get hold of the money, for after we are married, I shall just tell Lord Lake all about it."

D URING THE DAY Mr. Lake had sought an opportunity of speaking to Mr. Black.

"My dear sir," he said to him, "you don't seem well at all, and I shall insist that you do not trouble yourself to watch to-night by the door of the young lady, who has had so disagreeable a visitor."

"I am certainly not quite well," said Mr. Black. "The fact is, my health will not bear anything like a shock; a family occurrence has so shattered my nerves."

"My dear sir, say no more; you shall have no more trouble about us. My son, who loves his cousin, and is quite jealous of anybody defending her but himself,

will watch alone by her door. He has great courage when once his spirit is up, and it is now."

"I'm glad to hear it: it takes some time to get it up!"

"Why, a — a — yes, sometimes."

"I must be on the look out myself tonight, or the cowardly fellow will spoil all," thought Mr. Lake; "any unusual noise in the house, I suppose, will be almost sufficient to induce him to faint away. Confound his cowardice, it mars all."

Mr. Lake was not by any means so clear in his own mind as he pretended to be of the fact of the vampyre being only a delusion and a creation of the brain of his niece; so when the evening came, he did all that was in his power to keep the courage of his son to the mark.

He even took care that he should have a glass of something strong and hot, for he knew by personal experience that while they lasted, the fumes of hot alcohol did something for a weak heart.

But what pleased Mr. Lake most of all was the ease with which he had thus managed matters with Mr. Miller and his clerk, who, he had no doubt, would fabricate such a story as would convince the single-minded Annetta of his claims to be her father.

"Then," thought the old Lake, "we can surely among us badger her into marrying my son. Oh, it will be all right. Let no plot henceforward hope to succeed if this one does not. It must, and it shall; it shall, and it must."

It's all very well of any one to say that a scheme shall succeed; —

But how light a breath of air will chase away,

The darkly woven fancies of a thousand plots!

Mr. Lake stood upon a precipice which he little saw, or the terrific height of it would have driven him distracted.

MISS LAKE WAS in a great state of mental depression; if anything more than another was calculated to thoroughly break down the spirits of a young and innocent girl, it certainly would be such circumstances as those which now surrounded her, and deprived too, as she was, of that aid and sympathy she would have received at the hands of a father or a mother; it was only a wonder that she did not sink under the affliction most completely.

She made no objection to young Lake watching by the outside of her door. Indeed, she was weeping and depressed, so that she could scarcely know what proposal was made to her.

"I shall not sleep," she said. "God knows what will become of me."

"Do not despair, all may be well; it was a very sad thing that my brother Lord Lake ever found out that you were not his daughter. I'm sure I would have given freely all I possessed to have averted any such news, for it has attacked both his happiness and yours."

The young girl made no reply to this, but the look she gave him was quite sufficient to show him how much she doubted the sincerity of the professions of friendship and affection for her that fell from his lips. There was a *something* in his hollow, heartless character which, young and innocent and unknowing in the ways of the world even as that young girl was, she saw through, and he felt that she did so.

This was the most provoking thing of all that his heartlessness and selfishness should be transparent to one so young as she was.

But the night came at last, and with it the fidgetty fears of young Lake increased mightily. He was all of a shake, as Slop the waiter said, like a lot of jelly.

It was only by repeated doses of brandy-and-water that he kept himself from declaring off the adventure altogether, so that by eleven o'clock at night he was in a terrible state between fear and intoxication; and as any two impulses will each do its best to defeat the other, he was prevented from getting entirely drunk by his fears, and from getting entirely afraid by the liquor.

But at last he did actually take his place by the door of the chamber occupied by his cousin, and then with a table before him on which were lights, brandy-and-water, and cigars, he prepared to go through what to him was a terrible ordeal.

"You — you — really think," he whispered to his father, who came to promise him that he would not undress himself, but remain in his own room within call, "you really think there is no vampyre?"

"Tut, tut."

"Well, but really now, really —"

"Have I not told you before? Come, come, nonsense, there's the old grey travelling cloak, put it under the table, and now I shall leave you; it's about half-past eleven, and you have nothing in the world to do but just to enjoy yourself, you know. Good night."

CXC.

THE VAMPYRE DISCOVERED. — THE ESCAPE ON THE THAMES.

"ENJOY MYSELF!" muttered the young Lake, "enjoy myself! That may be his idea of staying here vampyre-catching, but it ain't mine. What a fool I was to consent to come here, to be sure, and all alone too. Eh, what was that? Oh! I'm all of a shake. I though I heard somebody, but I suppose it was nothing. Oh dear, what a disagreeable affair this is; what an infernal fool I am, to be sure. Eh? eh?"

The hair on his head nearly stood up as he heard, or fancied he heard, a low groan. He shook so while he arose from his seat that he was glad to sit down again as quickly as he possibly could, for he found his strength evaporating along with the Dutch courage, or rather as it should be called, French courage, as it had been instilled into him by brandy.

"What shall I do," he gasped, "what shall I do? Oh, what will become of me? I'm in for a row, I'm in for it to a certainty; I — I think I'll call the old man."

He did not, however, call his father, whom he designated the old man, more familiarly than respectfully, but as all continued now quiet, he thought he would wait until the next alarm, at all events, before he made a piece of work and thoroughly exhibited his own pusillanimity.

"It may be nothing," he said, "after all; perhaps only the wind coming through some chink in a door or window. Lord bless us, I've read of such things in romances till my blood had turned to curds and whey. There was *The Bloody Spectre of the Tub of Blood, or The Smashed Gore*. Eh? eh? I thought somebody spoke. No, no — oh, it's all what-do-they-call-it, imagination, that's what it is, and the sooner I get the job over the better, so I'll just pop on the cloak, and do the business."

With trembling hands Mr. Lake junior drew the cloak from under the table and put it on, bringing the collar of it right up to the top of his head, so that but a small portion of his head was at all visible when he was thus equipped, and he certainly might look like a vampyre, for he did not look like anything human by any means.

"Now, I wonder if she's asleep," he muttered as he laid his hand gently on the lock of the door, "if she ain't, it would be a pity; but still I can say, I only wanted to know how she was, so I'll just make the trial at all events. Here goes."

He opened the door of the bedroom a very short distance, and said, —

"Hist! hist! are you awake, eh? eh? What did you say? — nothing, oh, she's asleep, and now here goes — upon my life when one comes to think of it, it ain't by any means a bad plan. But just before I begin, I'll have another dram."

About two-thirds of a glass of brandy-and-water were in the tumbler on the table, and that he tossed down at once, and feeling very much fortified by laying in such a stratum of courage, he drew up the cloak to its proper vampyre-like position, as he considered it, and advanced two steps within the chamber of the sleeping girl.

She was sleeping, and slightly moaning in her sleep. It was a great satisfaction to young master Lake, to hear her so moaning, for it convinced him that such were the sounds which he previously heard, and which had gone near to terrifying him out of his project.

He had no compunction whatever regarding the amount of alarm which this dastardly project was likely to give to Miss Lake. No, all he looked to and thought of was himself. A light was burning in the chamber, and that according to the directions of his father he blew out, and then groping his ways towards the bed, he laid his hands upon the young girl's face, and said, —

"The vampyre! the vampyre has come! — blood, blood, blood! — the vampyre!"

She awoke with a cry of terror as usual, and then master Lake moved off to the door, and said in his natural voice,

"I'll protect you — I'm coming — I'll soon clear the room of the vampyre. Come on, you wretch! Oh, I'll do for him. Take that — and that — and that."

Then he commenced kicking about the chairs, and nearly upset the washing-stand, all by way of making the necessary disturbance, and convincing his cousin what a sanguinary conflict he was having with the vampyre. In the midst of this something laid hold of him by the ears and whiskers on each side of his head, and the door swinging open, his own light that was upon the table in the corridor shone upon a hideous countenance within half an inch of his own — the long fang-like teeth of which, with the lips retracted from them, were horrible to look upon; and a voice like the growl of an enraged hyena said, —

"What want you with the vampyre, rash fool? He is here."

Master Lake was absolutely petrified with horror and astonishment. The hair bristled up upon his head. His eyes opened the width of saucers, and when in a low voice the vampyre said again, — "What want you, reptile, with the vampyre?" he let his feet slide from under him, and had he not been upheld by the horrible being who grasped him, he would have fallen.

Bang went a pistol out of the corridor, and the vampyre uttered a cry and let go his hold of Lake, who then fell, and being out of the way, showed his father standing on the threshold of his own door, with a pistol in his hand recently discharged, and another apparently ready.

In another moment the vampyre kicked the insensible form of young Lake out of the way, and shut himself in the girl's bedroom. The father heard him lock the door, and although he instantly sent another pistol shot through the panelling, he heard no sound indicating its having done any execution.

"Help, help, help," he cried, "help here. The vampyre, the vampyre, the vampyre!"

All this had not taken above two or three minutes, and the whole house was now alarmed by the sound of fire-arms, and as nobody had completely undressed themselves to go to bed since the first alarm of the vampyre, the landlord and several of the waiters, and the night watchman ran with all speed to the spot, looking full of consternation, and all asking questions together.

"Force the door, force the door," cried Mr. Lake, "a hammer, a hatchet, anything, so that we may get the door forced; the vampyre is inside."

"Oh lor'!" cried one of the waiters who had gone close to the door, but who now made a precipitate retreat, treading upon the stomach of young Lake as he did so.

"If you'll pay for the door, Sir," said the landlord, "I'll soon have it open."

"Damn it, I'll pay for twenty doors."

The landlord took a short run at the door, probably he knew its weakness, and burst it open at once. There was the pause of about a moment, and then Mr. Lake, snatching up the candle, the light of which had first revealed the hideous features of the vampyre to his son, rushed into the room.

In these cases all that is wanted is a leader, so he was promptly enough followed. The state of affairs was evident at a glance. The young lady had fainted, and the window was wide open, indicating the mode of retreat of the vampire.

"I thought you told us," said Mr. Lake "that this window was too far from the ground to anticipate any danger from—"

"Yes, so I did, sir. But don't you see he could easy enough jump off the sill on to those leads there. Nobody could get in by the window, but anybody that wasn't afraid could get out. But we have him, sir, we have him now as sure as a gun."

"Have him. How?"

"Why don't you see sir, there's nothing but high walls. He must be among our stables, and he can't get out, for I have the keys of the outer doors myself, we shall not lose him now, sir, I'm not a little thankful for it. Come on, everybody, round to the stables, and nothing now can prevent us catching him if he is flesh and blood. Come on, come on."

By this time Mrs. Lake had reached the scene of action, and although the first thing she did was to tumble, sprawling, over her hopeful son, who lay in the door-way of his cousin's chamber, she gathered herself up again, and remained in charge of Annetta and the chamber, while Mr. Lake accompanied the landlord and the waiters to the stables of the hotel, which were surrounded by high walls and only to be approached by a pair of large gates, which were quite satisfactorily fastened, and there was not a chink large enough for a cat to get through.

The landlord had the keys, and he opened a small wicket in one of the large gates.

"Now be careful," he said, "for fear he bounces out."

At this everybody but Mr. Lake—who, to do him but justice, had certainly the quality of courage—looked as alarmed as possible, but he said,—

"I have re-loaded my pistols, and he shall not escape me."

The wicket was opened, and in an instant out walked Mr. Black! He appeared at first somewhat agitated, but speedily recovered his self-possession, and looking at the group, he said,—

"Have you caught him? I have been upon the look out, notwithstanding my indisposition, and jumped out of the bedroom window after him; I cannot see him anywhere. Have you caught him."

"Yes," cried Mr. Lake, "I saw you in

the room when I fired at you — *you* are the vampyre!"

He made a rush forward as he spoke, but Mr. Black got dexterously out of the way, and seizing the landlord by the hair of the head he cast him so fairly in Mr. Lake's way that they both fell down together; with amazing rapidity the vampyre then fled from the spot.

"After him, after him," cried Mr. Lake, as he scrambled to his feet, "don't let him escape, after him, whatever you do; alarm the whole city, rather than let the monster elude you. This way — this way, I see him. Follow me, a vampyre, a vampyre; help — help, seize him, a vampyre!"

"Fire," cried the landlord, and he too ran.

But all the running was in vain, the vampyre had fairly got the start of them, and he took good care to keep it, for with the most wonderful fleetness he ran on, until, to his great relief, he found his pursuers were distanced.

He made his way to the Strand, and diving down one of the narrow streets terminated by the river, and at the end of which was a landing place, he called aloud,—

"Boat, boat!"

An old waterman answered the hail.

"Where to, your honour?"

"Up the river, I will tell you where to land me, row quick, and row well, and you may name your own fare, without a chance of its being questioned."

"That's the customer for me," said the waterman.

CXC.

THE PLOT DISCOVERED. — THE LETTER LEFT AT THE HOTEL BY THE VAMPYRE.

THE FURTHER PURSUIT of the vampyre was very soon given up by those who had commenced it with, as they had vainly imagined, such an assurance of success.

Probably with the exception of Mr. Lake himself, none were really very eager in it at all, and they were not sorry for a good excuse to drop it.

There sat upon the countenance of Mr. Lake an appearance of great anger, and when they got back to the hotel, he said to the landlord,

"This is a very disagreeable affair, and I cannot think of remaining here over to-morrow."

"But sir, the vampyre has gone now!"

"Yes, and may come again, for all I know."

"Oh, dear me, surely not now, sir. After what has happened, I should be inclined to say that you will find this the quietest hotel in London."

Mr. Lake would not be moved from his determination, however, and briefly again announced that he would on the morrow remove.

"How very vexatious," thought the landlord, but he could do nothing in the matter. His only hope, and that was a very slight one indeed, was, by the morning the exasperated feelings of Mr. Lake would be somewhat assuaged, and therefore, he thought it would be, at all events, a prudent thing to say no more to him just then, when he was in such a mood.

When Mr. Lake retired to his own apartment he was in anything but a pleasant frame of mind, for he found that things were not exactly turning out as he wished, and he much feared that all his schemes would turn out abortive, in which case they would recoil upon his own head in their consequences.

It was quite by accident, that happening to cast his eyes upon the dressing-table, he saw a sealed letter lying there, and upon looking at the superscription he was surprised to find that Annetta was the person for whom it was intended.

It was not, as the reader may suppose from what he knows of Mr. Lake, from any honourable scruples that he hesitated at once to open the letter addressed to his niece, but he was for a time considering whether he might not, by doing so, be getting himself into some scrape from which he might find it very difficult to extricate himself.

"Who the deuce can it come from?" he said.

He turned the epistle about in all directions, but such an inquiry did not assist him, and finally he made up his mind that come what might, he would break the seal and look at the contents.

He soon, after coming to the determination, carried it into effect, and to his surprise he found that the letter contained the following statement.—

To THE LADY ANNETTA LAKE:—

Fear nothing, lady. He who disturbed your repose will disturb it no longer. Be happy, and do not let the dread of such another visitation ever disturb your pure imaginings. Your father will rescue you from your present unhappy circumstances, and you will, likewise, soon see one who ere this would have been with you, had he known of your being in London.

This comes from —
VARNEY THE VAMPYRE.

P.S. If Mr. Lake, your bad uncle, upon whose dressing table this note is placed, delivers it not to you, woe be to him, for I will make his nights hideous

with realities, and his days horrible with recollection and anticipation.

Mr. Lake was superstitious. Are not the unprincipled always so?

He read the postscript to the note with a shudder; and he felt that he could no more muster courage enough to destroy the letter, than he could to lay violent hands upon himself. There he was with an epistle that he would fain have kept from Annetta, and yet he dared not do so.

"Confound my unlucky destiny," he said, "for bringing me to this hotel. Perhaps if I had gone elsewhere, all this would not have happened. Oh, if I could but have suspected what this Mr. Black really was, I would have tried some means for his extermination."

He paced his chamber in an agitated manner until Mrs. Lake made her appearance from the chamber of the lady Annetta, where she had been staying, and to her then he at once communicated the letter that gave him so much uneasiness.

"I don't know what to do," he said, "or what to think."

"Indeed!"

"Yes, indeed. Perhaps you can suggest something?"

"And can you allow yourself to be made a slave of such fears. There is but one course to pursue, and that is, tomorrow to put the affair altogether in a different shape, by overwhelming Annetta with the seeming evidence that she is the daughter of an attorney's clerk, instead of her real father, Lord Lake. I know of no other way; and then when she finds such, as she will think, to be the case, it's my opinion that she will no longer hesitate to marry our son."

"You think so?"

"Indeed do I. The girl is not an absolute fool surely."

"Well, of course, I should be very glad if that daring project could be, after all, brought about; but what is to be done with this letter?"

"Can you ask?"

"I do, when I consider the threat that is in it. That threat, recollect, is to me, and you can afford to think lightly of it."

"I will take the consequences. It is hardly likely that you will be punished for what you can't help. I will take good care that this letter never reaches Annetta, and as you have it not, why of course you cannot deliver it, and so cannot be blamed."

"But I might have it."

"No such thing," said the lady snatching it up. "You know me rather too well, I should think, to hope that I would give it up to you, and as for your taking it by force, I should think you knew me too well likewise to make such a ridiculous attempt."

"Well, then I wash my hands of it."

"Ah! you may as well. I don't know what has come over you of late, you are as mean spirited as you can be, and formerly you used to be able to cope with anything."

"We never played for such a stake as we have now upon the board, and I confess that I am rather nervous for the consequences."

"Pshaw! I see that I must guide you, or all will be lost. To-morrow let the whole affair be settled. Let this attorney Miller, as you call him, come here, and bring with him the person who is to claim Annetta as his own daughter. Let him have all the evidence that you tell me he has been so ingenious in getting up, ready, in order that he may be in a position to answer any questions."

"Yes, yes."

"And then, when all is settled, our son must come forward, and make a speech, saying, he don't care a bit, who or what she is, that he loves her and will make her his wife, although she has not a penny piece in the world."

"I see, I see."

"I think, from what I know of her, that such a course of proceeding will have a great effect upon her."

"Well, I hope so."

"You hope so! How despondingly you talk."

"Why the honest truth — "

"Good God! what do you mean by making use of such words? I never told the honest truth in all my life; you may depend that won't do in this world, on any consideration. Never let me hear you say such a thing again, I beg of you."

"I was merely going to remark that this vampyre business had really so completely unsettled my whole nervous system, that I could not act with all the tact and the determination that used to characterise my proceedings, and for which you were ever disposed to give me so much credit."

"Really."

"Yes. But I cannot regret such a state of things so much as I should otherwise do, because I see that you are unmoved and as energetic as ever."

"Well, well, say no more."

"I am done."

"I will prepare our boy for the part he is to act to-morrow; and mind, I shall rely upon you to see your associates and get all the affair in train. Let it be all over by twelve in the morning, so that if you like you can send to Lord Lake where he is staying, at Florence still I presume, an account of the matter by post that same night; only let me see the letter before you send it."

"I will, I will; you are my guardian angel."

"Pho, pho; you are getting quite romantic and foolish; we have both made up our minds to get money, and we have likewise known so much the want of it, in abundance that is to say, that we have resolved to get it in any way we can."

"Yes, that I rather think is our principle of action."

"And has it not succeeded hitherto? Have we not lived well without troubling ourselves to earn the means by which we have done so? Earn, indeed! I leave that to a parcel of sleepy drones of people who have not the wit to live upon others as we have; so now go to bed and sleep off some of the unmanly fears that seem of late to be continually pressing upon you. It is well you have me to look after you as I do."

CXCII.

THE MEETING IN THE MORNING AT THE HOTEL. — THE PREPARATIONS OF THE ATTORNEY.

IT IS NO LESS THAN STRANGE, the difference that takes place in people's feelings with regard to precisely the same circumstances in the morning, from what they really felt and thought in the evening, and when the shadows of night were upon them.

This mental phenomenon was not wanting in the case of Mr. Lake.

He felt as he rose the next day, and the sun was shining in at the window of his bedroom, most thoroughly ashamed of his fears and his nervous tremours of the preceding night.

His wife saw with a smile the change in his feelings.

"You are no longer," she said, "afraid of the vampyre."

"Oh, say no more about it," was his reply. "I shall go immediately after breakfast and see Mr. Miller, and with him make such arrangements as will bring the affair upon which we have set our hearts to a crisis, and while I am gone you can instruct our son in what he has to do."

"I will."

The breakfast passed over in rather a constrained manner. Mrs. Lake had made an attempt to persuade Annetta that she was really too unwell to get up for an hour or two, but that Annetta would not submit to, as she felt herself, notwithstanding all her sufferings and all her fright, really capable of rising.

The consequence was, that she appeared at the breakfast table, and stopped most effectually anything in the shape of a confidential discourse taking place among the Lakes.

The meal therefore passed off rather

silently, and there were only a few remarks made, incidentally, about the preceding night's alarm.

Annetta was evidently in a state of great nervousness, as well she might be, for the idea that she would be again subjected to the frightful visits of the vampyre, was ever present to her, and she was denied the consolation which the letter of Varney might, and most probably would have, given her.

After the morning meal, Mr. Lake gave his wife a significant look to intimate that he was then going to Mr. Miller's, and that in his absence she was to play her part.

She perfectly understood him, and nodded in return, and thus this worthy pair separated.

We will follow Mr. Lake:

THE ATTORNEY DID NOT live in one of the most respectable haunts of the profession, but he was a man of his word, and by the time Mr. Lake reached his chambers he was there, it being then not much above ten o'clock.

There was some delay in admitting Mr. Lake to the private room of the attorney, and he thought that the clerk who was in the outer office looked a little confused.

"Is anybody with Mr. Miller?" asked Lake.

"Yes — that is to say — I mean no."

"A strange answer. Yes, and you mean no."

"Why, Sir, I only meant that Mr. Miller was rather busy, and we are so much in the habit when that is the case, of saying that he has some one with him that

it slipped out unawares, only as we would not deceive you, sir, for the world, you understand that that was why, you perceive, sir, that in a manner of speaking, I corrected myself."

This explanation was rather more wordy than satisfactory to Mr. Lake; however, for want of a better, he was compelled to put up with it, and he said nothing, but waited with the most exemplary patience, until Mr. Miller's bell rang.

The clerk answered it, and in a few moments returned to say that Mr. Miller had got through a legal document he had been engaged upon, and the he much regretted having kept Mr. Lake waiting, but was then quite at his disposal.

Now Lake could have sworn that he had heard the sound of a voice from the private room of the attorney, and he consequently did not feel quite easy.

When he went in he found Mr. Miller with a number of letters before him.

"Ah, my dear sir," cried the lawyer, "sit down."

"Thank you. I thought somebody was with you?"

"Oh, dear no, not at all. I was going through a lease, you see, and from long experience in such matters, I have found that I have a better and clearer understanding of the matter, if I read it aloud to myself, but perhaps that is only a peculiarity of mine."

"Then it was your voice I heard just now?"

Mr. Lake's suspicions were about half removed, certainly not more than half, but he could say no more about it, although he cast now and then suspicious glances round the room; yet if he had been asked what he was suspicious of, he would hardly have been able to give a clear and understandable answer to the question.

It is one of the curses of conscious guilt ever to live in an atmosphere of doubt and dread, and to the full did Mr. Lake feel that curse.

"Well, Mr. Miller," he said, after a pause, "I have called upon you to say that I hope it will suit your convenience to settle a little affair to-day at twelve o'clock at the hotel."

"Twelve — let me see — twelve. Not at the hotel, my dear sir, I am compelled to be in chambers in case of a letter coming on very particular business, but if you will bring her here, I can manage it very nicely; if she don't leave this place with a conviction that she has a father in London, I'll eat my boots."

"Well, I don't see why we should not come here, as you give me great satisfaction, Mr. Miller, by avowing yourself to be so confident of the result."

"I am as confident as that I sit on this three legged stool."

"Good — then you may depend upon our coming here at twelve o'clock precisely. There will be myself, Mrs. Lake, my son and the young lady. Mind she is no fool, she must be perfectly overwhelmed with proofs of what we wish to make her believe."

"Exactly, that she is not the daughter of Lord Lake, but a mere changling imposed upon him as his own child — the said own child being dead."

"Precisely."

"Agreed, sir, agreed. With respect to my reward, I have been thinking that I should like, you know, to have some acknowledgment. You tell me you have no money now, but that this obstacle once removed you will come in for all the Lake estates, and that Lord Lake cannot live long."

"That's the state of the case."

"Then sir, will you give me a note for two thousand pounds, payable on demand."

"On demand?"

"Yes; of course it would be needless folly of me to present it until you have money, you know."

"True, true."

We need not pursue the conversation further, but satisfy the reader by stating the result, which was, that the attorney got the note for two thousand pounds from Lake, likewise a paper signed, which admitted the debt more fully still, and effectually barred Lake from objecting to any proceedings on account of want of consideration for the promissory note, or that it had not been fairly obtained of him, pleas which might have inconvenienced Mr. Miller if he chose to pursue Lake for the amount.

IN THE MEANTIME Mrs. Lake had not been idle, but had spoken to her booby and cowardly son, making him aware of what he had to do in the business, namely, to shew his great disinterestedness in taking for his wife Annetta after she was supposed to be proved not the daughter of Lord Lake, but quite a different personage, and altogether destitute of pecuniary resources.

He managed pretty well always to understand any villany, and so entered life and soul into the scheme of his mother.

"Ah! I like that a monstrous deal better than keeping watch for a vampyre, which is a sort of job that don't at all suit such a constitution as mine, do you see?"

Mrs. Lake not being aware of the alteration of arrangements by which they were all to proceed to the lawyer's chambers, instead of coming to the hotel, took no trouble with Annetta, conceiving that it would perhaps be better at twelve o'clock, when the parties were assembled, to take her by surprise, than to say anything to her beforehand, which might have the effect of preparing her for what was to come, and so getting up a spirit of resistance and of inquiry which it might be difficult to resist or satisfactorily to meet.

When Mr. Lake came home from Gray's Inn, she was made aware of the alteration, and consultations ensued as to how Annetta was to be got there at all. At length after several modes of managing the matter had been discussed, Mrs. Lake said,

"You two can walk there, and then I can say to Annetta that I am going for a drive and to make a few purchases, so that she will have no objection to go with me for an airing, and I will take good care to be with you at the hour of twelve."

"That will do prime," said the son. "Leave mother alone for managing things."

"Well," said Mr. Lake, "it shall be so, I don't see any objection to the scheme, nor can I suggest a better one, so we will look upon that as settled. — All you have to do," turning to his son, "is to play your part well."

"Oh! never fear me, I like the girl and I like money."

CXCIII.

THE VAMPYRE'S VISIT TO THE BARRACKS AT KINGSTON. — THE YOUNG OFFICER.

WE DO NOT WISH altogether to lose sight of Varney in these proceedings, and it so happens that he is sufficiently mixed up in what further occurred to make it desirable that we should now again refer to him.

It was not the least singular fact in the character of that mysterious being, to notice how he always endeavoured to make some sort of amends or reparation to those whom he had so much terrified by his visitations.

We have seen in the case of the family of the Bannerworths how eventually he was most anxious to do them a service, as a recompense for the really serious injury he had inflicted upon them, and how it was really and eventually through him that they emerged from the circumstances of difficulty and danger in which they had been pecuniarily engaged.

We shall now see if Varney, who really in his way is a very respectable sort of a personage, is about good or evil.

We left him on the river, after promising, in his usual liberal spirit, a handsome reward to the waterman whom he employed to row the boat in which he embarked.

After going some distance, the

waterman, finding his fare was silent, thought it would be as well again to ask him where he was going.

Accordingly, with a preparatory hem, he began by saying,

"About as nice a tide, sir, as we could have for going up the stream."

"Very likely," was the brief reply.

"Do you land near hand, sir?"

"I want to go to Kingston; take me to some quay on the river as near as you can, for the purpose of my walking there."

"Kingston?" said the waterman, with a look rather of surprise. "It's a long pull to Kingston, and if your honour could get a conveyance, your best way would be to get out at Putney."

"Wherefore?"

"Why after that, the river takes such a plaguey lot of windings and turnings that you have to go treble the actual distance before you reach Teddington."

"I said Kingston."

"Well that's close by Teddington; but I'll row your honour if you like, only it will take us some hours to get there, that's all."

"Go on."

"Very good, pull away, pull a — way."

Having now, as he knew, a long job before him, the waterman husbanded his strength, he did not row near so fast, but to a low kind of tune he muttered to himself he worked away at his sculls, slowly and surely, and got through the water at a moderate easy rate, while rather a quick jerking one would soon have exhausted him.

The boat went slowly onward, and many an interesting sight was passed upon the banks of the river, but none appeared in the least to attract the attention of the man who sat in the boat, apparently deeply absorbed in his own meditations.

The boatman began much to wonder who he had got as a fare, and to think that it would be but a dull and wearisome job to row all the way to Teddington without any amusing gossip by the way, so he made yet another attempt to break the stillness that reigned around.

"The river up this way, sir," he said, "is quiet enough at night; it's different below bridge, though, for there there is always some bustle going on."

"Ah!" said Varney.

"But here, somehow, it is dull to my mind."

"Ah!"

"Though the gentry and those as is book-learned find a deal of pleasure in looking at the old places on the banks, where things have been done and said by folks many a long year since, whose heads don't ache now, sir."

"Ah!"

There was no getting on at this rate, so, after two or three more remarks and getting nothing by "Ah!" as a reply, the waterman gave it up as a bad job altogether, and pulled away, chaunting in a low tone his song again, without making another attempt to disturb the taciturnity of his fare, who sat as still as a statue in the boat, and looking as if he did not breathe, so rigid and strange were his attitude, and the lifeless-like appearance he had.

The waterman was really a little alarmed by the time they reached Teddington, for he thought that it might be possible his fare was dead, and the horrid idea that he had stiffened in that attitude as he sat, began to find a place in the boatman's imagination.

When, however, he boat's keel grated on the landing-place, he cried,—

"Here we are, your honour."

The vampyre rose and stepped on shore. He held out his hand and dropped a guinea into the extended palm of the waterman, and then stalked off.

After he had walked some distance he spoke to a watchman whom he met, saying,—

"Are there not military barracks somewhere hereabout?"

"Oh, yes."

"Thank you. Can you direct me?"

"Certainly. You have only to go on, and take the second turning to your left, and you will see the gate; it's horse soldiers that's there now—the 4th Light Dragoons."

By keeping to the directions which the watchman had given, Varney soon reached the gate of the barracks, and then it was three o'clock in the morning. A sentinel was pacing to and fro at the gate. To him Varney at once went, and with a lofty kind of courtesy, that made the man at once respectful to him, he said,—

"Is Lieutenant Rankin in barracks?"

"Yes, sir,—on duty."

"Indeed! Is he on guard to-night?"

"Yes, sir, to four o'clock. He will be relieved then."

"That's fortunate, I want to see him. It is on business of the very first importance, or of course I would not trouble him or myself. You must send to him somehow."

The sentinel hesitated.

"I hardly know," he said, "how the lieutenant will take it—he is on duty."

"But I suppose he is human for all that, and is liable to all the accidents and alternations of human affairs, which may make it absolutely necessary he should be communicated with, even at such an hour as this. I will hold you harmless."

This was so reasonable, and there was such an air of quiet gentlemanly authority about Varney, that the soldier began to think he should run less risk of offending somebody of importance if he consented to disturb the lieutenant than if he refused. Accordingly he stepped a pace or two within the gate and called out.

"Guard!"

A soldier from the guard-room answered the summons.

"Aye," he said, "what is it?—a strange cat I suppose."

"No, none of your nonsense. Here is a gentleman, I think a general officer, by Jove, wants to see Lieutenant Rankin. Go and tell him."

"And give him this," said Varney, as he handed the soldier a card, on which was written,—

"A friend to a friend of Lieutenant Rankin, whose initials are A. L."

"I know that this young soldier loves the Lady Annetta," muttered the vampyre to himself, "and he shall be given the opportunity of flying to her rescue from her villanous relations. So far, I will make reparation to her."

In less than three minutes, Lieutenant Rankin came hurriedly to the gate.

"Where is the gentleman?" he said.

"Here sir," said Varney, "step aside with me."

The young officer did so, and then Varney said to him,—

"It matters not how I became acquainted with the fact, but I know that you love the Lady Annetta Lake, and that you are far from being indifferently regarded by her. She is in London at the London Hotel. A vile plot is formed to marry her to her cousin, the gist of which is to make her both her and her father believe that she is a changeling and not the daughter of Lord Lake. You love her, young man. Go and rescue her."

"Annetta in London!"

"Yes, what I tell you you may rely upon, as if it were a voice from heaven that spoke to you. Go and snatch her whom you love from the base hands of those who, under the mask of pretended friendship, would betray her."

"And you," cried the young soldier; "who are you, and how can I repay you for bringing me this intelligence of her whom I —"

"Enough," said the vampyre. "I have performed my mission. It is for you, young sir, to take a due advantage of that which I have told to you."

In another moment he was gone.

CXCIV.

AN ECLAIRCISSEMENT. — THE INNOCENT TRIUMPHANT.

IT IS ELEVEN O'CLOCK. Mr. and Mrs. Lake are standing by one of the windows at the hotel conversing in whispers, while the hopeful son is brushing his hat.

"It is time, you think?" said Mrs. Lake.

"Yes," was the reply. "and I will be off now at once, and depend upon you following with Annetta to Mr. Miller's."

"That you may be sure of. She has had a refreshing night's rest, and this morning she eagerly enough caught at the proposal to take a drive round the principal thoroughfares in the carriage we have hired so that that is no longer a difficulty."

"What is to be done if she rejects?"

Mr. Lake gave a jerk with his head in the direction of his son, to signify that it was of him he talked.

"It can't be helped if she does. Then I should say all we have to do, is to persevere in making her out no child of Lord Lake's, and wait for his decease. We must be careful what we are about, though, or he may take it into his head to make some ample provision for her, to the decrease of his personal means, which I hope to see all ours."

"The only way to stop that will be getting Miller and the pretended father to make it as a complete part of the plan that Annetta herself should seem latterly to have been a party to palming herself off upon him as his daughter when she knew the contrary quite well."

"Ah, if that could be done."

"It must and shall; Miller's ingenuity in such matters is immense. He will accomplish anything in the world — aye, seeming impossibilities — for money."

"He is just the man for us, so now be off with you at once, and expect me in good time."

In a few moments afterwards, Mr. Lake set off with this booby son to the lawyer's, enjoining him all the way as they went, to be especially careful how he maintained the character of a disinterested suitor, which had been marked out for him in the programme of the family proceedings.

"Oh, never fear me, father."

"Well, I hope that you will do and say the right things, and what is as important, I hope you will do and say them at the right time, otherwise you will spoil all."

Thus armed at all points, as they thought, for conquest, old Lake and young Lake, than whom all London could not have produced two more unprincipled persons, arrived at Gray's Inn*, and were received in the outer room of Mr. Miller's chambers with every demonstration of respect.

"Walk in, gentlemen, walk in to the clients' private-room if you please," said the clerk. "Mr. Miller left directions with me that when you came, you should be shown in at once."

All this was very gratifying indeed, and the solicitor was there, seated in his easy chair, looking as full of serenity as possible, and as if the least affair in the world was on *tapis*.

Scarcely had the usual salutations passed, when the clerk announced Mrs. Lake and a young lady.

"My wife with Annetta!" exclaimed Lake; and in a moment his words were verified by the appearance of the parties he had named.

"Tell me at once," said Annetta, "why I am brought here?"

"My dear young lady," said Mr. Miller, "if you will condescend to take a seat, I will explain."

---

* One of the four Inns of Court at the Temple in London, where barristers had their offices.

"Be brief, sir."

The party was seated, and then Mr. Miller, clearing his throat said,—

"Ahem! You are of course aware, miss, that great doubt arose in the mind of Lord Lake with regard to your proper identity, and he sent you over to this country from Italy with his brother and family, to have those doubts resolved — ahem! They are resolved, and you are found to be the daughter of a gentleman now in London."

"The proofs, sir," said Annetta, with a dignity and a calmness that surprised the whole party.

"Ah, ah — the proofs. Let me see, oh yes; there are the papers. No. 1, copy of a confession made by —"

"Stop, sir," said young Lake, "stop. This is — it must be painful to the feelings of this young lady, and very, very painful is it to my feelings, for I have been long fervently attached to her, and let her be whose daughter she may, she is to me all perfection. I love her and would gladly make her my wife, let her be named whatever she may."

"But she is destitute, — quite destitute," said Miller.

"It don't matter to me," cried young Lake — he was playing his part famously — "it don't matter to me; I love her, and will work for her — she shall never want while I have life-blood in my veins."

"If this now were sincere," said Annetta, "I should begin for the first time to respect you. But you will excuse me for doubting it very much. I likewise doubt much the pretended evidence that you bring forward regarding my birth."

A tremendous knock at the outer door of the chambers now disturbed the

party. An altercation was heard with the clerk — then a shout for police, and a heavy fall as if somebody had been knocked down, and in another moment the door of Mr. Miller's private room was dashed open, and Lieutenant Rankin, in his undress military uniform, stood upon the threshold.

"Annetta!" he cried.

"Rankin — oh, George, George!" shrieked Annetta, and in another moment she was in his arms.

"Here's a go," cried young Lake; "I say, young fellow, this won't do."

"Oh, George, George!" said Annetta, "they will have it that I am not my own father's child, that I am some nameless, houseless thing."

"They lie, Annetta who say so," replied the young soldier; "you shall be mine, and the proudest that ever stepped shall treat you with becoming respect, or shall rue the consequences."

"Well, I think it's time!" cried Mr. Miller in a marked manner, and throwing open the door of an inner room, he added, "my Lord Lake, come forth; no doubt you have heard all."

Lord Lake himself — the Mr. Blue of the London Hotel, the sham confidential clerk of Miller — made his appearance, to the utter confusion of the Lakes.

"My father," said Annetta, "my dear father!"

"Hold," said Lord Lake, gravely, "I suspected, Annetta, from the first that your birth was impugned by my brother from the most interested motives, and I followed you from Italy — Mr. Miller disclosed all to me, and the infamous plot is discovered."

"Then I am your child?"

"Confusion," muttered Lake, "death and the devil, what a *contretemps*."

"Stop," added Lord Lake, "the strangest thing of all has yet to be told. This plot to make out that you are not my child is but a plot, but it is not baseless as to the fact. You are not my daughter. I have by mere chance found out that lately, and I cannot provide for you, as the resources I have must go to him who will inherit my title. What say you, Master Lake, this girl with all her beauty is destitute, her name is Smith — will you have her?"

"Not I in faith, thank you for nothing."

"Will you, young soldier, knowing what she is?"

"Ay, will I with all my heart! she is the highest, brightest treasure this world can offer me. Any name or no name — poor or rich — noble or commoner — she is still my own dear girl, and her resting place shall be my heart, the whole world shall not tear her from it."

"God's blessings on you," cried Lord Lake, grasping his hands; "I did but this to give yon shrinking coward a chance of creeping into favour with me, because he boasted so of his disinterested affection a while ago. She is my child, the Lady Annetta Lake — I never doubted it, and she is yours — George Rankin, and you shall be the dear son of my adoption."

"I say, father," said young Lake, "I — I think we had better go."

"Curse you all," cried Lake, "and doubly curse you, lawyer Miller, you have betrayed me; but I'll be revenged."

"Through the bars of a prison," said the lawyer. "An officer is down stairs to arrest you for two thousand pounds. Ha, ha, ha!"

T HUS THEN WAS IT that this episode in the life of Varney the Vampyre terminated. But still he lived, and still there existed all the strange and fearful mixture of good and evil that was in his disposition. There he was yet upon the earth's surface, looking like one of the great world, and yet possessing so few feelings in common with its inhabitants.

Surely to him there must have been periods of acute suffering, of intense misery, such as would have sufficed to drive any ordinary mind to distraction, and yet he lived, although one cannot, upon reviewing his career, and considering what he was, consider that death would have been other than a grateful release to him from intense suffering.

Perhaps, of all the suffering that, in consequence of his most awful and singular existence, was inflicted upon human nature, he suffered the most, for that he was a man of good intellect no one who has followed us thus far can doubt, and one cannot help giving in almost at times to as strange and fanciful theory of his own, namely that this world was to him the place of perdition for crimes done in some other sphere.

"It must be so!" he would say, "but as the Almighty Master of all things is all merciful, as he is all powerful, the period of my redemption will surely come at last."

This was the most consolate thought that Varney could have, and it showed that even yet there was a something akin to humanity lingering at his heart.

This showed that despite the dreadful power he had — a power, as well as an awful propensity — he had some yearnings after a better state.

What had he been? How did he become a vampyre? Did the voice of fond affection ever thrill in his ears? Had little children ever climbed the knee of that wretched man? Fearful questions, if he could have answered them the affirmative — if he bore about with him, deep in his memory, a remembrance of such joys gone by.

"*I sprung upon her. There was a shriek, but not before I had secured a draught of life-blood from her neck. It was enough. I felt it dart through my veins like fire, and I was restored. From that moment I found out what was to be my sustenance; it was blood — the blood of the young and the beautiful.*" (see page 1339)

PART XI:

The Vampyre's Corpse-Bride.

CXCV.

THE VAMPYRE HAS SERIOUS THOUGHTS. — THE DREAM. — THE RESOLUTION.

THE NEXT DAY AFTER the events that we have detailed, Varney found himself in a hotel in London. He did not even make the effort to inquire how the affair connected with the Lady Annetta, in which towards the last he had played a generous part, prospered.

He was too spirit-broken himself to do so.

For nearly the whole day he remained in a room by himself, and although to avoid uncomfortable and ungracious remarks being made by the people of the house, he ordered from time to time food and wine, he, in accordance with his horrible nature, which forbade him any nourishment but human blood, touched neither.

During that day he seemed to be suffering acutely, for now and then as the waiters of the hotel passed the door of the private room he occupied, they heard deep agonising groans, and when once or twice they went in, fancying that he must be very ill or dying, they found him seated at a table on which his head was resting.

He would start up on these occasions, and sternly question them for interrupting him, so at last they left him alone.

Let us look at him in his solitude.

It is getting towards the dim and dusky hours of late twilight, and he can only barely be descried as he sits bolt upright in a high-backed arm-chair, looking at vacancy, while his lips move, and he appears to be conversing with the spirits of another world, that in their dim intangibility are not visible to mortal eyes.

Now and then he would strike his breast, and utter a dull groan as if some sudden recollection of the dreadful past had come over him, with such a full tide of horror that it could not be resisted.

It was not until a considerable time had elapsed, and the darkness had greatly increased, that he at length spoke.

"And I was once happy," he said mournfully, "once happy, because I was innocent. Oh! gracious Heaven, how long am I to suffer?"

A spasmodic kind of movement of his whole features ensued, that was quite dreadful to look upon, and would have terrified any one who could have seen them. Then he spoke again.

"I was happy one hundred and eighty years ago," he said, "for that has been the awful duration my life as yet; yes, a hundred and eighty years have, with their sunshine of summer, and their winter storms, passed over my head; and I had a wife and children, who, with innocent and gladsome prattle, would climb my knee and nestle in my bosom. Oh! where are they all now?"

He wrung his hands, but he did not weep; the fount of tears had dried up for a hundred years in his bosom.

"Yes, yes! the grave holds them — holds them? said I. No, no, long since have they crumbled into dust, and nothing of them remains as a faint indication even of who once was human. I, I it was who listened to the councils of a fiend, and destroyed her who had give up home, kindred, associations, all for me."

He rose up from the chair, and seemed to think that he would find some relief in pacing the room to and fro, but he soon threw himself again into the seat.

"No, no," he said, "no peace for me; and I cannot sleep, I have never slept what mortals call sleep, the sleep of rest and freedom from care, for many a long year. When I do seem to repose, then what dreadful images awake to my senses. Better, far better that my glaring eyeballs should crack with weariness, than that I should taste such repose."

The sympathetic shudder with which he uttered these words was quite proof sufficient of his deep and earnest sincerity. He must indeed have suffered much before he could have give such a sentiment such an utterance. We pity thee, Varney!

"And when, oh, when will my weary pilgrimage be over," he ejaculated; "Oh when will the crime of murder be cleansed from my soul? I killed her. Yes, I killed her who loved me. A fiend, I know it was a fiend, whispered suspicion in my ear, suspicion of her who was as pure as the first ray of sunlight that from heaven shows itself to chase away the night, but I listened and then created from my own fevered brain the circumstances that gave suspicion strength and horrible consistency — and I killed her."

After the utterance of these words he was silent for a time, and then in heart-rending accents he again repeated them.

"I killed her — I killed her, and she was innocent. Then I became what I am. There was a period of madness, I think, but I became a vampyre; I have died many deaths, but recovered from them all; for ever, by some strange accident or combination of circumstances, the cold moonbeams have had access to my lifeless form, and I have recovered."

B Y THIS TIME the landlord of the hotel in which Varney was staying, had got in a fearful fidget, for he began to think that he had a madman in his house, and that it would turn out that his guest had made his escape from some lunatic asylum.

"I wonder now," he thought, "if a little soothing civility would do any good; I will try it. It can't surely do any harm."

With this intent the landlord went up stairs to the room in which Varney the Vampyre was, and he tapped gently at the door.

There was no reply, and after a few moments' consideration, the landlord opened the door and peeped in, when he saw his customer sitting in an arm-chair, in the manner in which we have described him to sit.

"If you please, sir," said the landlord, "would you not like —"

"Blood!" said Varney, rising.

The landlord did not wait for any more, but bustled down stairs again with all the promptitude in his power.

It was a bed-room and sitting-room that Varney occupied at the hotel, the one adjoining the other, and now although he groaned and sighed at the idea of repose, he flung himself upon the bed, full dressed, as he was, and there he lay as still as death itself.

One of those strange fitful kind of slumbers, such as he had himself described as being so full of dread, came over him.

For a time he was still, as we have said, but then as various images of agony began to chase each other through his brain, he tossed about his arms, and more than once the word "mercy" came from his lips in accents of the most soul-harrowing nature.

This state of things continued for some considerable time, and then in his sleep a great change came over him, and he fancied he was walking in a garden replete with all the varied beauties of a southern clime, and through the centre of which meandered a stream, the crystal music of which was delightfully calming and soothing to his senses.

All around seemed to speak of the peace and loveliness of an Eden.

As he wandered on, he fancied that some form was walking by his side, and that he heard the gentle fall of its feet, and

the flutter of garments.

"Varney," it said, "you have suffered much."

"I have. Oh, God knows I have."

"You would die, Varney, if the moonbeams could be prevented from reaching you."

"Yes, yes. But how — how?"

"The ocean. The deep, deep sea hides many a worse secret than the corpse of a vampyre."

It might have been that, after all, his sleep was to some extent refreshing to him, or that the dream he had, had instilled a hope into him of a release from what, in his case, might truly be called the bondage of existence; but he certainly arose more calm, cool, and collected, than he had been for some time past.

"Yes," he said, "the deep sea holds a secret well, and if I could but be washed into some of its caverns, I might lie there and rot until the great world itself had run its course."

This idea took great possession of him. He thought over various modes of carrying it out. At one time he thought that if he bought a boat on the sea coast, and went out alone, sailing away as far from land as he could, he might be able to accomplish his object. But then he might not be able to get far enough.

At length he thought of a more feasible and a better plan than that, and it was to take his passage in some ship for any port, and watch his opportunity, some night when far from land, to steal up upon the deck and plunge in the waves.

The more he considered of this plan the better he liked it, and the more it wore an appearance of probability and an aspect of success, so at length the thought grew into a resolution.

"Yes, yes," he muttered, "who knows but that some friendly spirit — for the mid air that floats 'twixt earth and heaven is peopled with such — may have whispered such counsel in my ears. It shall be done; I will no longer hesitate, but make this attempt to shake off the dreadful weight which mere existence is to me."

CXCVI.

THE SCOTCH PACKET SHIP. — THE SUICIDE.

IT WAS IN PURSUANCE of this resolution, so strangely and suddenly formed, that the unhappy Varney rose on the following morning and went to that region of pitch, slop clothing, red herrings, and dirt — the docks.

But yet, somehow, although the docks may not be the cleanest or the most refined part of the vast city of London, the coarseness and the litter there — for after all it is more litter than dirt — are by no means so repulsive as those bad addenda to other localities.

There is a kind of rough freshness induced by the proximity of the water which has a physical and moral effect, we are inclined to think, upon the place and the people, and which takes off much of what would otherwise wear the aspect of what is called low life.

But this is all by the way, and we will at once proceed to follow the fortunes of Varney, in carrying out his plan of self-annihilation.

The hour was an early one, and many a curious glance was cast at him, for although he had humanised and modernised his apparel to a great extent, he could not get rid of the strange, unworld-like (if we may use the phrase) look of his face. He was very pale, too, and jaded-looking, for the thoughts that had recently occupied him were not such as to do good to the looks of any one.

He cared little in what vessel he embarked. He had but one object in embarking at all, and that was to get out to sea, so that the ultimate destination of the ship that should receive so very odd and equivocal a passenger was a matter of no moment.

Stopping a personage who had about him a sea-faring look, Varney, pointing to a bustling place of embarkation, said, —

"Does any vessel start from there today?"

"Yes, there's one going now, or as soon as the tide serves her. She is for Leith."

"On the coast of Scotland, I think?"

"Yes, to be sure."

Varney walked on until he came to a kind of counting-house, where sat a man with books before him, and, not to take up more valuable space, he secured what was called a berth on board the *Ocean*, a dirty, small, ill-convenient ship bound for the port near the Scotch metropolis of Edinburgh.

Not wishing to be himself much noticed, and having no desire to notice anybody, Varney went down below, and seated himself in a dark corner of the generally dingy cabin, and there, amid all the noise, bawling, abuse, and bustle contingent upon getting the ill-conditioned bark under way, he never moved or uttered a word to any one, although the cabin was frequently visited.

But Varney had no idea of the amount of annoyance to which he was likely, in the course of the evening, to be subjected.

The vessel was got under way, and as both wind and tide happened to be favourable, she dropped down the river rapidly, and soon was clear of the Nore-light, and holding on her course northward.

The cabin now began to fill with the passengers, and extraordinary as the fact may appear, there were many Scotchmen actually going back again. They were, however, only going to pay visits, for it is one of the popular delusions that Scotchmen try to keep up in this country, that they have left something dear and delightful behind them in Scotland, and that, take it altogether, it is one of the most desirable spots in the whole world. It becomes, therefore, quite necessary for them to go back now and then, in order to keep up that delusion.

Personal vanity, too, is one of the great characteristics of the nation; and many a Scotchman goes back to Edinburgh, for example, to make an appearance among his old friends and family connexions, totally incompatible with his real position in London.

By about nine o'clock at night, when the shore to the west could only be discovered as a dim, grey line on the horizon, the cabin of the *Ocean* packet was crammed.

Whisky was produced, and a drink that the Scotch call "bottled yell," meaning ale; and as these two heady liquids began to take effect "Auld Lang Syne" was chaunted in the vernacular by the whole party.

At length a feeling of annoyance began to grow up from the fact of the isolated aspect of Varney, and the quiet, unobtrusive manner in which he looked on at the proceedings, appearing not in the smallest degree enthusiastic, even when the most uproarious Scotch songs, in the most unintelligible of all jargons, were sung, for strange to say, the authors of that nation take a pride in slaughtering the English language. *

At length a Scotchman approached Varney and said,—

"Ye'll take a glass to auld Reekie, mon?"

(Edinburgh is called Reekie in consequence of the absence of drainage, giving it a horrible foetid smell, a reeky atmosphere, in a manner of speaking; which may be illustrated by the Scotchman, who was returning to that place from England, on the top of a stage coach, when within about fifty miles he began sniffing and working his nose in an extraordinary manner.—"What are you doing that for?" said an Englishman.—"Eh! mon, I can smell the gude auld toon.")

"I do not understand your language," said Varney, and he walked from the cabin to the deck of the vessel. He recoiled an instant, for the moon was rising.

---

* *Likely intended as a pot-shot at Robert Burns.*

"Ever thus, even thus," he said, "how strange it is that I never dream of ridding myself of the suffering of living, but the moon is shining brightly. Can its rays penetrate the ocean?"

The deck was very still and silent indeed. The man at the helm, and one other pacing to and fro, were all that occupied it, save Varney himself, and he stood by the side gazing in the direction, where he had last seen the dim grey speck of land.

"A pleasant run, sir, we shall have of it," said the man who had been pacing the deck, "if this kindly wind continues."

"It blows from the west."

"Yes, nearly due-west; but that suits us. We keep her head a few points in shore, and do well with such a wind, although a south-west-by-south is our choice."

"How far are we from land?"

"It's the coast of Suffolk that is to our left, but we are I hope a good thirty miles or more from it."

"You hope?"

"Yes, sir. Perhaps you are not sufficient of a sailor to know that we never hug the shore if we can possibly help it."

"I understand. And there?"

"Oh, there lies the German Ocean."

"How deep now should you say the sea was here?"

"Can't say, sir, but it's blue water."

This was not much information to Varney, but he bowed his head and walked forward, as much as to say that he had had enough of the information and conversation of the man, who was the mate of the vessel, and quite disposed to be communicative. Perhaps in the very dim light he did not see exactly what a strange-looking personage he was talking to.

"Thirty miles from land," thought Varney, "surely that is far enough, and I need have no dread of floating to the shore through such a mass of water as that thirty miles. The distance is very great; I can to-night in another hour make the attempt."

To his great joy some heavy clouds climbed up the sky along with the moon, and congregating around the beautiful satellite, effectually obscured the greater number of its beams. There was in fact, no absolute moonlight, but a soft reflected kind of twilight coming through the clouds, and dispersed far and wide.

"This will do," muttered Varney. "All I have to fear are the direct moonbeams. It is they that have the effect of revivifying such as I am."

The man who had been pacing the deck finally sat down, and appeared to drop off to sleep, so that all was still, and as Varney kept to the head of the vessel, the man at the wheel could see nothing of him, there being many intervening obstacles. He was perfectly alone.

Now and then, with a loud roaring-about, he heard some boisterous drinking chorus come from the cabin, and then a rattle of glasses as fists were thumped upon the tables in token of boisterous approbation, and then all would be still again.

Varney looked up to the sky and his lips moved, but he uttered no sound. He went closer to the vessel's side and gazed upon the water as it lazily rippled past. How calm and peaceful, he thought, he ought to be, far beneath that tide.

A sudden plunge into the sea would have made a splash that would have been heard, and that he wished of all things to avoid. He clambered slowly over the side, and only held on by his hands for a moment. The cool night air tossed about his long elfin locks, and in another moment he was gone.

CXCVII.

THE OLD MANOR-HOUSE. — THE RESCUE. — VARNEY'S DESPAIR.

AT ABOUT TEN O'CLOCK on that same night on which Varney the Vampyre plunged into the sea with hopes of getting rid of the world of troubles that oppressed him, a small fishing boat might have been seen a distance of about twenty-five miles from the Suffolk coast, trying to make for land, and baffled continually by the wind that blew off shore.

In this boat were two young men, and from their appearance they evidently belonged to the wealthier class of society. They were brothers.

From their conversation we shall gather the circumstances that threw them into such situation, not by any means divested of peril as it was.

"Well, Edwin," said one, "here we have been beating about for five hours, trying to get in shore, and all our little bark permits us to do is I think not materially to increase our distance from home."

"That is about the truth, Charles," said the other, "and it was my fault."

"Come, Edwin, don't talk in that way. There is no fault in the matter; how could you know that the wind would stiffen into such a breeze as it has, so that we cannot fight out against it; or if there be fault, of course it's as much mine as yours, for am not I here, and do I not know full well what an amount of consternation there will be at the Grange?"

"There will indeed!"

"Well, their joy when we get back will be all the greater."

"Shall we get back?"

"Can you ask? Look at our little boat, is she not sea-worthy? Does she not dance on the waves merrily? It is only the wind after all that baffles us, if it would drop a little, we could, I think make head against it with the oars.

The brothers were silent now for a few moments, for they were each looking at the weather. At length Edwin spoke, saying,—

"We shall have the moon up, and that may make a change."

"Very likely — very likely. There is not, I think, quite so much sea as there was; suppose we try the oars again?"

The other assented, and the two young men exerted themselves very much to decrease their distance from the Suffolk coast by pulling away right manfully, but it was quite evident to them that they did no good, and that they had just as well dropped westward as they had been doing, by keeping the sail set, and steering as near as possible to the wind.

"Why, if this goes on, Charles, where shall we get to by the morning?"

"To Northumberland, perhaps."

"Or further."

"Well, if we go far enough, what say you to attempting the *vexata questio* of the north-west passage?" *

"Nay, I cannot jest — it's a sad thing this — more sad a good deal for those who are at home, than for us. To-morrow is Clara's wedding day, and what a damper it will be upon all to suppose that we have perished at sea."

"They will never suppose that we would do anything so ridiculous. Why, at the worst, you know, we could go before the wind and run on to Holland."

"Yes, if no storm arises or such a gale as might founder our boat. There, there is the moon."

"Yes, and she will soon be overtaken by yon bank of clouds that seem to be scudding after her in the blue heavens. Ha! a sail, by Jove!"

"Where? where?"

"Not I think above four miles there to the east, by our little compass which it is a thousand mercies we have with us. Look, you may see her sails against that light cloud — there."

"I see her. Think you she will see us?"

"There is every chance, for her swell of canvass will be all the other way. Fire your fowling-piece and the sound may reach her, the wind is good for carrying it."

Charles took a fowling-piece from the bottom of the boat. The brothers had merely gone out at sunset or a little before

it, to shoot gulls, and he tried to discharge the piece, but several seas that they had shipped, while they were thinking of other things than keeping the gun dry, had, for the time being, most effectively prevented it from being discharged.

"Ah!" said Edwin as he heard the click of the lock, "that hope is lost."

"It is indeed, and to my thinking the ship is distancing us rapidly. You see our mast and sail, will, at even this distance, lie so low in the horizon that they will hardly see us unless they are sweeping the sky with a night glass."

"And that is not likely."

"Certainly not, so we have nothing for it but to hold on our way. I am getting hungry if you are not."

"I certainly am not getting hungry, for I have felt half famished these last two hours; but I suppose we may hold out against the fiend hunger some hours yet. What are you looking at so earnestly, eh?"

"I hardly know."

"You hardly know? Let me see — why — why what is it?"

"There seems to me to be something now and that much darker than the waves, tiding on their tops; there, do you not see it? There it is again. There!"

"Yes, yes."

"What on earth can it be?"

"A dead body."

"Indeed! ah! it drifts towards us. There is some current hereabouts, for you see it comes to us against the wind."

"Don't deceive yourself, brother. It is we who are going with the wind towards it, and now you can see there is no doubt about what it is. Some poor fellow, who has been drowned. Get out the boat-hook, get it out."

---

* *Through northern Canada to the Pacific. The search for a northwest passage had been luring explorers to North America for centuries. A passage was discovered shortly after* Varney *was published, but it was unnavigable to the ships of the era.*

"Why, you would not take in such a cargo, Edwin."

"God forbid! but I feel some curiosity to see who and what sort of a personage it is. Here we have him. What a length he is to be sure."

The body was nearly alongside the boat, and one of the brothers detained it with a boat-hook, while they both looked earnestly at it.

It was the body of a man, remarkably well dressed, and had no appearance of having been under the water long. The features, as far as they could see them, were calm and composed. The hands were clenched, and some costly looking rings glittered on the fingers through the salt spray that foamed and curled around the insensible form.

"Charles," said Edwin; "what we shall do?"

Edwin shook his head.

"I — I don't like."

"Like what?"

"I don't like to cast it adrift again, and not take it ashore, where it can rest in an honest man's grave if he be one. Fancy it being one of us, would it not be a consolation to those who love us to know that we rested in peace among our ancestors, in preference to rotting in the sea, tossed and mangled by every storm that blows. I do not like to cast the body adrift again."

"It's a ghastly passenger."

"It is, but that ghastliness is only an idea, and we should remember that we ourselves —"

"Stop, brother, stop. Do not fancy that I oppose your wish to convey this body to the shore, and place it in some sanctified spot. What I expressed concerning it was merely the natural feeling that must arise on such an occasion, nothing more."

"Then you are willing?"

"I am."

The two brothers now, without further doubts or remarks upon the subject, got the body into the boat, and laid it carefully down. Then Edwin folded and tied a handkerchief over the face, for as he truly enough said, —

"There is no occasion to have to encounter that dead face each moment that one turns one's eyes in that direction; it is sufficient that we have, by taking the body in at all done, all that humanity can dictate to us."

To this Charles agreed, and it was remarked by them both as a strange thing that from the moment of their taking in the dead body to the boat, the wind dropped, and finally there was almost a calm, after which there came soft gentle air from the south-east, which enabled them with scarcely any exertion on their own parts to make great progress towards their own home, from which they found they had not by any means been driven so far northward as they had at first thought.

The brothers looked at each other, and it was Edwin who broke the silence, and put into words what both thought, by saying, —

"Charles, there is something more in this whole affair than what lies just upon its surface."

"Yes, it seems as if we were driven out to sea by some special providence to do this piece of work, and that having done it, the winds and the waves obeyed the hand of their mighty Master, and allowed of our return."

"It does seem so," said the other.

CXCVIII.

A FAMILY SCENE. — THE SISTERS. — THE HORRIBLE ALARM.

IN THE COURSE OF TWO HOURS more, the young men were so close in shore that they could see the lights flashing along the coast, and they even fancied they could catch a glimpse of human forms moving along with torches; and if such were the case, they doubted not but that these people were sent to serve as a guide to them should they with their little bark be hovering near the coast.

"Look, Edwin," said Charles, "we are expected, are we not?"

"Yes, yes."

"I am certain that those lights are meant as guides for us."

"They may spare themselves the trouble, for do you not see that the clouds are wearing away, and that in a few minutes more we shall have the undimmed lustre of a full moon looking down upon us."

"It will be so."

The boat had now got so far within a large natural inlet of the ocean that but very little wind caught its gently flapping sail, so that the brothers bent manfully to their oars, and got the boat through the water at a rapid rate.

Oh, how very different their sensations were now to what they had been when they were beating about at the mercy of the winds and waves, but a few short hours since, and when it certainly was but an even chance with death whether they would ever see their home again!

If a gale had sprung up, accompanied by anything in the shape of a very heavy sea, they must have been lost.

Soon they saw that their boat was descried, and at a particular portion of the coast there stood a complete cluster of men with torches, inviting them there to land, and they knew that such landing place was upon their father's property, and that in a few minutes they would be safe on shore.

Neither of them spoke, but reflection was busy in the hearts of both.

There was a loud and thoroughly English shout, as the boat grated upon the sandy beach, and Edwin and Charles jumped on shore. They were in another moment pressed in their father's arms.

"Why, why, boys," he said, "what a fright you have given us all; there's Clara and Emma have been forced — I say forced, for nothing but force would do it — to go home, and the whole country has been in an uproar. You were blown out to sea, I suppose?"

"Yes, father, but we have not been in any danger."

"Not in any danger with such a cockleshell of a boat fairly out into the German Ocean! — But we will say no more about it, lads. Not another word, come home at once, and make all hearts glad at the old Grange-house."

"There's something in the boat," cried one of the men who held a light.

"Good God, yes!" exclaimed Charles.

"We had forgotten," said Edwin, "we

met with a little adventure at sea, and picked up a dead body."

"A dead body?"

"Yes, father, we could not find it in our hearts to let it be, so we brought it on shore that it might have the rites of Christian burial in the village church-yard. Somebody who loved the man may yet thank us for it, and feel a consolation to know that such had been done."

"You are right boys, you are right," said the father, "you have done in that matter just as I would wish you; I will give orders for the body to be taken to the dead house by Will Stephens, and to-morrow it shall be decently interred."

This being settled, the father, accompanied by his two sons, who were not a little pleased to be safe upon *terra firma* again, walked together up a sloping pathway, which led to the Grange-house, as it was called.

The joy that the return of the brothers caused in the family, our readers may well imagine. The sisters Clara and Emma wept abundantly, and the mother, who had let her fears go further than any one else, was deeply affected.

But it is time that we should inform the reader who these people were, whom we have introduced upon the scene of our eventful history.

Sir George Crofton, for such was the name of the father of Edwin and Charles, was a wealthy warm-hearted country gentleman, and constantly resided upon his own estate all the year round,* being a good landlord to his tenantry, and a good father to his four children, who have already been to some extent presented to the reader.

The mother was a kind-hearted, but rather weak woman, with an evangelical bias that at times was rather annoying to the family.

This, however, was perhaps the good lady's only fault, for with that one exception, she was fond of her children to excess, notwithstanding, as Sir George sometimes jestingly said he verily

---

* As opposed to the absentee landlords which were growing more common in the 1840s, who lived in fancy London flats on the revenue from their country estates, neglecting their tenants and shirking their duties as squires.

believed, she in her heart considered they were all "on the high road to a nameless abode."

The night was so far advanced when the young men got home that, of course, not much was said or done, and among other things that were put off until the following morning, was the story of the finding of the body.

"There is no occasion," whispered Sir George, "to say anything to your mother about it."

"Certainly not, father."

"At least not till to-morrow, for if you do, I shall not get a wink of sleep for her reflections on the subject."

The two young men knew very well that this was no exaggeration, and that their mother would, like any divine, eagerly seize the opportunity of what is called "improving the occasion" by indulging in a long discourse upon the most dismal of all subjects that the mind of any human being can conceive, namely, the probability of everybody going to eternal perdition unless they believe in a particular set of doctrines that to her seem orthodox.

The consequence of this was that the dead body was quietly taken out of the boat by men who did not possess the most refined feelings in the world, and carried to the bone house.

"He seems a decent sort of chap," said one, as he looked at the very respectable habiliments of the corpse.

"Ah! look at the gold rings."

"Yes, you may, look, Abel, but eyes on, hands off."

"Why?"

"Why, you gowk, do you think as young Master Charles and Edwin don't know of 'em, and more besides, who would touch dead man's gold off of his fingers?"

"Is it unlucky?"

"Horrid!"

"Then I'll have nought to do with un."

The body was placed on the ground, for there was no coffin of any sort to put it in, and the door was shut upon it in the dead house, and then the party who had brought it there thought it a part of their duty to wake up Will Stephens the sexton, to tell him that there was such a thing as a dead body placed in his custody, as it were, by being put into the dead house, which was not above a hundred yards from the cottage occupied by Will.

They hammered away rather furiously at his door, and no wonder that he felt a little, or perhaps not a little, alarmed upon the occasion.

In a few moments a casement was opened and out popped a head.

"Hilloa! you ragamuffins, what do you mean by hammering away at an honest man's door at this rate, eh? Am I to have any sleep?"

"Ragamuffin yourself," cried one; "there's a dead body of a drowned man in the bonehouse. All you have got to do is to look after it, and there's a lot of gold rings on its fingers with diamonds in them, for all we know, worth God knows how much. You may make the most of it now that you know it."

"A dead man! Who is he?"

"Ah, that's more than we can tell. Good night, or rather good morning, old crusty."

"Stop! stop! — tell me —"

The men only laughted, for they had no desire to protract a conversation with the sexton, and he called in vain after them to give him some further information upon the subject of this rather mysterious information.

"A drowned man," he pondered to himself, "a drowned man, and with fingers loaded with gems, and brought to the bonehouse! Oh, pho! pho! It's a hoax, that's what it is, and I won't believe it. It's done to get me up in the cold, that's all, and then there will be some trick played off upon me safe, and I shall be only laughed at for my pains."

Full of this idea, the sexton turned into his bed again, and hoped that by speedily going to sleep, he should get the laugh of his tormentors, instead of they getting it of him, as well as lose the shivering that had come on him through standing at the open window, exposed to the night air so very indifferently clad.

CXCIX.

THE SEXTON'S AVARICE. — THE DEAD AND THE LIVING. — THE RING.

IT WAS ALL VERY WELL for the sexton to wish, and to try to got to sleep, but actually to succeed in procuring "Nature's sweet oblivion" was quite another matter.

In vain he tossed and turned about, there was no rest for him of any kind or description, dreamless or dreamful, and still he kept repeating to himself,—

"A dead body, with gold and diamond rings in the bone-house."

These were the magic words which, like a spell that he was compelled by some malign influence continually to repeat, kept Will Stephens awake, until at last he seemed to lose entirely his first perception of the fact that he might be only hoaxed, and all his imagination became concentrated on the idea of how came the dead body in the bone-house, and how was it that gold and diamond rings were left on its fingers in such a place?

These were mental ruminations, the result of which was transparent from the first, for that result in the natural order of things was sure to be that the passion of curiosity would get the better of all other considerations, and he, Will Stephens, would rise to ascertain if such were really the state of things.

"It ain't far off morning, now," he reasoned with himself, "so I may as well get up at once as lie here tossing and tumbling about, and certainly unable to get another wink of sleep, and besides after all I may be wrong in thinking this a

hoax. There may really be such a dead body as those fellows mentioned in the bone-house and if there be, I ought certainly to go and look after it."

We easily reason ourselves into what is our pleasure, and so while these cogitatory remarks were uttered by the sexton, he rose.

He found that if he drew back the blind from before his window, the moon which was now sailing through a nearly cloudless sky, would give him amply sufficient light to enable him to go through the process of dressing, so he at once began that operation.

"Yes," he said, "I ought to go, it's my positive duty to do so, after getting the information I have, and if that information be untrue, let it recoil on the heads of those who invented the falsehood. I shall go, that's settled. What a sweet moonlight."

It was a sweet moonlight indeed. The floods of soft silvery light fell with an uncommon radiance upon all objects, and the minutest thing could have been seen upon the ground, with the same clearness and distinctness as at mid-day.

The only difference was that a soft preternatural looking atmosphere seemed to be around everything, and a kind of marble like look was imparted to all objects far and near on which those soft silvery rays rested in beauty and sublimity.

The sexton was full dressed, and although the moonlight guided him well, he thought that he might in the bone-house require another mode of illumination, and he lighted and took with him a small lantern which had a darkening shade to it.

Thus prepared, he walked at a rapid pace from his own house towards the small shedlike building which served as a receptacle for the unowned dead, and for such human remains as were from time to time cast ashore by the waves, or flung up from new graves by the spade and the mattock.

Familiar as he was and had been for many a year with that bone-house, and often in contact with the dead, he yet on this occasion felt as if a strange fear was creeping over him, and then a flutter of his heart and the fiery feel that was in his brain were circumstances quite novel to him.

"Well, this is odd," he said, "and I suppose it is what they call being nervous I can't make it out to be anything else, I'm sure."

Thus reasoning with himself upon his own unwonted timidity, he reached the bone-house.

The door of the dilapidated building which was known by that name, was only secured by a latch, for it was not considered that the contents of the place were sufficiently interesting for any one's cupidity to be excited by it.

The sexton paused a moment before he lifted the latch, and glanced around him. Even then he half expected to hear a loud laugh expressive of the triumph of those who had combined to play him the trick, if it were one, of getting him out of his bed on a bootless errand. But all was still around him — still as the very grave itself — and muttering then in a hurried

tone, "it is true, there is no trick," he hastily opened the door, and went into the bone-house.

All was darkness save one broad beam of moonlight that came in at the door-way, but the sexton closed the entrance, and applied to his lantern for a light.

He slid the darkening piece of metal from before the magnifying glass, and then a rather sickly ray of light fell for a moment upon the corpse that lay then upon its back — a ray only sufficiently strong and sufficiently enduring to enable the sexton to make quite sure that there was a body before him, and then his lantern went out.

"Confound the lantern!" he said, "I ought to have looked to it before I started, instead of lighting it on the mere hazard of its going on comfortably. What's to be done? Ah, I have it, I remember."

What the sexton remembered was that on the same wall in which the door was situated, there was a large square aperture only covered by a kind of shutter of wood, the withdrawal of a bolt from which would cause it to fall in a moment on its hinges.

The sexton knew the place well, and drawing back the somewhat rusty bolt, down went the shutter, and a broad flood of moonlight fell at once upon the corpse.

"Ah," said Will Stephens, "there it is sure enough. What a long odd-looking fellow to be sure, and what a face — how thin and careworn looking. I do very much wonder now who he really is?"

As he continued to gaze upon the dead body, his eyes wandered to the hands, and then sure enough he saw the bright and glittering gems the men had spoken of, and which the salt water had not been able to tarnish into dimness. Perceiving that the setting was gold and the stones real,—

"Ahem!" said Stephens, softly; "they will not bury the corpse with those rings on his fingers. Why, he must have half a dozen on at least; they will be somebody's perquisite of course, and that somebody won't be me. The idea of leaving such property unprotected in a bone-house!"

Will Stephens remained now silent for a short time, moving his head about in different directions, so that he caught the bright colours of the jewels that adorned the dead man's hands, and then he spoke again.

"What's more easy," said he, "than for some of the very fellows who brought him here, to slip back quietly, and take away every one of those rings?"

After this much, he went to the door of the bone-house and listened, but all was perfectly still; and then his cogitations assumed another shape.

"Who saw me come from my house?" he said.— "Nobody. Who will see me go back to it?— Nobody. Then what is to hinder me from taking the rings, and—and letting the blame lie on some one else's shoulders, I should like to know? Nothing will be easier than for me to say in the morning that owing to the strange and insolent manner in which the information was given me of the arrival of the dead body in the bone-house, I did not believe it and therefore did not rise, and so—so I think I may as well, eh?"

He thought he heard something like a faint sigh, and the teeth chattered in his head, and he shook in every limb as he bent all his energies to the task of listening

if there were really any one in or at hand, playing the spy upon him.

All was as before profoundly still, and with a long breath of relief, he cast off his terror.

"What a fool I am to be sure," he said; "it was but the wind after all, no doubt, making its way through some one of the numerous chinks and crevices in this shed; it did sound like a sigh from some human lips, but it wasn't."

The propriety of making short work of the affair, if he wished to do it at all, now came forcibly to the mind of the sexton, and arming himself with all the courage he could just then summon to his aid, he advanced close to the corpse.

Kneeling on one knee he took up one of the hands from which he wished to take the rings, and when he saw them closer, he felt convinced that they did not belie their appearance, but were in reality what they seemed to be—jewels of rarity and price.

The hand was cold and clammy and damp to the touch, and the knuckles were swollen, so that there was great difficulty in getting the rings over them, and the sexton was full five minutes getting one of them off.

When he had done so, he wiped the perspiration of fear and excitement from his brow, as he muttered,—

"That's always the case with your drowned folks, they are so swelled when first they come out of the water, and so I shall have quite a job, I suppose."

The sexton's cupidity was, however, now sufficiently awakened, to make him persevere, despite any such obstacles, in what he was about, and accordingly, kneeling on both knees he clasped the wrist of the dead man in one hand, and with the other strove to coax off, by twisting the hoop of gold round and round, a ring that had one diamond, apparently of great value, set in it, and which the robber of the dead thought was a prize worth some trouble in the obtaining.

In an instant, the dead hand clasped him tight.

CC.

THE RECOVERY. — THE SEXTON'S FRIGHT. — THE COMPACT.

WHAT PEN SHALL describe the abject fright of Master Will Stephens, the sexton, as the cold clammy fingers of the supposed corpse closed upon his hand?

The blood seemed to curdle at his very heart — a film spread itself before his eyes — he tried to scream, but his tongue clove to the roof of his mouth, and he could utter no sound.

In good truth he was within an ace of fainting, and it was rather a wonder that he did not go clean off.

Power to withdraw his hand from the horrible grasp he had not, and there he knelt, shivering and shaking, and with his mouth wide open, and the hair literally bristling upon his head.

How long he and the dead man remained in this way together in silence, he knew not, but he was aroused from the state of almost frenzy in which he was, by a deep sepulchral voice — the voice of the apparently dead.

"What has happened?" it said, "what has happened? Is this the world which was to come?"

"M-m-mer-cy — help," stammered the sexton. "I — I — I — am a poor man — I — I don't want your rings, good Mr. — Mr. Ghost. Oh — oh — oh — have mercy upon me I — I — implore you."

The only reply was a frightful groan.

The perspiration rolled down the sexton's face.

"Oh, don't — oh, pray don't — hold — hold me so — so tight."

"Now," said the dead man, "I know all. The die is cast; my fate has again spoken. Steel shall not slay me, the bullet shall kill me not, fire shall not burn me, and water will not drown while yon bright satellite sails on 'twixt earth and heaven."

"Yes — yes, sir."

"The fiat has gone forth, and I am wretched, oh, Heaven, so unutterably wretched!"

"Perhaps, good Mr. Ghost, you — you will let me go now. Here's your ring, I don't want to keep it. Here's the only one I took off your worshipful fingers, good Mr. Ghost."

A very thin filmy sort of cloud had been going over the moon's disc, but now had passed completely away, and such a flood of unchecked untempered brillancy poured in at the open window, if it might be so called of the dead-house that it became quite radiant with the silvery beams.

The drowned man rose with a wild howling cry of rage, and springing at the throat of the sexton, bore him down to the earth in an instant, and placed his knee upon his chest.

"Villain," he groaned out between his clenched teeth, "you shall die, although you have made me live. There shall be one victim to the fell destroyer."

The sexton thought his hour was come.

"Wretch!" pursued the revived corpse, "wretch, what devil prompted you to do this most damnable deed? Speak — speak, I say, who are you?"

"What — what deed?" gasped the sexton.

"The deed of restoring me to life — of dragging me from the ocean, and forcing me to live again."

"I — I — oh dear."

"Speak. Go on."

"I didn't do anything of the sort. The truth is, I only came to — to — to —"

"To what?"

"To borrow a ring of you, that's all, and the greatest calamity that ever happened to me is your coming to life."

"How came I here?"

"That I can't tell your worship. I am the sexton of this place, it's called Culburn, and is in Suffolk, and they picked your worship up at sea, and brought you here. That's all I know about it, as I hope for mercy. It can't do you any good to kill a poor fellow like me. I don't think you are a ghost now, but some ugly — no I mean handsome fellow — supposed only to be drowned."

"Do you tell me truth?"

"As I live, and hope your worship will let me live I do. And here's the ring, I came to borrow of you, sir, as a proof."

"Of what?"

"Of — of — of — I hardly know what to say to you, sir."

"If you are not the great enemy to me that I thought you — you are a mere thief. You came to steal the jewels I had upon my fingers. Is not that the truth?"

"I — I rather think it is, sir."

"You may save your wretched life if you like. If you promise me that you will keep all that has happened a secret, except so much of it as I shall empower you to reveal, I will spare you; but if after having so promised, you break faith with me, and let your tongue wag further than I wish it, you will not live twenty-four hours afterwards, be assured, for I will find you out, and twist your head from your shoulders."

"Anything, sir, I will promise anything, I will swear if you like."

"I heed no oaths. Consideration for your own safety will keep you silent. Rise."

He took his knee off the chest of the sexton and his hand off his throat, and then Will Stephens tremblingly rose to his feet. The idea did cross him for a moment of measuring his strength with the resuscitated man, but when he beheld the tall, bony, gaunt figure before him, he saw he had not the shadow of a chance in a personal struggle.

Moreover, he had a lively remembrance of a most vice-like pressure upon his throat, which seemed to say that the ugly stranger was by no means in an exhausted state.

Upon the whole, then, the sexton was glad to have escaped so well.

"You have only to say, sir, what you would have me do," he said.

"Answer me first. Have you always lived here? Is this your native place?"

"Oh, no, sir, I came from London; but then it's years ago."

"Very well. You must say that you remember me in London, as a gentleman of good repute, and you must add that you came to the bone-house here, and found me reviving, and that you took measures to complete my recovery."

"Yes, sir. And here is your ring."

"Keep it as a memento of this affair."

"Many thanks, sir. Will it please you to tell me your name and condition?"

"John Smith, a foreign merchant; and now tell me, minutely, how I was rescued from the ocean, or did the waves themselves give up their dead?"

The sexton who was now assured in his own mind that it was no ghost he was speaking to, entered as far as he knew into the story of the finding the body, and bringing it to the bone-house, but as that information was not great, he volunteered, if Mr. Smith would go with him to his cottage, to get him all the particulars.

To this the other consented, and they both left the bone-house together.

On the short bit of road, the sexton began to think that his companion must be some madman, for ever and anon when the moon was brightest, he saw him lift up both his arms to it, as if he were worshipping it, and at those times too, he heard him mutter some words in a language that he did not comprehend. At length the singular being spoke in English.

"Henceforth," he cried, as if quite forgetful of the presence of another, "henceforth, begone remorse, begone despair. The great sea has rejected me, and not again will I seek destruction; I will live, and I will live to be the bane and curse of the beautiful."

"Sir," said the sexton, "here is my house, sir; if you will step in, I will soon dish you up a little something in the way of refreshment. You see, sir, I live alone, that is to say, an old woman who keeps my cottage in order and waits upon me goes away at night, and comes again in the morning, but as it is not her time yet, I will get you anything you like to eat or to drink."

"I never eat nor drink."

"Not eat! — nor — drink! Never, sir?"

"Never. I shall cost you nothing to entertain me. I want some rest, and while I am taking it, do you go and get me such information as you can regarding me. Make no concealment that I am alive, but go at once, and return with what expedition you may, and remember that your fate is in my hands."

"I will, sir."

The sexton was quite terrified enough to do what he was bidden, and perhaps, the consciousness that the strange and mysterious man whom he had for a guest might accuse him of the projected robbery of the jewellery he had about his person influenced him more than the rather obscure threat of personal vengeance by the promised screwing his head off.

But the matter, take it for all in all, was anything but an agreeable one for Master Will Stephens, and most heartily did he wish he had remained in his bed and left the stranger to recover, if was to recover, by himself. Will did not attribute that recovery to the moonlight he had himself let in.

CCI.

THE NIGHT ALARM. — THE VAMPYRE'S ATTACK UPON THE BRIDE.

THE PARTICULARS CONCERNING the bringing-in of the body that had been picked up at sea by the brothers Edwin and Charles Crofton, were to be learnt from many mouths so soon as the sexton evinced a disposition to know them, and in a very short time, and as the daylight was making the fainter and more spiritual light of the moon fade away, he again reached his own abode, where he had left a guest of whom the reader knows much, but of whom Will Stephens knew but little.

He found the self-christened Mr. Smith waiting for him rather impatiently.

"Well," he cried, "your news? your news?"

"May be told, sir, in a few words," replied the sexton, and then he made his new friend acquainted with the whole story, just as he had heard it of the fishermen on the coast.

Mr. Smith, or as we may as well call him at once the vampyre, hesitated for a few moments as if he had not exactly and accurately made up his mind what to do, and then he said,—

"You will go to the Grange-house and tell the story that I have before informed you I would have told. Be sure that you expatiate upon my gentility and respectability, for I want to be upon good terms with the Crofton family."

"Well, but sir, I'm a tenant of Sir George Crofton's and so you see —"

"What," said the vampyre, his eyes flashing with indignation as he spoke "dare you dispute my positive commands?"

"No, sir, I — I only —"

"Peace, caitiff, and know that I hold thy life in my hands for your attempted robbery of me."

The sexton trembled. That was indeed the weak point now of all his defences against whatever commands might be put upon him by his master, as we may now call the vampyre, although after all it was but the usual dominion of a strong mind over a weak one, for there was not so much in reality for the sexton to be afraid of as his own guilty conscience dictated to him.

It were easy enough for the vampyre to charge him with robbery, but not at all so easy for him to prove such a charge, and at the same time to substantiate, as by some inquisitive counsel he might be called upon to do, his own position in society.

But it is most true that —

*"Conscience doth make cowards of us all."**

And feeling that his intention regarding the rings of the supposed drowned man had been of a dishonest character, he could not summon courage sufficient to defy him now.

"I will go," he said, "I am going."

" 'Tis well."

In far from the pleasantest train of thought the sexton went to the Grange,

---

* *A line from Shakespeare's* Hamlet, *Act III Scene I.* "Conscience" *refers to a sense of guilt.*

and asked to see Mr. Charles Crofton, and to him he related the version of the resuscitating of the supposed drowned man. It was heard with, as might be expected, the most profound astonishment, and the sexton soon found himself confronted with the whole assembled family, and force to repeat the wonderful facts over again.

It seemed, as indeed it might well do, a something quite beyond belief.

"Why, Edwin," said Charles, "he must

have been in the water far beyond the length of time that it mostly takes to drown any one before we saw him."

"I think so too."

"It must be so, for this reason, that he was a considerable distance from land, and there was no vessel near enough for him to have come from."

"Hold!" said Sir George Crofton, "my dear boys, you are forgetting the most important fact of all."

"Are we, father?"

"Yes, and that is that the gentleman is alive. You cannot get over that, you know, and as I have often heard that whatever is is natural, why there's no use in disputing any more about it; and besides how do we know but that he was in some boat which was swamped a few minutes before you saw him."

"That is a most rational supposition," said Edwin.

"And that we can say nothing against," added Charles; "what is to be done, father?"

"Why, do not let us do good by inches, we know that this is the only decent house within a considerable distance for a gentleman to remain in, if he have the habits of comfort about him. So Master Stephens, if you will go and give our compliments to the stranger, and ask him to come here, I shall be much obliged to you."

"I will, Sir George."

"And you can tell him that we are plain folks, but assure him of a hearty welcome."

Will Stephens made his bow and exit.

"Well," said Edwin, "it's very odd, although of course, it must be all right, and I am the last person who would wish to make anything out of a common-place

event, but to all appearances dead he was when we took him into the boat, and I never before heard of a spontaneous recovery like this from such a state."

"Then you have added to your stock of experience," said his father, laughing, "and I must own, for my own part, that I am rather curious to see this person, who was a curiosity in appearance, according to your accounts when he was dead or supposed to be dead."

"He was so," remarked Charles, "for I am certain you might travel the world over without meeting a more singular-looking man than he was; in the first place, he looked particularly tall, but that might have arisen from the fact that we only saw him in a horizontal position, and then there was a something about the expression of his face which was perfectly indescribable, and yet at the same time filled you with feelings of curiosity and dread."

The sisters heard this account of the mysterious stranger with feelings of great interest.

"Why," said Emma, "we have all of us often complained of being dull here, but such an animal as this will be quite an acquisition."

"And just as Clara is going, too, what a pity," laughed Edwin.

"I shall endeavour to survive the horrid disappointment," said Clara, for she was to be married on that day, to one who had been the chosen companion of her heart for many a day, and was to leave the home of her childhood to proceed far away to his house in Wales, where she was to be the light of joy to another admiring and loving circle.

"Ah, well, I pity you," said Emma.

"Then you had better at once," remarked Clara, "forbid the occasional visits here of a certain young officer who, I'm afraid, has some audacious intentions."

The ready colour flushed to the cheek of the younger sister, who had scarcely expected such a retort, although she had fairly provoked it.

"Come, girls," said the father, "we will have no more lance-breaking between you about your lovers."

"Certainly not, father," said Clara, "but then, you know, unless Emma is made to see that she is vulnerable, she will go on tormenting me."

"In other words, Emma," said Edwin, "you see that people who live in glass houses should not throw stones — a most useful maxim."

"I don't care for any of you," said Emma, half crying, as she ran out of the room.

Clara followed her, for there was really the very best understanding and the kindest feeling between the two young girls, although occasionally a smart repartee would be uttered upon some such occasion as the present, but all that was soon forgotten.

The sexton, who was getting each moment more and more uneasy about the share he had in the affair of the resuscitated man of the bone-house, went back to the cottage, and there informed the self-named Mr. Smith of the success of his mission to the Grange-house.

"You think they will welcome me," said the vampyre.

"I am sure of it, sir. They are the frankest, freest family I ever knew, and they would not have asked you to got to the Grange if they did not mean to use you well."

"And there are two daughters?"

"Yes, sir."

"And young and fair, you tell me."

"They are two as handsome girls as you will find in this part of the country, sir. They have always been much admired. One of them, as I before mentioned, is going to be married and taken away, but the other stays at home."

"'Tis well, now you will not fail to remember the awkward situation in which you are. Keep the ring which you took from my finger, and with it keep your own counsel, for any babbling upon your part will most assuredly lead to your destruction."

"Yes, sir, I know."

"And although that destruction might not be immediate, you would lead a life of trembling terror until your doom was accomplished, and that doom should be a dreadful one in its manner. Now farewell! farewell! and remember me."

"I shall never forget you the longest day I have got to live," said the sexton, with a shudder, as he saw the tall, angular, gaunt-looking form of his most mysterious new acquaintance leave his cottage, and make his way towards the Grange.

CCII.

THE DEFILE IN THE ROCKS. — THE HORSEMAN AND THE ACCIDENT.

THE GRANGE-HOUSE WAS visible from the cottage of the sexton, and so the vampyre had declined the offer of Will Stephens to be his guide.

As it happened, though, it would have been better regarding his reaching the Grange quickly that he should have taken the sexton with him, for the cliffs that were close at hand concealed to the eye many deep gulleys and frightful precipices that had to be coasted round, before any one could reach the Grange-house by that route.

If he could have gone directly onward, about half a mile's walking would have sufficed to enable him to reach the place, but before he had proceeded a quarter of that distance, he came upon a deep ravine or splitting in the cliff, too wide to jump across, and with all the appearance of extending inland a considerable distance without narrowing.

"I had indeed better have brought a guide with me," muttered Varney.

He then paused for a few moments, as if he was debating with himself whether or not he should return back and get the sexton. But the mental hesitation did not last long, and accustomed as he was to trust to his own sagacity and his own resources more than to other people, he walked along by the side of the fissure in the cliff, muttering to himself,—

"Were all the guides in the country here, they could but do as I am doing, namely, walk on until the ravine closes."

With this idea he pursued it, but to his mortification he found that it widened instead of presenting the least symptoms of closing, and suddenly it opened to his eyes to a width of about fifty feet, and he paused again irresolute.

"How am I to proceed?" he said; "this is a perplexity."

He advanced close to the brink, and looked down. The depth was very considerable, and at the bottom there was evidently a road made of sand and chalk, which wound down somewhere from the interior of the country to the sea-beach.

As he looked, he heard the rapid sound of a horse's feet.

In another moment there dashed down the road towards the sea, a horse bearing on his back a man, who was exerting himself in every possible way to stop the maddened, headlong career of the animal, but it would not be checked.

With starting eyes and dilated nostrils, and with its flanks covered with foam, the frighted steed, which had evidently come some distance in that state, rushed on, but the broken nature of the ground made it almost impossible that it should make such great speed then as it had been making, at least with any degree of safety.

This was what occurred to the thoughts of Varney, and it was sufficiently proved to be a correct idea, by the horse stumbling the next moment, and throwing his rider heavily upon the sand

and broken rock that was strewn around.

The steed, now disencumbered of its load, recovered itself in a moment, and with a snort of rage and probably of pain likewise, dashed and disappeared from the sight, round the abrupt corner of the ravine to the left hand on the beach.

"So be it," said the vampyre, calmly; "another being is snatched away from the muster roll of the living, one who perhaps would gladly have preserved his existence, while I — I remain and cannot, let me do what I will to accomplish such a purpose, shake off the cumbrous load of life that will cling to me."

Suddenly quite a whirlwind of passion seemed to come on him, and, standing on the brink of the ravine with his arms extended, he cried, —

"Since death is denied to me, I will henceforward shake off all human sympathies. Since I am compelled to be that which I am, I will not be that and likewise suffer all the pangs of doing deeds at which a better nature that was within me revolted. No, I will from this time be the bane of all that is good and great and beautiful. If I am forced to wander upon the earth, a thing to be abhorred and accursed among men, I will perform my mission to the very letter as well as the spirit, and henceforth *adieu* all regrets, *adieu* all feeling — all memory of goodness — of charity to human nature, for I will be a dread and a desolation! Since blood is to be my only sustenance, and since death is denied to me, I will have abundance of it — I will revel in it, and no spark of human pity shall find a home in this once racked and tortured bosom. Fate, I thee defy!"

He continued for some few moments after uttering this speech in the same attitude in which he had spoken the words. Then, suffering his hands slowly to fall, again he looked cold, and passionless, as he had been before.

But his determination was made.

By looking carefully about him, he saw that there was a kind of footpath down the side of the ravine, which an active person might descend by, although, probably, not altogether without some risk, for the least false step might precipitate him to the bottom.

The vampire, however, had no such fears. He seemed to feel that he possessed a kind of charmed life, and that he might adventure to do what others might well shrink from.

This feeling begot a confidence which was almost certain to be his protection, even if it had been only founded upon imagination, for it fortified his nerves, and when he began the descent down the side of the ravine, it was without the smallest terror.

He found, however, that when he was fairly on the path, it was a better and a wider one than he had a first supposed it to be, and in the course of five minutes he had got completely down to the narrow road, on which, apparently dead, lay the wounded man, for he was only grievously hurt by his fall, although he was quite insensible.

The vampyre strode up to him.

"Ah," he said, "young, and what the world would call handsome. Ha! ha! Heaven takes but little care sometimes of its handiwork."

After a few moments' contemplation of the still form that lay at his feet, he knelt on one knee by its side, and placed his hand upon the region of the heart, after roughly tearing open the vest of the stranger.

"He lives — he lives. Well, shall I crush the fluttering spirit that now is hovering 'twixt life and death, or shall I let it linger while it may within its earthly prison? Let it stay. The worst turn that any one can do another in this world, is surely to preserve existence after once the pang of what would be all the agony of death is past."

The vampyre rose, and was moving away up the ravine, when a sudden thought seemed to strike him, and he turned back again.

"Gold," he said, "is always useful to me, and I think with my new thoughts and feelings it will now be more so than ever. This insensible man may have some about him."

Again he knelt by the side of the young man, and soon possessed himself of a tolerably well-stocked purse that he found upon him. Round his neck, too, by a thin chain of gold, hung a small portrait of a young and beautiful girl, upon which Varney gazed intently.

"She is fair," he said, "very fair — she would make a fit victim for me. I will take this portrait; it might stand me in some stead should I encounter the original."

He placed the portrait in his pocket, and was in the act of rising, when he heard the sound of a footstep.

"Ah, some one comes; it will be no part of my plan to have been seen by the body."

He darted forth down the narrow gorge or ravine, and was soon sufficiently hidden from the sight of those who were advancing. They proved to be some fishermen going to spread their nets upon the beach, which just below the spot where the seemingly fatal accident had taken place, was as level as a carpet, screened from the wind, and composed of the finest sand.

Of course, it was impossible to avoid seeing the body that lay in their path, and Varney had no need to be fearful that he would be seen, when an object of so much greater and more absorbing interest lay in their direct and unavoidable path.

He heard from the sudden exclamations that fell from them, that they had seen the body, and upon advancing a step or two, he found that they were collected round it in a dense throng, for there were about a dozen men in all.

"'Tis well," said Varney, "it matters not to me if he be living or dead. I can doubtless now find my way to the Grange-house by this path along the shore. I will pursue it at all events, and see whither it will lead me."

He did so, and after going about half a mile, he found another ravine, which, upon entering and ascending for a time, led him quite close to one of the entrances of the Grange-house, as it was called, and which he was so anxious to reach.

CCIII.

THE DISAPPOINTMENT AT THE GRANGE. — THE NEWS OF DESPAIR. — THE FINDING OF THE BODY.

IT WAS A FINE OLD PLACE, the Grange, view it from what aspect you might, and had not the mind of Varney, the vampyre, been so fearfully irritated by the circumstances of his horrible existence, he must have paused to admire it.

It was one of those ancient English edifices, which, alas, are fast disappearing from the face of once merry England. Railways have gone tearing and screaming through the old parks and shady glens. Alas, all is altered now, and for the sake of getting to some abominable place, such as Manchester, or Birmingham, in a very short space of time, many a lonely spot of nature's own creating is marred by noise and smoke.

"So," said Varney, "this then is the home of these young men who have done me such an injury as to rescue me from the sea."

He ground his teeth together as he spoke, and it was quite clear that he felt disposed to consider that a most deadly injury had been done to him by Edwin and Charles Crofton, who had only followed the proper dictates of humanity in rescuing him from the waves.

"It shall go hard with me," added Varney, "but I will teach such meddling fools to leave the great sea in charge of its dead. Oh, had I but been allowed to remain until now, which but for these officious persons might still have been the case, I should have sunk deep — deep into

the yellow sands, and there rotted."

His passion as he uttered these words had in it something fearful, but in a few moments the external symptoms of it passed away, and he walked slowly and to all appearance calmly enough towards the Grange.

The distance he had to go was still as before, a deceiving one, for he had to wind round a clump of trees before he really got to the gate, which appeared to be just in sight, but at length he reached it, and paused as he saw an old man, who was a kind of warder there.

"Is this Sir George Crofton's?" he said, and he threw into his voice all that silvery softness which at times had been so fascinating to the Bannerworth family.

"It is, sir."

"Will you announce me?"

"I do not leave this gate, sir, but if you go down this avenue, you will reach the mansion, and some of the servants will attend to you."

Varney walked on.

The avenue was one formed by two stately rows of chestnuts, the spreading branches of which met over head, forming a beautiful canopy, and notwithstanding that they were so near the sea — that foe to vegetation — these trees were in good truth most luxuriantly beautiful.

"There was a time," muttered Varney, "when I should have admired such a spot as this, but all that has long since passed away. I am that which I am."

He now arrived in front of the house itself, and being perceived by one of the domestics, he was politely asked what he wanted.

"Say that Mr. Smith is here," was the message that Varney gave.

The servant had already heard that such was the name of the person who had been rescued from the sea by his young masters Edwin and Charles, he now hastened with the information to the drawing-room, where the family was assembled.

"Oh, if you please, sir, he has come."

"Who has come?"

"The drowned man, Mr. Smith."

"Admit him instantly."

The servant ran back to Varney, and then politely ushered him into the large and really handsome room, in which the family sat awaiting his arrival with no small share of curiosity. What the sexton had said of him had excited much speculation, and the eagerness to see a man who was, as it were, a present from the sea, was extreme.

"Mr. Smith," announced the servant; and Varney with one of his courtly bows, and a smile that was half hideous, half charming, entered.

There was a decided effect produced by his appearance, and perhaps that effect is best described by the word awe. They all seemed as if they were in the presence of something very peculiar, if not something very superior.

Sir George Crofton broke the rather awkward silence that ensued by addressing his visitor with all the frankness that was a part of his nature.

"Sir," he said, "I am glad to see you and hope you will make yourself as much at home as if you were in a house of your own."

"Sir," said Varney, "you know how much I owe your family already, and I fear to increase the heavy debt of gratitude."

"Oh, you are welcome, most welcome. Stay here as long as you like; we are rather dull at times in this isolated house, and the arrival of an intelligent guest is always an event."

Varney bowed, and Edwin advanced.

"Mr. Smith," he said, "I suppose I may almost call myself an old acquaintance."

"And I," said Charles.

"Gentlemen, if you be those to whom I am indebted for my preservation, I owe you my warmest thanks."

"Oh, think nothing of it," said Sir George; "it was not at all likely that my two boys would see a fellow creature in such a situation, and not, dead or alive, take possession of him. Your recovery is the only remarkable thing in the whole affair."

"Very remarkable," said Varney.

They waited a moment as if he was expected to make some sort of explanation of that part of the business, but as he did not, Sir George said —

"You have no idea of how you became resuscitated."

"Not the least."

"Well, that is strange indeed."

"Perhaps the good fellow who afforded me an immediate shelter, applied before that, some means of recovering suspended vitality."

"Oh no. Will Stephens is to the full as much surprised as any one. But, however, I dare say, to you, sir, that is not the most entertaining subject in the world, so we will say no more about it, except that we are very glad to have a living guest instead of a dead one."

"I much fear, from what I have heard," said Varney, "that I shall be intruding at a time like this into your family circle."

"Oh, you allude to the marriage to-day of one of my daughters, and that puts me in mind of really quite an omission on my part. Mr. Smith — my daughters, Clara and Emma."

The vampyre bowed low, and the young ladies went with established grace through the ceremony of the introduction to the remarkable personage before them.

At this moment there came upon the ears of all assembled there the sound of hurried footsteps, and a servant without any ceremony burst into the apartment, exclaiming —

"Oh, Sir George — Oh, oh, sir — "

"What is it? Speak!"

"Oh, oh. They have found him — killed in the ravine."

"Who, who?"

"Mr. Ringwood, as was to be married —"

"My daughter."

Clara uttered a cry of despair, and sank into a chair in a state of insensibility.

The scene of confusion and general consternation that now ensued baffles all description, and the only person who looked calm and collected upon the occasion was Mr. Smith, although it was not the insulting calmness of seeming indifference.

In a few minutes, however, Sir George himself recovered from the first shock which the intelligence had given to him, and he said, —

"Where is he? Where is he? Let me to the spot."

"And allow me, sir, to accompany you," said Varney. "Believe me, sir, I feel deeply for the family misfortune. Let me be useful."

"Thank you, sir, thank you — Edwin, Charles, come with me and this gentleman, and we will see if this dreadful report be true. Let us hope that fear and ignorance have exaggerated a very simple affair into so seemingly dreadful a circumstance.

Leaving Clara to the care of her sister and some of the female domestics of the Grange, who were hastily summoned to attend upon her, the little party, consisting of Sir George, his two sons, Varney, and several of the men-servants, turned from the Grange in the direction of the ravine.

Their intimate acquaintance with all the neighbourhood enabled them to reach the place much sooner than Varney thought it possible to do, and as they came within sight of the spot where the accident had occurred, they saw a crowd of villagers and fishermen assembled.

They quickened their pace, and forcing through the throng, Sir George Crofton saw his intended son-in-law, to all appearance, lying dead and bleeding on the sands.

Such a sight was enough, for a moment, to paralyse every faculty, and it really had, for a time, that effect upon Sir George.

CCIV.

THE SICK-CHAMBER AT THE GRANGE. — THE NIGHT.

"Is he dead? Is he dead?" cried Sir George.

"We don't know, sir," replied one of the fishermen; "some of us think he is, and some of us think he is not."

"What is to be done?"

"Have him taken at once to the Grange, father," said Charles, "and let us get medical assistance; who knows but the affair may turn out in reality very different from what it first appeared. He may be only stunned by a fall."

"I hope to Heaven it may be so. Can you, among you, my men, make anything like a litter to carry him on?"

This was soon done. Some of the loose seats from some boats close at hand, and a rough cloak or two, made a capital couch for the dead or wounded man, as the case might be. They lifted him carefully into it, and then four of them lifted the rude but easy and appropriate conveyance, and carried him towards the hall.

"How could this have happened?" said Sir George.

"Perhaps I may be able to throw some light upon it," said Varney. "As I came here to your hospitable house, a horse without a rider, but caparisoned for one, passed me furiously."

"That must have been his horse then," said Charles. "You may depend, father, he was riding on to see Clara before the hour appointed for their marriage, and has met with this accident. Come, there is some consolation in that. A fall from his horse is not likely to kill him."

"Where is Edwin?"

"Oh, he went off at once for Dr. North, and no doubt he will get to the Grange about as soon as we shall."

"That was right—that was right. I really have been taken so much by surprise that I hardly know what I am about. It was very right of Edwin."

Nothing of any importance now passed in the way of conversation, nor did any incident worth recording take place until the melancholy little procession reached the Grange, and by the advice of Varney, the young bridegroom was carried direct to a bed-chamber before he was removed from the litter on which he had been carried.

The operation was scarcely performed, and he laid upon a bed, when Dr. North came, having mounted his horse upon hearing the information from Edwin that he was wanted in a case of such great emergency at the Grange, and ridden hard all the way.

He was at once introduced to his patient, and upon a cursory examination, he said,—

"This is a concussion of the brain, but don't let that alarm you. It may be very slight, although it certainly has an awkward sound, and a little rest and blood-letting may put him all to rights."

This was to some extent cheering, and the doctor at once proceeded to bleed his patient. As the ruddy stream fell into a crystal goblet, the young man gradually opened his eyes, and looked round him with a bewildered glare.

"Darken the room," said Dr. North; "he is right enough, but he must be kept quiet for a day or two at all events."

"What has happened?" said the wounded man.

"Nothing particular," replied Dr. North, "nothing particular. You have had a fall from your horse."

"Clara!"

"Ah, I know, and now listen to me. If you remain quiet and don't speak, you will see Clara soon; but if you are willful and disobey orders, you will bring on a brain fever and you won't see her at all in this world; so now you can judge for yourself."

"You are rather harsh," said Sir George.

"Pardon me sir, I am not. There is nothing like making a patient thoroughly understand his own position; and I give this young gentleman credit for sufficient wisdom to enable him to profit by what I say to him."

Mr. Ringwood nodded.

"There, you see, all's right; now he will go to sleep, and as all will depend upon the state in which he awakens, I will, if you please, wait here, unless I should be urgently sent for from home, for I have left word where I am."

"Pardon me, doctor, for finding any fault with you."

"Don't mention it; what I said did sound harsh."

Sir George went now at once to the room where his daughter Clara had been taken to, for the purpose of informing her of the hopeful state of affairs. He found her just recovered from her swoon, so that recollection had not yet sufficiently returned to give her all the agony of thinking that the news so heedlessly and so suddenly communicated by the servant might be true in its full intensity.

"My dear, you must not distress yourself," said Sir George. "Ringwood was riding over here, it seems, to see you, and his horse, getting restive, has thrown him; Dr. North says, there is nothing particular the matter, and that after a little rest he will recover."

Clara tried to speak, but she could not — she burst into tears.

"Ah!" said the old nurse, who was attending her, and who had been in her family many years, "ah, poor dear, she will be all right now. I was just wishing that she would have a good cry; it does any one a world of good, it does."

"What an agitating night and day this has been, to be sure," said Sir George. "First the terror of losing both my boys, then their return with the dead man, who so oddly comes to life again; then this dreadful accident to Ringwood; upon my word the incidents of a whole year have been crammed into a few hours. I only hope this is the last of it."

"And I shall see him again, father," sobbed Clara.

"Of course you will."

"You — you have sent him home very carefully?"

"Home? no. He is here under this roof and here he shall stay till he recovers, poor lad. Oh dear no, I never thought of sending him home, but I must send some one, by-the-bye, with the news of what has happened. This is well thought of."

The knowledge that her lover, and

her affianced husband, was doing well, and that he was under the same roof with her, gave Clara the most unalloyed satisfaction, and she recovered rapidly her good and healthful looks. It was duly explained to her, that she must not go near Ringwood to disturb him, as rest was so very essential to his recovery; so she did not attempt it. The whole household was commanded to be unusually quiet, and never had the Grange before presented such a collection of creeping domestics, for they went up and down stairs like so many cats.

Clara did not omit to thank Mr. Smith for the assistance he had rendered them in this evil emergency, and Dr. North stood with the family in the dining room waiting, perhaps with greater anxiety than he chose to express, the awaking of his patient.

A servant was left in the adjoining chamber to that occupied by Ringwood, who was told to bring to the dining-room the first intimation that the wounded man was living.

ABOUT TWO HOURS ELAPSED when the servant came in with an air of affright.

Dr. North sprang to his feet in a moment.

"What is it, is he awake?"

"Not exactly awake, sir, but he is speaking in his sleep, and it's all about a—a—"

"A what?"

"A vampyre."

"Stuff."

"Well, sir, he's a having some horrid dream, I can tell you, sir, and he said, 'Keep off the vampyre; save her, oh, save her from the vampyre!'"

"How singular!" said Varney, "what an absurd belief that is! A vampyre! what on earth could have put such a thing in his head, I wonder?"

"I will go to him," said Dr. North, "if he should be very much disturbed, perhaps I shall think it preferable to awake him; but I can inform you all that such dreams show that there is much excitement going on in the brain."

"Then you do not consider the symptom favourable, doctor?"

"Certainly not; quite the reverse of favourable."

Dr. North rose, and as Varney offered very politely to accompany him, he made no sort of objection, and they proceeded to the chamber of the bridegroom.

During the time that the doctor had been in the society of Varney, he had been much pleased with him, for he found that he possessed a vast store of knowledge upon almost any subject that could be touched upon, besides no small amount of skill and theoretical information upon medical matters, so he let him come with him, when perhaps he would have objected to any one else.

Varney the vampyre could fascinate when he liked.

When they reached the chamber the young man was quiet, but in a few minutes he began to toss about his head, and mutter in his sleep,—

"The vampyre, the dreadful vampyre. Oh, save her! Help, help, help!"

"This won't do," said the doctor.

He went to the toilette table, and procuring a large towel he soaked it well in cold water, and then wrapped it round

the head of Ringwood, and so carefully too as not to arouse him.

The effect was almost instantaneous. The vexed sleeper relapsed into a much easier attitude, the breathing was more regular, and the distressing fancies that had tortured his fevered brain were chased away.

"A simple plan," said Varney.

"Yes, but a most efficacious one."

CCV.

A MIDNIGHT ALARM. — THE CHASE. — THE MYSTERY.

YOUNG RINGWOOD DID awaken about two hours afterwards, and the state he was in, although not such as to create alarm, was not pleasing to Dr. North. That gentleman desired that he should be carefully watched and kept quiet, while he went to his own house for some medicines.

He returned as soon as he possibly could, and administered such remedies as he considered the urgency of the case required, and having, as he always made a practice of doing, left word at his own house where he was, he offered to remain at the Grange the whole of the night.

It is scarcely necessary to say, that such an offer was most gratefully accepted.

Clara was profuse in her acknowledgements of the doctor's kindness, and they all passed the evening together in the large dining room, to which Varney was first introduced.

Not, however, for a long time had so gloomy an evening been passed at the Grange as that; nobody was in spirits, and although there was a great deal of conversation, it somehow assumed always a very sombre shape, let it commence on what subject it might.

Half past ten o'clock was the usual hour at which the family retired for the night, and it was quite a relief to every one, when that hour came, and Sir George ordered lights for the bed chambers.

Clara, indeed, being much oppressed, had retired some time before, and so had Emma, so that there were none but gentlemen in the dining room at half past ten.

"I have ordered a bed to be prepared for you close to your patient's," said Sir George to Dr. North.

"Oh, thank you, but I shall only lie down in my clothes, a couch would have done just as well, I am used to sitting up all night upon occasion."

"No doubt, but I hope you will not be disturbed, and that tomorrow-morning we shall have a better account of your patient."

"I hope so too; a good calm night's rest may do much."

"You speak doubtingly."

"Why in these cases it is difficult to know the extent of injury. There is no fracture of the skull, but it is as yet impossible to say what amount of shaking he has had."

"Well, we can but hope for the best. Mr. Smith, although we retire at this early hour, there is no sort of occasion for you to do so. Order what wines you please, and sit as long as you please."

"By no means, Sir George; I am a great patron of early hours myself."

Varney was shown into a bed-room which was upon the same floor with those of the family, and which formed one of a range of chambers, all opening from a corridor that ran the entire length of the house, and which in the daytime was lighted by a very large, handsome window at one end, while at the other was a broad flight of stairs ascending from the lower part of the house.

The sisters occupied contiguous chambers, and then there was an empty room, and next to that again was the bed-room in which was Ringwood, and then Dr. North's.

Exactly opposite was Varney's room, and close at hand slept the sons, while Sir George himself occupied a room at the furthest corner of the corridor.

Emma made Clara an offer to sleep with her that night, as she was in grief and anxiety, but this Clara would not permit, for she could not think of sacrificing her sister's repose to attend upon her.

"No, Emma," she said," I will hope for the best, and strive to rest."

The bade each other affectionately good night, and shortly afterwards retired to their separate apartments.

B Y ELEVEN O'CLOCK all was still in the house.

Dr. North had begged a book from the library, for he thought it likely enough that he should not be able to get much repose, and with that he sat in his room, the only one, as he thought, in all the house who was not in bed.

He continued reading for about an hour, and then, after visiting his patient, and finding him asleep, he thought it would be just as well for him to pull off his boots and his coat, and lie down on the bed to snatch a few hours' sleep.

He performed all the operations but the final one — the sleeping — for scarcely had he lain down, when he heard a soft sliding sort of noise close to the room door, he thought, and he sprung up in a sitting posture to listen to it.

"Who's there!" he cried.

There was no answer, and jumping off his bed, he took the light which he had not put out, and opened his door. All was deserted and still in the corridor.

"Imagination, or some accidental noise that I am not familiar with," said the doctor, as he closed his door again.

Down he laid himself, and he was just upon the point of getting to sleep, when he heard a scratching sound as he thought upon the very panel of the door of his room.

Up he sprang again, and this time without the delay of asking who was there; he opened his door, and looked out into the corridor, holding the light above his head so as to diffuse its rays as much as possible, but he saw no one, and all the other doors were close shut.

"A plague take it," he said, "I may keep myself at this sort of thing all night, if I am foolish enough. It's a cat, perhaps, for all I know; however it may scratch away, I won't move again."

Shutting the door, he lay down, now fully determined that he would not move, unless something very much out of the common way, indeed, should take place.

Again he started. There was a curious sound about the lock of his door, and he listened intently.

"Now, what on earth can that be?"

All was still, and he nearly dropped asleep. Twice, however, he thought he heard the sound again, but he would not move, and in a few moments more, he was enjoying a sound repose.

How long this repose lasted, he had no means of telling, for he was suddenly awakened by such a cry, that at first he lay overpowered completely by it, and unable to move. It was a loud shrieking cry, such as might come form any one in a most dreadful agony.

"Good Heaven!" he cried, "what's that?"

Now, Dr. North was not a fearful man, nor a nervous one, and he soon recovered. Besides, such a cry as that, he knew very well, must have the effect of arousing everybody in the house, so he sprung out of his bed, and rushed to the door.

It was fast.

In vain he tried the lock, and hammered at it and pushed. The door was a thick and a heavy one, and it was quite clear he was a prisoner.

This was serious, and he cried out,—

"Help! help! here, undo the door, undo the door. Who has locked me in?"

He heard the scraping of feet, the sound of voices, the ringing of bells, and all the symptoms of a suddenly disturbed and alarmed household, but nobody paid any attention to him. He dragged on his boots, in order that he might be able to keep up a constant kicking on the lower part of his door, and he did keep it up with a vengeance.

At length he heard voices close to his door, and some one cried,—

"Open the door, sir, open the door!"

"Open it yourself," said Dr. North, "you have fastened it on the outside, I suppose."

There was some further running about, and then with a crash the door was forced open with a crowbar, and upon emerging from the apartment, the doctor found assembled in the corridor, the whole family, with the exception of the two girls, and several servants half-dressed bearing lights.

"What's the matter," cried Sir George, "what's the matter?"

"Ah," said the doctor, "that's what I want to know."

"Yes, why—why you made all the disturbance."

"I beg your pardon, there was a scream came from somewhere, and when I tried to come out to find what it was, my room door was fast. That's all I know about it."

Bang—bang, bang, bang, came now a sound. Bang, bang, bang; and all eyes were turned in the direction of the chamber occupied by Mr. Smith, and they heard his voice from within shouting in loud and frightened tones.

"Help! help! is it fire! Open my door, help—help. Do you lock in your guests here? Help!"

"Why, God bless me," said Dr. North, "that gentleman is locked in likewise."

"But it can't be," said Sir George, "for the keys of all these doors are in the library in a drawer. The fact is, we none of us fasten up our bed-rooms, and the keys were all removed years ago."

"Help! help! help!" cried Mr. Smith.

"Break the door open," said Sir George, "this is inexplicable to me, I cannot make it out in the least."

The same crow-bar that had been brought by one of the servants to bear upon the door of Dr. North's room, was now applied to that of Mr. Smith, and it soon yielded to the force of the lever that was used with strength and judgment.

Mr. Smith partially dressed, and with rather a terrified look, emerged.

"Good God," he cried, "I wish you wouldn't lock one in; what has happened? I heard a shriek that awoke me up, as if the last trumpet had sounded."

"My daughters, are they safe?" cried Sir George.

He flew to the door of Clara's room, it yielded to his touch.

"Clara, Clara," he called.

CCVI.

THE SIGHT OF TERROR. — THE DOCTOR'S SUSPICIONS. — THE NIGHT WATCH.

THE SIGHT THAT MET the eyes of the father in his daughter's chamber, was, indeed, one calculated in every respect to strike him with horror and misery.

Emma was lying insensible at the side of the bed, and Clara seemed to be dead, for she was ghastly pale, and there was blood upon her neck.

The father staggered to a seat, but Dr. North at once rushed forward, and held the light to the eyes of Clara, at the same time, that he placed his finger on her wrist to note if there was any pulsation.

"Only a fainting fit," he said.

"But the blood — the — the blood," cried Sir George.

"That I know nothing about, just at present, but let us see what's the matter here."

He raised Emma from the floor, and found that she too had fainted, but as she appeared to be perfectly uninjured. She slightly recovered as he lifted her up, and he resigned her at once to the care of some of the female servants, who now made their appearance in the chamber, all terribly alarmed at the shriek that had awakened them.

"This is strange," said Dr. North, "here is a small puncture upon the throat of your daughter Clara, that almost looks like the mark of a tooth."

"A tooth!"

"Yes, but of course that cannot be."

"Hear me, oh, hear me," cried Emma, at this moment. "Horror — horror!"

"What would you say — speak at once, and clear up this mystery if you can. What has happened?"

"I heard a noise, and came from my own chamber to this. There was some one bending over the bed. 'Twas I who shrieked."

"You?"

"Yes, oh yes! 'Twas I. I know not what then happened, for I either fell or was struck down, and I felt that my senses left me. What has happened? I too ask; oh, Clara! What was it? what was it?"

"Imagination, most likely," said the doctor. "You had better go to your room

"I am paralysed," said Dr. North, "and so are you, sir. Come in."

He seized a light from one of the servants, and with a presentiment that there was to be found a solution of, at all events, the mystery of the dreadful shriek that had alarmed all the house, he dashed into the chamber of the young girl, followed by the father.

again, Miss Emma, for you are trembling with cold and apprehension. Perhaps in the morning, all this affair will assume a different shape. At present we are all to much flurried to take proper cognisance of it. There your sister is rapidly recovering. How do you feel now, Miss Clara?"

"I — I — am mad!"

"Oh, pho! pho! nonsense!"

"Oh, God help me! How horrifying ! How more than dreadful! That awful face! Those hideous teeth! — I am mad! — I am mad!"

"Why, my dear child, you will drive me mad," cried Sir George, "if you talk in such a strain. Oh, let me beg of you not."

"Don't heed her," said Dr. North. "This will soon pass away. Come, Miss Clara, you must tell me freely, as your medical man, what has happened. Let us hear the full particulars, and then you know well, that if any human means can aid you, you shall be aided."

This calm mode of discourse had evidently a great effect upon her, and after the silence of a few moments, she spoke much more collectedly than before, saying, —

"Oh, no — no! I cannot think it a dream."

"What a dream?"

"You — you shall hear. But do not drag me from my home, and from all I love, if I am mad; I pray you do not — I implore you!" *

"You are quite safe. Why, what a ridiculous girl you are, to be sure. Nobody wants to drag you from your home, and

nobody will attempt such a thing, I assure you. You have only to tell us all unreservedly, and you will then be quite safe. If you refuse us you confidence how can we act for you in any way?"

This argument seemed to be effective, and to reach her understanding quite, so that after a shudder, and a glance around her of great dread and dismay, she spoke, saying in a low, faltering voice, —

"Something came; something not quite human, yet having the aspect of a man. Something that flew at me, and fastened its teeth upon my neck."

"Teeth! everbody says 'teeth!' " exclaimed the father.

"Hush!" said the doctor, with an admonitory wave of his hand; "keep that a secret from her, whatever you do. I implore you, keep quiet on that head. Well, is that all, Clara?"

"Yes — yes."

"Then it was a dream, and nothing else, I can assure you. Nothing but a dream; make yourself comfortable, and think no more of it. I dare say you will have a quiet sleep now, after this. But you had better let your sister Emma lay with you, as your nerves are a little shattered."

"Oh, yes, yes."

Emma, who truth to tell, was very little better than her sister, professed her readiness to stay, and the doctor giving Sir George a nod, as much as to say, "Let no more be said about it just now," led the way from the room at once.

When he reached the corridor, where Varney and the two sons were waiting, he said, —

"We shall none of us after this, I am certain, feel inclined to sleep; suppose we go down stairs at once and think and talk

---

* *In the 1840s it was all too common for women deemed to have fallen into "madness" to be shipped off to an asylum for the rest of their lives.*

this matter over together; there is more in it, perhaps, than meets the eye; I will follow you in a moment, when I have just seen that my patient is all right."

They all proceeded down stairs to the dining-room, and in a few minutes, the doctor followed; lights were procured, and they sat down, all looking at the doctor who had taken the lead in the affair, and who evidently had some very disagreeable, if not very true, ideas upon the subject matter of the evening's disturbance.

"Well, doctor," said Sir George, "we rely upon you to give us your opinion upon this business, and some insight into its meaning."

"In the first place then," said the doctor, "I don't understand it."

"Well, that's coming to the point."

"Stop a bit; it was no dream."

"You think not."

"Certainly not a dream, two people don't dream of the same thing at the same time; I don't of course deny the possibility of such a thing, but it is too remarkable a coincidence to believe all at once; but Emma avows that she saw a somebody in her sister's room."

"Ah," said Sir George; "she did, I had in my confusion forgotten that horrible confirmation of Clara's story. She did so, and before Clara was well recovered too, so she could not have put the idea into her head. Good God! what am I to think? For the love of Heaven some of you tell me what are your opinions upon this horrible affair, which looks so romantically unreal, and yet so horribly real."

All except the doctor looked at each other in surprise.

"Well," he said, "I will tell you what the thing suggests; not what it is, mind you, for the affair to me is too out of the way of natural causes to induce me to come to a positive conclusion. Before I speak, however, I should like to have your opinion, Mr. Smith; I am convinced it will be valuable."

"Really I have formed none," replied Varney; "I am only exceedingly surprised that somebody should have fastened me in my bed-room. I know that that circumstance gave me a terrible fright, for when I heard all the outcry and confusion, I thought the house was on fire."

"Ah! the locking of us in our rooms, too," said the doctor, "there's another bit of reality. Who did that?"

"It puzzles me beyond all comprehension," said Sir George; "how the doors could be locked I cannot imagine; for as I told you the keys are in a drawer in my library."

"At all events, the doors could not lock themselves, with or without keys," said Charles; "and that circumstance shows sufficiently evidently that some one has been at work in the business whom we have still to discover."

"True," said Mr. Smith.

"Well, gentlemen," added the doctor, "I will tell you what I suggest; and that is contained in a letter, written a long while ago by a distant relation of mine, likewise a surgeon. Mind, I do not of course pledge myself at the present time, for the truth and accuracy of a man who was dead long before I was born; he might too have been a very superstitious man."

"But what did he suggest?"

"He did more than suggest; he wrote for a medical publication of that day an account, only of course suppressing names, of the appearance of a vampyre."

"A what?"

"A vampyre!"

"I have heard of such horrors," said Mr. Smith, "but really at the present day, no one can think of believing such things. Vampyres indeed! No — that is too great a claim upon one's credulity. These existences, or supposed existences, have gone the same way as the ghosts, and so on."

"One would think so, but you shall hear."

Sir George Crofton and his sons looked curious, and thought that the doctor was going to draw upon his memory in the matter to which he alluded, but he took from his pocket a memorandum book, and from it extracted some printed papers.

"The communication was so curious," he said, "that I cut it out of the old volume in which it appeared, and kept it ever since."

"Pray," said Mr. Smith, "what was the name of your distant relation, the medical man?"

"Chillingworth."

"Oh, indeed; an odd name rather, I don't recollect ever hearing of it."

"No, sir, it is not likely you should. Dr. Chillingworth has been dead many years, and no one else of his name is at present in the medical profession to my knowledge. But you shall hear, at all events, what he says about it."

The doctor then opened the folded paper, and read as follows: —

"Notwithstanding the incredulity that has been shown regarding vampyres, I am in a condition from my own knowledge to own the existence of one, I think he is dead now. His name was Varney, at least that was the name he went by, and he came strangely enough under my observation, in connection with some dear friends of mine named B —"

"Is that all?" said Mr. Smith.

"Not quite," replied Dr. North, "He goes on to say that but for touching the feeling of living persons, he could and would unfold some curious particulars respecting vampyres, and that if he lived long enough he will perhaps do so, by which I suppose he meant if he outlived the parties whose feelings he was afraid of hurting by any premature disclosures."

"And — and," faltered Sir George, "do you draw a conclusion from all that, that my daughter has been visited by one of these persons — surely not."

"May be, Sir George; I draw no conclusions at all, I merely throw out the matter for your consideration. It is always worth while considering these matters in any possible aspect. That is all."

"A most horrible aspect," said Sir George.

"Truly dreadful," said Mr. Smith.

"This shall be settled," said Charles, "Edwin and I will take upon ourselves to-morrow night to set this question completely at rest."

At this moment there was a loud cry of "Help, help, help," in the voice of Emma, and they all rushed up stairs with great speed.

"Oh, this way, this way," she cried, meeting them at the head of the stairs. "Come to Clara."

They followed her, and when they reached the room, they found to their horror and surprise that Clara was dead!

CCVII.

FAMILY TROUBLES. — THE HOUSE OF MOURNING.

IT WAS TOO TRUE. It was not the mere appearance of death, but the reality of the fell destroyer that the Crofton family had to mourn. She who, but a few short hours since, was in all the bloom of apparent health, and youth, and beauty was now no more.

The poor father, the sisterless sister, the astonished, indignant, and agonised brothers formed a group that was too sad to contemplate.

As they gazed upon the wreck of her whom they had all loved so fondly, they could scarcely believe that death had indeed claimed her as her own; they —

"Thought her more beautiful than death,"

— and could not, as they gazed tremblingly upon her still form, bring themselves to believe that she had indeed gone from them for ever.

Dr. North, however, soon put all doubt upon the subject to rest by an announcement that her spirit had really fled. In vain he tried all the means that his art suggested. That mysterious and mighty something which we call life, which we miss and yet see no loss, which is so great, yet so evanescent and impalpable, was gone.

"Come away," he said, "we can do no good here now. Come away, all of you!"

"Oh, no, no," cried Sir George. "Why should we leave my child?"

"That," said the doctor, as he pointed to the corpse, "that is not your child."

The old man shuddered, and with an aspect upon his face, as if ten years of added age had at least passed over him in those few moments, he suffered them to lead him from the room. They all passed down stairs again, leaving Emma in her own chamber along with the female servants, so hastily again called up to remain with her.

When the dining-room was reached once more, Mr. Smith, who bore all the appearance of being quite thunder-struck by what had passed, spoke in the most feeling manner, saying, —

"This is truly one of the most affecting circumstances I ever remember. It is dreadful; a young girl to be at once snatched from a circle of admiring and loving friends in this manner, is too sad a picture for any one with a heart to feel for the distresses of others to contemplate. What, sir, is your opinion," to Dr. North, "of the actual cause of death?"

"The shock to the nervous system I suspect has induced some sudden action of the heart that has been too much for vitality."

"Dreadful!"

"Alas, alas!" sobbed Sir George. "What have I done, that Heaven should thus launch against me the bolts of its bitterest vengeance? Why should I be robbed of my child? Surely there were angels enough in Heaven without taking mine from me."

"Hush, hush," said Dr. North; "you are in grief, sir, and know not what you say. These were not else the words that would fall from the lips of such a man as you are."

The bereaved father was silent, and the sons looked at him with countenances in which dismay was most strongly pictured. They seemed as if as yet they had not become fully alive to the loss they had sustained, or of what had really happened within the once happy domestic circle, of which the fairest portion was now so ruthlessly dragged from them.

"It is like a dream," said Edwin, addressing his brother Charles in a whisper. "It is much more like a dream than aught else in the world."

"It is, it is. Oh, tell me that this is not real."

"It is too real," said the doctor, "you must bow with what amount of resignation you can call to your aid to that stroke of destiny which you cannot control; you should consider that as regards her who has gone from you, that she is now no object of pity. Death is an evil to you in your loss, but it is the end of all evil and pain to her; and then again, she has but gone a few years, after all, earlier than usual, for how long shall we — aye, the best and strongest of us — be behind her?"

This was consolation of the right sort, and was sure to have its effect upon persons in the habit of conversing coolly and calmly upon general subjects, so that in a short time, the father even felt much better, and although the sons were quite convinced of their loss they no longer looked at each other with such bewildered aspects, but exhibited the rational grief of men.

Charles spoke after a time with great energy, saying, —

"It is true that we may call our reason to our aid, and contrive to rid ourselves of our grief in a great measure; but there is another duty we have to perform, and that is, to diligently inquire why and how it was, that our sister got this horrible fright, that has had the effect of hurrying her into eternity."

"Yes, brother," said Edwin, "you are right! our sister's memory shall be vindicated, and woe be to him who has brought this desolation and grief upon us."

Sir George looked from one of his sons to the other, but said nothing; he appeared to be prostrated too much by his feelings, and the doctor strongly urging him to retire to rest, he shortly did so, where we will leave him for a time, hoping that he will find the oblivion of sleep creep over him, and —

Knit up the ravelled sleeve of care. *

"Now," said Dr. North, "here we are four men with cool heads, and active enough judgments. For God's sake, let us try to come to some sort of conclusion about this dreadful affair. What do you say, Charles?"

"In the first place, I should recommend that the house be searched diligently, in order that we may see if any stranger is in it, or discover any means by which an entrance to the premises has been effected. We don't know but that after all some robbery may be the aim, and that the fright of our sister which has had so fatal an effect, may be the consequence merely of the appearance of a thief in her room."

---

* *A line from Shakespeare's* Macbeth, *Act II Scene II.*

"Agreed," said Edwin, "let the search of the house be our first step."

Two of the new servants were summoned with lights, and the party of four proceeded to an examination of the house, which on account of its size was not a very short process, for there was so many staircases and rooms opening the one into the other, that the hiding places were numerous enough.

At length, however, they were not only satisfied that no one was concealed on the premises, but likewise that all the fastenings were quite secure, and had been made so before the servants retired to rest. The mystery therefore was rather increased.

Had there not been the collateral evidence of Emma and the singular fact of the fastening up of the doors of the doctor's and Mr. Smith's bed-chambers, no doubt the whole affair would have rested where it was, and have been put down as a remarkable death arising from the influence of a dream.

But that was out of the question — somebody had been seen, and whether that somebody was really not an inhabitant of this world was the question.

In the midst of all this, the day began to dawn.

Sir George had had no sleep, but he had done himself some good in the solitude of his own chamber. He had prayed long and earnestly, and his prayers had had the effect which they almost invariably have upon all imaginative persons, namely, of bringing him an amount of mental calmness, peace, and resignation, highly desirable in his circumstances.

The breakfast table was laid in silence by the servants, and when Sir George met his sons and his guests, he spoke calmly enough, saying to them, —

"You will no more hear from me the accents of grief or of despair. I accept what consolation I can find, but as a man, and a father I will have justice; my child has been terrified to death, and I will find who has done the deed, for let him be whom he may, he is as much her murderer as though he had plunged a dagger in her heart."

"It is so," said Mr. Smith.

"Being so, then let him beware."

Varney thought that as the father uttered these last words, he glanced in a peculiar manner at him, but he was not quite sure that such was the case. Had he been sure, perhaps, he would have taken other steps than he did.

Little more passed during the breakfast, but when the meal was over, Sir George said, —

"Edwin, we are but dull and poor company to Mr. Smith; it will amuse him, perhaps, if you take him through the grounds, and show him the estate."

Edwin made no objection, and as the thing was put in the shape of an amusement to him, Varney could only say some civil things, and rise to go.

"I regret," he said, "to be of so much trouble."

"Not at all," said Edwin, "no trouble, sir; my own mind, God knows, wants something to distract it from too close a contemplation of its own thoughts. If you will accompany me in a walk over the estate, it will, perhaps, put me into better spirits."

They left the room, and when they were gone, Sir George Crofton rose and shut the door, fastening it on the inside carefully, rather to the surprise of the doctor and his son Charles, who looked at him in silence.

"Charles," he then said, "and you, doctor, I have something particular to say to you."

"What is it? What is it?"

"God forgive me if I am wrong, but I suspect our guest."

"Mr. Smith?"

"Yes, I don't like his looks at all; now we know nothing of him but from his own report; we have searched the house right through, or at least you have, you tell me, and found nothing. He is the only stranger within our doors. Perhaps it is uncharitable to suspect him, but I cannot help it, the thought came too strongly upon me last night, as I was alone in my chamber, for me to overcome it. I have now spoken to you both frankly, and tell me what are your thoughts."

"I don't like him," said Charles.

"He is a singular man," said Dr. North.

"What—what now if he were— were—"

"Why do you hesitate, father? what would you say?"

"Go on, sir," said Dr. North, with a nod, that signified, I know very well what you are going to say. "Go on, sir."

"What, then, if it were really true, that there were such things, and he is a vampyre?"

Edwin sprang to his feet in surprise, and said,—

"Good God! you put a frightful idea into my brain that will now never leave it. A vampyre?"

"Heaven forbid," added Sir George, "that I should say such a thing heedlessly,

or that I should take upon myself to assert that such is the case; I merely throw it out as a supposition—a horrible one, I grant, but yet one that perhaps deserves some consideration."

"Get rid of him," said Dr. North.

"It is difficult after telling him he was welcome to stay, to now tell him that we want him to go. I would much prefer watching him closely, and endeavouring by such means, either to confirm or to do away entirely with my suppositions. And you can take an opportunity of speaking to Edwin upon the subject, quietly and carefully."

"I will, father."

"Then we can be all upon the alert; but above all things I charge you say nothing to Emma of the really terrific idea. Only I should say that to-night it is in the direction of her chamber that I would wish to keep the closest watch."

"And that, too, without her knowing it," said the doctor. "If she is aware of anything of the sort, there is no knowing what tricks her imagination might play her, and now, Sir George, I must say that I take the greatest interest in the matter, and will with your permission remain here until I am sent for. Poor Ringwood still reminds insensible, and I take it that under the circumstances that it is really a mercy, for what a sad communication has to be made to him, when he does recover sufficiently to hear it."

"Sad, indeed."

It was now finally agreed among them that there was to be no variation whatever in their conduct towards Mr. Smith, but that after they had taken leave of him for the night, and had all gone to bed, they should each glide out of his chamber, and wait at the extreme end of the corridor in silence, to mark if anything should happen.

This was duly announced to Edwin, who with a shudder announced that he had his suspicions, too, of Mr. Smith, so he of course came into the scheme at once; and now they waited rather anxiously for the night to come again.

CCVIII.

THE NIGHT WATCH. — THE SURPRISE. — THE CHASE.

EVERYTHING WAS NOW SAID and done that could induce a feeling in the mind of Varney, that he was perfectly welcome at the Grange, and to dispel the least idea of anything in the shape of supposition that he might have had, that he was suspected, although he had not himself by word or look betrayed such a feeling.

The day to all parties seemed a frightfully long one. Ringwood remained in the same state of unconsciousness as he had been in the day previous, and the only circumstance that served to break the monotony of the time, was the arrival of some of his friends to see him.

It is not essential to our story that we should take up space in detailing what they said and what they did; suffice it that all the grief was exhibited that was to be expected, and that finally they left the Grange with a conviction that the wounded man was in as kind hands as they could possibly wish him, and everything would be done, that kindness and skill could suggest, to recover him and preserve his life.

Probably the dreadful catastrophe that had happened in the family of the Croftons had an effect in reconciling the Ringwoods to the lesser calamity, for Dr. North gave them strong hopes of his ultimate recovery.

And so the time passed on, until the dim shadows of the evening began to creep over the landscape, and the distant trees imperceptibly mingled together in a chaotic mass. The song of the birds was over — the herds and flocks had sought their shelter for the night, and a solemn and beautiful stillness was upon the face of nature.

Assembled once more in the dining-room of the Grange, were the Croftons — but not Emma, she was in her chamber — the doctor, and Mr. Smith.

Varney had exerted himself much to be entertaining, and yet not obtrusively so, as under the calamitous and extraordinary circumstances in which the family was placed, that would have been bad taste; but he led the conversation into the most interesting channels, and he charmed those who listened to him, in spite of themselves.

Dr. North was peculiarly pleased with so scientific a companion, and one who had travelled so much, for Varney spoke of almost every portion of the globe as familiar to him.

In this kind of way, the evening sped on, and more than once, as Varney was giving some eloquent and comprehensive description of some natural phenomenon that he had witnessed in some other clime, not only were the suspicions entertained against him forgotten, but even the grief of the family faded away for a brief space before the charm of his discourse.

At length the time for rest came.

Sir George rose, and bowing to Varney, said,—

"Do not let our example influence you, sir. We retire now."

"I shall be glad to do so," said Varney, "likewise; last night was a disturbed as well as a melancholy one for all in this house."

"It was indeed."

In another five minutes, the dining-room was vacant, and all that could be heard in the house was the noise of putting up extra bars, and shooting into their places long-unused bolts in order that it should be quite beyond all doubt that no one could get into the premises.

After that, all was still.

THE MOON WAS IN her last quarter now, but only at the commencement of it, so if the night proved not to be cloudy, it would be rather a brilliant one, which might, or might not be of service to those who were going to watch in the corridor the proceedings of Mr. Smith.

An hour elapsed before there was any movement whatever, and then it was Dr. North who first, with great care, emerged from his room.

He had drawn on his stockings over his shoes, so that his footsteps might not be heard, and he took his station in a dark corner by the large window we have before spoken of as lighting the corridor.

The moon was up, but it only shone in obliquely at the window, so that one side of the corridor was enveloped in the deepest gloom, while on the other the pale rays fell.

A few minutes more, for half-past eleven was the hour on which they had all agreed, and Sir George, with Edwin and Charles joined the doctor, who merely nodded to them, as they could faintly see him.

Sir George spoke in a very faint whisper, saying,—

"We are well armed."

"Good," replied the doctor, in a similar cautious tone, "but let me implore you to be careful how you use your arms. Do nothing hastily, I beg of you; you don't know what cause of regret the imprudence of a moment may give rise to."

"Depend upon us, we will be very careful indeed."

"That is right."

"We had better not talk," said Charles, "these corridors carry sound sometimes too well; if we are to do any good, it must be by preserving the profoundest silence."

This advice was too practical and evidently good to be neglected, and consequently they were all as still as they could be, and stood like so many statues for the next half hour.

They heard a clock that hung in the hall below strike the hour of twelve, and when the reverberations of sound were over, a stillness even more profound than before seemed to pervade the whole house. The half hour they had waited in such silence appeared to them to be of four times the usual length, and they were

glad to hear twelve strike.

Still they said nothing, for if silence before twelve o'clock was a thing to be desired, it was much more so after that hour, for it was then that the alarm of the preceeding evening had taken place. Their watchfulness, and their anxiety momentarily increased.

The old clock in the hall chimed the quarter past twelve, and yet all was as still as the grave; not the smallest sound disturbed the repose of the house.

The moon had shifted round a little, so that the gloom of the corridor was not so complete as it had been, and Dr. North was aware that in another hour the spot where they all stood would be visited by some rays which would render their concealment out of the question.

But as yet all was right, and there was no need to shift their position in the least.

Suddenly Sir George Crofton laid his hand upon the arm of the doctor, and an exclamation involuntarily escaped him, but not in a loud tone.

"Hush, for God's sake," whispered the doctor.

They had all heard a slight noise, like the cautious opening of a door. They looked eagerly in the direction from whence it came, and to their surprise they found it proceed from the chamber of the dead!

Yes, the door of the room in which lay the corpse of Clara slowly opened.

"God of Heaven!" said Sir George.

"Hush — hush," again whispered the doctor, and he held him by the arm compulsively.

All was still. The door creaked upon its hinges a little, that was all.

A quarter of an hour passed, and then Sir George was about to say something, when he started as if a shock of electricity had been applied to him, for the door of Varney's room was swung wide open, and he appeared, full dressed.

All the doors opening from the corridor creaked unless they were flung open smartly and quickly, and there could be no doubt but that Varney knew this, and hence the apparent precipitancy of his appearance.

There he stood in the moonlight, close by the threshold of his room, gazing about him. He bent himself into an attitude of intense listening, and remained in it for some time, and then he with slow sliding steps made his way towards the door of Emma's room.

His hand was actually upon the lock, when Sir George, who could stand the scene no longer, levelled a pistol he had taken from his pocket, and without giving any intimation to those who were with him of what he was going to do, he pulled the trigger.

The pistol only flashed without being fully discharged.

"How imprudent," said the doctor. "You have done it now! Follow me!"

He rushed forward, but he was too late, Varney had taken the alarm, and in a moment he regained his own room and fastened it securely on the inside.

"We must have him," cried Charles. "He cannot escape from that room. There is no other door, and the window is a good thirty feet from the garden below. Alarm the servants, we will soon open his door. It can't be very secure, for the lock was broken last night."

As he spoke, Charles made a vigorous effort to open the door, but it resisted as if it had been a part of the solid wall, while within the chamber all was perfectly still, as if Mr. Smith had quite satisfied himself by shutting out his assailants, and meant to take no further notice of them.

"This is strange," said the doctor, "but we shall soon find out what he means by it. The door must be forced as quickly as possible."

Edwin ran down stairs by his father's orders to arouse some of the men servants, besides getting some weapon or tool by the assistance of which the door might be forced, and he soon returned with several of the men, and one armed with the identical crow-bar that had been used with such effect on the preceding evening. They brought lights with them too, so that the capture of Mr. Smith appeared to be no longer a matter of doubt with such a force opposed to him.

"Now," cried Sir George, "do not mind what mischief you do, my men, so that you break open the door of that room, and quickly too."

People somehow are always glad to be engaged in anything that has a destructive look about it, and when the servants heard that they might break away at the door as much as they liked, they set about it with a vengeance that promised soon to succeed in the object.

The door yielded with a crash.

"Come on, come on. Yield yourself," cried Sir George, and he rushed into the room followed by his sons and by Dr. North.

There was no Mr. Smith there.

"Escaped," said Dr. North.

"Impossible, — impossible! and yet this open window. He must be lying dashed to pieces below, for no one could with safety drop or jump such a height. Run round to the garden some of you, at once."

"Stop," said Charles. "There is no occasion. He has had ample time to escape. Look here."

Charles pointed out the end of a thick rope, firmly fastened to the ledge of the window, and by which it was quite clear any one could safely descend into the garden, it only requiring a little nerve to do so with perfect ease.

"This has all been prepared," said Dr. North.

"Still," cried Sir George, "I will not give the affair up. Mind I offer a reward of twenty guineas to any one of my household who succeeds in catching Mr. Smith."

"Lor', sir! what has he done?" said a groom.

"Never you mind what he has done. Bring him in, and you shall have the reward."

"Very good, sir. Come on, Dick, and you Harry; let's all go, and you know it will be all the pleasanter to share the reward among us. Come on."

Thus stimulated by their companion, the servants ran out of the house into the moonlit park in search of Varney the Vampyre.

CCIX.

THE FUNERAL. — A STRANGE INCIDENT.

IT WAS ALL VERY WELL for Sir George Crofton to offer his twenty guineas for the taking of Mr. Smith, and nothing could be more legitimate than his servants making active exertions to endeavour to earn that amount of money, but the really succeeding in doing so was quite another thing.

To be sure they went out into the park, and did the best to catch him, and being well acquainted with every turn and every pathway within it, they considered they had a fair chance of succeeding, but after their pains they were at length obliged to give up the affair as a bad job, after an hour or two's most active search.

While they were away though, there was something that occurred at the Grange which gave a great additional shock to Sir George and his sons.

It will not fail to be remembered that the first door they saw move while they were keeping watch and ward in the moonlit gallery was the door of the chamber in which lay the corpse of Clara, who had met with so melancholy an end.

This circumstance recurred to them all with fearful force when they felt convinced that the now more suspected Mr. Smith had really and truly made his escape.

Upon proceeding to that room of the dead, Dr. North being first, they found some difficulty in opening the door, but upon using force they succeeded, when to their absolute horror they saw that the

dead body was lying upon the floor close to the door, and that it had been the obstruction to moving it.

Dr. North would fain have spared the feelings of Sir George this affecting sight, but the baronet was so close behind him that he could not do so.

"Oh, God!" cried the father, "my child, my child."

"Take your father away, boys, for heaven's sake," said Dr. North to the two young men; "this is no sight for him to see."

It appeared too as if it was no sight for any one to see unmoved, for both Charles and Edwin stood like statues gazing at it, and for a time incapable of motion.

"My sister — is it indeed my sister?" said Charles.

The doctor fairly closed the door upon them all, and turned them so out of the room. Then he having professionally lost all dread of the dead, lifted the body upon the bed again, and disposed of it properly, after which, without saying a word, he walked down to the dining-room.

"Tell me, tell me," said Sir George "what does all this mean?"

"Do not ask me," replied Dr. North, "I cannot tell you; I confess I do not know what advice to give you, or indeed what to say to you."

The old man rested his head upon his hands, and wept bitterly, while his two sons sat looking at each other perfectly aghast, and unable to think anything of a rational import concerning the most mysterious proceedings that had taken place.

LET OUR READERS THEN suppose that a week has passed away, and that the morning has arrived when the body of Clara is to be placed in a vault appropriated as the resting place of the Croftons, beneath the church that was close at hand.

During that time nothing whatever had been heard of Mr. Smith. He seemed to have completely disappeared from the neighbourhood as well as from the Grange-house.

Fortunately, although Sir George had offered twenty guineas for the apprehension of Mr. Smith to his servants, he had said nothing of the cause why he offered such a reward, and the neighbourhood was left to its own conjectures upon the subject.

Those conjectures were of course sufficiently numerous, but it was quite agreed between Sir George, Doctor North, and the two sons that nothing more should be said upon the subject.

They of course did not wish "to fill the ear of idle curiosity" with such a tale as they might tell, but had a thousand reasons, each good and substantial of its kind, for withholding.

Young Ringwood was sufficiently recovered to be about, and to have told him the story that widowed his heart. He fell into a profound melancholy which nothing could alleviate, and as his recovery went on, he asked permission to remain at the Grange.

Sir George, and indeed all the Crofton family, gladly pressed him to remain with them as long as he would do so, for it was some alleviation of their own distress to have him about them.

He begged permission to be present at the funeral, and it is of that funeral we have now to speak, for it took place on that day-week on which the vampyre had first taken up his dreadful residence at the old Grange-house, where all before had been so happy.

The church, as we have remarked, was not very distant, and a mournful procession it was, consisting of the funeral equipages, followed by Sir George Crofton's carriage, that at twelve o'clock in the day started to place the youngest and the fairest of the name of Crofton that had ever reposed in the family vault.

The whole neighbourhood was in a state of commotion, and by the time the funeral cortege reached the churchyard, there was not a person capable of being out, for some miles around, that was not congregated about the spot.

The old church bell tolled a melancholy welcome to the procession, and the clergyman met the corpse a the entrance of the graveyard, and preceded it to the church, where it was placed by the altar while he made an impressive prayer.

This brief ceremony over, the coffin was carried to the part of one of the aisles, where upon the removal of a large stone slab, the resting-place of the Croftons was visible.

"I have not looked upon these stone steps," said Sir George, "since my poor wife went down there in the sleep of death."

"Compose yourself," whispered Dr.

North, who was present. "You ought not, sir, to have been present at such a scene as this."

"Nay, it surely was my duty to follow my own child to her last resting-place."

The body was lowered into the vault, and the funeral service was read impressively over the cold and still remains of Clara.

"All is over," said the doctor.

"Yes," faltered Sir George; "all is over. Farewell, my dear child, but not a long farewell to thee; this blow has nearly stricken me into the grave."

Leaning on the arm of his son Charles, who as well as Edwin was deeply affected, the old man now allowed himself to be led from the church. He met at the door Will Stephens, the sexton, who seemed desirous of speaking to him.

"What is it, Will?"

"Will your honour have some fresh sawdust put down in the vault? It wants it, Sir George; there ain't been any put in for many a long day."

"Very well. It will be ready for me when I go. It won't be long before the vault is again opened."

"Oh, do not say that, father," said Edwin. "Do not leave us; think that if you have lost one child who loved you, you have others who ought to be as dear to you."

"That's right, Edwin," said the doctor.

Sir George made no distinct reply to this, but he pressed the hand of his son, and looked kindly upon him, to signify that he felt the full justice of what he had just said, so they had hopes that time would soon produce its usual effects upon that feeling which of all others is, while it lasts, the most poignant, at the same time

that it is the most evanescent — grief for the dead.

And well it is that it should be so, otherwise we should be a world of weepers and mourners, for who is there that has not felt the pang of losing some fond heart in which we have garnered up the best affections of human nature.

Emma since her sister's death had been terribly broken down in spirit, and when they all got home to the Grange, they found her looking so ill, that the old baronet took Dr. North on one side, and said to him in tones expressive of the deepest anguish, —

"Am I to lose both my girls?"

"Oh no — no; certainly not," was the decided reply. "Why, my old friend, you used to be a man of great moral courage. Where has it all gone to now?"

"It is in the grave of my child."

"Come, come, you must for your own sake, as well as for the sake of others, who are near and dear to you, rouse yourself from this state of mental torpor, as I may call it. You can do so, and it is worthy of you to make the effort. Only think what would have been your situation if you had had but one child, and that had been snatched away from you; but you have yet three to comfort you, and yet you talk despairingly, as if every tie that bound you to the world had been suddenly burst asunder."

After this Sir George Crofton was almost ashamed to make such an exhibition of his grief, and whatever his thoughts were he kept them to himself, as well as exercising a much greater control over his voice, and the external expression of the feelings, which were still busy at his heart.

The despondency of Ringwood was great. He could not help but fancy that if he had not met with the unlucky accident in the ravine, Clara would have been saved, and in some obscure way to his mind, the circumstances seemed to be connected together. He could not account either for the loss of her miniature, which he had been in the habit of wearing but which he missed upon his convalescence, so that he was irresistibly led to the conclusion that some unfriendly hands had been about him during his insensibility.

So highly did he prize the miniature, that he offered a sum of money, exceeding its intrinsic value by twenty times, for its recovery and pledged himself to make no inquiry as to how it came into the possession of the party who should restore it to him; but for all that it was not forthcoming.

The reader of this narrative knows very well in whose possession it was. Varney the Vampyre had possessed himself of it in the ravine, when he saw the young bridegroom lying insensible at his feet, and he kept it, although why he did so does not as yet appear, for surely the sight of it could only remind him of one of his victims; but then Varney had other thoughts and feelings than he used to have.

Alas, what a thousand pities it was that the ocean had presented him to the two brothers? Why did he not sink — why did not some wave hide him from their observation? What misery would have been spared to them, and to all dear to them. And what misery would have been spared to the wretched Varney himself!

It is true that he had given expression to sentiments, and declared intentions which would go far to prove that he had for ever given up and got rid of all human feelings and influences, but has he really so got rid of such feelings? It is a question which time alone can answer.

We shall soon see in his now very short career whether he is most to suffer or to inflict suffering, and what will be the result of his new principles of action — those principles which he had in the despair and the agony of his heart painted to himself as the main springs of a combined existence, he had with such vain and such fruitless perseverance strove to rid himself of. It was sad — very sad, indeed, that such a being could not die when he chose, the poor privilege of all.

CCX.

THE STRANGE VISITOR TO THE OLD CHURCH AT NIGHT.

THE REQUEST OF Will Stephens to be allowed to put some sawdust in the vault of the Croftons, was one of those regular things that he always propounded to any one who had a vault opened beneath the old church, and he generally made a very good thing of it.

People were always too much taken up with thinking of the loss of the relation who had just been placed in that dismal repository, to think much of a guinea to Will for a shilling's worth of sawdust, and if they did ever intimate that they thought it rather too much, he always had his answer ready at the tip of his tongue.

"How should you like, sir, or madam, as the case may be, to go into a vault among the dead, to lay the sawdust for 'em."

That argument was generally conclusive, and Will would get his guinea.

With Sir George Crofton he was quite sure and safe, so he had no scruples upon the subject, and the little bit of sawdust he meant to carry in when he had time, was more for the say of the thing, than for any utility it was at all likely to be of, but then as he said,—

"Where's the odds, the dead 'uns can't see it, and living 'uns won't go to see it, so it does very well, and I pockets my guinea, which does better still, for after all a sexton's ain't the most agreeable life in the world, and he ought to be paid well; not that I care much about it, being used to it, but there was a time when I had my

qualms, and I've had to get over 'em the best way I could, somehow, if I am now all right."

These were Will's arguments and reflections to himself before night, when he meant to go and place the little bag of saw-dust in the Croftons' family vault.

But, before we follow Will Stephens on his saw-dust expedition, as we intend to do, we wish first to draw the attention of the reader to another circumstance, the relation of which to Will Stephen's proceedings will very shortly appear indeed.

As the night came on there was some appearance of stormy weather. The wind blew in a strange, gusty and uncertain manner, shifting about from point to point of the compass in an odd way, as though it had not made up its mind from whence to blow. The most weather-wise personages of the neighbourhood were puzzled, for just as they prognosticated one species of weather from the particular direction whence the wind came, it shifted and came from some other quarter very nearly directly opposite.

This was extremely provoking, but at all events it was generally agreed that the moon would not on that night, shed its soft light upon the earth.

How far they were mistaken in this surmise we shall presently see.

Will Stephens had an opinion, from certain admonitory symptoms arising from his corns, that it would rain; so he delayed going to the church until he should see what sort of weather it was going to be, inwardly deciding that it would be a capital excuse not to go at all that night if the rain should come down pretty sharply.

This period of indecision he passed at a public house, known as the Blue Lion, the charms of the excellent ale of that establishment materially assisting him in coming to the conclusion that if it should rain ever so little it would be better to put off his job until the morning.

Now it was not that Will was afraid that he hesitated. He was too used to death to feel now any terrors of fear. It was nothing but the ale. Why then was the hurry? Simply that the flat stone which was over the vault of the Croftons was left unfastened until the aforesaid saw-dust was placed within the receptacle of the dead, and the next day was Sunday, so that the job must be finished before the service should commence.

At night, therefore, or very early the following morning, Will must seem to earn his guinea by going to the vault. He did not like to venture saying he had been and yet neglect going, for he knew there were too many gossips about the village to make that safe.

WHILE HE IS, however, regaling himself at the ale house, another person totally, to all appearance heedless of wind and threatening rain, is abroad in the neighbourhood of the church.

A tall figure enveloped in a large murky-looking cloak is moving slowly past the few cottages in the immediate vicinage of the church, and so noiselessly that it looks like a spirit of the dead rather than a living person.

It was unseen by any one, for it was a time of the night — half-past eleven — now at which few persons in that little quiet place were abroad, and as we have said, Will Stephens, perhaps the only inhabitant who had any real business to be abroad at such an hour, was still solacing himself at the Blue Lion with the ale that seemed to get better with every glass he took.

The figure moved on at a slow and steady pace among the old tomb stones that lay so thick around in the circuit of the church-yard, until it reached the church itself, and then it walked slowly around the sacred edifice, looking with a curious eye at the windows that presented themselves to observation, and apparently scanning the height from the ground.

Finally he paused at a rugged-looking part of the wall, and commenced, with great muscular power and most wonderful agility, climbing up to one of the windows.

To look at that wall it would have seemed that nothing human could possibly have succeeded in ascending it, and yet this stranger, catching at asperities which scarcely seemed to be such, did, with a wonderful power and strength, drag himself up until he grasped an iron bar, close to the window immediately above him, and then he had a firm hold.

After this his progress was easy, assuming that his object was merely to get up to the window of the old church, for he stood upon the narrow ledge without in a few moments.

There was a slight noise, it was of the breaking of a pane of glass; and then the stranger introduced his hand into the church, and succeeded in removing a rude, primitive-looking fastening which held the window in its place.

In another moment he disappeared from external observation within the sacred building.

What could he want there at such an hour, and who was he? Did he contemplate disturbing the repose of the dead with some unhallowed purpose? Was robbery his aim?

Let us be patient, and probably we shall soon enough perceive that some affairs are in progress that require the closest attention, and which in the vaults are calculated to fill the reflecting mind with the most painful images, and awake sensations of horror at the idea that such things can really be, and are permitted tacitly by Heaven to take place on the beautiful earth destined for the dwelling place of man.

CCXI.

WILL STEPHENS' VISIT TO THE FAMILY VAULT WITH THE SAW-DUST, AND WHAT HE SAW THERE.

WILL STEPHENS WAITED at the ale-house much longer than he intended. To be sure the rain cleared off, but what of that? It was not a circumstance that made the ale anything worse, and so he waited to drink it with a gusto that improved each glass amazingly, and then some of those who were present — jolly topers like himself — began to laugh and to say, —

"Ah, Will, you may as well poke that bag of saw-dust into some corner; you won't do anything with it to-night, old fellow, we know."

Now, some people get good tempered and complying when they have had the drop too much, and others again, get particularly obstinate and contradictory. Will of the two, certainly had more pretensions to belong to the latter class than the former, so when he heard such a prophecy concerning his movements and knew it was all an assumption based upon the ale he had drunk, he felt indignant.

"Not go!" he cried. "Not go. You may fancy if you please that I will not go, but you will find yourselves mistaken, I will go."

"What, so late."

"What's the odds to me. Any of you now would be frightened out of your lives to set foot in the old church at such a time as this, I know; but I'm none of the timid sort, I'm afraid of nobody living, and it ain't likely that I am now going to be afraid of anybody dead."

"Then you really will go."

The only reply that he made to this was to finish off the glass of ale that was before him, shouldering the bag of saw-dust, and sally out into the open air. Will Stephens felt highly indignant and touchy about his honour, and as he had said he would go and then somebody chose to imply a doubt still, he was grievously offended.

When he got out, he found that the night was anything but an inviting one. He was still sober enough to see that, and to feel that although the heavy rain had ceased, there was a little disagreeable misty sort of vapour in the air.

He staggered at the first turning he came to, for rather an uncomfortable gust of wind blew in his face, carrying along with it such a shower of small cold rain that he was, or fancied himself to be, wet through in a moment.

"Pleasant, this," thought Will, "but I won't go back to be laughed at."

As for the saw-dust he was carrying, its weight was by no means any great consideration, for it was just as light as it could be.

"No, I won't go back — back indeed, not I; they would make me stand a pot of ale to a certainly if I were to go back, and besides it would be all over the parish tomorrow that Will Stephens after he got half way to the church was afraid to go any further. Confound the small rain, it pricks like pins and needles."

Nothing is more sobering than rain, and as he, Will, gradually got saturated with the small aqueous particles, the effect of the strong ale gradually wore off, until by the time the dim, dusky outline of the church rose before him he was almost as sober as need be.

"Ah," he said, "here I am at last at any rate. I do hate this sort of rain, you can hardly make up your mind that it is raining at all, and yet somehow you get soaked before you know where you are. It's just like going through a damp cloud, that it is, and yet somehow or another, I don't much mind it; I'm earning a guinea easy enough. Ha, ha!"

This was by no means an unpleasant reflection.

"Yes," he added, "I am earning a guinea easily enough, that's quite clear; but then it's not everybody who would, for a guinea, go into anybody's family vault at such a time. By-the-bye, I wonder now what the time is exactly."

Scarcely had Will spoken those words when the old church-clock struck twelve.

It was a very serious, deliberate sort of clock that, and it took a long time to strike twelve, and Will listened with the greatest attention with the hope of persuading himself that it was only eleven, but there could be no mistake; twelve it was.

"Really," he said, "is it so late, well, I didn't think —"

Will stood within the porch of the church door, and he gave a sort of shiver, and then, with the bag of sawdust in his hand, he stopped to listen attentively, for he thought he heard a slight sound.

"What was that, eh? what — I thought, nay, I am sure I heard something; it's very odd — very odd indeed."

As if then to afford Will an excuse for resolving the sound to something else, the wind at this moment came in such a sudden gale round the ancient edifice, that he quite congratulated himself that he was within the porch and protected from its fury, and besides it to his mind was a sufficing explanation of the noise he had heard.

"Some of the old doors," he muttered, "rattled by the wind, that's all. Now I suppose we shall have a clear night after all the rain. Such a gale will soon blow off the damp clouds."

Will was right. The gale, for a gale it was, blew from the north, and away went the rain clouds as if a curtain had been drawn aside by some invisible hand.

After some rummaging Will found in his pocket the key of the church; it was not the key of the principal door, but of a smaller side entrance, at which the officials, who required at all times free ingress and egress, made application. The little arched door creaked upon its hinges and then Will stood in a sort of vestibule, for another door that was never fast had to be opened before he could be fairly said to be within the church.

This second door was covered with green baize, and could be opened and shut very noiselessly indeed.

Will Stephens stood in the vestibule until he had got a small lantern out of one pocket, and some matches from another. Then, in a few moments, he had a light, and once again shouldering the bag of sawdust, he pushed open the inner door, and stood in the church.

It might have been fancy — nay, he felt certain, it could be nothing else — but he thought as he opened the door that a faint sort of sigh came upon his ears.

Fancy or not, though, it was an uncomfortable thing at such an hour, and in such a place too, and he had never before heard anything of the sort upon his visits to the church, and he had visited it at all hours, many and many a time.

"It's odd," he said, "it's uncommonly odd, I never felt so uncomfortable in the church before. I — I never used to mind coming to it in the middle of the night. But now, I — eh? — what was that?"

Again an odd sort of noise came upon his ears, and he dropped the bag of sawdust.

All was still again, save the regular roar of wind, as it swept round the sacred building, and although Will Stephens stood for nearly ten minutes in an attitude of listening, he heard nothing to augment his terrors. But let an impulse once be given to fear, and it will go on accumulating material from every trivial circumstance. The courage of the sexton was broken down, and there was no knowing, now, what tricks his awakened imagination might play him.

He began to wish he had not come, and from that wish, to think that he might as well go back, only shame forbade him, for it would be easily known on the morrow, that he had not placed the sawdust in the vault, and lastly, he began to think that some one might be playing him a trick.

This last supposition, probably, had more effect in raising his courage than any preceding one. Indignation took possession of him, and he no longer thought of retreating. He went forward at once, and fell over the bag of sawdust.

"Murder!" shouted Will.

The moment he did so, he recollected what it was that had occasioned his fall, and being ashamed of himself he called out impulsively, as if somebody was there to hear him, —

"No — no, it's only the sawdust. No — no."

He rose to his feet again, heartily ashamed of his own fears. Luckily, his lantern had not been broken or extinguished in his fall, and now, without another word, he prepared himself to execute the work he came to do, and leave the church to its repose as quickly as possible.

At one end of the church, the

southern end, there was a large window, which might be said to light the whole of the interior, for the little windows at the sides were more ornamental than useful, being nothing but lattices; and across this window was drawn a heavy cloth curtain, so that when the sun shone too brightly upon the congregation on a summer's day, it could be wholly or partially excluded upon a sign from the clergyman.

The curtain was drawn close on the window now, at night, and Will just glanced up to it, as he walked on towards the aisle where the opening to the family vault of the Croftons was situated.

"All's right," he said, "what a fool I have been, to be sure. Upon my word I might have saved frightening myself all night, and some people would too, but that's not my way of doing business. So here we are, all right. The door on one side, so that I have just room enough to go down into the vault. Oh! when one comes to think of it, it was rather a melancholy thing, the death of such a young girl as she was, going to be married too. Well, that's the way the world goes."

The stone steps leading down to the vault were rather steep, and Will threw down the bag of sawdust first, in preference to carrying it, and then with his lantern in his hand, he commenced his own descent.

"That'll do," said Will, when he felt his feet upon the soft old sawdust that was on the floor of the vault. "That'll do — now for it, I shall soon have this job settled, and then I'll get home no faster than I can."

Somehow, or another, he felt very much inclined to talk; the sound of his own voice, conversing, as he might be said to be, with himself, gave him a sort of courage, and made the place not appear to be altogether so desperately lonely as it really was.

That, no doubt, was the feeling that brought forth so many indifferent remarks from Will Stephens. He held up his light to look round him, and turned gradually upon his heels as he did so.

The light shook in his hand. The hair almost stood on end on his head — his teeth chattered, and he tried to speak in vain, as he saw lying at his feet, a coffin lid.

It was new. The nails that held the blue cloth upon it, were bright, and fast — the plate shone like silver. Yes, it was the lid of the coffin of Miss Clara Crofton; but how came it off — unsecured, and lying upon the floor of the vault, while the coffin was in its proper niche?

"Gracious goodness!" gasped Will at length. "What does this mean?"

The question was easy to ask, but most difficult to answer, and he stood trembling and turning over in his mind all the most frightful explanations of what he saw, that could occur to any one.

"Has she been buried alive? Have the body-snatchers been after her? How is it — what — what has happened?"

Then it occurred to Will, that it would be just as well to look into the coffin, and see if it was tenantless or not. If it were, he thought, he should know what to think, or if the dead body was there, then he could only conclude that she had been buried alive, and had had just strength enough to force open the coffin, and cast the lid of it on the floor of the vault, and then to die in that horrible place.

It required almost more courage than Will could muster, to go and look into the coffin, for now that his usual indifference was completely broken down, he was as timid as any stranger to graves and vaults would have been. But curiosity is, after all, a most exciting passion, and that lent him power.

"Yes," he said, "I — I will look in the coffin, I shall have but a poor tale to tell to Sir George Crofton, if I do not look in the coffin. I — I — have nothing to be afraid of."

He advanced with trembling steps, the light shaking in his hands as he did so. He reached the coffin, and with eyes unusually wide he looked in:

It was empty.

CCXII.

THE APPARITION IN THE CHURCH. — WILL STEPHENS'S SWOON. — THE MORNING.

FOR SOME MINUTES, Will Stephens continued to gaze in the empty coffin, as if there was something peculiarly fascinating in it, and most attractive, and yet nothing was in it, no vestige even of the vestments of the dead. If Clara Crofton had herself risen, and left the vault, it was quite clear she had taken with her the apparel of the grave.

Will had thought that if he found the coffin empty, all his fears would vanish, and that he should be able to come at once to the conclusion, that she had become the prey of resurrectionists. But new ideas, as he gazed at that abandoned receptacle of the dead, began to creep across him.

"I — I — don't know," he muttered, "but she may in a ghost-like kind of way be going about. I don't know whether ghosts is corpses or not. I — I wish I was out of this."

The idea of spreading the sawdust in the vault now completely left him; all he thought of was to get away, and the dread that Clara Crofton was, perhaps, hiding somewhere, and might come suddenly out upon him with a yell, got so firm a hold of him, that several times he thought he should faint with excess of terror.

"That would be too horrible," he said, "I am sure I should go mad — mad — mad."

He retreated backward to the stairs, for the coffin, empty though it was, held his gaze with a strange kind of fascinating power. He thought that if he turned round something would be sure to lay hold of him. It was a most horrifying and distressing idea that, and yet he could not conquer it.

Of course, he must turn round, it would be an awkward thing to attempt ascending the staircase, short as it was, backward; so he felt the necessity of turning his back upon the vault.

"I — I will do so," he thought, "and then make such a rush up the steps, that I shall be in the church in a moment, I — I can surely do that, and — and after all it's nothing really to be afraid of — it's only a matter of imagination, after all! oh, yes, that's all, I — I will do that."

He put this notable scheme into execution by turning suddenly round and making a dash at the stairs, but as people generally do things badly when they do them in a hurry, he stumbled when about half-way and felt himself at the mercy of the whole of the supernatural world.

"Have mercy on me," he cried, "I am going. Have mercy on me."

He had struck the lantern so hard against the stone stairs that he had broken it into fragments, and now all was intense darkness around him.

He gave himself up for lost.

He lay, expecting each moment to feel some dead bony fingers clutching him, and he only groaned, thinking that surely now his last hour was come; and it is a wonder that his fancy, excited as it was, did not conjure up to him the very effect he dreaded, but it did not do so, strange to say, and he lay for full five minutes without anything occurring to add to his terrors.

Then he began gradually to recover.

"If — if," he gasped, "I could but reach the church, I — I think I should be safe. Yes, I should surely be safe in the body of the church. Have mercy on me, good ghosts; I never harmed any of you, I — I respect you very much, indeed I do. Let me go, and — I'll never say a light word of any of you again, no, never, if I were to live for a thousand years."

As he uttered these words, he crawled up the remaining stairs, and to his great satisfaction, made his way fairly into the church.

But then a new surprise, if it was not exactly a new fright, perhaps it was something of both, awaited him.

The curtain that had been, as he had observed when he was walking down the aisle, closely drawn across the large south window was now drawn on one side, so that a large portion of that window was exposed, and the north wind having chased away by this time entirely the damp clouds, the moon was sailing in a cloudless sky, and sending into the old church a glorious flood of light.

"What a change," said Will Stephens.

It was indeed a change; the church was as light as day, save in some places where shadows fell, and they, in contrast to the silvery lightness of the moonbeams, were of a jetty blackness.

But still, let the moon shine ever so brightly, there is not that distinctness and freshness of outline produced as in the direct daylight. A strange kind of hazy vapour seems to float between the eye and all objects — an indistinctness and mysteriousness of aspect, which belongs not to the sun's unreflected rays. Thus it was, that although the church was illuminated by the moon, it had a singular aspect, and would scarcely have been recognised by any one who had only seen it by the mild searching light of day.

But of course Will Stephens the sexton knew it well, and as he wiped the perspiration from his face, he said, —

"What a relief to get out of that vault and find now that the night has turned out so fair and beautiful. I — I begin to think I have frightened myself more than I need have done — but it was that coffin-lid that did the business; I wasn't my own man after that. But now that I have got out of the vault, I feel quite different — oh, quite another thing."

Suddenly, then, it occurred to him, that the curtain had been close on the window, when he came into the church, and following upon that thought came another, namely, that it could not very well remove itself from before the casement, and that consequently some hands, mortal or ghostly, must have done that part of the business.

Here there was ample food again for all his fears, and Will Stephens almost on the instant relapsed into his former trembling and nerveless state.

"What shall I do?" he said; "it ain't all over yet. What will become of me? There's something horrid going to happen, I feel certain, and that curtain has only been drawn aside to let the moonlight come in for me to see it."

With a painful expectation of his eyes being blasted by some horrible sight, he glared round him, but he saw nothing, although the dense little mass of pews before him might have hidden many a horror.

His next movement was to turn his eyes to the gallery, and all round it he carried them until he came to the window again, but he saw nothing.

"Who knows," he muttered, "who knows after all, but that the wind, in some odd sort of way, may have blown the curtain on one side. I — I wish I had the courage to go up to the gallery, and see, but I — I don't think I should like to do that."

He hesitated. He knew that it would sound well on the morrow for him to be able to say that he went up, and yet it was rather a fearful thing.

"A — hem!" he said at length, "is any one here?"

As he made this inquiry, he took care to keep himself ready to make a dart out at the door into the churchyard, but as there was no response to it, he was a little

encouraged. The gallery staircase was close to where he stood, and after the not unnatural hesitation of a few moments more, he approached them, and began slowly to ascend.

Nothing interrupted him; all was profoundly still, and at length he did reach the south window, and he found that the curtain was most deliberately drawn on one side, and that the window was fast, so that no vagary of the wind could have accomplished the purpose.

"Now I'll go — I'll go at once," he said; "I can't stand this any longer! I'll go and alarm the village — I'll — I'll make a disturbance of some sort."

"Awake!" said a deep, hollow voice.

Will sunk upon his knees with a groan, and mechanically his eyes wandered to the direction from whence the sound came, and he saw in a pew just beneath him, and on which the moonlight now fell brightly, a human form.

It was lying in a strange huddled-up position in the pew, and a glance showed the experienced eyes of the sexton that it was arrayed in the vestments of the dead.

He tried to speak — he tried to scream — he tried to pray, but all was in vain. Intense terror froze up every faculty of his body, and he could only kneel there with his face resting upon the front of the gallery, and glare with aching eyes, that would not close for a moment, upon the scene below.

"Awake!" said a deep, strange voice again, "awake."

It was quite clear that that voice did not come from the figure in the pew, but from some one close at hand. The sexton soon saw another form.

In the adjoining pew, standing upright

as a statue, with one hand pointing upwards to the window, where came in the moonlight, was a tall figure, enveloped in a cloak. It was from the lips of that figure, that the sound came, so deeply, and so solemnly.

"Sister," it said, "be one of us — let the cold chaste moonbeams endow thee with thy new, and strange, and horrible existence. Be one of us. Be one of us! Hours must yet elapse, ere the faint flash of morning will kill the moonbeams.

There is time, sister. Awake, be one of us."

There was a passing cloud that swept for an instant over the face of the moon obscuring its radiance, and the figure let its arm fall to its side. But when the silvery beams streamed into the church, it again pointed to the window.

"'Tis done. She moves," he said. "I have fulfilled my mission. Ha! ha! ha!"

The laugh was so terrific and unmirthful that it froze the very blood in the veins of Will, and he thought he was surely at that moment going mad.

But still he did not close his eyes, still he moved not from the position which he had first assumed when the horrible noise met his ears.

"'Tis done," said the figure, and the arm that had been outstretched was let fall to his side.

Will Stephens looked in the pew, where he had seen what appeared to be a corpse. It had altered its position. He saw it move and wave its arms about strangely, and deep sighs came from its lips. It was a dreadful sight to see, but at length it rose up in the grave clothes, and moved to the door of the pew.

The figure in the adjoining pew opened the door and stood on one side, and the revivified corpse passed out.

Slowly and solemnly it passed down the aisle. It reached the door at which Will Stephens had entered, and then it passed away from his sight. The tall figure followed closely, and Will Stephens was alone in the church.

What could he do? How could he give a sufficient alarm? Would the two horrible personages return or not? Alas! poor Will Stephens, never was an unhappy mortal sexton in such frightful tribulation before. He knelt and shook like an aspen. At length a lucky thought entered his head.

"The bell. The bell," he cried, all at once finding his voice. "To the bell."

He sprang to his feet, for what he was now about to do, did not involve the necessity of going down again into the body of the church. There was a narrow staircase at the corner of the gallery, leading to the belfry. It was up that staircase that Will now struggled and tore.

CCXII.

THE ALARM FROM THE BELFRY. — THE BEADLE IN A QUANDARY.

"THE BELFRY," CRIED Will Stephens. "Oh! if I could but reach the belfry."

He went stumbling on, now falling, then gathering himself up again to renewed exertions, for the stairs were steep and narrow, and although the little church tower was by no means very high, yet the place where the bell hung was not to be reached in a moment.

Perseverance, however, will do wonders, and it was reached at last. Yes, he stood panting in a little square building in the very centre of which hung a thick rope. It was the means of tolling the bell. To seize it was the work of a moment.

The bell swung round and its iron tongue gave forth a loud and stunning sound. Again and again — bang — bang — bang! went the bell, and then, feeling that at all events he had given an alarm, Will Stephens turned to retrace his steps.

He was half stupefied by his previous fears. The noise of the bell, so close as he had been to it, had been stunning and bewildering, and Will Stephens reeled like a drunken man. The ale, too, might have had a little to do with that, but certainly he made a false step, and down he went head foremost from top to bottom of those old steep, narrow belfry stairs.

WILL STEPHENS WAS RIGHT when he considered that the tolling of the bell would give an alarm. Most persons in the neighbourhood were awakened by it, and they listened to the seven or eight pealing sounds in surprise. What could they mean? Who was doing it? It could not be fire. Oh dear, no. The alarm would not leave off it it were. Somebody dead — ah, yes, it was some great person in the state dead, and the news had been brought there, and so the bell was tolled, and we shall hear all about it in the morning.

And so those who had been awakened went to sleep again, and the unhappy sexton was left to his fate at the foot of the little stairs leading up to the belfry, where he had gone with so much trouble, and produced so little effect.

The long weary hours of the night crept on, and at last the faint dawn of early morning showed itself upon the ocean, and in faint streaks of light in the glowing east.

The fishermen began to ply their hazardous and hardy trade. The birds in the gardens, and in the old lime and yew trees that shaded the church-yard, shook off their slumbers. Gradually the light advanced, and a new day began.

But there lay poor Stephens, the victim of what he had seen and heard in the old church, and there he was doomed to lie some time longer yet.

There was a Mr. Anthony Dorey, who was parish beadle, and he had awakened, and heard the sound of the tolling of the well-known bell.

"I say, mother Dorey," he had said to his better half, "what's that?"

"How should I know, idiot," was the polite rejoinder.

"Oh, very good."

"You had better get up and see."

"Oh dear no. It's no business of mine; Master Wiggins is bell-ringer; I dare say it's something, though."

This was a wise conclusion for the beadle to come to, and he turned to go to sleep again, which was wise likewise, only more easy in the conception than in the execution, for his mind was more disturbed than he had thought it possible anything could disturb it, by the tolling of the bell.

Whenever he found himself just going off to sleep, he jumped awake again quite wide, crying, —

"Eh! eh! Was that the bell?"

This sort of thing, varied by a great number of punches in the ribs from Mrs. Dorey, went on until the morning had sufficiently advanced to make it quite light enough to see objects with ordinary distinctness, and then, fancying that all his attempts to sleep would be futile, the vexed beadle rose.

"I can't sleep, that's a clear case," he said, "so I will go and see what the bell was tolled for at such an odd time of the night. The more I think of it, the more I don't know what to think."

Full of this resolution, he went post-haste to Mr. Wiggins's and knocked loudly at his cottage door.

"Hilloa! hilloa! Wiggins."

"Well," said Wiggins, looking out of his bed-room window with his head picturesquely adorned by a red night-cap, "Well, what's the matter now?"

"That's what I want to know. Why did you toll the bell in the middle of the night?"

"I toll the bell!"

"Yes, to be sure; I heard it."

"Yes, and I heard it too, but it was none of my tolling, and if I had not been rather indisposed, Mr. Dorey, I should have got up myself and seen what it was all about. As it is you find me cleaning myself rather early."

"I'll wait for you, then," said Dorey.

Wiggins soon made his appearance, and he and Dorey walked off together to the church, much pondering as they went, upon the mysterious circumstance that took them there, for if neither had rung the bell they could not think who had; for although the name of Will Stephens certainly occurred to them both, they thought it about one of the most unlikely things in the world that he would take the trouble to perform upon the great bell in the middle of the night, when it was none of his business to do so under any circumstances whatever.

"Nonsense," said the beadle; "I hardly ever knew him do a very civil thing."

"Nor I either, so you may depend, neighbour Dorey, it's not him."

"It's a great mystery, neighbour Wiggins. That's what it is, and nothing else."

"I hope it don't bode none of us no harm, that's all. Times are quite bad enough, without anything happening to make 'em worse."

This sentiment, as any grumbling one always is, was acceded to by the beadle, and so they went on conversing until they reached the church door; and then the surprise of finding the smaller entrance open struck them, and they stood staring at each other for some moments in profound silence.

"There's somebody here," said Wiggins at last.

"In course."

"What shall we do, Mr. Dorey? Do you think it's our duty to — to go in and see who it is, or — or run away? You know I ain't a constable, but you are, so perhaps it alters the case so far as you are concerned, you see."

"Not at all; you are a strong man, Mr. Wiggins, a very strong man; but suppose we try to make some one answer us. Here goes."

The beadle advanced close to the threshold of the door, and in as loud a tone of voice as he could command, he said, —

"Ahem! — ahem! — Hilloa, hilloa! — What are you at there? — Come, come, I'm down upon you."

"What do they say?" inquired Wiggins.

"Nothing at all."

"Then, perhaps, it's nobody."

"Well, do you know, if I thought that, I'd go in at once, like a roaring lion — I would — and show 'em who I was — ah!"

"So would I — so would I."

After listening for some short time longer, most intently, and hearing nothing, they came to the conclusion that, although someone had evidently been there, there was no one there now; so it would be quite safe to go into the church, always taking care to leave the door open, so that, in the event of any alarm, they could run away again, with all the precipitation in the world.

It certainly was not one of the most hazardous exploits in the whole history of chivalrous proceedings to enter a church in day-light, as it then was, in search of someone who it was very doubtful was there. But to have seen the beadle and Mr. Wiggins, anybody would have thought them bound upon an enterprise of life or death, and the latter the most likely of the two, by a great deal.

"Ahem!" cried Mr. Dorey again; "we are two strong, bold fellows, and we have left our six companions — all six feet high — at the door — ahem!"

No effect was produced by this speech, which Mr. Dorey fully intended should strike terror into somebody, and after a few minutes' search, they both felt convinced that there was no one hidden in the lower part of the church, and there was only the gallery to search.

And yet that was a ticklish job, for the nearer they approached the belfry, of course the nearer they approached the spot from whence the alarm had been given. It was therefore with rather a backwardness in going forward, that they both slowly proceeded up the staircase, and finally reached the gallery, where they saw no one; and much to their relief the want of any discovery was.

"It's all right," said the beadle. "There's nobody here. Oh, how I do wish the rascals had only stayed, that's all. I'd a shewn them what a beadle was — I'd a took 'em up in a twinkling — I would. Lord bless you, Mr. Wiggins, you don't know what a desperate man I am, when I'm put to it, that you don't."

"Perhaps not, but there don't seem to be any danger."

"Not the least. Eh? eh? — oh, the Lord have mercy upon us! I give in — what's that? — take my everything, but, oh! spare my life — oh! oh! oh!"

This panic of the beadle's was all owing to hearing somebody give a horrible groan — such a groan that it was really dreadful to hear it. Mr. Wiggins, too, was much alarmed, and leant upon the front rail of the gallery, looking dreadfully pale and wan. The beadle's face looked quite of a purple hue, and he shook in every limb.

"I — I thought I saw a groan," he said.

"So — so — did — I — oh, look — then don't you hear a horrible bundle up in that corner. Oh, mercy! I begin to think we are as good as dead men — that we are — oh, that we are. What will become of us? — what will become of us?"

By this time, Will Stephens, who, the reader is aware, was there to make the groan, had got up from the foot of the belfry-stairs, and he began to drag his bruised and stiffened frame towards the beadle and Mr. Wiggins, which they no sooner perceived than they set off as hard as they could scamper from the place, crying out for help, as if they had been pursued by a thousand devils.

In vain Stephens called after them; they did not hear his voice, nor did they stop in their headlong flight until they reached the door of the clergyman, concerning whose power to banish all evil spirits into the Red Sea, they had a strong belief, and as the reverend gentleman was at breakfast, the first thing they both did was to rush in, and upset the tea-tray which the servant had just brought in.

CCXIV.

THE CLERGYMAN'S VISIT TO THE VAULT. — RESCUE OF THE SEXTON.

"WHAT THE DEVIL! Zounds!"

Yes; that was what the parson said. With all due respect for his cloth, we cannot help recording the fact that the words at the commencement of this chapter were precisely those that came from the lips of the reverend gentleman upon the occasion of the sudden and rather alarming irruption of the beadle and the bell-ringer into his breakfast parlour at the parsonage.

"We beg your pardon, sir," said the beadle, "but —"

"Yes, sir, we beg your pardon," added the bell-ringer, "but —"

"What?" cried the parson, as he looked at the remains of his breakfast lying upon the hearth-rug in most admired disorder at his feet.

"The bell, sir — the church — the gallery — a groan — a ghost — a lot of ghosts."

Such were the incoherent words that came, thick as hail, from the beadle and the bell-ringer. In vain the clergyman strove to get to the rights of the story. He was compelled to wait until they were both very nearly tired out, and then he said, —

"Very well, I don't understand, so you may both go away again."

"But, sir —"

"But, sir —"

"If one of you will speak while the other listens I will attend, and not otherwise. This is Sunday morning, and I neither can, nor will waste any more time upon you."

Nothing is so terrible to a professed story teller, and the beadle was something of that class, as to tell him you won't listen to him, so Mr. Dorey at once begged that Wiggins would either allow him to tell what had happened, or tell it properly himself. Mr. Wiggins gave way, and the beadle as diffusely as possible told the tale of the bell tolling, and the visit to the church, with the awful adventure that there occurred.

"What do you think of it, sir?" he concluded by asking.

"I have no opinion formed as yet," replied the clergyman, "but I will step down to the church now, and see."

"You'll take plenty o' people with you, sir."

"Oh dear no, I shall go alone. I don't gather from what you have said that there is any danger. Your own fears, too, I am inclined to think, have much exaggerated the whole affair. I dare say it will turn out, as most of such alarms usually do, some very simple affair indeed."

The parson took his hat, and walked away to the church as coolly as possible, leaving Mr. Dorey and Mr. Wiggins to stare at each other, and to wonder at a temerity they could not have thought it possible for any human being to have practised.

But the clergyman was supported by a power of which they knew little — the power of knowledge, which enabled him at once in his own mind to divide the probable from the impossible, and therefore was it that he walked down to the church fully prepared to hear from somebody a very natural explanation of the mysterious bell-ringing in the night, which was the only circumstance that made him think that there was anything to explain, for he had heard that himself.

When he reached the sacred building, he found the door open, as the beadle and the bell-ringer had left it, and the moment he got into the body of the church, he heard a voice say, —

"Help! help! will nobody help me?"

"Yes," he replied, "of course, I will."

"Oh! thank Heaven!"

"Where are you?"

"Here, sir, I think that's your voice, Mr. Bevan."

"Ah, and I think that's your voice, Will Stephens; I thought this would turn out some very ordinary piece of business, so you are up stairs; and did you ring the bell in the night?"

"I did, sir."

"Just so — come down then."

"I'm afraid I can't, sir, without some help. I have had a very bad fall, and although, thank God, no bones are broken, I am sadly shaken and bruised, so that it is

with great pain, sir, I can crawl along, and as for getting down the stairs, why — I — I rather think I couldn't by myself, if there was a hundred pound note waiting for me below, just for the trouble of fetching, sir."

"Very well, I'm coming, don't move."

Mr. Bevan ascended the staircase, and without "a bit of pride," as Will Stephens said afterwards, in telling the story, helped the bruised sexton down the gallery steps to the body of the church, and then he made him sit down on one of the forms, and tell him all that had happened, which Will did from first to last, quite faithfully, not even omitting how he had stayed rather late at the ale-house, and how terrified he had been by the curious events that took place while he was in the church, ending by his fall from the stairs leading up to the belfry.

"Will, Will," said Mr. Bevan, "the ringing of the bell is good proof that you have been in the belfry, but you will scarcely expect me to believe the remainder of your dream."

"Dream, sir?"

"Yes, to be sure. You surely don't think now, in broad daylight, that it is anything else, do you?"

"I — I don't know, sir; of course, sir, if you say its a dream — why — why — "

"There, that will do. I will convince you that it was nothing more, or else you will go disturbing the whole neighbourhood with this story, that it is quite a mercy, I have first heard."

"Convince me, sir?"

"Yes; come with me to the vault."

Will Stephens shrunk from this proposal and his fear was so manifest, that Mr. Bevan was, at all events, convinced that he had told him nothing but what he himself believed, and accordingly he felt still more anxious to rid Will of his nervous terror.

"You surely," he said, "cannot be timid, while I am with you. Come at once, and if you do not find that the late Miss Crofton, poor girl, is quiet enough in her coffin, I promise you upon my sacred word, that I will never cease investigating this affair, and bringing it to some conclusion. Come at once, before any curious persons arrive at the church."

So urgent a request from the clergyman of the parish to Will Stephens, the sexton of the parish, almost might be said to amount to a command, so Will did not see how he could get out of it, without confessing an amount of rank cowardice that even he shrunk from.

"Well, sir," he said, "of course with you I can have no objection."

"That's right. Come along; there are means of getting a light into the vestry; wait here a moment."

Will would not wait; he stuck close by Mr. Bevan, who went into the vestry, and soon procured a candle, lighted from materials he kept there under lock and key; and they went together to the vault, the stone of which was just as it had been left when Will emerged with so much fright.

"I will go first," said Mr. Bevan.

"Thank you, sir."

The clergyman descended, and Will Stephens followed, trembling, about two stairs behind him. Little did he expect when he emerged from that vault previous to his adventures in the church, that he should revisit it again so quickly. Indeed he had made a mental resolve that nothing should induce him to go down those stairs

again, and yet there he was actually descending them.

So weak are the resolutions of mortals!

"Needs must," thought Will, "when the — parson, I mean, drives!"

"Come on, Will," said Mr. Bevan.

Will looked about him, but no coffin-lid was visible. There was Miss Crofton's coffin in its proper niche, with the lid on, and looking as calm and undisturbed as any respectable coffin could look. Will was amazed. He looked at the coffin, and he looked at the parson, and then he looked uncommonly foolish.

"Never mind it, Will," said Mr. Bevan, "never mind it, I say. The story need go no further. You can keep your own counsel if you like. You have come here under the influence of strong ale, and you have gone to sleep most likely in this very vault, and in your sleep, having a very vivid dream, you have walked up into the gallery, and thence into the belfry, where no doubt you did ring the bell under the influence of your dream; and then you fell down the belfry stairs, I believe, as you say you did."

"Ah!" said Will, "bless you, sir. It may be so, but —"

"You are not convinced."

"Not quite, sir,"

"Well, Will, you are quite right never to pretend to be convinced when you are not. I do not blame you for that, but in a short time, when the effect of the affair has worn off, you will entertain my opinion."

"I hope, sir, I may."

"That will do. Now the stone must be put over this vault."

"Sir, if you wouldn't mind, sir."

"What, Will?"

"Staying a moment or two, while I

empty the bag of sawdust on the floor, sir, I shan't be a minute, no — not half a minute, and then I shall have done with the vault altogether I hope, sir."

"Very well."

Will set to work, and although at any other time he would have been rather ashamed of letting Mr. Bevan see what a wonderfully small quantity of sawdust made up a guinea's worth, superior considerations now prevailed, and he would not have spared the clergyman's company on any account.

"Now I've done, sir."

"Very well, follow me."

Will did not like to ask the clergyman to follow him, so in that difficulty, for as to his remaining behind it was out of the question, he made a rush and reached the church before Mr. Bevan could ascend two of the steps. When that gentleman did reach the church he made no remark about the precipitancy, and apparent disrespect of Will, for he put it down to its right cause, but he left the church in order to make the usual preparations for the morning service, which would now commence in an hour-and-a-half.

Will walked home with his empty bag, for the little exercise he had had sufficed to convince him that he was not so much hurt as he thought, and that the stiffness of his limbs would soon pass away.

"It's all very well," he said to himself, "for Mr. Bevan to talk about dreams, but if that was one, nothing real has ever happened to me yet, that's all."

CCXV.

THE YOUNG LOVER'S MIDNIGHT WATCH.

DID THE CLERGYMAN really think what he said? Had he no suspicions, that after all there was a something more even than he was quite willing to admit in the story told by Will Stephens?

We shall see in good time, but at all events one thing is evident, that the parson thought it good sound policy, and it was, to endeavour to nip the thing in the head, and by ascribing it to a dream, put it down as a subject of speculation in the place.

He knew that nothing could be more dangerous than allowing any such story to pass current as a wonderful fact, and well he knew that in a short time, if such were the case, it would receive so many additions and so many embellishments, that the mischief it might produce upon the mind of an ignorant population might be extreme, and of a most regretful character indeed.

All this he felt hourly, and therefore Will Stephens' story was to be put down as a dream.

Now Mr. Bevan, it will be recollected, had urged Will to keep his own counsel, and to say nothing of the affair to any one, but he had faint hopes only that Will would do that, very faint hopes indeed, for after all he, Will, was the hero of the story, and there would be a something

extremely gratifying in telling it, and in stating what he would have done, had not his foot slipped as he came down the narrow stairs from the old belfrey, and so completely stunned him by the fall. Mr. Bevan therefore had very few if any compunctions in adopting the course he did, which was, in the evening, when there was no service at the church, to call at the Grange, to see Sir George Crofton upon the subject.

Mr. Bevan was always a welcome guest at the Grange, and he was on those intimate and good terms with the family, that he could always call whenever he pleased, so that a mere announcement of his presence by no means had the effect of preparing Sir George for any communication.

"Ah, Mr. Bevan," he said, when the clergyman entered the room, "I am glad to see you."

"And I to see you, Sir George."

"You come to a house of mourning, sir. But that will be the case here for a long, long time. Time may and will, no doubt, do much to assuage our grief, but the blow is as yet too recent."

Tears started to the eyes of Sir George Crofton, as he made this allusion to his daughter, and he turned his head aside to hide such evidences of emotion from the parson, from whom, however, he need have expected nothing but the most friendly sympathy that one human being could bestow upon another. Mr. Bevan was a man of refinement and consideration, and he let grief aways have its way, seldom doing more than merely throw out, in the form of a suggestion for consideration as it were, that death was not the great evil it was thought to be.

In such a way he generally succeeded in bring persons smarting under the infliction of the loss of dear friends and relations much sooner to proper sense of the subject, than if he had indulged in all the canting religious exhortations that some divines think applicable to such occasions.

Sir George Crofton was alone, for his two sons had gone for a stroll in the grounds. Ringwood, who still remained with the family, was in the library, where now he passed most of his time, in trying by reading to withdraw his mind from a too painful and fixed contemplation of his loss.

He was still weak, but might be considered now quite convalescent.

"Pray be seated, Mr. Bevan," said Sir George. "Believe me, I take it very kindly of you to come so often."

"Pray dear sir, don't say another word about it — I — I am very sorry to feel myself obliged to allude to anything of an uncomfortable nature."

"Think nothing of doing so, my friend. Think nothing of it, I have a master grief which drowns all others."

"But it is concerning that master grief, sir, that I come to speak."

"Indeed!"

"Yes, sir, will you kindly hear me?"

"Certainly, certainly."

"You told me on the day following the melancholy death of your daughter, as a friend, the peculiar circumstances attendant upon that death. Now I do not mean to say that what I am going to relate to you has any connection at all with those circumstances, nor would I tell you what I come to tell at all, were I not fearful that the same story with some of the usual exaggerations of ignorance would reach you from other quarters, for it is not a matter consigned to my bosom only, or there it should remain."

"You alarm me."

"That I feared, but deeply regret. Listen to me, and remember always as you do so, that I think the whole affair is a mere dream — a disturbed slumberer's vision — nothing more."

Sir George Crofton did listen with breathless eagerness, and Mr. Bevan, without detracting anything or adding anything to the narrative of Will Stephens, told him the whole story just as Will had told it to him, concluding by saying, —

"That is all, my dear sir, and I felt that my duty powerfully called upon me to be your informant upon the subject, simply that we might be forewarned against any coarse version of the story."

Sir George drew a long breath.

"More horrors! More horrors!"

"Nay, why should you say that?"

"Is it not so?"

"Nay I have already given my opinion, by saying, that I look upon the whole affair as but the phantasma of dream."

"Oh! Mr. Bevan, do not trifle with me. Is that really and truly your opinion, sir, or only said from kindness to me."

"It is the best opinion that I can come to."

"I thank you, sir; I thank you. Clara, Clara, my child, my child!"

The old man was overcome with grief, and at the interesting moment, Ringwood entered the room, with a book in his hand. He was astonished, as well he might be to see such a fearful relapse of grief on the part of Sir George Crofton, and he looked from him to Mr. Bevan, and from Mr. Bevan to him, for some few moments in silence, and then he said, —

"Surely all here have suffered enough, and there is no new calamity come upon this house."

"Tell him all," cried Sir George; "tell him all. It is fit that he should know; he is one of us now, he loved my child, and

loves her memory still. I pray you, Mr. Bevan, to tell all to Ringwood, for I have not the heart to do so."

"I wonder," said Ringwood, calmly, "to hear you speak thus. I wonder to see that any new grief can come so near to that which we have already suffered. The image of my lost one fills up each crevice of my heart. I shall listen to you Mr. Bevan with respect, but my grief, I fear is selfish, and cannot feel more than its own miseries."

Ringwood seemed to imagine that what the parson had to say referred to something with which Clara had nothing to do; but when, as the story proceeded, he found how intimately connected she was with the affair, his cheek flushed for a moment, and then grew of a death-like paleness, and he sat trembling and looking in the face of Mr. Bevan, as he proceeded with his most strange relation.

When he had concluded Ringwood gave a deep groan.

"You are much affected, sir," said Mr. Bevan.

"Crushed! crushed!" was the reply. "Oh God!"

"Nay now this is not manly, sir, you feel this thing too much; if you are so crushed how can any one expect that from you is to proceed the necessary exertion to prove that the story in all its particulars is but a falsehood?"

Ringwood caught at this idea in a moment.

"Exertion from me?" he said. "What exertions would I not make to prove such a horror to be but a creation of the fancy? What would I not do! What would I not suffer? You have warned me, sir. Yes, I have a duty to do — a duty to Clara's memory; a duty to you, Sir George, and a duty to myself, for did I not love her, and does not her gentle image still sit in my inmost heart enshrined? I will prove that this most monstrous story is a delusion. Bear with me, gentlemen, I must think. To-morrow you shall know more, but not until to-morrow."

He rose, and left the room.

"What does he mean," said Sir George, vacantly.

"I cannot tell you, sir; but wait until to-morrow. Perhaps by then he may have proposed some plan of action, that you or I may not think of. You will use your own discretion, about communicating the strange affair to your sons or not, sir. Upon such a point as family confidence, I never venture an opinion. Allow me to call upon you to-morrow morning, sir, when I hope to find you in better spirits."

The clergyman would not have been in such haste to leave Sir George; but as he saw Ringwood leave the room; that young man made a sign to him, that he wished to see him before he left, and accordingly Mr. Bevan was anxious to know what it was he had to say to him.

When he left Sir George, he asked a servant where Mr. Ringwood was, and being told he was in the library, Mr. Bevan, being quite familiar with the house, followed him there at once, and found him pacing that apartment in great agitation, and with disordered steps.

"Thank heaven you have come, sir," cried Ringwood, "tell me, oh, tell me, what would you advise me to do, Mr. Bevan."

"I think," replied the clergyman, "you have already half decided upon a course."

"I have, I have."

"Then follow it, if it be such a one as in its result will produce a conviction of the truth. Do not, Mr. Ringwood, allow anything to turn you aside from a course which you feel to be right; you will always find strength enough to persevere if you have that strong conviction upon you. What is your plan?"

"It is this night to watch in the church."

"Be it so; I will, if you like, keep watch with you."

"Oh, no, no! let me be alone. All I ask of you, sir, is to provide me with the means of getting into the sacred edifice at midnight."

"That I will do. You shall have a private key that I have for my own use; you can let yourself in without any one knowing of your presence. But do you think you have nerve enough to go alone? if you have the smallest doubt or hesitation, let me accompany you."

"No, no — I thank you, but let me go alone, and say nothing of this to Sir George. I had it in my mind when I told him I would speak to him to-morrow about what you had communicated. I would fain, if these horrors be really true, keep him in ignorance that I have verified them. But if I keep my night watch quite undisturbed, then he shall have the satisfaction of knowing that it has been so kept."

"You are right in that; I will send the key to you in the course of another hour and remember I am at your service if you should alter your mind, and wish for company. Do not hesitate about disturbing my rest."

CCXVI.

THE HORRORS OF THE GRAVE. — A FRIGHTFUL ADVENTURE.

ONE WOULD HAVE THOUGHT that young Ringwood might with effect and with discretion have disclosed his plan of watching in the old church to one of the brothers of Clara, but he shrunk from doing that.

In the first place he thought he should be put down as a visionary, and as one who was disposed to insult the memory of Clara by imagining that the story of the sexton could be true; and in the second place, if anything did happen, he was afraid that the feelings of the brother might clash with his.

"No," he said, "I will go alone — I will not rest again until I have thoroughly satisfied myself that this tale is but a fabrication of the fancy. Oh, Clara! can it be possible — no, no. The thought is by far too — too horrible."

It may really be considered a fortunate thing that the communication of the clergyman was made in the evening, for had it been earlier in the day, the hours of frightful anxiety which Ringwood would have endured until the night came must have been most painful.

As it was, however, the hours that would elapse ere he could venture to go to the church on his strange and melancholy errand were not many, and they passed the more quickly, that during some of them, he was making up his mind as to what he should do.

"Yes, Clara, my best beloved Clara," he said, "I will rescue your sweet memory from this horrible doubt that is cast upon it, or I will join you in the tomb. Welcome, a thousand times welcome death, rather than that I should live to think that you are — God, no — no! I cannot pronounce the dreadful word. Oh, what evil times are these, and what a world of agony do I endure. But courage, courage; let fancy sleep, I must not allow my imagination to become sufficiently excited to play me any pranks to-night. Be still my heart, and let me go upon this expedition as a spectator merely. Time enough will it be to become an actor, when I know more, if indeed there be more to know."

The clergyman sent the key, according to his promise, by a confidential servant, who had orders to ask for Mr. Ringwood and to give it into his own hands, so that the young man was fully prepared to go, when the proper time should arrive for him to start upon his expedition.

He purposely kept very much out of the way of Sir George Crofton and his two sons during the remainder of the evening, for such was the ingenuous nature of young Ringwood, and so unused was he to place any curb upon his speech, that he dreaded letting slip some information regarding his intention to keep watch in the old church that night; in such a case it would have been difficult to refuse company.

Sir George took the advice of the clergyman and said nothing to any one of the dreadful communication that had been made to him. But he could not conceal from the family and his servants, that some unusual grief was preying upon him, beyond even the sadness that had remained after the death of his daughter. He retired to rest unusually early, that he might escape their curious and inquiring glances.

THE CLOCK STRUCK eleven.

"It is time," said Ringwood, as he sprung from his seat in his bed-room. "It is time. For the love of thee, my Clara, I go to brave this adventure, Mine are you in death as in life. My heart is widowed, and can know no other love."

He armed himself with a pair of loaded pistols, for he made up his mind that if any trickery was at the bottom of the proceeding, the authors of such a jest should pay dearly for their temerity; and then, cautiously descending from his bed-room, he crossed the dining-room, and passing through a conservatory, easily made his way out of the house, and into a flower-garden that was beyond.

He thought that if he went out of the grounds by the way of the porter's lodge, it might excite some remark, his not returning again, so he went to a part of the wall which he knew was low and rugged.

"There," he said, "I can easily climb over, and by getting into the meadows make my way into the road."

This, to a young man, was not by any means a difficult matter, and he in a few minutes more found himself quite free of the house and grounds, and making his way very rapidly towards the church, the tower of which he could just see.

The night was again a cloudy one; although nothing had as yet fallen, the wind was uncertain, and no one could with any safety have ventured to predict whether it would be fair, or rain. Of the two, certainly, Ringwood would have preferred moonlight, for he wished in the church to be able to see well about him, without thinking of the necessity of a light.

"No," he said, as he pursued his way, "I must have no light; that would ruin all."

By the time he reached the church, he had a better opinion of the weather, and from a faint sort of halo that was in the sky, he was led to believe that the moon's light would soon be visible, and enable him to see everything that might take place.

The key that the parson had given him opened the same little door by which Will Stephens, the sexton, had entered, and there was no difficulty in turning the lock, for it was frequently used.

The young man paused for a moment, debating with himself, whether he should fasten the door securely on the inner side, or leave it open, and at last he thought, that considering all things, the latter was the best course to pursue."

"I do not wish," he said, "to stop any proceedings, so much as I wish to see what they are. There shall therefore be every facility for any one coming into the church, who may chance to have an intention so to do."

He still, it will be seen, clung a little to the hope that it was a trick.

When he pushed open the door that was covered with green baize, he found that in consequence of the cloth curtain being entirely drawn aside from before the south window, that there was not near the amount of darkness within the building that he had anticipated finding there.

When his eyes got a little accustomed to it, he could even see, dimly to be sure, but still, sufficiently to distinguish the several shapes of the well-known objects in the church. The pulpit, the communion table, the little rails before it, and some of the old monuments against the walls.

The stone slab that covered the opening to the vault of the Crofton family, had been before the commencement of the morning service properly secured, so that that entrance could be walked over with perfect safety, and Ringwood carefully ascertained that such was the fact.

"Surely, surely," he said, "it is as Mr. Bevan says. That man must have come here half stupefied by ale, and have gone to sleep. The only thing that gives the slightest semblance to such a tale, is the adventure of that most mysterious man who was reclaimed from the sea."

Yes, Ringwood was right. That was the circumstance, full of dread and awful mystery as it was, which sufficed to make anything else probable, and possible.

And what had become of him? Since the time when he made his escape from the Grange—nothing had been seen or heard of him unless that were he indeed, who was in the church pointing to the moonlight when the terrified Will Stephens was there.

And yet Stephens, although he might be supposed to be in a position to know him, did not recognise him, for we do not find in his account of the affair that he made any mention of him, or insinuated any opinion even, that the Mr. Smith of

the bone-house, was the same person who had played so strange a part in the church.

The reader will have his own opinion.

"Where shall I bestow myself," thought Ringwood, "I ought to be somewhere from whence I can get a good view of the whole church."

After some little consideration, and looking about him as well as the semi-darkness would permit him, he thought that he could not by any possibility do better than get into the pulpit. From there he could readily turn about in any direction from whence any noise might proceed, at the same time, that it was something like a position which could not be very well attacked except with fire arms, and if such weapons were used against him, he should have the great advantage of seeing who was his assailant.

Accordingly he ascended the pulpit stairs, and soon ensconced himself in that elevated place.

There was something very awful, and solemn, and yet beautiful about the faint view he got of the old conventicle-looking church from its pulpit, and irresistible had he chosen to resist it, there came to his lips a prayer to Heaven for its aid, its protection, and its blessing upon his enterprise.

How much calmer, and happier he felt after that. How true it is, as Prospero says, that prayer,—

Pierces so that it assaults
*Mercy itself, and frees all faults.**

---

* *A line from Shakespeare's* The Tempest, *from Prospero's final monologue in the epilogue to the play.*

Who is there in the wide world who has not felt the benign influence of an appeal to the great Creator of all things, under circumstances of difficulty, and of distress? Let us pity the heart, if there be such a one in existence, that is callous to such a feeling.

But there are none. A reliance upon divine mercy is one of the attributes of humanity, and may not be turned aside, by even all the wickedness and the infidelity that may be arrayed against it.

"All is still," murmured Ringwood. "The stillness of the very grave is here, Oh, my Clara; methinks without a pang of mortal fear, I could converse, in such an hour as this, with thy pure and unsullied spirit!"

In the enthusiasm of the moment, no doubt, Ringwood could have done so, and it is a wonder that his most excited imagination did not conjure up some apparent semblance of the being whom he loved so devotedly, and whose image he so fondly cherished, even although she had gone from him.

"Yes, my Clara," he cried, in tones of enthusiasm. "Come to me, come to me, and you will not find that in life or in death the heart that is all your own, will shrink from you!"

This species of mental exaltation was sure soon to pass away, and it did so. The sound of his own voice convinced him of the impropriety of such speeches, when he came there as an observer.

"Hush! hush!" he said. "Be still, be still."

It was evident to him that many clouds were careering over face of the moon, for at times the church would get very dark indeed, and everything assumed a pitchy blackness, and then again a soft kind of light would steal in, and give the whole place a different aspect.

This continued for a long time, as he thought, and more than once he tried to ascertain the progress of the hours by looking at his watch, but the dim light baffled him.

"How long have I been here?" he asked himself; "I must not measure the time by my feelings, else I should call it an age."

At that moment the old church clock began to chime, and having proclaimed the four quarters past eleven, it with its deep-toned solemn bell struck the hour of twelve — Ringwood carefully counted the strokes, so that, although it was too dark to see his watch, he could not be deceived.

CCXVII.

THE MIDNIGHT HOUR. — THE STONE SLAB. — THE VAMPYRE.

YES, IT WAS TWELVE o'clock, that mysterious hour at which it is believed by many that —

Graves give up their dead,
And many a ghost in church-yard decay,
Rise from their cold, cold bed
To make night horrible with wild vagary.

Twelve, that hour when all that is human feels a sort of irksome dread, as if the spirits of those who have gone from the great world were too near, loading the still night air with the murky vapours of the grave. A chilliness came over Ringwood and he fancied a strange kind of light was in the church, making objects more visible than in their dim and dusky outlines they had been before.

"Why do I tremble?" he said, "why do I tremble? Clouds pass away from before the moon, that is all. Soon there may be a bright light here, and lo, all is still; I hear nothing but my own breathing; I see nothing but what is common and natural. Thank heaven, all will pass away in quiet. There will be no horror to recount — no terrific sight to chill my blood. Rest Clara, rest in Heaven."

Ten minutes passed away, and there was no alarm; how wonderfully relieved was Ringwood. Tears came to his eyes, but there were the natural tears of regret, such as he had shed before for her who had gone from him to the tomb, and left no trace behind, but in the hearts of those who loved her.

"Yes," he said, mournfully "she has gone from me, but I love her still. Still does the fond remembrance of all that she was to me, linger at my heart. She is my own, my beautiful Clara, as she ever was, and as, while life remains, to me she ever will be."

At the moment that he uttered these words a slight noise met his ears.

In an instant he sprung to his feet in the pulpit, and looked anxiously around him.

"What was that?" he said. "What was that?"

All was still again, and he was upon the point of convincing himself, that the noise was either some accidental one, or the creation of his own fancy, when it came again.

He had no doubt this time. It was a perceptible, scraping, strange sort of sound, and he turned his whole attention to the direction from whence it came. With a cold creeping chill through his frame, he saw that that direction was the one where was the family vault of the Croftons, the last home of her whom he held still in remembrance, and whose memory was so dear to him.

He felt the perspiration standing upon his brow, and if the whole world had been the recompense to him for moving away from where he was he could not have done so. All he could do was to gaze with bated breath, and distended eyes upon the aisle of the church from whence the sound came.

That something of a terrific nature was now about to exhibit itself, and that the night would not go off without some terrible and significant adventure to make it remembered, he felt convinced. All he dreaded was to think for a moment what it might be.

His thoughts ran on Clara, and he murmured forth in the most agonising accents, —

"Anything — any sight but the sight of her. Oh, no, no, no!"

But it was not altogether the sight of her that he dreaded; oh no, it was the fact that the sight of her on such an occasion would bring the horrible conviction with it, that there was some truth in the dreadful apprehension that he had of the new state of things that had ensued regarding the after death condition of that fair girl.

The noise increased each moment, and finally there was a sudden crash.

"She comes! she comes!" gasped Ringwood.

He grasped the front of the pulpit with a frantic violence, and then slowly and solemnly there crossed his excited vision a figure all clothed in white. Yes, white flowing vestments, and he knew by their fashion that they were not worn by the living, and that it was some inhabitant of the tomb that he now looked upon.

He did not see the face. No, that for a time was hidden from him, but his heart told him who it was. Yes, it was his Clara.

It was no dream. It was no vision of a too excited fancy, for until those palpable sounds, and that most fearfully palpable form crossed his sight, he was rather inclined to go the other way, and to fancy what the sexton had reported was nothing but a delusion of his overwrought brain. Oh, that he could but for one brief moment have found himself deceived.

"Speak!" he gasped; "speak! speak!"

There was no reply.

"I conjure you, I pray you though the sound of your voice should hurl me to perdition — I implore you, speak."

All was silent, and the figure in white moved on slowly but surely towards the door of the church; but ere it passed out, it turned for a moment, as if for the very purpose of removing from the mind of Ringwood any lingering doubt as to its identity.

He then saw the face, oh, so well-known, but so pale. It was Clara Crofton!

"'Tis she! 'tis she!" was all he could say.

It seemed, too, as if some crevice in the clouds had opened at the moment, in order that he should with an absolute certainty see the countenance of that solemn figure, and then all was more than usually silent again. The door closed, and the figure was gone.

He rose in the pulpit, and clasped his hands. Irresolution seemed for a few moments to sway him to and fro, and then he rushed down into the body of the church.

"I'll follow it," he cried, "though it lead me to perdition. Yes, I'll follow it."

He made his way to the door, and even as he went he shouted, —

"Clara! Clara! Clara!"

He reached the threshold of the ancient church; he gazed around him distractedly, for he thought that he had lost all sight of the figure. No — no, even in the darkness and against the night sky, he saw it once again in its sad-looking death raiments. He dashed forward.

The moonbeams at this instant being freed from some dense clouds that had interposed between them and this world, burst forth with resplendent beauty.

There was not a tree, a shrub, nor a flower, but what was made distinct and manifest, and with the church, such was the almost unprecedented lustre of the beautiful planet, that even the inscriptions upon the old tablets and tombs were distinctly visible.

Such a refulgence lasted not many minutes, but while it did, it was most beautiful, and the gloom that followed it seemed doubly black.

"Stay, stay," he shouted, "yet a moment, Clara; I swear that what you are, that will I be. Take me over to the tomb with you, say but that it is your dwelling-place, and

I will make it mine, and declare it a very palace of the affections."

The figure glided on.

It was in vain that he tried to keep up with it. It threaded the churchyard among the ancient tombs, with a gliding speed that soon distanced him, impeded, as he continually was, by some obstacle or another, owing to looking at the apparition he followed, instead of the ground before him.

Still, on he went, heedless whether he was conveyed, for he might be said to be dragged onward, so much were all his faculties both of mind and body intent upon following the apparition of his beloved.

Once, and once only, the figure paused, and seemed to be aware that it was followed, for it flitted round an angle made by one of the walls of the church, and disappeared from his eyes.

In another moment he had turned the same point.

"Clara, Clara!" he shouted. "'Tis I — you know my voice, Clara, Clara."

She was not to be seen, and then the idea struck him that she must have re-entered the church, and he too, turned, and crossed the threshold. He lingered there for a moment or two, and the whole building echoed to the name of Clara, as with romantic eagerness, he called upon her by name to come forth to him.

Those echoes were the only reply.

Maddened — rendered desperate beyond all endurance, he went some distance into the building in search of her, and again he called.

It was in vain; she had eluded him, and with all the carefulness and all the energy and courage he had brought to bear upon that night's proceedings, he was foiled. Could anything be more agonising than this to such a man as Ringwood? — he who loved her so, that he had not shrunk from her, even in death, although she had so shrunk from him?

"I will find her — I will question her," he cried. "She shall not escape me; living or dead, she shall be mine. I will wait for her, even in the tomb."

Before he carried out the intention of going actually into the vault to await her return, he thought he would take one more glance at the churchyard with the hope of seeing her there, as he could observe no indications of her presence in the church.

With this view he proceeded to the door, and emerged into the dim light. He called upon her again by name, and he thought he heard some faint sound in the church behind him. To turn and make a rush into the building was the work of a moment.

He saw something — it was black instead of white — a tall figure — it advanced towards him, and with great force, before he was aware that an attack was at all intended, it felled him to the ground.

The blow was so sudden, so unexpected, and so severe, that it struck him down in a moment before he could be aware of it. To be sure, he had arms with him, but the anxiety and agony of mind he endured that night, since seeing the apparition come from the tomb, had caused him to forget them.

CCXVIII.

THE YOUNG GIRL IN THE VILLAGE, AND THE AWFUL VISIT.

IT IS NOW NECESSARY that we draw the reader's attention to a humbler place of residence than the Grange, with its spacious chambers and lordly halls.

Situated not very far from the church, and almost close to the churchyard, upon which its little garden abutted, was a cottage, the picture of rural neatness and beauty. In the winter it was beautiful and picturesque, but in the summer time, when its porch was overrun with the woodbine and the sweet clematis, it was one of the sweetest of abodes that content and happiness could ever live in.

This cottage was inhabited by an old woman and her only child, a young girl of sixteen, beautiful as a rose, and as guileless as an angel. They contrived to live upon a small annuity that the mother had from a family in whose service she spent the best years of her life, and who, with a generosity that would be well to be abundantly and extensively imitated, would not see their old dependent want.

These two innocent and blameless persons had retired to rest at nine o'clock, their usual hour, and had slept the calm sleep of contentment until about half-past one, when the mother was awakened by a loud and piercing shriek from her daughter's chamber.

To spring from her humble couch was the work of a moment.

"Anna, Anna! my child, Anna!" she shrieked.

As she did so, she rushed across the small stair landing which separated the two, and the only two upper rooms of the cottage, and was about to enter her daughter's room, when the door of it was opened from within, and the old dame's heart died within her, as she saw a figure upon the threshold, attired in the vestments of the grave, and opposing her entrance.

Was it a dream, or did she really see such a sight?

Aghast and trembling the mother stood, unable for a moment or two to speak, and as she fell fainting upon the landing, she thought that something passed her, but she could not be quite sure, as it was at the instant her faculties were flitting from her.

How long she lay in that seeming death she knew not, and when she recovered, it was some few minutes before recollection came back to her, and she really remembered what had so completely overpowered her.

But when her reason did resume its sway, and she recollected that it was some danger to Anna, which had first alarmed her, she called her loudly by her name.

"Anna, Anna, speak to me."

"Mother, mother," replied the young girl. "Oh, come to me."

These words supplied strength to the old woman, and rising she made her way immediately into the chamber of her daughter, whom she found in an agony of fear; a light was procured, and then Anna flung herself upon her mother's neck, and wept abundantly.

"Oh, mother, tell me, convince me that it was only a dream."

"What, my child? oh what?"

The girl trembled so much that it was only by the utmost persuasion that the following account was got from her, of the cause of her fright.

She said that she had gone to sleep as usual within a very few minutes after going to bed, that she enjoyed a calm, and uninterrupted slumber, the duration of which she had no means whatever of guessing, but she was partially awakened by a noise at the window of her room.

She instantly rose and stood looking at the window, on which a sort of shadow seemed to pass without, which alarmed her exceedingly.

Still as it did not come gain, and as she certainly had not been fully awake when she sprung from her bed, she had thought it quite possible that all might be a dream, and had forborne from making any alarm upon the subject.

After some hesitation she had persuaded herself to go to bed again, and when there, although she sometimes started awake fancying she heard something, she at length yielded to sleep, and again slept, soundly for a time, until a new circumstance awakened her.

She thought she felt something touching her about the neck, and after opening her eyes, the moonlight, which at that moment happened to be very bright, disclosed to her a white figure standing by the side of her bed, the face of which figure was leaning over her, and within a very few inches of her own.

Terror at first deprived her of all power of speech or motion, but as the figure did not move, she at length gave utterance to her fears in that shriek which had come from her lips, and so much alarmed the mother.

This was all the young girl could say, with the exception that the figure when she shrieked appeared to glide away, but where to she had no means of telling, for some clouds at that moment came again over the face of the moon.

The mother was much affected and terrified, and at first she thought of calling up her neighbours, but at length as the night was considerably advanced, and the intruder gone, they agreed to let the matter rest till morning, and the mother retired to her room again.

How long it was before the shriek from her daughter's room came again she did not know, but come again it did.

Yes, again came the dreadful shriek. It was — it could be no delusion now — and the mother once more sprung from her couch to rush to the rescue of her child.

Confused and bewildered, she darted onward to the chamber, but the door was fast, nor could all her exertions suffice to open it.

"Anna, Anna!" she shouted, "speak to me. One word only, my child, my child."

All was still. The trembling mother placed her ear to the door, and she heard a strange sucking sound, as if an animal was drinking with labour and difficulty. Her head seemed to be on fire, and her senses were upon the point of leaving her, but she did manage to reach her own room. She flew to the little casement — she dashed it open.

"Help! help! help! — for the love of God, help!"

There was no reply.

Again she raised her voice in shrieking wild accents.

"Help! — murder! — help!"

"What is it?" shouted a man's voice. It was one who was going some distance to take in his fishing nets.

"Oh! thank God, some human being hears me. Come in, come in."

"How am I to get in?"

"Stay a moment, and I will come down and open the cottage door for you. For the love of mercy do not go away."

Trembling and terrified to a dreadful excess, the old woman went down stairs and let the man into the cottage, when they both proceeded up to the chamber of the daughter.

"What do you suppose is the matter?" asked the fisherman.

"Oh! I know not — I know not; but twice to-night — twice has this dreadful alarm happened. Do not leave us — oh, do not."

"I don't want; but I should hardly think thieves would find it worth their while to come here at all for what they would get. You must have been dreaming."

"Oh, that I could think so!"

Anna's chamber was reached; and there, to the horror of the mother, she was found lying perfectly insensible on her bed, with a quantity of blood smeared about her neck.

"Why, it's a murder!" cried the fisherman; and firmly impressed with such a belief, he ran out of the house to spread an alarm.

The window of the chamber was wide open, and from that the mother now cried aloud for help; so that between her and the fisherman, such a disturbance was made all over the neighbourhood, that they were soon likely to have more assistance than could be useful.

The people living the nearest were soon roused, and they roused others, while the distracted woman, who believed Anna was dead, called for justice and for vengeance.

The alarm spread from house to house — from cottage to hall — and, in the course of half-an-hour, most of the inhabitants of the village had risen to hear the old dame's account of the horrible proceeding that had taken place that night in the cottage.

Exaggeration was out of the question. The fact itself was more than sufficient to induce the greatest amount of horror in the minds of all who heard it, and there was one, and only one, whose information enabled him to give a name to the apparition that had assaulted Anna. That one was the schoolmaster of the place, and he, after hearing the story, said, —

"If one could persuade oneself at all of the existence of such horrors, one would suppose that a vampire had visited the cottage."

This was a theme that was likely to be popular. The schoolmaster foolishly gave way to the vanity, and explained what a vampire was — or was supposed and said to be; and soon the whole place was in a state of the most indescribable alarm upon the subject.

As yet the horrible news had not reached the Grange, but it was destined soon to do so; and better would it have been that any one had at once plunged a dagger in the heart of poor Sir George Crofton than that there should be thought to be such a horrible confirmation of his worst fears.

To be sure, his daughter was not named, but he received the news with a scream of anguish, and fell insensible into the arms of his son.

All was confusion. The servants ran hither and thither, not knowing what to do, and it was not until Mr. Bevan arrived that something like order was restored. He as a privileged friend assumed for the nonce a kind of dictatorship at the Grange, and gave orders, which were cheerfully and promptly obeyed. Then he desired a strictly private interview with Sir George.

It was, or course, granted to him; but the old baronet begged that Charles and Edwin might now know all. It was Emma alone from whom he wished to keep the awful truth.

CCXIX.

THE AWFUL SUPPOSITION. — A RESOLUTION.

IT WAS WITH SOME reluctance that the clergyman spoke.

"Sir," he said to the old baronet, "and you, my young gentleman, I am afraid — very much afraid, that I am doing anything but right in countenancing a supposition so utterly at variance with all my own notions and feelings; but my abhorrence of a secret impels me to speak."

"Say on, sir — say on," cried Sir George. "Perhaps we are better prepared to hear what you have to tell, than you imagine."

After this Mr. Bevan had less reluctance to speak, he said, —

"I was aware, although you all were not, that Mr. Ringwood intended to keep watch last night in the church, in order to test the truth of what had been told by Will Stephens, the sexton. I did all I could to persuade him from making the attempt, but when I found that nothing else would satisfy him, I thought it prudent to give him the means of carrying out what had become such a fixed intention with him, that to oppose it was to do far more mischief than to grant it all the aid I had in my power to do."

Sir George gave a nod of assent.

"He went there," continued Mr. Bevan, "with a private key of my own, and took his place in the church."

"I wish, sir, you had been with him," said Edwin.

"Yes," added Charles. "If you, with your cool, calm, unbiased judgment had been there, we should have been much better able to come to a correct conclusion about what occurred; for that something did occur, or was supposed by Ringwood to do so, we can well guess."

"I wish, indeed, I had been there," said Mr. Bevan, "but he begged so earnestly to be allowed to go alone, that I had not the heart to refuse him."

"And what happened, sir?"

"I will tell you. I gave him a key which admitted him to the church, by the small private entrance, at which I usually go in myself; in fact, it was my own private key, for I at times visit the church, and wish to do so, when I am not expected by those who have the ordinary charge of it."

"We have heard as much."

"No doubt. Well, then, I say I gave him that key, but it was my sympathy with his evident distress rather than my judgment which consented to do so, and I had hardly done it, when I began to busy myself with conjectures, and to deeply regret that I had yielded to him so easily. 'What if he, in his excited and grief-stricken state of mind, should come to some serious mischief?' I said to myself, 'should not I be very much to blame? Would not all prudent persons say that I did very wrong to send a man in such a condition of mind into a church at midnight, alone?'"

"Your motives and your known character, sir, would protect you," said Charles.

"I hope so," continued Mr. Bevan. "I think it would from all other charges, but imprudence; and if any great mischance had befallen Ringwood, I should not so readily have forgiven myself, as others might have been induced to forgive me."

"I understand that feeling," said Sir George.

"Well, then, with such sensations tugging at my heart, no wonder I could not rest, and so at a little after twelve, I rose, and hastily dressing myself, I left my house as noiselessly as possible, and made my way towards the church. The moon's light was at that time obscured, but every spot was so familiar to me, that I was able to go with speed, and I soon reached the venerable building. I walked round it, until I came to the door, the key of which I had given to Mr. Ringwood; it was open,

but the moment I crossed the threshold, I stumbled on his insensible form."

"Go on! go on! He had seen something terrible," gasped Sir George; "I am nerved, I think, for the very worst; I pray you, sir, go on, and tell me all."

"I will, Sir George, because I feel convinced it is my duty to conceal nothing in this transaction, and because I think you had better more calmly and dispassionately, and without exaggeration, hear from me all that is to be told."

"That is a good reason, sir," said Edwin. "We should, of course, hear all from other sources, and probably, with all the aids that a feeling for the marvellous could append to it."

"That is my impression. When, then, I stumbled over a person lying just within the little private door of the church, I had no immediate means of knowing who it was; I tell you it was Ringwood, because I afterwards discovered as much. I had the means of getting a light; when I did so, I found Ringwood lying in a swoon, while at the same time, I could not but notice a large bruise upon his forehead.

"Of course, my first duty was to look after him, instead of troubling myself about his assailant, and having placed him in as convenient a posture as I could, I hurried home again, and roused up my servants. With their assistance I got him to my house, and placed him in bed."

"And did you search the church, sir?"

"I did. I went back and searched it thoroughly, but found nothing at all suspicious. Everything was in its right place, and I could not account for the affair at all, because of the wound that Ringwood had. I was most anxious to hear from him that he had had a fall."

"But—but," said Sir George, falteringly, "he told a different story."

"He did."

"A story which you will not keep from us."

"I do not feel myself justified, as I have said, in keeping it from you. This is it."

The clergyman then related to the family of the Croftons what is already known to the reader concerning the adventures of Ringwood in the old church, and which that morning, upon his recovery, Ringwood had told to him most circumstantially.

We need scarcely say that this recital was listened to with the most agonized feelings. Poor Sir George appeared to be most completely overcome by it. He trembled excessively, and could not command himself sufficiently to speak.

The two brothers looked at each other in dismay.

"Now, I pray you all to consider this matter more calmly," said Mr. Bevan, "than you seem inclined to do."

"Calmly," gasped Sir George, "calmly."

"Yes—what evidence have we after all that the whole affair is anything more than a dream of Mr. Ringwood's?"

"Does he doubt it?"

"No—I am bound to tell you that he does not; but we may well do so for all that. He is the last person who is likely to give in to the opinion that it is a mere vision, so strangely impressed as it is upon his imagination. Recollect always that he went to the church prepared to see something."

"Oh, if we could but think it unreal," said Sir George, glancing at his sons, as if to gather their opinions of the matter from their countenances.

"I will cling to such a thought," said Charles, "until I am convinced otherwise through the medium of my own senses."

"And I," said Edwin.

"You are right," added Mr. Bevan, "I never in the whole course of my experience heard of anything of which people should be so slow of believing in, as this most uncomfortable affair. You now know all, and it is for yourselves, of course, to make whatever determination you think fit. If I might advise, it would be that you all take a short tour, perhaps on the continent for a time."

"Mr. Bevan," said Sir George, in a kindly tone, "I am greatly obliged to you. The suggestion I know springs from the very best and friendly motives; but it carries with it a strong presumption that you really do think there is something in all this affair which it would be as well to have settled in my absence."

The clergyman could not deny but that some such feeling was at the bottom of his advice; but still he would not admit that he was at all convinced of the reality of what was presumed to have happened, and a short pause in the conversation ensued, after which Sir George spoke with a solemn air of determination, saying to his sons, as well as to his friend and pastor, Mr. Bevan,

"When I tell you that I have made a determination from which nothing but the hand of heaven visiting me with death shall move me, I hope no one here will try to dissuade me from carrying it out."

After such an exordium it was a difficult thing to say anything to him, so he continued,—

"My child was dear—very dear to me

in life, and I have no superstitious fears concerning one who held such a place in my affections. I am resolved that to-night I will watch her poor remains, and at once convince myself of a horror that may drive me mad or take a mountain of grief and apprehension off my heart."

"Father," cried Charles, "you will allow me to accompany you."

"And me," added Edwin.

"My sons, you are both deeply interested in this matter — you would be miserable while I was gone if you were not with me. Moreover, I will not trust my own imagination entirely — we will all three go, and then we cannot be deceived. This is my most solemn resolution."

"I have only one thing to say regarding it," said Mr. Bevan, "that is, to prefer an earnest request that you will allow me to be one of the party — you shall sit in a pew of the church, that shall command a view of the whole building."

"Accompany us, Mr. Bevan, if you will," said Sir George, "but I sit in no pew."

"No pew?"

"No. But my child's coffin, in the vault where repose the remains of more than one of my race who had been dear to me in life, will I take my place."

There was an earnest resolved solemnity about Sir George's manner, which showed that he was not to be turned from his purpose, and Mr. Bevan

accordingly did not attempt to do so. He had done what he scarcely expected, that is, got a consent to accompany him to the night vigil, and at all events let what would happen, he as a more disinterested party than the others, would be able, probably to interfere and prevent any disastrous circumstances from arising.

"Say nothing of what has been determined on to any one," said Sir George, "keep it a profound secret, sir, and this night will put an end to the agony of doubt."

"Depend upon me. Will you come to my house at eleven o'clock, or shall I come here?"

"We will come to you; it is in the way."

Thus then the affair was settled, so far satisfactorily, that there was to be a watch actually now in the vault, so that there could be no delusion, no trick practised.

What will be the result will be shown very shortly; in the meantime we cannot but tremble at what that attached and nearly heart-broken father may have still to go through.

The excitement too in the village was immense; for the story of the vampyre's attack upon the young girl was fresh in everybody's mouth, and it lost nothing of its real horrors by the frequency with which it was repeated, and the terror-stricken manner in which it was dilated upon.

CCXX.

THE GRAND CONSULTATION IN THE ALE-HOUSE. — THE AWFUL SUGGESTION.

SIR GEORGE CROFTON and his family could form no idea, owing to not being in a position to know, of the state of excitement produced in the village by the mysterious and frightful attack which had been made upon the widow's daughter.

When people are very much absorbed with their own grief, they are apt to set a lighter value upon those of others, and thus it was that the family of the Croftons was so entirely taken up with what itself felt and had to do that there was little room for sympathy with others.

Mr. Bevan likewise, from his peculiar and respectable position, was not likely to be made the depository of gossiping secrets; the inhabitants of that little place were in the habit of approaching him with respect, so that, although, as we are aware, he had heard from Will Stephens, the sexton, a full and particular account of what had happened to him in the old church, and was likewise cognizant of the story of the midnight attack upon the widow's daughter, he was not fully aware of the startling effect which those circumstances had had upon the small population of that fishing village.

We are bound to believe that if he had had any idea of the real result of those operations or of what was contemplated as their result — he would have done his best to adopt some course to prevent any disastrous collision.

We, however, with all the data and materials of this most singular narrative before us, are enabled to detail to the reader facts and occurrences as they took place actually, without waiting the arrival of those periods at which they reached the knowledge of those actors in the gloomy drama of real life.

Our readers, then, will please to know that the excitement among the inhabitants of the place was of that violent and overbearing description, that all the occupations of the villagers were abandoned, and a spirit of idleness, sadly suggestive of mischief, began to be prevalent among them.

This feeling was increased by frequent visits to the ale-house, the liquor of which was well esteemed by Will Stephens, as may be readily imagined; and towards evening the large old-fashioned parlour of that place of entertainment became crowded with a motley assemblage, whose sole purpose in meeting together was to drink strong ale, and discuss the irritating and exciting subject of the appearance of the vampyre in the village.

This discussion, from being at first a sober, serious, and alarmed one, became noisy and violent; and at length a blacksmith, who was a great man in the politics of the place, and who of all things in the world most admired to hear his own voice, rose and addressed his compeers in something of a set speech.

"Listen to me," he said; "are we to have the blood sucked out of all our bodies by a lot of vampyres? Is our wives and daughters to be murdered in the middle of the night?"

"No, no, no," cried many voices; "certainly not."

"Is we to be made into victims, or isn't we? What's Sir George Crofton and his family to us? To be sure he's the landlord of some of us, and a very good landlord he is, too, as long as we pay our rent."

"Hear, hear, hear."

"But there's no saying how long he might be so, if we didn't."

"Bravo, Dick!" cried the master of the place, handing the orator a pot; "bravo, Dick! take a pull at that, old fellow."

"Thank you, Muggins. Now, what I proposes is —"

"Stand on a chair, and let's all hear you."

"Thank you," said the blacksmith; and getting upon a chair, he was about to commence again, when some one advised him to get upon the table, but in an effort to accomplish that feat, he unfortunately trod upon what was a mere flap of the table, which had not sufficient power to support his weight, and down he came amid an assemblage of pots, jugs, and glasses, which made a most alarming crash.

This roused the fury of the landlord, who had no idea of being made such a sufferer in the transaction, and he accordingly began to declaim heavily at his loss.

A dispute arose as to how he was to be repaid, and it was finally settled that a general subscription would be the best mode of reimbursing him.

If anything was wanting to work up the feelings of the topers at the public-house to the highest pitch of aggravation, it certainly was their having to disburse for breakages a sum of money which, if liquefied, would have trickled most luxuriously down their throats. They were consequently ripe and ready for anything which promised vengeance upon anybody.

The blacksmith was not discomfited by his fall — when is a man who is fond of hearing himself talk discomfited by anything? — and he soon resumed his oration in the following words: —

"Is we to be put upon in this kind of way? Why, we shan't be able to sleep in our beds. All I asks is, is we to put up with it?"

"But what are we to do?" said one.

"Ah! there's the question," said the blacksmith, "I don't know exactly."

"Let's ask old Timothy Brown," said the butcher, "he's the oldest man here."

This was assented to; and accordingly the individual mentioned was questioned as to his ideas of the way of avoiding the alarming catastrophe which seemed to be impending over them. He advised them to wait patiently till the next night, and keep awake till the unwelcome nocturnal visitor made its appearance, when whoever it might visit was boldly to assail it, without any fear of the consequences to himself, till further assistance could be procured.

After Timothy Brown had delivered himself of this piece of advice, a dead silence ensued among the late boisterous company. There were many dissentients, and a few who seemed in favour of a trial of the practicability of the plan. Both parties seemed to give some consideration to the proposition, and they were by far too much engaged in thinking of the advice which had been given them, to pay much attention to the quarter from whence it had emanated; more particularly, too, as from his age and infirmities, he was incapacitated from carrying it out or from giving any active assistance to those who were disposed to do so.

A great many efforts were made to get him to say more, particularly with reference to the case under consideration, as being no common one; but the octogenarian had made his effort, and he only replied to the remonstrances of those who, alternately by coaxing and bullying, strove to get information from him, by a vacant stare.

"It's of no use," said the butcher, "you'll get nothing more now from old Timothy; he's done up now, that's quite clear, and ten to one if the excitement of to-night won't go a good way towards slaughtering him before his time."

"Well, it may be so," cried the blacksmith, "but still it's good advice, and as I said before it comes to this — is we to be afraid to lay down in our beds at night, or isn't we?"

Before any reply could be made to this interrogatory, the old clock that was in the public-house parlour struck the hour of eleven, and another peal of thunder seemed to be answering to the tinkling sounds.

"It's a rough night," said one, "I thought there would be a storm before morning by the look of the sun at setting — it went down with a strange fiery redness behind a bank of clouds. I move for going home."

"Who talks of going home," cried the blacksmith, "when vampires are abroad? hasn't old Timothy said, that a stormy night was the very one to settle the thing in."

"No," cried another, "he did not say night at all."

"I don't care whether he said night or day; I've made up my mind to do something; there's no doubt about it but that a vampyre is about the old church. Who'll come with me and ferret it out? it will be good service done to everybody's fireside."

CCXXI.

THE NIGHT WATCH. — THE VAULT.

IT WAS EACH MOMENT becoming a more difficult affair to carry on any conversation in the public-house parlour, for not only did the thunder each moment almost interrupt the speakers with its loud reverberations, but now and then such a tremendous gust of wind would sweep round the house that it would be quite impossible for any one to make himself heard amidst its loud howling noise.

These were circumstances, however, which greatly aided, no doubt, in the getting-up of a superstitious feeling in the minds of the people there assembled, which made them ripe for any proposition, which perhaps in their soberer moments they would have regarded with considerable dismay; hence when the blacksmith rushed to the door, crying,—

"Who will follow me to the old church and lay hold of the vampyre?" about half-a-dozen of the boldest and most reckless,—and be it told to their honour (if there be any honour in such an enterprise, which after all, was a grossly selfish one,) they were the worst characters in the village—started to their feet to accompany him thither.

There are many persons who waver about an enterprise, who will join it when it has a show of force, and thus was it with this affair. The moment it was found that the blacksmith's proposition had some half-dozen stout adherents, he got as many more—some of whom joined him from curiosity, and some from dread of being thought to lack courage by their companions if they held off.

There was now a sufficiently large party to make a respectable demonstration, and quite elated with his success, and caring little for the land storm that was raging, the blacksmith, closely followed by the butcher, who had no objection in life to the affair, especially as he was at variance with the parson concerning the tithes of a little farm he kept, called out,—

"To the church—to the church!" and followed by the rabble, rushed forward in the direction of the sacred edifice.

A S THE HOUR OF ELEVEN has struck, and as the reader is aware that at that hour Sir George Crofton and his two sons, accompanied by Mr. Bevan, had agreed to go to the church on their melancholy errand, we will leave the noisy brawlers of the alehouse for the purpose of detailling the proceedings of those whose fortunes we feel more closely interested in.

The baronet was by no means wavering in his determination, notwithstanding it had been made at a time of unusual excitement, when second thoughts might have been allowed to step in, and suggest some other course of proceeding.

Now, Mr. Bevan was not without his own private hopes that such would be the case; for what he dreaded above all other things was, the truth of the affair, and that Sir George would have the horror of discovering that there was much more in the popular superstition than, without ocular demonstration, he would have been inclined to admit.

Although a man of education and of refined abilities, the evidence that had already showed itself to him of the existence at all events of some supernatural being, with powers analogous to those of the fabled vampyre, was such that he could not wholly deny, without stultifying his intellect, that there might be such things.

It is a sad circumstance when the mind is, as it were, compelled to receive undeniable evidence of a something which the judgment has the strongest general reasons for disputing, and that was precisely the position of Mr. Bevan, and a most unenviable one it was.

That night's proceedings, however, in the vault, he felt must put an end to all doubts and perplexity upon the subject, and so, with a fervent hope that in some at-present-inexplicable manner, the thing would be found to be a delusion, he waited more anxiously the arrival of the Croftons at the parsonage.

At half past ten o'clock, instead of eleven, for as the evening advanced, Sir George Crofton had shown such an amount of nervousness that his sons had thought it would be better to bring him to the parsonage, they arrived; and Mr. Bevan perceived at once what a remarkable effect grief and anxiety had already had upon the features of the baronet.

He was a different man to what, but a few days since, he had been, and more than ever the kind clergyman felt inclined to doubt the expediency of his being present on such an occasion, and yet how to prevent him if he were really determined, was a matter of no small difficulty.

"My dear friend," said Mr. Bevan, "will you pardon me if I make an effort now to persuade you to abandon this enterprise?"

"I can pardon the effort easily," said Sir George Crofton, "because I know it is dictated by the best of motives, but I would fain be spared it, for I am determined."

"I will say no more, but only with deep sincerity hope that you may return to your dwelling, each relieved from the load of anxiety that now oppresses you."

"I hope to Heaven it may be so."

"The night looks strange and still," said Charles, who wished to draw his father's attention as much as possible from too close a contemplation of the expedition on which they were bound.

"It does," said Edwin; "I should not be surprised at a storm, for there is every indication of some disturbance of the elements."

"Let it come," said Sir George, who fancied that in all those remarks he detected nothing but a wish to withdraw him from his enterprise; "Let it come. I have a duty to perform, and I will do it, though Heaven's thunders should rock the very earth—the forked lightning is not launched at the father who goes to watch at the grave of his child."

Charles and Edwin, upon finding that Sir George was in the mood to make a misapplication of whatever was said to him, desisted from further remarks, but left Mr. Bevan quietly to converse with him, in a calm and unirritating manner.

It was the object of the clergyman to put off as much time as possible before proceeding to the church, so that the period to be spent in the family vault of the Croftons should be lessened as much as possible, for he felt assured that each minute there wasted would be one of great agony to the bereaved father, who would feel himself once again in such close approximation to that daughter on whom he had placed some of his dearest affections.

Sir George, however, defeated this intention, by promptly rising when his watch told him that the hour of eleven had arrived, and it was in vain to attempt to stultify him into a belief that he was wrong as regarded the time, for the church was sufficiently near for them to hear the hour of eleven pealed forth from its ancient steeple.

"Come," said Sir George, "the hour has arrived. I pray you do not delay. I know you are all anxious and fearful concerning me, but I have a spirit of resolution and firmness in this affair which shall yet stand me in good stead. I shall not shrink, as you imagine I shall shrink. Come, then, at once—it is suspense and delay which frets me, and not action."

These words enforced a better spirit into both his sons and Mr. Bevan, and in a few moments the party of four, surely sufficiently strong to overcome any unexpected obstacles, or to defeat any trickery that might be attempted to be passed off upon them, proceeded towards the church.

It will be recollected that it was just a little after that time that the storm commenced, and, in fact, the first clap of thunder, that seemed to shake the heavens, took place just as they reached the old grave-yard adjoining to the sacred building.

"There!" exclaimed Charles, "I thought that it would come."

"What matter?" said Sir George, "come on."

"Humour him in everything," said Mr. Bevan, "It is madness now to contradict him — he will not recede under any circumstances."

The natural senses of Sir George Crofton appeared to be preternaturally acute, for he turned sharply, and said quickly, but not unkindly,—

"No, he will not recede — come on."

After this, nothing was said until they reached the church door, and then while Mr. Bevan was searching in his pockets for the little key which opened the small private entrance, some vivid flashes of lightning lit up with extraordinary brilliancy the old gothic structure — the neighbouring tombs and the melancholy yew trees that waved their branches in the night air.

Perhaps the delay which ensued before Mr. Bevan could find the key, likewise arose from the wish to keep Sir George as short a time as possible within the vault; but he at length produced it, for any further delay could only be accounted for by saying that he had it not.

The small arched doorway was speedily cleared, and as another peal of thunder broke overhead in awful grandeur of sound, they entered the church.

Mr. Bevan took the precaution this time to close the door, so that there could be no interruption from without.

"Now, Sir George," he said, "remember your promise. You are to come away freely at the first dawn of day, and if nothing by then has occurred to strengthen the frightful supposition which, I suppose I may say, we have all indulged in, I do hope that for ever this subject will be erased from your recollection."

"Be it so," said Sir George; "be it so."

Mr. Bevan then busied himself in lighting a lantern, and from beneath one of the pews, where they were hidden, he procured a couple of crowbars, with which to raise the stone that covered the entrance to the vault.

These preparations took up some little time, so that the old clock had chimed the quarter past eleven, and must have been rapidly getting on to the half-hour, before they stood in the aisle close to the vault.

"This marble slab," said Sir George, as he cast his eyes upon it, "always hitherto has been cemented in its place. Why is it not so now?"

"Is it not?" said Mr. Bevan.

"No — lend me the light."

Mr. Bevan was averse to lending him the light, but he could not very well refuse it; and when Sir George Crofton had looked more minutely at the marble slab, he saw that it had been cemented, but that the cement was torn and broken away, as if some violence had been used for the purpose of opening the vault; but whether that violence came from within or without was a matter of conjecture.

CCXXII.

THE MADMAN. — THE VAMPYRE.

"WHAT DOES THIS mean?" cried Sir George Crofton, excitedly.

"Hush!" said Mr. Bevan, "I pray you be calm, sir. If you are to make any discovery that will give you peace of mind, rest assured it will not be made by violence."

"You do not answer my question."

"I cannot answer it. Remember that I know no more than you do, and that, like yourselves, I am an adventurer here in search of the truth."

Sir George said no more upon that head, but with clasped hands and downcast eyes he stood in silence, while his two sons, armed with the crowbars that Mr. Bevan had provided for the occasion, proceeded to lift up the marble slab that covered the vault where lay their sister's remains.

The work was not one of great difficulty, for the slab was not very large, and as it was not cemented down, it yield at once to the powerful leverage that was brought to play against it, and in a few minutes it was placed aside, and the yawning abyss appeared before them.

"Oh! sir," said Mr. Bevan, "even now at this late hour, and when the proceedings have commenced, I pray you to pause."

"Pause!" cried Sir George, passionately, "pause for what?"

"Disturb not the dead, and let them rest in peace. Absolve your mind from the dangerous and perhaps fatal fancies that possess it, and let us say a prayer, and close again this entrance to the tomb."

The sons hesitated, and they probably would have taken the clergyman's advice, but Sir George was firm.

"No, sir," he said, "already have I suffered much in coming thus far; I will not retreat until I have effected all my purpose. I swear it, by Heaven, whose temple we now are in. You would not, Mr. Bevan, have me break such an oath."

"I would not; but I regret you made it. Since, however, it must be so, and this rash adventure is determined upon, follow me; I will lead you the way into these calm regions, where you can sleep, I trust, in peace."

Sir George Crofton made a step forward, as if he would have arrested Mr. Bevan's progress and lead the way himself, but already the clergyman had descended several steps, so he had nothing to do but to follow him.

This they all did, Sir George going immediately after him, and his two sons, with pale anxious-looking faces, as if they had a suspicion that the adventure would end in something terrific, came last. They glanced nervously and suspiciously about them; but they said not a word, for if they had spoken, it would have been to express great apprehension, and that was what they were ashamed to do.

Mr. Bevan carried the light, and when he felt that he was at the bottom of the stone steps, by finding that he was treading upon the sawdust that was strewn on the floor of the vault, he turned and held the lamp up at arm's length, so that his companions might see their way down the steps.

In another minute they all stood on the floor of the vault.

The light burnt with rather a faint and sickly glare, for so rapidly were noxious gases evolved in that receptacle for the dead, that notwithstanding it had been so frequently opened as it had been lately, they had again accumulated.

In a few moments, however, this was partially remedied by the air from the church above, and the light burnt more brilliantly — indeed, quite sufficiently so to enable them to look around them in the vault.

Sir George Crofton's feelings at that moment must have been of the most painful and harrowing description. He had lived long enough to be a witness of the death and the obsequies of many members of his family whom he had loved fondly, and there he stood in that chamber of death, surrounded by all the remains of those beings, the memory of whose appearance and voices came now freshly upon his mind.

Mr. Bevan could well guess the nature of the sad thoughts that transpired in the breast of the baronet, and the sons having by accident cast their eyes upon the coffin that contained the remains of their mother, regarded it in silence, while memory was busy, too, within them in conjuring up her image.

"And it has come to this," said Sir George, solemnly.

"We must all come to this," interposed Mr. Bevan; "this is indeed a place for solemn and holy thoughts — for self-examination, for self-condemnation."

"But there is peace here."

"There is — the peace that shall be eternal."

"Hark! hark!" said Charles; "what is that?"

"The wind," said Mr. Bevan; "nothing but the wind howling round and through the old belfry — you will remember that it is a boisterous night."

"Turn, turn, father."

Sir George turned and looked at Charles, who pointed in silence to the coffin which contained the corpse of his mother. The light gleamed upon the plate on which was engraved her name. Sir George's features moved convulsively as he read it, and he turned aside to hide a sudden gush of emotion that came over him.

After a few minutes, he touched Mr. Bevan on the arm, and said in a whisper, —

"Where did they place my child?"

The clergyman pointed to the narrow shelf on which was the coffin of Clara Crofton, and then Sir George, making a great effort to overcome his feelings, said, —

"Mr. Bevan, our worthy minister and friend, and you, likewise, my boys, hear me. You can guess to some extent, but not wholly — that can only be known by God — the agony that a sight of the poor remains of her who has gone from me in all the pride of her youth and beauty, must be to me; yet now that I am here I consider it to be my duty to look once again upon the face of my child—my—my lost Clara."

"Oh! father, father," said Edwin, "forego this purpose."

"You will spare us this," cried Charles.

"Repent you, sir," said Mr. Bevan, "of the wish. Let her rest in peace. The dead are sanctified."

"The dead are sanctified,—but I am her father."

"Nay, Sir George, let me implore you."

"Implore me to what, sir? Not to look upon the face of my own child? Peace—peace. It is no profanation for one who loved her as I loved her to look upon her once again. Urge me no more."

"This is in vain," said Charles.

"You are right—it is in vain."

A shriek burst from the lips of Edwin at this moment, and flinging his arms around his father, he held him back. Mr. Bevan, too, gave a cry of terror, and Charles stood with his hands clasped, as if turned to stone.

Their eyes were all bent upon Clara's coffin.

The lid moved, and a strange sound was heard from within that receptacle for the dead—the clock of the old church struck twelve—the coffin lid moved again, and then sliding on one side, it eventually fell upon the floor of the vault.

The four spectators of this scene were struck speechless for the time with terror. Then they stood gazing at the coffin as if they were so many statues.

And now the light which Mr. Bevan still for a miracle held in his trembling grasp, shone on a mass of white clothing within the coffin, and in another moment that white clothing was observed to be in motion. Slowly the dead form that was there rose up, and they all saw the pale and ghastly face. A streak of blood was issuing from the mouth, and the eyes were open.

Sir George Crofton lifted up both his hands, and struck his head, and then he burst into a wild frightful laugh. It was the laugh of insanity.

Mr. Bevan dropped the light, and all was darkness.

"Ha, ha, ha, ha, ha!" laughed Sir George Crofton. "Ha, ha, ha, ha, ha!" and the horrible laugh was taken up by many an echo in the old church, and responded to with strange and most unearthly reverberations. "Ha, ha, ha, ha!" Oh what a dreadful sound that was coming at such a time from the lips of the father.

"Fly Edwin—oh, fly," cried Charles.

Edwin screamed twice, for he was full of horror, and then he fell on the floor of the vault in a state of insensibility.

Charles had just sense left him to spring towards the steps, and make a frantic effort to reach the church; in his hurry he fell twice, but each time rising again with a shout of despair, he resumed his efforts, and all the while the horrible laugh of his maniac father sounded in his ears, a sound which he felt that he should never forget.

By a great effort he did reach the aisle of the church, and when there, he called aloud.

"Mr. Bevan, Mr. Bevan, help—oh help! For the love of God speak. Help, help, Mr. Bevan, where are you, speak, I

and it would appear that immediately upon dropping in his horror the light in the vault, he had ran up the stairs with the intent of getting another.

"Who calls me? Who calls me?" he cried.

""I — I," said Charles. "Oh God, what a dreadful night is this."

The clergyman was trembling violently, and was very pale, but he made his way up to Charles, from whose brow the perspiration was falling in heavy drops, and then again they heard the mad Sir George laughing in the vault.

"Ha, ha, ha! ha, ha, ha! ha, ha, ha!"

"Oh God, is not that horrible?" said Charles.

"Most horrible," responded Mr. Bevan.

Bang — bang — bang! at this moment came a violent knocking at the church

implore you? Am I too going mad? Oh yes, I shall — I must. What mortal intellect can stand such a scene as this. Help, help — oh, help!"

The church was suddenly lit up by a flash of light, and turning in the direction from whence it proceeded, Charles saw Mr. Bevan approaching with a light, which he had procured from the chancel, door, and then several voices were heard without shouting.

"The vampyre — the vampyre — the vampyre."

"What is that? What is that?" said Charles.

"Nay, I know not," replied Mr. Bevan, "I am nearly distracted already. Where is your brother? Did he not escape from the vault? Where is he? Oh, that horrible laugh. Good God! that knocking too at the church door. What can be the meaning of it? Heaven in its mercy guide us now what to do."

The reader will understand the meaning of the knocking, although those bewildered persons who heard it in the church did not. The fact is, that the party from the alehouse headed by the valiant blacksmith, and heated by their too liberal potations had just arrived at the church, and were clamouring for admission.

They had seen through one of the old pointed windows, the reflection of the light which Mr. Bevan carried, and that it was that convinced them some one was there who might if he would pay attention to the uproarious summons.

The knocking lasted with terrible effect, for the old door of the sacred edifice shook again, it seemed as if certainly it could not resist the making of such an attack.

Mr. Bevan was confounded. A horrible suspicion came across him, of what was meant by those violent demands for admission, and he shook with brutal trepidation as he conjectured what might be the effect of the proceedings of a lawless mob.

"Now Heaven help us," he said, "for we shall soon I fear be powerless."

"Good God! what mean you?" said Charles.

"I scarcely know how to explain to you all my fears. The are too dreadful to think of, but while that knocking continues, what can I think?"

"I understand! they call for my sister."

"Oh call her not now by that name. Remember, and remember with a shudder, what she now is."

CCXXIII.

THE HUNT OF THE VAMPYRE.

ALL THESE OCCURRENCES which have taken a considerable time in telling, occurred as simultaneously, that although it would appear Mr. Bevan and Charles Crofton, rather neglected Sir George and Edwin who were still in the vault, they had really not had time to think of them, to say nothing of making any effort to extricate them from the frightful situation in which they were placed.

Probably, after procuring a light, Mr. Bevan would have rushed to their rescue had not that incessant knocking at the church door suggested a new and more horrible danger, still, from the evil passions of an infuriated multitude.

"Oh, Mr. Charles," he said, "if we

could but get your father away from the church, there is no knowing what an amount of misery he might be spared."

"Misery, sir; surely there is no more misery in store for us — have we not suffered enough — more than enough. Oh, Mr. Bevan, we have fallen upon evil times, and I dread to think what will yet be the end of those most frightful transactions."

The knocking at the church door continued violently, and Charles indicated a wish to proceed there to ascertain what it was, but Mr. Bevan stopped him, saying, —

"No, Charles — no — let them be, I hardly think they will venture to break into the sacred edifice, but whether they do or not, remember that your duty and mine, yours being the duty of a son, and mine that of a friend, should take us now to your father's vault."

"That is true, sir," said Charles, "lead on I will follow you."

Mr. Bevan, who had all the intellectual courage of a man of education, and of regular habits, led the way again to the vault, with the light in his hand. It was a great relief that the insane and horrible laugh of Sir George Crofton had ceased, the best friend of any man could almost have wished him dead ere their ears had drunk in such horrible sounds.

The shouts and cries from without now became incessant, and it seemed as if some weapon had been procured, wherewith to hammer violently upon the church door, for the strokes were regular and incessant, and it was evident that if they continued long that frail defence against the incursions of the rabble rout without must soon give way.

The only effect, however, which these sounds had upon Mr. Bevan was to make him hasten his progress towards the vault, for anything in the shape of a collision between those who wanted to take the church by storm, and Sir George Crofton, was indeed most highly to be deprecated.

The steps were not many in number, and once again the clergyman and Charles Crofton stood upon the sawdust that covered the flooring of the vault.

At first, in consequence of the flaring of the light, the state of affairs in that dismal region could not be ascertained; but as soon as they could get a view, they found Sir George lying apparently in a state of insensibility across the coffin of his daughter Clara, while Edwin was in a swoon close to his feet.

"Sir George, Sir George," cried Mr. Bevan, "arouse yourself; it is necessary that you leave this place at once."

The baronet got up and glanced at the intruders. Charles uttered a deep groan, for the most superficial observation of his father's face was sufficient to convince him that reason had fled, and that wildness had set up his wild dominion in his brain.

"Father — father," he cried, "speak to me, and dissipate a frightful thought."

"What would you have of me," said Sir George; "I am a vampyre, and this is my tomb — you should see me in the rays of the cold moon gliding 'twixt earth and heaven, and panting for a victim. I am a vampyre."

At this moment Edwin seemed to be partially recovering, for his eyes opened as he lay upon the floor, and he looked around him with a bewildered gaze, which soon settled into one of more intelligence as memory resumed her sway, and he recollected the various circumstances that had brought him into his present position.

"Rouse yourself, Edwin, rouse yourself," cried Mr. Bevan, "you must aid us to remove your father."

"Do you talk of me?" said Sir George, "know you not that I am one of those supernatural existences known as the death and despair-dealing vampyres — it's time I took my nightly prowl to look for victims. I must have blood — I must have blood."

"Gracious Heaven! he raves," said Charles.

"Heed him not," said Mr. Bevan — "heed him not, and touch him not, so that he leave the place — when we have him once clear of the church we can procure assistance, and take him to his own home."

"Edwin," whispered Charles, "what of our sister."

Edwin shook his head and shuddered. "I know nothing but that I saw her — oh, horrible sight, rising from her coffin, and then in a convulsion of terror my senses fled — a frightful ringing laugh came on my ears, and from that time till now, be the period long or short, I have been blessed by a death-like trance."

"Blessed indeed," said Mr. Bevan; "tarry one moment."

Sir George Crofton was ascending the steps of the vault, but his two sons paused for an instant at the request of Mr. Bevan, and then the latter approaching Clara's coffin slightly removed the lid, and was gratified as far as any feeling could be considered gratification under such circumstances, to find that the corpse occupied an ordinary position in its narrow resting place.

"All's right," he said, "let us persuade ourselves that this too has been but a dream, that we have been deceived, and that imagination has played us tricks it is accustomed to play to those who give it the rein at such hours as these — let us think and believe anything rather than that what we have seen to-night is real."

As he spoke these words, he ascended hastily the steps in pursuit of Sir George, who, by this time had alone reached the top.

The heavy strokes against the door of the church had ceased, but an odd sort of scraping, rattling sound at the lock convinced the clergyman that a workman of more skill than he who had wielded the hammer, was now at work, endeavouring to force an entrance.

"Oh, if we could but get out," he said, "by the small private entrance, all might be well; Charles, urge your father, I pray you."

Charles did so to the best of his ability, but the blacksmith who had originally incited the crowd to attack the church, in order to get possession of the body of the vampyre, had sent to his workshop for the tools of his craft, and soon quietly accomplished by skill what brute force would have been a long time about, namely, the opening of the church-door.

It was flung wide open, before Sir George Croton and his sons could reach the small private entrance, of which Mr. Bevan had the key.

The sight of the multitude of persons, for they looked such crowds in the church porch, materially increased the incipient sadness of the bereaved father.

CCXXIV.

THE FATE OF SIR GEORGE. — THE CROSS-ROAD.

SIR GEORGE, WHEN HE SAW the crowd of persons, seemed to have some undefined idea that they were enemies, but this would not have been productive of any serious consequences, if it had not most unfortunately happened that a most formidable weapon was within his grasp.

That weapon consisted of one of the long iron crowbars which had been successfully used by his own sons in order to force a passage to the family vault, where such horrors had been witnessed.

Suddenly, then, seizing this weapon, which, in the hands of a ferocious man was a most awful one, he swung it once round his head, and then rushed upon those he considered his foes.

He dealt but three blows, and at each of those one of the assailants fell lifeless in the church porch.

To resist, or, to attempt to contend with a man so armed, and apparently possessed of such preternatural strength, was what none of the party wished, and accordingly a free passage was left for him, and he rushed out of the church into the night air shouting for vengeance, and still at interval, accusing himself of being a vampyre, a most dangerous theme to touch upon, considering the then state of feeling in that little district.

Anxiety for the safety of Sir George induced his sons and Mr. Bevan to rush after him, regardless of all other consequences, so that the church, the vaults, and everything they contained, were left to the mercy of a mob infuriated by superstition, rendered still more desperate by the loss of three of their number in so sudden and exampled a manner.

They opposed no obstacle to the leaving of those persons, who thus for dearer considerations abandoned the old church, but they rushed with wild shouts and gesticulations into the building.

"The vampyre, the vampyre," cried the blacksmith, "death to the vampyre — death and destruction to the vampyre."

"Hurrah!" cried another, "to the vaults; this way to Sir George Crofton's vault."

There seemed to be little doubt now, but that this disorderly rabble would execute summary vengeance upon the supposed nocturnal disturber of the peace of the district.

Ever and anon, too, as these shouts of discord, and of threatening vengeance, rose upon the night air, there would come the distant muttering of thunder, for the storm had not yet ceased, although its worst fury had certainly passed away.

Dark and heavy clouds were sweeping up from the horizon, and it seemed to be tolerably evident that some heavy deluge of rain would eventually settle the fury of the elements, and reconcile the discord of wind and electricity.

Several of the rioters were provided with links and matches, so that in a few moments the whole interior of the church was brilliantly illuminated, while at the same time it presented a grotesque appearance, in consequence of the unsteady and wavering flame from the links, throw myriads of dancing shadows upon the walls.

There would have been no difficulty under any ordinary circumstances in finding the entrance to the vault, where the dead of the Crofton family should have lain in peace, but now since the large flagstone that covered the entrance to that receptacle of the grave was removed, it met their observation at once.

It was strange now to perceive how, for a moment, superstition having led them on so far, the same feeling should induce them to pause, ere they ventured to make their way down these gloomy steps.

It was a critical moment, and probably if any one or two had taken a sudden panic, the whole party might have left the church with precipitation, having done a considerable amount of mischief, and yet as it is so usual with rioters, having left their principal object unaccomplished.

The blacksmith put an end to this state of indecision, for, seizing a link from the man who was nearest to him, he darted down the steps, exclaiming as he did so, —

"Whoever's afraid, need not follow me."

This was a taunt they were not exactly prepared to submit to, and the consequence was, that in a very few moments the ancient and time-honoured vault of the Croftons was more full of the living than of the dead.

The blacksmith laid his hand upon Clara's coffin.

"Here it is," he said, "I know the very pattern of the cloth, and the fashion of the nails, I saw it at Grigson's the undertaker's before it was taken to the Grange."

"Is she there — is she there," cried half a dozen voices at once.

Even the blacksmith hesitated a moment ere he removed the lid from the receptacle of death, but when he did so, and his eyes fell upon the face of the presumed vampyre, he seemed rejoiced to find in the appearances then exhibited some sort of justification for the act of violence of which already he had been the instigator.

"Here you are," he said, "look at the bloom upon her lips, why her cheeks are fresher and rosier than ever they were while she was alive, a vampyre my mates, this is a vampyre, or may I never break bread again; and now what's to be done?"

"Burn her, burn her," cried several.

"Well," said the blacksmith, "mind it's as you like. I've brought you here, and shown you what it is, and now you can do what you like, and of course I'll lend you a hand to do it."

Any one who had been very speculative in this affair, might have detected in these last words of the blacksmith, something like an inclination to creep out of the future consequences of what might next be done, while at the same time shame deterred him from exactly leaving his companions in the lurch.

After some suggestions then, and some argumentation as to the probability or possibility of interruption — the coffin itself, was with its sad and wretched occupant, lifted from the niche where it should have remained until that awful day when the dead shall rise for judgement, and carried up the steps into the graveyard; but scarcely had they done so, when the surcharged clouds burst over their heads, and the rain came down in perfect torrents.

The deluge was of so frightful and continuous a character, that they shrank back again beneath the shelter of the church porch, and there waited until its first fury had passed away.

Such an even down storm seldom lasts long in our climate, and the consequence was that in about ten minutes the shower had so far subsided that although a continuous rain was falling it bore but a very distant comparison to what had taken place.

"How are we to burn the body on such a night as this?"

"Aye, how indeed," said another; "you could not so much as kindle a fire, and if you did, it would not live many minutes."

"I'll tell you what to do at once," said one who had as yet borne but a quiet part in the proceedings; "I'll tell you what to do at once, for I saw it done myself; a vampyre is quite as secure buried in a cross-road with a stake through its body, as if you burned it in all the fires in the world; come on, the rain won't hinder you doing that."

This was a suggestion highly approved of, and the more so as there was a cross road close at hand, so that the deed would be done quick, and the parties dispersed to their respective homes, for already the exertion they had taken, and the rain that had fallen, had had a great effect in sobering them.

And even now the perilous and disgusting operation of destroying the body, by fire or any other way, might have been abandoned, had any one of the party suggested such a course — but the dread of a future imputation of cowardice kept all silent.

Once more the coffin was raised by four of the throng, and carried through the church-yard, which was now running in many little rivulets, in consequence of the rain. The cross-road was not above a quarter of a mile from the spot, and while those who were disengaged from carrying the body, were hurrying away to get spades and mattocks, the others walked through the rain, and finally paused at the place they though suitable for that ancient superstitious rite, which it was thought would make the vampyre rest in peace.

It is hard to suppose that Sir George Crofton, his sons, and Mr. Bevan were all deceived concerning these symptoms of vitality which they had observed in the corpse of Clara; but certainly now, there was no appearance of anything of the kind, and the only suspicious circumstances appeared to be the blood upon the lips, and the very fresh-like appearance of the face.

If it were really a fact that the attack of Varney the Vampyre upon this fair young girl had converted her into one of those frightful existences, and that she had been about to leave her tomb for the purpose of seeking a repast of blood, it would appear that the intention had been checked and frustrated by the presence of Sir George and his party in the vault.

At last a dozen men now arrived well armed with spades and picks, and they commenced the work of digging a deep, rather than a capacious grave, in silence.

A gloomly and apprehensive spirit

seemed to come over the whole assemblage, and the probability is that this was chiefly owing to the fact that they now encountered no opposition, and that they were permitted unimpeded to accomplish a purpose which had never yet been attempted within the memory of any of the inhabitants of the place.

The grave was dug, and about two feet depth of soil was thrown in a huge mound upon the surface; the coffin was lowered, and there lay the corpse within that receptacle of poor humanity, unimprisoned by any lid for that had been left in the vault, and awaiting the doom which they had decreed upon it, but which they now with a shuddering horror shrunk from performing.

A hedge-stake with a sharp point had been procured, and those who held it looked around them with terrified countenances, while the few links that had not been extinguished by the rain, shed a strange and lurid glare upon all objects.

"It must be done," said the blacksmith, "don't let it be said that we got thus far and then were afraid."

"Do it then yourself," said the man that held the stake, "I dare not."

"Aye, do," cried several voices; "you brought us here, why don't you do it — are you afraid after all your boasting."

"Afraid — afraid of the dead; I'm not afraid of any of you that are alive, and it's not likely I'm ging to be afraid of a dead body; you're a pretty set of cowards. I've no animosity against the girl, but I want that we shall all sleep in peace, and that our wives and children should not be disturbed nocturnally in their blessed repose. I'll do it if none of you'll do it, and then you may thank me afterwards for the act, although I suppose if I get into trouble I shall have you all turn tail upon me."

"No, we won't — no, we won't."

"Well, well, here goes, whether you do or not. I — I'll do it directly."

"He shrinks," cried one.

"No," said another; "he'll do it — now for it, stand aside."

"Stand aside yourself — do you want to fall into the grave."

The blacksmith shuddered as he held the stake in an attitude to pierce the body, and even up to that moment it seemed to be a doubtful case, whether he would be able to accomplish his purpose or not; at length, when they all thought he was upon the point of abandoning his design, and casting the stake away, he thrust it with tremendous force through the body and the back of the coffin.

The eyes of the corpse opened wide — the hands were clenched, and a shrill, piercing shriek came from the lips — a shriek that was answered by as many as there were persons present, and then with pallid fear upon their countenances they rushed headlong from the spot.

CCXXV.

THE SOLITARY MAN. — VARNEY'S DESPAIR.

THERE LAY THE DEAD, alone, in that awful grave, dabbled in blood, and the victim of the horrible experiment that had been instituted to lay a vampire. The rain still fell heavily.

On, surely, pitying Heaven sent those drops to wash out the remembrance of such a deed. The grave slowly began to be a pool of water; it rose up the sides of the coffin, and in a few minutes, more nothing of the ghastly and the terrible contents of that grave could have been seen.

Before that took place, a man of tall stature and solemn gait stepped up and stood upon the brink of the little excavation.

For a time he was as still as that sad occupant of the little space of earth that served her for a resting place, but at length in a tone of deep anguish he spoke, —

"And has it come to this?" he said, "is this my work? Oh, horror! horror unspeakable. In this some hideous dream or a reality of tragedy, so far transcending all I looked for, that if I had tears I should shed them now; but I have none. A hundred years ago that fount was dry. I thought that I had steeled my heart against all gentle impulses; that I had crushed — aye, completely crushed dove-eyed pity in my heart, but it is not so, and still sufficient of my once human feelings clings to me to make me grieve for thee, Clara Crofton, thou victim!"

We need not tell our readers now, that it was no other than Varney the Vampyre himself from whom these words came.

After thus, then, giving such fervent utterance to the sad feeling that had overcome him, he stood for a time silent, and then glancing around him as well as he could by the dim light, he found the spades, by the aid of which the grave had been dug, and which the men had in their great fright left behind them.

Seizing one, he commenced, with an energy and perseverance that was well adapted to accomplish the object, to fill up the grave.

"You shall now rest in peace," he said.

In the course of about ten minutes the grave was levelled completely, so that there were no signs or indications of any one having been there interred.

The rain was still falling, and notwithstanding that circumstance, he continued at his work, until he had stamped down the earth to a perfect level; and then, even, as if he was still further anxious to thoroughly destroy any indication of the deed that had been done, he took the loose earth that was superfluous, and scattered it about.

"This done," he said, "surely you will now know peace."

He cast down the spade with which he had been working, and lingered for a few brief moments. Suddenly he started, for he heard, or thought he heard, an approaching footstep.

His first impulse appeared to be to fly, but that he soon corrected, and folding his

who had been the guest of Sir George Crofton, and from whom it was supposed had sprung all he mischief and horror that had fallen upon the family, at the Grange.

"Who are you?" he cried; "can you give me information of an outrage that has been committed hereabouts."

"Many," said Varney.

"Ah! I know the voice. Are you not he who was rescued from the sea by the two sons of Sir George Crofton?"

"Well."

"Now I know you, and I am glad to have met with you."

"You will try to kill me?"

"No, no — peace is my profession."

"Ah! you are the priest of this place.

arms solemnly across his breast, he waited for the man that was now evidently making speed towards that spot.

In a few moments more he saw the dusky outline of the figure, and then Mr. Bevan, the clergyman, stood before him.

Mr. Bevan did not at the moment recognize in the form before him the man

Well, sir, what would you with me?"

"I would implore you to tell me if it be really true that — that —"

Mr. Bevan paused, for he disliked to show that the fear that it might be true there were such creatures as vampyres, had taken so strong a hold of him.

"Proceed," said Varney.

"I will. Are you then a vampyre?"

"A strange question for one living man to put to another! Are you?"

"You are inclined to trifle with me. But I implore you to answer me. I am perhaps the only man in all this neighbourhood to whom you can give an answer in the affirmative with safety."

"And why so?"

"Because I question not the decrees of Heaven. If it seems fit to the great Ruler of Heaven and of earth that there should be ever such horrible creatures as vampyres, ought I, His creature, to question it?"

"You ought not — you ought not. I have heard much from priests, but from your lips I hear sound reason. I am a vampyre."

Mr. Bevan shrunk back, and shook for a moment, as he said in a low faltering tone, —

"For how long — have you —"

"You would know how long I have endured such a state of existence. I will tell you that I have a keen remembrance of being hunted through the streets of London in the reign of Henry the Fourth."

"Henry the Fourth?"

"Yes, I have seen all the celebrities of this and many other lands from that period. More than once have I endeavoured to cast off this horrible existence, but it is my destiny to remain in it. I was picked up by the brothers Crofton after one of my attempts to court death. They have been repaid."

"Horribly!"

"I cannot help it — I am what I am."

There was a strange and mournful solemnity about the tones of Varney that went to the heart of Mr. Bevan, and after a few moments pause, he said, —

"You greatly, very greatly awake my interest. Do not leave me. Ask yourself if there is anything that I can do to alleviate your destiny. Have you tried prayer?"

"Prayer?"

"Yes. Oh! there is great virtue in prayer."

"I pray? What for should I pray but for that death which whenever it seems to be in my grasp has them flitted from me in mockery, leaving me still a stranded wretch upon the shores of this world. Perhaps you have at times fancied you have suffered some great amount of mental agony. Perhaps you have stood by the bed-side of dying creatures, and heard them howl their hopelessness of Heaven's mercy, but you cannot know — you cannot imagine — what I have suffered."

As he spoke, he turned away, but Mr. Bevan followed him, saying, —

"Remain — remain, I implore you,"

"Remain — and wherefore?"

"I will be your friend — it is my duty to be such; remain, and you shall if you wish it, have an asylum in my house. If you will not pray yourself, to Heaven, I will pray for you, and in time to come you will have some hope. Oh, believe me, earnest prayer is not in vain."

"My friend!"

"Yes, your friend; I am, I ought to be the friend of all who are unhappy."

"And is there really one human being

who does not turn from me in horror and disgust? Oh, sir, you jest."

"No — on my soul, that which I say I mean. Come with me now, and you shall if you please, remain in secret in my house — no one shall know you are with me — from the moment that you cross the threshold you shall hope for happier days."

The vampyre paused, and it was evident that he was deeply affected by what Mr. Bevan said to him, for his whole frame shook.

CCXXVI.

THE STRANGE GUEST. — THE LITTLE CHAPEL. — VARNEY'S NARRATIVE.

Mr. Bevan could not but see that he had made some impression, even upon the obdurate heart of Varney, and he was determined to follow that impression up by every means in his power.

"Always have in mind," he said, "that by trusting me, you trust one who is not in the habit of condemning his fellows. You will be safe from anything like sanctified reproach, for to my thinking, religion should be a principle of love and tenderness, and not a subject upon which people who, perhaps are themselves liable and obnoxious to all sorts of reproach, should deal forth denunciations against their neighbours."

"Is that indeed your faith?"

"It is; and it is the real faith, taught by my Great Master."

"You are as one among many thousands."

"Nay, you may have been unfortunate in meeting with bad specimens of those who are devoted in the priesthood. Do not condemn hastily."

"Hastily! I have been some hundreds of years in condemning."

"You will come with me."

"I will for once again put faith in human nature."

"Tell me then, before we leave this spot, if you know aught of what has happened to, or become of the body of Clara Croton."

"I can tell you; it was left here buried, but uncovered."

"Indeed — the ground is level, and I see no trace of a grave."

"No; I have obliterated all such traces, I have placed the earth upon her — may she now rest in peace. Oh, that such a flower should have been so rudely plucked, and I the cause. Is not that enough to make Heaven's angels mutiny if I should essay to pass the golden gates?"

"Say no more of that. I thank God that the body is so disposed of, and that it will not come in the way of any of the Crofton family. This affair had far better now be let sink into oblivion — alas! poor Sir George is now the most pitiable sufferer."

"Indeed!"

"Yes; madness has seized upon him. He only sits and smiles to himself, weaving in his imagination strange fancies."

"And call you that unhappy?"

"It is called, and considered so."

"Oh, fatal error—he is happy. Reason! boasted, God-like reason—what are you but the curse of poor humanity. The maniac, who will in his cell, fancy it a gorgeous hall, and of the damp straw that is his couch make up a glittering coronet, is a king indeed, and most happy."

"This is poetical," said Mr. Bevan, "if not true."

"It is true."

"Well, well; we will talk on that as well as other themes at our leisure. Come on, and I will at once take you to my home, where you will be safe, and I hope more happy."

"Are you not afraid?"

"I am not."

"You are right, confidence is safety—lead on, sir, I'll follow you, although I little thought to make any human companionship to-night."

Mr. Bevan walked only about a step in advance as they proceeded towards the parsonage house, and on the way he conversed with Varney with calmness which considering the very peculiar circumstances, few men could have brought to bear upon the occasion.

But Mr. Bevan was no common man. He looked upon nature, and all the living creatures that make up its vital portion with peculiar eyes, and if the bishop of his diocese had known one half of what Mr. Bevan thought, he would not have suffered him to remain in his religious situation.

But he kept the mass of his liberal opinions to himself, although he always acted upon them, and a man more completely free from sectarian dogmas, and illiberal fancies of superstition, which are nicknamed faith, could not be.

There was still, notwithstanding all the circumstances, a hope lingering in his mind that Varney might after all not be even what he thought himself to be, but some enthusiast who had dreamt himself into a belief of his own horrible powers.

We know that such was not the case. But it was natural enough for Mr. Bevan to hold as long as he could by such an idea.

And so those two most strangely assorted beings, the clergyman and the vampyre, walked together towards the pretty and picturesque dwelling of the former.

"The distance is short," said Mr. Bevan.

"Nay, that matters not," replied Varney.

"I spoke because I thought you seemed fatigued."

"No, my frame is of iron. My heart is bowed down with many griefs, but the physical structure knows no feeling of dejection. The life I possess is no common one. Oh! would that it were so, that I might shuffle it off as any ordinary men can do."

"Do not say that. Who knows but that after all your living accomplishes better things?"

"I cannot say that it accomplishes aught completely but one thing."

"And that?"

"That is my most exquisite misery."

"Even that may pass away. But here we are at my little garden gate. Come in, and fear nothing; for if you will seek Heaven, as I would wish you, you will find this place such a haven of peace, and such a refuge against the storms of life, as you hardly fancied existed, I dare say, in this world."

"Not for me. I did not fancy that there existed a spot on earth on which I could lie down in peace, and yet it may be here."

————

CCXXVII.

VARNEY OPENS THE VAST STORE-HOUSE OF HIS MEMORY.

A MORE SINGULAR CONVERSATION than that which took place between Varney, the Vampyre, and this minister of religion, could not be conceived. If there was any one particle of goodness existing in Varney's disposition, we may suspect it would now be developed.

Perhaps the whole domestic history of the world never yet exhibited so remarkable an association as that between Mr. Bevan and Varney; and when they sat down together in the little cheerful study of the former, never had four walls enclosed two beings of the same species, and yet of such opposite pursuits.

But we can hardly call Varney, the Vampyre, human — his space of existence had been lengthened out beyond the ordinary routine of human existence, and the kind of vitality that he now enjoyed, if one might be allowed the expression, was something distinct and peculiar.

It speaks volumes, however, for the philanthropy and liberality of the minister of any religion who could hold out the hand of fellowship to so revolting and to so horrible an existence.

But Mr. Bevan was no common man. His religion was doctrinal, certainly, but it was free from bigotry; and his charity to the feelings, opinions, and prejudices of others was immense.

He was accustomed to say "may not my feelings be prejudices," and one of the sublimest precepts of the whole Scriptures was to him that which says, "Judge not, lest ye, too, should be judged."

Hence it was that he would not allow himself to revolt at Varney. It had seemed right to the great Creator of all things that there should be such a being, and therefore, he, Mr. Bevan, would neither question nor contemn it.

"Look about you," he said to Varney with a disordered gaze; "you seem to look very about you as if there was danger in the atmosphere you breathe, but be assured you are safe here; it shall be my life for your life if any harm should be attempted to be done you."

Varney looked at him for a few moments silence, and then in his deep and sepulchral voice he spoke, saying, —

"My race is run."

"What mean you by that expression?"

"I mean I shall no longer be a terror to the weak, nor a curiosity to the strong. In time past, more than once I have tried to shuffle off the evil of this frightful existence, but some accident, strange, wild, and wonderful, has brought me back to life again."

"Perhaps not an accident," said Mr. Bevan.

"You may be right, but when I have sought to rid the world of my own bad company, I have been moved to do so by some act of kindness and consideration, most contrary to my deserts; and then again when I have been cast back by the waves of fate upon the shores of existence, my heart is burdened, and I have begun to plan to work mischief and misery and woe to all."

"I can understand how your feelings have alternated, but I hope that out association will have better result."

"Yes, a better result, for with consummate art, with cool perseverance and extended knowledge, I trust I may think of some means which cannot fail of changing this living frame to that dust from which it sprung, and to which it should long since have returned."

"You believe in that, but do you not think there is a pure spirit that will yet live, independent of the grovelling earth?"

"There are times when I have hoped that even that fable were true; but you have promised me rest, will you keep your word?"

"That will I most certainly; but will you keep yours? You have promised me some details of your extraordinary existence, and as a divine, and I hope in some degree as a philosopher, I look for them with some degree of anxiety."

"You shall have them — leave me pens, ink and paper, and in the solitude of this room, until to-morrow morning, and you shall have what I believe to be the origin of this most horrible career."

"Your wishes shall be consulted — but, will you not take refreshment?"

"Nothing — nothing. My refreshment is one I need not name to you, and when,

forced by the world's customs and considerations of my own safety, I have partaken of man's usual food, it has but ill accorded with my preternatural existence, I eat not — drink not — here. You know me as I am."

As he continued speaking, Varney evidently grew weaker, and Mr. Bevan could scarcely persuade himself that it was not through actual want of nourishment, but the Vampyre assured him that it was not so, and that rest would recruit him, to which opinion, as the experience of human nature generally afforded no index to Varney's peculiar habits, he was forced to subscribe.

There was a couch in the room, and upon that Varney laid himself, and as he seemed indisposed for further conversation, Mr. Bevan left him, promising to return to him as he himself requested in the morning, with the hope of finding that he had completed some sort of narrative to the effect mentioned.

It can scarcely be said that Mr. Bevan had thoroughly made up his mind to leave his guest for so long a period, and as there was a window that looked from the study in his little garden, he thought, that by now and then peeping in, to see that all was right, he could scarcely be considered as breaking faith with his mysterious guest.

"He will surely attempt nothing against his own life," thought Mr. Bevan, "for already he seems to be impressed with the futility of such an attempt, and to think that when he has made them he has been made the sport of circumstances that had forced him back to life again, despite all his wishes to the contrary."

Mr. Bevan reasoned thus, but he little

knew what was passing in the mind of Varney the Vampire.

After about two hours more, when the night was profoundly dark, the liberal-minded but anxious clergyman went into his garden, for the purpose of peeping into his study, and he then saw, as he supposed, his visitor lying enveloped in his large brown cloak, lying upon the couch.

He was better pleased to see he was sleeping, and recovering from the great fatigue of which he complained, instead of writing, although that writing promised to be of so interesting a character, and he crept softly away for fear of awakening him.

The hour had now arrived at which Mr. Bevan usually retired to rest, but he delayed doing so, and let two hours more elapse, after which, he again stole out of his garden, and peeped into the study.

There lay the long, gaunt, slumbering figure upon the couch.

"I am satisfied," said Mr. Bevan to himself; "fatigue has completely overcome him, and he will sleep till morning now. I long much to become acquainted with his strange eventful history."

After this, Mr. Bevan retired to rest, but not until in prayer he had offered up his thanks, and stated his hopes of being able to turn aside from the wicked path he had been pursuing, the wretched man who at that moment was slumbering peacefully beneath his roof.

We should have less of opposition to churchmen, if they were all like Mr. Bevan, and not the wily, ravenous, illiberal, grasping crew they really are. There was no priestcraft in him, he was almost enough to make one in love with his doctrines, be they what they might, so that they were his.

Although we say that he retired to rest, we should more properly say he retired to try to rest; for, after all, there were feelings of excitement and anxiety about him which he could not repress wholly; and although he had every reason to believe his guest was sleeping, and calmly sleeping too, yet he found he was becoming painfully alive to the slightest sound.

He became nervously alive to the least interruption, and kept fancying that he heard the slightest indications of movements in the house, such as at any other time he would have paid no attention to.

It always happened too, provokingly, that just as he was dropping into a slight slumber, that he thought he heard one of these noises, and then he would start, awake, and sit up in his bed, and listen attentively, until tired nature forced him to repose again.

Those who have passed such a night of watchfulness need not be told how very very exciting it becomes, and hour after hour becomes more intense and acute, and the power of escaping its fell influence less and less.

Indeed, it was not until the dawn of morning that Mr. Bevan tasted the sweets of sound repose, then, as is generally usual after nights of fever and disquietude, the cool, pure, life-giving air of early morn, produced quite a different state of feeling, and his repose was calm and serene.

CCXXVIII.

THE FLIGHT OF THE VAMPYRE. — THE MASS.

As was to be expected, in consequence of the sleepless state in which he had been in the early part of the night, Mr. Bevan did not awaken at his usually early hour; and as his confidential servant had stolen into his room upon tip-toe, and seeing that he was sleeping quietly and soundly, she did not think proper to disturb him.

An autumnal sun was gleaming into his lattice window when he spontaneously awoke, and the reflection of the sunlight upon a particular portion of the wall convinced him that it was late.

For a moment or two, he lay in that dreamy state when we are just conscious of where we are, without having the smallest pretensions to another idea; and probably he would have dropped to sleep again had it not been that his servant again opened the door, the lock of which had the infirmity of giving a peculiar snap every time it was used, and that thoroughly awakened him.

"Oh, you are awake, sir?" said his old servant, "I never knew you sleep so long. Breakfast has been ready an hour and a half. It's a cool morning, sir, and what's worse, I can't get into your study to light you a bit of fire, which I thought you would want."

The interruption altogether, and the mention of the study, served completely to arouse Mr. Bevan to a remembrance of the events of the preceding evening, and he cried,—

"What's the time? What's the time?"

"It's after nine, and as for the study—"

"Never mind the study—never mind the study, I will be down directly."

Scarcely ever had Mr. Bevan dressed himself with such precipitation as he now did.

"How provoking," he thought, "that upon this particular occasion, when I should like to have been up and stirring earlier than usual, I am a good hour and a half later. It can't be helped, though, and if my guest of last night is to be credited, he won't be waiting for his breakfast."

The simple toilet of the kind-hearted clergyman was soon completed, and then he ran down stairs to the lower part of his house, and finding that his servant was in the kitchen, he thought he might at once proceed to his study, to speak to the extraordinary inmate.

He had furnished Varney with the means of locking himself in for the night, and it would seem that the vampyre had fully availed himself of those means, for when Mr. Bevan tried the door, he found himself as much at fault as his servant had been, and could not by any means effect an admittance.

"He said his fatigue was great," remarked Mr. Bevan, "and so it seems it was, for surely he is yet sleeping. It is a comfort when one oversleeps oneself that the necessity for one's rising has been put off by the same means."

Unwilling to disturb Varney, and not hearing from the slightest movement from within that he had yet done so, Mr. Bevan went to his breakfast, much better satisfied than he had been a quarter of an hour since, and as the breakfast room adjoined the study, he had every opportunity if the vampyre should be stirring, of hearing and attending to him.

Not above ten minutes elapsed in this kind of way, when Mr. Bevan, although he saw nothing of his guest, heard something of the approach of a visitor, by the trampling of feet upon the gravel walk, and upon looking through the window, he saw that it was his friend Sir George Crofton from the hall.

It was rather an early hour for visitors, but still under the peculiar circumstances, Sir George might be supposed not to stand upon ceremony in calling upon the clegyman of his parish and upon his old friend, combining, as Mr. Bevan did, both these characters in one.

It was rather, though, placing the clergyman in a situation of difficulty, for while there was nothing he so much hated as mystery and concealment, he yet could not, upon the spur of the moment, decide whether he ought to inform Sir George of the presence of Varney or not.

After the frightful manner in which the baronet and his family had suffered from what might be called the machinations of the vampyre, it could scarcely be supposed that his feelings were otherwise than in a most exasperated state, and it might, for all he knew, be actually dangerous for the personal safety of that guest whom he had pledged his honour to protect, to allow Sir George Crofton to know at all that he was beneath his roof.

While he was engaged in these considerations, and before he could come to anything like a conclusion concerning them, Sir George was announced, and shown as a privileged visitor into the parlour.

We cannot but pause to make a remark upon the stupendous change that had taken place in the appearance of that unhappy man. When first we presented him to the reader, he was as good a specimen of the hale hearty English gentleman, as we could wish to see; good humour and good health beamed forth on every feature of his face; and well they might do so, for although the past had not been unchequered by trials, the future wore to him a sunny aspect, and some of the feelings of his youth were returning to him, in the happiness of his children.

But what a change was now. Twenty years of ordinary existence, with extraordinary vicissitudes, would scarcely have produced the effect that the events of the last fortnight had upon that unhappy father.

He appeared to be absolutely sinking into the grave with grief, and not only was his countenance strangely altered, but the tones of his voice were completely changed from what they had been.

Alas! poor Sir George Crofton, never will the light of joy again illumine your face. There are griefs, inevitable griefs, which time will heal, griefs which the more we look upon them the more we find our reason array itself against them. But his sorrows were of a different complexion, and were apt to grow more gigantic from thought.

"Good morning, Mr. Bevan," he said, "I am an early visitor, sir."

"Not more early than welcome, Sir George. I pray you to be seated."

"You are very good," said the baronet, "but when one comes at an hour like this, I am of opinion that he ought to come with something like a good excuse for his intrusion."

"There is none needed, I assure you."

"But I have been thinking upon the advice which you have given me, Mr. Bevan, to leave this part of the country, and try the endeavour, by the excitement and changes of foreign travel, to lessen the weight of my calamities."

"I think your determination is a good one, Sir George."

"Probably it is the best I could adopt, but I must confess that I should set about it in better spirit, but I am haunted by apprehensions."

"Apprehensions, Sir George! is not the worst passed?"

"It may be, and I hope to Heaven it is, but I have another child, another daughter, fair and beautiful as my lost Clara; but what security have I that that dreadful being may not pursue her, and with frightful vindictiveness drive her to the grave."

Mr. Bevan was silent two or three minutes, and the idea crossed him that if he could get Sir George in the proper state of mind, it would be, perhaps, better that he should know that the vampyre was in the house, and in such a state of mind as not to renew any outrages against him or his family, than that he should go abroad with the dread clinging to him of being still followed and persecuted by that dreadful being.

"Sir George," said Mr. Bevan, in an extremely serious voice, "Sir George, did you ever reason with yourself calmly and seriously, and in a Christian spirit, about this affair."

"Calmly, Mr. Bevan! how could I reason calmly?"

"I have scarcely put my question as I ought; what I meant to ask was, what are your personal feelings towards the vampyre? We must recollect that even he, dreadful existence as he is, was fashioned by the same God that fashioned us; and who shall say but he may be the victim of a horrible and stern necessity? Who shall say but he may be tortured by remorse, and that the circumstances connected with your daughter, of which you so justly complain, may be to him sources of the bitterest reflection? What if you were to be assured that never more would that mysterious man cross your path, if man we can call him? Do you think that you could then forgive him?"

"It is hard to say, but the feeling that my other child was safe would prompt me much."

"Sir George, I could make a communication to you if I thought you would listen to it patiently; if you will swear to me to be calm."

"I swear, tell me — oh, tell me!"

"The vampyre is in this house."

CCXXIX.

THE MYSTERIOUS DISAPPEARANCE.

ONE MAY FORM some sort of judgment of the astonishment with which Sir George Crofton heard this statement. He looked indeed a few moments at Mr. Bevan, as if he had a stong suspicion that he could not possibly have heard aright, so that the good clergyman was induced to repeat his statement, which he did, by saying,—

"Sir George, I assure you, however remarkable such a circumstance may be, and however much you may feel yourself surprised at it, that in the extreme bitterness of spirit, and feeling all the compunction that you could possibly wish him to feel, Varney the Vampyre is now an inmate of this house."

Had a bomb-shell fallen at his feet, Sir George Crofton could not have felt more surprised, and he exhibited that surprise by several times repeating to himself,—

"Varney the Vampyre an inmate of this house! Varney the Vampyre here!"

"Yes," said Mr. Bevan, "here, an inmate of this house. He is within a few paces of you, slumbering in the next apartment, and from his own lips you shall have the assurance that never again will you have any trouble on his account, and that he most bitterly and most deeply regrets the suffering he had brought upon you and yours."

"Will that regret," said Sir George, excitedly, "restore the dead? Will that regret give me my child again? Will it open the portals of the grave, and restore her to me who was the life and joy of my existence? Tell me, will it do that? If not, what is his regret to me?"

"No, Sir George, no, his regret will not do that. There is such power, but it is not upon earth. Heaven delegates not such fearful responsibilities to any of its creatures, and the only reason which has induced me to make this confidence was to take from you the fearful anxiety of fancying yourself followed by that dreadful being."

"Vengeance," replied Sir George Crofton, "vengeance shall be mine. In the name of my lost child, I cry for vengeance. Shall he not perish who has made her whom I love perish? Make way, Mr. Bevan, make way."

"No, Sir George, no; this is my house. I, as a Christian minister, offered the hospitality of its roof to Varney the Vampyre, and I cannot violate my word."

"You speak, sir, to a desperate man," cried "Sir George; "no roof to me is sanctified, beneath which the murderer of my child finds a shelter. Mr. Bevan, the respect that one man has for another, or ever has had for another, cannot exceed the respect I have for you; but with all that, sir, I cannot forget my own personal wrongs; the shade of my murdered Clara beckons me."

"Fly, Varney, fly," cried Mr. Bevan, "fly."

"Is it so?" said Sir George; "do you then side with my direst foe?"

"No — no, I side with Sir George Crofton against his own furious unbridled passions."

Neither from profession nor practice was Mr. Bevan one who was likely to force to resist Sir George, and at the moment the baronet was about to lay hands upon him to hurl him from his path, he slipped aside.

"Rash man," he said, "the time will come when you will repent this deed."

The door of the study was still fast, but to the infuriated Sir George, that opposed but a very frail obstacle, and with the effort of a moment he forced it open, and rushed into the apartment.

"Varney, monster," he cried, "prepare to meet your doom. Your career is at an end."

Mr. Bevan was after him, and in the room with him in a moment, fully expecting that some very dreadful scene would ensue, as a consequence of the unbridled passion of Sir George Crofton.

Sir George Crofton was standing in the centre of the apartment with Varney's large brown cloak in his grasp, which he had dragged from the sofa, but the vampyre himself was not to be seen.

"Escaped!" he cried, "escaped!"

"Thank Heaven, then," said Mr. Bevan, "that this roof has not been desecrated by an act of violence. Oh, Sir George, it is a mercy that time has been given to think he has escaped."

"I'll follow him, were it to perdition."

Sir George was about to open the window and rush into the garden, thinking, of course, it was by that means by which the vampyre escaped, but Mr.

Bevan pointed his hand upon the smooth gravel path that was immediately below the casement.

"Behold," he said, "one of the first results of an autumnal night. That this coating of fleecy sleet, you see, is undisturbed; it fell about midnight; nine hours have since elapsed, and you perceive there is no foot mark upon it, and in what direction would you chase Varney the Vampyre while he has such a start of you?"

Infuriated with passion, as was Sir George Crofton, the reasonableness of this statement struck him forcibly, and he became silent. A revulsion of feeling took place; he staggered to a seat, and wept.

"Yes, he is gone," he said. "Yes, the murderer of my child is gone; vengeance is delayed, but perhaps not altogether stopped. Oh, Mr. Bevan, Mr. Bevan, why did you tell me he was here?"

"I do now regret having done so, but I believed him to be here, and his departure is as mysterious to me as it can be to you."

Mr. Bevan cast his eyes upon the table, and there he saw a large packet addressed to himself. Sir George saw it too, at the same moment, and pointing to it, said, —

"Is that the vampyre's legacy to his new friend?"

"Sir George," said Mr. Bevan, "let it suffice that the packet is addressed to me."

All the good breeding of the gentleman returned, and Sir George Crofton bowed as he left the room, closely followed by the clergyman, who was as much bewildered by the disappearance of Varney as even Sir George could possibly be. He had a most intense desire to examine the packet, with the hope that there he should find some explanation or

solution of the mystery; but not being aware, of course, of what it contained, he could not tell if it would be prudent to trust Sir George at that time with its contents.

As may be well supposed, there was a sort of restraint in the manner of both of them after what had happened, and they did what was very rare with them both, parted without making any appointment for the future.

But whatever might be the feelings of Sir George Crofton then, a little reflection would be quite sure to bring him back again to a proper estimation of what was due to such a friend as Mr. Bevan, and we cannot anticipate any serious interruption to their general friendly intercourse.

THE MOMENT THE clergyman found himself alone, he with eager steps went into his study, and eagerly seized upon the packet that was left to him by the vampyre, the outside of which merely bore the superscription of—"These to the Rev. Mr. Bevan, and strictly private."

With eagerness he tore open the envelope, and the first thing that attracted his attention was a long, narrow slip of paper, on which were written the following words:—

It was not my intention to trespass largely upon your hospitality; it would have been unjust—almost approaching to criminality so to do. I could only think of taking a brief refuge in your house, so brief as should just enable me to avail myself of the shadows of night to escape from a neighbourhood where I knew I should be hunted.

The few hours which I have quietly remained beneath your roof have been sufficient to accomplish that object, and the wee papers that I leave you accompanying this, contain the personal information concerning me you asked. They had been previously prepared, and are at your service.

To attempt to follow me would be futile, for I have as ample means of making a rapid journey as you could possibly call to your aid, and I have the

advantage of many hours' start; under these circumstances I have no hesitation in telling you that my destination is Naples, and that perhaps the next you hear of me will be, that some stranger in a fit of madness has cast himself into the crater of a burning mountain, which would at once consume him and all his sorrows. —

VARNEY THE VAMPYRE.

One may imagine the feelings with which Mr. Bevan read this most strange and characteristic epistle—feelings that for some moments kept him a prisoner to the most painful thoughts.

All that he had hoped to accomplish by the introduction of Varney to his house was lost now. He had but in fact given him a better opportunity of carrying out a terrible design—a design which now there really did not appear to be any means of averting the consummation of.

"Alas! alas!" he said, "this is most grievous, and what can I do now, to avert the mischief—nothing, absolutely nothing. If it be true that he has, as he says he has, the means of hastening on his journey, all pursuit would be utterly useless."

This was taking a decidedly correct view of the matter. Varney was not the sort of man, if he really intended to reach Naples quickly, to linger on his route, and then there was another view of the subject which could not but occur to Mr. Bevan, and that was, that his mentioned destination might be but a blind to turn off pursuit.

CCXXX.

VARNEY GIVES SOME PERSONAL ACCOUNT OF HIMSELF.

NEVER HAD MR. BEVAN in all his recollection been in such a state of hesitation as now.

He was a man usually of rapid resolves, and very energetic action; but the circumstances that had recently taken place were of so very remarkable a nature, that he was not able to bring to bear upon them any portion of his past experience.

He felt that he could come to no determination, but was compelled by the irresistible force of events to be a spectator instead of an actor in what might ensue.

"I shall hear," he thought, "if any such event happens at Naples as that to which Varney has adverted, and until I do so, or until a sufficient length of time has elapsed to make me feel certain that he will not plunge into that burning abyss, I shall be a prey to every kind of fear; and then again as regards Sir George Crofton. What am I to say to him? Shall I show him this note or not?"

Even that was a question which he could not absolutely decide in his own mind, although he was strongly inclined to think that it would be highly desirable to do so, and while he was considering the point, and holding the note in his hand, his eye fell upon the other papers which had been enclosed with it, and addressed to him.

Hoping and expecting that there he should find something that would better qualify him to come to an accurate conclusion, he took up the packet, and found that the topmost paper bore the following endorsement:—

SOME   PARTICULARS CONCERNING MY OWN LIFE.

"There, then," said Mr. Bevan, "is what he has promised me."

It was to be expected that Mr. Bevan should take up those papers with a very considerable amount of curiosity, and as he could not think what course immediately to pursue that would do good to Varney or anybody else, he thought he had better turn his attention at once to the documents that the vampyre had left to his perusal.

Telling his servant, then, not to allow him to be disturbed unless the affair was a very urgent one indeed, he closed the door of his study, and commenced reading one of the most singular statements that ever was created by being placed upon paper. It was as follows:—

During my brief inter-course—and it has always been brief when of a confidential nature with various persons—I have created surprise by talking of individuals and events long since swallowed up in the almost forgotten past. In these few pages I declare myself more fully.

In the reign of the First Charles, I resided in a narrow street, in the immediate neighbourhood of Whitehall. It was a straggling, tortuous thoroughfare, going down to the Thames; it matters little what were my means of livelihood, but I have no hesitation in saying that I was a well-paid agent in some of the political movements which graced and disgraced that period.

London was then a mass of mean-looking houses; with here and there one that looked like a palace, compared with its humbler neighbours. Almost every street appeared to be under the protection of some great house situated somewhere in its extent, but such of those houses as have survived the wreck of time rank now with their neighbours, and are so strangely altered, that I, who knew many of them well, could now scarcely point to the place where they used to stand.

I took no prominent part in the commotions of that period, but I saw the head of a king held up in its gore at Whitehall as a spectacle for the multitude.*

There were thousands of persons in England who had aided to bring about that result, but who were very far from expecting it, and who were the first to fall under the ban of the gigantic power they had themselves raised.

Among these were many of my employers; men, who had been quite willing to shake the stability of a throne so far as the individual occupying it was concerned, but who certainly never contemplated the destruction of monarchy; so the death of the First Charles, and the

---

* *A reference to the execution of King Charles I, who was tried and convicted of high treason and beheaded by Oliver Cromwell's Commonwealth government in 1649 during the English Civil War.*

dictatorship of Cromwell, made royalists in abundance.

They had raised a spirit they could not quell again, and this was a fact which the stern, harsh man, Cromwell, with whom I had many interviews, was aware of.

My house was admirably adapted for the purposes of secrecy and seclusion, and I became a thriving man from the large sums I received for aiding the escape of distinguished loyalists, some of whom lay for a considerable time perdu at my house, before an eligible opportunity arrived of dropping down the river quietly to some vessel which would take them to Holland.

It was to offer me so much per head for these royalists that Cromwell sent for me, and there was one in particular who had been private secretary to the Duke of Cleveland, a young man merely, of neither family nor rank, but of great ability, whom Cromwell was exceedingly anxious to capture.

I think there likewise must have been some private reasons which induced the dictator of the Commonwealth to be so anxious concerning this Master Francis Latham, which was the name of the person alluded to.

It was late one evening when a stranger came to my house, and having desired to see me, was shown into a private apartment, when I immediately waited upon him.

"I am aware," he said, "that you have been confidentially employed by the Duke of Cleveland, and I am aware that you have been very useful to distressed loyalists, but in aiding Master Francis Latham, the duke's secretary, you will be *permitted almost to name your own terms."*

I named a hundred pounds, which at that time was a much larger sum than now, taking into consideration the relative value. One half of it was paid to me at once, and the other promised within four-and-twenty hours after Latham had effected his escape.

I was told that at half-past twelve o'clock that night, a man dressed in common working apparel, and with a broom over his shoulder would knock at my door and ask if he could be recommended to a lodging, and that by those tokens I should know him to be Francis Latham. A Dutch lugger, I was further told, was lying near Gravesend, on board of which, to earn my money, I was expected to place the fugitive.

All this was duly agreed upon; I had a boat in readiness, with a couple of watermen upon whom I could depend, and I was far from anticipating any extraordinary difficulties in carrying out the enterprise.

I had a son about twelve years of age, who being a sharp acute lad, I found very useful upon several occasions, and I never scrupled to make him acquainted with any such affair as this that I am recounting.

Half-past twelve o'clock came, and in a very few minutes after that period of time there came a knock at my door, which my son answered, and according to arrangement, there was the person with a broom, who asked to be recommended to a lodging, and who was immediately requested to walk in.

He seemed rather nervous, and asked me if I thought there was much risk.

"No," said I, "no more than ordinary risk in all these cases, but we must wait half an hour till the tide turns. For just now to struggle against it down the river would really be nothing else but courting observation."

To this he perfectly agreed, and sat down by my fireside.

I was as anxious as he to get the affair over, for it was a ticklish job, and Oliver Cromwell, if he had brought anything of the kind exactly home to me, would as lief order me to be shot as he would have taken his luncheon in the name of the Lord.

I accordingly went down to the water-side to speak to the men who were lying there with the boat, and had ascertained from them that in about twenty minutes the tide would begin to ebb in the centre of the stream, when two men confronted me.

Practised as I was in the habits and appearances of the times, I guessed at once who they were. In fact, a couple of Oliver Cromwell's dismounted dragoons were always well known.

"You are wanted," said one of them to me.

"Yes, you are particularly wanted," said the other.

"But, gentlemen, I am rather busy," said I. "In an hour's time I will do myself the pleasure, if you please, of waiting upon you anywhere you wish to name."

The only reply they made to this was the practical one, of getting on each side of me, and then hurrying me on, past my own door.

I was taken right away to St. James's at a rapid pace, being hurried through one of the court yards; we paused at a small door, at which was a sentinel.

My two guides communicated something to him, and he allowed us to pass. There was a narrow passage without any light, and through another door, at which was likewise a sentinel, who turned the glare of a lantern upon me and my conductors. Some short explanation was given to him likewise, during which I heard the words "His Highness," which was the title which Cromwell had lately assumed.

They pushed me through this doorway, closed it behind me, and left me alone in the dark.

CCXXXI.

A SINGULAR INTERVIEW, AND THE CONSEQUENCES OF PASSION.

Being perfectly ignorant of where I was, I thought the most prudent plan was to stand stock still, for if I advanced it might be into danger, and my retreat was evidently cut off.

Moreover, those who brought me there must have some sort of intention, and it was better for me to leave them to develop it than to take any steps myself, which might be of a very hazardous nature.

That I was adopting the best policy I was soon convinced, for a flash of light suddenly came upon me, and I heard a gruff voice, say, —

"Who goes there? come this way."

I walked on, and passed through an open door way into a small apartment, in the centre of which, standing by a common deal table on which his clenched hand was resting, I found Oliver Cromwell himself.

"So, sirrah," he said, "royalists and pestilent characters are to ravage the land, are they so? Answer me."

"I have no answer to make, your highness," said I.

"God's mercy, no answer, when in your own house the Duke of Cleveland's proscribed secretary lies concealed."

I felt rather staggered, but was certain I had been betrayed by some one, and Cromwell continued rapidly, without giving me time to speak.

"The Lord is merciful, and so are we, but the malignant must be taken by the beloved soldiers of the Commonwealth, and the gospel God-fearing men, who always turn to the Lord, with short carbines, will accompany you. The malignant shall be taken from your house, by you, and the true God-fearing dragoons shall linger in the shade behind. You will take him to the river side, where the Lord willing, there will be a boat with a small blue ensign, on board of which you will place him, wishing him good speed."

He paused, and looked fixedly upon me by the aid of the miserable light that was in the apartment.

"What then, your highness?" I said.

"Then you will probably call upon us to-morrow for a considerable sum, which will be due to you for this good service to the Commonwealth; yes, it shall be profitable to fight the battles of the Lord."

I must confess, I had expected a very

different result from the interview, which I had been greatly in fear would have resulted in greatly endangering my liberty. Cromwell was a man not to be tampered with; I knew my danger, and was not disposed to sacrifice myself for Master Latham.

"Your highness shall be obeyed," I said.

"Aye, verily," he replied, "and if we be not obeyed, we must make ourselves felt with a strong arm of flesh. What ho! God-fearing Simkins, art thou there?"

"Yes, the Lord willing," said a dragoon, making his appearance at the door.

Cromwell merely made him a sign with his hand, and he laid hold of the upper part of my arm, as though it had been in a vice, and led me out into the passage again where the sentinels were posted.

In the course of a few moments, I was duly in custody of my two guards again, and we were proceeding at a very rapid pace towards my residence.

It was not a very agreeable affair, view it in whatever light I might; but as regarded Cromwell, I knew my jeopardy, and it would be perceived that I had not hesitated a moment in obeying him. Moreover, I considered, for I knew he was generous, I should have a good round sum by the transaction, which added to the fifty pounds I had received from the royalists, made the affair appear to me in a pleasant enough light. Indeed, I was revolving in my mind as I went along, whether it would not be worth while, almost entirely to attach myself to the protector.

"If," I reasoned with myself, "I should do that, and still preserve myself a character with the royalists, I should thrive."

But it will be seen that an adverse circumstance put an end to all those dreams.

When we reached the door of my house, the first thing I saw was my son wiping his brow, as if he had undergone some fatigue; he ran up to me, and catching me by the arm, whispered to me.

I was so angered at the moment, that heedless of what I did, and passion getting the mastery over me, I with my clenched fist struck him to the earth. His head fell upon one of the hard round stones with which the street was paved, and he never spoke again. I had murdered him.

I don't know what happened immediately subsequent to this fearful deed; all I can recollect is, that there was a great confusion and a flashing of lights, and it appeared to me as if something had suddenly struck me down to the earth with great force.

When I did thoroughly awaken, I found myself lying upon a small couch, but in a very large apartment dimly lighted, and where there were many such couches ranged against the walls. A miserable light just enabled me to see about me a little, and some dim dusky-looking figures were creeping about the place.

It was a hospital that the protector had lately instituted in the Strand.

I tried to speak, but could not; my tongue seemed glued to my mouth, and I could not, and then a change came upon my sense of sight, and I could scarcely see at all the dim dusky-looking figures about me.

Some one took hold of me by the wrist, and I heard one say, quite distinctly, —

"He's entirely going, now."

Suddenly it seemed as if something had fallen with a crushing influence upon my chest, and then a consciousness that I was gasping for breath, and then I thought I was at the bottom of the sea. There was a moment, only a moment, of frightful agony, and then came a singing sound, like the rush of waters, after which, I distinctly felt some one raising me in their arms. I was dropped again, my limbs felt numbed and chill, an universal spasm shot through my whole system; I opened my eyes, and found myself lying in the open air, by a newly opened grave.

A full moon was sailing through the sky and the cold beams were upon my face; a voice sounded in my ears, a deep and solemn voice — and painfully distinct was every word it uttered.

"Mortimer," it said, for that was my name, "Mortimer, in life you did one deed which at once cast you out from all hope that anything in that life would be remembered in the world to come to your advantage. You poisoned the pure font of mercy, and not upon such as you can the downy freshness of Heaven's bounty fall. Murderer, murderer of that being sacredly presented to your care by the great Creator of all things, live henceforth a being accursed. Be to yourself a desolation and a blight, shunned by all that is good and virtuous, armed against all men, and all men armed against thee, Varney the Vampyre."

I staggered to my feet; the scene around me was a churchyard, I was gaunt and thin, my clothes hung about me in tattered remnants. The damp smell of the grave hung about them.

I met an aged man, and asked him where I was. He looked at me with a shudder, as though I had escaped from some charnel-house.

"Why this is Isledon," said he.

A peal of bells came merrily upon the night air.

"What means that?" said I.

"Why, this is the anniversary of the Restoration."

"The Restoration! What Restoration?"

"Why, of the royal family to the throne, to be sure, returned this day last year. Have you been asleep so long that you don't know that?"

I shuddered and walked on, determined to make further inquiries, and to make them with so much caution, that the real extent of my ignorance should scarce be surmised, and the result was to me of the most astonishing character.

I found that I had been in the trance of death for nearly two years, and that during that period, great political changes had taken place. The exiled royal family had been restored to the throne, and the most remarkable revulsion of feeling that had ever taken place in a nation had taken place in England.

But personally I had not yet fully awakened to all the horror of what I was. I had heard the words addressed to me, but I had attached no very definite meaning to them.

CCXXXII.

VARNEY'S NARRATIVE CONTINUED.

MR. BEVAN PAUSED when he had got thus far, to ask himself if he ought to give credence to what he read, or put it down as the raving of some person, whose wits had become tangled and deranged by misfortune.

Had the manuscript come to him without other circumstances to give it the air of truthfulness, he would have read it only as a literary curiosity; but it will be remembered that he had been a spectator of the resuscitation of Clara Crofton, which afforded of itself a very frightful verification of Varney's story — a story so horrible in all its details, that but for the great interest which it really possessed, he would have deeply regretted mixing it up in his memory with brighter subjects.

There was something yet to read in the papers before him, and thinking that it was better to know all at once than to leave his imagination to work upon matters so likely seriously to affect it, he resumed his perusal of these papers, which might be considered the autobiography of Varney:

I have already said that I was not yet fully alive to the horror of what I was, but I soon found what the words which had been spoken to me by the mysterious being who had exhumed me meant; I was a thing accursed, a something to be shunned by all men, a horror, a blight, and a desolation.

I felt myself growing sick and weak, as I traversed the streets of the city, and yet I loathed the sight of food, whenever I saw it.

I reached my own house, and saw that it had been burned down; there lay nothing but a heap of charred ruins where it once stood.

But I had an interest in those ruins, for from time to time I had buried considerable sums of money beneath the flooring of the lowest apartments, and I had every reason to believe, as such a secret treasure was only known to myself, that it remained untouched.

I waited until the moon became obscured by some passing clouds, and then having a most intimate knowledge of the locality, I commenced groping about the ruins, and removing a portion of them, until I made my way to the spot where my money was hidden.

The morning came, however, and surprised me at my occupation; so I hid myself among the ruins of what had once been my home for a whole day, and never once stirred from my concealment.

Oh, it was a long and weary day. I could hear the prattle of children at play, an inn or change-house was near at hand, and I could hear noisy drinkers bawling forth songs that had been proscribed in the Commonwealth.

I saw a poor wretch hunted nearly to death, close to where I lay concealed, because from the fashion of his garments, and the cut of his hair, he was supposed to belong to the deposed party.

But the long expected night came at last. It was a dark one, too, so that it answered my purpose well.

I had found an old rusty knife among the ruins, and with that I set to work to dig up my hidden treasure; I was successful, and found it all. Not a guinea had been removed, although in the immediate neighbourhood, there were those who would have sacrificed a human life for any piece of gold that I had hoarded.

I made no enquiries about any one that had belonged to me. I dreaded to receive some horrible and circumstantial answer, but I did get a slight piece of news, as I left the ruins, although I asked not for it.

"There's a poor devil," said one; "did you ever see such a wretch in all your life?"

"Why, yes," said another, "he's enough to turn one's canary sour, he seems to have come up from the ruins of Mortimers's house. By-the-bye, did you ever hear what became of him?"

"Yes, to be sure, he was shot by two of Cromwell's dragoons in some fracas or another."

"Ah, I recollect now, I heard as much. He murdered his son, didn't he?"

I passed on. Those words seemed to send a bolt of fire through the brain, and I dreaded that the speaker might expatiate upon them.

A slow misty rain was falling, which caused the streets to be very much deserted, but being extremely well acquainted with the city, I passed on till I came to that quarter which was principally inhabited by Jews, who I knew would take my money without any

troublesome questions being asked me, and also I could procure every accommodation required; and they did do so, for before another hour had passed over my head, I emerged richly habited as a chevalier of the period, having really not paid to the conscientious Israelite much more than four times the price of the clothing I walked away with.

And thus I was in the middle of London, with some hundreds of pounds in my pocket, and a horrible uncertainty as to what I was.

I was growing fainter and fainter still, and I feared that unless I succeeded in housing myself shortly, I should become a prey to some one who, seeing my exhausted condition, would, notwithstanding I had a formidable rapier by my side, rob me of all I possessed.

My career has been much too long and too chequered an one even to give the briefest sketch of. All I purpose here to relate is how I became convinced I was a vampyre, and that blood was my congenial nourishment and the only element of my new existence.

I passed on until I came to a street where I knew the houses were large but unfashionable, and that they were principally occupied by persons who made a trade by letting out apartments, and there I thought I might locate myself in safety.

As I made no difficulty about terms, there was no difficulty at all of any sort, and I found myself conducted into a tolerably handsome suite of rooms in the house of a decent-looking widow woman, who had two daughters, young and blooming girls, both of whom regarded me, as the new lodger, with looks of anything *but favour, considering my awful and cadaverous appearance most probably as promising nothing at all in the shape of pleasant companionship.*

This I was quite prepared for — I had seen myself in a mirror — that was enough; and I could honestly have averred that a more ghastly and horrible looking skeleton, attired in silks and broad-cloth, never yet walked the streets of the city.

When I retired to my chamber, I was so faint and ill, that I could scarcely drag one foot after the other; and was ruminating what I should do, until a strange feeling crept over me that I should like — what? Blood! — raw blood, reeking and hot, bubbling and juicy, from the veins of some gasping victim.

A clock upon the stairs struck one. I arose and listened attentively; all was still in the house — still as the very grave.

It was a large old rambling building, and had belonged at one time, no doubt, to a man of some mark and likelihood in the world. My chamber was one of six that opened from a corridor of a considerable length, and which traversed the whole length of the house.

I crept out into this corridor, and listened again for full ten minutes, but not the slightest sound, save my own faint breathing, disturbed the stillness of the house; and that emboldened me so that, with my appetite for blood growing each moment stronger, I began to ask myself from whose veins I could seek strength and nourishment.

But how was I to proceed? How was I to know in that large house which of the sleepers I could attack with safety, for it had now come to that, that I was to attack somebody. I stood like an evil spirit,

pondering over the best means of securing a victim.

And there came over me the horrible faintness again, that faintness which each moment grew worse, and which threatened completely to engulf me. I feared that some flush of it would overtake me, and then I should fall to rise no more; and strange as it may appear, I felt a disposition to cling to the new life that had been given to me. I seemed to be acquainted already with all its horrors, but not all its joys.

Suddenly the darkness of the corridor was cleared away, and soft and mellow light crept into it, and I said to myself, —

"The moon has risen."

Yes, the bright and beautiful moon, which I had felt the soft influence of when I lay among the graves, had emerged from the bank of clouds along the eastern sky, its beams descending through a little window. They streamed right through the corridor, faintly but effectually illuminating it, and letting me see clearly all the different doors leading to the different chambers.

And thus it was that I had light for anything I wished to do, but not information.

The moonbeams playing upon my face seemed to give me a spurious sort of strength. I did not know until after experience what a marked and sensible effect they would always have upon me, but I felt it even then, although I did not attribute it wholly to the influence of the queenly planet.

I walked on through the corridor, and some sudden influence seemed to guide me to a particular door. I know not how it was, but I laid my hand upon the lock, and said to myself, —

"I shall find my victim here."

CCXXXIII.

THE NIGHT ATTACK. — THE HORRIBLE CONCLUSION.

I paused yet a moment, for there came across me even then, after I had gone so far, a horrible dread of what I was about to do, and a feeling that there might be consequences arising from it that would jeopardise me greatly. Perhaps even then if a great accession of strength had come to my aid — mere bodily aid I mean — I should have hesitated, and the victim would have escaped; but, as if to mock me, there came that frightful feeling of exhaustion which felt so like the prelude to another death.

I no longer hesitated; I turned the lock of the door, and I thought that I must be discovered. I left it open about an inch, and then flew back to my own chamber.

I listened attentively; there was no alarm, no movement in any of the rooms — the same death-like stillness pervaded the house, and I felt that I was still safe.

A soft gleam of yellow looking light had come through the crevice of the door when I had opened it. It mingled strangely with the moonlight, and I concluded correctly enough, as I found afterwards, that a light was burning in the chamber.

It was at least another ten minutes before I could sufficiently re-assure myself to glide from my own room and approach that of the fated sleeper; but at length I told myself that I might safely do so, and the night was waning fast, and if anything was to be accomplished it must be done at once, before the first beams of early dawn should chase away the spirits of the night, and perhaps should leave me no power to act.

"What shall I be," I asked myself; "after another four-and-twenty hours of exhaustion? Shall I have power then to make the election of what I will do or what I will not? No, I may suffer the pangs of death again, and the scarcely less pangs of another revival."

This reasoning — if it may be called reasoning — decided me; and with cautious and cat-like footsteps, I again approached the bed-room door which I had opened.

I no longer hesitated, but at once crossed the threshold, and looked around me. It was the chamber of the youngest of my landlady's daughters, who, as far as I could judge, seemed to be about sixteen years of age; but they had evidently been so struck with my horrible appearance, that they had placed themselves as little as possible in my way, so that I could not be said to be a very good judge of their ages or of their looks.

I only knew she was the youngest, because she wore her hair long, and wore it in ringlets, which were loose and streaming over the pillow on which she slept, while her sister, I remarked, wore her hair plaited up, and completely off her neck and shoulders.

I stood by the bed-side, and looked upon this beautiful girl in all the pride of her young beauty, so gently and quietly slumbering. Her lips were parted, as though some pleasant images were passing in her mind, and induced a slight smile even in her sleep. She murmured twice, too, a word, which I thought was the name of some one — perchance the idol of her young heart — but it was too indistinct for me to catch it, nor did I care to hear; that which was perhaps a very cherished secret, indeed, mattered not to me. I made no pretentions to her affections, however strongly in a short time I might stand in her abhorrence.

One of her arms, which was exquisitely rounded, lay upon the coverlet; a neck, too, as white as alabaster, was partially exposed to my gaze, but I had no passions — it was food I wanted.

I sprung upon her. There was a shriek, but not before I had secured a draught of life-blood from her neck. It was enough. I felt it dart through my veins like fire, and I was restored. From that moment I found out what was to be my sustenance; it was blood — the blood of the young and the beautiful.

The house was thoroughly alarmed, but not before I had retired to my own chamber. I was but partially dressed, and those few clothes I threw off me, and getting into my bed, I feigned to be asleep; so that when a gentleman who slept likewise in the house, but of whose presence I knew nothing, knocked hardly at my door, I affected to awaken in a fright, and called out, —

"What is it? what is it? — for God's sake tell me if it is a fire."

"No, no — but get up, sir, get up. There's some one in the place. An attempt at murder, I think, sir."

I arose and opened the door; so by the light he carried he saw that I had to dress myself — he was but half attired himself, and he carried his sword beneath his arm.

"It is a strange thing," he said; "but I have heard a shriek of alarm."

"And I likewise," said I; "but I thought it was a dream."

"Help! help! help!" cried the widow, who had risen, but stood upon the threshold of her own chamber; "thieves! thieves!"

By this time I had got on sufficient of my apparel that I could make an appearance, and, likewise with my sword in my hand, I sallied out into the corridor.

"Oh, gentlemen — gentlemen," cried the landlady, "did you hear anything?"

"A shriek, madam," said my fellow-lodger; "have you looked into your daughters' chambers?"

The room of the youngest daughter was the nearest, and into that she went at once. In another moment she appeared on the threshold again with a face as white as a sheet, then she wrung her hands, and said, —

"Murder! murder! — my child is murdered — my child is murdered, Master Harding," — which I found was the name of my fellow-lodger.

"Fling open one of the windows, and call for the watch," said he to me. "and I will search the room, and woe be to any one that I may find within its walls unauthorised."

I did as he desired, and called the watch, but the watch came not, and then, upon a second visit to her daughter, the landlady found she had only fainted, and that she had been deceived in thinking she was murdered by the sudden sight of the blood upon her neck, so the house was

restored to something like quiet again, and the morning begin now near at hand, Mr. Harding retired to his chamber, and I to mine, leaving the landlady and her eldest daughter assiduous in their attentions to the younger.

How wonderfuly revived I felt — I was quite a new creature when the sunlight came dancing into my apartment.

I dressed and was about to leave the house, when Mr. Harding came out of one of the lower rooms, and intercepted me.

"Sir," he said, "I have not the pleasure of knowing you, but I have no doubt that an ordinary feeling of chivalry will prompt you to do all in your power to obviate the dread of such another night as the past."

"Dread, sir," said I, "the dread of what?"

"A very proper question," he said, "but one I can hardly answer; the girl states, she was awakened by some one biting her neck, and in proof of the story she actually exhibits the marks of teeth, and so terrified is she, that she declares that she shall never be able to sleep again."

"You astonish me."

"No doubt—it is sufficiently astonishing to excuse even doubts; but if you and I, who are both inmates of the house, were to keep watch to-night in the corridor, it might have the effect of completely quieting the imagination of the young girl, and perhaps result in the discovery of this nocturnal disturber of the peace."

"Certainly," said I, "command me in any way, I shall have great pleasure."

"Shall it be understood, then, that we meet at eleven in your apartment or in mine."

"Whichever you may please to consider the most convenient, sir."

"I mention my own then, which is the furthest door in the corridor, and where I shall be happy to see you at eleven o'clock."

There was a something about this young man's manner which I did not altogether like, and yet I could not come to any positive conclusion as to whether he suspected me, and therefore I thought it would be premature to fly, when perhaps there would be really no occasion for doing so; on the contrary, I made up my mind to wait the result of the evening, which might or might not be disastrous to me. At all events, I considered that I was fully equal to taking my own part, and if by the

decrees of destiny I was really to be, as it were, repudiated from society, and made to endure a new, strange, and horrible existence, I did not see that I was called upon to be particular how I rescued myself from difficulties that might arise.

Relying, then, upon my own strength, and my own unscrupulous use of it, I awaited with tolerable composure the coming of night.

During the day I amused myself by walking about, and noting the remarkable changes which so short a period as two years had made in London. But these happened to be two years most abundantly prolific in change. The feelings and habits of people seemed to have undergone a thorough revolution, which I was the more surprised at when I learned by what thorough treachery the restoration of the exiled family was effected. *

The day wore on; I felt no need of refreshment, and I began to feel my own proper position, and to feel that occasionally a draught of delicious life-blood, such as I had quaffed the night before, was fresh marrow to my bones.

I could see, when I entered the house where I had made my temporary home, that notwithstanding that I considered my appearance wonderfully improved, that feeling was not shared in by others,

---

* Lord Protector Oliver Cromwell's death in 1658 was widely rumoured not to have been a natural one, although it probably was. In the 1840s, readers of Varney the Vampyre would have been thoroughly familiar with the history of the Restoration, and would have understood this reference without any further explanation, but it's beyond the scope of these footnotes to go into it, so modern readers must do a little remedial reading if they want more context here.

for the whole family shrunk from me as though there had been a most frightful contamination in my touch, and as though the very air I had breathed was hateful and deleterious. I felt convinced that there had been some conversation concerning me, and that I was rather more than suspected. I certainly could then have left the place easily and quietly, but I had a feeling of defiance, which did not enable me to do so.

I felt as if I were an injured being, and ought to resist a something that looked like oppression.

"Why," I said to myself, "have I been rescued from the tomb to be made the sport of a malignant destiny? My crime was a great one, but surely I suffered enough, when I suffered death as an expiation of it, and I might have been left to repose in the grave."

The feelings that have since come over me held no place in my imagination, but with a kind of defiant desperation I felt as if I should like to defeat the plan by which I was attempted to be punished, and even in the face of Providence itself, to show that it was a failure entailing far worse consequences upon others than upon me.

This was my impression, so I would not play the coward, and fly upon the first flash of danger.

I sat in my own room until the hour came for my appointment with Mr. Harding, and then I walked along the corridor with a confident step, and let the hilt end of my scabbard clank along the floor. I knocked boldly at the door, and I thought there was a little hesitation in his voice as he bade me walk in, but this might have been only my imagination.

He was seated at a table, fully dressed, and in addition to his sword, there was lying upon the table before him a large holster pistol, nearly half the size of a carbine.

"You are well prepared," said I, as I pointed to it.

"Yes," he said, "and I mean to use it."

"What do they want now?" I said.

"What do who want?"

"I don't know," I said, "but I thought I heard some one call you by name from below."

"Indeed, excuse me a moment, perhaps they have made some discovery."

There was wine upon the table, and while he was gone, I poured a glass of good Rhenish down the barrel of the pistol. I wiped it carefully with the cuff of my coat, so there was no appearance upon the barrel of anything of the sort, and when he came back, he looked at me very suspiciously, as he said, —

"Nobody called me, how could you say I was called."

"Because I thought I heard you called; I suppose it is allowable for human nature to be fallible now and then."

"Yes, but then I am so surprised how you could make such a mistake."

"So am I."

It was rather a difficult thing to answer this, and looking at me very steadily, he took up the pistol and examined the priming. Of course, that was all right, and he appeared to be perfectly satisfied.

"There will be two chairs and a table," he said, "placed in the corridor, so that we can sit in perfect ease. I will not anticipate that anything will happen, but if it should, I can only say that I will not *be backward in the use of my weapons."*

"I don't doubt it," said I, "and commend you accordingly. That pistol must be a most formidable weapon. Does it ever miss fire?"

"Not that I know of," he said, "I have loaded it with such extraordinary care that it amounts to almost an impossibility that it should. Will you take some wine?"

At this moment there came a loud knocking at the door of the house. I saw an expression of satisfaction come over his face and he sprung to his feet, holding the pistol in his grasp.

"Do you know the meaning of that knocking," said I, "at such an hour?" and at the same time with a sweep of my arm I threw his sword off the table and beyond his reach.

"Yes," he said, rather excitedly; "you are my prisoner, it was you who caused the mischief and confusion last night. The girl is ready to swear to you, and if you attempt

to escape, I'll blow your brains out."

"Fire at me," said I, "and take the consequences — but the threat is sufficient, and you shall die for your temerity."

I drew my sword, and he evidently thought his danger imminent, for he at once snapped the pistol in my face. Of course it only flashed in the pan, but in one moment my sword went through him like a flash of light. It was a good blade the Jew had sold me — the hilt struck against his breast bone, and he shrieked.

Bang! bang! bang! came again at the outer door of the house. I withdrew the reeking blade, dashed it into the scabbard just in time to prevent my landlady from opening the door, which she was almost in the act of doing. I seized her by the back of the neck, and hurled her to a considerable distance, and then opening the door myself, I stood behind it, and let three men rush into the house. After which I quietly left it, and was free.

CCXXXIV.

VARNEY DETAILS HIS SECOND DEATH.

THE CLERGYMAN WAS perfectly amazed, as well he might be, at these revelations of the vampyre. He looked up from the manuscript that Varney had left him, with a far more bewildered look than he had ever worn when studying the most abstruse sciences or difficult languages.

"Can I," he said, — "ought I to believe it?"

This was a question more easily asked than answered, and after pacing the little

room for a time, he thought he had better finish the papers of the vampyre, before he tortured his mind with any more suppositions upon the subject.

The papers continued thus, and the clergyman was soon completely absorbed in the great interest of the strange recital they contained:

I cared nothing as regarded my last adventure, so that it had one termination which was of any importance to me, namely, that termination which insured my safety. When I got into the street, I walked hurriedly on, never once looking behind me, until I was far enough off, and I felt assured all pursuit was out of the question.

I then began to bethink me what I had next to do.

I was much revived by the draught of blood I had already had, but as yet I was sufficiently new to my vampyre-like existence not to know how long such a renewal of my life and strength would last me.

I certainly felt vigorous, but it was a strange, unearthly sort of vigour, having no sort of resemblance whatever to the strength which persons in an ordinary state of existence may be supposed to feel, when the faculties are all full of life, and acting together harmoniously and well.

When I paused, I found myself in Pall Mall, and not far off from the palace of St. James, which of late had seen so many changes, and been the witness of such remarkable mutations in the affair of monarchs, that its real chronicles would even then have afforded an instructive volume.

I wandered right up to the gates of the royal pile, but then as I was about to enter the quadrangle called the colour court, I was rudely repulsed by a sentinel.

It was not so in the time of Cromwell, but at the same moment I had quite forgotten all that was so completely changed.

I always bow to authority when I cannot help it, so I turned aside at once, without making any remark; but as I did so I saw a small door open, not far from where I was, and two figures emerged muffled up in brown cloaks.

They looked nothing peculiar at the first glance, but when you came to examine the form and features, and to observe the manners of those two men, you could not but come to a conclusion that they were what the world would estimate as something great.

Adventure to me was life itself, now that I had so strangely shuffled off all other ties that bound me to the world, and I had a reckless disregard of danger, which arose naturally enough from my most singular and horrible tenure of existence. I resolved to follow these two men closely enough, and yet, if possible, without exciting their observation.

"Shall we have any sport?" said one.

"I trust that the ladies," replied the other, "will afford us some."

"And yet they were rather coy, do you not think, on the last meeting, Rochester?"

"Your majesty — "

"Hush, man — hush! why are you so imprudent as to 'majesty' me in the public streets. Here would be a court scandal if any eaves-dropper had heard you. You were wont to be much more careful than that."

"I spoke," said the other, "to recall your majesty to care. The name of Rochester, which you pronounced, is just as likely in the streets at such a time to create court scandal as that of — "

"Hush, hush! Did I say Rochester? Well — well, man, hold your peace if I did, and come on quickly — if we can but persuade them to come out, we can take them into the garden of the palace; I have the key of that most handy little door in the wall, which has served us more than once."

Of course, after this, I had no difficulty in knowing that the one speaker was the restored monarch, Charles the Second, and the other was his favourite, and dissolute companion, Rochester, of whom I had heard something, although I had been far too short a time in the land of the living **again**, to have had any opportunity of seeing either of them before; but since they had now confessed themselves to be what they were, I could have no sort of difficulty in their recognition at any other time. *

I had carefully kept out of sight while the little dialogue I have just recorded took place, so that although they more than once glanced **around** them suspiciously and keenly, they saw me not, and having quite satisfied **them** that their imprudent speech had **done** them no harm, they walked on hurriedly in the direction of Pimlico.

Little did Charles and his companion guess how horrible a being was following close upon their track. If they had done so they might have paused, aghast, and pursued another course to that which was occupying their **attention** I had a difficult part to play in following them, for although the king was incautious enough to have been **safely** and easily followed by

any one, Rochester was not, but kept a wary eye around him, so that I was really more than once upon the point of being detected, and yet by dint of good management I did escape.

Pimlico at that time was rather a miserable neighbourhood, and far, very far indeed from being what it is now, but both the king and Rochester appeared to be well acquainted with it and they went on for a considerable distance until they came to a turning of a narrow dismal-looking character bounded on each side not by houses but by the garden walls of houses, and to judge from the solidity and the height of those walls, the houses should have been houses of some importance.

"Bravo, bravissimo!" said the king, "we are thus far into the enemy territory without observation."

"So it seems," replied Rochester; "and now think you we can find the particular wall again."

"Of a surety, yes. Did I not ask them to hang out a handkerchief or some other signal, by which we might be this night guided in our search, and there it flutters."

The king pointed to the top of the wall, where a handkerchief waved and something certainly in the shape of a human head appeared against the night sky, and as sweet a voice as ever I heard in my life, said, —

"Gentlemen, I pray you to go away."

"What," said the king; "go away just as the sun has risen?"

"Nay, but gentlemen," said the voice, "we are afraid we are watched."

"We!" said Rochester, "you say we, and yet your fair companion is not visible."

"Fair sir," said the lady, "it is not the

---

* James II was of the House of Stuart, which held the Throne until the death of Queen Anne in 1714. After that, the Throne passed to the House of Hanover, which still held it when Varney the Vampyre was written; however, Stuart relatives (known as Jacobites) spent a century or so scheming and intriguing to get it back. Queen Victoria was a Hanoverian monarch, so it was perfectly acceptable for James Malcolm Rymer, writing in 1847 or so, to tell a story like this about James II.

easiest task in the world for one of us to stand upon a ladder. It certainly will not hold two."

"Fair lady," said the king, "and if you can but manage to come over the wall, we will all four take one of the pleasantest strolls in the world; a friend of mine, who is a captain in the Royal Guard, will at my request, allow us to walk in the private garden of St. James's palace."

"Indeed."

"Yes, fair one. That garden of which you may have heard as the favourite resort of the gay Charles."

"But we are afraid," said the lady; "our uncle may come home. It's very improper indeed — very indiscreet — we ought not to think of such a thing for a moment. In fact, it's decidedly wrong, gentlemen; but how are we to get over the wall?"

The party all laughed out together.

CCXXXV.

THE PALACE GARDEN IN ST. JAMES'S.

It was certainly a very ingenious speech which the lady on the wall had given utterance to, and sufficiently exemplified how inclination was struggling with prudence. It was just the sort of speech which suited those to whom it was addressed.

After the laughter had subsided a little Charles spoke, —

"By the help of the ladder we have," he said, "you can easily leave where you are, and as easily return, but I perceive you lack the strength to lift it over this side so as to descend."

"Just so," said the lady, in a low voice.

"Well, I think that by the aid of my friend Smith here, I can get up to the top of the wall, and assist you."

Charles, by the aid of Rochester, contrived to scramble to the top of the wall, to the assistance of the two damsels who were so fearful, and yet so willing, to risk a little danger to their reputations, for the purpose of enjoying a walk in the king's garden at St. James's.

The idea came across me of doing some mischief, but I did not just then interfere as I wanted to see the result of the affair. The ladder was duly pulled over by the monarch after both the ladies had got on the top of the wall, and while Rochester steadied it below they descended in perfect safety, and the party walked hastily from the place in the direction of St. James's.

I followed them with great caution, after having removed the ladder to the wall of a garden several doors from the proper one. They went on talking and laughing in the gayest possible manner, until they reached Buckingham house, and then they took a secluded path that led them close to the gardens of St. James's.

Some overhanging trees shed such an impervious shadow upon all objects that I found I might as well be quite near to the party as far off, so I approached boldly and heard that the ladies were beginning to get a little alarmed at this secret and strictly private mode of entrance to the garden.

"Gentlemen," said one, "don't go into the garden if you have no proper leave to do so."

"Oh, but we have," said the king. "Lately I have had proper leave, I assure you; it did happen that for some time the leave was taken away, but I have it again along with a few other little privileges that I wanted much."

"You need fear nothing," said Rochester.

They all four stood in a group by the little door, while the king fumbled about with a key for some few minutes, before he could open the lock. At length, however, he succeeded in doing so, and the door swung open. The king dropped the key and was unable to find it again; so leaving the door as close as they could, the party passed onwards, and I soon followed in their footsteps.

The place was profoundly dark.

I could feel the soft grating of fine gravel under my feet, and feeling that such a sand might betray me, I stepped aside until I trod upon a border, as I found it to be, of velvet turf. The odour of sweet flowers came upon my senses, and occasionally as the night wind swept among the trees, there would be a pleasant murmuring sound quite musical in its effect.

The soft soil effectually prevented my footsteps from being heard, and I soon stood quite close to the parties, and found that they were at the entrance of a little gaudy pavilion, from a small painted window in which streamed a light.

The ladies seemed to be rather in a flutter of apprehension, and yet the whole affair no doubt to them presented itself in the shape of such a charming and romantic adventure, that I very much doubt if they would have gone back now, had they had all the opportunity in the world so to do.

Finally they all went into the pavillion. I then advanced, and finding a window, that commanded a good view of the interior I looked in and was much amused at what passed.

The place was decorated in a tasteful manner, although a little approaching to the gaudy, and the pictures painted in fresco upon the walls were not precisely what the strictest prudery would have considered correct, while at the same time there was nothing positively offensive in them.

A table stood in the centre, and was covered with rich confectionery, and wine, while the lamp that had sent the stream of light through the painted window was dependent from the ceiling by three massive gilt chains.

Take it for all in all, it certainly was a handsome place.

The king and Rochester were urging the ladies to drink wine, and now that for the first time I had an opportunity of seeing the countenances of the different persons whom I had followed so far, I confess that I looked upon them with much curiosity. The ladies were decidedly handsome, and the youngest who had fallen to the lot of the king was very pretty indeed, and had a look of great innocence and sweetness upon her face. I pitied her.

The king was a small, dark, sharp-featured man, and I thought that there was an obliquity in his vision. As for

Rochester, he was decidedly ugly. His face was rather flat, and of a universal dirty-looking white colour. He certainly was not calculated to win a lady's favour. But then for all I knew, he might have a tongue to win an angel out of heaven.

Such a capacity goes much further with a woman who has any mind than all the physical graces, and women of no mind are not worth the winning.

CCXXXVI.

AN ADVENTURE. — THE CARBINE-SHOT. — THE DEATH.

"Nay," I heard the king say, "they ought, and no doubt do, keep choice wine here; drink, fair one."

The young girl shook her head.

"Nay, now," said Charles with a laugh, as he finished off himself the glass that the young girl took so small a sip of, "I will convince you that I think it good."

The lady with whom Rochester was conversing in a low tone, had no such scruples, for she tossed off a couple of glasses as fast as they were tendered to her, and talked quite at her ease, admiring the pavilion, the pictures, the hangings and furniture, and wondering whether the king ever came there himself.

Rochester began mystifying her, talking to her in a low tone, while I turned my attention to the king, and the younger, and certainly more estimable, female of the two.

The king had been talking to her in a low tone, when she suddenly started to her feet, her face flushed with anger and alarm.

"Louisa," she said, "I claim your protection; you were left in care of me. Take me home, or I will tell my uncle how you basely betrayed your trust, by pursuading me there was no harm in meeting those gentlemen."

"Pho! the child's mad," said Louisa.

"Quite mad," said the king, as he advanced towards her again; she fled to the door of the pavilion.

I knew not what impulse it was that urged me on, but I left the window hastily, and met her, she fell into my arms, and the light fell strongly upon me as I confronted the king.

"The guard. The guard," he shouted.

"Louisa pretended to faint, and the young girl clung to me as her only protector, exclaiming, —

"Save me! save me; Oh save me!"

"The garden door is open," I whispered to her, "follow me quickly, not a moment is to be lost." We both fled together.

I was about to pass through the doorway, when a shot from one of the guards struck me, and I fell to the ground as if the hand of a giant had struck me down. There was a rush of blood from my heart to my head, a burning sensation of pain for a moment or two, that was most horrible, and then a sea of yellow light seemed to be all around me.

I remembered no more.

It was afterwards that I found this

was my second death, and that the favourite, Rochester, had actually directed that I should be shot rather than permitted to escape, for he dreaded more than the monarch did the exposure of his vices. I do not think that Charles, in like manner, had he been at hand, would have had my life taken, although it is hard to say what kings will do or what they will not when they are thwarted.

CCXXXVII.

THE TOTAL DESTRUCTION OF VARNEY THE VAMPYRE, AND CONCLUSION.

THE MANUSCRIPT which the clergyman had read with so much interest, here abruptly terminated. He was left to conclude that Varney after that had been resuscitated; and he was more perplexed than ever to come to any opinion concerning the truth of the narration which he had now concluded.

IT WAS ONE WEEK after he had finished the perusal of Varney's papers that the clergyman read in an English newspaper the following statement: —

We extract from the Algemeine Zeitung *the following most curious story, the accuracy of which of course we cannot vouch for, but still there is a sufficient air of probability about it to induce us to present it to our readers.*

Late in the evening, about four days since, a tall and melancholy-looking stranger arrived, and put up at one of the principal hotels at Naples. He was a most peculiar looking man, and considered by the persons of the establishment as about the ugliest guest they had ever had within the walls of their place.

"In a short time he summoned the landlord, and the following conversation ensued between him and the strange guest.

"I want,' said the stranger, 'to see all the curiosities of Naples, and among the rest Mount Vesuvius. Is there any difficulty?"

"None," replied the landlord, "with a proper guide."

A guide was soon secured, who set out with the adventurous Englishman to make the ascent of the burning mountain.

They went on then until the guide did not think it quite prudent to go any further, as there was a great fissure in the side of the mountain, out of which a stream of lava was slowly issuing and spreading itself in rather an alarming manner.

"The ugly Englishman, however, pointed to a secure mode of getting higher still, and they proceeded until they were very near the edge of the crater itself. The stranger then took his purse from his pocket and flung it to the guide saying, —

"You can keep that for your pains, and for coming into some danger with me. But the fact was, that I wanted a witness to an act which I have set my mind upon performing."

The guide says that these words were spoken with so much calmness, that he verily believed the act mentioned as about to be done was some scientific experiment of which he knew that the English were very fond, and he replied, —

"Sir, I am only too proud to serve so generous and so distinguished a gentleman. In what way can I be useful?"

"You will make what haste you can," said the stranger, "from the mountain, inasmuch as it is covered with sulphurous vapours, inimical to human life; and

when you reach the city you will cause to be published an account of my proceedings, and what I say. You will say that you accompanied Varney the Vampyre to the crater of Mount Vesuvius, and that, tired and disgusted with a life of horror, he flung himself in to prevent the possibility of a reanimation of his remains."

Before then the guide could utter anything but a shriek, Varney took one tremendous leap, and disappeared into the burning mouth of the mountain.

Made in United States
Troutdale, OR
01/10/2024

16864119R00399